**B**arker is so good I am almost tongue-tied. What Barker does makes the rest of us look like we've been asleep for the last ten years . . . His stories are compulsorily readable and original. He is an important, exciting and enormously saleable writer."—*STEPHEN KING*

"Monstrous imagination . . . WEAVEWORLD is a high drama, with every emotion known to man woven through its complex pattern . . . In WEAVEWORLD anything can, and does, happen." —*NEW MUSICAL EXPRESS*

"WEAVEWORLD confirms Clive Barker as a formidable talent in British dark fantasy." —*Q MAGAZINE*

"Recommended . . . a fantastic tale of imagination." —*JONATHAN ROSS, SUNDAY EXPRESS*

"Extremely readable . . . WEAVEWORLD is a rich and cunning book." —*THE LIST*

"His new dark fantasy, an epic tale of a magic carpet and the wondrous world within its weave, towers above his earlier work . . . it manages, via its powerful and giddy torrent of invention, to grasp the golden ring as the most ambitious and visionary horror novel of the decade . . . Like Barker's earlier fiction, this complex work erupts with explicit sex and violence—but now the shocks punctuate a raging flood of image and situation so rich as to overflow . . . Here Barker has unleashed literary genius." —*KIRKUS REVIEWS*

C live Barker was born in Liverpool in 1952. In addition to his work as a short story writer and novelist, he also illustrates, and writes and directs for the stage and screen (most recently with HELLRAISER). WEAVEWORLD is his second novel. Clive Barker now lives in London.

"The most important horror writer of the decade." —*RAMSEY CAMPBELL*

"Quintessential Barker; graphic, grotesque, and yet compellingly readable ... its energy is unstoppable." —*WASHINGTON POST*

"Something new, something unique, a powerful and powerfully disturbing new voice who tells us things we don't necessarily want to know about ourselves, and whispers them so eloquently that we can't stop listening." —*GEORGE R. R. MARTIN*

"Barker's visions are at one turn horrifying and at the next flickering with brilliant invention that leaves the reader shaking not with fear, but with wonder." —*SOUNDS MAGAZINE*

"From the start it's clear that Barker is in a class by himself." —*LOCUS*

" pop-fiction classic." - *MACLEAN'S*

"An epic contemporary fantasy."
- *OTTAWA CITIZEN*

"All the elements of WEAVEWORLD - questing, hidden magical world, human protagonists, magical beings, evil antagonists - are the staples of fantasy." - *OTTAWA CITIZEN*

"The writing qualities of JRR Tolkien, Edgar Allan Poe and Stephen King all rolled into one."
- *WATERLOO CHRONICLE*

"No wonder even Stephen King is impressed."
- *KINGSTON WHIG-STANDARD*

"A wondrous excursion into the imagination."
- *TORONTO SUN*

"Flamboyantly original." - *MACLEAN'S*

"Latter-day, upbeat Poe."
- *KINGSTON WHIG-STANDARD*

"An irresistible yarn." - *TIME*

**W**EAVEWORLD is Clive Barker's second novel. It follows the enormous international success of his previous novel, THE DAMNATION GAME, and his six collections of short stories, THE BOOKS OF BLOOD. Both his stories and his novel have been widely acclaimed on both sides of the Atlantic. Already, Clive Barker's fellow-writers have begun the chorus of critical acclaim his new novel is bound to generate:

"A powerful and fascinating writer with a brilliant imagination. WEAVEWORLD reveals Clive Barker as an outstanding storyteller."
—*J.G. BALLARD*

"All that you expect from Clive Barker and more—terrifying, shocking, audaciously imaginative, moving and ruthlessly unputdownable." —*RAMSEY CAMPBELL*

"Clive Barker has been an amazing writer from his first appearance with the great gifts of invention and commitment to his own vision stamped on every page. WEAVEWORLD is pure dazzle, pure storytelling. The mixed tricky country where fantasy and horror overlap has been visited before—though not very often—and WEAVEWORLD will be a guide for everyone who travels there in the future. I think it'll probably be imitated for the next decade or so, as lesser talents try to crack its code and tame its insights." —*PETER STRAUB*

# Clive Barker

# WEAVEWORLD

COLLINS    TORONTO

First published in hardcover 1987
by Collins Publishers
This edition published 1988
by Collins Paperbacks
100 Lesmill Road, Don Mills, Ontario

Drawings by Tim White

The publishers would like to acknowledge permission to quote
from the following material.
Lines from *The Tryst* by Walter de la Mare published by
permission of the Literary Trustees of Walter de la Mare and the
Society of Authors as their representatives.
Lines from *Stopping by Woods on a Snowy Evening* from THE
POETRY OF ROBERT FROST edited by Edward Connery
Lathem by permission of the Estate of Robert Frost and Jonathan
Cape Ltd.
Lines from *The Two* from THE COLLECTED POEMS OF W. H.
AUDEN reprinted by permission of Faber and Faber Ltd.

**Canadian Cataloguing in Publication Data**
Barker, Clive, 1952–
  Weaveworld

ISBN 0-00-223294-4

I. Title.

PR6052.A6475W43 1988     823'.914     C88-093877-3

Printed and bound in Canada

To D.J.D.

*' . . . the spirit has its homeland, which is the realm of the meaning of things.'*

Saint Exupéry
*The Wisdom of the Sands*

# CONTENTS

BOOK ONE
## IN THE KINGDOM OF THE CUCKOO

### Part One: Wild Blue Yonder

| | | |
|---|---|---|
| I | Homing | 5 |
| II | The Pursuers | 10 |
| III | Who Moved the Ground? | 14 |
| IV | Contact | 26 |
| V | Before the Dark | 30 |
| VI | Mad Mooney | 41 |

### Part Two: Births, Deaths and Marriages

| | | |
|---|---|---|
| I | The Suit of Lights | 51 |
| II | The Skin of the Teeth | 62 |
| III | Selling Heaven | 70 |
| IV | Nuptials | 74 |
| V | In the Arms of Mama Pus | 84 |
| VI | Sick Souls | 91 |
| VII | The Tall-Boy | 99 |
| VIII | Following the Thread | 106 |
| IX | Finders Keepers | 112 |
| X | The Menstruum | 118 |

### Part Three: The Exiles

| | | |
|---|---|---|
| I | The River | 127 |
| II | Waking in the Dark | 130 |
| III | What She Told | 138 |

| IV | Night Terrors | 148 |
| V | From the Mouths of Babes | 155 |
| VI | Events in a High Wind | 163 |
| VII | The Aftermath | 171 |
| VIII | Necessary Evils | 175 |
| IX | On the Might of Princes | 178 |
| X | Humankindness | 180 |
| XI | Three Vignettes | 188 |

*Part Four: What Price Wonderland?*

| I | To Sell is To Own | 195 |
| II | Tell Me No Lies | 199 |
| III | So Near, So Far | 202 |
| IV | Breaking the Law | 208 |
| V | Threshold | 215 |

BOOK TWO
THE FUGUE

*Part Five: Revels*

| I | Cal, Amongst Miracles | 231 |
| II | At the Lake, and Later | 238 |
| III | Delusions | 243 |
| IV | Allegiances | 246 |
| V | The Orchard of Lemuel Lo | 251 |
| VI | Capra's House | 263 |
| VII | Shadwell on High | 274 |
| VIII | The Virgin Blooded | 276 |
| IX | Never, and Again | 281 |
| X | The Summons | 283 |
| XI | At the Gazebo | 286 |
| XII | A Vanishing Breed | 293 |
| XIII | A Proposal | 294 |

*Part Six: Back Among the Blind Men*

| Time's Gone by | | 305 |

| II | Despair | 313 |
| III | Forgetfulness | 315 |
| IV | The Nomads | 320 |
| V | Our Lady of the Bones | 328 |
| VI | The Brittle Machine | 341 |
| VII | Tales of Spook City | 337 |

## Part Seven: The Demagogue

| I | The Messenger | 345 |
| II | Seeing the Light | 350 |
| III | Charisma | 355 |
| IV | As Good Men Go | 363 |
| V | The Hours Pass | 367 |
| VI | Hello, Stranger | 370 |
| VII | Lost Causes | 378 |
| VIII | New Eyes for Old | 383 |
| IX | A Secret Place | 387 |
| X | Fatalities | 392 |
| XI | Cal, Travelling North | 399 |
| XII | Resolution | 401 |

## Part Eight: The Return

| I | Strategy | 407 |
| II | The Burial Party | 410 |
| III | The Horse Unharnessed | 414 |
| IV | The Rope-Dancers | 422 |
| V | Nonesuch | 428 |
| VI | The Flesh is Weak | 435 |
| VII | An Open Book | 443 |
| VIII | The Essential Dragon | 450 |
| IX | The Fire | 459 |
| X | Unearthly Delights | 468 |
| XI | A Witness | 476 |
| XII | One Fell Swoop | 482 |
| XIII | A Fleeting Glimpse | 493 |
| XIV | The Narrow Bright | 497 |

*Part Nine: Into the Gyre*

| I | Trespassers | 505 |
| II | The Temple | 513 |
| III | The Miracle of the Loom | 519 |
| IV | Shadwell | 536 |
| V | A Fragile Peace | 539 |

BOOK THREE
## OUT OF THE EMPTY QUARTER

*Part Ten: The Search for the Scourge*

| I | No Rest for the Wicked | 549 |
| II | Oblivion | 556 |
| III | The Wall | 562 |
| IV | Uriel | 566 |

*Part Eleven: The Dream Season*

| I | Portrait of the Hero as a Young Lunatic | 581 |
| II | Representations | 587 |
| III | No Lullabies | 599 |
| IV | The Shrine of the Mortalities | 604 |
| V | The Naked Flame | 614 |
| VI | Death Comes Home | 622 |

*Part Twelve: Stalking Paradise*

| I | A Chapter of Accidents | 633 |
| II | Dust and Ashes | 640 |
| III | The Secret Isle | 649 |
| IV | Past Hope | 660 |

*Part Thirteen: Magic Night*

| I | Blizzard | 667 |
| II | Shelter from the Storm | 676 |

| III | On the Hill | 688 |
| IV | Symmetry | 700 |
| V | The Sleepwalker | 711 |
| VI | Rapture | 716 |

BOOK ONE

# IN THE KINGDOM
# OF
# THE CUCKOO

# Part One

# Wild Blue Yonder

'I, for one, know of no
sweeter sight for a man's
eyes than his own country . . .'

Homer
*The Odyssey*

# I

## HOMING

### 1

**N**othing ever begins.

There is no first moment; no single word or place from which this or any other story springs.

The threads can always be traced back to some earlier tale, and to the tales that preceded that; though as the narrator's voice recedes the connections will seem to grow more tenuous, for each age will want the tale told as if it were of its own making.

Thus the pagan will be sanctified, the tragic become laughable; great lovers will stoop to sentiment, and demons dwindle to clockwork toys.

Nothing is fixed. In and out the shuttle goes, fact and fiction, mind and matter, woven into patterns that may have only this in common: that hidden amongst them is a filigree which will with time become a world.

It must be arbitrary then, the place at which we choose to embark.

Somewhere between a past half forgotten and a future as yet only glimpsed.

This place, for instance.

This garden, untended since the death of its protector three months ago, and now running riot beneath a blindingly bright late August sky; its fruits hanging unharvested, its herbaceous borders coaxed to mutiny by a summer of torrential rain and sudden, sweltering days.

This house, identical to the hundreds of others in this street alone, built with its back so close to the railway track that the passage of the slow train from Liverpool to Crewe rocks the china dogs on the dining-room sill.

And with this young man, who now steps out of the back door and makes his way down the beleaguered path to a ramshackle hut from which there rises a welcoming chorus of coos and flutterings.

His name is Calhoun Mooney, but he's universally known as Cal. He is twenty-six, and has worked for five years at an insurance firm in the city centre. It's a job he takes no pleasure in, but escape from the city he's lived in all his life seems more unlikely than ever since the death of his mother, all of which may account for the weary expression on his well-made face.

He approaches the door of the pigeon loft, opens it, and at that moment – for want of a better – this story takes wing.


2


Cal had told his father several times that the wood at the bottom of the loft door was deteriorating. It could only be a matter of time before the planks rotted completely, giving the rats who lived and grew gross along the railway line access to the pigeons. But Brendan Mooney had shown little or no interest in his racing birds since Eileen's death. This despite, or perhaps because, the birds had been his abiding passion during her life. How often had Cal heard his mother complain that Brendan spent more time with his precious pigeons than he did inside the house?

She would not have had that complaint to make now; now Cal's father sat most of every day at the back window, staring out into the garden and watching the wilderness steadily take charge of his wife's handiwork, as if he might find in the

6

spectacle of dissolution some clue as to how his grief might be similarly erased. There was little sign that he was learning much from his vigil however. Every day, when Cal came back to the house in Chariot Street – a house he'd thought to have left for good half a decade ago, but which his father's isolation had obliged him to return to – it seemed he found Brendan slightly smaller. Not hunched, but somehow *shrunken*, as though he'd decided to present the smallest possible target to a world suddenly grown hostile.

Murmuring a welcome to the forty or so birds in the loft, Cal stepped inside, to be met with a scene of high agitation. All but a few of the pigeons were flying back and forth in their cages, near to hysteria. Had the rats been in, Cal wondered? He cast around for any damage, but there was no visible sign of what had fuelled this furore.

He'd never seen them so excited. For fully half a minute he stood in bewilderment, watching their display, the din of their wings making his head reel, before deciding to step into the largest of the cages and claim the prize birds from the mêlée before they did themselves damage.

He unlatched the cage, and had opened it no more than two or three inches when one of last year's champions, a normally sedate cock known, as were they all, by his number – 33 – flew at the gap. Shocked by the speed of the bird's approach, Cal let the door go, and in the seconds between his fingers slipping from the latch and his retrieval of it, 33 was out.

'Damn you!' Cal shouted, cursing himself as much as the bird, for he'd left the door of the loft itself ajar, and – apparently careless of what harm he might do himself in his bid – 33 was making for the sky.

In the few moments it took Cal to latch the cage again, the bird was through the door and away. Cal went in stumbling pursuit, but by the time he got back into the open air 33 was already fluttering up above the garden. At roof-height he flew around in three ever larger circles, as if orienting himself. Then

7

he seemed to fix his objective and took off in a North-North-Easterly direction.

A rapping drew Cal's attention, and he looked down to see his father standing at the window, mouthing something to him. There was more animation on Brendan's harried face than Cal had seen in months; the escape of the bird seemed to have temporarily roused him from his despondency. Moments later he was at the back door, asking what had happened. Cal had no time for explanation.

'*It's off* –' he yelled.

Then, keeping his eye on the sky as he went, he started down the path at the side of the house.

When he reached the front the bird was still in sight. Cal leapt the fence and crossed Chariot Street at a run, determined to give chase. It was, he knew, an all but hopeless pursuit. With a tail wind a prime bird could reach a top speed of 70 miles an hour, and though 33 had not raced for the best part of a year he could still easily outpace a human runner. But he also knew he couldn't go back to his father without making some effort to track the escapee, however futile.

At the bottom of the street he lost sight of his quarry behind the rooftops, and so made a detour to the foot bridge that crossed the Woolton Road, mounting the steps three and four at a time. From the top he was rewarded with a good view of the city. North towards Woolton Hill, and off East, and South-East, over Allerton towards Hunt's Cross. Row upon row of council house roofs presented themselves, shimmering in the fierce heat of the afternoon, the herringbone rhythm of the close-packed streets rapidly giving way to the industrial wastelands of Speke.

Cal could see the pigeon too, though he was a rapidly diminishing dot.

It mattered little, for from this elevation 33's destination was perfectly apparent. Less than two miles from the bridge the air was full of wheeling birds, drawn to the spot no doubt by some concentration of food in the area. Every year brought at least one such day, when the ant or gnat population suddenly boomed, and the bird life of the city was united in its

8

gluttony. Gulls up from the mud banks of the Mersey, flying tip to tip with thrush and jackdaw and starling, all content to join the jamboree while the summer still warmed their backs.

This, no doubt, was the call 33 had heard. Bored with his balanced diet of maize and maple peas, tired of the pecking order of the loft and the predictability of each day – the bird had wanted out; wanted up and away. A day of high life; of food that had to be chased a little, and tasted all the better for that; of the companionship of wild things. All this went through Cal's head, in a vague sort of way, while he watched the circling flocks.

It would be perfectly impossible, he knew, to locate an individual bird amongst these riotous thousands. He would have to trust that 33 would be content with his feast on the wing, and when he was sated do as he was trained to do, and come home. Nevertheless, the sheer spectacle of so many birds exercised a peculiar fascination, and crossing the bridge, Cal began to make his way towards the epicentre of this feathered cyclone.

## II

## THE PURSUERS

The woman at the window of the Hanover Hotel drew back the grey curtain and looked down at the street below.

'Is it possible . . . ?' she murmured to the shadows that held court in the corner of the room. There was no answer to her question forthcoming, nor did there need to be. Unlikely as it seemed the trail had incontestably led here, to this dog-tired city, lying bruised and neglected beside a river that had once borne slave ships and cotton ships and could now barely carry its own weight out to sea. To Liverpool.

'Such a place,' she said. A minor dust-dervish had whipped itself up in the street outside, lifting antediluvian litter into the air.

'Why are you so surprised?' said the man who half lay and half sat on the bed, pillows supporting his impressive frame, hands linked behind his heavy head. The face was wide, the features upon it almost too expressive, like those of an actor who'd made a career of crowd-pleasers, and grown expert in cheap effects. His mouth, which knew a thousand variations of the smile, found one that suited his leisurely mood, and said:

'They've led us quite a dance. But we're almost there. Don't you feel it? I do.'

The woman glanced back at this man. He had taken off the jacket that had been her most loving gift to him, and thrown it over the back of the chair. The shirt beneath was sweat-

10

sodden at the armpits, and the flesh of his face looked waxen in the afternoon light. Despite all she felt for him – and that was enough to make her fearful of computation – he was only human, and today, after so much heat and travel, he wore every one of his fifty-two years plainly. In the time they had been together, pursuing the Fugue, she had lent him what strength she could, as he in his turn had lent her his wit, and his expertise in surviving this realm. The Kingdom of the Cuckoo, the Families had always called it, this wretched human world which she had endured for vengeance's sake.

But very soon now the chase would be over. Shadwell – the man on the bed – would profit by what they were so very close to finding, and she, seeing their quarry besmirched and sold into slavery, would be revenged. Then she would leave the Kingdom to its grimy ways, and happily.

She turned her attentions back to the street. Shadwell was right. They had been led a dance. But the music would cease soon enough.

From where Shadwell lay Immacolata's silhouette was clear against the window. Not for the first time his thoughts turned to the problem of how he would sell this woman. It was a purely academic exercise, of course, but one that pressed his skills to their limits.

He was by profession a salesman; that had been his business since his early adolescence. More than his business, his genius. He prided himself that there was nothing alive or dead he could not find a buyer for. In his time he had been a raw sugar merchant, a small arms salesman, a seller of dolls, dogs, life-insurance, salvation rags and lighting fixtures. He had trafficked in Lourdes water and *hashish*, in Chinese screens and patented cures for constipation. Amongst this parade of items there had of course been frauds and fakes aplenty, but nothing, *nothing* that he had not been able to foist upon the public sooner or later, either by seduction or intimidation.

But *she* – Immacolata, the not quite woman he had shared his every waking moment with these past many years – she, he knew, would defy his talents as a salesman.

For one, she was paradoxical, and the buying public had

11

little taste for that. They wanted their merchandise shorn of ambiguity: made simple and safe. She was not safe; oh, certainly not; not with her terrible rage and her still more terrible alleluias; nor was she simple. Beneath the incandescent beauty of her face, behind eyes that concealed centuries yet could be so immediate they drew blood, beneath the deep olive skin, the Jewess' skin, there lay feelings that would blister the air if given vent.

She was too much herself to be sold, he decided – not for the first time – and told himself to forget the exercise. It was one he could never hope to master; why should he torment himself with it?

Immacolata turned away from the window.

'Are you rested now?' she asked him.

'It was you wanted to get out of the sun,' he reminded her. 'I'm ready to start whenever you are. Though I haven't a clue where we begin . . .'

'That's not so difficult,' Immacolata said. 'Remember what my sister prophesied? Events are close to crisis-point.'

As she spoke, the shadows in the corner of the room stirred afresh, and Immacolata's two dead sisters showed their ethereal skirts. Shadwell had never been easy in their presence, and they in their turn had always despised him. But the old one, the Hag, the Beldam, had skills as an oracle, no doubt of that. What she saw in the filth of her sister, the Magdalene's after-birth, was usually proved correct.

'The Fugue can't stay hidden much longer,' said Immacolata. 'As soon as it's moved it creates vibrations. It can't help itself. So much life, pressed into such a hideway.'

'And do you feel any of these . . . vibrations?' said Shadwell, swinging his legs over the edge of the bed and standing up.

Immacolata shook her head. 'No. Not yet. But we should be ready.'

Shadwell picked up his jacket, and slipped it on. The lining shimmered, casting filaments of seduction across the room. By their momentary brightness he caught sight of the Magdalene and the Hag. The old woman covered her eyes against the spillage from the jacket, fearful of its power. The Magdalene did

12

not concern herself; her lids had long ago been sewn closed over sockets blind from birth.

'When the movements begin it may take an hour or two to pin-point the location,' said Immacolata.

'An hour?' Shadwell replied.

– the pursuit that had finally led them here seemed today to have been a lifetime long –

'I can wait an hour.'

# III

## WHO MOVED THE GROUND?

### 1

The birds did not stop their spiralling over the city as Cal approached. For every one that flew off, another three or four joined the throng.

The phenomenon had not gone unnoticed. People stood on the pavement and on doorsteps, hands shading their eyes from the glare of the sky, and stared heavenwards. Opinions were everywhere ventured as to the reason for this congregation. Cal didn't stop to offer his, but threaded his way through the maze of streets, on occasion having to double back and find a new route, but by degrees getting closer to the hub.

And now, as he approached, it became apparent that his first theory had been incorrect. The birds were not feeding. There was no swooping nor squabbling over a six-legged crumb, nor any sign in the lower air of the insect life that might have attracted these numbers. The birds were simply circling. Some of the smaller species, sparrows and finches, had tired of flying and now lined rooftops and fences, leaving their larger brethren — carrion-crows, magpies, gulls — to occupy the heights. There was no scarcity of pigeons here either; the wild variety banking and wheeling in flocks of fifty or more, their shadows rippling across the rooftops. There were some domesticated birds too, doubtless escapees like 33. Canaries and budgerigars: birds called from their millet and their bells by whatever force had summoned the others. For these birds being here was effectively suicide. Though their fellows were at present too excited by this ritual to take note of the pets in their midst, they would not be so indifferent when the circling spell no longer bound them. They would be cruel and quick. They'd fall on the canaries and the budgerigars and peck out their eyes, killing them for the crime of being tamed.

But for now, the parliament was at peace. It mounted the air, higher, ever higher, busying the sky.

The pursuit of this spectacle had led Cal to a part of the city he'd seldom explored. Here the plain square houses of the council estates gave way to a forlorn and eerie no-man's-land, where streets of once-fine, three-storey terraced houses still stood, inexplicably preserved from the bulldozer, surrounded by areas levelled in expectation of a boom-time that had never come; islands in a dust sea.

It was one of these streets – *Rue Street* the sign read – that seemed the point over which the flocks were focused. There were more sizeable assemblies of exhausted birds here than in any of the adjacent streets; they twittered and preened themselves on the eaves and chimney tops and television aerials.

Cal scanned sky and roof alike, making his way along Rue Street as he did so. And there – a thousand to one chance – he caught sight of his bird. A solitary pigeon, dividing a cloud of sparrows. Years of watching the sky, waiting for pigeons to return from races, had given him an eagle eye; he could recognize a particular bird by a dozen idiosyncrasies in its flight pattern. He had found 33; no doubt of it. But even as he watched, the bird disappeared behind the roofs of Rue Street.

He gave chase afresh, finding a narrow alley which cut between the terraced houses half way along the road, and let on to the larger alley that ran behind the row. It had not been well kept. Piles of household refuse had been dumped along its length; orphan dustbins overturned, their contents scattered.

But twenty yards from where he stood there was work going on. Two removal men were manœuvring an armchair out of the yard behind one of the houses, while a third stared up at the birds. Several hundred were assembled on the yard

15

walls and window sills and railings. Cal wandered along the alley, scrutinizing this assembly for pigeons. He found a dozen or more amongst the multitude, but not the one he sought.

'What d'you make of it?'

He had come within ten yards of the removal men, and one of them, the idler, was addressing the question to him.

'I don't know,' he answered honestly.

'Maybe they're goin' to migrate,' said the younger of the two armchair carriers, letting drop his half of the burden and staring up at the sky.

'Don't be an idiot, Shane,' said the other man, a West Indian. His name – Gideon – was emblazoned on the back of his overalls. 'Why'd they migrate in the middle of the fuckin' summer?'

'Too hot,' was the idler's reply. 'That's what it is. Too fuckin' hot. It's cookin' their brains up there.'

Gideon had now put down his half of the armchair and was leaning against the back yard wall, applying a flame to the half-spent cigarette he'd fished from his top pocket.

'Wouldn't be bad, would it?' he mused. 'Being a bird. Gettin' yer end away all spring, then fuckin' off to the South of France as soon as yer get a chill on yer bollocks.'

'They don't live long,' said Cal.

'Do they not?' said Gideon, drawing on his cigarette. He shrugged. 'Short and sweet,' he said. 'That'd suit me.'

Shane plucked at the half-dozen blond hairs of his would-be moustache. 'Yer know somethin' about birds, do yer?' he said to Cal.

'Only pigeons.'

'Race 'em, do you?'

'Once in a while –'

'Me brother-in-law keeps whippets,' said the third man, the idler. He looked at Cal as though this coincidence verged on the miraculous, and would now fuel hours of debate. But all Cal could think of to say was:

'Dogs.'

'That's right,' said the other man, delighted that they were of one accord on the issue. 'He's got five. Only one died.'

16

'Pity,' said Cal.

'Not really. It was fuckin' blind in one eye and couldn't see in the other.'

The man guffawed at this observation, which promptly brought the exchange to a dead halt. Cal turned his attention back to the birds, and he grinned to see – there on the upper window-ledge of the house – *his* bird.

'I see him,' he said.

Gideon followed his gaze. 'What's that then?'

'My pigeon. He escaped.' Cal pointed. 'There. In the middle of the sill. See him?'

All three now looked.

'Worth something is he?' said the idler.

'Trust you, Bazo,' Shane commented.

'Just asking,' Bazo replied.

'He's won prizes,' said Cal, with some pride. He was keeping his eyes glued to 33, but the pigeon showed no sign of wanting to fly; just preened his wing feathers, and once in a while turned a beady eye up to the sky.

'Stay there . . .' Cal told the bird under his breath, '. . . don't move.' Then, to Gideon: 'Is it all right if I go in? Try and catch him?'

'Help yourself. The auld girl who had the house's been carted off to hospital. We're taking the furniture to pay her bills.'

Cal ducked through into the yard, negotiating the bric-a-brac the trio had dumped there, and went into the house.

It was a shambles inside. If the occupant had ever owned anything of substance it had long since been removed. The few pictures still hanging were worthless; the furniture was old, but not old enough to have come back into fashion; the rugs, cushions and curtains so aged they were fit only for the incinerator. The walls and ceilings were stained by many years' accrual of smoke, its source the candles that sat on every shelf and sill, stalactites of yellowed wax depending from them.

He made his way through the warren of pokey, dark rooms, and into the hallway. The scene was just as dispiriting here. The brown linoleum rucked up and torn, and everywhere the

17

pervasive smell of must and dust and creeping rot. She was well out of this squalid place, Cal thought, wherever she was; better off in hospital, where at least the sheets were dry.

He began to climb the stairs. It was a curious sensation, ascending into the murk of the upper storey, becoming blinder stair by stair, with the sound of birds scurrying across the slates above his skull, and beyond that the muted cries of gull and crow. Though it was no doubt self-deception, he seemed to hear their voices *circling*, as though this very place were the centre of their attentions. An image appeared in his head, of a photograph from *National Geographical*. A study of stars, taken with a slow release camera, the pin-point lights describing circles as they moved, or appeared to move, across the sky, with the Pole Star, the Nail of Heaven, steady in their midst.

The wheeling sound, and the picture it evoked, began to dizzy him. He suddenly felt weak, even afraid.

This was no time for such frailties, he chided himself. He had to claim the bird before it flew off again. He picked up his pace. At the top of the stairs he manœuvred past several items of bedroom furniture, and opened one of the several doors that he was presented with. The room he had chosen was adjacent to the one whose sill 33 occupied. Sun streamed through the curtainless window; the stale heat brought fresh sweat to his brow. The room had been emptied of furniture, the only souvenir of occupancy a calendar for the year 1961. On it, a photograph of a lion beneath a tree, its shaggy, monolithic head laid on vast paws, its gaze contemplative.

Cal went out on to the landing again, selected another door, and was this time delivered into the right room. There, beyond the grimy glass, was the pigeon.

Now it was all a question of tactics. He had to be careful not to startle the bird. He approached the window cautiously. On the sun-drenched sill 33 cocked its head, and blinked its eye, but made no move. Cal held his breath, and put his hands on the frame to haul the window up, but there was no budging it. A quick perusal showed why. The frame had been sealed up years ago, a dozen or more nails driven deep into the wood.

18

A primitive form of crime prevention, but no doubt reassuring to an old woman living alone.

From the yard below, he heard Gideon's voice. Peering down, he could just see the trio dragging a large rolled-up carpet out of the house, Gideon giving orders in a ceaseless stream.

'– to my left, Bazo. *Left!* Don't you know which is your left?'

'I'm going left.'

'Not *your* left, yer idiot. *My* left.'

The bird on the sill was undisturbed by this commotion. It seemed quite happy on its perch.

Cal headed back downstairs, deciding as he went that the only option remaining was to climb up on to the yard wall and see if he couldn't coax the bird down from there. He cursed himself for not having brought a pocketful of grain. Coos and sweet words would just have to do.

By the time he stepped out into the heat of the yard once more, the removal men had successfully manhandled the carpet out of the house, and were taking a rest after their exertions.

'No luck?' said Shane, seeing Cal emerge.

'The window won't budge. I'll have to try from down here.'

He caught a deprecating look from Bazo. 'You'll never reach the bugger from here,' the man said, scratching the expanse of beer-gut that gleamed between T-shirt and belt.

'I'll try from the wall,' said Cal.

'Watch yerself –' Gideon said.

'Thanks.'

'– you could break yer back –'

Using pits in the crumbling mortar for footholds, Cal hauled himself up on to the eight-foot wall that divided this yard from its neighbour.

The sun was hot on his neck and the top of his head, and something of the giddiness he'd experienced climbing the stairs returned. He straddled the wall as though it were a horse, until he got used to the height. Though the perch was the width of a brick, and offered ample enough walking space, heights and he had never been happy companions.

'Looks like it's been a nice piece of handiwork,' said Gideon, in the yard below. Cal glanced down to see that the West Indian was now on his haunches beside the carpet, which he'd rolled out far enough to expose an elaborately woven border.

Bazo wandered over to where Gideon crouched, and scrutinized the property. He was balding, Cal could see, his hair scrupulously pasted down with oil to conceal the spot.

'Pity it's not in better nick,' said Shane.

'Hold yer horses,' said Bazo. 'Let's have a better look.'

Cal returned his attention to the problem of standing upright. At least the carpet would divert his audience for a few moments; long enough, he prayed, for him to get to his feet. There was no breath of wind here to alleviate the fury of the sun; he could feel sweat trickle down his torso and glue his underwear to his buttocks. Gingerly, he started to stand, bringing one leg up into a kneeling position – both hands clinging to the brick like grim death.

From below, there were murmurs of approval as more of the carpet was exposed to light.

'Look at the work in that,' said Gideon.

'Are you thinkin' what I'm thinkin'?' said Bazo, his voice lowered.

'I don't know 'til you tell me,' came Gideon's reply.

'What say we take it down to Gilchrist's. We might get a price for this.'

'The Chief'll know it's gone,' Shane protested.

'Keep it down,' said Bazo, quietly reminding his companions of Cal's presence. In fact Cal was far too concerned with his inept tight-rope act to bother himself with their petty theft. He had finally got the soles of both feet up on to the top of the wall, and was about to try standing up.

In the yard, the conversation went on.

'Take the far end, Shane, let's have a look at the whole thing . . .'

'D'you think it's Persian?'

'Haven't a fuckin' clue.'

20

Very slowly, Cal stood upright, his arms extended at ninety degrees from his body. Feeling as stable as he was ever going to feel, he chanced a quick look up at the window sill. The bird was still there.

From below he heard the sound of the carpet being unrolled further, the men's grunts punctuated with words of admiration.

Ignoring their presence as best he could, he took his first faltering step along the wall.

'Hey there . . .' he murmured to the escapee '. . . remember me?'

33 took no notice. Cal advanced a second trembling step, and a third, his confidence growing. He was getting the trick of this balancing business now.

'Come on down,' he coaxed, a prosaic Romeo.

The bird finally seemed to recognize his owner's voice, and cocked his head in Cal's direction.

'Here, boy . . .' Cal said, tentatively raising his hand towards the window as he risked another step.

At that instant either his foot slipped or the brick gave way beneath his heel. He heard himself loose a yell of alarm, which panicked the birds lining the sill. They were up and off, their wing-beats ironic applause, as he flailed on the wall. His panicked gaze went first to his feet, then to the yard below.

No, not the yard; that had disappeared. It was the carpet he saw. It had been entirely unrolled, and it filled the yard from wall to wall.

What happened next occupied mere seconds, but either his mind was lightning fast, or the moments played truant, for it seemed he had all the time he needed –

Time to appreciate the startling intricacy of the design laid out beneath him; an awesome proliferation of exquisitely executed detail. Age had bled brightness from the colours of the weave, mellowing vermilion to rose, and cobalt to a chalky blue, and here and there the carpet had become thread-bare, but from where Cal teetered the effect was still overwhelming.

Every inch of the carpet was worked with motifs. Even the

21

border brimmed with designs, all subtly different from their neighbours. The effect was not over-busy; every detail was clear to Cal's feasting eyes. In one place a dozen motifs congregated as if banded together; in another, they stood apart like rival siblings. Some kept their station along the border; others spilled into the main field, as if eager to join the teeming throng there.

In the field itself ribbons of colour described arabesques across a background of sultry browns and greens, forms that were pure abstraction – bright jottings from some wild man's diary – jostling with stylized flora and fauna. But this complexity paled beside the centre piece of the carpet: a huge medallion, its colours as various as a summer garden, into which a hundred subtle geometries had been cunningly woven, so that the eye could read each pattern as flower or theorem, order or turmoil, and find each choice echoed somewhere in the grand design.

He saw all of this in one prodigious glance. In his second the vision laid before him began to change.

From the corner of his eye he registered that the rest of the world – the yard, and the men who'd occupied it, the houses, the wall he'd been toppling from – all were winking out of existence. Suddenly he was hanging in the air, the carpet vaster by the moment beneath him, its glorious configurations filling his head.

The design was shifting, he saw. The knots were restless, trembling to slip themselves, and the colours seemed to be merging into each other, new forms springing from this marriage of dyes.

Implausible as it seemed, the carpet was coming to life.

A landscape – or rather a confusion of landscapes thrown together in fabulous disarray – was emerging from the warp and the weft. Was that not a mountain he could see below him, pressing its head up through a cloud of colour?; and was that not a river?; and could he not hear its roar as it fell in white water torrents into a shadowed gorge?

There was a *world* below him.

And he was suddenly a bird, a wingless bird hovering for a

breathless instant on a balmy, sweet-scented wind, sole witness to the miracle sleeping below.

There was more to claim his eye with every thump of his heart.

A lake, with myriad islands dotting its placid waters like breaching whales. A dappled quilt of fields, their grasses and grains swept by the same tides of air that kept him aloft. Velvet woodland creeping up the sleek flank of a hill, on whose pinnacle a watchtower perched, sun and cloud-shadow drifting across its white walls.

There were other signs of habitation too, though nothing of the people themselves. A cluster of dwellings hugging a river bend; several houses beetling along the edge of a cliff, tempting gravity. And a town too, laid out in a city-planner's nightmare, half its streets hopelessly serpentine, the other half cul-de-sacs.

The same casual indifference to organization was evident everywhere, he saw. Zones temperate and intemperate, fruitful and barren were thrown together in defiance of all laws geological or climatic, as if by a God whose taste was for contradiction.

How fine it would be to walk there, he thought, with so much variety pressed into so little space, not knowing whether turning the next corner would bring ice or fire. Such complexity was beyond the wit of a cartographer. To be there, in that world, would be to live a perpetual adventure.

And at the centre of this burgeoning province, perhaps the most awesome sight of all. A mass of slate-coloured cloud, the innards of which were in perpetual, spiralling motion. The sight reminded him of the birds wheeling above the house in Rue Street – an echo of this greater wheel.

At the thought of them, and the place he'd left behind, he heard their voices – and in that moment the wind that had swept up from the world below, keeping him aloft, faltered.

He felt the horror in his stomach first, and then his bowels: he was going to fall.

The tumult of the birds grew louder, crowing their delight at his descent. He, the usurper of their element; he, who had snatched a glimpse of a miracle, would now be dashed to death upon it.

He started to yell, but the speed of his fall stole the cry from his tongue. The air roared in his ears and tore at his hair. He tried to spread his arms to slow his descent but the attempt instead threw him head over heels, and over again, until he no longer knew earth from sky. There was some mercy in this, he dimly thought. At least he'd be blind to death's proximity. Just tumbling and tumbling until –

– the world went out.

He fell through a darkness unrelieved by stars, the birds still loud in his ears, and hit the ground, hard.

It hurt, and went on hurting, which struck him as odd. Oblivion, he'd always assumed, would be a painless condition. And soundless too. But there were voices.

'Say something . . .' one of them demanded, '. . . if it's only goodbye.'

There was laughter now.

He opened his eyes a hair's breadth. The sun was blindingly bright, until Gideon's bulk eclipsed it.

'Have you broken anything?' the man wanted to know.

Cal opened his eyes a fraction wider.

'Say something, man.'

He raised his head a few inches, and looked about him. He was lying in the yard, on the carpet.

'What happened?'

'You fell off the wall,' said Shane.

'Must have missed your footing,' Gideon suggested.

'Fell,' Cal said, pulling himself up into a sitting position. He felt nauseous.

'Don't think you've done much damage,' said Gideon. 'A few scrapes, that's all.'

Cal looked down at himself, verifying the man's remark. He'd taken skin off his right arm from wrist to elbow, and there was tenderness down his body where he'd hit the ground, but there were no sharp pains. The only real harm was to his dignity, and that was seldom fatal.

He got to his feet, wincing, eyes to the ground. The weave

was playing dumb. There was no tell-tale tremor in the rows of knots, no sign that hidden heights and depths were about to make themselves known. Nor was there any sign from the others that they'd seen anything miraculous. To all intents and purposes the carpet beneath his feet was simply that: a carpet.

He hobbled towards the yard gate, offering a muttered thanks to Gideon. As he stepped out into the alley, Bazo said:

'Yer bird flew off.'

Cal gave a small shrug and went on his way.

What had he just experienced? An hallucination, brought on by too much sun or too little breakfast? If so, it had been startlingly real. He looked up at the birds, still circling overhead. *They* sensed something untoward here too; that was why they'd gathered. Either that, or they and he were sharing the same delusion.

All, in sum, that he could be certain of was his bruising. That, and the fact that though he was standing no more than two miles from his father's house, in the city in which he'd spent his entire life, he felt as homesick as a lost child.

# IV

## CONTACT

As Immacolata crossed the width of heat-raddled pavement between the steps of the hotel and the shaded interior of Shadwell's Mercedes, she suddenly let out a cry. Her hand went to her head, the sunglasses she always wore in the Kingdom's public places falling from her face.

Shadwell was swiftly out of the car, and opening the door, but his passenger shook her head.

'Too bright,' she murmured, and stumbled back through the swing-doors into the vestibule of the hotel. It was deserted. Shadwell came in swift pursuit, to find Immacolata standing as far from the door as her legs would carry her. The wraith-sisters were guarding her — their presences distressing the stale air — but he couldn't prevent himself from snatching the opportunity, in the guise of legitimate concern, to reach and touch the woman. Such contact was anathema to her, and a joy to him made more potent because she forbade it. He was obliged therefore to exploit any occasion when he might pass such contact off as accidental.

The ghosts chilled his skin with their disapproval, but Immacolata was quite able to protect her inviolability. She turned, her eyes raging at his presumption. He immediately removed his hand from her arm, his fingers tingling. He would count the minutes until he had a private moment in which to put them to his lips.

'I'm sorry,' he said. 'I was concerned.'

A voice intervened. The receptionist had emerged from his room, a copy of *Sporting Life* in hand.

'Can I be of help?' he offered.

'No, no . . .' said Shadwell.

The receptionist's eyes were not on him, however, but on Immacolata.

'Touch of heat stroke, is it?' he said.

'Maybe,' said Shadwell. Immacolata had moved to the bottom of the stairs, out of the receptionist's enquiring gaze. 'Thank you for your concern –'

The receptionist made a face, and returned to his armchair. Shadwell went to Immacolata. She had found the shadows; or the shadows had found her.

'What happened?' he said. 'Was it just the sun?'

She didn't look at him, but she deigned to speak.

'I felt the Fugue . . .' she said, so softly he had to hold his breath to catch her words '. . . then something else.'

He waited for further news from her, but none came. Then, as he was about to break the silence, she said:

'At the back of my throat . . .' She swallowed, as if to dislodge some remembered bitterness '. . . the Scourge . . .'

The Scourge? Had he heard her correctly?

Either Immacolata sensed his doubt, or shared it, for she said:

'It was *there*, Shadwell,'

and when she spoke even her extraordinary self-control couldn't quite tame the flutter in her voice.

'Surely you're mistaken.'

She made a tiny shake of her head.

'It's dead and gone,' he said.

Her face could have been chiselled from stone. Only her lips moved, and he longed for them, despite the thoughts they shaped.

'A power like that doesn't die,' she said. 'It can't ever die. It sleeps. It waits.'

'What for? *Why?*'

'Till the Fugue wakes, maybe,' she said.

Her eyes had lost their gold; become silvery. Motes of the

27

menstruum, turning like dust in a sun-beam, dropped from her lashes and evaporated inches from his face. He'd never seen her like this before, so close to exposing her feelings. The spectacle of her vulnerability aroused him beyond words. His prick was so hard it ached. She was apparently dead to his arousal however; or else chose to ignore it. The Magdalene, the blind sister, was not so indifferent. She, Shadwell knew, had an appetite for what a man might spill, and horrid purposes to put it to. Even now he saw her form coagulating in a recess in the wall, one hunger from scalp to sole.

'I saw a wilderness,' Immacolata said, calling Shadwell's attention from the Magdalene's advances. 'Bright sun. *Terrible* sun. The emptiest place on earth.'

'And that's where the Scourge is now?'

She nodded. 'It's sleeping. I think . . . it's forgotten itself.'

'It'll stay that way, then, won't it?' Shadwell replied. 'Who the hell's going to wake it?'

His words failed to convince even himself.

'Look –' he said, '– we'll find the Fugue and sell it before the Scourge can so much as roll over. We haven't come so far to stop now.'

Immacolata said nothing. Her eyes were still fixed on that nowhere she'd sighted, or tasted – or both – minutes earlier.

Only very dimly did Shadwell comprehend what forces were at work here. Finally, he was only a Cuckoo – a human being – and that limited his vision; for which fact, as now, he was sometimes grateful.

One thing he *did* comprehend: the Fugue trailed legends. In the years of their search he'd heard it reported so many ways, from cradle-song to death-bed confession, and he'd long ago given up attempting to sort fact from fiction. All that mattered was that the many and the mighty longed for that place, spoke of it in their prayers, without knowing – most of them – that it was real; or had been. And what a profit he would turn when he had that dream on the block; there had never been a sale its like, or ever would be again. They could not give up now. Not for fear of something lost in time and sleep.

'It *knows*, Shadwell,' Immacolata said. 'Even in its sleep, it knows.'

Had he had the words to persuade her from her fear she would have been contemptuous of them. Instead, he played the pragmatist.

'The sooner we find the carpet and dispose of it the happier we'll all be,' he said.

The response seemed to stir her from the wilderness.

'Maybe in a while,' she replied, her eyes flickering towards him for the first time since they'd stepped off the street. 'Maybe then we'll go looking.'

All sign of the menstruum had abruptly vanished. The moment of doubt had passed, and the old certainty was back. She would pursue the Fugue to the end, he knew, as they had always planned. No rumour – even of the Scourge – would deflect her from her malice.

'We may lose the trail if we don't hurry.'

'I doubt that,' she said. 'We'll wait. Until the heat dies down.'

Ah, so this was to be his punishment for that ill-considered touch. It was *his* heat she made mocking reference to, not that of the city outside. He would be obliged to wait her pleasure, as he had waited before, and bear his stripes in silence. Not just because she alone could track the Fugue by the rhythm of its woven life, but because to wait another hour in her company, bathing in the scent of her breath, was an agony he would gladly endure.

For him it was a ritual of crime and punishment which would keep him hard for the rest of the day.

For her, the power his desire lent her remained a diverting curiosity. Furnaces, after all, grew cold if left unstoked. Even stars went out after a millennium. But the lust of Cuckoos, like so much else about that species, defied all the rules. The less it was fed, the hotter it became.

# V

## BEFORE THE DARK

### 1

In all, Suzanna had probably met her maternal grandmother less than a dozen times. Even as a child, before she'd fully understood the words, she'd been taught that the old woman was not to be trusted, though she could not remember ever hearing a reason offered as to why. The mud had stuck however. Though in her early adulthood – she was now 24 – she had learned to view her parents' prejudices with a critical eye, and come to suspect that whatever their anxiety regarding her grandmother it was likely to be perfectly irrational – she could nevertheless not entirely forget the mythology that had grown up around Mimi Laschenski.

The very name was a stumbling block. To the ear of a child it sounded more like a faery-tale curse than a name. And indeed there had been much about the woman that supported such a fiction. Suzanna remembered Mimi as being small, with skin that was always slightly jaundiced, her black hair (which with hindsight, was probably dyed) drawn back tightly from a face which she doubted capable of a smile. Perhaps Mimi had reason for grief. Her first husband, who had been some sort of circus performer, had disappeared before the Great War; run away, the family gossip went, because Mimi was such a harridan. The second husband, Suzanna's grandfather, had died of lung cancer in his early forties; smoked himself to death. Since then the old woman had lived in increasingly eccentric isolation, alienated from her children and grandchildren alike, in a house in Liverpool; a house to which – at Mimi's enigmatic request – Suzanna was about to pay a long-delayed visit.

As she drove North she turned over her memories of Mimi, and of that house. She recalled it being substantially larger than her parents' place in Bristol had been; and darker. A house that had not been painted since before the Flood, a stale house; a house in mourning. And the more she remembered, the gloomier she became.

In the private story-book of her head this trip back to Mimi's was a return to the mire of childhood; a reminder not of blissful, careless years, but of an anxious, blinkered state from which adulthood had liberated her. And Liverpool had been that state's metropolis; a city of perpetual dusk, where the air smelt of cold smoke and a colder river. When she thought of it she was a child again, and frightened of dreams.

Of course she'd shrugged off those fears years ago. Here she was, at the wheel of her car, perfect mistress of herself, driving in the fast lane with the sun on her face. What hold could those old anxieties have over her now? Yet as she drove she found herself drawing to her keepsakes from her present life, like talismans to keep that city at bay.

She thought of the studio she'd left behind in London, and the pots she'd left to be glazed and fired when – in just a little while – she got back. She remembered Finnegan, and the flirtatious dinner she'd had with him two nights ago. She thought of her friends, robust and articulate people, any of a dozen of whom she'd trust her life and sanity to. With so much *clarity* to arm her, she could surely re-tread the paths of her childhood and remain untainted. She travelled a broader, brighter highway now.

Yet the memories were still potent.

Some, like her picturing of Mimi and the house, were images she'd recalled before. One in particular, however, emerged from some hidden niche in her head, unvisited since the day she'd sealed it up there.

The episode didn't come, as many had, piece by piece. It flashed before her all at once, in astonishing particularity –

She was six. They were in Mimi's house, she and her mother, and it was November — wasn't it always? — drear and cold. They'd come on one of their rare visits to Gran'ma, a duty which father had always been spared.

She saw Mimi now, sitting in an armchair near to a fire that barely warmed the soot in the grate. Her face — soured and sad to the brink of tragedy — was pale with powder, the brows meticulously plucked, the eyes glittering even in the dour light through the lace curtains.

She spoke; and her soft syllables drowned out the din of the motorway.

*'Suzanna . . .'*

Addressed from the past, she listened.

*'. . . I've something for you.'*

The child's heart had fallen from its place, and thumped around in her belly.

*'Say thank you, Suzie,'* her mother chided.

The child did as she was told.

*'It's upstairs,'* Mimi said, *'in my bedroom. You can go and get it for yourself, can't you? It's all wrapped up, at the bottom of the tall-boy.'*

*'Go on, Suzie.'*

She felt her mother's hand on her arm, pushing her away towards the door.

*'Hurry up now.'*

She glanced at her mother, then back at Mimi. There was no mercy to be had from either: they would have her up those stairs, and no protest would mellow them. She left the room, and went to the bottom of the stairs. They were a mountain-face before her; and the darkness at the summit a terror she tried not to contemplate. In any other house she would not have been so fearful. But this was Mimi's house; Mimi's darkness.

She climbed, her hand clinging to the bannister, certain that something terrible awaited her on every stair. But she reached the top without being devoured, and crossed the landing to her grandmother's bedroom.

The drapes were barely parted: what little light fell between was the colour of old stone. A clock ticked on the mantelpiece, at a quarter the speed of her pulse. On the wall above the clock, gazing down the length of the head-high bed was an oval portrait photograph of a man in a suit that was buttoned up to the neck. And to the left of the mantelpiece, across a carpet that killed her footsteps, was the tall-boy, twice her size and more.

She went to it quickly, determined – now that she was in the room – to do the deed and be out before the ticking had its way with her and slowed her heart 'til it stopped.

Reaching up, she turned the chilly handle. The door opened a little. From inside bloomed the smell of moth-balls, shoe-leather and lavender water. Ignoring the gowns that hung in the shadows she plunged her hand amongst the boxes and tissue paper at the bottom of the tall-boy, hoping to chance upon the present.

In her haste, she pushed the door wide – and something wild-eyed lurched out of the darkness towards her. She screamed. It mocked her, screaming back in her face. Then she was running towards the door, tripping on the carpet in her flight, before hurtling downstairs. Her mother was in the hallway –

'What is it, Suzie?'

There were no words to tell. Instead she threw herself into her mother's arms – though, as ever, there was that moment when they seemed to hesitate before choosing to hold her – and sobbed that she wanted to go home. Nor would she be placated, even after Mimi had gone upstairs and returned saying something about the mirror in the tall-boy door.

They'd left the house soon after that, and, as far as she could now recall, Suzanna had never since entered Mimi's bedroom. As for the gift, it had not been mentioned again.

That was the bare bones of the memory, but there was much else – perfumes; sounds; nuances of light – that fleshed those bones. The incident, once exhumed, had more authority than events both more recent and ostensibly more significant. She could not now conjure – nor would ever, she suspected – the

33

face of the boy to whom she'd given her virginity, but she could remember the smell from Mimi's tall-boy as though it were still in her lungs.

Memory was so strange.

And stranger still, the letter, at the beck of which she was making this journey.

It was the first missive she'd received from her grandmother for over a decade. That fact alone would have been sufficient to have her foresake the studio and come. But the message itself, spindly scrawlings on an air-mail paper page, had lent her further speed. She'd left London as soon as the summons had arrived, as if she'd known and loved the woman who'd written it for half a hundred years.

*Suzanna*, it had begun. Not *Dear* nor *Dearest*. Simply:

> *Suzanna,*
> *Forgive my scribbles. I'm sick at the moment. I feel weak some hours, and not so weak others. Who knows how I'll feel tomorrow?*
> *That's why I'm writing to you now, Suzanna, because I'm afraid of what may happen.*
> *Will you come to see me, at the house? We have very much to say to each other, I think. Things I didn't want to say, but now I have to.*
> *None of this will make much sense to you, I know, but I can't be plain, not in a letter. There are good reasons.*
> *Please come. Things are different to the way I thought they'd be. We can talk, the way we should have talked many years ago.*
>
> > *My love to you, Suzanna,*
> > *Mimi.*

The letter was like a midsummer lake. Its surface placid, but beneath?; such darkness. *Things are different to the way I thought they'd be*, Mimi had written. What did she mean? That life was over too soon, and her sunlit youth had contained no clue as to how bitter mortality would be?

The letter had been delayed, through the vagaries of the

34

postal service, by over a week. When, upon getting it, she'd rung Mimi's house she'd received only the number disconnected tone. Leaving the pots she was making unfinished, she had packed a bag and driven North.

## 2

She went straight to Rue Street, but number eighteen was empty. Sixteen was also deserted, but at the next house a florid woman by the name of Violet Pumphrey was able to offer some explanation. Mimi had fallen sick a few days earlier, and was now in Sefton General Hospital, close to death. Her creditors, which included the Gas and Electricity Boards, and the Council, in addition to a dozen suppliers of food and drink, had immediately made moves to claim some recompense.

'Like vultures, they were,' said Mrs Pumphrey, 'and her not even dead yet. It's shameful. There they were, taking everything they could lay their hands on. Mind you, she was difficult. Hope you don't mind my being plain, love? But she was. Kept herself hidden away in the house most of the time. It was a bloody fortress. That's why they waited, see? 'til she was peggin' out. If they'd tried to get in with her there they'd have still been tryin'.'

Had they taken the tall-boy? Suzanna idly wondered. Thanking Mrs Pumphrey for her help, she went back to have another look at number eighteen − its roof so covered in bird-shit it looked to have had its own private blizzard − then went on to the hospital.

## 3

The nurse wore her show of compassion indifferently well. 'I'm afraid Mrs Laschenski's very sick. Are you a close relative?'

'I'm her grand-daughter. Has anybody else been to see her?'

35

'Not that I know of. There really isn't that much point. She's had a major stroke, Miss —'

'Parrish. Suzanna Parrish.'

'Your grandmother's unconscious most of the time, I'm afraid.'

'I see.'

'So please don't expect too much.'

The nurse led her down a short corridor to a room that was so quiet Suzanna could have heard a petal drop, but that there were no flowers. She wasn't unfamiliar with death rooms; her mother and father had died three years before, within six months of each other. She recognized the scent, and the hush, as soon as she stepped inside.

'She's not been awake today,' said the nurse, as she stood back to let Mimi's visitor approach the bed.

Suzanna's first thought was that there'd been some colossal error. This couldn't be Mimi. This poor woman was too frail; too white. The objection was on the tip of her tongue when she realized that the error was hers. Though the hair of the woman in the bed was so thin that her scalp gleamed through, and the skin of her face was draped slackly on her skull like wet muslin, this was, nevertheless, Mimi. Robbed of power; reduced by some malfunction of nerve and muscle to this unwelcome passivity; but still Mimi.

Tears rose in Suzanna, seeing her grandmother tucked up like a child, except that she was sleeping not in preparation for a new day but for endless night. She had been so fierce, this woman, and so resolute. Now all that strength had gone, and forever.

'Shall I leave you alone awhile?' said the nurse, and without waiting for a reply, withdrew. Suzanna put her hand to her brow to keep the tears at bay.

When she looked again, the old woman's blue-veined lids were flickering open.

For a moment it seemed Mimi's eyes had focused somewhere beyond Suzanna. Then the gaze sharpened, and the look that found Suzanna was as compelling as she had remembered it.

Mimi opened her mouth. Her lips were fever-dried. She passed her tongue across them to little effect. Utterly unnerved, Suzanna approached the bedside.

'Hello,' she said softly. 'It's me. It's Suzanna.'

The old woman's eyes locked with Suzanna's. I *know* who you are, the stare said.

'Would you like some water?'

A tiny frown nicked Mimi's brow.

'Water?' Suzanna repeated, and again, the tiniest of frowns by way of reply. They understood each other.

Suzanna poured an inch of water from the plastic jug on the bedside table into a plastic glass, and took the glass to Mimi's lips. As she did so the old woman lifted her hand a fraction from the crisp sheet and brushed Suzanna's arm. The touch was feather-light, but it sent such a jolt through Suzanna that she almost dropped the glass.

Mimi's breath had suddenly become uneven, and there were tics and twitches around her eyes and mouth as she struggled to shape a word. Her eyes blazed with frustration, but the most she could produce was a grunt in her throat.

'It's all right,' said Suzanna.

The look on the parchment face refused such platitudes. *No*, the eyes said, it *isn't* all right, it's very far from all right. Death is waiting at the door, and I can't even speak the feelings I have.

'What is it?' Suzanna whispered, bending closer to the pillow. The old woman's fingers still trembled against her arm. Her skin tingled at the contact, her stomach churned. 'How can I help you?' she said. It was the vaguest of questions, but she was shooting in the dark.

Mimi's eyes flickered closed for an instant, and the frown deepened. She had given up trying to make words, apparently. Perhaps she had given up entirely.

And then, with a suddenness that made Suzanna cry out, the fingers that rested on her arm slid around her wrist. The grip tightened 'til it hurt. She might have pulled herself free, but she had no time. A subtle marriage of scents was filling

37

her head; dust and tissue-paper and lavender. The tall-boy of course; it was the perfume from the tall-boy. And with that recognition, another certainty: that Mimi was somehow reaching into Suzanna's head and putting the perfume there.

There was an instant of panic – the animal in her responding to this defeat of her mind's autonomy. Then the panic broke before a vision.

Of what, she wasn't certain. A pattern of some kind, a design which melted and reconfigured itself over and over again. Perhaps there was colour in the design, but it was so subtle she could not be certain; subtle too, the shapes evolving in the kaleidoscope.

This, like the perfume, was Mimi's doing. Though reason protested, Suzanna couldn't doubt the truth of that. This image was somehow of vital significance to the old lady. That was why she was using the last drops of her will's resources to have Suzanna share the sight in her mind's eye.

But she had no chance to investigate the vision.

Behind her, the nurse said:

'*Oh my god.*'

The voice broke Mimi's spell, and the patterns burst into a storm of petals, disappearing. Suzanna was left staring down at Mimi's face, their gazes momentarily locking before the old woman lost all control of her wracked body. The hand dropped from Suzanna's wrist, the eyes began to rove back and forth grotesquely; dark spittle ran from the side of her mouth.

'You'd better wait outside,' the nurse said, crossing to press the call button beside the bed.

Suzanna backed off towards the door, distressed by the choking sounds her grandmother was making. A second nurse had appeared.

'Call Doctor Chai,' the first said. Then, to Suzanna, '*Please*, will you wait outside?'

She did as she was told: there was nothing she could do inside but hamper the experts. The corridor was busy; she had to walk twenty yards from the door of Mimi's room before she found somewhere she could take hold of herself.

Her thoughts were like blind runners; they rushed back and

forth wildly, but went nowhere. Time and again, she found memory taking her to Mimi's bedroom in Rue Street, the tall-boy looming before her like some reproachful ghost. What had Gran'ma wanted to tell her, with the scent of lavender?; and how had she managed the extraordinary feat of passing thoughts between them? Was it something she'd always been capable of? If so, what other powers did she own?

'Are you Suzanna Parrish?'

Here at least was a question she could answer.

'Yes.'

'I'm Doctor Chai.'

The face before her was round as a biscuit, and as bland.

'Your grandmother, Mrs Laschenski . . .'

'Yes?'

'. . . there's been a serious deterioration in her condition. Are you her only relative?'

'The only one in this country. My mother and father are dead. She has a son. In Canada.'

'Do you have any way of contacting him?'

'I don't have his telephone number with me . . . but I could get it.'

'I think he should be informed,' said Chai.

'Yes, of course,' said Suzanna. 'What should I . . . ? I mean, can you tell me how long she's going to live?'

The Doctor sighed. 'Anybody's guess,' he said. 'When she came in I didn't think she'd last the night. But she did. And the next. And the next. She's just kept holding on. Her tenacity's really remarkable.' He halted, looking straight at Suzanna. 'My belief is, she was waiting for you.'

'For me?'

'I think so. Your name's the only coherent word she's spoken since she's been here. I don't think she was going to let go until you'd come.'

'I see,' said Suzanna.

'You must be very important to her,' he replied. 'It's good you've seen her. So many of the old folks, you know, die in here and nobody ever seems to care. Where are you staying?'

'I hadn't thought. A hotel, I suppose.'

'Perhaps you'd give us a number to contact you at, should the necessity arise.'

'Of course.'

So saying, he nodded and left her to the runners. They were no less blind for the conversation.

Mimi Laschenski did not love her, as the Doctor had claimed; how could she? She knew nothing of the way her grandchild had grown up; they were like closed books to each other. And yet something in what Chai had said rang true. Perhaps she *had* been waiting, fighting the good fight until her daughter's daughter came to her bedside.

And why? To hold her hand and expend her last ounce of energy giving Suzanna a fragment of some tapestry? It was a pretty gift, but it signified either too much or too little. Whichever, Suzanna did not comprehend it.

She went back to Room Five. The nurse was in attendance, the old lady still as stone on her pillow. Eyes closed, hands laid by her side. Suzanna stared down at the face, slack once more. It could tell her nothing.

She took hold of Mimi's hand and held it for a few moments, tight, then went on her way. She would go back to Rue Street, she decided, and see if being in the house jogged a memory or two.

She'd spent so much time forgetting her childhood, putting it where it couldn't call the bluff of hard-won maturity. And now, with the boxes sealed, what did she find? A mystery that defied her adult self, and coaxed her back into the past in search of a solution.

She remembered the face in the tall-boy mirror, that had sent her sobbing down the stairs.

Was it waiting still? And was it still her own?

# VI

## MAD MOONEY

### 1

Cal was frightened as he had never been frightened in his life before. He sat in his room, the door locked, and shook.

The shaking had begun a few minutes after events at Rue Street, almost twenty-four hours ago now, and it hadn't shown much sign of stopping since. Sometimes it made his hands tremble so much he could hardly hold the glass of whisky he'd nursed through an all but sleepless night, other times it made his teeth chatter. But most of the shaking didn't go on outside, it was *in*. It was as if the pigeons had got into his belly somehow, and were flapping their wings against his innards.

And all because he'd seen something wonderful, and he knew in his bones that his life would never be the same again. How could it? He'd climbed the sky and looked down on the secret place that he'd been waiting since childhood to find.

He'd always been a solitary child, as much through choice as circumstance, happiest when he could unshackle his imagination and let it wander. It took little to get such journeys started. Looking back, it seemed he'd spent half his school days gazing out of the window, transported by a line of poetry whose meaning he couldn't quite unearth, or the sound of someone singing in a distant classroom, into a world more pungent and more remote than the one he knew. A world whose scents were carried to his nostrils by winds mysteriously warm in a chill December; whose creatures paid him homage on certain nights at the foot of his bed, and whose peoples he conspired with in sleep.

But despite the familiarity of this place, the comfort he felt there, its precise nature and location remained elusive, and though he'd read every book he could find that promised some rare territory, he always came away disappointed. They were too perfect, those childhood kingdoms; all honey and summer.

The true Wonderland was not like that, he knew. It was as much shadow as sunlight, and its mysteries could only be unveiled when your wits were about used up and your mind close to cracking.

That was why he trembled now, for that was how he felt. Like a man whose head was about to split.

## 2

He'd woken early, gone downstairs and cooked himself a fried egg and bacon sandwich, then sat with the ruins of his gluttony until he heard his father stirring above. He quickly called the firm, and told Wilcox that he was sick, and wouldn't be in work today. He told the same to Brendan – who was about his morning ablutions and, with the door locked, couldn't see the ashen, anxious face his son was wearing this morning. Then, these duties done, he went back to his room and sat on his bed to examine the events at Rue Street afresh, hoping that the nature of yesterday's mysteries could eventually be made to come clear.

It did little good. Whichever way he turned events they seemed impervious to rational explanation, and he was left only with the same razor-sharp memory of the experience and the ache of longing that came with it.

Everything he'd ever wanted had been in that land; he knew it. Everything his education had taught him to disbelieve – all miracles, all mystery, all blue shadow and sweet-breathed spirits. All the pigeon knew, all the wind knew, all the human world had once grasped and now forgotten, all of it was waiting in that place. He'd seen it with his own eyes.

Which probably made him insane.

How else could he explain an hallucination of such precision and complexity? No, he was insane. And why not? He had lunacy in his blood. His father's father, Mad Mooney, ended his life crazy as a coot. The man had been a poet, according to Brendan, though tales of his life and times had been forbidden in Chariot Street. *Hush your nonsense*, Eileen had always said, whenever Brendan mentioned the man, though whether this taboo was against Poetry, Delirium or the Irish Cal had never decided. Whichever, it was an edict his father had often broken when his wife's back was turned, for Brendan was fond of Mad Mooney and his verses. Cal had even learned a few, at his father's knee. And now here he was, carrying on that family tradition: seeing visions and crying into his whisky.

The question was: to tell or not to tell. To speak what he'd seen, and endure the laughter and the sly looks, or to keep it hidden. Part of him badly wanted to talk, to spill everything to somebody (Brendan, even) and see what they made of it. But another part said: be quiet, be careful. Wonderland doesn't come to those who blab about it, only to those who keep their silence, and *wait*.

So that's what he did. He sat, and shook, and waited.

3

Wonderland didn't turn up, but Geraldine did, and she was in no mood for lunatics. Cal heard her voice in the hall below; heard Brendan telling her that Cal was ill, and didn't want to be disturbed, heard *her* tell Brendan that she intended to see Cal whether he was sick or not; then she was at the door.

'Cal?'

She tried the handle, found the door locked and rapped on it. 'Cal? It's me. Wake up.'

He feigned bleariness, aided by a tongue now well whisky-sodden.

43

'Who is it?' he said.

'Why's the door locked? It's *me*. Geraldine.'

'I'm not feeling too good.'

'Let me in, Cal.'

He knew better than to argue with her in such a mood. He shambled to the door, and turned the key.

'You look terrible,' she said, her voice mellowing as soon as she set eyes on him. 'What's wrong with you?'

'I'm all right,' he protested. 'Really. I just had a fall.'

'Why didn't you ring me? I was expecting you at the wedding rehearsal last night. Had you forgotten?'

The following Saturday Geraldine's elder sister Teresa was to marry the love of her life, a good Catholic boy whose fertility could scarcely be in question: his beloved was four months pregnant. Her swelling belly was not being allowed to over-shadow proceedings however: the wedding was to be a grand affair. Cal, who'd been courting Geraldine for two years, was a valued guest, given the general expectation that he'd be the next to exchange vows with one of Norman Kellaway's four daughters. Doubtless his missing the rehearsal had been viewed as minor heresy.

'I did remind you, Cal,' Geraldine said. 'You know how important it is to me.'

'I had a bit of trouble,' he told her. 'I fell off a wall.'

She looked incredulous.

'What were you doing climbing on a wall?' she said, as though at his age he should be well beyond such indignities.

He told her briefly about the escape of 33, and the chase to Rue Street. It was a bowdlerized account, of course. In it there was no mention of the carpet or what he'd seen there.

'Did you find the bird?' she asked, when he'd finished recounting the chase.

'In a manner of speaking,' he told her. In fact, he'd come home to Chariot Street, only to be told by Brendan that 33 had flown back to the loft in the late afternoon, and was now back beside his speckled wife. This he told Geraldine.

'So you missed the rehearsal looking for a pigeon that came home anyway?' she said.

44

He nodded. 'But you know how Dad loves his birds,' he said.

Mention of Brendan softened Geraldine further still; she and Cal's father had been fast friends since Cal had first introduced them. 'She sparkles,' his father had told Cal, 'hold on to her, 'cause if you don't, somebody else will.' Eileen had never been so certain. She'd always been cool with Geraldine, a fact which had only made Brendan's praise more lavish.

The smile she offered now was gently indulgent. Though Cal had been loath to let her in and have her spoil his reverie, he was suddenly grateful for her company. He even felt the shaking fade a little.

'It's stale in here,' she said. 'You need some fresh air. Why don't you open the window?'

He did as she suggested. When he turned round she was sitting cross-legged on the bed, her back to the collage of pictures he'd put up there in his youth, and which his parents had never removed. The Wailing Wall, Geraldine called it; it had always upset her, with its parade of movie stars and mushroom clouds, politicians and pigs.

'The dress is beautiful,' she said.

He puzzled over the remark a moment, his mind sluggish.

'*Teresa's* dress,' she prompted.

'Oh.'

'Come and sit down, Cal.'

He lingered by the window. The air was balmy, and clean. It reminded him —

'What's wrong?' she said.

The words were on the tip of his tongue. '*I saw Wonderland,*' he wanted to say. That was it, in sum. The rest — the circumstances, the description — those details were niceties. The three essential words were easy enough, weren't they? *I saw Wonderland.* And if there was anybody in his life to whom he should say them, it was this woman.

'Tell me, Cal,' she said. 'Are you ill?'

He shook his head.

'I saw . . .' he began.

She looked at him with plain puzzlement.

'What?' she said. 'What did you see?'

'I saw . . .' he began again, and again faltered. His tongue refused the instruction he gave it; the words simply wouldn't come. He looked away from her face at the Wailing Wall. 'The pictures . . .' he said finally, '. . . they're an eyesore.'

A strange euphoria swept over him as he sailed so close to telling, then away. The part of him that wanted what he'd seen kept secret had in that moment won the battle, and perhaps even the war. He could not tell her. Not now, not ever. It was a great relief to have made up his mind.

*I'm Mad Mooney*, he thought to himself. It wasn't such a bad idea at that.

'You're looking better already,' she said. 'It must be the fresh air.'


4


And what lessons could he learn from the mad poet, now that they were fellow spirits? What would Mad Mooney do, were he in Cal's shoes?

He'd play whatever game was necessary, came the answer, and then, when the world turned its back, he'd *search*, search until he found the place he'd seen, and not care that in doing so he was inviting delirium. He'd find his dream and hold on to it and never let it go.


They talked a little while longer, until Geraldine announced that she had to leave. There was wedding business to do that afternoon.

'No more pigeon-chasing,' she said to Cal. 'I want you there on Saturday.'

She put her arms around him.

'You're too thin,' she said. 'I'm going to have to feed you up.'

She expects to be kissed now, the mad poet whispered in his ear; oblige the lady. We don't want her to think you've

46

lost interest in copulation, just because you've been half way to Heaven and back. Kiss her, and say something fetching.

The kiss Cal could deliver, though he was afraid the fact that his passion was prompted would show. He needn't have feared. She returned his fake fervour with the genuine article, her body warm and tight against his.

That's it, said the poet, now find something seductive to say, and send her off happy.

Here Cal's confidence faltered. He had no skill with sweet-talk, nor ever had. 'See you Saturday,' was all he could muster. She seemed content with that. She kissed him again, and took her leave.

He watched her from the window, counting her steps until she turned the corner. Then, with his lover out of sight, he went in search of his heart's desire.

# Part Two

# Births, Deaths and Marriages

*'The iron tongue of midnight hath told twelve;*
*Lovers to bed; 'tis almost fairy time.'*

Shakespeare:
*A Midsummer Night's Dream*

# I

---

# THE SUIT OF LIGHTS

## 1

**T**he day Cal stepped out into was humid and stale. It could not be long before the summer let fall take its toll. Even the breeze seemed weary, and its condition was contagious. By the time Cal reached the vicinity of Rue Street his feet felt swollen in his shoes and his brain in his skull.

And then, to add insult to injury, he couldn't find the damn street. He'd made his way to the house the previous day with his eyes on the birds rather than on the route he was following, so he had only an impressionistic notion of its whereabouts. Knowing he could well wander for several hours and not find the street, he asked the way from a gaggle of six-year-olds, engaged in war games on a street corner. He was confidently re-directed. Either through ignorance or malice, however, the directions proved hopelessly incorrect, and he found himself wandering around in ever more desperate circles, his frustration mounting.

Any sixth sense he might have hoped for – some instinct that would lead him unerringly to the region of his dreams – was conspicuous by its absence.

It was luck then, pure luck, that brought him finally to the corner of Rue Street, and to the house that had once belonged to Mimi Laschenksi.

51

## 2

Suzanna had spent much of the morning attempting to do as she had promised Doctor Chai: notifying Uncle Charlie in Toronto. It was a frustrating business. For one thing, the small hotel she'd found the previous night only boasted a single public telephone, and other guests wanted access to it as well as she. For another, she had to call round several friends of the family until she located one who had Charlie's telephone number, all of which took the best part of the morning. When, around one, she finally made contact, Mimi's only son took the news without a trace of surprise. There was no offer to drop his work and rush to his mother's bedside; only a polite request that Suzanna call back when there was 'more news'. Meaning, presumably, that he didn't expect her to ring again until it was time for him to send a wreath. So much for filial devotion.

The call done, she rang the hospital. There was no change in the patient's condition. She's hanging on, was the duty nurse's phrase. It conjured an odd image of Mimi as mountaineer, clinging to a cliff-face. She took the opportunity to ask about her grandmother's personal effects, and was told that she'd come into hospital without so much as a nightgown. Most probably the vultures Mrs Pumphrey had spoken of would by now have taken anything of worth from the house – the tall-boy included – but she elected to call by anyway, in case she could salvage anything to make Mimi's dwindling hours a little more comfortable.

She found a small Italian restaurant in the vicinity of the hotel to lunch in, then drove to Rue Street.

## 3

The back yard gate had been pushed closed by the removal men, but left unbolted. Cal opened it, and stepped into the yard.

If he had expected some revelation, he was disappointed. There was nothing remarkable here. Just parched chickweed sprouting between the paving stones, and a litter of chattels the trio had discarded as worthless. Even the shadows, which might have hidden some glory, were wan and unsecretive.

Standing in the middle of the yard — where all of the mysteries that had overturned his sanity had been unveiled — he doubted for the first time, *truly* doubted, that anything had in fact happened the previous day.

Maybe there would be something inside the house, he told himself; some flotsam he could cling to that would bear him up in this flood of doubt.

He crossed the ground where the carpet had lain, to the back door. The removal men had left it unlocked; or else vandals had broken in. Either way, it stood ajar. He stepped inside.

At least the shadows were heavier within; there was some room for the fabulous. He waited for his eyes to accommodate the murk. Was it really only twenty-four hours since he'd been here, he thought, as his sharpening gaze scanned the grim interior; only yesterday that he'd entered this house with no more on his mind than catching a lost bird? This time he had so much more to find.

He wandered through to the hallway, looking everywhere for some echo of what he'd experienced the day before. With every step he took his hopes fell further. Shadows there were, but they were deserted. The place was shorn of miracles. They'd gone when the carpet was removed.

Half way up the stairs he halted. What was the use of going any further? It was apparent he'd missed his chance. If he was to rediscover the vision he'd glimpsed and lost he'd have to search elsewhere. It was mere doggedness, therefore — one of Eileen's attributes — that made him continue to climb.

At the top of the stairs the air was so leaden it made drawing breath a chore. That, and the fact that he felt like a trespasser today — unwelcome in this tomb — made him anxious to confirm his belief that the place had no magic to show him, then get gone.

As he went to the door of the front bedroom something moved behind him. He turned. The labourers had piled several articles of furniture at the top of the stairs, then apparently decided they weren't worth the sweat of moving any further. A chest of drawers, several chairs and tables. The sound had come from behind this furniture. And now it came again.

Hearing it, he imagined rats. The sound suggested several sets of scurrying paws. Live and let live, he thought: he had no more right to be here than they did. Less, perhaps. They'd probably occupied the house for rat generations.

He returned to the job at hand, pushed open the door, and stepped into the front room. The windows were grimy, and the stained lace curtains further clogged the light. There was a chair overturned on the bare boards, and three odd shoes had been placed on the mantelpiece by some wit. Otherwise empty.

He stood for a few moments and then, hearing laughter in the street and needing its reassurance, crossed to the window and drew the curtain aside. But before he found the laughter's source he foresook the search. His belly knew before his senses could confirm it that somebody had entered the room behind him. He let the curtain drop and looked around. A wide man in late middle-age, dressed too well for this dereliction, had joined him in the half-light. The threads of his grey jacket were almost iridescent. But more eye-catching still, his smile. A practised smile, belonging on an actor, or a preacher. Whichever, it was the expression of a man looking for converts.

'Can I be of help?' he said. His voice was resonant, and warm, but his sudden appearance had chilled Cal.

'Help me?' he said, floundering.

'Are you perhaps interested in purchasing property?' the other man said.

'Purchasing? No . . . I . . . was just . . . you know . . . looking around.'

'It's a fine house,' said the stranger, his smile as steady as a surgeon's handshake, and as antiseptic. 'Do you know much about houses?' The line was spoken like its predecessors,

54

without irony or malice. When Cal didn't reply, the man said: 'I'm a salesman. My name's Shadwell.' He teased the calf-skin glove from his thick-fingered hand. 'And yours?'

'Cal Mooney. Calhoun, that is.'

The bare hand was extended. Cal took two steps towards the man – he was fully four inches taller than Cal's five foot eleven – and shook hands. The man's cool palm made Cal aware that he was sweating like a pig.

The handshake broken, friend Shadwell unbuttoned his jacket, and opened it, to take a pen from his inside pocket. This casual action briefly revealed the lining of the Salesman's garment, and by some trick of the light it seemed to shine, as though the fabric were woven of mirrored threads.

Shadwell caught the look on Cal's face. His voice was feather-light as he said:

'Do you see anything you like?'

Cal didn't trust the man. Was it the smile or the calf-skin gloves that made him suspicious? Whichever, he wanted as little time in the man's company as possible.

But there *was* something in the jacket. Something that caught the light, and made Cal's heart beat a little faster.

'Please . . .' Shadwell coaxed. 'Have a look.'

His hand went to the jacket again, and opened it.

'Tell me . . .' he purred, '. . . if there's anything there that takes your fancy.'

This time, he fully opened the jacket, exposing the lining. And yes, Cal's first judgment had been correct. It *did* shine.

'I am, as I said, a salesman,' Shadwell was explaining. 'I make it a Golden Rule always to carry some samples of my merchandise around with me.'

Merchandise. Cal shaped the word in his head, his eyes still fixed on the interior of the jacket. What a word that was: *merchandise*. And there, in the lining of the jacket, he could almost see that word made solid. Jewellery, was it, that gleamed there? Artificial gems with a sheen that blinded the way only the fake could. He squinted into the glamour, looking to make sense out of what he saw, while the Salesman's voice went about its persuasions:

'Tell me what you'd like and it's yours. I can't say fairer than that, can I? A fine young man like you should be able to pick and choose. The world's your oyster. I can see that. Open in front of you. Have what you like. Free, gratis and without charge. You tell me what you see in there, and the next minute it's in your hands . . .'

*Look away*, something in Cal said; nothing comes free. Prices must be paid.

But his gaze was so infatuated with the mysteries in the folds of the jacket that he couldn't have averted his eyes now if his life depended upon it.

'. . . tell me . . .' the Salesman said, '. . . what you see . . .'

Ah, *there* was a question –

'. . . and it's yours.'

He saw forgotten treasures, things he'd once upon a time set his heart upon, thinking that if he owned them he'd never want for anything again. Worthless trinkets, most of them; but items that awoke old longings. A pair of X-ray spectacles he'd seen advertised at the back of a comic book (see thru walls! impress your friends!) but had never been able to buy. There they were now, their plastic lens gleaming, and seeing them he remembered the October nights he'd lain awake wondering how they worked.

And what was that beside them? Another childhood fetish. A photograph of a woman dressed only in stiletto heels and a sequinned G-string, presenting her over-sized breasts to the viewer. The boy two doors down from Cal had owned that picture, stolen it from his uncle's wallet, he'd claimed, and Cal had wanted it so badly he thought he'd die of longing. Now it hung, a dog-eared memento, in the glittering flux of Shadwell's jacket, there for the asking.

But no sooner had it made itself apparent than it too faded, and new prizes appeared in its place to tempt him.

'What is it you see, my friend?'

The keys to a car he'd longed to own. A prize pigeon, the winner of innumerable races, that he'd been so envious of he'd have happily abducted –

'. . . just tell me what you see. Ask, and it's yours . . .'

56

There was so much. Items that had seemed – for an *hour*, a *day* – the pivot upon which his world turned, all hung now in the miraculous store-room of the Salesman's coat.

But they were fugitive, all of them. They appeared only to evaporate again. There was something else there, which prevented these trivialities from holding his attention for more than moments. What it was, he couldn't yet see.

He was dimly aware that Shadwell was addressing him again, and that the tone of the Salesman's voice had altered. There was some puzzlement in it now, tinged with exasperation.

'Speak up, my friend . . . why don't you tell me what you want?'

'I can't . . . quite . . . *see* it.'

'Then try harder. Concentrate.'

Cal tried. The images came and went, all insignificant stuff. The mother-lode still evaded him.

'You're not trying,' the Salesman chided. 'If a man wants something badly he has to zero in on it. Has to make sure it's clear in his head.'

Cal saw the wisdom of this, and re-doubled his efforts. It had become a challenge to see past the tinsel to the real treasure that lay beyond. A curious sensation attended this focusing; a restlessness in his chest and throat, as though some part of him were preparing to be gone; out of him and along the line of his gaze. Gone into the jacket.

At the back of his head, where his skull grew the tail of his spine, the warning voices muttered on. But he was too committed to resist. Whatever the lining contained, it teased him, not quite showing itself. He stared and stared, defying its decorum until the sweat ran from his temples.

Shadwell's coaxing monologue had gained fresh confidence. It's sugar coating had cracked and fallen away. The nut beneath was bitter and dark.

'Go on . . .' he said. 'Don't be so damn weak. There's something here you want, isn't there? Very badly. Go on. Tell me. *Spit it out.* No use waiting. You wait, and your chance slips away.'

Finally, the image was coming clear –

*'Tell me and it's yours.'*

Cal felt a wind on his face, and suddenly he was flying again, and wonderland was spread out before him. Its deeps and its heights, its rivers, its towers – all were displayed there in the lining of the Salesman's jacket.

He gasped at the sight. Shadwell was lightning swift in his response.

'What is it?'

Cal stared on, speechless.

*'What do you see?'*

A confusion of feelings assailed Cal. He felt elated, seeing the land, yet fearful of what he would be asked to give (was *already* giving, perhaps, without quite knowing it) in return for this peep-show. Shadwell had harm in him, for all his smiles and promises.

*'Tell me . . .'* the Salesman demanded.

Cal tried to keep an answer from coming to his lips. He didn't want to give his secret away.

*'. . . what do you see?'*

The voice was so hard to resist. He wanted to keep his silence, but the reply rose in him unbidden.

'I . . .' (*Don't say it*, the poet warned), 'I see . . .' (*Fight it. There's harm here.*) 'I . . . see . . .'

'He sees the Fugue.'

The voice that finished the sentence was that of a woman.

'Are you sure?' said Shadwell.

'Never more certain. Look at his eyes.'

Cal felt foolish and vulnerable, so mesmerized by the sights still unfolding in the lining he was unable to cast his eyes in the direction of those who now appraised him.

'He *knows*,' the woman said. Her voice held not a trace of warmth. Even, perhaps, of humanity.

'You were right then,' said Shadwell. 'It's been here.'

'Of course.'

'Good enough,' said Shadwell, and summarily closed the jacket.

The effect on Cal was cataclysmic. With the world – *the*

*Fugue*, she'd called it – so abruptly snatched away he felt weak as a babe. It was all he could do to stand upright. Queasily, his eyes slid in the direction of the woman.

She was beautiful: that was his first thought. She was dressed in reds and purples so dark they were almost black, the fabric wrapped tightly around her upper body so as to seem both chaste, her ripeness bound and sealed, and, in the act of sealing, eroticized. The same paradox informed her features. Her hair-line had been shaved back fully two inches, and her eye-brows totally removed, which left her face eerily innocent of expression. Yet her flesh gleamed as if oiled, and though the shaving, and the absence of any scrap of make-up to flatter her features, seemed acts in defiance of her beauty, her face could not be denied its sensuality. Her mouth was too sculpted; and her eyes – umber one moment, gold the next – too eloquent for the feelings there to be disguised. What feelings, Cal could only vaguely read. Impatience certainly, as though being here sickened her, and stirred some fury Cal had no desire to see unleashed. Contempt – for him most likely – and yet a great focus upon him, as though she saw through to his marrow, and was preparing to congeal it with a thought.

There were no such contradictions in her voice however. It was steel and steel.

'How long?' she demanded of him. 'How long since you saw the Fugue?'

He couldn't meet her eyes for more than a moment. His gaze fled to the mantelpiece, and the tripod's shoes.

'Don't know what you're talking about,' he said.

'You've seen it. You saw it again in the jacket. It's fruitless to deny it.'

'It's better you answer,' Shadwell advised.

Cal looked from mantelpiece to door. They had left it open. 'You can both go to Hell,' he said quietly.

Did Shadwell laugh? Cal wasn't certain.

'We want the carpet,' said the woman.

'It belongs to us, you understand,' Shadwell said. 'We have a legitimate claim to it.'

'So, if you'd be so kind . . .' the woman's lip curled at this courtesy, '. . . tell me where the carpet's gone, and we can have the matter done with.'

'Such easy terms,' the Salesman said. 'Tell us, and we're gone.'

Claiming ignorance would be no defence, Cal thought; *they* knew that *he* knew, and they wouldn't be persuaded otherwise. He was trapped. Yet dangerous as things had become, he felt inwardly elated. His tormentors had confirmed the existence of the world he'd glimpsed: the Fugue. The urge to be out of their presence as fast as possible was tempered by the desire to play them along, and hope they'd tell him more about the vision he'd witnessed.

'Maybe I did see it,' he said.

'No *maybe*,' the woman replied.

'It's hazy . . .' he said. 'I remember *something*, but I'm not quite sure what.'

'You don't know what the Fugue is?' said Shadwell.

'Why should he?' the woman replied. 'He came on it by luck.'

'But he saw,' said Shadwell.

'A lot of Cuckoos have some sight, it doesn't mean they *understand*. He's lost, like all of them.'

Cal resented her condescension, but in essence she was right. Lost he was.

'What you saw isn't your business,' she said to him. 'Just tell us where you put the carpet, then forget you ever laid eyes on it.'

'I don't *have* the carpet,' he said.

The woman's entire face seemed to darken, the pupils of her eyes like moons barely eclipsing some apocalyptic light.

From the landing, Cal heard again the scuttling sounds he'd previously taken to be rats. Now he wasn't so sure.

'I won't be polite with you much longer,' she said. 'You're a thief.'

'No –' he protested.

'*Yes*. You came here to raid an old woman's house and you got a glimpse of something you shouldn't.'

'We shouldn't waste time,' said Shadwell.

Cal had begun to regret his decision to play the pair along. He should have run while he had half a chance. The noise from the other side of the door was getting louder.

'Hear that?' said the woman. 'Those are some of my sister's bastards. Her by-blows.'

'They're vile,' said Shadwell.

He could believe it.

'Once more,' she said. 'The carpet.'

And once more he told her. 'I don't have it.' This time his words were more appeal than defence.

'Then we must make you tell,' said the woman.

'Be careful, Immacolata,' said Shadwell.

If the woman heard him, she didn't care for his warning. Softly, she rubbed the middle and fourth fingers of her right hand against the palm of her left, and at this all but silent summons her sister's children came running.

# II

## THE SKIN OF THE TEETH

### 1

Suzanna arrived in Rue Street a little before three, and went first to tell Mrs Pumplrey of her grandmother's condition. She was invited into the house with such insistence she couldn't refuse. They drank tea, and talked for ten minutes or so: chiefly of Mimi. Violet Pumphrey spoke of the old woman without malice, but the portrait she drew was far from flattering.

'They turned off the gas and electricity in the house years ago,' Violet said. 'She hadn't paid the bills. Living in squalor, she was, and it weren't for want of me keeping a neighbourly eye. But she was rude, you know, if you enquired about her health.' She lowered her voice a little. 'I know I shouldn't say it but ... your grandmother wasn't entirely of sound mind.'

Suzanna murmured something in reply, which she knew would go unheard.

'All she had was candles for light. No television, no refrigerator. God alone knows what she was eating.'

'Do you know if anyone has a key to the house?'

'Oh no, she wouldn't have done that. She had more locks on that house than you've had hot dinners. She didn't trust anybody, you see. Not anybody.'

'I just wanted to look around.'

'Well there's been people in and out since she went; probably find the place wide open by now. Even thought of having a look myself, but I didn't fancy it. Some houses ...

they're not quite *natural*. You know what I mean?'

She knew. Standing finally on the doorstep of number eighteen Suzanna confessed to herself that she'd welcomed the various duties that had postponed this visit. The episode at the hospital had validated much of the family suspicion regarding Mimi. She *was* different. She could give her dreams away with a touch. And whatever powers the old woman possessed, or was possessed by, would they not also haunt the house she'd spent so many years in?

Suzanna felt the grip of the past tighten around her: except that it was no longer that simple. She wasn't here hesitating on the threshold just because she feared a confrontation with childhood ghosts. It was that here – on a stage she'd thought to have made a permanent exit from – she dimly sensed dramas waiting to be played, and that Mimi had somehow cast her in a pivotal role.

She put her hand on the door. Despite what Violet had said, it was locked. She peered through the front window, into a room of debris and dust. The desolation proved oddly comforting. Maybe her anxieties would yet prove groundless. She went around the back of the house. Here she had more luck. The yard gate was open, and so was the back door.

She stepped inside. The condition of the front room was reprised here: practically all trace of Mimi Laschenski's presence – with the exception of candles and valueless junk – had been removed. She felt an unhappy mixture of responses. On the one hand, the certainty that nothing of value would have survived this clearance, and that she'd have to go back to Mimi empty-handed; and on the other, an undeniable relief that this was so: that the stage was deserted. Though her imagination hung the missing pictures on the walls, and put the furniture back in place, it was all in her mind. There was nothing here to spoil the calm good order of the life she lived.

She moved through from the parlour into the hallway, glancing into the small sitting room before turning the corner to the stairs. They were not so mountainous; nor so dark. But

63

before she could climb them she heard a movement on the floor above.

'Who's there?' she called out –

## 2

– the words were sufficient to break Immacolata's concentration. The creatures she'd summoned, the by-blows, halted their advance towards Cal, awaiting instruction.

He took his opportunity, and threw himself across the room, kicking at the beast closest to him.

The thing lacked a body, its four arms springing straight from a bulbous neck, beneath which clusters of sacs hung, wet as liver and lights. Cal's blow connected, and one of the sacs burst, releasing a sewer stench. With the rest of the siblings close upon him, Cal raced for the door, but the wounded creature was fastest in pursuit, sidling crab-like on its hands, and spitting as it came. A spray of saliva hit the wall close to Cal's head, and the paper blistered. Revulsion gave heat to his heals. He was at the door in an instant.

Shadwell moved to intercept him, but one of the beasts got beneath his feet like an errant dog, and before he could regain his equilibrium Cal was out of the room and on to the landing.

The woman who'd called out was at the bottom of the stairs, face upturned. She stood as bright day to the night he'd almost succumbed to in the room behind him. Wide grey-blue eyes, curls of dark auburn hair framing her pale face, a mouth upon which a question was rising, but which his wild appearance had silenced.

'Get out of here!' he yelled as he hurtled down the stairs.

She stood and gaped.

'The *door*!' he said. 'For God's sake open the door.'

He didn't look to see if the monsters were coming in pursuit, but he heard Shadwell cry out:

'*Stop, thief!*'

from the top of the stairs.

The woman's eyes went to the Salesman, then back to Cal, then to the front door.

'Open it!' Cal yelled, and this time she moved to do so. Either she distrusted Shadwell on sight or she had a passion for thieves. Whichever, she flung the door wide. Sunlight poured in, dust dancing in its beams. Cal heard a howl of protest from behind him, but the girl did nothing to arrest his flight.

'Get out of here!' he said to her, and then he was over the threshold and into the street outside.

He took half a dozen steps from the door and then turned around to see if the woman with the grey eyes was following, but she was still standing in the hallway.

'Will you come on?' he yelled at her.

She opened her mouth to say something to him, but Shadwell was at the bottom of the stairs by now, and pushing her out of the way. He couldn't linger; there were only a few paces between him and the Salesman. He ran.

The man with the greased-back hair made no real attempt at pursuit once his quarry was out in the open. The young man was whippet-lean, and twice as fleet; the other was a bear in a Savile Row suit. Suzanna had disliked him from the moment she'd set eyes on him. Now he turned and said:

'Why'd you do that, woman?'

She didn't grace the demand with a reply. For one thing, she was still trying to make sense of what she'd just seen; for another, her attention was no longer on the bear but on his partner – or keeper – the woman who had now followed him down the stairs.

Her features were as blank as a dead child's, but Suzanna had never seen a face that exercised such fascination.

'Get out of my way,' the woman said as she reached the bottom of the stairs. Suzanna's feet had already begun to move when she cancelled her acquiescence and instead stepped directly into the woman's path, blocking her route to the door. A flood of adrenalin surged through her system as she did so,

65

as though she'd stepped in front of a speeding juggernaut.

But the woman stopped in her tracks, and the hook of her gaze caught Suzanna and raised her face to be scrutinized. Meeting the woman's eyes Suzanna knew the adrenalin rush had been well timed: she had just skirted death. That gaze had killed, she'd swear to it; and would again. But not now; now the woman studied Suzanna with curiosity.

'A friend of yours, was he?' she finally said.

Suzanna heard the words spoken, but she couldn't have sworn that the woman's lips had moved to form them.

At the door behind her the bear said:

'Damn thief.'

Then he poked at Suzanna's shoulder, hard.

'Didn't you hear me telling you?' he said.

Suzanna wanted to turn to the man and tell him to take his hands off her, but the woman hadn't done with her study, and held her with that gaze.

'She heard,' the woman said. This time her lips did move, and Suzanna felt the hold on her relax. But the mere proximity of the other woman made her body tremble. Her groin and breasts felt pricked by tiny thorns.

'Who are you?' the woman demanded.

'Leave it be,' said the bear.

'I want to know who she is. Why she's here.' The gaze, which had briefly flitted to the man, settled on Suzanna afresh, and the curiosity had murder in its shadow.

'There's nothing here we need . . .' the man was saying.

The woman ignored him.

'Come on now . . . leave it be . . .'

There was something in the tone of his voice of one coaxing an hysteric from the brink of an attack, and Suzanna was glad of his intervention.

'. . . it's too public . . .' he said, '. . . especially here . . .'

After a long, breathless moment the woman made the tiniest of nods, conceding the wit of this. She suddenly seemed to completely lose interest in Suzanna, and turned back towards the stairs. At the top of the flight, where Suzanna had once imagined terrors to be in wait for her, the gloom was not quite at rest. There were ragged forms moving up there, so insubstantial she could not be certain whether she saw them or merely sensed their presence. They were spilling down the stairs like poison smoke, losing what little solidity they might have owned as they approached the open door, until, by the time they reached the woman who awaited them at the bottom, their vapours were invisible.

She turned from the stairs and walked past Suzanna to the door, taking with her a cloud of cold and tainted air, as though the wraiths that had come to her were now wreathed about her neck, and clinging to the folds of her dress. Carried unseen into the sunlit human world, until they could congeal again.

The man was already out on the pavement, but before his companion stepped out to join him she turned back to Suzanna. She said nothing, either with her lips or without. Her eyes were quite expressive enough: their promises were all joyless.

Suzanna looked away. She heard the woman's heel on the step. When she looked up again the pair had gone. Drawing a deep breath, she went to the door. Though the afternoon was growing old, the sun was still warm and bright.

Not surprisingly the woman and the bear had crossed over, so as to walk on the shadowed side of the street.

### 3

Twenty-four years was a third of a good span; time enough to form some opinions on how the world worked. Up until mere hours ago, Suzanna would have claimed she'd done just that.

Certainly there were sizeable gaps in her comprehension: mysteries, both inside her head and out, that remained un-illuminated. But that had only made her the more determined not to succumb to any sentiment or self-delusion that would give those mysteries power over her – a zeal that touched both her private and professional lives. In her love-affairs she had always tempered passion with practicality, avoiding the

67

emotional extravagance she'd seen so often become cruelty and bitterness. In her friendships she'd pursued a similar balance: neither too cloying nor too detached. And no less in her craft. The very appeal of making bowls and pots was its pragmatism; the vagaries of art disciplined by the need to create a functional object.

The question she would ask, viewing the most exquisite jug on earth, would be: *does it pour?* And it was in a sense a quality she sought in every facet of her life.

But here was a problem which defied such simple distinctions; that threw her off-balance; left her sick and bewildered.

First the memories. Then Mimi, more dead than alive but passing dreams through the air.

And now this meeting, with a woman whose glance had death in it, and yet had left her feeling more alive than perhaps she'd ever felt.

It was that last paradox that made her leave the house without finishing her search, slamming the door on whatever dramas it had waiting for her. Instinctively, she made for the river. There, sitting awhile in the sun, she might make some sense of the problem.

There were no ships on the Mersey, but the air was so clear she could see cloud shadows moving over the hills of Clwyd. There was no such clarity within her, however. Only a chaos of feelings, all unsettlingly familiar, as though they'd been inside her for years, biding their time behind the screen of pragmatism she'd established to keep them from sight. Like echoes, waiting on a mountain-face for the shout they were born to answer.

She'd heard that shout today. Or rather, met it, face to face, on the very spot in the narrow hallway where as a six-year-old she'd stood and trembled in fear of the dark. The two confrontations were inextricably linked, though she didn't know how. All she knew was that she was suddenly alive to a space inside herself where the haste and habit of her adult life had no dominion.

She sensed the passions that drifted in that space only vaguely, as her fingertips might sense fog. But she would come to know them better with time, those passions, and the acts that they'd engender: she was certain of that as she'd been certain of nothing in days. She'd know them – and, God help her – she'd love them as her own.

# SELLING HEAVEN

**M**r Mooney? Mr *Brendan* Mooney?'

'That's right.'

'Do you happen to have a son by the name of Calhoun?'

'What business is it of yours?' Brendan wanted to know. Then, before the other could answer, said: 'Nothing's happened to him?'

The stranger shook his head, taking hold of Brendan's hand and pumping it vigorously.

'You're a very lucky man, Mr Mooney, if I may make so bold.'

That, Brendan knew, was a lie.

'What do you want?' he said. 'Are you selling something?' He withdrew his hand from the grip of the other man. 'Whatever it is, I don't want it.'

'Selling?' said Shadwell. 'Perish the thought. I'm *giving*, Mr Mooney. Your son's a wise boy. He volunteered your name – and lo and behold, you've been selected by computer as the recipient of –'

'I told you I don't want it,' Brendan interrupted, and tried to close the door, but the man already had one foot over the threshold.

'Please –' Brendan sighed, '– will you just leave me alone? I don't want your prizes. I don't want anything.'

'Well that makes you a very remarkable man,' the Salesman said, pushing the door wide again. 'Maybe even unique. There's really nothing in all the world you want? That's remarkable.'

Music drifted from the back of the house, a recording of Puccini's Greatest Hits which Eileen had been given several years ago. She'd scarcely listened to it, but since her death Brendan – who had never stepped inside an opera-house in his life, and was proud of the fact – had become addicted to the *Love Duet* from *Madam Butterfly*. If he'd played it once he'd played it a hundred times, and the tears would always come. Now all he wanted to do was get back to the music before it finished. But the Salesman was still pressing his suit.

'Brendan,' he said. 'I may call you Brendan –?'

'Don't call me anything.'

The Salesman unbuttoned his jacket.

'Really, Brendan, we have a great deal to discuss, you and I. Your prize, for one.'

The lining of the jacket scintillated, drawing Brendan's eye. He'd never in his life seen a fabric its equal.

'Are you sure there's nothing you want?' the Salesman said. 'Absolutely sure?'

The *Love Duet* had reached a new plateau, the voices of Butterfly and Pinkerton urging each other on to fresh confessions of pain. Brendan heard, but his attention was increasingly focused on the jacket. And *yes*, there was something there that he wanted.

Shadwell watched the man's eyes and saw the flame of desire ignited. It never failed.

'You *do* see something, Mr Mooney.'

'Yes,' Brendan admitted softly. He saw, and the joy he felt at what he saw made his heavy heart light.

Eileen had said to him once (when they were young, and mortality was just another way to express their devotion to each other): '– if I die first, Brendan, I'll find some way to tell you what Heaven's like. I swear I will.' He'd hushed her with kisses then, and said that if she were to die he would die too, of a broken heart.

But he hadn't died, had he? He'd lived three long, empty months, and more than once in that time he'd remembered her frivolous promise. And now, just as he felt despair would undo him utterly, here on his doorstep was this celestial messenger. An odd choice, perhaps, to appear in the shape of a salesman, but no doubt the Seraphim had their reasons.

'Do you *want* what you see, Brendan?' the visitor asked.

'Who are you?' Brendan breathed, awe-struck.

'My name's Shadwell.'

'And you brought this for me?'

'Of course. But if you accept it, Brendan, you must understand there'll be a small charge for the service.'

Brendan didn't take his eyes off the prize the jacket housed. 'Whatever you say,' he replied.

'We may ask for your help, for instance, which you'd be obliged to furnish.'

'Do angels need help?'

'Once in a while.'

'Then of course,' said Brendan. 'I'd be honoured.'

'Good.' The Salesman smiled. 'Then please –' he opened the jacket a little wider, '– help yourself.'

Brendan knew how the letter from Eileen would smell and feel long before he had it in his hands. It did not disappoint him. It was warm, as he'd expected, and the scent of flowers lingered about it. She'd written it in a garden, no doubt; in the paradise garden.

'So, Mr Mooney. We have a deal, do we?'

The *Love Duet* had ended; the house behind Brendan was silent. He held the letter close to his chest, still fearful that this was all a dream, and he'd wake to find himself empty-handed.

'Whatever you want,' he said, desperate that this salvation not be snatched from him.

'Sweetness and light,' came the smiling reply. 'That's all a wise man ever wants, isn't it? Sweetness and light.'

Brendan was only half-listening. He ran his fingers back and forth over the letter. His name was on the front, in Eileen's cautious hand.

'So tell me, Mr Mooney –' the Seraphim said, 'about Cal.'

'Cal?'

'Can you tell me where I can find him?'

'He's at a wedding.'

'A wedding. Ah. Could you perhaps furnish me with the address?'

'Yes. Of course.'

'We've got a little something for Cal too. Lucky man.'

# IV

# NUPTIALS

## 1

Geraldine had spent many long hours giving Cal a working knowledge of her family tree, so that come Teresa's wedding he'd know who was who. It was a difficult business. The Kellaway family was heroically fecund, and Cal had a poor memory for names, so it wasn't surprising that many of the hundred and thirty guests who packed the reception hall this balmy Saturday evening were unknown to him. He didn't much mind. He felt safe amongst such numbers, even if he didn't know who they were; and the drink, which had flowed freely since four in the afternoon, further allayed his anxieties. He didn't even object when Geraldine presented him before a parade of admiring aunts and uncles, every one of whom asked him when he was going to make an honest woman of her. He played the game; smiled; charmed; did his best to seem sane.

Not that a little lunacy would have been noticeable in such a heady atmosphere. Norman Kellaway's ambition for his daughter's wedding day seemed to have been upped a notch for every inch her waist-line had swelled. The ceremony had been grand, but necessarily decorous; the reception, however, was a triumph of excess over good taste. The hall had been decorated from floor to ceiling with streamers and paper lanterns; ropes of coloured lights were looped along the walls and in the trees out at the back of the hall. The bar was supplied with beer, spirits and liqueurs sufficient to intoxicate a modest army; food was in endless supply, carried to the

74

tables of those content to sit and gorge by a dozen harassed waitresses.

Even with all the doors and windows open, the hall soon grew hot as Hell, the heat in part generated by those guests who'd thrown inhibitions to the wind and were dancing to a deafening mixture of country and western and rock and roll, the latter bringing comical exhibitions from several of the older guests, applauded ferociously from all sides.

At the edge of the crowd, lingering by the door that led out behind the hall, the groom's younger brother, accompanied by two young bucks who'd both at some point courted Teresa, and a fourth youth whose presence was only countenanced because he had cigarettes, stood in a litter of beer cans and surveyed the talent available. The pickings were poor; those few girls who were of beddable age were either spoken for or judged so unattractive that any approach would have been evidence of desperation.

Only Elroy, Teresa's penultimate boy-friend, could lay claim to any hint of success tonight. Since the ceremony he'd had his eyes on one of the bridesmaids, whose name he'd yet to establish but who'd twice chanced to be at the bar while he was there: a significant statistic. Now he leaned against the door and watched the object of his lust across the smoky room.

The lights had been dimmed inside the hall, and the mood of the dancing had changed from cavortings to slow, smoochy embraces.

This was the moment, he judged, to make his approach. He'd invite the woman onto the dance floor, then, after a song or two, take her out for a breath of fresh air. Several couples had already retired to the privacy of the bushes, there to do what weddings were made to celebrate. Beneath the pretty vows and the flowers they were here in the name of fucking, and he was damned if he was going to be left out.

He'd caught sight of Cal chatting with the girl earlier on; it'd be simplest, he thought, to have Cal to introduce them. He pressed through the crush of dancers to where Cal was standing.

'How you doin', mate?'

Cal looked at Elroy blearily. The face before him was flushed with alcohol.

'I'm doing fine.'

'Didn't much like the ceremony,' Elroy said. 'I think I'm allergic to churches. Do us a favour, will yer?'

'What is it?'

'I'm in lust.'

'Who with?'

'One of the bridesmaids. She was over by the bar. Long blonde hair.'

'You mean Loretta?' Cal said. 'She's a cousin of Geraldine's.'

It was odd, but the drunker he got the more of his lessons on the Kellaway family he remembered.

'She's a fucking cracker. And she's been giving me the eye all night.'

'Is that right?'

'I was wondering . . . will you introduce us?'

Cal looked at Elroy's panting eyes. 'I think you're too late,' he said.

'Why?'

'She went outside –'

Before Elroy could voice his irritation Cal felt a hand on his shoulder. He turned. It was Norman, the father of the bride.

'A word, Cal, m'boy?' he said, glancing across at Elroy.

'I'll catch you later,' Elroy said, retreating in case Norman nabbed him too.

'Are you enjoying yourself?'

'Yes, Mr Kellaway.'

'Less of this Mr Kellaway shit, Cal. Call me Norm.'

He poured a generous measure of whisky from the bottle he was armed with into Cal's lager glass, then drew on his cigar.

'So tell me,' he said. 'How long before I have to give my other little girl away? Don't think I'm pushing, son. I'm not. But one bride in labour's enough.'

Cal swilled the whisky around the bottom of his glass, hoping for a prompt from the poet. None came.

'I've got a job for you at the works,' Norm went on, unfazed by Cal's silence. 'I want to see my baby live in a little style. You're a good lad, Cal. Her mother likes you a lot, and I always trust her judgment. So you think on it . . .'

He transferred the bottle to his cigar-wielding right hand, and reached into his jacket.

The gesture, innocent as it was, brought a chill of recognition. For an instant Cal was back in Rue Street, gazing into the enchanted cave of Shadwell's jacket. But Kellaway had simpler gifts to give.

'Have a cigar,' he said, and went off to his duties as host.

## 2

Elroy picked up another can of beer from the bar then headed out into the garden in search of Loretta. The air was considerably cooler than inside, and as soon as it hit him he felt sick as a flea in a leper's jock strap. He tossed the beer aside and headed towards the bottom of the garden, where he could throw up unseen.

The coloured lights stopped a few yards from the hall, where the cable petered out. Beyond was a welcoming darkness, which he plunged into. He was used to vomiting; a week in which his stomach didn't rebel through some excess or other was poorly spent. He efficiently discharged the contents of his belly over a rhododendron bush, then turned his thoughts back to the lovely Loretta.

A little way from where he stood the leaf-shadow, or something concealed by it, moved. He peered more closely, trying to interpret what he saw, but there was not sufficient illumination to make sense of it. He heard a sigh however: a woman's sigh.

There was a couple in the shelter of the tree, he decided, doing what darkness had been created to conceal. Perhaps it was Loretta, her skirt up and her knickers down. It would break his heart, but he had to see.

Very quietly, he advanced a couple of paces.

On his second step, something grazed his face. He stifled a cry of shock and put his hand up to find strands of matter in the air around his head. For some reason he thought of phlegm – cold, wet threads of phlegm – except that they *moved* against his flesh as if they were a part of something larger.

A heart-beat later this notion was confirmed, as the matter, which was adhering now to his legs and body, pulled him off his feet. He would have let out a cry, but the filthy stuff had already sealed up his lips. And then, as if this were not preposterous enough, he felt a chill around his lower belly. His trousers were being torn open. He started to fight like fury, but resistance was fruitless. There was a weight bearing down on his abdomen and hips, and he felt his manhood drawn up into a channel that might have been flesh, but that it was corpse cold.

Tears of panic blurred his vision, but he could see that the thing astride him had a human form. He could see no face, but the breasts were heavy the way he liked them, and though this was far from the scene he'd pictured with Loretta his lust ignited, his little length responding to the chilly ministrations of the body that contained him.

He raised his head slightly, wanting a better view of those sumptuous breasts, but in doing so he caught sight of another figure behind the first. She was the antithesis of the ripe, gleaming woman that rode him: a stained, wretched thing, with gaping holes in her body where cunt and mouth and navel should have been, so large the stars showed through from the other side.

He started to fight afresh, but his thrashings did nothing to slow his mistress' rhythm. Despite his panic he felt the familiar tremor in his balls.

In his head half a dozen pictures collided, becoming one monstrous beauty: the ragged woman, a necklace of coloured lights hanging between her sister's breasts, raised her skirts, and the mouth between her legs was Loretta's mouth, flicking its tongue. He could not resist this pornography: his prick spat its load. He howled against the seal at his mouth. The pleasure was short, the pain that followed, agonizing.

'What's your fuckin' problem?' somebody said in the darkness. It took him a moment to realize that his cry for help had been heard. He opened his eyes. The silhouettes of the trees loomed over him, but that was all.

He started to shout again; not caring that he was lying in the muck with his trousers around his ankles. Just needing to know he was still in the land of the living –

### 3

The first glimpse Cal had of trouble was through the bottom of his glass, as he upped it to drain the last of Norman's malt whisky. At the door two of the printers from the Kellaway factory, who were acting as bouncers for the night, were engaged in friendly conversation with a man in a well-cut suit. Laughing, the man glanced into the hall. It was Shadwell.

The jacket was closed and buttoned. There was no need, it seemed, for supernatural seductions; the Salesman was buying his entrance with charm alone. Even as Cal watched he patted one of the men on the shoulder as if they'd been bosom-buddies since childhood, and stepped inside.

Cal didn't know whether to stay still and hope that the crowd would conceal him, or make a move to escape and so risk drawing the enemy's attention. As it was he had no choice in the matter. A hand was over his, and at his side stood one of the aunts Geraldine had introduced him to.

'So tell me,' she said, apropos of nothing, 'have you been to America?'

'No,' he said, looking away from her powdered face towards the Salesman. He was entering the hall with flawless confidence, bestowing smiles hither and thither. His appearance won admiring eyes on all sides. Somebody extended a hand to be shaken; another asked him what he was drinking. He played the crowd with ease, a smiling word offered to every ear, all the while his eyes ranging back and forth as he sought out his quarry.

As the distance between them narrowed Cal knew he

79

couldn't long avoid being seen. Claiming his hand from the grip of the aunt he headed off into the thickest part of the crowd. A hubbub drew his attention to the far end of the hall, where he saw somebody – it looked to be Elroy – being carried in from the garden, his clothes in filthied disarray, his jaw slack. Nobody seemed much bothered by his condition – every gathering had its share of professional drunkards. There was laughter, and some disapproving looks, then a rapid return to jollification.

Cal glanced back over his shoulder. Where was Shadwell? Still close to the door, pressing the flesh like an aspirant politician? No; he'd moved. Cal scanned the room nervously. The noise and the dancing went on unabated, but now the sweating faces seemed a mite too hungry for happiness; the dancers only dancing because it put the world away for a little time. There was a desperation in this jamboree, and Shadwell knew how to exploit it, with his stale bonhomie and that air he pretended of one who'd walked with the great and the good.

Cal itched to get up onto a table and tell the revellers to stop their cavortings; to see for themselves how foolish their revels looked, and how dangerous the shark they'd invited into their midst.

But what would they do, when he'd shouted himself hoarse? Laugh behind their hands, and quietly remind each other that he had a madman's blood in his veins?

He'd find no allies here. This was Shadwell's territory. The safest thing would be to keep his head down, and negotiate a route to the door. Then get away, as *far* as possible as *fast* as possible.

He acted upon the plan immediately. Thanking God for the lack of light, he began to slip between the dancers, keeping his eyes peeled for the man with the coat of many colours.

There was a shout behind him. He glanced round, and through the milling figures caught sight of Elroy, who was thrashing about like an epileptic, yelling blue murder. Somebody was calling for a doctor.

Cal turned back towards the door, and the shark was suddenly at his side.

'*Calhoun*,' said Shadwell, soft and low. 'Your father told me I'd find you here.'

Cal didn't reply to Shadwell's words, merely pretended he hadn't heard. The Salesman wouldn't dare do anything violent in such a crowd, surely, and he was safe from the man's jacket as long as he kept his eyes off the lining.

'Where are you going?' Shadwell said, as Cal moved off. 'I want a word with you.'

Cal kept walking.

'We can help each other . . .'

Somebody called Cal's name, asking him if he knew what was wrong with Elroy. He shook his head, and forged on through the crowd towards the door. His plan was simple. Tell the bouncers to find Geraldine's father, and have Shadwell thrown out.

'. . . tell me where the carpet is,' the Salesman was saying, 'and I'll make sure her sisters never get their hands on you.' His manner was placatory. 'I've no argument with you,' he said. 'I just want some information.'

'I told you,' said Cal, knowing even as he spoke that any appeal was a lost cause. 'I don't know where the carpet went.'

They were within a dozen yards of the vestibule now, and with every step they took Shadwell's courtesy decayed further.

'They'll drain you dry,' he warned. 'Those sisters of hers. And I won't be able to stop them, not once they've got their hands on you. They're dead, and the dead don't take discipline.'

'Dead?'

'Oh yes. She killed them herself, while the three of them were still in the womb. Strangled them with their own cords.'

True or not, the image was sickening. And more sickening still, the thought of the sisters' touch. Cal tried to put both from his mind as he advanced, Shadwell still at his side. All pretence to negotiation had vanished; there were only threats now.

'You're a dead man, Mooney, if you don't confess. I won't lift a finger to help you –'

Cal was within hailing distance of the men.

81

He shouted across to them. They broke off their drinking, and turned in his direction.

'What's the problem?'

'This man −' Cal began, looking towards Shadwell.

But the Salesman had gone. In the space of seconds he'd left Cal's side and melted into the crowd, an exit as skilful as his entrance.

'Got some trouble?' the bigger of the two men wanted to know.

Cal glanced back at the man, fumbling for words. There was no use his trying to explain, he decided.

'No . . .' he said, '. . . I'm all right. I just need some air.'

'Too much to drink?' said the other man, and stood aside to let Cal step out into the street.

It was chilly after the suffocation of the hall, but that was fine by Cal. He breathed deeply, trying to clear his head. Then, a familiar voice.

'Do you want to go home?'

It was Geraldine. She was standing a short way from the door, a coat draped over her shoulders.

'I'm all right,' he told her. 'Where's your father?'

'I don't know. Why do you want him?'

'There's somebody in there who shouldn't be,' said Cal, crossing to where she stood. To his drunken gaze she seemed more glamorous than he'd ever seen her; eyes shining like dark gems.

'Why don't we walk together a little way?' she said.

'I have to speak to your father,' he insisted, but she was already turning from him, laughing lightly. Before he could voice a protest she was away around the corner. He followed. There were a number of lamps not working along the street, and the silhouette he dogged was fitful. But she trailed her laughter still, and he went after it.

'Where are you going?' he wanted to know.

She only laughed again.

Above their heads the clouds were moving quickly, stars glimmering between, their fires too feeble to illuminate much below. They caught Cal's eye for an instant, and when he looked back at Geraldine she was turning to him, making a sound somewhere between a sigh and a word.

The shadows that embraced her were dense, but they unfolded even as he watched, and what they revealed made his gut somersault. Geraldine's face had dislodged somehow, her features running like heated wax. And now, as the facade fell away, he saw the woman beneath. Saw, and knew: the browless face, the joyless mouth. Who else but Immacolata?

He would have run then, but that he felt the cold muzzle of a gun against his temple, and the Salesman's voice said:

'Make a sound and it's going to hurt.'

He kept his silence.

Shadwell gestured towards the black Mercedes that was parked at the next intersection.

'Move,' he said.

Cal had no choice, scarcely believing, even as he walked, that this scene was taking place on a street whose paving cracks he'd counted since he was old enough to know one from two.

He was ushered into the back of the car, separated from his captors by a partition of heavy glass. The door was locked. He was powerless. All he could do was watch the Salesman slide into the driver's seat, and the woman get in beside.

There was little chance he'd be missed from the party, he knew, and littler chance still that anyone would come looking for him. It would simply be assumed that he'd tired of the festivities and headed off home. He was in the hands of the enemy, and helpless to do anything about it.

What would Mad Mooney do now, he wondered.

The question vexed him only a moment, before the answer came. Taking out the celebratory cigar Norman had given him, he leaned back in the leather seat, and lit up.

*Good*, said the poet; take what pleasure you can, while there's still pleasure to be had. And breath to take it with.

# V

# IN THE ARMS OF MAMA PUS

In the haze of fear and cigar smoke he soon lost track of their route. His only clue to their whereabouts, when they finally came to a halt, was that the air smelt sharply of the river. Or rather, of the acreage of black mud that was exposed at low tide; expanses of muck which he'd had a terror of as a child. It wasn't until he'd reached double figures that he'd been able to walk along Otterspool Promenade without an adult between him and the railings.

The Salesman ordered him from the car. He got out obediently — it was difficult not to be obedient with a gun in his face. Shadwell immediately snatched the cigar from Cal's mouth, grinding it beneath his heel, then escorted him through a gate into a walled compound. Only now, as he laid eyes on the canyons of household refuse ahead did Cal realize where they'd brought him: the Municipal Rubbish Tip. In former years, acres of parkland had been built on the city's detritus, but there was no longer the money to transform trash into lawns. Trash it remained. Its stench — the sweet and sour of rotting vegetable matter — even overpowered the smell of the river.

'Stop,' said Shadwell, when they reached a place that seemed in no way particular.

Cal looked round in the direction of the voice. He could see very little, but it seemed Shadwell had pocketed his gun. Seizing the instant, he began to run, not choosing any particular direction, merely seeking escape. He'd covered

84

maybe four paces when something tangled with his legs, and he fell heavily, the breath knocked from him. Before he had a chance to get to his feet forms were converging on him from every side, an incoherent mass of limbs and snarls that could only be the wraith-sister's children. He was glad of the darkness; at least he couldn't see their deformities. But he felt their limbs upon him; heard their teeth snapping at his neck.

They didn't intend to devour him, however. At some cue he neither saw nor heard, their violence dwindled to mere bondage. He was held fast, his body so knotted up his joints creaked, while a terrible spectacle unfolded a few yards in front of him.

It was one of Immacolata's sisters, he had no doubt of that: a naked woman whose substance flickered and smoked as though her marrow was on fire, except that she could have no marrow, for surely she had no bones. Her body was a column of grey gas, laced with strands of bloody tissue, and from this flux fragments of finished anatomy emerged: a seeping breast, a belly swollen as if by a pregnancy months beyond its term, a smeared face in which the eyes were sewn-up slits. That explained, no doubt, her hesitant advance, and the way her smoky limbs extended from her body to test the ground ahead: the ghost was blind.

By the light this unholy mother gave off, Cal could see the children more clearly. No perversion of anatomy had been overlooked amongst them: bodies turned inside out to parade the bowel and stomach; organs whose function seemed simply to seep and wheeze lining the belly of one like teats, and mounted like a coxcomb on another's head. Yet despite their corruptions, their heads were all turned adoringly upon Mama Pus, their eyes unblinking so as not to miss a moment of her presence. She was their mother; they her loving children.

Suddenly, she started to shriek. Cal turned to look at her again. She'd taken up a squatting posture, her legs splayed, her head thrown back as she voiced her agony.

Behind her there now stood a second ghost, as naked as the first. More so perhaps, for she could scarcely lay claim to flesh.

85

She was obscenely withered, her dugs like empty purses, her face collapsed upon itself in a jumble of tooth-shard and hair. She'd taken hold of her squatting sister, whose scream had now reached a nerve-shredding height. As the swollen belly came close to bursting, there was an issue of smouldering matter from between the mother's legs. The sight was greeted with a chorus of welcomes from the children. They were entranced. So, in his horrified way, was Cal.

Mama Pus was giving birth.

The scream became a series of smaller, rhythmic shouts as the child began its journey into the living world. It was less born than shat, dropping from between its parent's legs like a vast mewling turd. No sooner had it hit the ground than the withered midwife was about her business, coming between mother and spectators to draw away veils of redundant matter from the child's body. The mother, her labours over, stood up, the flame in her flesh dying, and left the child to her sister's ministrations.

Now Shadwell came back into view. He looked down at Cal.

'Do you see?' he said, his voice all but a whisper, 'what kind of horrors these are? I warned you. Tell me where the carpet is and I'll try to make sure the child doesn't touch you.'

'I don't know. I swear I don't.'

The midwife had withdrawn. Shadwell, a sham of pity on his face, now did the same.

In the dirt a few yards from Cal the child was already standing up. It was the size of a chimpanzee, and shared with its siblings the appearance of something traumatically wounded. Portions of its inner workings were teased out through its skin, leaving its torso to collapse upon itself in places and in others sport ludicrous appendages of gut. Twin rows of dwarf limbs hung from its belly, and between its legs a sizeable scrotum depended, smoking like a censer, uncompanioned by any organ to discharge what boiled within.

The child knew its business from its first breath: to terrorize.

Though its face was still wreathed with afterbirth, its gummy eyes found Cal, and it began to shamble towards him.

'Oh Jesus . . .'

Cal began looking for the Salesman, but the man had vanished.

'I told you,' he yelled into the darkness, 'I don't know where the fucking carpet is.'

Shadwell didn't respond. Cal shouted again. Mama Pus' bastard was almost upon him.

'Jesus, Shadwell, listen to me, will you?'

Then, the by-blow spoke.

'*Cal . . .*' it said.

He stopped struggling against his restraints a moment, and looked at it in disbelief.

It spoke again. The same syllable.

'*Cal . . .*'

Even as it pronounced his name its fingers pulled at the muck about its head. The face that appeared from beneath lacked a complete skull, but it was recognizably that of its father: *Elroy*. Seeing familiar features in the midst of such deformity was the crowning horror. As Elroy's child reached to touch him Cal started yelling again, scarcely aware of what he was saying, only begging Shadwell to keep the thing from touching him.

The only reply was his own voice, echoing back and forth until it died. The child's arms jerked forward, and its long fingers latched onto Cal's face. He tried to fight it off, but it drew closer to him, its sticky body embracing him. The more he struggled the more he was caught.

The rest of the by-blows loosed their hold on him now, leaving him to the new child. It was only minutes old, but its strength was phenomenal, the vestigial hands on its belly raking Cal's skin, its grip so tight his lungs laboured for breath.

With its face inches from Cal's, it spoke again, but the voice that came from the ruined mouth was not its father's this time, but that of Immacolata.

'*Confess*,' she demanded. '*Confess what you know.*'

'I just saw a place —' he said, trying to avoid the trail of spittle that was about to fall from the beast's chin. He failed. It hit his cheek, and burned like hot fat.

'Do you know *what* place?' the Incantatrix demanded.

'No . . .' he said. 'No, I don't —'

'But you've dreamt it, haven't you? *Wept* for it . . .'

*Yes*, was the answer; of course he'd dreamt it. Who hadn't dreamt of paradise?

Momentarily his thoughts leapt from present terror to past joy. To his floating over the Fugue. The sight of that Wonderland kindled a sudden will to resist in him. The glories he saw in his mind's eye had to be preserved from the foulness that embraced him, from its makers and masters, and in such a struggle his life was not so hard to forfeit. Though he knew nothing about the carpet's present whereabouts he was ready to perish rather than risk letting anything slip that Shadwell might profit by. And while he had breath, he'd do all in his power to confound them.

Elroy's child seemed to read this new-found resolution. It drew its arms more tightly about him.

'I'll confess!' he yelled in its face. 'I'll tell you everything you want to know.'

Immediately, he began to talk.

The substance of his confession was not, however, what they wanted to hear. Instead he began to recite the train timetable out of Lime Street, which he knew by heart. He'd first started learning it at the age of eleven, having seen a Memory Man on television who'd demonstrated his skills by recalling the details of randomly chosen football matches – teams, scores, scorers – back to the 1930s. It was a perfectly useless endeavour, but its heroic scale had impressed Cal mightily, and he'd spent the next few weeks committing to memory any and every piece of information he could find, until it struck him that his magnum opus was passing to and fro at the bottom of the garden: the trains. He'd begun that day, with the local lines, his ambition elevated each time he successfully remembered a day's times faultlessly. He'd kept his information up to date for several years, as services were cancelled or stations closed. And his mind, which had difficulty putting names to faces, could still spew this perfectly redundant information out upon request.

That's what he gave them now. The services to Manchester, Crewe, Stafford, Wolverhampton, Birmingham, Coventry,

Cheltenham Spa, Reading, Bristol, Exeter, Salisbury, London, Colchester; all the times of arrival and departure, and footnotes as to which services only operated on Saturdays, and which never ran on Bank Holidays.

I'm Mad Mooney, he thought, as he delivered this filibuster, listing the services with a bright, clear voice, as if to an imbecile. The trick confounded the monster utterly. It stared at Cal while he talked, unable to understand why the prisoner had forsaken fear.

Immacolata cursed Cal through her nephew's mouth, and offered up new threats, but he scarcely heard them. The timetables had their own rhythm, and he was soon carried along by it. The beast's embrace grew tighter; it could not be long before Cal's bones began to break. But he just went on talking, drawing in gulps of breath to start each day, and letting his tongue do the rest.

It's poetry, my boy, said Mad Mooney. Never heard its like. Pure poetry.

And maybe it was. Verses of days, and lines of hours, transmuted into the stuff of poets because it was all spat into the face of death.

They'd kill him for this defiance, he knew, when they finally realized that he'd never exchange another meaningful word with them. But Wonderland would have a gate for ghosts.

He had just begun the Scottish services – to Edinburgh, Glasgow, Perth, Inverness, Aberdeen and Dundee – when he caught sight of Shadwell from the corner of his eye. The Salesman was shaking his head, and now exchanged some words with Immacolata – something about having to ask the old woman. Then he turned, and walked into the darkness. They'd given up on their prisoner. The coup de grace could only be seconds away.

He felt the grip relax. His recitation faltered for an instant, in anticipation of the fatal blow. It didn't come. Instead, the creature withdrew its arms from around him, and followed behind Shadwell, leaving Cal lying on the ground. Though released, he could scarcely move; his bruised limbs were rigid with cramp after being held fast for so long.

And now he realized that his troubles were not over. He felt the sweat on his face turning cold, as the mother of Elroy's terrible infant drew herself towards him. He could not escape her. She straddled his body, then reached down and drew his face up towards her breasts. His muscles complained at this contortion, but the pain was forgotten an instant after, as she put her nipple to his lips. A long-neglected instinct made him accept it. The breast spurted a bitter fluid down his throat. He wanted to spit it out, but his body lacked the strength to reject it. Instead he felt his consciousness flee from this last degeneracy. A dream eclipsed the horror.

He was lying in darkness on a scented bed, while a woman's voice sang to him, some wordless lullaby whose cradle rhythms were shared by a feather-light touch upon his body. Fingers were playing on his abdomen and groin. They were cold, but they knew more tricks than a whore. He was hard in a heart-beat; gasping in two. He'd never felt such caresses, coaxed by agonizing degrees to the point of no return. His gasps became cries, but the lullaby drowned them out, mocking his manhood with its nursery lilt. He was a helpless infant, despite his erection; or perhaps because of it. The touch grew more demanding, his cries more urgent.

For an instant his thrashings shook him from his dream, and his eyes flickered open long enough to see that he was still in the sister's sepulchral embrace. Then the smothering slumber claimed him again, and he discharged into an emptiness so profound it devoured not only his seed but the lullaby and its singer; and, finally, the dream itself.

He woke alone, and weeping. Every ligament tender, he untied the knot he'd made of himself, and stood up.

His watch read nine minutes after two. The last train of the night had left Lime Street long ago; and the first of Sunday morning would not run for many hours yet.

# VI

# SICK SOULS

## 1

Sometimes Mimi woke; sometimes she slept. But one was much like the other now: sleep marred by distress and discomfort – wakefulness full of unfinished thoughts that faded into scraps of nonsense, like dreams. One moment she was certain there was a small child crying in the corner of the room, until the night nurse came in, and wiped the tears from her patient's eyes. Another moment she could see, as if through a dirtied window, some place she knew, but had lost, and her old bones ached with wanting to be there.

But then came another vision, and this one she hoped against hope was a dream. It was not.

'Mimi?' said the dark woman.

The stroke that had crippled Mimi had dimmed her eyes, but she had sight enough to recognize the figure standing at the bottom of her bed. After years of being alone with her secret, somebody from the Fugue had finally found her. But there would be no tearful reunions tonight, not with this visitor, nor her dead sisters.

The Incantatrix Immacolata had come here to fulfil a promise she'd made before the Fugue had been hidden: that, if she could not rule the Seerkind, she'd destroy them. She was Lilith's descendant, she'd always claimed: the last pure line from the first state of magic. Her authority over them was therefore unquestionable. They'd laughed at her for her presumption. It wasn't their nature to be ruled, nor to count much on genealogy. Immacolata had been humiliated; a fact a woman like her – possessed, it had to be admitted, of powers that were purer than most – would not easily forget. Now she'd found the carpet's last Custodian, and she'd have blood if she could get it.

An age ago the Council had bequeathed Mimi some of the tactics of the Old Science to arm her against a situation such as this. They were minor raptures, no more; devices to distract an enemy. Nothing fatal. That took more time to learn than they'd had. She'd been grateful for them at the time, however: they'd offered some smidgen of comfort as she faced life in the Kingdom without her beloved Romo. But the years had gone by and nobody had come, either to tell her that the waiting was over and the Weave could give up its secrets, or to try and take the Fugue by force. The excitement of the early years, knowing she stood between magic and its destruction, dwindled to a weary watchfulness. She became lazy and forgetful; they all did.

Only towards the end, when she was alone, and she realized just how frail she was becoming, did she shake off the stupor that living amongst the Cuckoos had brought on, and try to set her beleaguered mental powers to the problem of the secret she'd protected for so long. But by that time her mind was wandering – the first symptoms of the stroke that would incapacitate her. It took her a day and a half to compose the short letter she'd written to Suzanna, a letter in which she'd risked saying more than she wanted to, because time was getting short, and she sensed danger close.

She'd been right; here it was. Immacolata had probably sensed the signal Mimi had sent up at the very last: a summons to any Kingdom-bound Seerkind who might have come to her aid. That, with hindsight, had probably been her greatest error. An incantatrix of Immacolata's strength would not have missed such alarms.

Here she was, come to visit Mimi like a dispossessed child, eager to make good at the death-bed, and so claim her inheritance. It was an analogy not lost on the creature.

'I told the nurse I was your daughter,' she said, 'and that I needed some time with you. Alone.'

Mimi would have spat in disgust, had she had the strength or the spittle.

'– I know you're going to die, so I've come to say goodbye, after all these years. You've lost the power of speech, I hear; so I'm not to expect you to babble your confession. There are other ways. We know how the mind can be laid bare without words, don't we?'

She stepped a little closer to the bed.

Mimi knew what the Incantatrix said was true; there were ways a body – even one as wretched and close to death as her own – could be made to give up its secrets, if the interrogator knew the methods. And Immacolata did. She, the slaughterer of her own sisters; she, the eternal virgin, whose celibacy gave her access to powers lovers were denied: she had ways. Mimi would have to turn some final trick, or all would be lost.

From the corner of her eye Mimi saw the Hag, the withered sister, hunched up beside the wall, her toothless maw wide. The Magdalene, Immacolata's second sister, was occupying the visitor's chair, her legs splayed. They were waiting for the fun to begin.

Mimi opened her mouth, as if to speak.

'Something to say?' Immacolata asked.

As the Incantatrix spoke Mimi used what little strength she had to turn her left hand palm up. There, amid the grid of her life and love lines, was a symbol, drawn in henna, and reworked so often that her skin was now irredeemably stained; a symbol taught to her hours before the great weaving by a Babu in the Council.

She'd long ago forgotten what it meant or did – if she'd ever been told – but it was one of the few defences they'd given her that she was in any condition to use.

The raptures of the Lo were physical, and her body was too paralysed to perform them; those of the Aia were musical, and, being tone deaf, had been the first she'd forgotten. The Ye-me, the Seerkind whose genius was weaving, hadn't given her raptures at all. They'd been too busy, during those last, hectic days, with the business of their magnum opus: the carpet that was soon to conceal the Fugue from sight for an age.

Indeed, most of what that Babu had taught her was beyond her present power to use – word raptures were valueless if your lips couldn't shape them. All she had left was this obscure sign – little more than a dirt-mark on her palsied hand – to keep the Incantatrix at bay.

But nothing happened. There was no release of power; not even a breath. She tried to recall if the Babu had given her some specific instruction about activating the rapture, but all her mind would conjure was his face; and a smile he'd given her; and the trees behind his head sieving sunlight through their branches. What days they'd been; and she so young; and it all an adventure.

No adventure now. Just death on a stale bed.

Suddenly, a roar. And from her palm – released by the memory, perhaps – the rapture broke.

A ball of energy leapt from her hand. Immacolata stepped back as a humming net of light came down around the bed, keeping malice at bay.

The Incantatrix was quick to respond. The menstruum, that stream of bright darkness which was the blood of her subtle body, spilled from her nostrils. It was a power Mimi had seen manifested no more than a dozen times, always and only by women: an etheric solution in which it was said the wielder could dissolve all experience, and make it again in the image of her desire. While the Old Science was a democracy of magic, available to all – independent of gender, age or moral standing – the menstruum seemed to choose those it favoured. It had driven a fair number of those chosen to suicide with its demands and its visions; but it was undeniably a power – perhaps even a condition of the flesh – that knew no bounds.

It took a few droplets only, their spheres becoming barbed in the air, to lacerate the net that the Babu rapture had created, leaving Mimi utterly vulnerable.

Immacolata stared down at the old woman, fearful of what would come next. Doubtless the Council had left the Custodian

94

with some endgame rapture which, in extremis, she'd unleash. That was why she'd counselled Shadwell that they try other routes of investigation first: in order to avoid this potentially lethal confrontation. But those routes had all been cul-de-sacs. The house in Rue Street had been robbed of its treasure. The sole witness, Mooney, had lost his wits. She'd been obliged to come here and face the Custodian, not fearing Mimi herself, but rather the scale of the defences the Council had surely lodged with her.

'Go on . . .' she said, '. . . do your worst.'

The old woman just lay there, her eyes full of anticipation.

'We haven't got forever,' Immacolata said. 'If you've got raptures, show them.'

Still she just lay there, with the arrogance of one who had power in plentiful supply.

Immacolata could bear the waiting no longer. She took a step towards the bed, in the hope of making the bitch show her powers; whatever they were. There was still no response.

Was it possible that she'd misread the signs? Was it perhaps not arrogance that made the woman lie so still, but despair? Dare she hope that the Custodian was somehow, miraculously, *defenceless*?

She touched Mimi's open palm, brushing the spent calligraphy. The power there was defunct; and nothing further came to meet her from the woman on the bed.

If Immacolata knew pleasure, she knew it then. Unlikely as it seemed, the Custodian was unarmed. She possessed no final, devastating rapture. If she'd ever had such authority, age had decayed it.

'Time to unburden yourself,' she said, and let a dribble of torment climb into the air above Mimi's trembling head.

2

The night nurse consulted the clock on the wall. It was thirty minutes since she'd left the tearful daughter with Mrs Laschenski. Strictly speaking she should have told the visitor to return the following morning, but the woman had travelled through the night, and besides there was every chance the patient would not make it to first light. Rules had to be tempered with compassion; but half an hour was enough.

As she started down the corridor, she heard a cry issuing from the old lady's room, and the sound of furniture being overturned. She was at the door in seconds. The handle was clammy, and refused to turn. She rapped on the door, as the noise within grew louder still.

'What's going on?' she demanded.

Inside, the Incantatrix looked down at the bag of dry bones and withered flesh on the bed. Where did this woman find the will-power to defy her?; to resist the needles of interrogation the menstruum had driven up through the roof of her mouth, into her very thoughts?

The Council had chosen well, electing her as one of the three guardians of the Weaveworld. Even now, with the menstruum probing the seals of her brain, she was preparing a final and absolute defence. She was going to die. Immacolata could see her willing death upon herself before the needles pricked her secrets out.

On the other side of the door the nurse's enquiries rose in pitch and volume.

'Open the door! Please, will you open the door!'

Time was running out. Ignoring the nurse's calls, Immacolata closed her eyes and dug into the past for a marriage of forms that she hoped would unseat the old woman's reason long enough for the needles to do their work. One part of the union was easily evoked: an image of death plucked from her one true refuge in the Kingdom, the Shrine of the Mortalities. The other was more problematic, for she'd only seen the man Mimi had left behind in the Fugue once or twice. But the menstruum had its way of dredging the memory up, and what better proof of the illusion's potency than the look that now came over the old woman's face, as her lost love appeared to her at the bottom of the bed, raising his rotting arms? Taking her cue, Immacolata pressed the points of her enquiry into the Custodian's cortex, but before she had a chance to find the carpet there, Mimi – with one last gargantuan effort – seized hold of the sheet with her good hand and flung it towards the phantom, a punning call on the Incantatrix's bluff.

Then she fell sideways from the bed, dead before she hit the floor.

Immacolata shrieked her fury; and as she did so, the nurse flung the door open.

What the woman saw in Room Six she would never tell, not for the rest of her long life. In part because she feared the derision of her peers; in part because if her eyes told the truth, and there were in the living world such terrors as she glimpsed in Mimi Laschenski's room, to talk of them might invite their proximity, and she, a woman of her times, had neither prayers nor wit enough to keep such darkness at bay.

Besides, they were gone even as her eyes fell upon them – the naked woman and the dead man at the foot of the bed – gone as if they'd never been. And there was just the daughter, saying: 'No . . . no . . .' and her mother dead on the floor.

'I'll get the Doctor,' said the nurse. 'Please stay here.'

But when she got back to the room, the grieving woman had made her final farewells, and left.

3

'What happened?' said Shadwell, as they drove from the hospital.

'She's dead,' said Immacolata, and said no more until they'd driven two miles from the gates.

Shadwell knew better than to press her. She would tell what she had to tell in her own good time.

Which she did, saying:

'She had no defence, Shadwell, except some poxy trick I learned in my cot.'

'How's that possible?'

'Maybe she just grew old,' came Immacolata's reply. 'Her mind rotted.'

'And the other Custodians?'

'Who knows? Dead, maybe. Wandered off into the Kingdom. She was on her own, at the last.' The Incantatrix smiled; an expression her face was not familiar with. 'There was I, being cautious and calculating, afraid she'd have raptures that'd undo me, and she had nothing. *Nothing.* Just an old woman dying in a bed.'

'If she's the last, there's no-one to stop us, is there? No-one to keep us from the Fugue.'

'So it'd seem,' Immacolata replied, then lapsed into silence again, content to watch the sleeping Kingdom slide past the window.

It still amazed her, this woeful place. Not in its physical particulars, but in its unpredictability.

They'd grown old here, the Keepers of the Weave. They — who'd loved the Fugue enough to give their lives to keep it from harm — they'd finally wearied of their vigil, and withered into forgetfulness.

Hate remembered though; hate remembered long after love had forgotten. She was living proof of that. Her purpose — to find the Fugue and break its bright heart — was undimmed after a search that had occupied a human life-time.

And that search would soon be over. The Fugue found and put up for auction, its territories playgrounds for the Cuckoos, its peoples — the four great families — sold into slavery or left to wander in this hopeless place. She looked out at the city. A fidgety light was washing brick and concrete, frightening off what little enchantment the night might have lent.

The magic of the Seerkind could not survive long in such a world. And, stripped of their raptures, what were they? A lost people, with visions behind their eyes, and no power to make them true.

They and this tarnished, forsaken city would have much to talk about.

# VII

## THE TALL-BOY

### 1

**E**ight hours before Mimi's death in the hospital, Suzanna had returned to the house in Rue Street. Evening was falling, and the building, pierced from front to back with shafts of amber light, was almost redeemed from its dreariness. But the glory didn't last for long, and when the sun took itself off to another hemisphere she was obliged to light the candles, many of which remained on the sills and the shelves, set in the graves of their predecessors. The illumination they offered was stronger than she'd expected, and more glamorous. She moved from room to room accompanied everywhere by the scent of melting wax, and could almost imagine Mimi might have been happy here, in this cocoon.

Of the design which her grandmother had shown her, she could find no sign. It was not in the grain of the floorboards, nor in the pattern of the wallpaper. Whatever it had been, it was gone now. She didn't look forward to the melancholy task of breaking that news to the old lady.

What she did find, however, all but concealed behind the stack of furniture at the top of the stairs, was the tall-boy. It took a little time to remove the items piled in front of it, but there was a revelation waiting when she finally set the candle on the floor before it, and opened the doors.

The vultures who'd picked the household clean had forgotten to rifle the contents of the tall-boy. Mimi's clothes still hung on the rails, coats and furs and ball-gowns, all, most likely, unworn since last Suzanna had opened this treasure trove. Which thought reminded her of what she'd sought on that occasion. She went down on her haunches, telling herself that it was folly to think her gift would still be there, and yet *knowing* indisputably that it was.

She was not disappointed. There, amongst the shoes and tissue, she found a package wrapped in plain brown paper and marked with her name. The gift had been postponed, but not lost.

Her hands had begun to tremble. The knot in the faded ribbon defied her for half a minute, and then came free. She pulled the paper off.

Inside: a book. Not new, to judge by its scuffed corners, but finely bound in leather. She opened it. To her surprise, she found it was in German. *Geschichten der Geheimen Orte* the title read, which she hesitatingly translated as *Stories of the Secret Places.* But even if she hadn't had a smattering of the language, the illustrations would have given the subject away: it was a book of faery-tales.

She sat down at the top of the stairs, candle at her side, and began to study the volume more closely. The stories were familiar, of course: she'd encountered them, in one form or another, a hundred times. She'd seen them re-interpreted as Hollywood cartoons, as erotic fables, as the subject of learned theses and feminist critiques. But their bewitchment remained undiluted by commerce or academe. Sitting there, the child in her wanted to hear these stories told again, though she knew every twist and turn, and had the end in mind before the first line was spoken. That didn't matter, of course. Indeed their inevitability was part of their power. Some tales could never be told too often.

Experience had taught her much: and most of the news was bad. But these stories taught different lessons. That sleep resembled death, for instance, was no revelation; but that death might with kisses be healed into mere sleep . . . that was knowledge of a different order. Mere wish-fulfilment, she chided herself. Real life had no miracles to offer. The devouring beast, if cut open, did *not* disgorge its victims unharmed. Peasants were not raised overnight to princedom, nor was evil ever vanquished by a union of true hearts. They were the kind of illusions that the pragmatist she'd striven so hard to be had kept at bay.

Yet the stories moved her. She couldn't deny it. And they moved her in a way only *true* things could. It wasn't sentiment that brought tears to her eyes. The stories weren't sentimental. They were tough, even cruel. No, what made her weep was being reminded of an inner life she'd been so familiar with as a child; a life that was both an escape from, and a revenge upon, the pains and frustrations of childhood; a life that was neither mawkish nor unknowing; a life of mind-places — haunted, soaring — that she'd chosen to forget when she'd took up the cause of adulthood.

More than that; in this reunion with the tales that had given her a mythology, she found images that might help her fathom her present confusion.

The outlandishness of the story she'd entered, coming back to Liverpool, had thrown her assumptions into chaos. But here, in the pages of the book, she found a state of being in which nothing was fixed: where magic ruled, bringing transformations and miracles. She'd walked there once, and far from feeling lost, could have passed for one of its inhabitants. If she could recapture that insolent indifference to reason, and let it lead her through the maze ahead, she might comprehend the forces she knew were waiting to be unleashed around her.

It would be painful to relinquish her pragmatism, however: it had kept her from sinking so often. In the face of waste and sorrow she'd held on by staying cool; rational. Even when her parents had died, separated by some unspoken betrayal which kept them, even at the last, from comforting each other, she'd coped; simply by immersing herself in practicalities until the worst was over.

Now the book beckoned, with its chimeras and its sorceries; all ambiguity; all flux; and her pragmatism would be worthless. No matter. Whatever the years had taught her about loss, and compromise, and defeat she was here invited back into a

101

forest in which maidens tamed dragons; and one of those maidens still had her face.

Having scanned three or four of the stories, she turned to the front of the book, in search of an inscription. It was brief.

'*To Suzanna,*' it read. '*Love from M.L.*'

It shared the page with an odd epigram:

*Das, was man sich vorstellt, braucht man nie zu verlieren.*

She struggled with this, suspecting that her rusty German might be missing the felicities. The closest approximation she could make was:

*That which is imagined need never be lost.*

With this oblique wisdom in mind, she returned to the stories, lingering over the illustrations, which had the severity of woodcuts but on closer inspection concealed all manner of subtleties. Fish with human faces gazed up from beneath the pristine surface of a pool; two strangers at a banquet exchanged whispers that had taken solid form in the air above their heads; in the heart of a wild wood figures all but hidden amongst the trees showed pale, expectant faces.

The hours came and went, and when, having been through the book from cover to cover, she briefly closed her eyes to rest them, sleep overcame her.

When she woke she found her watch had stopped a little after two. The wick at her side flickered in a pool of wax, close to drowning. She got to her feet, limping around the landing until the pins and needles had left her foot, and then went into the back bedroom in search of a fresh candle.

There was one on the window ledge. As she picked it up, her eye caught a movement in the yard below. Her heart jumped; but she stood absolutely still so as not to draw attention to herself, and watched. The figure was in shadow, and it wasn't until he forsook the corner of the yard that the starlight showed her the young man she'd seen here the day before.

She started downstairs, picking up a fresh flame on the way. She wanted to speak to the man; wanted to quiz him on the reasons for his flight, and the identity of his pursuers.

As she stepped out into the yard he rose from his hiding place and made a dash for the back gate.

'*Wait!*' she called after him. 'It's Suzanna.'

The name could mean little to him, but he halted nevertheless.

'Who?' he said.

'I saw you yesterday. You were running –'

The girl in the hall, Cal realized. The one who'd come between him and the Salesman.

'What happened to you?' she said.

He looked terrible. His clothes were ripped, his face dirtied; and, though she couldn't be sure, bloodied too.

'I don't know,' he said, his voice scraping gravel. 'I don't know anything any longer.'

'Why don't you come inside?'

He didn't move.

'How long have you been here?' he said.

'Hours.'

'And the house is empty?'

'Except for me, yes.'

With this ascertained, he followed her through the back door. She lit several more candles. The light confirmed her suspicions. There *was* blood on him; and a cess-pit smell.

'Is there any running water?' he said.

'I don't know; we can try.'

They were in luck; the Water Board had not turned off the supply. The kitchen tap rattled and the pipes roared but finally a stream of icy water was spat forth. Cal slung off his jacket and doused his face and arms.

'I'll see if I can find a towel,' said Suzanna. 'What's your name, by the way?'

'Cal.'

She left him to his ablutions. With her gone he stripped off his shirt and sluiced down his chest, neck and back with chilly water. She was back before he was done, with a pillow-slip.

'Nearest thing I can find to a towel,' she said.

She had set two chairs in the lower front room, and lit several candles there. They sat together, and talked.

'Why did you come back?' she wanted to know. 'After yesterday.'

'I saw something here,' he said, cautiously. 'And you? Why are you here?'

'This is my grandmother's house. She's in hospital. Dying. I came back to look around.'

'The two I saw yesterday,' Cal said. 'Were they friends of your grandmother's?'

'I doubt it. What did they want with you?'

Here Cal knew he got into sticky ground. How could he begin to tell her what joys and fears the last few days had brought?

'It's difficult . . .' he said. 'I mean, I'm not sure anything that's happened to me recently makes much sense.'

'That makes two of us,' she replied.

He was looking at his hands, like a palmist in search of a future. She studied him; his torso was covered in scratches, as though he'd been wrestling wolves.

When he looked up his pale blue eyes, fringed with black lashes, caught her scrutiny. He blushed slightly.

'You said you saw something here,' she said. 'Can you tell me what?'

It was a simple question, and he saw no reason not to tell her. If she disbelieved him, that was her problem, not his. But she didn't. Indeed, as soon as he described the carpet her eyes grew wide and wild.

'Of course,' she said. 'A carpet. *Of course.*'

'You know about it?' he said.

She told him what had happened at the hospital; the design Mimi had tried to show her.

Now any lingering doubts about telling the whole story were forgotten. He gave her the adventure from the day the bird had escaped. His vision of the Fugue; Shadwell and his coat; Immacolata; the by-blows; their mother and the midwife; events at the wedding, and after. She punctuated his narrative with insights of her own, about Mimi's life here in the house, the doors bolted, the windows nailed down, living in a fortress as if awaiting siege.

'She must have known somebody would come for the carpet sooner or later.'

'Not for the carpet,' said Cal. 'For the Fugue.'

She saw his eyes grow dreamy at the word, and envied him his glimpse of the place: its hills, its lakes, its wild woods. And were there maidens amongst those trees, she wanted to ask, who tamed dragons with their song? That was something she would have to discover for herself.

'So the carpet's a doorway, is it?' she said.

'I don't know,' he replied.

'I wish we could ask Mimi. Maybe she –'

Before the sentence was out, Cal was on his feet.

'*Oh my God.*' Only now did he recall Shadwell's words on the rubbish tip, about going to speak to the old woman.

He'd meant Mimi, who else? As he pulled on his shirt he told Suzanna what he'd heard.

'We have to go to her,' he said. 'Christ! Why didn't I think?'

His agitation was infectious. Suzanna blew out the candles, and was at the front door before him.

'Surely Mimi'll be safe in a hospital,' she said.

'Nobody's safe,' he replied, and she knew it was true.

On the step, she about-faced and disappeared into the house again, returning seconds later with a battered book in her hands.

'Diary?' he said.

'Map,' she replied.

# VIII

# FOLLOWING THE THREAD

## 1

imi was dead.

Her killers had come and gone in the night, leaving an elaborate smoke-screen to conceal their crime.

'There's nothing mysterious about your grandmother's death,' Doctor Chai insisted. 'She was failing fast.'

'There was somebody here last night.'

'That's right. Her daughter.'

'She only had one daughter; my mother. And she's been dead for two and a half years.'

'Whoever it was, she did Mrs Laschenski no harm. Your grandmother died of natural causes.'

There was little use in arguing, Suzanna realized. Any further attempt to explain her suspicions would end in confusion. Besides, Mimi's death had begun a new spiral of puzzles. Chief amongst them: what had the old woman known, or been, that she had to be dispatched?; and how much of her part in this puzzle would Suzanna now be obliged to assume? One question begged the other, and both, with Mimi silenced, would have to go unanswered. The only other source of information was the creature who'd stooped to kill the old woman on her death-bed: Immacolata. And that was a confrontation Suzanna felt far from ready for.

They left the hospital, and walked. She was badly shaken.

'Shall we eat?' Cal suggested.

It was still only seven in the morning, but they found a cafe

106

that served breakfast and ordered glutton's portions. The eggs and bacon, toast and coffee restored them both somewhat, though the price of a sleepless night still had to be paid.

'I'll have to 'phone my uncle in Canada,' said Suzanna. 'Tell him what happened.'

'All of it?' said Cal.

'Of course not,' she said. 'That's between the two of us.'

He was glad of that. Not just because he didn't like the thought of the story spreading, but because he wanted the intimacy of a secret shared. This Suzanna was like no woman he had ever met before. There was no facade, no games-playing. They were, in one night of confessionals – and this sad morning – suddenly companions in a mystery which, though it had brought him closer to death than he'd ever been, he'd happily endure if it meant he kept her company.

'There won't be many tears shed over Mimi,' Suzanna was saying. 'She was never loved.'

'Not even by you?'

'I never knew her,' she said, and gave Cal a brief synopsis of Mimi's life and times. 'She was an outsider,' Suzanna concluded. 'And now we know why.'

'Which brings us back to the carpet. We have to trace the house cleaners.'

'You need some sleep first.'

'No. I've got my second wind. But I do want to go home. Just to feed the pigeons.'

'Can't they survive without you for a few hours?'

Cal frowned. 'If it weren't for them,' he said, 'I wouldn't be here.'

'Sorry. Do you mind if I come with you?'

'I'd like that. Maybe you can give Dad something to smile about.'

As it was, Brendan had smiles aplenty today; Cal had not seen his father so happy since before Eileen's illness. The change was uncanny. He welcomed them both into the house with a stream of banter.

'Coffee, anybody?' he offered, and went off into the kitchen. 'By the way Cal, Geraldine was here.'

'What did she want?'

'She brought some books you'd given her; said she didn't want them any longer.' He turned from the coffee-brewing and stared at Cal. 'She said you've been behaving oddly.'

'Must be in the blood,' said Cal, and his father grinned. 'I'm going to look at the birds.'

'I've already fed them today. And cleaned them out.'

'You're really feeling better.'

'Why not?' said Brendan. 'I've got people watching over me.'

Cal nodded, not quite comprehending. Then he turned to Suzanna.

'Want to see the champions?' he said, and they stepped outside. The day was already balmy.

'There's something off about Dad,' said Cal, as he led the way down the clogged path to the loft. 'Two days ago he was practically suicidal.'

'Maybe the bad times have just run their course,' she said.

'Maybe,' he replied, as he opened the loft door. As he did so, a train roared by, making the earth tremble.

'Nine-twenty-five to Penzance,' Cal said, as he led her inside.

'Doesn't it disturb the birds?' she asked. 'Being so close to the tracks?'

'They got used to it when they were still in their shells,' he replied, and went to greet the pigeons.

She watched him talking to them, paddling his fingers against the wire mesh. He was a strange one, no doubt of that; but no stranger than she, probably. What surprised her was the casual way they dealt with the imponderables which had suddenly entered their lives. They stood, she sensed, on a threshold; in the realm beyond a little strangeness might be a necessity.

Cal suddenly turned from the cage.

'*Gilchrist*,' he said, with a fierce grin. 'I just remembered. They talked about a guy called Gilchrist.'

'Who did?'

'When I was on the wall. The removal men. God, yes! I looked at the birds and it all came back. I was on the wall and they were talking about selling the carpet to someone called *Gilchrist*.'

'That's our man then.'

Cal was back in the house in moments.

'I don't have any cake –' Brendan said as his son made for the telephone in the hallway. 'What's the panic?'

'It's nothing much,' said Suzanna.

Brendan poured her a cup of coffee, while Cal rifled through the directory. 'You're not a local lass, are you?' Brendan said.

'I live in London.'

'Never liked London,' he commented. 'Soulless place.'

'I've got a studio in Muswell Hill. You'd like it.' When Brendan looked puzzled at this, she added: 'I make pottery.'

'I've found it,' said Cal, directory in hand. '*K. W. Gilchrist*,' he read, '*Second-Hand Retailer*.'

'What's all this about?' said Brendan.

'I'll give them a call,' Cal said.

'It's Sunday,' said Suzanna.

'Lot of these places are open Sunday morning,' he replied, and returned to the hallway.

'Are you buying something?' Brendan said.

'In a manner of speaking,' Suzanna replied.

Cal dialled the number. The receiver at the other end was picked up promptly. A woman said:

'Gilchrist's?'

'Hello,' said Cal. 'I'd like to speak to Mr Gilchrist please.'

There was a beat's silence, then the woman said:

'Mr Gilchrist's dead.'

Jesus, Shadwell was fast, Cal thought.

But the telephonist hadn't finished:

'He's been dead eight years,' she said. Her voice had less colour than the speaking clock. 'What's your enquiry concerning?'

'A carpet,' said Cal.

'You want to buy a carpet?'

'No. Not exactly. I think a carpet was brought to your saleroom by mistake —'

'By *mistake*?'

'That's right. And I have to have it back. Urgently.'

'I'm afraid you'll have to speak to Mr Wilde about that.'

'Could you put me through to Mr Wilde then, please?'

'He's in the Isle of Wight.'

'When will he be back?'

'Thursday morning. You'll have to ring back then.'

'Surely that must be —'

He stopped, realizing the line was dead.

'Damn,' he said. He looked up too see Suzanna standing at the kitchen door. 'Nobody there to talk to.' He sighed. 'Where does that leave us?'

'Like thieves in the night,' she replied softly.


3


When Cal and the woman had gone, Brendan sat awhile watching the garden. He'd have to get to work on it soon: Eileen's letter had chastized him for being so lax in its upkeep.

Musing on the letter inevitably led him back to its carrier, the celestial Mr Shadwell.

Without analysing why, he got up and went to the 'phone, consulting the card the angel had given him, then dialled. His memory of the encounter with Shadwell had almost been burned away by the brightness of the gift the Salesman had brought, but there'd been a bargain made, that he *did* remember, and it somehow concerned Cal.

110

'Is that Mr Shadwell?'

'Who is this please?'

'It's Brendan Mooney.'

'Oh Brendan. How good to hear your voice. Do you have something to tell me? About Cal?'

'He went to a warehouse, for furniture and such . . .'

'Did he indeed. Then we shall find him, and make him a happy man. Was he alone?'

'No. There was a woman with him. A lovely woman.'

'Her name?'

'Suzanna Parrish.'

'And the warehouse?'

A vague twinge of doubt touched Brendan. 'Why is it you need Cal?'

'I told you. A prize.'

'Oh yes. A prize.'

'Something to take his breath away. The warehouse, Brendan. We have a deal, after all. Fair's fair.'

Brendan put his hand into his pocket. The letter was still warm. There was no harm in making bargains with angels, was there? What could be safer?

He named the warehouse.

'They only went for a carpet –' Brendan said.

The receiver clicked.

'Are you still there?' he said.

But the divine messenger was probably already winging his way.

## IX

# FINDERS KEEPERS

## 1

**G**ilchrist's Second-Hand Furniture Warehouse had once been a cinema, in the years when cinemas were still palatial follies. A folly it remained, with its mock-rococo facade, and the unlikely dome perched on its roof; but there was nothing remotely palatial about it now. It stood within a stone's throw of the Dock Road, the only property left in its block that remained in use. The rest were either boarded up or burned out.

Standing at the corner of Jamaica Street, staring across at the dereliction, Cal wondered if the late Mr Gilchrist would have been proud to have his name emblazoned across such a decayed establishment. Business could not flourish here, unless they were the kind of dealings best done out of the public eye.

The opening times of the warehouse were displayed on a weather-beaten board, where the cinema had once announced its current fare. Sundays, it was open between nine-thirty and twelve. It was now one-fifteen. The double-doors were closed and bolted, and a pair of huge ironwork gates, a grotesque addition to the facade, padlocked in front of the doors.

'What are your house-breaking skills like?' Cal asked Suzanna.

'Under-developed,' she replied. 'But I'm a fast learner.'

They crossed Jamaica Street for a closer inspection. There was little need to pretend innocence; there had been no pedestrians on the street since they'd arrived, and traffic was minimal.

'There must be some way in,' said Suzanna. 'You head round the far side. I'll go this way.'

'Right. Meet you at the back.'

They parted. Whereas Cal's route had taken him into shadow, Suzanna's left her in bright sunlight. Oddly, she found herself longing for some clouds. The heat was making her blood sing, as though she was tuned in to some alien radio-station, and its melodies were whining around her skull.

As she listened to them Cal stepped around the corner, startling her.

'I've found a way,' he said, and led her round to what had once been the cinema's emergency exit. It too was padlocked, but both chain and lock were well rusted. He had already found himself half a brick, with which he now berated the lock. Brick-shards flew off in all directions, but after a dozen blows the chain surrendered. Cal put his shoulder to the door, and pushed. There was a commotion from inside, as a mirror and several other items piled against the door toppled over; but he was able to force a gap large enough for them to squeeze through.

## 2

The interior was a kind of Purgatory, in which thousands of household items — armchairs, wardrobes, lamps large and small, curtains, rugs — awaited Judgment, piled up in dusty wretchedness. The place stank of its occupants; of things claimed by woodworm and rot and sheer usage; of once fine pieces now so age-worn even their makers would not have given them house room.

And beneath the smell of decrepitude, something more bitter and more human. The scent of sweat perhaps, soaked up by the boards of a sick bed, or in the fabric of a lamp that had burned through a night whose endurer had known no morning. Not a place to linger too long.

They separated once more, for speed's sake.

113

'Anything that looks promising,' Cal said, 'holler.'

He was now eclipsed by piles of furniture.

The whine in Suzanna's skull did not die down once she was out of the sun; it worsened. Maybe it was the enormity of the task before them that made her head spin, like an impossible quest from some faery-tale, seeking a particle of magic in the wilderness of decay.

The same thought, though formulated differently, was passing through Cal's mind. The more he searched, the more he doubted his memory. Maybe it hadn't been Gilchrist they'd named; or perhaps the removal men had decided the profit made bringing the carpet here would not repay their effort.

As he turned a corner, he heard a scraping sound from behind a stack of furniture.

'Suzanna?' he said. The word went out and returned unanswered. The noise had already faded behind him, but it had sent adrenalin rushing through his system, and it was with speedier step that he made his way to the next mountain of goods and chattels. Even before he came within five yards of it his eyes had alighted upon the rolled carpet that was all but concealed beneath half a dozen dining chairs and a chest of drawers. All of these items lacked price-tags, which suggested they were recent, unsorted acquisitions.

He went down on his knees and pulled at the edge of the carpet, in an attempt to see the design. The border was damaged, the weave weak. When he pulled he felt strands snap. But he could see enough to confirm what his gut already knew: that this was the carpet from Rue Street, the carpet which Mimi Laschenski had lived and died protecting; the carpet of the Fugue.

He stood up and started to unpile the chairs, deaf to the sound of approaching footsteps at his back.

3

The first thing Suzanna saw was a shadow on the ground. She looked up.

114

A face appeared between two wardrobes, only to move off again before she could call it by its name.

*Mimi! It was Mimi.*

She walked over to the wardrobes. There was no sign of anyone. Was she losing her sanity? First the din in her head, now hallucinations?

And yet, why were they here if they didn't believe in miracles? Doubt was drowned in a sudden rush of hope – that the dead might somehow break the seal on the invisible world and come amongst the living.

She called her grandmother's name, softly. And she was granted an answer. Not in words, but in the scent of lavender water. Off to her left, down a corridor of piled tea-chests, a ball of dust rolled and came to rest. She went towards it, or rather towards the source of the breeze that had carried it, the scent getting stronger with every step she took.

## 4

'That's my property, I believe,' said the voice at Cal's back. He turned. Shadwell was standing a few feet from him. His jacket was unbuttoned.

'Perhaps you'd stand aside, Mooney, and let me claim what's mine.'

Cal wished he'd had the presence of mind to come here armed. At that moment he'd have had no hesitation in stabbing Shadwell through his gleaming eye and calling himself a hero for it. As it was, all he had were his bare hands. They'd have to suffice.

He took a step towards Shadwell, but as he did so the man stood aside. There was somebody standing behind him. One of the sisters, no doubt; or their bastards.

Cal didn't wait to see, but turned and picked up one of the chairs from those dumped on the carpet. His action brought a small avalanche; chairs spilling between him and the enemy. He threw the one he held towards the shadowy form that had taken Shadwell's place. He picked up a second, and threw it

115

the way of the first, but now the target had disappeared into the labyrinth of furniture. So had the Salesman.

Cal turned, his muscles fired, and put his back into shifting the chest of drawers. He succeeded; the chest toppled backwards, knocking over several other pieces as it fell. He was glad of the commotion; perhaps it would draw Suzanna's attention. Now he reached to take possession of the carpet, but as he did so something seized him from behind. He was dragged bodily from his prize, a small section of the carpet coming away in his hand, then he was flung across the floor.

He came to a halt against a pile of ornately framed paintings and photographs, several of which toppled and smashed. He lay amid the litter of glass for a moment to catch his breath, but the next sight snatched it from him again.

The by-blow was coming at him out of the gloom.

'Get up!' it told him.

He was dead to its instruction, his attention claimed by the face before him. It wasn't Elroy's off-spring, though this monstrosity also had its father's features. No; this child was *his*.

The horror he'd glimpsed, stirring from the lullaby he'd heard lying in the dirt of the rubbish tip, had been all too real. The sisters had squeezed his seed from him, and this beast with his face was the consequence.

It was not a fine likeness. Its naked body was entirely hairless, and there were several horrid distortions – the fingers of one hand were twice their natural length, and those of the other half-inch stumps, while from the shoulder blades eruptions of matter sprang like malformed wings – parodies, perhaps, of the creatures his dreams envied.

It was made in more of its father's image than the other beasts had been, however, and faced with himself, he hesitated.

It was enough, that hesitation, to give the beast the edge. It leapt at him, seizing his throat with its long-fingered hand, its touch without a trace of warmth, its mouth sucking at his as if to steal the breath from his lips.

116

It intended patricide, no doubt of that; its grip was unconditional. He felt his legs weaken, and the child allowed him to collapse to his knees, following him down. The knuckles of his fingers brushed against the glass shards, and he made a fumbling attempt to pick one up, but between mind and hand the instruction lost urgency. The weapon dropped from his hand.

Somewhere, in that place of breath and light from which he was outcast, he heard Shadwell laughing. Then the sound stopped, and he was staring at his own face, which looked back at him as if from a corrupted mirror. His eyes, which he'd always liked for the paleness of their colour; the mouth, which though it had been an embarrassment to him as a child because he'd thought it too girlish, he'd now trained into a modicum of severity when the occasion demanded, and which was, he was told, capable of a winning smile. The ears, large and protuberant: a comedian's ears on a face that warranted something sleeker . . .

Probably most people slip out of the world with such trivialities in their heads. Certainly it was that way for Cal.

Thinking of his ears, the undertow took hold of him and dragged him down.

# X

# THE MENSTRUUM

Suzanna knew the instant before she stepped into what had once been the cinema foyer that this was an error. Even then, she might have retreated, but that she heard Mimi's voice speak her name and before any argument could stay her step her feet had carried her through the door.

The foyer was darker than the main warehouse, but she could see the vague figure of her grandmother standing beside the boarded-up box-office.

'Mimi?' she said, her mind a blur of contrary impressions.

'Here I am,' said the old lady, and opened her arms to Suzanna.

The proffered embrace was also an error of judgment, but on the part of the enemy. Gestures of physical affection had not been Mimi's forte in life, and Suzanna saw no reason to suppose her grandmother would have changed her habits upon expiring.

'You're not Mimi,' she said.

'I know it's a surprise, seeing me,' the would-be ghost replied. The voice was soft as a feather-fall. 'But there's nothing to be afraid of.'

'Who are you?'

'You *know* who I am,' came the response.

Suzanna didn't linger for any further words of seduction, but turned to retrace her path. There were perhaps three yards between her and the exit, but now they seemed as many miles. She tried to take a step on that long road, but the commotion in her head suddenly rose to deafening proportions.

The presence behind her had no intention of letting her escape. It sought a confrontation, and it was a waste of effort to defy it. So she turned and looked.

The mask was melting, though there was ice in the eyes that emerged from behind it, not fire. She knew the face, and though she'd not thought herself ready to brave its fury yet, she was strangely elated by the sight. The last shreds of Mimi evaporated, and Immacolata stood revealed.

'My sister . . .' she said, the air around her dancing to her words, '. . . my sister the Hag had me play that part. She thought she saw Mimi in your face. She was right, wasn't she? You're her child.'

'Grandchild,' Suzanna murmured.

'*Child*,' came the certain reply.

Suzanna stared at the woman before her, fascinated by the masterwork of grief half-concealed in those features. Immacolata flinched at her scrutiny.

'How *dare* you pity me?' she said, as if she'd read Suzanna's thought, and on the words something leapt from her face.

It came too fast for Suzanna to see what it was; she had time only to throw herself out of its whining path. The wall behind her shook as it was struck. The next instant the face was spilling more brightness towards her.

Suzanna was not afraid. The display only elated her further. This time, as the brightness came her way, her instinct overruled all constraints of sanity, and she put her hand out as if to catch the light.

It was like plunging her arm into a torrent of ice-water. A torrent in which innumerable fish were swimming, fast, fast, against the flood; swimming to spawn. She closed her fist, snatching at this brimming tide, and *pulled*.

The action had three consequences. One, a cry from Immacolata. Two, the sudden cessation of the din in Suzanna's head. Three, all that her hand had felt — the chill, the torment and the shoal it contained — all of that was suddenly *within* her. *Her body was the flood.* Not the body of flesh and bone, but some other anatomy, made more of thought than of substance, and more ancient than either. Somehow it had recognized itself in Immacolata's assault, and thrown off its sleep.

Never in her life had she felt so complete. In the face of this feeling all other ambition – for happiness, for pleasure, for power – all others faded.

She looked back at Immacolata, and her new eyes saw not an enemy but a woman possessed of the same torrent that ran in her own veins. A woman twisted and full of anguish but for all that more like her than not.

'That was stupid,' said the Incantatrix.

'Was it?' said Suzanna. She didn't think so.

'Better you remained unfound. Better you never tasted the menstruum.'

'The menstruum?'

'Now you'll know more than you wish to know, feel more than you ever wanted to feel.' There seemed to be something approximating pity in Immacolata's voice. 'So the grief begins,' she said. 'And it will never end. Believe me. You should have lived and died a Cuckoo.'

'Is that how Mimi died?' said Suzanna.

The ice eyes flickered. 'She knew what risks she took. She had Seerkind blood, and that's always run freely. You're of their blood too, through that bitch grand-dam of yours.'

'*Seerkind?*' So many new words. 'Are they the Fugue people?'

'They're *dead* people,' came the reply. 'Don't look to them for answers. They're dust soon enough. Gone the way everything in this stinking Kingdom goes. To dirt and mediocrity. We'll see to that. You're alone. Like she was.'

That '*we*' reminded her of the Salesman, and the potency of the coat he wore.

'Is Shadwell a Seerkind?' she asked.

'*Him?*' The thought was apparently preposterous. 'No. Any power he's got's my gift.'

120

'*Why?*' said Suzanna. She understood little of Immacolata, but enough to know that she and Shadwell were not a perfect match.

'He taught me . . .' the Incantatrix began, her hand moving up to her face, '. . . he taught me, the *show*.' The hand passed across her features, and upon reappearing she was smiling, almost warmly. 'You'll need that now.'

'And for that you're his mistress?'

The sound that came from the woman might have been a laugh; but only might. 'I leave love to the Magdalene, sister. She's an appetite for it. Ask Mooney —'

*Cal.* She'd forgotten Cal.

'— if he has the breath to answer.'

Suzanna glanced back towards the door.

'Go on . . .' said Immacolata, '. . . go find him. I won't stop you.'

The brightness in her, the menstruum, knew the Incantatrix was telling the truth. That flood was part of them both now. It bonded them in ways Suzanna could not yet guess at.

'The battle's already lost, sister,' Immacolata murmured as Suzanna reached the threshold. 'While you indulged your curiosity, the Fugue's fallen into our hands.'

Suzanna stepped back into the warehouse, fear beginning for the first time. Not for herself, but for Cal. She yelled his name into the murk.

'Too late . . .' said the woman behind her.

'*Cal!*'

There was no reply. She started to search for him, calling his name at intervals, her anxiety growing with each unanswered shout. The place was a maze; twice she found herself in a location she'd already searched.

It was the glitter of broken glass that drew her attention; and then, lying face down a little way from it, Cal. Before she got close enough to touch him she sensed the profundity of his stillness.

He was too brittle, the menstruum in her said. You know how these Cuckoos are.

She rejected the thought. It wasn't hers.

121

'Don't be dead.'

*That* was hers. It slipped from her as she knelt down beside him, a plea to his silence.

'Please God, don't be dead.'

She was frightened to touch him, for fear of discovering the worst, all the while knowing that she was the only help he had. His head was turned towards her, his eyes closed, his mouth open, trailing blood-tinged spittle. Instinctively, her hand went to his hair, as if she might stroke him awake, but pragmatism had not entirely deserted her, and instead her fingers sought the pulse in his neck. It was weak.

*So the grief begins*, Immacolata had said, mere minutes before. Had she known, even as she offered that prophecy, that Cal was half way to dying already?

Of course she'd known. Known, and welcomed the grief this would bring, because she wanted Suzanna's pleasure in the menstruum soured from its discovery; wanted them sisters in sorrow.

Distracted by the realization she focused again on Cal to find that her hand had left his neck and was once again stroking his hair. Why was she doing this? He wasn't a sleeping child. He was hurt; he needed more concrete help. But even as she rebuked herself she felt the menstruum start to rise from her lower abdomen, washing her entrails, and lungs and heart, and moving – without any conscious instruction – down her arm towards Cal. Before, it had been indifferent to his wounding; *you know how these Cuckoos are*, it had said to her. But her rage, or perhaps her sadness, had chastened it. Now she felt its energies carry her need to wake him, to heal him, through the palm of her hand and into his sealed head.

It was both an extraordinary sensation, and one she felt perfectly at ease with. When, at the last moment, it seemed not to want to go, she pressed it forward and it obeyed her, its stream flowing into him. It was hers to control, she realized, with a rush of exhilaration, which was followed immediately by an ache of loss as the body below her drank the torment down.

He was greedy for healing. Her joints began to jitter as the

122

menstruum ran from her, and in her skull that alien song rose like a dozen sirens. She tried to take her hand from his head, but her muscles wouldn't obey the imperative. The menstruum had taken charge of her body, it seemed. She'd been too hasty, assuming control would be easy. It was deliberately depleting itself, to teach her not to press it.

An instant before she passed out, it decided enough was enough, and removed her hand. The flow was abruptly stemmed. She put her shaking hands up to her face, Cal's scent on her fingertips. By degrees the whine in her skull wound down. The faintness began to pass.

'Are you all right?' Cal asked her.

She dropped her hands and looked across at him. He'd raised himself from the ground, and was now gingerly investigating his bloodied mouth.

'I think so,' she said. 'You?'

'I'll do,' he replied. 'I don't know what happened . . .' The words trailed away as the memory came back, and a look of alarm crossed his face.

*'The carpet —'*

He hauled himself to his feet, looking all around.

'— I had it in my hand,' he said. 'Jesus, I had it in my hand!'

'They've taken it!' she said.

She thought he was going to cry, the way his features crumpled up, but it was rage that emerged.

'Fucking Shadwell!' he shouted, sweeping a copse of table-lamps off the top of a chest-of-drawers. 'I'll kill him! I swear —'

She stood up still feeling giddy, and her downcast eyes caught sight of something in the litter of broken glass beneath their feet — she stooped again; cleared the fragments, and there was a piece of the carpet. She picked it up.

'They didn't get it all,' she said, offering the find to Cal.

The anger melted from his face. He took it from her almost reverentially, and studied it. There were half a dozen motifs worked into the piece, though he could make no sense of them.

Suzanna watched him. He held the fragment so delicately,

as though it might bruise. Then he sniffed, hard, and wiped his nose with the back of his hand.

'Fucking Shadwell,' he said again, but softly now; numbly.

'What do we do now?' she wondered aloud.

He looked up at her. This time there were tears in his eyes.

'Get out of here,' he said. 'See what the sky says.'

'Huh?'

He offered a tiny smile.

'Sorry,' he said. 'Must be Mad Mooney talking.'

124

# Part Three

# The Exiles

*'Wandering between two worlds, one dead,*
*The other powerless to be born.'*

Matthew Arnold
*The Grande Chartreuse*

# I

## THE RIVER

The defeat they'd sustained was utter. The Salesman had snatched the Weave from Cal's very fingers. But, though they had nothing to be jubilant about, they had at least survived the clash. Was it simply that fact that made his spirits rise when they stepped out of the warehouse into the warm air?

It smelt of the Mersey; of silt and salt. And it was there – at Suzanna's instigation – they went. They walked without exchanging a word, down Jamaica Street to the Dock Road, then followed the high, black wall that bounded the docks until they found a gate that gave them access to the wharfs. The region was deserted. It was years since the last of the big cargo vessels had berthed here to unload. They wandered through a ghost-town of empty warehouses to the river itself, Cal's gaze creeping back, and back again, to the face of the woman at his side. There was some change in her, he sensed; some freight of hidden feeling which he couldn't unlock.

The poet had something to say on the subject.

'Lost for words, boy?' he piped up in Cal's head. 'She's a strange one, isn't she?'

That was certainly the truth. From his first sight of her at the bottom of the stairs, she'd seemed haunted. They had that in common. They shared too the same determination, fuelled perhaps by an unspoken fear that they'd lose sight of the mystery they'd dreamt of for so long. Or was he kidding himself, reading lines from his own story into her face? Was it just his eagerness to find an ally that made him see similarities between them?

She was staring into the river, snakes of sunlight from the water playing on her face. He'd known her only a night and a day, but she awoke in him the same contradictions – unease and profound contentment; a sense that she was both familiar and unknown – that his first glimpse of the Fugue had aroused.

He wanted to tell her this, and more, if he could just find the words.

But it was Suzanna who spoke first.

'I saw Immacolata,' she said, 'while you were facing Shadwell . . .'

'Yes?'

'. . . I don't quite know how to explain what happened . . .'

She began haltingly, still staring at the river as though mesmerized by its motion. He understood some of what she was telling him. That Mimi was part of the Seerkind, the occupants of the Fugue; and Suzanna, her granddaughter, had that people's blood in her. But when she began to talk about the menstruum, the power she'd somehow inherited, or plugged into, or both, he lost any hold on what she was saying. In part because her talk became vaguer, dreamier; in part because staring at her as she struggled to find the words for her feelings gave him the words for his own.

'I love you,' he said. She had stopped trying to describe the torrent of the menstruum; just given herself over to the rhythm of the water as it lapped against the wharf.

He wasn't sure she'd heard him. She didn't move; didn't speak.

Finally, she just said his name.

He suddenly felt foolish. She didn't want professions of love from him; her thoughts were somewhere else entirely. In the Fugue, perhaps, where – after this afternoon's revelations – she had more right to be than he.

'I'm sorry,' he muttered, attempting to cover his faux pas with further fumblings. 'I don't know why I said that. Forget I spoke.'

His denial stung her from her trance. Her gaze left the river,

128

and found his face, a look of hurt in her eyes, as though drawing her gaze from its brilliance pained her.

'Don't say that,' she said. 'Never say that.'

She stepped towards him, and put her arms around him, holding him hard. He answered the demand and hugged her in return. Her face was hot against his neck, wetting him not with kisses but with tears. They didn't speak, but stood like that for several minutes, while the river flowed on at their side.

Eventually he said:

'Shall we go back to the house?'

She stepped back and looked at him, seeming to study his face.

'Is it all over; or just beginning?' she asked.

He shook his head.

She made a tiny, sideways glance back at the river. But before its liquid life could claim her again he took hold of her hand and led her back towards the concrete and the brick.

# II

## WAKING IN THE DARK

They returned — through a dusk that had autumn in its hollows — to Chariot Street. There they scoured the kitchen for something to placate their growling stomachs — ate — then retired to Cal's room with a bottle of whisky they'd bought on the way back. The intended debate on what they should do next soon faltered. A mixture of tiredness, and an unease generated by the scene at the river, made the conversation hesitant. They circled the same territory over and over, but there were no inspirations as to how they should proceed.

The only token they had of their adventures to date was the carpet fragment, and it offered up no clues.

The exchange dwindled, half-finished sentences punctuated by longer and still longer silences.

Around eleven, Brendan came home, hailing Cal from below, then retired to bed. His arrival stirred Suzanna.

'I should go,' she said. 'It's late.'

The thought of the room without her made Cal's heart sink.

'Why not stay?' he said.

'It's a small bed,' she replied.

'But it's comfortable.'

She put her hand to his face, and brushed the bruised place around his mouth.

'We're not meant to be lovers,' she said quietly. 'We're too much alike.'

130

It was bluntly put, and it hurt to have it said, but in the same moment as having any sexual ambition dampened he had a different, and finally more profound, hope confirmed. That they belonged together in this enterprise: she the child of the Fugue, he the innocent trespasser. Against the brief pleasure of making love to her he set the grander adventure, and he knew – despite the dissension from his cock – that he had the better of the deal.

'Then we'll sleep,' he said. 'If you want to stay.'

She smiled. 'I want to stay,' she said.

They stripped off their dirty clothing, and slipped beneath the covers. Sleep was upon them before the lamp had cooled.

It was not empty sleep; far from it. There were dreams. Or rather, a particular dream which filled both their heads.

They dreamt a noise. A planet of bees, all buzzing fit to burst their honeyed hearts; a rising swell that was summer's music.

They dreamt smell. A confusion of scents; of streets after rain, and faded cologne, and wind out of a warm country.

But most of all, they dreamt *sight*.

It began with a pattern: a knotting and weaving of countless strands, dyed in a hundred colours, carrying a charge of energy which so dazzled the sleepers they had to shield their minds' eyes.

And then, as if the pattern was becoming too ambitious to hold its present order, the knots began to slide and slip. The colours at each intersection bled into the air, until the vision was obscured in a soup of pigments through which the loosed strands described their liberty in line and comma and dot, like the brushstrokes of some master calligrapher. At first the marks seemed quite arbitrary – but as each trace drew colour to itself, and another stroke was laid upon it, and another upon that, it became apparent that forms were steadily emerging from the chaos.

Where, dream-moments ago, there'd been only warp and weft, there were now five distinct human forms appearing

131

from the flux, the invisible artist adding detail to the portraits with insolent facility.

And now the voices of the bees rose, singing in the sleeper's heads gave names to these strangers.

The first of the quintet to be called was a young woman in a long, dark dress, her small face pale, her closed eyes fringed with ginger lashes. This, the bees said, is *Lilia Pellicia*.

As if waking to her name, Lilia opened her eyes.

As she did so a rotund, bearded individual in his fifties, a coat draped over his shoulders and a brimmed hat on his head, stepped forward. *Frederick Cammell* the bees said, and the eyes behind the coin-sized lenses of his spectacles snapped open. His hand went to his hat immediately, and took it off, to reveal a head of immaculately coiffured hair, oiled to his scalp.

'So . . .' he said, and smiled.

Two more now. One, impatient to be free from this world of dyes, was also dressed as if for a wake. (What happened, the dreamers wondered, to the brilliance that the strands had first bled? Were those colours hidden somewhere beneath this funereal garb: in parrot-bright petticoats?) The dour face of this third visitor did not suggest a taste for such indulgence.

*Apolline Dubois* the bees announced, and the woman opened her eyes, the scowl that instantly came to her face displaying teeth the colour of old ivory.

The last members of this assembly arrived together. One, a negro whose fine face, even in repose, was shaped for melancholy. The other, the naked baby he held in his arms, drooling on his protector's shirt.

*Jerichau St Louis* the bees said, and the negro opened his eyes. He immediately looked down at the child he held, who had begun to bawl even before his name was heard.

*Nimrod* the bees called, and though the baby was surely not yet a year old, he already knew the two syllables of his name. He raised his lids, to reveal eyes that had a distinctly golden cast to them.

His waking brought the process to an end. The colours, the bees and the threads all retreated, their tide leaving the five strangers stranded in Cal's room.

It was Apolline Dubois who spoke first.

'This can't be right,' she said, making for the window and pulling back the curtains. 'Where the Hell are we?'

'And where are the others?' said Frederick Cammell. His eyes had found the mirror on the wall, and he was scrutinizing himself in it. Tutting, he took a pair of scissors from his pocket and began to snip at some overlong hairs on his cheek.

'That's a point,' said Jerichau. Then, to Apolline: 'What does it look like out there?'

'Deserted,' said the woman. 'It's the middle of the night. And . . .'

'What?'

'Look for yourself,' she said, sucking spit through her broken teeth, 'there's something amiss here.' She turned from the window. 'Things aren't the way they were.'

It was Lilia Pellicia who took Apolline's place at the sill. 'She's right,' the girl said. 'Things *are* different.'

'And why's it only *us* who are here?' Frederick asked for the second time. 'That's the real point.'

'Something's happened,' said Lilia, softly. 'Something terrible.'

'No doubt you feel it in your kidneys,' Apolline remarked. 'As usual.'

'Let's keep it civil, Miss Dubois,' said Frederick, with the pained expression of a school master.

'Don't call me Miss,' Apolline said. 'I'm a married woman.'

Immersed in sleep, Cal and Suzanna listened to these exchanges, entertained by the nonsenses their imaginations had conjured up. Yet for all the oddity of these people – their antiquated clothes, their names, their absurd conversations – they were uncannily real; every detail perfectly realized. And as though to confuse the dreamers further, the man the bees had called Jerichau now looked towards the bed, and said:

'Perhaps *they* can tell us something.'

Lilia turned her pale gaze towards the slumbering pair.

'We should wake them,' she said, and reached to shake the sleepers.

'*This is no dream*,' Suzanna realized, as she pictured Lilia's

133

hand approaching her shoulder. She felt herself rising from sleep; and as the girl's fingers touched her, she opened her eyes.

The curtains had been pulled apart as she'd imagined they'd been. The street lamps cast their light into the little room. And there, standing watching the bed, were the five: her dream made flesh. She sat up. The sheet slipped, and the gaze of both Jerichau and the child Nimrod flitted to her breasts. She pulled the sheet over her and in so doing uncovered Cal. The chill stirred him. He peered at her through barely open eyes.

'What's going on?' he asked, his voice slurred by sleep.

'*Wake up*,' she said. 'We've got visitors.'

'I had this dream . . .' he muttered. Then, '*Visitors?*' He looked up at her, following her gaze into the room.

'Oh sweet Jesus . . .'

The child was laughing in Jerichau's arms, pointing a stubby finger at Cal's piss-proud groin. He snatched up a pillow and concealed his enthusiasm.

'Is this one of Shadwell's tricks?' he whispered.

'I don't think so,' said Suzanna.

'Who's Shadwell?' Apolline wanted to know.

'Another Cuckoo, no doubt,' said Frederick, who had his scissors at the ready should either of these two prove belligerent.

At the word *Cuckoo*, Suzanna began to understand. Immacolata had first used the term, speaking of Humankind.

'. . . the Fugue . . .' she said.

Naming the place had every eye upon her, and Jerichau demanding:

'What do you know about the Fugue?'

'Not much,' she replied.

'You know where the others are?' Frederick asked.

'What others?'

'And the land?' said Lilia. 'Where is it all?'

Cal had taken his eyes off the quintet and was looking at the table beside the bed, where he'd left the fragment of the Weave. It had gone.

134

'They came from that piece of carpet,' he said, not quite believing what he was saying.

'That was what I dreamt.'

'I dreamt it too,' said Suzanna.

'A *piece* of the carpet?' said Frederick, aghast. 'You mean we're separated?'

'Yes,' Cal replied.

'Where's the rest?' Apolline said. 'Take us to it.'

'We don't know where it is,' said Cal. 'Shadwell's got it.'

'Damn Cuckoos!' the woman erupted. 'You can't trust any of them. All twisters and cheats!'

'He's not alone,' Suzanna replied. 'His partner's one of your breed.'

'I doubt that,' said Frederick.

'It's true. Immacolata.'

The name brought an exclamation of horror from both Frederick and Jerichau. Apolline, ever the lady, simply spat on the floor.

'Have they not hanged that bitch yet?' she said.

'Twice to my certain knowledge,' Jerichau replied.

'She takes it as flattery,' Lilia remarked.

Cal shuddered. He was cold and tired; he wanted dreams of sun-lit hills and bright rivers, not these mourners, their faces riddled with spite and suspicion. Ignoring their stares, he threw away the pillow, walked over to where his clothes lay on the floor and started to pull on his shirt and jeans.

'And where are the Custodians?' said Frederick, addressing the entire room. 'Does anyone know that?'

'My grandmother . . .' said Suzanna. '. . . Mimi . . .'

'Yes?' said Frederick, homing in, 'where's she?'

'Dead, I'm afraid.'

'There were other Custodians,' said Lilia, infected by Frederick's urgency. 'Where are they?'

'I don't know.'

'You were right,' said Jerichau, his expression almost tragic. 'Something terrible *has* happened.'

Lilia returned to the window, and threw it open.

'Can you sniff it out?' Frederick asked her. 'Is it nearby?'

135

Lilia shook her head. 'The air stinks,' she said. 'This isn't the old Kingdom. It's *cold*. Cold and filthy.'

Cal, who'd dressed by now, pushed his way between Frederick and Apolline, and picked up the bottle of whisky.

'Want a drink?' he said to Suzanna.

She shook her head. He poured himself a generous measure, and drank.

'We have to find this Shadwell of yours,' Jerichau said to Suzanna, 'and get the weave back.'

'What's the hurry?' said Apolline, with a perverse nonchalance. She waddled over to Cal. 'Mind if I partake?' she said. Reluctantly, he handed her the bottle.

'What do you mean: *what's the hurry*?' Frederick said. 'We wake up in the middle of nowhere, alone –'

'We're not alone,' said Apolline, swallowing a gulletful of whisky. 'We've got our friends here.' She cocked a lopsided smile at Cal. 'What's your name, sweet?'

'Calhoun.'

'And *her*?'

'Suzanna.'

'I'm Apolline. This is Freddy.'

Cammell made a small formal bow.

'That's Lilia Pellicia over there, and the brat is her brother, Nimrod –'

'And I'm Jerichau.'

'There,' said Apolline. 'Now we're all friends, right? We don't need the rest of them. Let 'em rot.'

'They're our people,' Jerichau reminded her. 'And they need our help.'

'Is that why they left us in the Border?' she retorted sourly, the whisky bottle hovering at her lips again. 'No. They put us where we could get lost, and don't try and make any better of it. We're the *dirt*. Bandits and bawds and God knows what else.' She looked at Cal. 'Oh yes,' she said. 'You've fallen amongst thieves. We were a shame to them. Every one of us.'
Then, to the others:

'It's better we're separated. We get to have some wild times.'

As she spoke Cal seemed to see flashes of iridescence ignite in the folds of her widow's weeds. 'There's a whole world out there,' she said. 'Ours to enjoy.'

'Lost is still lost,' said Jerichau.

Apolline's reply was a bullish snort.

'He's right,' said Freddy. 'Without the weave, we're refugees. You know how much the Cuckoos hate us. Always have. Always will.'

'You're damn fools,' said Apolline, and returned to the window, taking the whisky with her.

'We're a little out of touch,' Freddy said to Cal. 'Maybe you could tell us what year this is? 1910? 1911?'

Cal laughed. 'Give or take eighty years,' he said.

The other man visibly paled, turning his face to the wall. Lilia let out a pained sound, as though she'd been stabbed. Shaking, she sat down on the edge of the bed.

'Eighty years . . .' Jerichau murmured.

'Why did they wait so long?' Freddy asked of the hushed room. 'What happened that they should wait so long?'

'Please stop talking in riddles –' Suzanna said, '– and explain.'

'We can't,' said Freddy. 'You're not Seerkind.'

'Oh don't talk such drivel,' Apolline snapped. 'Where's the harm?'

'Tell them, Lilia,' said Jerichau.

'I *protest*,' Freddy said.

'Tell them as much as they need to know,' said Apolline. 'If you tell it all we're here 'til Doomsday.'

Lilia sighed. 'Why me?' she said, still shaking. 'Why should I have to tell it?'

'Because you're the best liar,' Jerichau replied, with a tight smile. 'You can make it true.'

She threw him a baleful glance.

'Very well,' she said; and began to tell.

# III

## WHAT SHE TOLD

**W**e weren't always lost,' she began. 'Once we
lived in a garden.'

Two sentences in, and Apolline was inter-
rupting.

'That's just a story,' she informed Cal and
Suzanna.

'So let her *tell* it, damn you!' Jerichau told her.

'Believe nothing,' Apolline advised. 'This woman wouldn't
know the truth if it fucked her.'

In response, Lilia merely passed her tongue over her lips,
and took up where she'd left off.

'It was a garden,' she said. 'That's where the Families began.'

'What Families?' said Cal.

'The Four Roots of the Seerkind. The *Lo*; the *Ye-me*; the *Aia*
and *Babu*. The Families from which we're all descended. Some
of us came by grubbier roads than others, of course —' she
said, casting a barbed glance at Apolline. '— but all of us can
trace our line back to one of those four. Me and Nimrod; we're
Ye-me. It was our Root that wove the carpet.'

'And look where it got us,' Cammell growled. 'Serves us
right for trusting weavers. Clever fingers and dull minds. Now
the Aia — that's my Root — we have the craft *and* the grasp.'

'And you?' said Cal to Apolline, reaching over and retrieving
his bottle. It had at best two swallows of spirits left in it.

'Aia on my mother's side,' the woman replied. 'That's what
gave me my singing voice. And on my father's, nobody's really
sure. He could dance a rapture, could my father —'

'When he was sober,' said Freddy.

'What would you know?' Apolline grimaced. 'You never met my father.'

'Once was enough for your mother,' Freddy replied in an instant. The baby laughed uproariously at this, though the sense of it was well beyond his years.

'Anyhow,' said Apolline. 'He could dance; which meant he had Lo blood in him somewhere.'

'And Babu too, by the way you talk,' said Lilia.

Here, Jerichau broke in. '*I'm* Babu,' he said. 'Take it from me, breath's too precious to waste.'

Breath. Dancing. Music. Carpets. Cal tried to keep track of these skills and the Families who possessed them, but it was like trying to remember the Kellaway clan.

'The point is,' said Lilia, 'all the Families had skills that Humankind don't possess. Powers you'd call miraculous. To us they're no more remarkable than the fact that bread rises. They're just ways to delve and summon.'

'Raptures?' said Cal. 'Is that what you called them?'

'That's right,' said Lilia. 'We had them from the beginning. Thought nothing of it. At least not until we came into the Kingdom. Then we realized that your kind like to make laws. Like to decree what's what, and whether it's good or not. And the world, being a loving thing, and not wishing to disappoint you or distress you, indulges you. Behaves as though your doctrines are in some way absolute.'

'That's arguable metaphysics,' Freddy muttered.

'The laws of the Kingdom are the Cuckoo's laws,' said Lilia. 'That's one of Capra's Tenets.'

'Then Capra was wrong,' came Freddy's reply.

'Seldom,' said Lilia. 'And not about this. The world behaves the way the Cuckoos choose to describe it. Out of courtesy. That's been proved. Until somebody comes up with a better idea —'

'Wait a minute,' said Suzanna. 'Are you saying the earth somehow listens to us?'

'That was Capra's opinion.'

'And who's Capra?'

'A great man –'

'Or woman,' said Apolline.

'Who may or may not have lived,' Freddy went on.

'But, even if she didn't –' Apolline said, '– had a great deal to say for herself.'

'Which answers nothing,' said Suzanna.

'That's Capra for you,' said Cammell.

'Go on, Lilia,' said Cal. 'Tell the rest of the story.'

She began again:

'So there's you, Humankind, with all your laws and your perimeters and your bottomless envy; and there's us, the Families of the Seerkind. As different from you as day from night.'

'Not *so* different,' said Jerichau. 'We lived amongst them once, remember that.'

'And we were treated like *filth*,' said Lilia, with some feeling.

'True,' said Jerichau.

'The skills we had,' she went on, 'you Cuckoos called *magic*. Some of them wanted it for themselves. Some were afraid of it. But few loved us for it. Cities were small then, you must understand. It was difficult to hide in them. So we retreated. Into the forests and the hills, where we thought we'd be safe.'

'There were many of us who'd never ventured amongst the Cuckoos in the first place,' said Freddy. 'Especially the Aia. Nothing to sell, you see; no use suffering the Cuckoos if you had nothing to sell. Better be out in the great green.'

'That's pretension,' said Jerichau. 'You love cities as much as any of us.'

'True,' said Freddy. 'I like bricks and mortar. But I envy the shepherd –'

'His solitude or his sheep?'

'His pastoral pleasures, you cretin!' Freddy said. Then, to Suzanna: 'Mistress, you must understand that I do not belong with these people. Truly I don't. *He* –' (here he stabbed a finger in Jerichau's direction) '– is a convicted thief. *She* –' (now Apolline) '– ran a bordello. And *this* one –' (Lilia now) '– she and her little brother there have so much grief on their hands –'

140

'A child?' said Lilia, looking at the baby. 'How could you accuse an innocent –'

'Please spare us the histrionics,' said Freddy. 'Your brother may look like a babe in arms, but we know better. Masquers, both of you. Or else why were you in the Border?'

'I might ask you the same question,' Lilia retorted.

'I was conspired against,' he protested. 'My hands are clean.'

'Never did trust a man with clean hands,' Apolline muttered.

'*Whore!*' said Freddy.

'*Barber!*' said the other, which brought the outburst to a halt.

Cal exchanged a disbelieving look with Suzanna. There was no love lost between these people, that much was apparent.

'So . . .' said Suzanna. 'You were telling us about hiding in the hills.'

'We weren't hiding,' said Jerichau. 'We just weren't visible.'

'There's a difference?' said Cal.

'Oh certainly. There are places sacred to us which most Cuckoos could stand a yard from and not see –'

'And we had raptures,' said Lilia, 'to cover our tracks, if Humankind came too close.'

'Which they did, on occasion,' Jerichau said. 'Some got curious. Started to poke around in the forests, looking for trace of us.'

'They knew what you were then?' said Suzanna.

'No,' said Apolline. She'd thrown a pile of clothes off one of the chairs and was straddling it. 'No, all they knew was rumour and hearsay. Called us all kinds of names. Shades and faeries. All manner of shite. Only a few got really close, though. And that was only because we let them.'

'Besides, there weren't that many of us,' said Lilia. 'We've never been very fertile. Never had much of a taste for copulation.'

'Speak for yourself,' said Apolline, and winked at Cal.

'The point is, we were mostly ignored, and – like Apolline said – when we did make contact it was for our own reasons. Perhaps one of your Kind had some skill we could profit by.

Horse-breeders, wine-merchants . . . but the fact is as the centuries went by you became a lethal breed.'

'True,' said Jerichau.

'What little contact we had with you dwindled to almost nothing. We left you to your bloodbaths, and your *envy* –'

'Why do you keep harking on envy?' said Cal.

'It's what your Kind's notorious for,' said Freddy. 'Always after what isn't yours, just for the having.'

'You're a perfect bloody species, are you?' said Cal. He'd tired of the endless remarks about Cuckoos.

'If we were perfect,' said Jerichau, 'we'd be invisible, wouldn't we?' The response fazed Cal utterly. 'No. We're flesh and blood like you,' he went on, 'so of course we're imperfect. But we don't make such a song and dance about it. You people . . . you have to feel there's some tragedy in your condition, or you think you're only half alive.'

'So why trust my grandmother to look after the carpet?' said Suzanna. 'She was a Cuckoo, wasn't she?'

'Don't use that word,' said Cal. 'She was *human*.'

'She was of mixed blood,' Apolline corrected him. 'Seerkind on her mother's side and Cuckoo on her father's. I talked with her on two or three occasions. We had something in common you see. Both had mixed marriages. Her first husband was Seerkind, and my husbands were all Cuckoos.

'But she was only one of several Custodians. The only woman; the only one with any human blood too, if I remember rightly.

'We had to have at least one Custodian who knew the Kingdom, who would seem perfectly unremarkable. That way we hoped we'd be ignored, and finally forgotten.'

'All this . . . just to hide from Humankind?' said Suzanna.

'Oh no,' said Freddy. 'We might have continued to live as we had, on the margins of the Kingdom . . . but things changed.'

'I can't remember the year it began –' said Apolline.

'1896,' said Lilia. 'It was 1896, the year of the first fatalities.'

'What happened?' said Cal.

'To this day nobody's certain. But something appeared out

142

of the blue, some creature with only one ambition. To wipe us out.'

'What sort of creature?'

Lilia shrugged. 'Nobody ever saw its face and survived.'

'Human?' said Cal.

'No. It wasn't blind, the way the Cuckoos are blind. It could sniff us out. Even our most vivid raptures couldn't deceive it for long. And when it had passed by it would be as if those it had looked on had never existed.'

'We were trapped,' said Jerichau. 'On one side, Humankind, growing more ambitious for territory by the day, 'til we had scarcely a place left to hide; and on the other, the *Scourge*, as we called it, whose sole intention seemed to be genocide. We knew it could only be a matter of time before we were extinct.'

'Which would have been a pity,' said Freddy, drily.

'It wasn't all gloom and doom,' said Apolline. 'Seems odd to say it but I had a fine time those last years. Desperation, you know; it's the best aphrodisiac,' she grinned. 'And we found one or two places where we were safe awhile, where the Scourge never sniffed us out.'

'I don't remember being happy,' said Lilia. 'I just remember the nightmares.'

'What about the hill?' said Apolline, 'what was it called? The hill where we stayed, the last summer. I remember that as if it was yesterday . . .'

'Rayment's Hill.'

'That's right. Rayment's Hill. I was happy there.'

'But how long would it have lasted?' said Jerichau. 'Sooner or later, the Scourge would have found us.'

'Perhaps,' said Apolline.

'We had no choice,' said Lilia. 'We needed a hiding place. Somewhere the Scourge would never look for us. Where we could sleep awhile, until we'd been forgotten.'

'The carpet,' said Cal.

'Yes,' said Lilia. 'That was the refuge the Council chose.'

'After *endless* debate,' said Freddy. 'During which time hundreds more died. That final year, when the Loom was at work, there were fresh massacres every week. Terrible stories. Terrible.'

'We were vulnerable of course,' said Lilia. 'Because there were refugees coming from all over . . . some of them bringing fragments of their territories . . . things that had survived the onslaught . . . all converging on this country in the hope of finding a place in the carpet for their properties.'

'Like what?'

'Houses. Pieces of land. Usually they'd get a good Babu in, who could put the field or the house or whatever it was, into a screed. That way it could be carried, you see –'

'No, I don't see,' said Cal. 'Explain.'

'It's *your* Family,' said Lilia to Jerichau. '*You* explain.'

'We Babus can make hieroglyphs,' Jerichau said, 'and carry them in our heads. A great technician, like my master, Quekett . . . he could make a screed that could carry a small city, I swear he could, and speak it out again perfect down to the last tile.' Describing this, his long face brightened. Then a memory brought his joy down. 'My master was in the Low Countries when the Scourge found him,' he said. 'Gone.' He clicked his fingers. 'Like that.'

'Why'd you all gather in England?' Suzanna wanted to know.

'It was the safest country in the world. And the Cuckoos of course, were busy with Empire. We could get lost in the crowd, while the Fugue was woven into the carpet.'

'What is the Fugue?' said Cal.

'It's everything we could save from destruction. Pieces of the Kingdom that the Cuckoos had never truly seen, and so wouldn't miss when they were gone. A forest, a lake or two, a bend of one river, the delta of another. Some houses, which we'd occupied; some city squares, even a street or two. We put them together, in a township of sorts.'

'Nonesuch, they called it,' said Apolline. 'Damn fool name.'

'At first there was an attempt to put all this property into some kind of order,' said Freddy. 'But that soon fell by the wayside, as refugees kept arriving with more to be woven into the carpet. More every day. There'd be people waiting outside

144

Capra's House for nights on end, with some little niche they wanted kept from the Scourge.'

'That's why it took so long,' said Lilia.

'But nobody was turned away,' said Jerichau. 'That was understood from the beginning. Anyone who wanted a place in the Weave would be granted it.'

'Even us,' said Apolline, 'who weren't exactly lily-whites. We were granted our places.'

'But why a *carpet*?' said Suzanna.

'What's more easily overlooked than the thing you're standing on?' said Lilia. 'Besides, the craft was one we knew.'

'Everything has its pattern,' Freddy put in. 'If you find it, the great can be contained within the small.'

'Not everyone wanted to go into the Weave, of course,' said Lilia. 'Some decided to stay amongst the Cuckoos, and take their chance. But most went.'

'And what was it like?'

'Like sleep. Like dreamless sleep. We didn't age. We didn't hunger. We just waited until the Custodians judged that it was safe to wake us again.'

'What about the birds?' said Cal.

'Oh, there's no end of flora and fauna, woven in —'

'I don't mean in the Fugue itself. I mean my pigeons.'

'What have your pigeons got to do with this?' said Apolline.

Cal gave them a brief summary of how he'd first come to discover the carpet.

'That's the Gyre's influence,' said Jerichau.

'The Gyre?'

'When you had your glimpse of the Fugue,' said Apolline. 'You remember the clouds in its heart? That's the Gyre. It's where the Loom's housed.'

'How can a carpet contain the Loom it was woven on?' said Suzanna.

'The Loom isn't a machine,' said Jerichau. 'It's a state of making. It drew the elements of the Fugue into a rapture which resembles a common-place carpet. But there's a good deal there that denies your human assumptions, and the closer you get to the Gyre, the stranger things become. There are

145

places there in which ghosts of the future and past are at play –'

'We shouldn't talk about it,' said Lilia. 'It's bad luck.'

'How much worse can our luck become?' Freddy observed. 'So few of us . . .'

'We'll wake the Families, as soon as we recover the carpet,' said Jerichau. 'The Gyre must be getting restless, or else how did this man get a look? The Weave can't hold forever –'

'He's right,' said Apolline. 'I suppose we're obliged to do something about it.'

'But it isn't *safe*,' said Suzanna.

'Safe for what?'

'Out here, I mean, in the world. In England.'

'The Scourge must have given up –' said Freddy, '– after all these years.'

'So why didn't Mimi wake you?'

Freddy pulled a face. 'Maybe she forgot about us.'

'*Forgot?*' said Cal. 'Impossible.'

'Easy to say,' Apolline replied. 'But you have to be strong to resist the Kingdom. Get in too deep and next thing you can't even remember your name.'

'I don't believe she forgot,' said Cal.

'Our first priority,' said Jerichau, ignoring Cal's protest, 'is to retrieve the carpet. Then we get out of this city, and find a place where Immacolata will never come looking.'

'What about us?' said Cal.

'What *about* you?'

'Don't we get to see?'

'See what?'

'The Fugue, damn you!' Cal said, infuriated by the lack of anything approaching courtesy or gratitude from these people.

'It's not your concern now,' said Freddy.

'It damn well is!' he said. 'I *saw* it. Almost got killed for it.'

'Better you stay away then,' said Jerichau. 'If you're so concerned for your breath.'

'That's not what I meant.'

'Cal,' said Suzanna, putting her hand on his arm.

Her attempt to calm him merely inflamed him further.

146

'Don't side with them,' he said.

'It's not a question of sides –' she began, but he wasn't about to be placated.

'It's easy for you,' he said. 'You've got connections –'

'That's not fair –'

'– and the menstruum –'

'*What?*' said Apolline, her voice silencing Cal. 'You?'

'Apparently,' Suzanna said.

'And it didn't dissolve the flesh off your bones?'

'Why should it do that?'

'Not in front of *him*,' said Lilia, looking at Cal.

That was the limit.

'All right,' he said. 'You don't want to talk in front of me, that's fine. You can all go fuck yourselves.'

He started towards the door, ignoring Suzanna's attempts to call him back. Behind him, Nimrod was tittering.

'And you can shut the fuck up,' he told the child, and left the room to its usurpers.

147

# IV

## NIGHT TERRORS

### 1

**S**hadwell woke from a dream of Empire; a familiar fantasy, in which he owned a vast store, so vast indeed that it was impossible to see the far wall. And he was selling; doing trade to make an accountant weep for joy. Merchandise of every description heaped high on all sides — Ming vases, toy monkeys, sides of beef — and customers beating at the doors, desperate to· join the throngs already clamouring to buy.

It wasn't, oddly enough, a dream of profit. Money had become an irrelevancy since he'd stumbled upon Immacolata, who could conjure all they needed from thin air. No, the dream was one of *power*; he, the owner of the goods that people were bleeding to buy, standing back from the crowd and smiling his charismatic smile.

But suddenly he was awake, the clamour of customers was fading, and he heard the sound of breathing in the darkened room.

He sat up, the sweat of his enthusiasm chilling on his brow. 'Immacolata?'

She was there, standing against the far wall, her palms seeking some hold in the plaster. Her eyes were wide, but she saw nothing. At least, nothing that Shadwell could share. He'd known her like this before — most recently two or three days ago, in the foyer of this very hotel.

He got out of bed, and put on his dressing gown. Sensing his presence, she murmured his name.

148

'I'm here,' he replied.

'Again,' she said. 'I felt it again.'

'The Scourge?' he said, his voice grey.

'Of course. We have to sell the carpet, and be done with it.'

'We will. We will,' he said, slowly approaching her. 'The arrangements are underway, you know that.'

He spoke evenly, to calm her. She was dangerous at the best of times; but these moods scared him more than most.

'The calls have been made,' he said. 'The buyers'll come. They've been waiting for this. They'll come and we'll make our sale, and it'll all be over with.'

'I saw the place it lives,' she went on. 'There were walls; huge walls. And sand, inside and out. Like the end of the world.'

Now her eyes found him, and the hold this vision had on her seemed to deteriorate.

'*When*, Shadwell?' she said.

'When what?'

'The Auction.'

'The day after tomorrow. As we arranged.'

She nodded. 'Strange,' she said, her tone suddenly conversational. The speed with which her moods changed always caught him unawares. 'Strange, to have these nightmares after so long.'

'It's seeing the carpet,' said Shadwell. 'It reminds you.'

'It's more than that,' she said.

She went to the door that led through to the rest of Shadwell's suite, and opened it. The furniture had been pushed to the edges of the large room beyond, so that their prize, the Weaveworld, could be laid out. She stood on the threshold, staring at the carpet.

She didn't set her bare soles on it – some superstition kept her from that trespass – but paced along the border, scrutinizing every inch.

Half way along the far edge, she stopped.

'There,' she said, and pointed down at the Weave.

Shadwell went to where she stood.

'What is it?'

'A piece missing.'

He followed her gaze. The woman was right. A small portion of the carpet had been torn away; in the struggle at the warehouse, most likely.

'Nothing significant,' he commented. 'It won't bother our buyers, believe me.'

'I don't care about the value,' she said.

'What then?'

'Use your eyes, Shadwell. Every one of those motifs is one of the Seerkind.'

He went down on his haunches, and examined the markings in the border. They were scarcely recognizable as human; more like commas with eyes.

'These are *people*?' he said.

'Oh yes. Riff-raff; the lowest of the low. That's why they're at the edge. They're vulnerable there. But they're also useful.'

'For what?'

'As a first defence,' Immacolata replied, her eyes fixed on the tear in the carpet. 'The first to be threatened, the first —'

'*To wake*,' said Shadwell.

'— to wake.'

'You think they're out there now?' he said. His gaze went to the window. They'd closed the curtains, to keep anyone from spying on their treasure, but he could picture the benighted city beyond. The thought that there might be magic loose out there brought an unexpected charge.

'Yes,' the Incantatrix said. 'I think they're awake. And the Scourge smells them in its sleep. It knows, Shadwell.'

'So what do we do?'

'We find them, before they attract any more attention. The Scourge may be ancient. May be slow and forgetful. But its power . . .' Her voice faded away, as though words were valueless in the face of such terrors. She drew a deep breath before beginning again. 'A day's scarcely gone by,' she said, 'when I haven't watched the menstruum for a sign of it

150

coming. And it'll come, Shadwell. Not tonight maybe. But it'll come. And on that day there'll be an end to all magic.'

'Even to you?'

'Even to me.'

'So we have to find them,' said Shadwell.

'Not *we*,' said Immacolata. 'We needn't dirty our hands.' She started to walk back towards Shadwell's bedroom. 'They can't have gone far,' she said as she went. 'They're strangers here.'

At the door she stopped, and turned to him.

'On no account leave this room until we call you,' she said. 'I'm going to summon someone to be our assassin.'

'Who?' said Shadwell.

'Nobody you ever met,' the Incantatrix replied. 'He was dead a hundred years before you were born. But you and he had a good deal in common.'

'And where is he now?'

'In the Ossuary at the Shrine of the Mortalities, where he lost his life. He wanted to prove himself my equal you see, to seduce me. So he tried to become a necromancer. He might have done it too; there was nothing he wouldn't dare. But it went awry. He brought the Surgeons from some nether-world or other, and they weren't amused. They pursued him from one end of London to the other.

'At the last he broke into the Shrine. Begged me to call them off.' Her voice had become a whisper now. 'But how could I?' she said. 'He'd made his conjurations. All I could do was let the Surgeons perform what tricks Surgeons must. And at the end, when he was all blood, he said to me: *Take my soul.*'

She stopped. Then said:

'So I did.'

She looked at Shadwell.

'Stay here,' she said, and closed the door.

Shadwell didn't need any encouragement to stay clear of the sisters while they were plotting. If he never again set eyes on the Magdalene and the Hag he would count himself a lucky man. But the ghosts were inseparable from their living sister;

151

each, in some fashion incomprehensible to him, a part of the other. Their perverse union was only one of the mysteries that attended them; there were many others.

The Shrine of Mortalities, for one. It had been a gathering place for her Cult when she'd been at the height of her power and ambition. But she'd fallen from grace. Her desire to rule the Fugue, which had then still been a ragged collection of far-flung settlements, had been frustrated. Her enemies had assembled evidence against her, listing crimes that had begun in her mother's womb, and she and her followers had retaliated. There had been bloodshed, though Shadwell had never gathered the scale of it. The consequence however, he *had* gathered. Vilified and humiliated, Immacolata had been forbidden to tread the magic earth of the Fugue again.

She had not taken this exile well. Unable to mellow her nature, and so pass unseen amongst the Cuckoos, her history became a round of blood-lettings, pursuits and further blood-lettings. Though she was still known and worshipped by a cognoscenti, who called her by a dozen different names – the Black Madonna, the Lady of Sorrows, Mater Malifecorium – she became nevertheless a victim of her own strange purity. Madness beckoned; the only refuge from the banality of the Kingdom she was exiled in.

That was how she had been when Shadwell had found her. A mad woman, whose talk had been like none he'd heard before, and who spoke in her ramblings of things that, could he but lay his hands upon them, would make him mighty.

And now, here they were, those wonders. All contained within a rectangle of carpet.

He approached the middle of it, staring down at the spiral of stylized clouds and lightning called the Gyre. How many nights had he lain awake, wondering what it would be like in that flux of energies? Like being with God, perhaps?; or the Devil.

He was shaken from these thoughts by a howl from the adjacent room, and the lamp above his head suddenly dimmed as its light was sucked beneath the intersecting door, testament to the profundity of darkness on the far side.

He moved to the opposite end of the room, and sat down.

How long until dawn? he wondered.

There was still no sign of morning, when – hours later, it seemed – the door opened.

There was only blackness beyond. Out of it, Immacolata said:

'Come and see.'

He stood up, his limbs stiff, and hobbled to the door.

A wave of heat met him at the threshold. It was like stepping into an oven in which cakes of human dirt and blood had been cooking.

Dimly, he could see Immacolata, standing – floating, perhaps – a little way from him. The air pressed against his throat: he badly wanted to retreat. But she beckoned.

'Look,' she instructed him, staring off into the darkness. 'Our assassin came. This is the Rake.'

Shadwell could see nothing at first. Then a shred of fugitive energy skittered up the wall and upon contact with the ceiling threw down a wash of cankered light.

By it, he saw the thing she called the Rake.

Had this once been a man? It was difficult to believe. The Surgeons Immacolata had spoken of had re-invented his anatomy. He hung in the air like a slashed coat left on a hook, his body somehow drawn out to superhuman height. Then, as though a breeze had gusted up from the earth, the body moved, swelling and rising. Its upper limbs – pieces of what might once have been human tissue held in an uneasy alliance by threads of mercurial cartilage – were raised, as if it were about to be crucified. The gesture unwound the matter that blinded its head. They fell away, and Shadwell could not prevent a cry from escaping him, as he understood what surgery had been performed upon the Rake.

153

They'd filleted him. They'd taken every bone from his body and left a thing more fit for the ocean-bed than the breathing world, a wretched echo of humanity, fuelled by the raptures the sisters had devised to bring it from Limbo. It swayed and swelled, its skull-less head taking on a dozen shapes as Shadwell watched. One moment it was all bulging eyes, the next only a maw, which howled its displeasure at waking to this condition.

'*Hush . . .*' Immacolata told it.

The Rake shuddered and its arms grew longer, as if it wanted to kill the woman that had done this to it. But it fell silent nevertheless.

'Domville,' Immacolata said. 'You once professed love for me.'

It threw back its head then, as if despairing of what desire had brought it to.

'Are you afraid, my Rake?'

It looked at her, its eyes like blood blisters close to bursting.

'We've given you a little life,' she said. 'And enough power to turn these streets upside down. I want you to use it.'

The sight of the thing made Shadwell nervous.

'Is he in control of himself?' he whispered. 'Suppose he goes berserk?'

'Let him,' she said. 'I hate this city. Let him burn it up. As long as he kills the Seerkind, I don't care what he does. He knows he won't be allowed to rest until he's done as I ask. And Death's the best promise he's ever had.'

The blisters were still fixed on Immacolata, and the look in them confirmed her words.

'Very well,' Shadwell said, and turned away, heading back into the adjoining room. There was only so much of this magic a man could take.

The sisters had an appetite for it. They liked to immerse themselves in these rites. For himself, he was content to be human.

Well, *almost* content.

154

# V

## FROM THE MOUTHS OF BABES

### 1

Dawn crept over Liverpool cautiously, as if fearful of what it would find. Cal watched the light uncover the city, and it seemed to him it was grey from gutter to chimney stack. He'd lived here all his life; this had been his world. The television and the glossy magazines had shown him different vistas on occasion, but somehow he'd never quite believed in them. They were as remote from his experience, or indeed from what he hoped to know in his seventy years, as the stars that were winking out above his head.

But the Fugue had been different. It had seemed, for a short, sweet time, a place he might truly belong. He'd been too optimistic. The land might want him, but its people didn't. As far as they were concerned he was contemptibly human.

He loitered on the streets for an hour or so, watching another Liverpool Monday morning get started.

Were they so bad, these Cuckoos whose tribe he shared? They smiled as they welcomed their cats in from a night of philandering; they hugged their children as they departed for the day; their radios played love-songs at the breakfast table. As he watched them he became fiercely defensive. Damn it, he'd go back and tell the Seerkind what bigots they were.

As he approached the house he saw that the front door was wide open, and that a young woman he recognized as a local,

155

but didn't know by name, was standing at the top of the path staring into the house. It was only as he came within a couple of paces of the front gate that he set eyes on Nimrod. He was standing on the welcome mat, wearing a pair of sunglasses that he'd filched from beside Cal's bed, and a toga made from one of Cal's shirts.

'Is that your kid?' the woman asked Cal, as he opened the gate.

'In a manner of speaking.'

'He started banging on the window when I went past. Isn't there anyone to look after him?'

'There is now,' said Cal.

He looked down at the child, remembering what Freddy had said about Nimrod only *seeming* to be a babe in arms. Having slid the sunglasses up onto his forehead, Nimrod was giving his visitor a look that fully confirmed Cammell's description. Cal had little option, however, but to play the part of father. He picked Nimrod up.

'What are you doing?' he whispered to the child.

'Bussteds!' Nimrod replied. He was having some difficulty mastering the infantile palate. 'El killum.'

'Who?'

But as Nimrod went to answer, the woman, who'd come down the path and was standing half a yard from the door, spoke:

'He's adorable,' she cooed.

Before Cal could make his excuses and close the door, the child raised his arms and reached towards her, a stage-managed gurgle in his throat.

'Oh –' said the woman, '– sweet thing –'

and she'd claimed Nimrod from Cal before he could prevent her.

Cal caught a gleam in Nimrod's eyes as he was pressed to the woman's ample bosom.

'Where's his mother?' she asked.

'She'll be back in a while,' said Cal, making an attempt to claim Nimrod from his luxury. He didn't want to go. He was beaming as he was rocked, his pudgy fingers grappling with

156

the woman's breasts. As soon as Cal laid hands on him he began to bawl.

The woman hushed him, pressing him closer to her, at which Nimrod began to toy with her nipples through the thin fabric of her blouse.

'Will you excuse us?' said Cal, braving Nimrod's fists and taking the babe from his pillows before he began to suckle.

'Shouldn't leave him alone,' the woman said, absent-mindedly touching her breast where Nimrod had fondled her.

Cal thanked her for her concern.

'Bye bye, beautiful,' she said to the child.

Nimrod blew a kiss at her. A flash of confusion crossed her face, then she backed away towards the gate, the smile she'd offered the child sliding from her lips.

## 2

'What a damn fool thing to do.'

Nimrod was unrepentant. He stood in the hallway where he'd been set down and stared up at Cal defiantly.

'Where are the others?' Cal wanted to know.

'Out,' said Nimrod. 'We'll go too.'

He was gaining control of his tongue by the syllable. And of his limbs too. He tottered to the front door and reached up towards the handle. 'Em sick of here,' he said. 'Too much bad news.'

His fingers fell inches short of the handle however, and after several failed attempts to snatch at it he beat his fists against the wood.

'I want to see,' he said.

'All right,' Cal agreed. 'Just keep your voice down.'

'Take me *out*.'

The cry was genuinely forlorn. There was little harm in giving the child a brief tour of the neighbourhood, Cal decided. There was something perversely satisfying about the thought of carrying this miraculous creature out into the open air, for all to see; and more satisfying still, the knowledge that the

157

child, whom he'd left laughing at him, would be dependent upon him.

Any lingering anger towards Nimrod evaporated very quickly, however, as his powers of speech became more sophisticated. They were soon involved in a fluent and animated exchange, careless of the glances they were garnering.

'They left me there!' he protested. 'Told me to fend for myself.' He held up his miniscule hand. 'How, I ask you? *How?*'

'Why are you shaped like this in the first place?' Cal asked.

'It seemed like a good idea at the time,' Nimrod replied. 'I had an irate husband in pursuit of me; so I hid in the most unlikely form I could think of. I thought I'd keep my head down for a few hours, then loose myself again. Stupid, really. A rapture like this takes *power*. And of course once the final weave began, there was none to be had. I was obliged to go into the carpet like this.'

'So how do you get back to normality?' .

'I can't. Not until I'm back on Fugue soil. I'm helpless.'

He pushed the sunglasses up to take a look at a passing beauty.

'Did you see the hips on her?' he said.

'Don't slaver.'

'Babies are supposed to slaver.'

'Not the way you're doing it.'

Nimrod ground his gums. 'It's noisy, this world of yours,' he said. 'And dirty.'

'Dirtier than 1896?'

'Much. I like it though. You must tell me about it.'

'Oh Jesus,' said Cal. 'Where do I begin?'

'Anywhere you like,' Nimrod replied. 'You'll find me a fast learner.'

What he said was true. On their half-hour walk around the vicinity of Chariot Street he questioned Cal on a wild selection of topics, some stimulated by something they saw in the street, others more abstract. First they talked of Liverpool, then of cities in general, then of New York and Hollywood. Talk of America took them on to East-West relations, at which point

Cal listed all the wars and assassinations he could remember since 1900. They touched briefly on the Irish Question, and the state of English politics, then on to Mexico, which they both had a yearning to visit, and thence to Mickey Mouse, the basic principle of aerodynamics, and back, via Nuclear War and the Immaculate Conception, to Nimrod's favourite subject: women. Or rather, to two in particular, who'd caught his eye.

In return for this short introduction to the late twentieth century Nimrod gave Cal a beginner's guide to the Fugue, telling him first of Capra's House, which was the building in which the Council of the Families met to debate; then of the Mantle, the cloud that hid the Gyre, and the Narrow Bright, the passage that led into its folds; and from there to the Firmament, and the Requiem Steps. The very names filled Cal with yearning.

Much was learned on both sides, not least the fact that they might with time become friends.

'No more talk,' said Cal as they came full circle to the gate of the Mooney house. 'You're a baby, remember?'

'How could I forget?' said Nimrod with a pained look.

Cal let himself in and called out to his father. The house, however, was silent from attic to foundations.

'He's not here,' said Nimrod. 'For God's sake put me down.'

Cal deposited the baby on the hallway floor. He immediately began towards the kitchen.

'I need a drink,' he said. 'And I don't mean milk.'

Cal laughed. 'I'll see what I can find,' he said, and went through to the back room.

Cal's first impression, seeing his father sitting in the armchair with his back to the garden, was that Brendan had died. His stomach turned over; he almost cried out. Then Brendan's eyes flickered, and he looked up at his son.

'Dad?' said Cal. 'What's wrong?'

Tears were spilling down Brendan's cheeks. He made no attempt to brush them away, nor to stifle the sobs that shook him.

'Oh Dad . . .'

Cal crossed to his father and went down on his haunches beside the chair.

'It's all right . . .' he said, putting his hand on his father's arm. 'Been thinking about Mum?'

Brendan shook his head. The tears tumbled. Words would not come. Cal didn't ask any further questions, but held onto his father's arm. He'd thought Brendan's melancholy had been lifting; that the grief was blunted now. Apparently not.

At last Brendan said:

'I . . . I had a letter.'

'A letter?'

'From your mother,' Brendan's liquid gaze fell on his son. 'Am I mad, Cal?' he said.

'Of course not, Dad. Of course not.'

'Well, I swear . . .' he put his hand down the side of the chair and plucked out a sodden handkerchief. He wiped his nose. 'It's over there,' he said nodding towards the table. 'Look for yourself.'

Cal went to the table.

'It was in her handwriting,' Brendan said.

There was indeed a piece of paper lying on the table. It had been much folded and unfolded. And, more recently, wept upon.

'It was a lovely letter,' he said, 'telling me she was happy, and I wasn't to go on grieving. She said . . .'

He stopped as a new bout of sobs overtook him. Cal picked the sheet up. It was thinner than any paper he'd ever set eyes on, and it was blank on both sides.

'She said she was waiting for me, but that I shouldn't fret about that, because waiting was a joy up there, and . . . and I should just get on with enjoying life for a while, 'til I was called.'

It wasn't just that the paper was thin, Cal now realized; it seemed to be growing more insubstantial as he watched. He put it back on the table, the small hairs at the nape of his neck prickling.

160

'I was so happy, Cal,' Brendan was saying. 'It was all I wanted, knowing that she was happy, and I'd be with her again one day.'

'There's nothing on the paper, Dad,' Cal said softly. 'It's blank.'

'There *was*, Cal. I swear it. There was. It was in her hand-writing. I'd know it anywhere. Then – God in Heaven – it just faded away.'

Cal turned from the table to see his father practically folded up double in the chair, sobbing as though his grief was beyond bearing. He put his hand on his father's hand, which was gripping the thread-bare arm of the chair.

'Hold on, Dad,' he murmured.

'It's a nightmare, son,' Brendan said. 'It's like I lost her twice.'

'You haven't lost her, Dad.'

'Why did her writing disappear like that?'

'I don't know, Dad.' He glanced back at the letter. The sheet of paper had practically faded altogether.

'Where did the letter come from?'

The old man frowned.

'Do you remember?'

'No . . . no, not really. It's hazy. I remember . . . somebody came to the door. Yes. That was it. Somebody came to the door. He told me he had something for me . . . it was in his coat.'

*Tell me what you see and it's yours.*

Shadwell's words echoed in Cal's skull.

*Have what you like. Free, gratis and without charge.*

That was a lie of course. One of many. There was always a charge.

'What did he want, Dad? In exchange? Can you remember?'

Brendan shook his head, then, frowning as he tried to recollect:

'Something . . . about you. He said . . . I *think* he said . . . he knew you.'

He looked up at Cal.

'Yes he did. I remember now. He said he knew you.'

161

'It was a trick, Dad. A disgusting trick.'

Brendan narrowed his eyes, as if trying to comprehend this. And then, suddenly, the solution seemed to come clear.

'I want to die, Cal.'

'No, Dad.'

'Yes I do. Really I do. I don't want to bother any longer.'

'You're just sad,' Cal said softly. 'It'll pass.'

'I don't want it to,' Brendan replied. 'Not now. I just want to fall asleep and forget I ever lived.'

Cal reached and put his arms around his father's neck. At first Brendan resisted the embrace; he'd never been a demonstrative man. But then the sobs mounted again, and Cal felt his father's thin arms stretch around him, and they hugged each other tight.

'Forgive me, Cal,' Brendan said through his tears. 'Can you do that?'

'Shush, Dad. Don't be daft.'

'I let you down. I never said the things . . . all the things I felt. Not to her either. Never told her . . . how much . . . never could tell her how much I loved her.'

'She knew, Dad,' said Cal, his own tears blinding him now. 'Believe me, she knew.'

They held each other a little while longer. It was small comfort, but there was a heat of anger in Cal that he knew would dry his tears soon enough. Shadwell had been here; Shadwell and his suit of deceptions. In its folds, Brendan had imagined the letter from Heaven, and the illusion had lasted for as long as the Salesman had needed him. Now Brendan was redundant; the carpet had been found. So the magic no longer held. The words had faded, and finally the paper too, returned to that no-man's land between desire and consummation.

'I'll make some tea, Dad,' Cal said.

It was what his mother would have done in the circumstances. Boiled some fresh water, warmed the pot and counted out the spoonfuls of tea. Setting domestic order against the chaos, in the hope of winning some temporary reprieve from the vale of tears.

# VI

## EVENTS IN A HIGH WIND

### 1

As he stepped back into the hall, Cal remembered Nimrod.

The back door was ajar, and the child had tottered out into the wilderness of the garden, dwarfed by the bushes. Cal went to the door and called after him, but Nimrod was busy pissing into a bed of rampant Sweet William. Cal left him to it. In his present condition the most gratification Nimrod could hope for was a good piss.

As he set the kettle on the stove, the Bournemouth train (via Runcorn, Oxford, Reading and Southampton) thundered past. A moment later Nimrod was at the door.

'Good God,' he said. 'How did you ever sleep here?'

'You get used to it,' said Cal. 'And keep your voice down. My Dad'll hear you.'

'What happened to my drink?'

'It'll have to wait.'

'I'll bawl,' Nimrod warned.

'So bawl.'

His bluff called, Nimrod shrugged and turned back to survey the garden.

'I could get to love this world,' he announced, and stepped out again into the sunlight.

Cal picked up a soiled cup from the sink, and rinsed it clean for his father. Then he crossed to the refrigerator in search of milk. As he did so he heard Nimrod make a small sound. He turned, and went to the window. Nimrod was staring up at the sky, his face wide with wonder. He was watching a plane go over, no doubt. Cal retraced his steps. As he took the milk, which was practically the sole occupant of the refrigerator, off the shelf, there was a rapping on the front door. He looked up again, and two or three impressions hit him at the same time.

One, that a breeze had suddenly got up from somewhere. Two, that Nimrod was stepping back into the thicket of raspberry bushes, in search of a hiding place. And three, that it was not wonder on his face, but *fear* –

Then the rapping became a beating. Fists on the door.

As he made his way through the hall he heard his father say:

'Cal? There's a child in the garden.'

And from the garden, a shout.

'Cal? A child –'

From the corner of his eye he saw Brendan walk through the kitchen, heading for the garden.

'Wait, Dad –' he said, as he opened the front door.

Freddy was on the step. But it was Lilia – standing a little way behind him – who said:

'*Where's my brother?*'

'Out in the –'

*Garden*, he was going to say, but the street scene outside left him mute.

The wind had picked up every item not nailed down – litter, dustbin lids, pieces of garden furniture – and flung them into an aerial tarantella. It had uprooted flower beds, and was picking up the soil from the borders, staining the sun with a veil of earth.

A few pedestrians, caught in this hurricane, were clinging to lamp-posts and fences; some were flat on the ground, hands over their heads.

Lilia and Freddy stepped into the house; the wind followed, eager for fresh conquest, roaring through the house and out again into the back garden, its sudden gusts so strong Cal was almost flung off his feet.

'*Shut the door!*' Freddy yelled.

Cal pushed the door closed, and bolted it. It rattled as the wind beat on the other side.

'Jesus,' said Cal. 'What's happening?'

'Something's come after us,' said Freddy.

'*What?*'

'I don't know.'

Lilia was already half way to the kitchen. Through the open door at the back it was almost night, the air was so full of dirt, and Cal saw his father stepping over the threshold, shouting something against the banshee howl of the wind. Beyond him, only visible because of his toga, Nimrod was clinging to a bush as the wind tried to pick him up.

Cal followed Lilia at a run and overtook her at the kitchen door. There was a commotion on the roof, as a pack of slates were ripped away.

Brendan was in the garden now, all but eclipsed by the wind.

'*Wait, Dad!*' Cal yelled.

As he crossed the kitchen his eyes grazed the tea-pot and the cup beside it, and the utter absurdity of all this hit him like a hammer blow.

I'm dreaming, he thought; I fell from the wall and I've been dreaming ever since. The world isn't like this. The world is the tea-pot and the cup, it isn't raptures and tornadoes.

In that instant of hesitation, the dream became a nightmare. Through the gusting dirt he saw the Rake.

It hung on the wind for a moment, its form caught in a sliver of sun.

'*Done for,*' said Freddy.

The words stung Cal into moving. He was through the back door and out into the garden before the Rake could fall upon the pitiful figures below.

The beast drew Cal's astonished eyes. He saw the morbid fashioning of its skin, which made it billow and swell, and heard again the howl that he'd thought was simply the wind. It was nothing so natural; the sound came out of this phantasm from a dozen places, either the din or the breath it rose on

165

drawing most of the garden's contents out of the ground and throwing them into the air.

A rain of plants and stones came down on the occupants of the garden. Cal covered his head with his hands, and ran blindly towards the spot where he'd last seen his father. Brendan was flat on the ground, shielding himself. Nimrod was not with him.

Cal knew the route the garden path took like the back of his hand. Spitting out mud as he went, he headed away from the house.

Somewhere above, now mercifully hidden, the Rake howled again, and Cal heard Lilia cry out. He did not look behind him, for ahead he now saw Nimrod, who had reached the back fence and was attempting to tear at the rotted timbers. He was having some success too, despite his size. Cal ducked his head down as another rain of earth fell, and ran past the pigeon loft towards the fence.

The howls had stopped, but the wind was far from spent. To judge by the din from the other side of the house it was tearing Chariot Street apart. As he reached the fence, Cal turned round. The sun stabbed the veil of dirt, and he saw blue sky for an instant – then a form blocked the sight, and Cal threw himself at the fence and started to scramble over, as the creature moved towards him. At the top, his belt snagged on a nail. He reached to release it, certain that the Rake was at his neck, but Mad Mooney must have been pushing from behind, for as he pulled his belt from its mooring he fell over the far side of the fence, life and limb intact.

He stood up, and saw why. The boneless beast was hovering beside the loft, its head weaving back and forth as it listened to the pigeons within. Silently blessing the birds, Cal ducked down and tore another plank of the fence away, sufficient to pull Nimrod through.

As a child he'd had the dangers of this no-man's land between fence and railway track beaten into him. Now such dangers seemed negligible beside whatever it was that loitered at the loft. Picking Nimrod up in his arms, Cal climbed the gravel embankment towards the rails.

166

'Run,' said Nimrod. 'It's just behind us. *Run!*'

Cal looked North and South. The wind had reduced visibility to ten or fifteen yards in both directions. Heart in mouth he stepped over the first rail and onto the oil-slicked space between the sleepers. There were four tracks altogether, two in each direction. He was stepping towards the second when he heard Nimrod say:

'*Shit.*'

Cal turned, heels grinding in the gravel, to see that their pursuer had forsaken bird-fancying and was rising over the fence.

Behind the beast, he saw Lilia Pellicia. She was standing in the ruins of the Mooney garden, her mouth open as if to shout. But no sound emerged. Or at least none that Cal could hear. The beast was not so insensitive however. It halted in its advance, turning back towards the garden and the woman in it.

What happened next was confused both by the wind and Nimrod, who, forseeing his sister's slaughter, began to struggle in Cal's arms. All Cal saw was the billowing form of their pursuer suddenly flicker, and the next moment he heard Lilia's voice swoop into an audible register. It was a cry of anguish she let loose, echoed by Nimrod. Then the wind blew up again, shrouding the garden, just as Cal glimpsed Lilia's form swathed in white fire. The cry stopped abruptly.

As it did so, a tingling in the soles of his feet announced the approach of a train. Which direction was it coming from, and on which track? The murder of Lilia had further excited the wind. He could now see less than ten yards down the line in either direction.

Knowing there was no safety the way they'd come, he turned from the garden as the beast let out another scalp-crawling commotion.

*Think*, he told himself. In moments it would be after them again.

He wrenched his arm around Nimrod, and looked at his watch. It read twelve thirty-eight.

167

Where would the train be heading at twelve thirty-eight? *To* Lime Street Station, or *from* it?

*Think.*

Nimrod had begun to cry. Not an infantile bawling, but a deep, heart-felt sob of loss.

Cal glanced over his shoulder as the trembling in the gravel grew more insistent. Again, a tear in the veil of dust gave him a glimpse of the garden. Lilia's body had disappeared, but Cal could see his father standing in the devastation, as Lilia's killer rose above him. Brendan's face was slack. Either he failed to comprehend his danger, or didn't care. He moved not a muscle.

'The shout!' said Cal to Nimrod, lifting the child up so that they were face to snotty face. 'The shout she made –'

Nimrod just sobbed.

'Can you make that shout?'

The beast was almost upon Brendan.

'*Make it!*' Cal yelled at Nimrod, shaking him 'til his gums rattled. 'Make it or I'll fucking kill you!'

Nimrod believed him.

'*Go on!*' Cal said, and Nimrod opened his mouth.

The beast heard the sound. It swung its ballooning head around, and began to come at them again.

All this had taken seconds only, but seconds in which the reverberations had deepened. How far away was the train now? A mile? A quarter of a mile?

Nimrod had ceased the shout, and was fighting to be free of Cal.

'Christ, man!' he was yelling, eyes on the terror approaching through the smoke. 'It's going to kill us!'

Cal tried to ignore Nimrod's cries, and dug for access to that cool region of memory where the dates and destinations of the trains lay.

Which line was it on, and from which direction? His mind flipped through the numbers like a station announcement board, looking for a train six or seven minutes from departure or arrival at Liverpool Lime Street.

The beast was climbing the gravel embankment. The wind

gave it skirts of dust, and danced in and out of its lacerated frame, moaning as it went.

The percussion of the train's approach was enough to make Cal's belly tremble. And still the numbers flipped over.

Where to? Where from? Fast train or slow?

*Think*, damn you.

The beast was almost upon them.

*Think.*

He took a step backwards. Behind him the furthest track began to whine.

And with the whine came the answer. It was the Stafford train, via Runcorn. Its rhythm rose through his feet as it thundered to its destination.

'Twelve forty-six from Stafford,' he said, and stepped onto the humming line.

'What are you *doing*?' Nimrod demanded.

'Twelve forty-six,' he murmured; it was a prayer by numbers.

The slaughterer was crossing the first of the Northbound lines. It had nothing but death to give. No curse, no sentence; only death.

'Come and get us,' Cal yelled at it.

'Are you insane?' Nimrod said.

By way of reply Cal lifted the bait a little higher. Nimrod bawled. The pursuer's head grew vast with hunger.

'*Come on!*'

It had crossed both the Northbound lines; now it stepped onto the first of those headed South.

Cal took another stumbling step backwards, his heel hitting the furthest rail, the voice of the beast and the roar in the ground shaking the fillings loose in his teeth.

The last thing he heard as the creature came to fetch him was Nimrod running through a celestial checklist in search of a Redeemer.

And suddenly, as if in answer to his call, the veil of dirty air divided, and the train was upon them. Cal felt his foot catch on the rail, and raised it an inch higher to step back, then fell away from the track.

169

What followed was over in seconds. One moment the creature was on the line, its maw vast, its appetite for death vaster
still. The next, the train hit it.

There was no cry. No moment of triumph, seeing the monster undone. Just a foul stench, as if every dead man in the
vicinity had sat up and expelled a breath, then the train was
rushing by, smeared faces peering from the windows.

And just as suddenly as it had appeared, it was away through
the curtain on its way South. The whine in the rails receded
to a sibilant whisper. Then even that was gone.

Cal shook Nimrod from his roll-call of deities.

'It's over . . .' he said.

It took Nimrod a little while to accept the fact. He peered
through the smoke, expecting the Rake to come at them again.

'It's gone,' said Cal. 'I killed it.'

'The train killed it,' said Nimrod. 'Put me down.'

Cal did so, and without looking right or left Nimrod started
back across the tracks towards the garden where his sister had
perished. Cal followed.

The wind that had come with the boneless creature, or
borne it, had dropped completely. As there was not even a
light breeze to keep the dirt it had swept up aloft, a deluge
now descended. Small stones, fragments of garden furniture
and fencing, even the remains of several household pets who'd
been snatched away. A rain of blood and earth the like of
which the good people of Chariot Street had not expected to
see this side of Judgment Day.

170

# VII

## THE AFTERMATH

### 1

Once the dust had begun to settle, it was possible to assess the extent of the devastation. The garden had been turned upside down, of course, as had all the other gardens along the row; there were dozens of slates missing from the roof, and the chimney stack looked less than secure. The wind had been equally lethal at the front of the house. All along the street havoc had been wreaked: lamps toppled, walls demolished, car windows smashed by flying trash. Mercifully there seemed to be no serious casualties; just cuts, bruises and shock. Lilia – of whom no sign remained – was the only fatality.

'That was Immacolata's creature,' Nimrod said. 'I'll kill her for that. I swear I will.'

The threat sounded doubly hollow coming from his diminutive body.

'What's the use?' said Cal despondently. He was watching through the front window as the occupants of Chariot Street wandered around in a daze, some staring at the wreckage, others squinting up at the sky as if expecting some explanation to be written there.

'We won a substantial victory this afternoon, Mr Mooney –' said Frederick. 'Don't you understand that? And it was your doing.'

'Some victory,' said Cal, bitterly. 'My Dad sitting next door not saying a word; Lilia dead, half the street torn apart –'

171

'We'll fight again,' said Freddy, 'until the Fugue's safe.'

'Fight, will we?' said Nimrod. 'And where were you when the shit was flying?'

Cammell was about to protest, then thought better of it, letting silence confess his cowardice.

Two ambulances and several police cars had arrived at the far end of Chariot Street. Hearing the sirens, Nimrod joined Cal at the window.

'Uniforms,' he muttered. 'They always mean trouble.'

As he spoke the door of the lead police car swung open, and a sober-suited man stepped out, smoothing his thinning hair back with the palm of his hand. Cal knew the fellow's face – his eyes so ringed with shadow he seemed not to have slept in years – but, as ever, he could put no name to it.

'We should get gone,' said Nimrod. 'They'll want to talk with us –'

Already a dozen uniformed police were fanning out amongst the houses to begin their enquiries. What would his fellow Charioteers have to report, Cal wondered. Had they glimpsed anything of the creature that had killed Lilia, and if so, would they admit to it?

'I can't go,' said Cal. 'I can't leave Dad.'

'You think they won't sniff a rat if they speak to you?' said Nimrod. 'Don't be an imbecile. Let your father tell them all he has to tell. They won't believe it.'

Cal saw the sense in this, but he was still reluctant to leave Brendan alone.

'What happened to Suzanna and the others?' asked Cammell, as Cal turned the problem over.

'They went back to the warehouse to see if they could trace Shadwell from there,' said Freddy.

'Isn't likely, is it?' said Cal.

'It worked for Lilia,' said Freddy.

'You mean you know where the carpet is?'

'Almost. She and I went back to the Laschenski house, you see, to take bearings from there. She said the echoes were very strong.'

'Echoes?'

172

'Back from where the carpet now *is*, to where it *had been*.'

Freddy fished in his pocket and brought out three shiny new paperbacks, one of which was a Liverpool and District Atlas. The others were murder mysteries. 'I borrowed these from a confectioner's,' he said, 'to trace the carpet.'

'But you didn't succeed,' said Cal.

'As I said, *almost*. We were interrupted when she felt the presence of that thing that killed her.'

'She was always acute,' said Nimrod.

'That she was,' Freddy replied. 'As soon as she sniffed the beast on the wind she forgot about the carpet. Demanded we came to warn you. That was our error. We should have stayed put.'

'Then it would have picked us off one by one,' said Nimrod.

'I hope to God it didn't go after the others first,' said Cal.

'No. They're alive,' said Freddy. 'We'd feel it if they weren't.'

'He's right,' said Nimrod. 'We can pick up their trail easily. But we have to go *now*. Once the uniforms get here we're trapped.'

'All right, I heard you first time,' said Cal. 'Let me just say goodbye to Dad.'

He went next door. Brendan hadn't moved since Cal had settled him in the chair.

'Dad . . . can you hear me?'

Brendan looked up from his sorrows.

'Haven't seen a wind like that since the war,' he said. 'Out in Malaya. Saw whole houses blown down. Didn't think to see it here.'

He spoke distractedly, his gaze on the empty wall.

'The police are in the street,' said Cal.

'At least the loft's still standing, eh,' Brendan said. 'A wind like that . . .' his voice faded. Then he said: 'Will they come here? The police?'

'I would think so, Dad. Are you all right to speak to them? I have to go.'

'Of course you do,' Brendan murmured. 'You go on.'

'Do you mind if I take the car?'

173

'Take it. I can tell them —' Again, he halted, before picking up his thoughts. 'Haven't seen a wind like that since . . . oh, since the war.'

## 2

The trio left by the back door, climbing the fence and making their way along the embankment to the footbridge at the end of Chariot Street. From there they could see the size of the crowd that had already gathered from neighbouring streets, eager to view the spectacle.

Part of Cal itched to go down and tell them what he'd seen. To say: the world isn't just the tea-cup and the pot. I *know*, because *I've seen*. But he held onto his words, knowing how they'd look at him.

There'd maybe come a time to be proud, to tell his tribe about the terrors and miracles they shared with the world. But this wasn't it.

# VIII

## NECESSARY EVILS

The name of the man with the dark suit, whom Cal had seen getting out of the police-car, was Inspector Hobart. He had been in the force for eighteen of his forty-six years, but it was only recently – with the riots that had erupted in the city during the late spring and summer of the previous year – that his star had come into the ascendant.

The origins of those riots were still the subject of both Public Enquiry and private argument, but Hobart had no time for either. It was the Law and how to keep it that obsessed him, and in that year of civil disturbance his obsession had made him the man of the moment.

Not for him the niceties of the sociologist or the civic planner. His sacred task was to preserve the peace, and his methods – which his apologists described as uncompromising – found sympathy with his civic masters. He rose in the ranks within weeks, and behind closed doors he was offered *carte blanche* to deal with the anarchy that had already cost the city millions.

He was not blind to the politics of this manœuvre. No doubt the higher echelons, for whom he had utter but unspoken contempt, were fearful of the backlash should they wield too strong a whip themselves. No doubt too he would be the first to be sacrificed to the ferocity of public indignation should the techniques he brought to bear fail.

But they did not fail. The elite he formed – men chosen from the Divisions for their sympathy with Hobart's methods – was quickly successful. While the conventional forces kept the blue line unbroken on the streets, Hobart's Special Force, known – to those who knew of it at all – as the Fire Brigade, was acting behind the scenes to terrorize any suspected of fuelling the agitation, either by word or deed. Within weeks the riots died down, and James Hobart was suddenly a force to be reckoned with.

There had followed several months of inactivity, and the Brigade languished. It had not escaped Hobart that being the man of the hour was of little consequence once that hour had passed; and through the spring and early summer of this, the following year, that seemed to be the case.

Until now. Today he dared hope he still had a fight on his hands. There'd been chaos, and here, in front of him, the gratifying evidence.

'What's the situation?'

His right-hand man, Richardson, shook his head.

'There's talk of some kind of whirlwind,' he said.

'Whirlwind?' Hobart indulged a smile at the absurdity of this. When he smiled his lips disappeared, and his eyes became slits. 'No felons?'

'Not that we've had reported. Apparently it was just this wind –'

Hobart stared at the spectacle of destruction in front of him.

'This is England,' he said. 'We don't have whirlwinds.'

'Well something did this . . .'

'Some*body*, Bryn. Anarchists. They're like rats, these people. You find a poison that does the job, and they learn how to get fat on it.' He paused. 'You know, I think it's going to begin again.'

As he spoke, another of his officers – one of the blood-spattered heroes of the previous year's confrontations, a man called Fryer – approached.

'Sir. We've got reports of suspects seen crossing the bridge.'

'Get after them' said Hobart. 'Let's have some arrests. And Bryn, you talk to these people. I want testimonies from every-one in the street.'

The two officers went about their business, leaving Hobart to ponder the problem. There was no doubt in his mind that events here were of human making. It might not be the same individuals whose heads he'd broken last year, but it was essentially the same animal. In his years of service he'd confronted that beast in its many guises, and it seemed to him that it grew more devious and damnable every time he stared into its maw.

But the enemy was a constant, whether it concealed itself behind fire, flood or whirlwind. He took strength from that fact. The battlefield might be new, but the war was old. It was the struggle between the Law, of which he was the representative, and the rot of disorder in the human heart. He would let no whirlwind blind him to that fact.

Sometimes, of course, the war required that he be cruel, but what cause worth fighting for did not require cruelty of its champions once in a while? He had never shirked that responsibility and he would not shirk now.

Let the beast come again, in whatever fancy dress it chose. He would be ready.

# IX

# ON THE MIGHT OF PRINCES

T he Incantatrix did not look towards Shadwell when he entered; indeed it seemed she'd not moved a muscle since the night before. The hotel room was stale with her breath and sweat. Shadwell inhaled deeply.

'My poor libertine,' she murmured. 'He's destroyed.'

'How's that possible?' Shadwell replied. The image of the creature was still lodged in his head, in all its appalling magnificence. How could a thing so powerful be killed, especially as it had already been dead?

'It was the Cuckoos,' she said.

'Mooney, or the girl?'

'Mooney.'

'And the carpet crawlers?'

'All survived but one,' said Immacolata. 'Am I right, sister?'

The Hag was squatting in the corner, her body like phlegm on a wall. Her reply to Immacolata was so soft Shadwell missed it.

'Yes,' the Incantatrix said. 'My sister saw one of them dispatched. The rest escaped.'

'And the Scourge?'

'I hear only silence.'

'Good,' said Shadwell. 'I'll have the carpet moved this evening.'

'Where to?'

'A house across the river, that belongs to a man I once did

business with: Shearman. We'll hold the Auction there. This place is too public for our clients.'

'Are they coming then?'

Shadwell grinned. 'Of course they're coming. They've waited years, these people. Just for a chance to bid. And I'm going to give it to them.'

It pleased him, to think of how readily they sprang to his command, the seven mighty bidders whom he'd invited to this Sale of Sales.

Among their members were some of the wealthiest individuals in the world; between them, fortunes sufficient to trade in nations. None of the seven had a name that would have meant anything to the hoi-polloi – they were, like the truly mighty, anonymously great. But Shadwell had done his researches well. He knew that these seven had something else in common besides wealth beyond calculation. All, he knew, hungered for the miraculous. That was why they were even now leaving their chateaux and penthouses and hurrying to this grimy city, their palates dry, their palms sweaty.

He had something each of them wanted almost as much as life itself: and perhaps more than wealth. Mighty they were. But today, was he not mightier?

# X

# HUMANKINDNESS

**S**o much *desire*,' Apolline commented to Suzanna, as they walked the streets of Liverpool. They'd found nothing at Gilchrist's Warehouse but suspicious stares, and had made a quick exit before enquiries were made. Once out, Apolline had demanded to take a tour of the city, and had followed her nose to the busiest thoroughfare she could find, its pavements crammed with shoppers, children and dead-beats.

'Desire?' said Suzanna. It wasn't a motive that sprang instantly to mind on this dirty street.

'Everywhere,' said Apolline. 'Don't you see?'

She pointed across at a billboard advertising bed-linen, which depicted two lovers languishing in a post-coital fatigue; beside it a car advertisement boasted The Perfect Body, and made its point as much in flesh as steel. 'And there,' said Apolline, directing Suzanna to a window display of deodorants, in which the serpent tempted a fetchingly naked Adam and Eve with the promise of confidence in crowds.

'The place is a whorehouse,' said Apolline, clearly approving.

Only now did Suzanna realize that they'd lost Jerichau. He'd been loitering a few paces behind the woman, his anxious eyes surveying the parade of human beings. Now he'd gone.

They retraced their steps through the throng of pedestrians and found him standing in front of a video rental shop, entranced by bank upon bank of monitors.

'Are they prisoners?' he said, as he stared at the talking heads.

'No,' said Suzanna. 'It's a show. Like a theatre.' She plucked at his oversized jacket. 'Come on,' she said.

He looked around at her. His eyes were brimming. The thought that he had been moved to tears by the sight of a dozen television screens made her fear for his tender heart.

'It's all right,' she said, coaxing him away from the window. 'They're quite happy.'

She put her arm through his. A flicker of pleasure crossed his face, and together they moved through the crowd. Feeling his body trembling against hers it was not difficult to share the trauma he was experiencing. She'd taken the harlot century she'd been born into for granted, knowing no other, but now – seeing it with *his* eyes, hearing it with *his* ears – she understood it afresh; saw just how desperate it was to please, yet how dispossessed of pleasure; how crude, even as it claimed sophistication; and, despite its zeal to spellbind, how utterly unenchanting.

For Apolline, however, the experience was proving a joy. She strode through the crowd, trailing her long black skirts like a widow on a post-funereal spree.

'I think we should get off the main street,' said Suzanna when they'd caught up with her. 'Jerichau doesn't like the crowd.'

'Well he'd best get used to it,' said Apolline, shooting a glance at Jerichau. 'This is going to be *our* world soon enough.'

So saying, she turned and started away from Suzanna again.

'Wait a minute!'

Suzanna went in pursuit, before they lost each other in the throng.

'Wait!' she said, taking hold of Apolline's arm. 'We can't wander around forever. We have to meet with the others.'

'Let me enjoy myself awhile,' said Apolline. 'I've been asleep too long. I need some entertainment.'

'Later maybe,' said Suzanna. 'When we've found the carpet.'

'Fuck the carpet,' was Apolline's prompt reply.

They were blocking the flow of pedestrians as they debated,

receiving sour looks and curses for their troubles. One pubescent boy spat at Apolline, who promptly spat back with impressive accuracy. The boy retreated, with a shocked look on his bespittled face.

'I like these people,' she commented. 'They don't pretend to courtesy.'

'We've lost Jerichau again,' Suzanna said. 'Damn him, he's like a child.'

'I see him.'

Apolline pointed down the street, to where Jerichau was standing, striving to keep his head above the crowd as though he feared drowning in this sea of humanity.

Suzanna started back towards him, but she was pressing against the tide, and it was tough going. But Jerichau didn't move. He had his fretful gaze fixed on the empty air above the heads of the crowd. They jostled and elbowed him but he went on staring.

'We almost lost you,' Suzanna said when she finally reached his side.

His reply was a simple:

'Look.'

Though she was several inches shorter than he, she followed the direction of his stare as best she could.

'I don't see anything.'

'What's he troubling about now?' Apolline, who'd now joined them, demanded to know.

'They're all so sad,' Jerichau said.

Suzanna looked at the faces passing by. Irritable they were; and sluggish some of them, and bitter; but few struck her as sad.

'Do you see?' said Jerichau, before she had a chance to contradict him: 'The lights.'

'No she doesn't see them,' said Apolline firmly. 'She's still a Cuckoo, remember? Even if she has got the menstruum. Now come on.'

Jerichau's gaze now fell on Suzanna, and he was closer to tears than ever. 'You *must* see,' he said. 'I want you to see.'

'Don't do this,' said Apolline. 'It's not wise.'

'They have colours,' Jerichau was saying.

'Remember the Principles,' Apolline protested.

'Colours?' said Suzanna.

'Like smoke, all around their heads.'

Jerichau took hold of her arm.

'Will you listen?' Apolline said. 'Capra's Third Principle states –'

Suzanna wasn't attending. She was staring at the crowd, her hand now grasping Jerichau's hand.

It was no longer simply his senses she shared, but his mounting panic, trapped amongst this hot-breathed herd. An empathic wave of claustrophobia rose in her; she closed her lids and told herself to be calm.

In the darkness she heard Apolline again, talking of some Principle. Then she opened her eyes.

What she saw almost made her cry out. The sky seemed to have changed colour, as though the gutters had caught fire, and the smoke was choking the street. Nobody seemed to have noticed, however.

She turned to Jerichau, seeking some explanation, and this time she let out a yell. He had gained a halo of fireworks, from which a column of light and vermilion smoke was rising.

'Oh Christ,' she said. 'What's happening?'

Apolline had taken hold of her shoulder, and was pulling on her.

'Come away!' she shouted. 'It'll spread. *After three, the multitude.*'

'Huh?'

'The Principle!'

But her warning went uncomprehended. Suzanna – her shock becoming exhilaration – was scanning the crowd. Everywhere she saw what Jerichau had described. Waves of colour, plumes of it, rising from the flesh of Humankind. Almost all were subdued; some plain grey, others like plaited ribbons of grimy pastel; but once or twice in the throng she saw a pure pigment; brilliant orange around the head of a child carried high on her father's back; a peacock display from a girl laughing with her lover.

Again, Apolline tugged at her, and this time Suzanna acquiesced, but before they'd got more than a yard a cry rose from the crowd behind them – then another, and another – and suddenly to right and left people were putting their hands to their faces and covering their eyes. A man fell to his knees at Suzanna's side, spouting the Lord's prayer – somebody else had begun vomiting, others had seized hold of their nearest neighbour for support, only to find their private horror was a universal condition.

'Damn you,' said Apolline. 'Now look what you've done.'

Suzanna could see the colours of the haloes changing, as panic convulsed those who wore them. The vanquished greys were shot through with violent greens and purples. The mingled din of shrieks and prayers assaulted her ears.

'*Why?*' said Suzanna.

'Capra's Principle!' Apolline yelled back at her. '*After three, the multitude.*'

Now Suzanna grasped the point. What two could keep to themselves became public knowledge if shared by three. As soon as she'd embraced Apolline and Jerichau's vision – one they'd known from birth – the fire had spread, a mystic contagion that had reduced the street to bedlam in seconds.

The fear bred violence almost instantly, as the crowd looked for scapegoats on which to blame these visions. Shoppers forsook their purchases and leapt upon each others' throats; secretaries broke their nails on the cheeks of accountants; grown men wept as they tried to shake sense from their wives and children.

What might have been a race of mystics was suddenly a pack of wild dogs, the colours they swam in degenerating into the grey and umber of a sick man's shit.

But there was more to come. No sooner had the fighting begun than a well-dressed woman, her make-up smeared in the struggle, pointed an accusing finger at Jerichau.

'*Him!*' she shrieked. '*It was him!*'

Then she flung herself at the guilty party, ready to take out his eyes. Jerichau stumbled back into the traffic as she came after him.

*'Make it stop!'* she yelled. *'Make it stop!'*

At her cacophony, several members of the crowd forgot their private wars and set their sights on this new target.

To Suzanna's left somebody said: 'Kill him.' An instant later, the first missile flew. It hit Jerichau's shoulder. A second followed. The traffic had come to a halt, as the drivers, slowed by curiosity, came under the influence of the vision. Jerichau was trapped against the cars, as the crowd turned on him. Suddenly, Suzanna knew, the issue was life and death. Confused and frightened, this mob was perfectly prepared, *eager* even, to tear Jerichau and anyone who went to his rescue limb from limb.

Another stone struck Jerichau, bringing blood to his cheek. Suzanna advanced towards him, calling for him to *move*, but he was watching the advancing crowd as if mesmerized by this display of human rage. She pushed on, climbing over a car bonnet and squeezing between bumpers to get to where he stood. But the leaders of the mob – the smeared woman and two or three others – were almost upon him.

*'Leave him be!'* she yelled. Nobody paid the least attention. There was something almost ritualistic about the way victim and executioners were playing this out, as though their cells knew it of old, and had no power to re-write the story.

It was the police sirens that broke the spell. The first time Suzanna had heard that gut-churning wail and been thankful for it.

The effect was both immediate and comprehensive. Members of the crowd began to moan as though in sympathy with the sirens, those still in combat forsaking their enemies' throats, the rest staring down at their trampled belongings and bloodied fists in disbelief. One or two fainted on the spot. Several others began weeping again, this time more in confusion than fear. Many, deciding discretion bettered arrest, took to their heels. Shocked back into their Cuckoo blindness they fled in all directions, shaking their heads to dislodge the last vestiges of their vision.

Apolline had appeared at Jerichau's side, having

manœuvred her way round the back of the mob during the previous few minutes.

She bullied him from his trance of sacrifice, shaking him and shouting. Then she hauled him away. Her rescue attempt came not a moment too soon, for though most of the lynch-party had dispersed a dozen or so weren't ready to give up their sport. They wanted blood, and would have it before the law arrived.

Suzanna looked around for some escape route. A small street off the main road offered some hope. She summoned Apolline with a shout. The arrival of the patrol cars proved a useful distraction: there was a further scattering of the mob.

But the hard core of dedicated lynchers came in pursuit. As Apolline and Jerichau reached the street corner the first of the mob, the woman with the smeared face, snatched at Apolline's dress. Apolline let go of Jerichau and turned on her attacker, delivering a punch to the woman's jaw that threw her to the ground.

A couple of the officers had caught sight of the chase and were now chasing in their turn, but before they could step in to prevent violence, Jerichau stumbled. In that second the mob was on him.

Suzanna turned back to lend him a hand. As she did so a car raced towards her, skirting the kerb. The next second it was at her side, the door flung open, and Cal was yelling:

'Get in! Get in!'

'Wait!' she called to him, and looked back to see Jerichau being flung against a brick wall, cornered by the hounds. Apolline, who'd laid another of the mob out for good measure, was now making for the open car door. But Suzanna couldn't leave Jerichau.

She ran back towards the knot of bodies that now eclipsed him, blotting out the sound of Cal's voice calling her to get away while she could. By the time she reached Jerichau he'd given up all hope of resistance. He was just sliding down the wall, sheltering his bloodied head from a hail of spittle and blows. She shouted for the assault to stop but anonymous hands dragged her from his side.

186

Again she heard Cal shout, but she couldn't have gone to him now if she'd wanted to.

'*Drive!*' she yelled, praying to God he heard her and got going. Then she flung herself at the most vicious of Jerichau's tormentors. But there were simply too many hands holding her back, some covertly molesting her in the confusion of the moment. She struggled and shouted, but it was hopeless. In desperation she reached for Jerichau, and hung onto him for dear life, covering her head with her other arm as the bruising hail intensified.

Quite suddenly, the beating and the cursing and the kicks all ceased, as two officers broke into the ring of lynchers. Two or three of the mob had already taken the opportunity to slope away before they were detained, but most of them showed not the least sign of guilt. Quite the reverse; they wiped the spit from their lips and began to justify their brutality in shrill voices.

'They started it, officer,' said one of the number, a balding individual who, before the blood had stained his knuckles and shirt, might have been a bank cashier.

'Is that right?' said the officer, taking a look at the black derelict and his sullen mistress. 'Get the fuck up, you two,' he said. 'You've got some questions to answer.'

# XI

## THREE VIGNETTES

### 1

**W**e should never have left them,' Cal said, when they'd made a circuit of the block and come back up Lord Street again to find the street crawling with officers, and no sign of Jerichau or Suzanna. 'They've been arrested,' he said. 'Damn it, we shouldn't have –'

'Be practical,' said Nimrod. 'We had no choice.'

'They almost murdered us,' said Apolline. She was still panting like a horse.

'At this point, our priority has to be the Weave,' Nimrod said. 'I think we're agreed on that.'

'Lilia saw the carpet,' Freddy explained to Apolline. 'From the Laschenski house.'

'Is that where she is now?' Apolline enquired.

Nobody replied to the question for several seconds. Then Nimrod spoke.

'She's dead,' he said flatly.

'Dead?' Apolline replied. 'How? Not one of the Cuckoos?'

'No,' said Freddy. 'It was something Immacolata raised. Our man Mooney here destroyed it, before it killed us all.'

'She knows we're awake then,' said Apolline.

Cal caught her reflection in the mirror. Her eyes had become like black pebbles in the puffed dough of her face.

'Nothing's changed, has it?' she said. 'Humankind on one side, and bad raptures on the other.'

'The Scourge was worse than any rapture,' said Freddy.

188

'It's still not safe to wake the rest of them,' Apolline insisted. 'The Cuckoos are more dangerous than ever.'

'If we don't wake them, what happens to *us*?' said Nimrod.

'We become Custodians,' said Apolline. 'We watch over the carpet until times get better.'

'If they ever do,' said Freddy.

That remark put an end to the conversation for a good long while.

2

Hobart looked at the blood that was still bright on the paving stones of Lord Street, and knew for certain that the debris the anarchists had left on Chariot Street had been only a curtain-raiser. Here was something more graspable: a spontaneous eruption of lunacy amongst an ordinary cross-section of people, their violence whipped up by the two rebels who were now in custody awaiting his interrogation.

Last year's weapons had been bricks and home-made bombs. This year's terrorists had more access to more sophisticated equipment, it seemed. There'd been talk of a mass hallucination here, on this unremarkable street. The testimonies of perfectly sane citizens spoke of the sky changing colour. If the forces of subversion had indeed brought new weapons into the field – mind-altering gases, perhaps – then he'd be well placed to press for more aggressive tactics: heavier armaments, and a freer hand to use them. There would be resistance from the higher ranks, he knew from experience; but the more blood that was seen to be spilled the more persuasive his case became.

'*You*,' he said, calling one of the press photographers over. He directed the man's attention to the splashes on the paving underfoot. 'Show *that* to your readers,' he said.

The man duly photographed the splashes, then turned his lens towards Hobart. He had no opportunity to snatch a portrait before Fryer stepped in and wrenched the camera from his grip.

'No pictures,' he said.

'Got something to hide?' the photographer retorted.

'Give him his property back,' said Hobart. 'He's got a job to do, like all of us.'

The journalist took his camera and withdrew.

'Scum,' Hobart muttered as the man turned his back. Then: 'Anything from Chariot Street?'

'We've got some damn peculiar testimonies.'

'Oh?'

'Nobody's actually confessed to seeing anything, but apparently around the time of this whirlwind things got crazy. The dogs went wild; all the radios cut off. Something strange went on there, no doubt of that.'

'And here too,' said Hobart. 'I think it's time we spoke to our suspects.'

<h1 style="text-align:center">3</h1>

The haloes had faded by the time the officers threw open the back of the Black Maria, and ordered Suzanna and Jerichau out into the yard of Hobart's headquarters. All that was left of the vision she'd shared with Jerichau and Apolline was vague nausea and an aching skull.

They were taken into the bleak concrete building and separated; their belongings were taken from them. Suzanna had nothing she cared much about but Mimi's book, which she'd kept in either hand or pocket since finding it. Though she protested at its confiscation, it too was taken from her.

There was a brief exchange between the arresting officers as to where she was to be lodged, then she was escorted down a flight of stairs to a bare interrogation cell somewhere in the bowels of the building. Here an officer filled in a form of her personal details. She answered his questions as best she could, but her thoughts kept drifting off: to Cal, to Jerichau, and to the carpet. If things had looked bad at dawn they looked a good deal worse now. She told herself to cross each bridge as she came to it, and not fret uselessly about matters she could do nothing to influence. Her first priority was to get herself and Jerichau out of custody. She'd seen his fear and desperation when they were separated. He would be easy meat if anyone chose to get rough with him.

Her thoughts were interrupted by the door opening. A pale man in a charcoal-grey suit was staring at her. He looked not to have slept in a long while.

'Thank you, Stillman,' he said. The interviewing officer vacated the chair opposite Suzanna. 'Wait outside, would you?'

The man withdrew. The door slammed.

'I'm Hobart,' the newcomer announced. 'Inspector Hobart. We have some talking to do.'

She could no longer see even the merest shadow of a halo, but she knew, even before he sat down in front of her, the colour of this man's soul. It gave her no comfort.

# Part Four

# What Price Wonderland?

*Caveat Emptor*
*(Let the Buyer Beware)*

Latin Motto

# 1
---

# TO SELL IS TO OWN

## 1

That was the most important lesson Shadwell had learned as a salesman. If what you possessed was desired ardently enough by another person, then you as good as possessed that person too.

Even princes could be owned. Here they were now, or their modern equivalent, all assembled at his call: the old money and the new, the aristocracy and the *arrivistes*, watching each other warily, and eager as children for a glimpse of the treasure they were here to fight over.

Paul van Niekerk, reputed to own the finest collection of erotica in the world, outside the walls of the Vatican; Marguerite Pierce, who had with the death of her parents inherited at the tender age of nineteen one of the largest personal fortunes in Europe; Beauclerc Norris, the Hamburger King, whose company owned small states; the oil billionaire Alexander A., who was within hours of death in a Washington hospital but had sent his companion of many years, a woman who answered only to Mrs A., Michael Rahimzadeh, the origins of whose fortune were impossible to trace, its previous owners all recently, and suddenly, deceased; Leon Devereaux, who'd come hot-foot from Johannesburg, his pockets lined with gold dust; and finally, an unnamed individual whose features had been toyed with by a succession of surgeons, who could not take from his eyes the look of a man with an unspeakable history.

That was the seven.

# 2

They'd started to arrive at Shearman's house, which stood in its own grounds on the edge of Thurstaston Common, in the middle of the afternoon. By six-thirty they had all gathered. Shadwell played the perfect host – plying them with drinks and platitudes – but letting few hints drop as to what lay ahead.

It had taken him years, and much conniving, to get access to the mighty, and more trickery still to learn which of them had dreams of magic. When pressed, he'd used the jacket, seducing those who fawned upon the potentates into revealing all they knew. Many had no tales to tell; their masters made no sign of mourning a lost world. But for every atheist there was at least one who *believed*; one prone to moping over lost dreams of childhood, or to midnight confessions on how their search for Heaven had ended only in tears and gold.

From that list of believers Shadwell had then narrowed the field down to those whose wealth was practically unfathomable. Then, using the jacket once more, he got past the underlings and met his elite circle of buyers face to face.

It was an easier pitch to make than he'd imagined. It seemed that the existence of the Fugue had long been rumoured in both the highest places and the lowest; extremes which more than one of this assembly knew with equal intimacy; and he had enough detail of the Weaveworld from Immacolata to persuade them that he would soon enough be able to offer that place for sale. There was one from his short-list who would have no truck with the Auction, muttering that such forces could not be bought and sold, and that Shadwell would regret his acquisitiveness; another had died the previous year. The rest were here, their fortunes trembling in readiness to be spent.

'Ladies and gentlemen,' he announced. 'Perhaps the time has come for us to view the object under consideration.'

He led them like sheep through the maze of Shearman's

manse to the room on the first floor where the carpet had been laid. The curtains were drawn; a single light shed a warm illumination onto the Weave, which almost covered the floor.

Shadwell's heart beat a little faster as he watched them inspect the carpet. This was the essential moment, when the purchasers' eyes first alighted upon the merchandise; the moment when any sale was truly made. Subsequent talk might massage the price, but no words, however cunning, could compete with this first exchange of glance and goods. Upon that, everything pivoted. And he was aware that the carpet, however mysterious its designs, appeared to be simply that: a carpet. It required the client's imagination, stoked by longing, to see the geography that lay in wait there.

Now, as he scanned the faces of the seven, he knew his gambit had not failed. Though several of them were tactical enough to try and disguise their enthusiasm, they were mesmerized, each and every one.

'This is it,' Devereaux said, his usual severity confounded by awe. '. . . I didn't really think . . .'

'That it was real?' Rahimzadeh prompted.

'Oh it's real enough,' said Norris. He'd already gone down on his haunches to finger the goods.

'Take care,' said Shadwell. 'It's volatile.'

'What d'you mean?'

'The Fugue wants to show itself,' Shadwell replied. 'It's ready and waiting.'

'Yes,' said Mrs A. 'I can feel it.' She clearly didn't like the sensation very much. 'Alexander said it would look just like an ordinary carpet, and I suppose it does. But . . . I don't know . . . there's something odd about it.'

'It's moving,' said the man with the lifted face.

Norris stood up. 'Where?' he said.

'In the centre.'

All eyes studied the intricacies of the Gyre design, and yes, there did seem the subtlest eddying in the Weave. Even Shadwell had not noticed this before. It made him more eager than ever to have the business over and done with. It was time to sell.

'Does anybody have any questions?' he asked.

'How can we be certain?' said Marguerite Pierce. 'That this is *the* carpet.'

'You can't,' said Shadwell. He'd anticipated this challenge, and had his reply to hand. 'You either know in your gut that the Fugue is waiting in the Weave, or else you leave. The door is open. Please. Help yourself.'

The woman said nothing for several seconds.

Then: 'I'll stay,' she said.

'Of course,' said Shadwell. 'Shall we begin?'

## II

## TELL ME NO LIES

The room they'd put Suzanna in was cold and charmless enough, but it could have taken lessons from the man who sat opposite her. He handled her with an ironic courtesy that never quite concealed the hammer head beneath. Not once during the hour of their interview had he raised his voice above the conversational, nor shown the least impatience at repeating the same enquiries.

'What's the name of your organization?'

'I have none,' she'd told him for the hundredth time.

'You're in very serious trouble,' he said. 'Do you understand that?'

'I demand to see a solicitor.'

'There'll be no solicitor.'

'I have rights,' she protested.

'You forfeited your rights on Lord Street,' he said. 'Now. The name of your confederates.'

'I don't *have* any confederates, damn you.'

She told herself to be calm, but the adrenalin kept pumping. He knew it, too. He didn't take his lizard eyes off her for an instant. Just kept watching, and asking the same old questions, winding her up until she was ready to scream.

'And the nigger –' he said. 'He's in the same organization.'

'No. No, he doesn't know anything.'

'So you admit the organization exists.'

'I didn't say that.'

'You just admitted as much.'

'You're putting words in my mouth.'

Again, the sour civility: 'Then please . . . speak for yourself.'

'I've nothing to say.'

'We've witnesses that'll testify that you and the nigger –'

'Don't keep calling him that.'

'That you and the nigger were at the centre of the riot. Who supplies your chemical weapons?'

'Don't be ridiculous,' she said. 'That's what you are. You're ridiculous.'

She could feel herself flushing, and tears threatened. Damn it, she wouldn't give him the satisfaction of seeing her cry.

He must have sensed her determination, because he gave up that line of questioning and tried another.

'Tell me about the code,' he said.

This perplexed her utterly. 'What code?'

He took Mimi's book from the pocket of his jacket, and laid it on the table between them, his wide, pale hand placed proprietorially across it.

'What does this mean?' he said.

'It's a book . . .'

'Don't take me for a fool.'

'I don't,' she thought. 'You're dangerous, and you make me afraid.'

But she replied: 'Really, it's just a book of faery-tales.'

He opened it, flicking through the pages.

'You read German?'

'A little. The book was a present. From my grandmother.'

He paused here and here, to glance at the illustrations. He lingered over one – a dragon, its coils gleaming in a midnight forest – before passing on.

'You realize, I hope, that the more you lie to me the worse things will get for you.'

She didn't grace the threat with a reply.

'I'm going to take your little book apart –' he said.

'Please don't –'

She knew he'd read her concern as confirmation of her guilt, but she couldn't help herself.

'Page by page,' he said. 'Word by word if I have to.'

'There's nothing in it,' she insisted. 'It's just a book. And it's mine.'

'It's evidence,' he corrected her. 'It means something.'

'. . . faery-tales . . .'

'I want to know *what*.'

She hung her head, so as not to let him enjoy her pain.

He stood up.

'Wait for me, would you?' he said, as if she had any choice in the matter. 'I'm going to have a word with your nigger friend. Two of this city's finest have been keeping him company –' he paused to let the sub-text sink in, '– I'm sure by now he'll be ready to tell me the whys and the wherefores. I'll be back in a little while.'

She put her hand over her mouth to stop herself begging him to believe her. It would do no good.

He rapped on the door. It was unbolted; he stepped out into the corridor. The door was locked behind him.

She sat at the table for several minutes and tried to make sense of the feeling that seemed to narrow her wind-pipe and her vision, leaving her breathless, and blind to everything but the memory of his eyes. Never in her life had she felt anything quite like it.

It took a little time before she realized that it was hate.

## III

_____

# SO NEAR, SO FAR

## 1

**T**he echoes that Cammell had spoken of were still loud and clear in Rue Street when, as evening drew on, Cal and his passengers arrived there. It was left to Apolline, using pages torn from the atlas spread out like playing cards on the bare boards of the upper room, to compute the carpet's present location.

To Cal's untutored eye it seemed she did this much the same way his mother had chosen horses for her annual flutter on the Derby, with closed eyes and a pin. It was only to be hoped that Apolline's method was more reliable; Eileen Mooney had never chosen a winner in her life.

There was a burst of controversy half way through the process, when Apolline — who appeared to have entered a trance of some kind — spat a hail of pips onto the floor. Freddy made some scathing remark at this, and Apolline's eyes snapped open.

'Will you keep your damn silence?' she said. 'This is bloody hard work.'

'It's not wise to use the Giddies,' he said. 'They're unreliable.'

'You want to take over?' she challenged him.

'You know I've got no skill with that.'

'Then bite your tongue,' she snapped. 'And leave me to it, will you? Go on!' She got to her feet and pushed him towards the door. 'Go on. Get out of here. All of you.'

They withdrew to the landing, where Freddy continued to

complain. 'The woman's lazy,' he said. 'Lilia didn't need the fruit.'

'Lilia was special,' said Nimrod, sitting at the top of the stairs, still wrapped in his tattered shirt. 'Let her do it her way, will you? She's not stupid.'

Freddy sought solace with Cal. 'I don't belong to these people,' he protested. 'It's all a terrible error. I'm not a thief.'

'What is your profession then?'

'I'm a barber. And you?'

'I work in an insurance company.' It seemed odd to think of that; of his desk, the claim forms piling up in the tray; of the doodles he'd left on the blotting paper. It was another world.

The bedroom door opened. Apolline was standing there, with one of the pages from the atlas in her hand.

'Well?' said Freddy.

She handed the page to Cal.

'I've found it,' she said.


2


The trail of echoes led them across the Mersey, through Birkenhead, and over Irby Hill, to the vicinity of Thurstaston Common. Cal knew the area not at all, and was surprised to find such rural territory within a hop, skip and a jump of the city.

They circled the area, Apolline in the passenger seat, eyes closed, until she announced:

'It's here. Stop here.'

Cal drew up. The large house they had arrived outside was in darkness, although there were several impressive vehicles in the driveway. They vacated the car, climbed the wall, and approached.

'This is it,' Apolline announced. 'I can practically smell the Weave.'

Cal and Freddy made two complete circuits of the building, looking for an entrance that wasn't locked, and on the second trip found a window which, while too small for an adult, offered easy access to Nimrod.

'Softly, softly does it,' Cal counselled, as he hoisted Nimrod through. 'We'll wait by the front door.'

'What are our tactics?' Cammell enquired.

'We get in. We take the carpet. We bugger off again,' said Cal.

There was a muffled thump as Nimrod leapt or tumbled from the sill on the other side. They waited a moment. There was no further sound, so they returned to the front of the house, and waited in the darkness. A minute passed; and another, and yet another. Finally, the door opened, and Nimrod was standing there, beaming.

'Lost my way,' he whispered.

They slipped inside. Both lower and upper floors were unlit, but there was nothing restful about the darkness. The air was agitated, as if the dust couldn't quite bear to settle.

'I don't think there's anyone here,' said Freddy, going to the bottom of the stairs.

'Wrong,' Cal whispered. There was no doubting the origin of the chill in the air.

Freddy ignored him. He had already climbed two or three steps. It passed through Cal's head that his foolhardy show of indifference to danger, which was more than likely compensation for his cowardice at Chariot Street, would do no good to anyone. But Apolline was already accompanying Freddy upstairs, leaving Cal and Nimrod to investigate the ground floor.

Their route led them through a murky assault course, which Nimrod, being much the smaller, negotiated with more ease than Cal.

'Poll's right,' Nimrod whispered as they passed from room to room. 'The Weave's here. I can feel it.'

So could Cal; and at the thought of the Fugue's proximity he felt his courage bolstered. This time he wasn't alone against Shadwell. He had allies, with powers of their own, and they had the element of surprise on their side. With a little luck they might steal the Salesman's booty from under his nose.

Then there was a cry from the upper landing. It was unmistakably Freddy; his voice anguished. The next moment came the stomach-turning sound of his body tumbling down the stairs. Two minutes in, and the game was up.

Nimrod had already started back the way they'd come, apparently careless of the consequences. Cal followed, but stumbled into a table in the darkness, the corner of which found his groin.

As he stood upright, cupping his balls, he heard Immacolata's voice. Her whisper seemed to come from every direction at once, as though she was in the very walls.

'*Seerkind . . .*' she said.

The next moment he felt an icy air against his face. He knew the sour stench it carried, from that night in the trash canyons by the river. It was the smell of corruption – the sisters' corruption – and with it came a dismal light by which he could pick out the geography of the room he occupied. Of Nimrod there was no sign; he'd gone ahead into the hall, where the light was sourced. And now Cal heard him cry out. The light flickered. The cry stopped. The wind was chillier as the sisters came in search of further victims. He had to hide; and quickly. Eyes on the passage ahead, down which the light was spilling, he backed away towards the only exit door available.

The room he stepped into was the kitchen, and it offered nothing in the way of hiding places. His bladder aching, he went to the back door. It was securely locked. There was no key. Panic mounting, he glanced back through the kitchen door. The Magdalene was floating through the room he'd just left, her blind head moving back and forth as she scoured the air for a trace of human heat. It seemed he could feel her fingers at his throat already; her lips on his mouth.

Despairing, he scanned the kitchen one more time, and his gaze alighted on the refrigerator. As the Magdalene approached the kitchen, he crossed to the refrigerator and opened the door. Arctic air billowed out to greet him. He threw the door as wide as possible, and bathed himself in the chill.

The Magdalene was on the kitchen threshold now, trails of her poison milk seeping from her breasts. There she hovered, as if uncertain of whether she sensed life here or not.

Cal stood absolutely still, praying the cold air would cancel his warmth. His muscles had begun to jitter, and the urge to piss was near enough unbearable. Still she didn't move, except to put her hand on her perpetually swollen belly, and pat whatever slept there.

And then, from the next room, he heard the cracked voice of the Hag.

'Sister . . .' she whispered. She was coming through. He was lost if she entered.

The Magdalene advanced into the kitchen a little way, and her head turned with horrid intent in his direction. She glided a little closer. Cal held his breath.

The creature was within two yards of him now, her head still moving back and forth on a neck of mucus and ether. Beads of her bitter milk floated towards him and broke against his face. She sensed something, that was clear, but the cold air was confusing her. He set the muscles of his jaw to prevent his teeth from chattering, praying for some diversion from above.

The shadow of the Hag fell through the open door.

'Sister?' she said again. 'Are we alone?'

The Magdalene's head drifted forward, her neck becoming grotesquely long and thin, until her blind face hovered a foot from Cal's. It was all he could do to prevent himself from running.

Then, she seemed to make up her mind. She turned towards the door.

'All alone,' she said, and drifted back to join her sister. With every foot of ground she covered he was certain she'd think better of her retreat, and come in search of him again. But she disappeared through the kitchen door, and they left to get on with business elsewhere.

He waited for a full minute until the last vestiges of their phosphorescence had faded. Then, gasping for breath, he stepped away from the refrigerator.

From above he heard shouts. He shuddered to think what entertainments were afoot here. Shuddered too at the thought that he was now alone.

# IV

## BREAKING THE LAW

### 1

Itt was Jerichau's voice she heard, Suzanna had no doubt of that, and it was raised in wordless protest. The cry startled her from the murky pit that had claimed her since Hobart's departure. She was at the door in seconds, and beating on it.

'What's happening?' she demanded.

There was no reply from the guard on the other side; only another heart-rending shout from Jerichau. *What were they doing to him?*

She'd lived all her life in England, and — never having had more than a casual acquaintance with the law — had assumed it a fairly healthy animal. But now she was in its belly, and it was sick; very sick.

Again she beat a tattoo on the door, again it went unanswered. Tears of impotence began, stinging her sinuses and eyes. She put her back to the door and tried to stifle the sobs with her hand, but they wouldn't be quelled.

Aware that the officer in the corridor could hear her sorrows, she started across to the other side of the cell, but something stopped her dead in her tracks. Through her watery vision she saw that the tears she'd shed on the back of her hand no longer resembled tears at all. They were almost silvery; and bursting, as she watched, into tiny spheres of luminescence. It might have come from a story in Mimi's book: a woman who wept living tears. Except that this was no faery-tale. The

208

vision was somehow more real than the concrete walls that imprisoned her; more real even than the pain that had brought these tears to her eyes.

It was the menstruum she was weeping. She hadn't felt it move in her since she'd knelt beside Cal at the warehouse, and events had proceeded so speedily from there she had given little thought to it. Now she felt the torrent afresh, and a wave of elation swept her.

Down the corridor Jerichau cried out again, and in response, the menstruum, bright to blinding, brimmed in her subtle body.

Unable to prevent herself, she yelled, and the stream of brightness became a flood, spilling from her eyes and nostrils, and from between her legs. Her gaze fell on the chair which Hobart had occupied and it instantly flung itself against the far wall, rattling against the concrete as if panicking to be gone from her presence. The table followed, smashing itself to splinters.

From outside the door she heard voices, raised in consternation. She didn't care. Her consciousness was *in* and *of* the tide, her sight running to the edge of the menstruum's reach and looking back at herself, wild-eyed, smiling a river. She was looking down from the ceiling too, where her liquid self was rising in spume.

Behind her, they were unlocking the door. They'll come with cudgels, she thought. These men are afraid of me. And with reason. I'm their enemy, *and they're mine*.

She turned. The officer in the doorway looked pitifully frail, his boots and buttons a weak man's dream of strength. He gaped at the scene before him – the furniture reduced to tinder, the light dancing on the walls. Then the menstruum was coming at him.

She followed in its wake, as it threw the man aside. Parts of her consciousness trailed behind her, snatching the truncheon from his hand and breaking it in pieces; other parts surged ahead of her physical body, turning corners, seeking under doors, calling Jerichau's name –

## 2

The interrogation of the male suspect had proved disappointing for Hobart. The man was either an imbecile or a damn good actor – one minute answering his questions with more questions, the next, talking in riddles. He'd despaired of getting any sense from the prisoner, so he'd left him in the company of Laverick and Boyce, two of his best men. They'd soon have the man spitting the truth, and his teeth with it.

Upstairs at his desk he'd just begun a closer analysis of the book of codes when he heard the sound of breakage from below. Then Patterson, the officer he'd left guarding the woman, began yelling.

He was heading down the stairs to investigate when he was inexplicably seized by the need to void his bladder; an ache which became an agonizing pain as he descended. He refused to let it slow his progress, but by the time he reached the bottom of the stairs he was almost doubled up.

Patterson was sitting in the corner of the passageway, his hands over his face. The cell door was open.

'Stand up, man!' Hobart demanded, but the officer could only sob like a child. Hobart left him to it.

## 3

Boyce had seen the expression on the suspect's face change seconds before the cell door was blown open, and it had almost broken his heart to see a smile so lavish appear on features he'd sweated to terrorize. He was about to beat the smile to Kingdom Come when he heard Laverick, who'd been enjoying a mid-session cigarette in the far corner of the room, say: 'Jesus Christ', and the next moment –

What had happened in that next moment?

First the door had rattled as if an earthquake was waiting on the other side; then Laverick had dropped his cigarette and stood up, and Boyce, suddenly feeling sick as a dog, had reached out to take the suspect hostage against whatever was beating on the door. He was too late. The door was flung wide – brightness flooded in – and Boyce felt his body weaken to the point of near collapse. An instant later something took hold of him, and turned him round and round on his heels. He was helpless in its embrace. All he could do was cry out as the cool force made gushing entry into him through every hole in his body. Then, as suddenly as he'd been snatched, he was let go. He hit the cell floor just as a woman, who seemed both naked and dressed to him, stepped through the door. Laverick had seen her too, and was shouting something, which the rushing in Boyce's ears – as if his skull was being rinsed in a river – drowned out. The woman terrified him as he'd only been terrified in dreams. His mind struggled to recall a ritual of protection against such terrors, one he'd known before his own name. He had to be quick, he knew. His mind was close to being washed away.

Suzanna's gaze lingered on the torturers for only an instant – it was Jerichau that concerned her. His face was raw, and puffed up with repeated beatings, but smiling at the sight of his rescuer.

'Quickly,' she said, extending a hand to him.

He stood up, but he wouldn't approach her. He's afraid too, she thought. Or if not afraid, at least respectful.

'We must go –'

He nodded. She stepped out into the corridor again, trusting that he'd follow. In the scant minutes since the menstruum had flowed in her she'd begun to exercise some control over it, like a bride learning to trail and gather the length of her train. Now, when she left the cell, she mentally called the wash of energy after her, and it came to her.

She was glad of its obedience, for as she began along the corridor Hobart appeared at the far end. Her confidence momentarily faltered, but the sight of her – or whatever he saw in her place – was enough to make him stop in his tracks. He seemed to doubt his eyes, for he shook his head violently. Gaining confidence, she began to advance towards him. The lights were swinging wildly above her head. The concrete walls creaked when she laid her fingers on them, as though with a little effort she might crack them wide. The thought of such a thing began to make her laugh. The sound of her laughter was too much for Hobart. He retreated and disappeared up the stairs.

No further challenge was offered as they made their escape. They climbed the stairs, then crossed the abruptly deserted office. Her very presence threw mounds of paperwork into the air, that spiralled down around her like vast confetti. (*I'm married to myself*, her mind announced.) Then she was stepping through the doors into the evening beyond, Jerichau a respectful distance behind. There were no thanks forthcoming. He merely said:

'You can find the carpet.'

'I don't know how.'

'Let the menstruum show you,' he told her.

The reply didn't make much sense to her, until he extended his hand, palm up:

'I never saw the menstruum so strong in anyone,' he said. 'You can find the Fugue. It and I –'

He didn't need to finish his sentence; she understood. He and the carpet were made of the same stuff; the *Weave* was the *woven*, and vice versa. She seized hold of his hand. In the building behind them alarm bells had begun to ring, but she knew they would not come after her: not yet.

Jerichau's face was a knot of anguish. Her touch was not kind to him. But in her head lines of force spiralled and converged. Images appeared: a house, a room. And yes, *the carpet*, lying in splendour before hungry eyes. The lines twisted; other images fought for her attention. Was that blood spilled so copiously on the floor?; and Cal's heel slipping in it?

She let go of Jerichau's hand. He made a fist of it.

'Well?' he said.

Before she could reply a patrol car squealed into the yard. The driver's partner, alerted by the alarm, was already stepping from the car, demanding that the escapees halt. He began towards them, but the menstruum threw a ghost-wave

212

towards him which caught him up and washed him out into the street. The driver threw himself out of the car and fled towards the safety of bricks and mortar, leaving the vehicle free for the taking.

'The book,' said Suzanna as she slipped into the driver's seat. 'Hobart's still got my book.'

'We've no time to go back,' said Jerichau.

Easily said. It hurt to think of leaving Mimi's gift in the hands of Hobart. But in the time it would take her to find him and claim it back, the carpet might be lost. She had no choice; she'd have to leave it in his possession.

Odd as it seemed, she knew there were few hands in which it was more secure.

4

Hobart retired to the toilet and gave vent to his bladder before he filled his trousers, then went out to face the chaos that had turned his well-ordered headquarters into a battlefield.

The suspects had escaped in a patrol car, he was informed. That was some comfort. The vehicle would be easy to trace. The problem was not finding them again, but subduing them. The woman possessed the skill to induce hallucinations; what other powers might she evidence if cornered? With this and a dozen other questions in his head, he went down in search of Laverick and Boyce.

There were a few men lingering at the cell door, clearly unwilling to step inside. She's slaughtered them, he thought, and could not deny a spasm of satisfaction that the stakes were suddenly so much higher. But it was not blood he smelt as he reached the door, it was excrement.

Laverick and Boyce had stripped off their uniforms, and smeared themselves from head to foot with the product of their own bowels. Now they were crawling around like animals, grinning from ear to ear, apparently well content with themselves.

'Jesus Christ,' said Hobart.

At the sound of his master's voice, Laverick looked up, and tried to get his tongue around some words of explanation. But his palate wasn't the equal of it. Instead, he crawled into a corner and hid his head.

'You'd better get them hosed down,' Hobart told one of the officers. 'We can't have their wives seeing them like that.'

'What happened, sir?' the man asked.

'I don't know yet.'

Patterson had appeared from the cell where the woman had been held, tear-stains on his face. He had some words of explanation.

'She's possessed, sir,' he said. 'I opened the door and the furniture was half way up the wall.'

'Keep your hysteria to yourself,' Hobart told him.

'I swear it, sir,' Patterson protested. 'I *swear* it. And there was this light —'

'*No*, Patterson! You saw nothing!' Hobart wheeled round on the rest of the spectators. 'If any of you breathe a word of this, there'll be worse than shit to eat. *You understand me?*'

There were mute nods from the assembly.

'What about *them*?' said one, glancing back into the cell.

'I told you. Scrub them down and take them home.'

'But they're like children,' someone said.

'No children of mine,' Hobart replied, and took himself off upstairs where he could sit and look at the pictures in the book in private.

# V

## THRESHOLD

### 1

**W**hat's the disturbance?' van Niekerk demanded to know.

Shadwell smiled his smile. Though he was irritated by the interruption to the Auction, it had served to lend further heat to the buyers' eagerness.

'An attempt to steal the carpet –' he said.

'By whom?' Mrs A. asked.

Shadwell pointed to the border of the carpet.

'There is, you'll observe, a portion of the Weave missing,' he admitted. 'Small as it is, its knots concealed several inhabitants of the Fugue.' He watched the buyers' faces as he spoke. They were utterly mesmerized by his story, desperate for some confirmation of their dreams.

'And they came here?' said Norris.

'They did indeed.'

'Let's see them,' the Hamburger King demanded, 'if they're here, let's see them.'

Shadwell paused before replying. 'Maybe one,' he said.

He'd been fully prepared for the request, and had already planned with Immacolata which of the prisoners they'd display. He opened the door, and Nimrod, released from the Hag's embrace, tottered onto the carpet. Whatever the buyers had expected, the sight of this naked child was not it.

'What is this?' Rahimzadeh snorted. 'Do you think we're fools?'

Nimrod looked up from the Weave underfoot at the puzzled

215

faces that surrounded him. He would have set them right on any number of matters, but that Immacolata had laid her fingers on his tongue, and he couldn't raise a grunt from it.

'This is one of the Seerkind,' Shadwell announced.

'It's just a child,' said Marguerite Pierce, her voice betraying some tenderness. 'A poor child.'

Nimrod stared at the woman: a fine, big-breasted creature, he thought.

'He's no child,' said Immacolata. She had slipped into the room unseen; now all eyes turned to her. All except Marguerite's, which still rested on Nimrod. 'Some of the Seerkind are shape-changers.'

'*This?*' said van Niekerk.

'Certainly.'

'What crap are you trying to feed us, Shadwell?' Norris said. 'I'm not taking –'

'*Shut up*,' said Shadwell.

Shock closed Norris' mouth; a lot of beef had been minced since he'd last been talked to that way.

'Immacolata can undo this *rapture*,' he said, floating the word on the air like a valentine.

Nimrod saw the Incantatrix make a configuration of thumb and third finger, through which, with a sharp intake of breath, she nonchalantly drew the shape-changing rapture. It was not an unwelcome shudder that convulsed him now; he was weary of this hairless skin. He felt his knees begin to tremble, and he fell forward onto the carpet. Around him, he could hear awed whispers, becoming louder with every step of the undeceiving, and more astonished.

Inmacolata was not delicate in her undoing of his anatomy. He winced as his flesh was transformed. There was one delicious moment in this hasty unveiling, when he felt his balls drop once more. Then, his manhood re-established, a second sequence of growth began, his skin tingling as the hair sprouted on his belly and back. Finally his face appeared from the facade of innocence, and he was – balls and all – himself again.

Shadwell looked down at the creature lying on the carpet, its skin faintly blue, its eyes golden; then at the buyers. This spectacle had probably doubled the price they'd bid for the carpet. Here was *magic*, in the panting flesh; more real and more oddly bewitching than even he'd anticipated.

'You made your point,' said Norris, his voice flat. 'Let's get down to *numbers.*'

Shadwell concurred.

'Perhaps you'd remove our guest?' he said to Immacolata, but before she could make a move Nimrod was up and kneeling at the feet of Marguerite Pierce, covering her ankles with kisses.

This excited but mute entreaty did not go unnoticed. The woman stretched her hand down to touch the thick hair of Nimrod's head.

'Leave him with me,' she said to Immacolata.

'Why not?' said Shadwell. 'Let him watch . . .'

The Incantatrix made a muttered protest.

'No harm in it,' said Shadwell. 'I can handle him.' Immacolata withdrew. 'Now . . .' said the Salesman. 'Shall we re-open the bidding?'

2

Half way between the kitchen and the bottom of the stairs Cal remembered he was unarmed. He rapidly retraced his steps and dug around in the kitchen drawers until he located a wide knife. Although he doubted if the sister's ethereal bodies would prove susceptible to a mere blade, its weight in his hand offered some comfort.

His heel slid in blood as he began to climb the stairs; it was a sheer fluke that his outflung hand found the bannister and kept him from falling downstairs. He silently cursed his clumsiness, and took the rest of the ascent more slowly. Though there was no sign of the sisters' luminescence from above, he knew they were close. But frightened as he was, one conviction attended his every step: whatever horrors were

217

ahead he would find a way to kill Shadwell. Even if he had to open the bastard's throat with his own hands he'd do it. The Salesman had broken his father's heart, and that was a hanging offence.

At the top of the stairs, a sound; or rather several: human voices raised in argument. He listened more closely. It wasn't argument at all. They were bidding, and Shadwell's voice was clearly distinguishable, fielding the contesting bids.

Under the cover of the racket Cal slipped across the landing to the first of several doors that presented themselves. Cautiously, he opened it, and entered. The small room was unoccupied, but the connecting door was ajar, and a light burned beyond. Leaving the door to the landing open, in case he needed to beat a fast retreat, he padded across to the second and peered through.

On the floor lay Freddy and Apolline; there was no sign of Nimrod. He studied the shadows, to be certain they concealed no by-blow; then he pushed the door open.

The bids and counter-bids were still flying, and their commotion drowned out any sound he made crossing to where the prisoners lay. They were very still, their mouths stifled with clots of ethereal matter, their eyes closed. It was clearly Freddy who'd spilled the blood on the stairs; his body was much worse for the sisters' attentions, his face raked with their fingers. But the profoundest wound was between his ribs, where he'd been stabbed with his own scissors. They protruded from him still.

Cal pulled away Freddy's gag, which crawled on his hands as if maggoty, and was rewarded with a breath from the wounded man. But there was no sign of consciousness. He then performed the same service for Apolline. She showed more sign of life – moaning as if about to wake.

The clamour of bids was heating up in the adjacent room; it was clear from the din that there were a good number of would-be purchasers involved. How could he hope to bring the process to a halt with so many in Shadwell's faction, and he single-handed?

At his side, Freddy moved.

His lids flickered open, but there was little in the way of life behind them.

'Cal . . .' he tried to say. The word was a shape not a sound. Cal bent closer to him, putting his arms around his chilly, trembling body.

'I'm here, Freddy,' he said.

Freddy tried to speak again.

'. . . almost . . .' he said.

Cal tightened his embrace, as though he could keep the life from seeping out. But a hundred hands couldn't have kept it from going; it had better places to be. Still Cal couldn't help but say:

'Don't go.'

The man made a tiny shake of his head.

'. . . almost . . .' he said again, '. . . almost . . .'

The syllables seemed too much for him. His trembling stopped.

'Freddy . . .'

Cal put his fingers to the man's lips, but there was no trace of breath. As he stared at the empty features Apolline snatched hold of his hand. She too was cold. Her eyes turned skyward; he followed her gaze.

Immacolata was lying on the ceiling, staring down at him. She'd been hovering there all along, basking in his sorrow and helplessness.

A shout of horror had reached his lips before he could prevent it, and in that instant she swooped, her darkness reaching for him. For once, however, his clumsiness did him a kindness, and he fell backwards before her claws could connect. The door at his back gave inwards, and he pitched himself through it, his terror of her touch lending him speed.

'*What is this?*'

The speaker was Shadwell. Cal had thrown himself into the midst of the Auction. The Salesman was at one end of the room, while half a dozen others, dressed as if for a night at the Ritz, were standing around the room. Immacolata would surely hesitate to murder him in such company. He had a moment's grace, at least.

219

Then he looked down, and the sight before him made him sick with joy.

He was sprawled across the carpet: its warp and weft were tingling beneath his palms. Was that why he so suddenly and absurdly felt *safe* – as though all that had gone before had been a test, the prize for which this was sweet reunion?

'Get him out of here,' said one of the buyers.

Shadwell took a step towards him.

'Remove yourself, Mr Mooney,' the Salesman said. 'We've got business here.'

So have I, thought Cal, and as Shadwell approached he drew the knife from his pocket and sprang at the man. Behind him, he heard Immacolata cry out. He had seconds only in which to act. He thrust the blade at Shadwell, but despite his bulk, the Salesman neatly side-stepped it.

There was a commotion from the buyers, which Cal took to be an expression of horror, but no – he glanced towards them to see that they'd taken the sale into their own hands, and were shouting bids in each others' faces.

It was laughable to see, but Cal had little time to applaud them, for Shadwell had torn open his jacket. The lining blazed.

'*Anything you want?*' he said.

As he spoke he stepped towards Cal, blinding him with the glamour of the garment, and knocked the knife from his hand. With Cal disarmed, he resorted to less subtle tactics, delivering a knee to Cal's groin that dropped him groaning to the floor. There he lay for several seconds, unable to move until the nausea subsided. Through the daze of light and sickness he could see Immacolata, still waiting for him at the door. Behind her, the sisters. So much for his attack. He was weaponless now, and alone –

But no; not alone. Never alone.

He was lying on a *world*, wasn't he?, on a sleeping world. Miracles beyond counting were in the Weave beneath him, if he could just liberate them.

But how? There were raptures, no doubt, to stir the Fugue from its slumber, but he knew none of them. All he could do was lay his palms on the carpet and whisper:

'*Wake up* . . .'

Was he deluding himself, or was there already a restlessness in the knots?, as though the creatures there struggled against their condition, like sleepers desperate to wake themselves, knowing the day had broken, but powerless to stir.

Now, from the corner of his eye, he caught sight of a naked figure crouching at the feet of a buyer. It was undoubtedly one of the Seerkind, but no-one he recognized. Or at least not the body. But the eyes –

'Nimrod?' he murmured.

The creature had seen him, and crawled from its place of safety to the edge of the carpet. He wasn't noticed. Shadwell was already back amongst the buyers, trying to prevent the Auction from becoming a blood-bath. He'd forgotten Cal's existence.

'Is it you?' Cal said.

Nimrod nodded, pointing to his throat.

'You can't speak? *Shit!*'

Cal glanced towards the door. Immacolata was still in wait. She had the patience of a carrion-bird.

'The carpet . . .' said Cal. 'We have to wake it.'

Nimrod looked at him blankly.

'Don't you understand what I'm saying?'

Before Nimrod could signal any reply, Shadwell had settled the buyers and announced:

'We'll begin again.'

Then, to Immacolata: 'Remove the assassin.'

Cal had at best seconds before the Incantatrix stopped his life. He desperately scanned the room for an exit route. There were several windows, all heavily draped. Perhaps if he could reach one he might fling himself out. Even if the fall killed him it could not be worse than death at Immacolata's touch.

But before she reached him she halted. Her gaze, which had been fixed upon him, now drifted away. She turned to Shadwell and the word she said was:

'. . . *menstruum* . . .'

As she spoke the room beyond the door, where Apolline

221

and Freddy had been left, was washed with a radiance which splashed through onto the carpet. At its touch, the colours seemed to become more vivid.

And then a shriek of wrath – the voice of the Hag – rose from the room, followed by a further spillage of light.

These new sights and sounds were enough to set the buyers into a fresh spin. One went to the door – either as spectator or escapee – and fell back, his hands over his eyes, yelling that he was blinded. Nobody went to his aid. The rest of the party retreated to the far end of the room, while the fury at the other escalated.

A figure had appeared at the door, threads of brilliance describing spirals all about her. Cal knew her at once, despite her transformation.

It was Suzanna. Fluid fireworks ran like veins over her arms, and showered from her fingertips; they danced on her belly and breasts and ran out from between her legs to ignite the air.

Seeing her thus, it took several seconds for Cal to voice his welcome, and by that time the sisters were through the door in pursuit of her. The battle had done grievous harm on both sides. The display of the menstruum could not hide the bleeding wounds on Suzanna's neck and body; and, though pain was most likely beyond the experience of the wraith-sisters, they too were torn.

Whether weakened or not, they fell back when Immacolata raised her hand, leaving Suzanna to their living sister.

'You're late,' she said. 'We were waiting.'

'Kill her,' said Shadwell.

Cal studied the look on Suzanna's face. Try as she might she could not entirely disguise her exhaustion.

Now, perhaps feeling his eyes on her, she looked his way, her gaze locking with his, then moving to his hands, which were still palm down upon the Weave. Did she read his thoughts, he wondered. Did she comprehend that the only hope remaining to them lay asleep at her feet?

Again, their eyes met, and in them Cal saw that she understood.

222

Beneath his fingers, the Weave tingled as though a mild electric shock was passing through it. He didn't remove his hand, but let the energy use him as it so desired. He was just part of a process now: a circle of power that ran through the carpet from Suzanna's feet to his hands and up through his eyes and back along the line of their glance to her.

'Stop them . . .' said Shadwell, dimly comprehending this mischief, but as Immacolata moved towards Cal again one of the buyers said:

'The knife . . .'

Cal didn't break the look he shared with Suzanna, but the knife now floated into view between them, as if raised on the heat of their thoughts.

Suzanna had no more idea of why or how this was happening than Cal, but she too grasped, albeit vaguely, the notion of the circuit that ran through her, the menstruum, the carpet, him, the gaze, and back to her again. Whatever was occurring here it had seconds only to work its miracle, before Immacolata reached Cal and broke the circle.

The knife had begun to spin now, catching fresh speed with each turn. Cal felt a fullness in his testicles which was almost painful; and – more alarmingly – the feeling that he was no longer quite fixed in his body, but being teased out, out through his eyes, to meet Suzanna's gaze on the knife between them, which was moving at such a speed it resembled a silver ball.

And then, quite suddenly, it dropped out of the air like a felled bird. Cal followed its descent, as with a thud it buried its point in the centre of the carpet.

Instantly, a shock-wave ran through every inch of warp and weft, as if the knife-point had severed a strand upon which the integrity of the whole depended. And with that strand cut, the Weave was loosed.

3

It was the end of the world, and the beginning of *worlds*.

First, a column of dervish cloud rose from the middle of the

Gyre, flying up towards the ceiling. As it struck, wide cracks opened, bringing an avalanche of plaster onto the heads of all beneath. It momentarily occurred to Cal that what Suzanna and he had unleashed was now beyond their jurisdiction. Then the wonders began, and all such concerns were forgotten.

There was lightning in the cloud, throwing arcs out to the walls and across the floor. As they sprang forth, knots from one border of the carpet to the other slipped their configurations, and the strands grew like grain in mid-summer, spilling colour as they rose. It was much as Cal and Suzanna had dreamt several nights before, only multiplied a hundredfold; ambitious threads climbing and proliferating across the room.

The pressure of growth beneath Cal was enough to throw him off the carpet as the strands sprang from their bondage, spreading the seeds of a thousand forms to right and left. Some were swifter to rise than others, reaching the ceiling in seconds. Others chose instead to make for the windows, trailing streamers of colour as they broke the glass and raced out to meet the night.

Everywhere the eye went there were new and extraordinary displays. At first the explosion of forms was too chaotic to be made sense of, but no sooner was the air awash with colour than the strands began to shape finer details, distinguishing plant from stone, and stone from wood, and wood from flesh. One surging thread exploded against the roof in a shower of motes, each of which, upon contact with the humus of the decaying Weave, threw out tiny shoots. Another was laying zig-zag paths of blue-grey mist across the room; a third and a fourth were intertwining, and fire-flies were leaping from their marriage, sketching in their motion bird and beast, which their companions clothed with light.

In seconds the Fugue had filled the room, its growth so fast that Shearman's house could not contain it. Boards were uprooted as the strands sought new territories; the rafters were thrown aside. Nor were bricks and mortar any better defence against the threads. What they couldn't coax, they bullied; what they couldn't bully, they simply overturned.

Cal had no intention of being buried. Bewitching as these birth-pangs were, it could not be long before the house collapsed. He peered through the fireworks towards the place where Suzanna had been standing, but she'd already gone. The buyers were also making their escape, fighting like street dogs in their panic.

Scrambling to his feet, Cal started to make his way to the door, but he'd got no more than two steps when he saw Shadwell moving towards him.

'*Bastard!*' the Salesman was screeching. '*Interfering bastard!*'

He reached into his jacket pocket, drew out a gun, and took aim at Cal.

'*Nobody crosses me, Mooney!*' he screamed; then fired.

But even as he pulled the trigger somebody leapt at him. He fell sideways. The bullet flew wide of its target.

Cal's saviour was Nimrod. He raced towards Cal now, his expression all urgency. He had reason. The entire house had begun to shake; there were roars of capitulation from above and below. The Fugue had reached the foundations, and its enthusiasm was about to pitch the house over.

Nimrod seized hold of Cal's arm, and pulled him not towards the door but towards the window. Or rather, the wall that had once contained the window, for the burgeoning Weave had torn them all out. Beyond the wreckage, the Fugue was telling its long-silenced story hither and thither, filling the darkness with further magic.

Nimrod glanced behind him.

'Are we going to jump?' said Cal.

Nimrod grinned, and held on even tighter to Cal's arm. One backward glance told Cal that Shadwell had found his gun, and was aiming it at their backs.

'Look out!' he yelled.

Nimrod's face brightened, and he pressed his hand on the nape of Cal's neck, to make him tuck his head down. An instant later Cal understood why, as a wave of colour sprang from the Weave, and Nimrod threw them both before it. The force carried them out through the window, and for a panicky moment they trod thin air. Then the brightness seemed to

225

solidify and spread beneath them, and they were riding down it like surfers on a tide of light.

The ride was over all too soon. Mere seconds later they were rudely deposited in a field some distance from the house, and the wave was off into the night, parenting all manner of flora and fauna as it went.

Dizzied but exhilarated, Cal got to his feet, and was delighted to hear Nimrod exclaim:

'Ha!'

'You can speak?'

'It appears so,' said Nimrod, his grin wider than ever. 'I'm out of her reach here –'

'Immacolata.'

'Of course. She undid my rapture, to tempt the Cuckoos. And tempting I was. Did you see the woman in the blue dress?'

'Briefly.'

'She fell for me on sight,' said Nimrod. 'Perhaps I should find her. She's going to need some tenderness, things being what they are –' and without another word he turned back towards the house, which was well on its way to rubble. Only as he disappeared in the confusion of light and dust did Cal notice that in his true shape Nimrod possessed a tail.

Doubtless he could look after himself, but there were others Cal was still concerned for. Suzanna, for one, and Apolline, whom he'd last seen lying beside Freddy in the ante-chamber to the Auction Room. All was din and destruction, but he started back towards the house nevertheless, to see if he could find them.

It was like swimming against a technicolour tide. Strands, late-born, flew and burst about him, some breaking against his body. They were kinder by far to living tissue than they were to brick. Their touch didn't wound him, but lent him fresh energy. His body tingled as though he'd stepped from an ice-water shower. His head sang.

There was no sign of the enemy. He hoped Shadwell had been buried in the house, but he knew too much of the luck of the wicked to believe this likely. He did however glimpse several of the buyers wandering in the brightness. They didn't

226

aid each other, but made their way as solitaries, either gazing at the ground for fear it open beneath their feet, or stumbling, hands masking their tears.

As he came within thirty yards of the house there was a further burst of activity from within, as the great cloud of the Gyre, spitting lightning, shrugged off the walls that had confined it, and blossomed in all directions.

He had time enough to see the figure of one of the buyers consumed by the cloud, then he turned and ran.

A wave of dust threw him on his way; filaments of brightness flew to left and right of him like ribbons in a hurricane. A second wave followed, this time of brick-shards and furniture. His breath was snatched from his lips, and his legs from beneath him. Then he was performing acrobatics, head over heels, no longer knowing Heaven from Earth.

He didn't try to resist, even if resistance had been possible, but let the fast train take him wherever it chose to go.

# BOOK TWO

# THE FUGUE

## Part Five

# Revels

*'Flee into some forgotten night and be*
*Of all dark long my moon-bright company;*
*Beyond the rumour even of Paradise come,*
*There, out of all remembrance,*
*make our home.'*

Walter de la Mare
*The Tryst*

# I

# CAL, AMONGST MIRACLES

## 1

**T**rue joy is a profound remembering; and true grief the same.

Thus it was, when the dust storm that had snatched Cal up finally died, and he opened his eyes to see the Fugue spread before him, he felt as though the few fragile moments of epiphany he'd tasted in his twenty-six years – tasted but always lost – were here redeemed and wed. He'd grasped fragments of this delight before. Heard rumour of it in the womb-dream and the dream of love; known it in lullabies. But never, until now, the whole, the thing entire.

It would be, he idly thought, a fine time to die.

And a finer time still to live, with so much laid out before him.

He was on a hill. Not high, but high enough to offer a vantage point. He got to his feet and surveyed this new-found land.

The unknotting of the carpet had by no means finished; the raptures of the Loom were far too complex to be so readily reversed. But the groundwork was laid: hills, fields, forest, and much else besides.

Last time he'd set eyes on this place it had been from a bird's eye view, and the landscape had seemed various enough. But from the human perspective its profusion verged on the riotous. It was as if a vast suitcase, packed in great haste, had been upturned, its contents scattered in hopeless disarray.

There appeared to be no system to the geography, just a random assembling of spots the Seerkind had loved enough to snatch from destruction. Butterfly copses and placid water-meadows; lairs and walled sanctuaries; keeps, rivers and standing stones.

Few of these locations were complete: most were slivers and snatches, fragments of the Kingdom ceded to the Fugue behind humanity's back. The haunted corners of familiar rooms that would neither be missed nor mourned, where children had perhaps seen ghosts or saints; where the fugitive might be comforted and not know why, and the suicide find reason for another breath.

Amid this disorder, the most curious juxtapositions abounded. Here a bridge, parted from the chasm it had crossed, sat in a field, spanning poppies; there an obelisk stood in the middle of a pool, gazing at its reflection.

One sight in particular caught Cal's eye.

It was a hill, which rose almost straight-sided to a tree-crowned summit. Lights moved over its face, and danced amongst the branches. Having no sense of direction here, he decided to make his way down towards it.

There was music playing somewhere in the night. It came to him by fits and starts, at the behest of the breeze. Drums and violins; a mingling of Strauss and Sioux. And occasionally, evidence of people too. Whispers in the trees; shadowed figures beneath a canopy which stood in the middle of a waist-high field of grain. But the creatures were fugitive; they came and went too quickly for him to gain more than a fleeting impression. Whether this was because they knew him for the Cuckoo he was, or simply out of shyness, only time would tell. Certainly he felt no threat here, despite the fact that he was, in a sense, trespassing. On the contrary, he felt utterly at peace with the world and himself. So much so that his concern for the others here – Suzanna, Apolline, Jerichau, Nimrod – was quite remote. When his thoughts did touch upon them it was only to imagine them wandering as he was wandering, lost among miracles. No harm could come to them; not here. Here was an end to harm, and malice, and envy too. Having this living rapture wrapping him round, what was left to envy or desire?

He was within a hundred yards of the hill and stood before it in amazement. The lights he'd seen from a distance were in fact human fire-flies; wingless, but describing effortless arabesques around the hill. There was no communication between them that he could hear, yet they had the precision of daredevils, their manœuvres repeatedly bringing them within a hair's breadth of each other.

'You must be Mooney.'

The speaker's voice was soft, but it broke the hold the lights had on him. Cal looked off to his right. Two figures were standing in the shade of an archway, their faces still immersed in darkness. All he could see were the two blue-grey ovals of their faces, hanging beneath the arch like lanterns.

'Yes. I'm Mooney,' he said. *Show yourselves*, he thought. 'How do you know my name?'

'News travels fast here,' came the reply. The voice seemed slightly softer and more fluting than the first, but he couldn't be certain it wasn't the same speaker. 'It's the air,' said his informant. 'It gossips.'

Now one of the pair stepped into the night-light. The soft illumination from the hill moved on his face, lending it strangeness, but even had Cal seen it by daylight this was a face to be haunted by. He was young, yet completely bald, his features powdered to remove any modulation in skin-tone, his mouth and eyes almost too wet, too vulnerable, in the mask of his features.

'I'm Boaz,' he said. 'You're welcome, Mooney.'

He took Cal's hand, and shook it, and as he did so his companion broke her covenant with shadow.

'You can see the Amadou?' she said.

It took Cal several seconds to conclude that the second speaker was indeed a woman, the processes of his doubt in turn throwing doubt on the sex of Boaz, for the two were very close to being identical twins.

'I'm Ganza,' said the second speaker. She was dressed in the same plain black trousers and loose tunic as her brother, or

235

lover, or whatever he was; and she too was bald. That, and their powdered faces, seemed to confuse all the cliches of gender. Their faces were vulnerable, yet implacable; delicate, yet severe.

Boaz looked towards the hill, where the fire-flies were still cavorting.

'This is the Rock of the First Fatality,' he told Cal. 'The Amadou always gather here. This is where the first victims of the Scourge died.'

Cal looked back towards the Rock, but only for a moment. Boaz and Ganza fascinated him more; their ambiguities multiplied the more he watched them.

'Where are you going tonight?' said Ganza.

Cal shrugged. 'No idea,' he said. 'I don't know a yard of this place.'

'Yes, you do,' she said. 'You know it very well.'

While she spoke she was idly locking and unlocking her fingers, or so it seemed, until Cal's eyes lingered on the exercise for two or three seconds. Then it became apparent that she was passing her fingers *through* the palms of the other hand, left through right, right through left, defying their solidity. The motion was so casual, the illusion – if illusion it was – so quick, that Cal was by no means certain he was interpreting it correctly.

'How do they look to you?' she enquired.

He looked back at her face. Was the finger-trick some kind of test of his perception? It wasn't her hands she was talking about, however.

'The Amadou,' she said. 'How do they appear?'

He glanced towards the Rock again.

'. . . like human beings,' he replied.

She gave him a tiny smile.

'Why do you ask?' he wanted to know. But she didn't have time to reply before Boaz spoke.

'There's a Council been called,' he said. 'At Capra's House. I think they're going to re-weave.'

'That can't be right,' said Cal. 'They're going to put the Fugue back?'

'That's what I hear,' said Boaz.

236

It seemed to be fresh news to him; had he just lifted it off the gossiping air? 'The times are too dangerous, they're saying,' he told Cal. 'Is that true?'

'I don't know any other,' Cal said. 'So I've got nothing to compare them with.'

'Do we have the night?' Ganza asked.

'Some of it,' said Boaz.

'Then we'll go to see Lo; yes?'

'It's as good a place as any,' Boaz replied. 'Will you come?' he asked the Cuckoo.

Cal looked back towards the Amadou. The thought of staying and watching their performance a while longer was tempting, but he might not find another guide to show him the sights, and if time here was short then he'd best make the most of it.

'Yes. I'll come.'

The woman had stopped lacing her fingers.

'You'll like Lo,' she said, turning away, and starting off into the night.

He followed, already full to brimming with questions, but knowing that if indeed he only had hours to taste Wonderland he should not waste time and breath asking.

# II

## AT THE LAKE, AND LATER

### 1

There had been a moment, back in the Auction House, when Suzanna had thought her life was at an end. She'd been helping Apolline down the stairs when the walls had creaked, and it seemed the house had come down around their ears. Even now, as she stood watching the lake, she was not certain how they'd escaped alive. Presumably the menstruum had intervened on her behalf, though she had not consciously willed it to do so. There was much she had to learn about the power she'd inherited. Not least, how much it belonged to *her* and how much she to *it*. When she found Apolline, whom she'd lost in the furore, she would find out all the woman knew.

In the meantime, she had the islands, their backs crowned with cypress trees, to wonder about, and the lisp of the waves on the stones to soothe her.

'We should go.'

Jerichau broke her reverie as softly as he could, touching the back of her neck with his hand. She had left him at the house that stood along the shore, talking with friends he'd not seen in a human life-time. They had reminiscences to exchange, in which she had no place, and which, she sensed, the others had no desire to share. Criminal talk, she'd uncharitably concluded as she left them to it. Jerichau was a thief, after all.

'Why did we come here?' she asked him.

'I was born here. I know every one of these stones by name.'
His hand still rested on her shoulder. 'Or at least I *did*. It
seemed a good place to show you –'

She looked away from the lake towards him. His brow was
furrowed; 'But we can't stay,' he said.

'Why not?'

'They'll want to see you at Capra's House.'

'Me?'

'You unmade the Weave.'

'I had no choice,' she said. 'Cal was going to be killed.'

The furrow deepened.

'Forget Cal,' he said, his tone toughening. 'Mooney's a
Cuckoo. You're not.'

'Yes I am,' she insisted. 'Or least that's what I feel I am, and
that's the important thing . . .'

His hand dropped from her shoulder. He was suddenly
sullen.

'Are you coming or not?' he said.

'Of course I'm coming.'

He sighed.

'It wasn't meant to be this way,' he said, his voice recaptur-
ing some of its former gentility.

She wasn't sure what he was speaking of: the unweaving,
his reunion with the lake, or the exchange between them.
Perhaps a little of each.

'Maybe it was a mistake to unmake the Weave,' she said,
somewhat defensively, 'but it wasn't just me. It was the
menstruum.'

He raised his eyebrows.

'It's *your* power,' he said, not without rancour. 'Control it.'

She gave him a frosty look. 'How far is Capra's House?'

'Nothing's far in the Fugue,' he replied. 'The Scourge destroyed most of our territories. Only these few remain.'

'Are there more in the Kingdom?'

'A few maybe. But all we really care for is here. That's why
we have to hide it again, before morning.'

*Morning.* She'd almost forgotten that the sun would soon be
rising and, with it, Humankind. The thought of her fellow

239

Cuckoos – with their taste for zoos, freak-shows and carnivals – invading this territory did not much amuse her.

'You're right,' she said. 'We have to be quick,' and together they went up from the lake towards Capra's House.

2

As they walked Suzanna had answered several questions that had been vexing her since the unweaving. Chief amongst them: what had happened to the portion of the Kingdom that the Fugue had invaded? It was not well populated certainly – there was the considerable acreage of Thurstaston Common behind the Auction House, and fields to either side; but the area was not entirely deserted. There were a number of houses in the locality, and up towards Irby Heath the population grew denser still. What had happened to those residences? And indeed to their occupants?

The answer was quite simple: the Fugue had sprung up around them, accommodating their existence with a kind of wit. Thus a line of lamp-posts, their fluorescence extinguished, had been decorated with blossoming vines like antique columns; a car had been almost buried in the side of a hill, another two had been tipped on their tails and leaned nose to nose.

The houses had been less recklessly treated; most were still complete, although the flowerage of the Fugue reached to their very doorsteps, as if awaiting an invitation inside.

As to the Cuckoos, she and Jerichau encountered a few, all of whom seemed more puzzled than fearful. One man, dressed only in trousers and braces, was complaining loudly that he'd lost his dog – 'Damn fool mutt,' he said. 'You seen him?' – and seemed indifferent to the fact that the world had changed around him. It was only after he'd headed off, still calling after the runaway, that Suzanna wondered if the fellow was seeing what *she* saw, or whether the same selective blindness that kept the haloes from human eyes was at work here. Was the dog-owner wandering familiar streets, unable to see beyond the cell of his assumptions? Or perhaps just glimpsing the Fugue from the corner of his eye, a glory he'd remember in his dotage, and weep over?

Jerichau had no answers to these questions. He didn't know, he said, and he didn't care.

And still the visions unfurled. With every step she took her astonishment grew at the variety of places and objects the Seerkind had saved from the conflagration. The Fugue was not, as she'd anticipated, simply a collection of haunted groves and thickets. Holiness was a far more democratic condition; it informed fragments of every kind: intimate and momentous, natural and artificial. Each corner and niche had its own peculiar mode of rapture.

The circumstances of their preservation meant that most of these fragments had been torn from their context like pages from a book. Their edges were still raw with the violence of that removal, and the haphazard way they'd been thrown together only made their disunity seem more acute. But there were compensations. The very disparity of the pieces – the way the domestic abutted the public; the commonplace, the fabulous – created fresh conundrums; hints of new stories that these hitherto unconnected pages might tell.

Sometimes the journey showed them collisions of elements so unlikely they defied any attempt to synthesize them. Dogs grazing beside a tomb, from the fractured lid of which rose a fountain of fire that ran like water; a window set in the ground, its curtains billowing skyward on a breeze that carried the sound of the sea. These riddles, defying her powers of explanation, marked her profoundly. There was nothing here that she hadn't seen before – dogs, tombs, windows, fire – but in this flux she found them re-invented, their magic made again before her eyes.

Only once, having been told by Jerichau that he had no answers to her questions, did she press him for knowledge, and that was regarding the Gyre, whose covering of cloud was perpetually visible, its brightest lightning bursts throwing hill and tree into relief.

'That's where the Temple of the Loom is,' he said. 'The closer you get to it the more dangerous it becomes.'

She remembered something of this from that first night, when they'd talked of the carpet. But she wanted to know more.

'Why dangerous?' she asked.

'The raptures required to make the Weave were without parallel. It required great sacrifice, great purity, to control them and knit them. More than most of us would ever be capable of. Now the power protects itself, with lightning and storms. And wisely. If the Gyre's broken into, the Weave rapture won't hold. All we've gathered here will come apart; be destroyed.'

'Destroyed?'

'So they say. I don't know if it's true or not. I've got no grasp of the theoretical stuff.'

'But you can perform raptures.'

The remark seemed to baffle him. 'That doesn't mean I can tell you how,' he said. 'I just do 'em.'

'Like what?' she said. She felt like a child, asking for tricks from a magician, but she was curious to know the powers residing in him.

He made an odd face; one full of contradictions. There was a shyness there; something quizzical; something fond.

'Maybe I'll show you,' he said. 'One of these times. I can't sing or dance, but I've got ways with me.' He stopped speaking, and walking too.

She didn't need any sign from him to hear the bells that were in the air around them. They were not the bells of a steeple – these were light and melodic – but they summoned nevertheless.

'Capra's House,' he said, striding ahead. The bells, knowing they were heard, rang them on their way.

# III

## DELUSIONS

### 1

The bulletin that had gone out from Hobart's Division announcing the escape of the anarchists had not gone unheard; but the alarm had come a little before eleven, and the patrols were dealing with the nightly round of fist-fights, drunken driving and theft which climaxed about that time. In addition there'd been a fatal stabbing on Seel Street, and a transvestite had been the cause of a near-riot in a pub on the Dock Road. Thus, by the time any serious attention had been paid to the alarm-call, the escapees were long gone; slipped through the Mersey Tunnel on their way to Shearman's house.

But on the opposite side of the river, just outside Birkenhead, a vigilant patrolman by the name of Downey caught sight of them. Leaving his partner in a Chinese restaurant ordering Chop Suey and Peking Fried Duck, Downey gave chase. The radio alert warned that these miscreants were extremely dangerous, and that no attempt should be made to apprehend them single-handed. Patrolman Downey therefore kept a discreet distance, aided in this by a thorough knowledge of the area.

When the villains finally reached their destination, however, it became apparent that this was no ordinary pursuit. For one, when he reported his location to Division he was told that things there were in considerable disarray – could he hear a man sobbing in the background? – and that this matter would be dealt with by Inspector Hobart in person. He was to wait, and watch.

It was while he was waiting and watching that he had his second proof that something untoward was in the air.

It began with lights flickering in the second-storey windows of the house; then exploding into the outside world, taking wall and window with it.

He got out of his car and began to walk towards the house. His mind, used to filing reports, was already scrabbling for adjectives to describe what he was seeing, but he kept coming up empty-handed. The brilliance that spilled from the house did not resemble anything he had witnessed or dreamt of before.

He was not a superstitious man. He immediately sought a secular explanation for the things he saw, or *almost* saw, all around him; and seeking, found. He was viewing UFO activity; that was surely it. He'd read reports of similar events happening to perfectly ordinary Joes like himself. It was not God or lunacy he was facing, but a visitation from a neighbouring galaxy.

Content that he had some grasp on the situation, he hurried back to the car to put his report through to headquarters. He was stymied, however. There was white noise on all frequencies. No matter: he'd informed them of his location on first arriving. They'd come to his aid presently. In the meanwhile his task was to watch this landing like a hawk.

That task rapidly became more difficult, as the invaders began to bombard him with extraordinary illusions, designed, no doubt, to conceal their operations from human sight. The waves of force that had burst from the house threw the car on its side (or at least that's what his eyes informed him; he was not about to take it as Gospel); then vague forms began to roil about him. The tarmac beneath his feet seemed to sprout flowers; bestial forms were performing acrobatics above his head.

He saw several members of the public similarly ensnared by these projections. Some stared up at the sky, others were on their knees praying for sanity.

And it came, by and by. Knowing that these images were merely phantoms gave him strength to resist them. Over and over he told himself that what he was seeing was not real, and by degrees the visions bowed to his certainty, grew faint, and finally faded almost entirely.

He scrambled into the over-turned car and tried the radio again, though he had no idea if anybody was hearing it or not. Oddly, he wasn't that concerned. He'd beaten the delusions, and that conviction sweetened his vigil. Even if they came for him now – the monsters that had landed here tonight – he would not fear them. He would put out his own eyes rather than let them bewitch him afresh.

## 2

'Any further word?'

'There's nothing, sir,' said Richardson. 'Only din.'

'Forget it then,' said Hobart. 'Just drive. We'll sniff them out if it takes us all fucking night.'

As they travelled, Hobart's thoughts returned to the scene he'd left behind him. His men reduced to babbling idiots, his cells defiled with shit and prayers. He had a score to settle with these forces of darkness.

Once upon a time he would not have cast himself so readily in the role of avenger. He'd been squeamish in admitting to any degree of personal involvement. But experience had made an honest man of him. Now – at least in the company of his men – he didn't pretend to be removed from the issues at hand, but confessed freely the heat in his belly.

After all, the business of pursuit and punishment was just a way to spit in the eye of one who had already spat on you. The Law, just another word for *revenge*.

# IV

# ALLEGIANCES

## I

I t was eighty years, give or take half a decade, since the three sisters had trodden the earth of the Fugue. Eighty years of exile in the Kingdom of the Cuckoo, worshipped and reviled by turns, almost losing their sanity amongst the Adamaticals, but driven to endure countless mortifications by their hunger one day to have the Weaveworld in their avenging grasp.

Now they hung in the air above that rapturous earth – its touch so antithetical that walking upon it was a trial – and surveyed the Fugue from end to end.

'It smells too much alive,' said the Magdalene, lifting her head to the wind.

'Give us time,' Immacolata told her.

'What about Shadwell?' the Hag wanted to know. 'Where is he?'

'Out looking for his clients, probably,' the Incantatrix replied. 'We should find him. I don't like the thought of his wandering here unaccompanied. He's unpredictable.'

'Then what?'

'We let the inevitable happen,' said Immacolata, gently swinging round to take in every sacred yard of the place. 'We let the Cuckoos tear it apart.'

'What about the Sale?'

'There'll be no Sale. It's too late.'

'Shadwell's going to know you used him.'

'No more than he used me. Or would have liked to.'

A tremor passed through the Magdalene's uncertain substance.

'Wouldn't you like to give yourself to him once?' she enquired softly. 'Just once.'

'No. Never.'

'Then let *me* have him. I can use him. Imagine his children.'

Immacolata reached out and grasped her sister's fragile neck. 'You will never lay a hand on him,' she said. 'Not a finger.'

The wraith's face grew absurdly long, in a parody of remorse.

'I know,' she said. 'He's yours. Body and soul.'

The Hag laughed. 'The man's got no soul,' she said.

Immacolata released the Magdalene, filaments of her sister's matter decaying into sewer air between them.

'Oh, he has a soul,' she said, letting gravity claim her for the earth beneath. 'But I want no part of it.' Her feet touched the ground. 'When all this is over – when the Seerkind are in the Cuckoo's hands – I'll let him go his way. Unharmed.'

'And us?' said the Hag. 'What happens to us then? Will we be free?'

'That's what we agreed.'

'We can go into extinction?'

'If that's what you want.'

'More than anything,' said the Hag. 'More than anything.'

'There are worse things than existence,' said Immacolata.

'Oh?' the Hag replied. 'Can you name one?'

Immacolata thought for a short while.

'No,' she conceded, with a soft sigh of distress. 'You may be right, sister.'


2


Shadwell had fled from the disintegrating house moments after Cal and Nimrod had escaped through the window, and had barely avoided being caught by the cloud that had swallowed Devereaux. He'd ended up face down, his mouth filled with dust and with the sour taste of defeat. After so many years of anticipation, to have the Auction end in ruin and humiliation, it was enough to make him weep.

But he didn't. For one thing, he was an optimist by nature: in today's rejection the seeds of tomorrow's sale. For another, the spectacle of the Fugue solidifying about him was a fine distraction from his sorrows. And for a third, he had found one worse off than he.

'What the fuck is *happening*?' It was Norris, the Hamburger King. Blood and plaster dust vied for the right to paint his face, and somewhere in the maelstrom he'd lost both the back of his jacket and most of his trousers; also one of his fine Italian shoes. The other he carried.

'I'll sue the ass off you!' he screeched at Shadwell. 'You fucking asshole. Look at me! *Fucking asshole!*'

He began to beat Shadwell with the shoe, but the Salesman was in no mood to be bruised. He slapped the man back, hard. Within seconds they were brawling like drunkards, indifferent to the extraordinary scenes coming to life all around them. The tussle left them more breathless and bloody than they'd started out, and did nothing to resolve their differences.

'You should have taken precautions!' Norris spat.

'It's too late for accusations,' Shadwell replied. 'The Fugue's woken whether we like it or not.'

'I would have woken it myself,' said Norris. 'If I'd got to own it. But I would have been *ready* and *waiting*. Had some forces to go in and take control. But *this*? It's chaos! I don't even know which way is out.'

'Any way'll do. It's not that big. If you want out, just walk in any direction.'

This simple solution seemed to pacify Norris somewhat. He turned his gaze on the burgeoning landscape.

'I don't know though . . .' he said, '. . . maybe it's better this way. At least I get to see what I would have bought.'

'And what do you make of it?'

'It's not the way I'd thought it'd be. I'd expected something . . . tamer. Frankly, I'm not sure now I'd want to own the place.'

As his voice faltered an animal that could surely be found in no menagerie jumped from the flux of threads and snarled a welcome at the world before bounding off.

'See?' said Norris. 'What was that?'

Shadwell shrugged. 'I don't know,' he said. 'There's things here that probably died out before we were born.'

'*That?*' said Norris, staring after the hybrid beast. 'I never saw the like of that before, even in books. I tell you I want none of this fucking place. I want you to get me out.'

'You'll have to find your own way,' said Shadwell. 'I've got business here.'

'Oh no you don't,' said Norris, pointing his shoe at Shadwell. 'I need a body-guard. And you're it.'

The sight of the Hamburger King reduced to this nervous wreckage amused Shadwell. More than that, it made him feel – perhaps perversely – secure.

'Look,' he said, his manner softening. 'We're both in the same shit here –'

'Damn right we are.'

'I've got something that might help,' he said, opening his jacket, '– something to sweeten the pill.'

Norris looked suspicious. 'Oh yeah?'

'Have a peep,' said Shadwell, showing the man the jacket lining. Norris wiped off the blood that was running into his left eye, and stared into the folds. 'What do you see?'

There was a moment of hesitation, when Shadwell wondered if the jacket was still functioning. Then a slow smile broke over Norris' face, and a look familiar from countless other such seductions crept into his eyes.

'See something you like?' Shadwell asked him.

'Indeed I do.'

'Take it then. It's yours. Free, gratis and for nothing.'

Norris smiled, almost coyly. 'Wherever did you find him?' he asked, as he extended a trembling hand towards the jacket. 'After all these years . . .'

Tenderly, he drew his temptation from the folds of the lining. It was a wind-up toy: a soldier with a drum, so fondly and so accurately remembered by its owner that the illusion he now held in his hand had been recreated with every dent and scratch in place.

'*My drummer*,' said Norris, weeping for joy as if he'd taken possession of the world's eighth wonder. 'Oh my drummer.' He turned it over. 'But there's no key,' he said. 'Do you have it?'

'I may find it for you, by and by,' Shadwell replied.

'One of his arms is broken,' said Norris, stroking the drummer's head. 'But he still plays.'

'You're happy?'

'Oh yes. Yes thank you.'

'Then put it in your pocket, so that you can carry me awhile,' said Shadwell.

'Carry you?'

'I'm weary. I need a horse.'

Norris showed no trace of resistance to this notion, though Shadwell was a bigger and heavier man, and would constitute quite a burden. The gift had won him over utterly, and while it held him in thrall he would allow his spine to crack before disobeying the giftgiver.

Laughing to himself, Shadwell climbed onto the man's back. His plans might have gone awry tonight, but as long as people had dreams to mourn he could possess their little souls awhile.

'Where do you want me to take you?' the horse asked him.

'Somewhere high,' he directed. 'Take me somewhere high.'

# THE ORCHARD OF LEMUEL LO

## 1

Neither Boaz nor Ganza were voluble guides. They led the way through the Fugue in almost complete silence, only breaking that silence to warn Cal that a stretch of ground was treacherous, or to keep close to them as they moved down a colonnade in which he heard dogs panting. In a sense he was glad of their quietness. He didn't want a guided tour of the terrain, at least not tonight. He'd known, when he'd first looked down at the Fugue from the wall in Mimi's yard, that it couldn't be mapped, nor its contents listed and committed to memory like his beloved timetables. He would have to understand the Weaveworld in a different fashion: not as hard fact but as feeling. The schism between his mind and the world it was attempting to grasp was dissolving. In its place was a relationship of echo and counter echo. They were thoughts inside each other's heads, he and this world; and that knowledge, which he could never have found the words to articulate, turned the journey into a tour of his own history. He'd known from Mad Mooney that poetry was heard differently from ear to ear. Poetry was like that. The same, he began to see, was also true of geography.

## 2

They climbed a long slope. He thought maybe a tide of crickets leapt before their feet; the earth seemed alive.

At the top of the slope they looked across a field. At the far side of the field was an orchard.

'Almost there,' said Ganza, and they began towards it.

The orchard was the biggest single feature he'd seen in the Fugue so far; a plot of maybe thirty or forty trees, planted in rows and carefully pruned so that their branches almost touched. Beneath this canopy were passages of neatly clipped grass, dappled by velvet light.

'This is the orchard of Lemuel Lo,' Boaz said, as they stood on the perimeter. His gentle voice was softer than ever. 'Even amongst the fabled, it's fabled.'

Ganza led the way beneath the trees. The air was still and warm and sweet. The branches were laden with a fruit that Cal did not recognize.

'They're Jude Pears,' Boaz told him. 'One of the species we've never shared with the Cuckoos.'

'Why not?'

'There are reasons,' said Boaz. He looked around for Ganza, but she'd disappeared down one of the avenues. 'Help yourself to the fruit,' he said, moving away from Cal in search of his companion. 'Lem won't mind.'

Though Cal thought he could see all the way down the corridor of trees his eyes deceived him. Boaz took three steps from him, and was gone.

Cal reached towards one of the low-slung branches and put his hand on one of the fruits. As he did so there was a great commotion in the tree and something ran down the branch towards him.

'Not that one!'

The voice was bass profundo. The speaker was a monkey.

'They're sweeter upstairs,' the beast said, throwing its brown eyes skyward. Then it ran back the way it had come, its passage bringing leaves down around Cal. He tried to follow its progress, but the animal moved too fast. It was back in half a dozen seconds, with not one but two fruits. Perched in the branches, it threw them down to Cal.

'Peel them,' it said. 'One each.'

Despite their name, they didn't resemble pears. They were

the size of a plum, but with a leathery skin. It was tough, but it couldn't disguise the fragrance of the meat inside.

'What are you waiting for?' the monkey demanded to know. 'They're tasty, these Giddys. Peel it and see.'

The fact of the talking monkey – which might have stopped Cal dead in his tracks a week before – was just part of the local colour now.

'You call them Giddys?' he said.

'Jude Pears; Giddy Fruit. It's all the same meat.'

The monkey's eyes were on Cal's hands, willing him to peel the fruit. He proceeded to do just that. They were more difficult to skin than any fruit he'd encountered; hence the monkey's bargain with him, presumably. Viscous juice ran from the broken skin and over his hands; the smell was ever more appetizing. Before he'd quite finished peeling the first of them, the monkey snatched it from his grasp and wolfed it down.

'Good –' it said, between mouthfuls.

Its pleasure was echoed from beneath the tree. Somebody made a sound of appreciation, and Cal glanced away from his labours to see that there was a man squatting against the trunk, rolling a cigarette. He looked back up to the monkey, then down at the man, and the voice from the beast made new sense.

'Good trick,' he said.

The man looked up at Cal. His features were distressingly close to mongoloid; the smile he offered huge, and seemingly uncomprehending.

'What is?' said the voice from the branches.

Confounded as he was by the face below him, Cal pursued his assumption, and addressed his reply not to the puppet but the puppeteer.

'Throwing your voice like that.'

The man still grinned, but showed no sign that he'd understood. The monkey, however, laughed loudly.

'Eat the fruit,' it said.

Cal's fingers had worked at the peeling without his direction. The Giddy was skinned. But some lingering superstition about stolen fruit kept him from putting it to his lips.

'Try it,' said the monkey. 'They're not poisonous –'

The smell was too tantalizing to resist. He bit.

'– at least not to us,' the monkey added, laughing again.

The fruit tasted even better than its scent had promised. The meat was succulent, the juice strong as a liqueur. He licked it off his fingers, and the palms of his hand.

'Like it?'

'Superb.'

'Food and drink all in one.' The monkey looked at the man beneath the tree. 'Want one, Smith?' it asked.

The man put a flame to his cigarette and drew on it.

'D'you hear me?'

Getting no response, the monkey scampered back up into the higher reaches of the tree.

Cal, still eating the pear, had found the pips at its centre. He chewed them up. Their slight bitterness only complemented the sweetness of the rest.

There was music playing somewhere between the trees, he now noticed. One moment lilting, the next manic.

'Another?' said the monkey, re-appearing with not two but several fruit.

Cal swallowed the last of his first.

'Same deal,' the monkey said.

Suddenly greedy, Cal took three, and started to peel.

'There's other people here,' he said to the puppeteer.

'Of course,' said the monkey. 'This has always been a gathering place.'

'Why do you speak through the animal?' Cal asked, as the monkey's fingers claimed a peeled fruit from his hands.

'The name's Novello,' said the monkey. 'And who says he's speaking at all?'

Cal laughed, as much at himself as at the performance.

'Fact is,' said the monkey, 'neither of us is quite sure who does what any longer. But then love's like that, don't you find?'

It threw back its head and squeezed the fruit in its hand, so that the liquor ran down its throat.

The music had found a fresh intoxication. Cal was intrigued to find out what instruments it was being played upon. Violins certainly, and whistles and drums. But there were sounds amongst these that he couldn't place.

'Any excuse for a party,' said Novello.

'Must be the biggest breakfast in history.'

'I daresay. Want to go see?'

'Yes.'

The monkey ran along the branch, and scurried down the trunk to where Smith was sitting. Cal, chewing the seeds of his second Giddy, reached up and claimed a further handful of fruit from amongst the foliage, pocketing half a dozen against future hunger, and skinning another to be consumed on the spot.

The sound of monkey-chatter drew his gaze down to Novello and Smith. The beast was perched on the man's chest, and they were talking to each other, a babble of words and grunts. Cal looked from man to beast and back to man again. He could not tell who was saying what to whom.

The debate ended abruptly, and Smith stood up, the monkey now sitting on his shoulder. Without inviting Cal to follow, they threaded their way between the trees. Cal pursued, peeling and eating as he went.

Some of the visitors here were doing as he'd done, standing beneath the trees, consuming Jude Pears. One or two had even climbed up and were draped amongst the branches, bathing in the perfumed air. Others, either indifferent to the fruit or sated upon it, lay sprawled in the grass and talked together in low voices. The atmosphere was all tranquillity.

Heaven is an orchard, Cal thought as he walked; and God is plenty.

'That's the fruit talking,' said Novello. Cal wasn't even aware that he'd spoken aloud. He looked round at the monkey, feeling slightly disoriented.

'You should watch yourself,' the animal said, 'an excess of Judes isn't good for you.'

'I've got a strong stomach,' Cal replied.

'Who said anything about your stomach?' the monkey replied. 'They're not called Giddy Fruit for nothing.'

Cal ignored him. The animal's condescending tone irritated him. He picked up his pace, overtaking man and beast.

'Have it your way,' said the monkey.

Somebody darted between the trees a little way ahead of Cal, trailing laughter. To Cal's eyes the sound was momentarily *visible*; he saw the rise and fall of notes as splashes of light, which flew apart like dandelion heads in a high wind. Enchantment upon enchantment. Plucking and peeling yet another of Lo's remarkable fruits as he went, he hurried on towards the music.

And ahead of him, the scene came clear. A blue and ochre rug had been laid on the ground between the trees, with wicks in oil flickering along its borders; and at its edge the musicians he'd heard. There were five of them: three women and two men, dressed formally in suits and dresses, in the dark threads of which brilliant designs were somehow concealed, so that the subtlest motion of the folds in the flame-light revealed a glamour that brought to Cal's mind the iridescence of tropical butterflies. More startling, however, was the fact that this quintet had not a single instrument between them. They were *singing* these violins, pipes and drums, and offering in addition sounds no instrument could hope to produce. Here was a music which did not imitate natural sound – it was not bird or whale song, nor tree nor stream – but instead expressed experiences which lay between words: the off-beat of the heart, where intellect could not go.

Hearing it, shudders of pleasure ran down Cal's spine.

The show had drawn an audience of perhaps thirty Seerkind, and Cal joined them. His presence was noted by a few, who threw mildly curious glances in his direction.

Surveying the crowd, he attempted to allot these people to one or other of the four Families, but it was near enough impossible. The choral orchestra were presumably Aia; hadn't Apolline said that it was Aia blood that had given her a good singing voice? But amongst the rest, who was who? Which of these people were of Jerichau's Family, for instance: the

Babu? Which of the Ye-me, or the Lo? There were negro and caucasian faces, and one or two with an oriental cast; there were some who boasted traits not quite human – one with Nimrod's golden eyes (and tail too, presumably); another pair whose features carried symmetrical marking that crept down from the scalp; yet others who bore – either at the dictates of fashion or theology – elaborate tattoos and hair-styles. There was the same startling variety in the clothes they wore, the formal designs of their late nineteenth-century garb re-fashioned to suit the wearer. And in the fabrics of skirts, suits and waistcoats, the same barely concealed iridescence: threads of carnival brilliance in wait behind the monochrome.

Cal's admiring gaze went from one face to another, and he felt he wanted each of these people as a friend, wanted to know them and walk with them and share his pittance of secrets with them. He was vaguely aware that this was probably the fruit talking. But if so, then it was wise fruit.

Though his hunger was assuaged, he took another of the pears from his pocket and was about to peel it when the music came to an end. There was applause and whistling. The quintet took their bows. As they did so a bearded man with a face as lined as a walnut, who had been sitting on a stool close to the edge of the rug, stood up. He looked directly at Cal and said:

'My friends . . . my friends . . . we have a stranger amongst us . . .'

The applause was dying down. Faces turned in Cal's direction; he could feel himself blush.

'Come out, Mr Mooney! Mr *Calhoun Mooney*!'

Ganza told the truth: the air *did* gossip.

The man was beckoning. Cal made a murmur of protest.

'Come on. Entertain us a while!' came the reply.

At this Cal's heart started to thump furiously. 'I can't,' he said.

'Of course you can,' the man grinned. 'Of course you can!'

There was more applause. The shining faces smiled around him. Somebody touched his shoulder. He glanced round. It was Novello.

'That's Mr Lo,' said the monkey. 'You mustn't refuse him.'

257

'But I can't *do* anything —'

'Everybody can do *something*,' said the monkey. 'If it's only fart.'

'Come on, come on,' Lemuel Lo was saying. 'Don't be shy.'

Much against his will, Cal edged through the crowd towards the rectangle of wicks.

'Really . . .' he said to Lo. 'I don't think . . .'

'You've eaten freely of my fruit,' said Lo, without rancour. 'The least you can do is entertain us.'

Cal looked about him for some support, but all he saw were expectant faces.

'I can't sing, and I've two left feet,' he pointed out, still hoping self-depreciation might earn him an escape-route.

'Your great-grandfather was a poet, wasn't he?' said Lemuel, his tone almost rebuking Cal for not making mention of the fact.

'He was,' said Cal.

'And can you not quote your own great-grandfather?' said Lemuel.

Cal thought about this for a moment. It was clear he was not going to be released from this circle without at least making some stab at recompense for his greed, and Lemuel's suggestion was not a bad one. Many years ago Brendan had taught Cal one or two fragments of Mad Mooney's verse. They'd meant little enough to Cal at the time — he'd been about six years old — but their rhymes had been intriguing.

'The rug is yours,' said Lemuel, and stood aside to let Cal have access to the performing area. Before he'd had an opportunity to run any of the lines through his head — it was two decades since he'd learnt them; how much would he remember? — he was standing on the rug, staring across the flickering footlights at his audience.

'What Mr Lo says is true . . .' he said, all hesitation, '. . . my great-grandfather . . .'

'Speak up,' somebody said.

'. . . my great-grandfather was a poet. I'll try and recite one of his verses. I don't know if I can remember them, but I'll do my best.'

There was scattered applause at this, which made Cal more uneasy than ever.

'What's it called, this poem?' said Lemuel.

Cal wracked his brain. The title had meant even less than the lines when he'd first been taught it, but he'd learned it anyway, parrot-fashion.

'It's called *Six Commonplaces*,' he said, his tongue quicker to shape the words than his brain was to dust them off.

'Tell it, my friend,' said the orchard-keeper.

The audience stood with bated breath; the only movement now was that of the flames around the rug.

Cal began.

'*One part of love . . .*'

For a terrible instant his mind went totally blank. If somebody had asked him his name at that juncture he would not have been able to reply. Four words, and he was suddenly speechless.

In that moment of panic he realized that he wanted more than anything in the world to please this gracious gathering; to show them how glad he was to be amongst them. But his damn tongue –

At the back of his head, the poet said:

'Go on, boy. Tell them what you know. Don't try and remember. Just speak.'

He began again, not falteringly this time, but strongly, as though he knew these lines perfectly well. And damn it, he did. They flowed from him easily, and he heard himself speaking them in a voice he'd never have thought himself capable of. A bard's voice, declaiming.

> '*One part of love is innocence,*
> *One part of love is guilt,*
> *One part the milk, that in a sense*
> *Is soured as soon as spilt.*
> *One part of love is sentiment,*
> *One part of love is lust,*
> *One part is the presentiment*
> *Of our return to dust.*'

Eight lines, and it was all over; over, and he was standing, the lines buzzing in his head, both pleased that he'd got through the verse without fumbling, and wishing it could have gone on a while longer. He looked at the audience. They were not smiling any longer, but staring at him with an odd puzzlement in their eyes. For an instant he thought maybe he'd offended them. Then came the applause, hands raised above their heads. There were shouts and whistles.

'It's a fine poem!' Lo said, applauding heartily as he spoke. 'And finely delivered!'

So saying, he stepped out of the audience again and embraced Cal with fervour.

'Do you hear?' Cal said to the poet in his skull. 'They like you.'

And back came another fragment, as if fresh from Mad Mooney's lips. He didn't speak it this time: but he heard it clearly.

> Forgive my Art. On bended knees,
> I do confess: I seek to please.

And it was a fine thing, this pleasing business. He returned Lemuel's hug.

'Help yourself, Mr Mooney,' the orchard-keeper said, 'to all the fruit you can eat.'

'Thank you,' said Cal.

'Did you ever know the poet?' he asked.

'No,' said Cal. 'He was dead before I was born.'

'Who can call a man dead whose words still hush us and whose sentiments move?' Mr Lo replied.

'That's true,' said Cal.

'Of course it's true. Would I tell a lie on a night like this?'

Having spoken, Lemuel called somebody else out of the crowd: another performer brought to the rug. Cal felt a pang of envy as he stepped over the footlights. He wanted that breathless moment again: wanted to feel the audience held by his words, moved and marked by them. He made a mental note to learn some more of Mad Mooney's verses if and when he saw his father's house again, so that next time he was here he had new lines to enchant with.

His hand was shaken and his face kissed half a dozen times as he made his way back through the crowd. When he turned round to face the rug once more, he was surprised to find that the next performers were Boaz and Ganza. Doubly surprised: they were both naked. There was nothing overtly sexual in their nakedness: indeed it was as formal in its way as the clothes they'd shrugged off. Nor was there any trace of discomfort amongst the audience: they watched the pair with the same grave and expectant looks as they'd watched him.

Boaz and Ganza had gone to opposite sides of the carpet, halted there a beat, then turned and begun to walk towards each other. They advanced slowly, until they were nose to nose, lip to lip. It crossed Cal's mind that maybe some erotic display *was* in the offing, and in a way that confounded his every definition of erotic, that was true, for they continued to walk towards each other, or so his eyes testified, pressing into each other, their faces disappearing, their torsos congealing, their limbs too, until they were one body, the head an almost featureless ball.

The illusion was absolute. But there was more to come; for the partners were still moving forward, their faces appearing now to press through the back of each other's craniums, as though the bone was soft as marshmallow. And *still* they advanced, until they were like siamese twins born back to back, their single skull now teased out, and boasting two faces.

As if this weren't enough, there was a further twist to the trick, for somehow in the flux they'd exchanged genders, to stand finally – quite separate once more – in their partner's place.

Love's like that, the monkey had said. Here was the point proved, in flesh and blood.

As the performers bowed, and fresh applause broke out, Cal detached himself from the crowd and began to wander back through the trees. Several vague thoughts were in his head. One, that he couldn't linger here all night, and should soon

261

go in search of Suzanna. Another that it might be wise to seek a guide. The monkey, perhaps?

But first, the laden branches drew his eye again. He reached, took another handful of fruit, and began to peel. Lo's *ad hoc* vaudeville was still going on behind him. He heard laughter, then more applause, and the music began again.

He felt his limbs growing heavier; his fingers were barely the equal of the peeling; his eye-lids drooped. Deciding he'd better sit down before he fell down, he settled beneath one of the trees.

Drowsiness was claiming him, and he had no power to resist it. There was no harm in dozing for a while. He was safe here, in the wash of starlight and applause. His eyes flickered closed. It seemed he could see his dreams approaching – their light growing brighter, their voices louder. He smiled to greet them.

It was his old life he dreamt.

He stood in the shuttered room that lay between his ears and let the lost days appear on the wall like a lantern show; moments retrieved from some stock-pile he hadn't even known he'd owned. But the scenes that were paraded before him now – these passages from the unfinished book of his life – no longer seemed quite real. It was fiction, that book; or at best momentarily real, when some part of him had leapt from that stale story, and glimpsed the Fugue in waiting.

The sound of applause called him to the surface of sleep, and his eyes flickered open. The stars were still set amongst the branches of the Giddy trees; there was still laughter and flame-light near at hand; all was well with his new-found land.

I wasn't born 'til now, he thought, as the lantern show returned. I wasn't even born.

Content with that thought, his mind's eye peeled another of Lo's sweet fruits, and put it to his lips.

Somewhere, somebody was applauding him. Hearing it, he took a bow. But this time he did not wake.

# VI

# CAPRA'S HOUSE

## 1

In its way, Capra's House was as great a surprise as anything Suzanna had seen in the Fugue. It was a low building, in a state of considerable disrepair, the off-white plaster that clad its walls falling away to reveal large hand-made red bricks beneath. The tiles of the porch were much weather-beaten; the door itself barely hanging on its hinges. Myrtle trees grew all around it, and in their branches the myriad bells they'd heard were hanging, responsive to the merest breath of wind. Their sound, however, was all but cancelled by the raised voices from within. It sounded more like a riot than civilized debate.

There was a guard at the threshold, squatting on his haunches, making a ziggurat of rocks in front of him. At their approach he stood up. He was fully seven feet tall.

'What business have you got here?' he demanded of Jerichau.

'We have to see the Council –'

From within, Suzanna could hear a woman's voice, raised clear and strong.

'I will not lie down and sleep!' she said. The remark was followed by a roar of approval from her supporters.

'It's vital we talk to the Council,' said Jerichau.

'Impossible,' the guard pronounced.

'This is Suzanna Parrish,' said Jerichau. 'She –'

He had no need to go on.

'I know who she is,' the guard said.

'If you know who I am then you know I woke the Weave,' said Suzanna. 'And I've opinions the Council should hear.'

'Yes,' said the guard. 'I can see that.'

He glanced behind him. The din had, if anything, worsened.

'It's bedlam in there,' he warned. 'You'll be lucky if you're heard.'

'I can shout with the best,' said Suzanna.

The guard nodded. 'No doubt,' he said. 'It's straight ahead.' He stood aside, pointing down a short hallway to a half-closed door.

Suzanna took a deep breath, looking round at Jerichau to see that he was still in tow, then she walked down the passage and pushed the door.

The room was large, but filled with people; some sitting, some on their feet, some even standing on chairs to get a better view of the debate's chief protagonists. There were five individuals in the heat of it. One, a woman with wild hair and an even wilder look – whom Jerichau identified as Yolande Dor. Her faction were in a knot around her, egging her on. She was facing two men, one long-nosed individual whose face was beetroot with yelling, and his older companion, who had a restraining hand upon the first man's arm. They were clearly the opposition. In between was a negress, who was haranguing both parties, and an oriental, immaculately dressed, who looked to be the moderator. If so, he was failing in this function. It could only be moments before the fists replaced opinions.

The presence of the interlopers had been noted by a few of the assembly, but the lead players raged on, deaf to each other's arguments.

'What's the name of the man in the middle?' Suzanna asked Jerichau.

'That's Tung,' said Jerichau.

'Thank you.'

Without another word Suzanna stepped towards the debators.

'Mr Tung,' she said.

The man looked towards her, and the fretfulness on his face turned to panic.

'Who are you?' he demanded to know.

'Suzanna Parrish.'

The name was enough to hush the argument instantly. Those faces which were not already turned in Suzanna's direction were now.

'A Cuckoo!' the old man said. 'In Capra's House!'

'Shut up,' said Tung.

'You're the one,' said the negress. 'You!'

'Yes?'

'*Do you know what you've done?*'

The remark ignited a fresh outburst, but this time it wasn't confined to those at the centre of the room. *Everybody* was yelling.

Tung, whose calls for control went unheard, pulled a chair up, stood on it, and yelled:

'*Silence!*'

The ploy worked; the din died down. Tung was touchingly pleased with himself.

'Ha,' he said, with a little pout of self-satisfaction. 'I think that's a little better. Now . . .' he turned to the old man. 'You have an objection, Messimeris?'

'Indeed I do,' came the reply. He jabbed an arthritic finger in Suzanna's direction: 'She's trespassing. I demand she be removed from this chamber.'

Tung was about to reply, but Yolande was there before him.

'This is no time for constitutional niceties,' she said. 'Whether we like it or not, we're awake.'

She looked at Suzanna.

'And she's responsible.'

'Well I'm not staying in the same room as a Cuckoo,' said Messimeris, contempt for Suzanna oozing from his every word. 'Not after all they've done to us.' He looked at his red-faced companion. 'Are you coming, Dolphi?'

'I am indeed,' he replied.

'Wait,' said Suzanna. 'I don't want to break any rules –'

'You already have,' said Yolande, 'and the walls are still standing.'

'For how long?' said the negress.

'Capra's House is a sacred place,' Messimeris murmured. It was clear that this was no sham: he was genuinely offended by Suzanna's presence.

'I understand that,' said Suzanna. 'And I respect it. But I feel responsible —'

'And so you are,' said Dolphi, working himself up into a fresh lather. 'But that's little comfort now, is it? We're awake, damn you. And we're *lost*.'

'I know,' said Suzanna. 'What you say's right.'

This rather deflated him: he'd been expecting argument.

'You agree?' he said.

'Of course I agree. We're all vulnerable at the moment.'

'At least we can fend for ourselves now we're awake,' Yolande argued. 'Instead of just lying there.'

'We had the Custodians,' said Dolphi. 'What happened to them?'

'They're dead,' Suzanna replied.

'All of them?'

'What does she know?' Messimeris commented. 'Don't listen to her.'

'My grandmother was Mimi Laschenski,' said Suzanna.

For the first time since she'd entered the fray Messimeris looked her straight in the eye. He was no stranger to unhappiness, she thought; it was there in abundance now.

'So?' he said.

'And she was murdered,' Suzanna went on, returning his stare, 'by one of *your* people.'

'Never!' said Messimeris, without a trace of doubt.

'Who?' said Yolande.

'Immacolata.'

'Not ours!' Messimeris protested. 'Not one of ours.'

'Well she's certainly no Cuckoo!' Suzanna retorted, her patience beginning to wear thin. She took a step towards Messimeris, who took a firmer grip of Dolphi's arm, as if he might use his colleague as a shield should push come to shove.

'Every one of us is in danger,' she said, 'and if you don't see that then all your sacred places – not just Capra's House, *all of them* – they'll be wiped away. All right, you've got reason not to trust me. But at least give me a hearing.'

The room had fallen pin-drop quiet.

'Tell us what you know,' said Tung.

'Not all that much,' Suzanna admitted. 'But I know you've got enemies here in the Fugue, and God knows how many more outside.'

'What do you suggest we do about it?' said a new voice, from somewhere in Dolphi's faction.

'We fight,' said Yolande.

'You'll lose,' Suzanna replied.

The other woman's fine features grew tight. 'Defeatism from you too?' she said.

'It's the truth. You've got no defences against the Kingdom.'

'We have the raptures,' said Yolande.

'Do you want to make weapons of your magic?' Suzanna replied. 'Like Immacolata? If you do that, you may as well call yourself Cuckoos.'

This argument won some murmurs of assent from the assembly; and sour stares from Yolande.

'So we have to re-weave,' said Messimeris, with some satisfaction. 'Which is what I've been saying from the outset.'

'I agree,' said Suzanna.

At this, the room erupted afresh, Yolande's voice rising above the din: *'No more sleep!'* she said. *'I will not sleep!'*

'Then you'll all be wiped out,' Suzanna yelled back.

The din subsided a little.

'This is a cruel century,' said Suzanna.

'So was the last,' somebody commented. 'And the one before that!'

'We can't hide *forever*,' said Yolande, appealing to the room. Her call received considerable support, despite Suzanna's intervention. And indeed it was difficult not to sympathize with her case. After so much sleep, the idea of consigning themselves to the dreamless bed of the Weave could not be attractive.

'I'm not saying you should stay in the carpet for long,' said Suzanna. 'Just until a safe place can be –'

'I've heard all of this before,' Yolande broke in. '*We'll wait, we said, we'll keep our heads low 'til the storm blows over.*'

'There are storms and storms,' said a man somewhere at the back of the crowd. His voice penetrated the clamour with ease, though it was scarcely more than a whisper. This in itself was enough to make the argument die down.

Suzanna looked in the direction of the sound, though she could not yet see the speaker. It came again:

'If the Kingdom destroys you . . .' the voice said, '. . . then all my Mimi's pain was for nothing . . .'

The Councillors were stepping aside as the speaker moved through them towards the centre of the room. He came into view. It took Suzanna several seconds to realize that she'd seen this face before, and another beat to remember where: in the portrait on Mimi's bedroom wall. But the faded photograph had failed to convey more than a hint of the man's presence; or indeed of his physical beauty. It wasn't difficult, seeing the way his eyes flickered, and his close-cropped hair flattered the curve of his skull, to understand why Mimi had slept beneath his gaze all her lonely life. This was the man she'd loved. This was –

'Romo,' he said, addressing Suzanna. 'Your grandmother's first husband.'

How had he known, sleeping in the Weave, that Mimi had taken a human husband? Had the air told him that tonight?

'What do you want here?' said Tung. 'This isn't a public thoroughfare.'

'I want to speak on behalf of my wife. I knew her heart better than any of you.'

'That was years ago, Romo. Another life.'

Romo nodded.

'Yes . . .' he said. 'It's gone, I know. So's she. All the more reason I speak for her.'

Nobody made any attempt to silence him.

'She died in the Kingdom,' he said, 'to keep us from harm.

268

She died without trying to wake us. Why was that? She had every reason to want the unweaving. To be relieved of her duties; and be back with me.'

'Not necessarily –' Messimeris said.

Romo smiled. 'Because she married?' he said. 'I would have expected no less. Or because she'd forgotten? No. Never.' He spoke with such authority, yet so gently, everyone in the room attended to him. 'She didn't forget us. She simply knew what her granddaughter knows. That it isn't *safe*.'

Yolande went to interrupt, but Romo raised his hand.

'A moment, please,' he said. 'Then I'm going. I've got business elsewhere.'

Yolande closed her mouth.

'I knew Mimi better than any of you. As far as I'm concerned we parted only yesterday. I know she guarded the Weave as long as she had breath and wit to do so. Don't waste her agonies by throwing us into the hands of our enemies just because you get a whiff of freedom in your nostrils.'

'Easy for you to say,' Yolande replied.

'I want to live again as much as you do,' Romo told her. 'I stayed here because of my children, thinking – the way we all thought – that we'd be awake in a year or two. Now look. We open our eyes, and the world has changed. My Mimi died an old woman, and it's the child of her child who stands in her place to tell us that we are as close to extinction as ever. I believe she speaks with Mimi's blessing. We should listen to her.'

'What do you advise?' said Tung.

'*Advise?*' Yolande said. 'He's a lion-tamer, why should we listen to his advice?'

'I suggest we re-weave,' said Romo, ignoring her outburst. 'Re-weave before the Cuckoos come amongst us. Then we find somewhere *safe*, somewhere we can unweave again in our own time, where the Cuckoos won't be waiting at the border. Yolande's right,' he said, looking at her. 'We can't hide forever. But facing tomorrow morning in this chaotic state isn't courage, it's suicide.'

The speech was neatly argued, and it clearly impressed a good number of the assembly.

'And if we do?' said one of Yolande's clan. 'Who guards the carpet?'

'She does,' said Romo, looking at Suzanna. 'She knows the Kingdom better than anyone. And it's rumoured she's got access to the menstruum.'

'Is that true?' said Tung.

Suzanna nodded. The man took a half step away from her. A swell of comments and questions now rose in the room, many of them directed at Romo. He was having none of them, however.

'I've said all I have to say on the subject,' he announced. 'I can't leave my children waiting any longer.'

With that, he turned and started back the way he'd come. Suzanna pursued him, as the controversy escalated afresh.

'Romo!' she called after him.

He stopped, and turned back.

'Help me,' she said. 'Stay with me.'

'There's no time,' he said. 'I've got an appointment to keep, on your grandmother's behalf.'

'But there's so much I don't understand.'

'Didn't Mimi leave you instructions?' he said.

'I was too late. By the time I reached her, she couldn't . . .' She stopped. Her throat was tight; she felt the sorrow of losing Mimi rising up in her. '. . . couldn't speak. All she left me was a book.'

'Then consult that,' Romo said. 'She knew best.'

'It was taken from me,' Suzanna said.

'Then you have to get it back. And what answers you don't find there, put in for yourself.'

This last remark lost Suzanna entirely, but before she could question it Romo spoke again.

'Look *between*,' he said. 'That's the best advice I can offer.'

'Between what?'

Romo frowned. 'Simply *between*,' he said, as though the sense of this was self-evident. 'I know you're the equal of it. You're Mimi's child.'

He leaned towards her, and kissed her.

'You have her look,' he said, his hand trembling against her cheek. She suddenly sensed that his touch was more than friendly; and that she felt something undeniable towards him: something inappropriate between her and her grandmother's husband. They both stepped back from the touch, startled by their feelings.

He began to walk towards the door, his goodnight delivered with his back to her. She went after him a pace or two, but didn't try to delay him any longer. He had business, he'd said. As he pushed open the door there was a roar from the darkness and her heart jumped as beasts appeared around him. He was not under attack, however. He'd spoken of children, and here they were. Lions, half a dozen or more, welcoming him with growls, their golden eyes turned up towards him as they jockeyed for the place closest to his side. The door slammed, eclipsing them.

'They want us to take our leave.'

Jerichau was standing in the passageway behind her. She stared at the closed door for a moment longer, as the sound of the lions faded, then turned to him.

'Are we being thrown out?' she asked.

'No. They just want to debate the problem awhile,' he said. 'Without us.'

She nodded.

'I suggest we walk a little way.'

By the time they opened the door, Romo and the animals had gone; about Mimi's business.

## 2

So they walked.

He had his silence; she, hers. So many feelings to try and comprehend. Her thoughts went back to Mimi, and the sacrifice she'd made, knowing Romo, her beautiful lion-tamer, was sleeping in a place she could not trespass. Had she touched the knots where he was concealed, she wondered?; had she

271

knelt and whispered her love for him to the Weave? The very thought of it was beyond bearing. No wonder she'd been so severe, so stoical. She'd stood guard at the paradise gates, alone; unable to breathe a word of what she knew; fearful of dementia, fearful of death.

'Don't be afraid,' Jerichau said at last.

'I'm not afraid,' she lied, then, remembering that the colours from her would be contradicting her every word, said: 'Well . . . maybe a little. I can't be a Custodian, Jerichau. I'm not the equal of it.'

They'd emerged from the myrtle copse and walked out into a field. Several huge marble beasts stood in the knee-high grass, their species either mythical or extinct, but either way chiselled in loving detail; tusk and fur and tiny eye. She leaned against the flank of one and stared at the ground. They could hear neither the debate behind them nor the bells in the branches; only night-insects going about their business in the shadow of the beasts.

His gaze was upon her – she felt it – but she couldn't raise her head to meet it.

'I think maybe –' he began, then stopped.

The insects chattered on, mocking his struggle for words.

Again, he tried.

'I just wanted to say: I know you're the equal of anything.'

She was going to smile at this courtesy, but:

'No. That's not what I wanted to say.' He took a fresh breath, and with it said: 'I want to go with you.'

'With me?'

'When you go back to the Kingdom. Whether it's with the carpet or without it, I want to be with you.'

Now she looked up, and his dark face was that of an accused man awaiting verdict; hanging on every flicker of her lash.

She smiled, searching for a response. Finally she said:

'Of course. Of course. I'd like that.'

'Yes?' he gasped. 'You would?'

The anxiety fled from his face, replaced by a luminous grin.

'Thank you,' he said. 'I want so much that we should be friends.'

'Then friends we'll be,' she replied.

The stone was chilly against her back; he, in front of her, exuded warmth. And there was she, where Romo had advised her to be: between.

# VII

## SHADWELL ON HIGH

**L**et me down,' said the Salesman to his broken-backed mount. They'd climbed a steep-sided hill, the highest Shadwell could find. The view from the top was impressive.

Norris, however, wasn't much interested in the view. He sat down, labouring for breath, and clutched his one-handed drummer to his chest, leaving Shadwell to stand on the promontory and admire the moon-lit vista spread beneath him.

The journey here had offered a host of extraordinary sights; the occupants of this province, though plainly related to species outside the Fugue, had somehow been coaxed by magic into new forms. How else to explain moths five times the size of his hand, which yowled like mating cats from the tops of the trees? Or the shimmering snakes he'd seen, posing as flames in the niche of a rock? Or the bush the thorns of which bled onto its own blossoms?

Such novelties were everywhere. The pitch he'd offered to his clients when tempting them to the Auction had been colourful enough; but it had scarcely begun to evoke the reality. The Fugue was stranger by far than any words of his had suggested; stranger, and more distressing.

That was what he felt, looking down from the hill-top: distress. It had come over him slowly, as they'd journeyed here, beginning like dyspepsia, and escalating to the point where he felt a kind of terror. At first he'd tried not to admit its origins to himself, but such was its force the feeling could now no longer be denied.

It was *covetousness* that had come to birth in his belly; the one sensation that no true Salesman could ever indulge. He tried to get the better of the ache by viewing the landscape and its contents in strictly commercial terms: how much could he ask for that orchard?; or the islands in that lake?; or the moths? But for once the technique failed him. He looked down over the Fugue and all thought of commerce was swept away.

It was no use to struggle. He had to admit the bitter fact: he'd made a terrible error trying to sell this place.

No price could ever be put on such mind-wracking profusion; no bidder, however wealthy, had the wherewithal to purchase it.

Here he was, looking down on the greatest collection of miracles the world had ever seen, with all ambition to lord it over princes fled.

A new ambition had taken its place. He would be a prince himself. More than a prince.

Here was a country, laid before him. Why should he not be King?

# VIII

## THE VIRGIN BLOODED

Happiness was not a condition Immacolata was much familiar with, but there were places in which she and her sisters felt something close to it. Battlefields at evening, when every breath she drew was somebody else's last; mortuaries and sepulchres. Anywhere death was, they took their ease; played amongst cadavers, and picknicked there.

That was why, when they'd got bored with searching for Shadwell, they came to the Requiem Steps. It was the only place in the Fugue sacred to death. As a child Immacolata had come here day after day to bathe in the sorrow of others. Now her sisters had taken themselves off in search of some unwilling father, and she was here alone, with thoughts so black the night sky was blindingly bright beside them.

She slipped off her shoes, and went down the steps to the black mud at the edge of the river. Here it was the bodies were finally relinquished to the waters. Here the sobs had always been loudest, and faith in the hereafter had trembled in the face of cold fact.

It was many, many years since those rituals had been in vogue. The practice of giving the dead to this or any other river had been stopped; too many of the corpses were being found by the Cuckoos. Cremation had taken over as the standard method of disposal, much to Immacolata's chagrin.

The Steps had dramatized something true, in the way that they descended into mud. Standing there now, with the river moving fast before her, she thought how easy it would be to pitch herself into the flood, and go the way of the dead.

But she would leave too much unfinished business behind. She'd leave the Fugue intact, and her enemies alive. There was no wisdom in that.

No; she had to go on living. To see the Families humiliated; their hopes, like their territories, in dust; their miracles reduced to playthings. Destruction would be altogether too easy for them. It hurt for an instant only, then it was all over. But to see the Seerkind enslaved: that was worth living for.

The roar of the waters soothed her. She grew nostalgic, remembering the bodies she'd seen snatched beneath this tide.

But did she hear another roar, beneath that of the river? She looked up from the murky waters. At the top of the steps was a ramshackle building, little more than a roof supported by columns, in which the lesser mourners had loitered while the final farewells were made at the river-side. She could just see movement there now; fugitives in the shadows. Was it her sisters? She didn't sense their proximity.

Her unspoken question was answered as she crossed the mud back to the bottom step.

'I knew you'd be here.'

Immacolata halted, her foot on the step.

'Of all places . . . here.'

Immacolata felt a twinge of trepidation. Not because of the man who emerged from the shelter of the column, but because of the company he kept. They moved in the shadows behind him, their panting flanks silken. Lions! He'd come with lions.

'Oh yes,' Romo said, seeing the Incantatrix flinch, 'I'm not alone, like she was. This time *you're* the vulnerable one.'

It was true. The lions were unreflective creatures. Her illusions would not mislead them. Nor would her assaults easily touch the tamer, who shared that bestial indifference.

'Sisters . . .' she breathed. 'Come to me.'

The lions were moving into the moonlight, six in all; three male, three female. Their eyes were glued to their owner, awaiting his instructions.

She took a step backwards. The mud was slick beneath her

heel. She almost lost her balance. Where was the Magdalene, and the Hag? She sent another thought in hectic pursuit of them, but fear made it sluggish.

The lions were at the top of the steps now. She didn't dare take her eyes off them, though she loathed the sight. They were so effortlessly magnificent. Much as the thought appalled her, she knew she would have to flee before them. She would have the menstruum carry her up above the river before they reached her. But it was taking its time to flow through her, distracted as she was. She made an attempt to delay their approach.

'You shouldn't trust them . . .' she said.

'The lions?' said Romo, half-smiling.

'The Seerkind. They cheated Mimi as they cheated me. They left her in the Kingdom, while they took refuge. They're cowards and deceivers.'

'And you? What are you?'

Immacolata felt the menstruum begin to suffuse her shadow-self. With her escape certain, she could afford to tell the truth.

'I'm nothing,' she said, her voice now so soft it was almost lost in the din of the river. 'I'm alive as long as my hatred for them keeps me alive.'

It was almost as if the lions understood this last remark, for they came at her suddenly, leaping down the steps to where she stood.

The menstruum rippled about her; she started to rise. Even as she did so the Magdalene appeared from along the river, and let out a cry.

The call diverted Immacolata's attention, her feet inches from the mud. It was all that the first of the lions required. He launched himself from the steps towards her, and before she could avoid the attack, he clawed her from the air. She fell backwards into the mud.

Romo pushed his way through the rest of the pride, calling the animal back before Immacolata mustered her powers. The summons came too late. The menstruum was spiralling around the beast, tearing at its face and flanks; the animal could

278

not have disengaged itself now if it had wanted to. But the menstruum's attack left little in reserve for defence, and the lion landed blow after blow, each gouging a brutal wound. Immacolata shrieked and squirmed in the blood-streaked mud, but the lion would not let her alone.

As its claws opened her face, it let out a throttled roar, and its assault ceased. It stood over Immacolata for an instant, as steam rose from between them; then it staggered sideways. Its abdomen had been opened from throat to testicles. It was not the menstruum's doing, but that of the knife now dropping from Immacolata's hand. The beast, trailing its innards, stumbled a little way then keeled over in the mud.

The rest of the animals growled their distress, but held their positions at Romo's command.

As for Immacolata, the sisters were coming to her aid, but she spat some contemptuous words at them and dragged herself to her knees. The wounds she'd sustained would have left a human being, or indeed most Seerkind, dead in the dirt. Her flesh and upper chest had been traumatically mauled; the flesh hung in sickening ribbons. Still she hauled herself to her feet, and turned her agonized eyes, which were now set in a single wound, on Romo.

'I will destroy everything you ever loved . . .' she said, her voice throbbing, her hand clutching her face while the blood gushed between her fingers. 'The Fugue. The Seerkind. All of it! Wiped away. You have my promise. *You will weep.*'

If it had been in Romo's power he would have had no compunction about dispatching the Incantatrix on the spot. But delivering Immacolata to pastures new was beyond the power of lion or lion-tamer; weakened as the enemy was, she and her sisters would undoubtedly kill the rest of the animals before they reached her. He would have to be content with what their surprise attack had achieved, and hope that Mimi knew, in her resting place, that her torment had been avenged.

He moved towards the felled lion, speaking soft words. Immacolata made no attempt to harm him, but started up towards the steps, her sisters flanking her.

The lions stood their ground, waiting for the order that would unleash them. But Romo was too busy grieving. He had laid his cheek on the cheek of the dying animal, still murmuring to it. Then the words of comfort stopped, and a look scarcely less than tragic came over his face.

The lions heard his silence, and knew what it signified. They turned their heads to him, and as they did so Immacolata rose into the air, a saint of mud and wounds, the wraith-sisters trailing her like corrupted seraphim.

He looked up as they ascended into darkness, a patter of blood falling. Almost as the night erased them he saw Immacolata's head loll, and the sisters rise to her aid. This time the Incantatrix did not despise their support, but let them bear her away.

# IX

# NEVER, AND AGAIN

he ziggurat builder who'd stood guard outside Capra's House was shouting at them from the edge of the field, courtesy preventing him from coming any closer.

'They want you back at the House,' he called.

As they walked back towards the myrtle trees it became apparent that events of some moment were afoot. Members of the Council were already leaving Capra's House, urgency in their step and on their faces. The bells in the trees were all ringing, though there was no breeze moving, and there were lights above the House, like vast fire-flies.

'The Amadou,' said Jerichau.

The lights swooped and rose in elaborate configurations.

'What are they doing?' Suzanna asked.

'Signalling,' Jerichau replied.

'Signalling what?'

As he went to reply, Yolande Dor appeared between the trees and stood in front of Suzanna.

'They're fools to trust you,' she stated flatly. 'But I tell you now, *I'm* not sleeping. You hear me? We have a right to *live*! You damn Cuckoos don't own the earth!' Then she was away, cursing Suzanna as she went.

'That means they're taking Romo's advice,' said Suzanna.

'That's what the Amadou are saying,' Jerachau confirmed, still watching the sky.

'I'm not sure I'm ready for this.'

Tung was at the door, calling her in.

'Hurry, will you? We have precious little time.'

She hesitated. The menstruum offered her no courage now; her stomach felt like a cold furnace: ash and emptiness.

'*I'm* with you,' Jerichau reminded her, reading her anxiety.

His presence was some comfort. Together, they went inside.

When she stepped into the chamber she was greeted by an almost reverential hush. All eyes were turned on her. There was desperation in every face. Last time she'd been here, mere minutes ago, she'd been an invader. Now she was the one upon whom their fragile hopes for survival depended. She tried not to let her fear show, but her hands trembled as she stood before them.

'We're decided,' said Tung.

'Yes,' she replied. 'Yolande told me.'

'We don't like it much,' said one of the number, whom Suzanna recognized as a defector from Yolande's faction. 'But we've got no choice.'

'There are already disturbances at the border,' said Tung. 'The Cuckoos know we're here.'

'And it'll soon be morning,' said Messimeris.

So it would. Dawn could be no more than ninety minutes away. An hour after that, and every curious Cuckoo in the vicinity would be wandering in the Fugue – not quite seeing it perhaps, but knowing there was something to stare at, something to fear. How long after that before there was a reprise of the scene on Lord Street?

'Steps have been taken to begin the re-weaving,' said Dolphi.

'Is that difficult?'

'No,' said Messimeris. 'The Gyre has great power.'

'How long will it take?'

'We have perhaps an hour,' said Tung, 'to teach you about the Weave.'

An hour: what would she learn in an hour?

'Tell me only as much as I need to know for your safety,' she said. 'And no more than that. What I don't know I can't let slip.'

'Point taken,' said Tung. 'No time for formalities, then. Let's begin.'

# X

## THE SUMMONS

Cal woke suddenly.

There was a slight chill in the air, though that wasn't what had woken him. It was Lemuel Lo, calling his name.

'Calhoun . . . Calhoun . . .'

He sat up. Lemuel was at his side, smiling through the thicket of his beard.

'There's someone here asking for you,' he said.

'Oh?'

'We haven't much time, my poet,' he said as Cal struggled to his feet. 'The carpet's being rewoven. In little more than minutes all this'll be sleeping again. And me with it.'

'That can't be right,' said Cal.

'It is, friend. But I have no fear. You'll be watching over us, won't you?'

He clasped Cal's hand in a fierce grip.

'I dreamt something . . .' Cal said.

'What was that?'

'I dreamt that this was real and the other wasn't.'

Lemuel's smile faded. 'I wish what you dreamt were true,' he said. 'But the Kingdom's all too real. It's just that a thing that grows too certain of itself becomes a kind of lie. That's what you dreamt. That the other place is a place of lies.'

Cal nodded. The grip on his hand tightened, as though there was a pact in the making.

'Don't be lost to it, Calhoun. Remember Lo, eh? And the orchard? *Will you?* Then we'll see each other again.'

283

Lemuel embraced him.

'*Remember*,' he said, his mouth next to Cal's ear.

Cal returned the bear-hug as best he could, given Lo's girth. Then the orchard-keeper broke from him.

'Best go quickly,' he said. 'Your visitor has important business, she says,' and he strode away to where the rug was being rolled up, and some last melancholy songs sung.

Cal watched him thread his way between the trees, his fingers brushing against the bark of each as he passed. Commanding them to sweet sleep, no doubt.

'Mr Mooney?'

Cal looked round. There was a small woman with distinctly oriental features standing two trees' breadth from him. In her hand she held a lamp, which she raised as she approached him, her scrutiny both lengthy and unapologetic.

'Well,' she said, her voice musical, 'he told me you were handsome, and so you are. In a quirky kind of way.'

She cocked her head slightly, as if trying to make better sense of Cal's physiognomy.

'How old are you?'

'Twenty-six. Why?'

'Twenty-six,' she said. 'His mathematics is terrible.'

So's mine, Cal was about to say, but there were other more pressing questions. The first of which was:

'Who are you?'

'I'm Chloe,' came the woman's reply. 'I've come to fetch you. We should hurry. He gets impatient.'

'Who does?'

'Even if we had time to talk I'm forbidden to tell you,' Chloe replied. 'But he's eager to see you, that I can say. Very eager.'

She turned and started to walk away from the corridor of trees. She was still speaking, but Cal couldn't catch the words. He set off in pursuit of her, the end of a sentence drifting back to him.

'– not time by foot –'

'What did you say?' he asked, coming abreast of her.

'We have to travel quickly,' she said.

They had reached the perimeter of the orchard, and there

stood, of all things, a rickshaw. Leaning on the handles, smoking a thin black cigarette, was a wiry middle-aged man, dressed in bright blue pantaloons and a shabby vest. On his head, a bowler hat. 'This is Floris,' Chloe told Cal. 'Please get in.'

Cal did as he was told, settling himself amongst a litter of cushions. He could not have refused this adventure if his life had depended upon it. Chloe got in beside him.

'Hurry,' she said to the driver, and they took off like the wind.

# XI

## AT THE GAZEBO

### 1

He'd promised himself he wouldn't look back at the orchard, and he was as good as his promise until the very last when, before the surrounding night claimed the sight entirely, he weakened and glanced round.

He could just see the ring of light where he'd stood and recited Mad Mooney's verse; then the rickshaw turned a corner, and the sight was gone.

Floris was responsive to Chloe's imperative: hurry they did. The vehicle rocked and rolled, hauled over stone and pasture with equal gusto, and threatening all the while to pitch its passengers out. Cal held onto the side of the vehicle and watched the Fugue pass by. He cursed himself for sleeping as he had, and missing a night of exploration. When he'd first glimpsed the Weaveworld it had seemed so very familiar, but travelling these roads he felt like a tourist, ogling the sights of an alien country.

'It's a strange place,' he said, as they passed beneath a rock which had been carved in the form of a vast, teetering wave.

'What did you expect?' said Chloe. 'Your own back yard?'

'Not exactly. But I thought I knew it, in a way. At least in dreams.'

'Paradise always has to be stranger than you expect, doesn't it?, or it loses its power to enchant. And you are enchanted.'

'Yes,' he said. 'And afraid.'

'Of course you are,' said Chloe. 'It keeps the blood fresh.'

He didn't really comprehend the remark, but there were

other claims upon his attention. At every turn and brow a fresh vista. And ahead the most impressive sight of all: the roiling cloud-wall of the Gyre.

'Is that where we're headed?' he asked.

'Close to it,' said Chloe.

They plunged suddenly into a copse of birch-trees, the silver bark bright by the lightning flashes from the cloud, then headed up a small incline, which Floris took at an impressive rate. Beyond the copse the land abruptly changed character. The earth was now dark, almost black, and the vegetation seemed more appropriate to a hot-house than the open air. More than that, as they reached the top of the rise and began to make their way along its spine, Cal found himself subject to odd hallucinations. At either side of the road he kept glimpsing scenes that weren't quite *there*; like images on a mis-tuned television, slipping out of focus and back in again. He saw a house built like an observatory, with horses grazing around it; saw several women in dresses of watered silk, laughing together. There was much else he saw, but none of it for more than a few seconds.

'You find it unsettling?' said Chloe.

'What's going on?'

'This is paradoxical ground. Strictly speaking, you shouldn't be here at all. There are always dangers.'

'What dangers?'

If she offered a reply it was drowned out by a thunder-clap from the belly of the Gyre, which followed upon lilac lightning. They were within a quarter of a mile of the cloud now; the hairs on Cal's arms and nape stood up; his testicles ached.

But Chloe wasn't interested in the Mantle. She was gazing at the Amadou, moving in the sky behind them.

'The re-weaving's under way,' she said. 'That's why the Gyre's so restless. We have less time than I thought.'

On this cue Floris picked up his pace to a run, which threw loose earth up from his heels into the rickshaw.

'It's for the best,' said Chloe. 'This way he won't have time to get maudlin.'

Three minutes more of bruising travel and they came to a

small stone bridge, at which Floris brought the vehicle to a dusty halt.

'Here we disembark,' said Chloe, and led Cal up a short flight of well-trodden steps to the bridge. It spanned a narrow but deep gorge, the sides of which were mossy and plumed with ferns. Water rushed beneath, feeding a pool where fishes jumped.

'Come, come –' said Chloe, and hurried Cal over the bridge.

Ahead was a house, its doors and shutters flung wide. There were copious bird-droppings on the tiled roof, and several large black pigs slumbering against the wall. One raised itself as Cal and Chloe approached the threshold, snuffling at Cal's legs before returning to its porcine slumbers.

There were no burning lights inside; the only illumination came from the lightning, which this close to the Gyre was practically constant. By it, Cal surveyed the room Chloe had ushered him into. It was sparsely furnished, but there were papers and books on every available surface. On the floor lay a collection of thread-bare rugs; and on one of these a vast – and probably vastly ancient – tortoise. At the far end of the room was a large window, which looked onto the Mantle. In front of it a man was seated in a large, plain chair.

'Here he is,' said Chloe. Cal wasn't sure who was being introduced to whom.

Either the chair or its occupant creaked as the man stood up. He was old, though not as old as the tortoise; about Brendan's age, Cal guessed. The face, though clearly acquainted with laughter, had known pain too. A mark, like a smoke stain, ran from his hairline to the bridge of his nose, where it veered off down his right cheek. It didn't disfigure his face, rather lent it an authority his features wouldn't otherwise have possessed. The lightning came and went, burning the man's silhouette into Cal's mind, but his host said nothing. He just looked at Cal, and looked some more. There was pleasure on his face, though quite why Cal didn't know. Nor did he feel ready to ask, at least not until the other broke the silence between them. That didn't seem to be on the cards, however. The man just stared.

It was difficult to be certain of much in the flare of the lightning, but Cal thought there was something familiar about the fellow. Suspecting they'd stand there for hours unless he initiated a conversation, he voiced the question his mind had already asked.

'Do I know you from somewhere?'

The old man's eyes narrowed, as if he wanted to sharpen his sight to pin-point and pierce Cal's heart. But there was no verbal reply.

'He's not allowed to converse with you,' Chloe explained. 'People who live this close to the Gyre —' Her words died.

'What?' said Cal.

'There's not time to explain,' she said. 'Just believe me.'

The man had not taken his gaze off Cal for a second, not even to blink. The perusal was quite benign; perhaps even loving. Cal was suddenly overcome by a fierce desire to stay; to forget the Kingdom, and sleep in the Weave, here; pigs, lightning and all.

But already Chloe had her hand on his arm.

'We must go,' she said.

'So soon?' he protested.

'We're taking chances bringing you here in the first place,' she said.

The old man was now moving towards them, his step steady, his gaze the same. But Chloe intervened.

'Now don't,' she said.

He frowned, his mouth tight. But he came no closer.

'We have to be away,' she told him. 'You know we must.'

He nodded. Were there tears in his eyes? Cal thought so.

'I'll be back soon enough,' she told him. 'I'll just take him to the border. All right?'

Again, a single nod.

Cal raised his hand in a tentative wave.

'Well,' he said, more mystified than ever. 'It's . . . it's been . . . an honour.'

A faint smile creased the man's face,

'He knows,' said Chloe. 'Believe me.'

289

She took Cal to the door. The lightning blazed through the room; the thunder made the air shake.

At the threshold Cal gave his host one last look, and to his astonishment – indeed to his delight – the man's smile became a grin that had a subtle mischief about it.

'Take care,' Cal said.

Grinning even as the tears ran down his cheeks, the man waved him away and turned back towards the window.


2


The rickshaw was waiting on the far side of the bridge. Chloe bundled Cal into his seat, throwing the tasselled cushions out to lighten the load.

'Be swift,' she said to Floris. No sooner had she spoken than they were off.

It was a hair-raising journey. A great urgency had seized everything and everybody, as the Fugue prepared to lose its substance to pattern again. Overhead, the night sky was a maze of birds; the fields were rife with animals. There was everywhere a great readying, as if for some momentous dive.

'Do you dream?' Cal asked Chloe as they travelled. The question had come out of the blue, but was suddenly of great importance to him.

'Dream?' said Chloe.

'When you're in the Weave?'

'Perhaps –' she said. She seemed preoccupied. '– but I never remember my dreams. I sleep too deeply . . .' She faltered, then looked away from Cal before saying, '. . . like death.'

'You'll wake again soon,' he said, understanding the melancholy that had come upon her. 'It'll only be a few days.'

He tried to sound confident, but doubted that he was succeeding. He knew all too little of what the night had brought. Was Shadwell still alive; and the sisters? And if so *where*?

'I'm going to help you,' he said. 'That I *do* know. I'm part of this place now.'

'Oh yes,' she said with great gravity. 'That you are. But

290

Cal –' She looked at him, her hand taking his, and he felt a bond between them, an intimacy even, which seemed out of all proportion to the meagre time they'd known each other. 'Cal. Future history is full of tricks.'

'I don't follow.'

'Things can be so easily erased,' she said. 'And *forever*. Believe me. Forever. Entire lives gone, as if they'd never been lived.'

'Am I missing something?' he said.

'Just don't assume everything's guaranteed.'

'I don't,' he told her.

'Good. Good.' She seemed a little cheered by this. 'You're a fine man, Calhoun. But you'll forget.'

'Forget what?'

'All this. The Fugue.'

He laughed. 'Never,' he said.

'Oh but you will. Indeed maybe you have to. Have to, or your heart would break.'

He thought of Lemuel again, and his parting words. *Remember*, he'd said. Was it really so difficult?

If there were any further words to be said on the subject, they went unvoiced, for at this point Floris brought the rickshaw to an abrupt halt.

'What's the problem?' Chloe wanted to know.

The rickshaw driver pointed dead ahead. No more than a hundred yards from where the rickshaw stood the landscape and all it contained was losing itself to the Weave, solid matter becoming clouds of colour, from which the threads of the carpet would be drawn.

'So soon,' said Chloe. 'Get out, Calhoun. We can take you no further.'

The line of the Weave was approaching like a forest fire, eating up everything in its path. It was an awesome scene. Though he knew perfectly well what procedures were under way here – and knew them to be benevolent – the sight was almost chilling. A world was dissolving before his very eyes.

'You're on your own from here,' said Chloe. 'About turn, Floris! And *fly*!'

The rickshaw was turned.

'What happens to me?' said Cal.

'You're a Cuckoo,' Chloe shouted back at him, as Floris hauled the rickshaw away. 'You can simply walk out the other side!'

She shouted something else, which he failed to catch.

He hoped to God it wasn't a prayer.

# XII

## A VANISHING BREED

### 1

Despite Chloe's words, the spectacle ahead offered little comfort. The devouring line was approaching at considerable speed, and it left nothing unchanged. His gut feeling was to flee before it, but he knew that would be a vain manœuvre. This same transfiguring tide would be eating in from all compass points: sooner or later there would be nowhere left to run.

Instead of standing still and letting it come to fetch him, he elected to walk towards it, and brave its touch.

The air began to itch around him as he took his first hesitant steps. The ground squirmed and shook beneath his feet. A few more yards and the region he was walking through actually began to shift. Loose pebbles were snatched into the flux; leaves plucked from bush and tree.

'This is going to hurt,' he thought.

The frontier was no more than ten yards from him now, and he could see with astonishing clarity the processes at work: the raptures of the Loom dividing the matter of the Fugue into strands, then drawing these up into the air and knotting them – those knots in their turn filling the air like countless insects, until the final rapture called them into the carpet.

He could afford to wonder at this sight for seconds only before he and it met each other, strands leaping up around him like rainbow fountains. There was no time for farewells: the Fugue simply vanished from sight, leaving him immersed in the working of the Loom. The rising threads gave him the sensation of falling, as though the knots were destined for heaven, and he a damned soul. But it wasn't heaven above him: it was *pattern*. A kaleidoscope that defeated eye and mind, its motifs configuring and re-configuring as they found their place beside their fellows. Even now he was certain he'd be similarly metamorphosed; his flesh and bone become symbol, and he be woven into the grand design.

But Chloe's prayer, if that it had been, afforded him protection. The Loom rejected his Cuckoo-stuff and passed him by. One minute he was in the midst of the Weave. The next the glories of the Fugue were behind him, and he was left standing in a bare field.

## 2

He wasn't alone there. Several dozen Seerkind had chosen to step out into the Kingdom. Some stood alone watching their home consumed by the Weave, others were in small groups, debating feverishly; yet others were already heading off into the gloom before the Adamaticals came looking for them.

Among them, lit by the blaze of the Weave, a face he recognized: that of Apolline Dubois. He went to her. She saw him coming, but offered no welcome.

'Have you seen Suzanna?' he asked her.

She shook her head. 'I've been cremating Frederick, and setting my affairs to rights,' she said.

She got no further. An elegant individual, his cheeks rouged, now appeared at her side. He looked every inch a pimp.

'We should go, Moth,' he said. 'Before the beasts are upon us.'

'I know,' Apolline said to him. Then to Cal: 'We're going to make our fortunes. Teaching you Cuckoos the meaning of desire.'

Her companion offered a less than wholesome grin. More than half his teeth were gold.

'There are high times ahead,' she said, and patted Cal's cheek. 'So you come see me one of these days,' she said. 'We'll treat you well.'

She took the pimp's arm.

'*Bon chance*,' she said, and the pair hurried away.

The line of the Weave was by now a good distance from where Cal stood, and the numbers of Seerkind who'd emerged was well into three figures. He went amongst them, still looking for Suzanna. His presence was largely ignored; they had more pressing concerns, these people, delivered into the late twentieth century with only magic to keep them from harm. He didn't envy them.

Amongst the refugees he caught sight of three of the Buyers, standing dazed and dusty, their faces blank. What would they make of tonight's experiences he wondered. Would they pour the whole story out to their friends, and endure the disbelief and contempt heaped on their heads; or would they let the tale fester untold? The latter, he suspected.

Dawn was close. The weaker stars had already disappeared, and even the brightest were uncertain of themselves.

'It's over . . .' he heard somebody murmur.

He looked back towards the Weave; the brilliance of its making had almost flickered out.

But suddenly, a shout in the night, and a beat later Cal saw three lights – members of the Amadou – rising from the embers of the Weave at enormous speed. They drew together as they rose, until, high above the streets and fields, they collided.

The blaze of their meeting illuminated the landscape as far as the eye could see. By it Cal glimpsed Seerkind running in all directions, averting their eyes from the brilliance.

Then the light died, and the pre-dawn gloom that followed seemed so impenetrable by contrast that Cal was effectively blind for a minute or more. As, by slow degrees, the world re-established itself about him, he realized that there had been nothing arbitrary about the fireworks or their effect.

The Seerkind had disappeared. Where, ninety seconds ago, there had been scraggling figures all around him, there was now emptiness. Under the cover of light, they'd made their escape.

# XIII

## A PROPOSAL

### 1

Hobart had seen the blaze of the Amadou too, though he was still two and a half miles from the spot. The night had brought disaster upon disaster. Richardson, still jittery after events at Headquarters, had twice driven the car into the back of stationary vehicles, and their route, which had taken them all over the Wirral, had been a series of cul-de-sacs.

But at last, here it was: a sign that their quarry was close.

'What was that?' said Richardson. 'Looked like something exploding.'

'God knows,' said Hobart. 'I wouldn't put anything past these people. Especially the woman.'

'Should we call in some back-up, sir? We don't know their numbers.'

'Even if we could —' Hobart said, switching off the white noise which had swallowed Downey hours ago, '— I want to keep this quiet until we know what's what. Kill the headlights.'

The driver did so, and they drove on in the murk that preceded daybreak. Hobart thought he could see figures moving in the mist beyond the grey foliage that lined the road. There was no time to investigate however; he would have to trust his instinct that the woman was somewhere up ahead.

Suddenly there was somebody in the road ahead of them. Cursing, Richardson threw the wheel over, but the figure seemed to leap up and over the car.

The vehicle mounted the pavement, and ran a few yards before Richardson brought it under control again.

'*Shit*. Did you see that?'

Hobart had, and felt the same aching unease he'd felt back at Headquarters. These people were holding weapons that worked on a man's sense of what was real, and he loved reality more than his balls.

'*Did you see?*' said Richardson. 'The fucker just *flew*.'

'No,' Hobart said firmly. 'There was no flying. Understood?'

'Yes, sir.'

'Don't trust your eyes. Trust me.'

'Yes, sir.'

'And if anything else gets in your way, *run it down*.'

## 2

The light that had blinded Cal blinded Shadwell too. He fell from the back of his human horse, and scrabbled around in the dirt until the world began to come back into focus. When it did two sights greeted him. One, that of Norris, lying on the ground sobbing like an infant. The other, Suzanna, accompanied by two of the Kind, emerging from the rubble of Shearman's house.

They weren't empty-handed. They were carrying the carpet. God, the carpet! He looked about him for the Incantatrix, but there was no-one near to aid him except the horse, who was well past aiding anybody.

*Stay calm*, he told himself, *you've still got the jacket*. He brushed off the worst of the dirt he'd acquired, centred the knot of his tie, then walked over to intercept the thieves.

'Thank you so much,' he said as he approached them, 'for preserving my property.'

Suzanna gave him a single glance, then told the carpet-bearers:

'Ignore him.'

That said, she led them towards the road.

Shadwell went after them quickly, and took firm hold of the woman's arm. He was determined to preserve his politeness as long as possible; it always confused the enemy.

'Do we have a problem here?' he wondered.

'No problem,' Suzanna said.

'The carpet belongs to me, Miss Parrish. I insist that it remain here.'

Suzanna looked around for Jerichau. They'd become separated in the last minutes of her briefing at Capra's House, when Messimeris had taken her aside to offer her some words of advice. He had still been in full flow when the Weave had reached the doorstep of Capra's House: she had never heard his final remarks.

'Please . . .' said Shadwell, smiling. 'We can surely come to some arrangement. If you wish, I'll buy the item off you. How much shall we say?'

He opened his jacket, no longer directing his spiel at Suzanna but at the two who were carrying the carpet. Strong armed they might be, but easy fodder. Already they were staring into the folds of the jacket.

'Maybe you see something you like?' he said.

'It's a trick,' said Suzanna.

'But *look* –' one of them said to her, and damn it if she instinctively didn't do exactly that. Had the night not brought so many exhausting diversions she would have had the strength to avert her sight immediately, but she wasn't fast enough. Something glimmered in the mother-of-pearl lining, and she could not quite unhook her gaze.

'You *do* see something –' Shadwell said to her. 'Something pretty, for a pretty woman.'

She did. The raptures of the jacket had seized her in two seconds flat, and she couldn't resist its mischief.

At the back of her head a voice called her name, but she ignored it. Again, it called. *Look away*, it said, but she could see something taking shape in the lining, and it tantalized her.

'*No, damn you!*' the same voice shouted, and this time a blurred figure came between her and Shadwell. Her reverie broke, and she was thrown from the jacket's soothing embrace

298

to see Cal in front of her, throwing a barrage of punches at the enemy. Shadwell was much the bigger of the two men, but the heat of Cal's fury had momentarily cowed him.

'Get the fuck out of here!' Cal yelled.

By now Shadwell had overcome his shock, and launched himself upon Cal, who reeled before the retaliation. Knowing he'd lose the bout in seconds, he ducked beneath Shadwell's fists and took hold of the Salesman in a bear-hug. They wrestled for several seconds: precious time which Suzanna seized to lead the carpet-carriers through the rubble and away.

Their escape came not a moment too soon. In the time she'd been distracted by the jacket, day had almost come upon them. They'd soon be easy targets for Immacolata, or indeed anyone else who wanted to stop them.

Hobart, for instance. She saw him now, as they reached the edge of Shearman's estate, stepping out of a car parked in the street. Even in this dubious light – and at some distance – she knew it was he. Her hatred smelt him. And she knew too, with some prophetic sense the menstruum had undammed in her, that even if they escaped him now, the pursuit would not stop here. She'd made an enemy for the millennium.

She didn't watch him for long. Why bother? She could perfectly recall every nick and pore upon his barren face; and if the memory ever grew a little dim all she would have to do was look over her shoulder.

Damn him, he'd be there.


3


Though Cal held onto Shadwell with the tenacity of a terrier, the Salesman's superior weight rapidly gained the day. Cal was thrown down amongst the bricks, and Shadwell closed in. No quarter was given. Shadwell began to kick him, not once but a dozen times.

'*Fucking bastard!*' he yelled.

The kicks kept coming, timed to prevent Cal getting up.

'*I'm going to break every bone in your fucking body*,' Shadwell promised. '*I'm going to fucking kill you.*'

He might have done it too, but that somebody said:

'You –'

Shadwell's assault stopped momentarily, and Cal looked past the Salesman's legs to the man in dark glasses who was approaching. It was the policeman from Chariot Street.

Shadwell turned on the man.

'Who the hell are you?' he said.

'Inspector Hobart,' came the reply.

Cal could imagine the wave of guilelessness that would now be breaking over Shadwell's face. He could hear it in the man's voice:

'Inspector. Of course. Of *course*.'

'And you?' Hobart returned. 'Who are *you*?'

Cal didn't hear the rest of the exchange. He was occupied with the business of making his bruised body crawl away through the rubble, hoping the same good fortune that had let him escape alive had speeded Suzanna on her way.


'Where is she?'

'Where's who?'

'The woman who was here,' said Hobart. He took off his glasses, the better to see this suspect in the half-light. The man has dangerous eyes, thought Shadwell. He has the eyes of a rabid fox. And he wants Suzanna too. How interesting.

'Her name is Suzanna Parrish,' said Hobart.

'Ah,' said Shadwell.

'You know her?'

'Indeed I do. She's a thief.'

'She's a good deal worse than that.'

*What's worse than a thief?* thought Shadwell. But said: 'Is that so?'

'She's wanted for questioning on charges of terrorism.'

'And you're here to arrest her?'

'I am.'

'Good man,' said Shadwell. What better? he thought: an

300

upstanding, fine-principled, Law-loving despot. Who could ask for a better ally in such troubled times?

'I have some evidence,' he said, 'that may be of value to you. But strictly for your eyes only.'

On Hobart's instruction Richardson retired a little way.

'I'm in no mood for games,' Hobart warned.

'Believe me,' said Shadwell, 'upon my mother's eyes: *this is no game.*'

He opened his jacket. The Inspector's fretful glance went immediately to the lining. He's hungry, thought Shadwell; he's *so* hungry. But what for? That would be interesting to see. What would friend Hobart desire most in all the wide world?

'Maybe . . . you see something there that catches your eye?'

Hobart smiled; nodded.

'You do? Then take it, please. It's yours.'

The Inspector reached towards the jacket.

'Go on,' Shadwell encouraged him. He'd never seen such a look on any human face: such a wilderness of innocent malice.

A light ignited within the jacket, and Hobart's eyes suddenly grew wilder still. Then he was drawing his hand out of the lining, and Shadwell almost let out a yelp of surprise as he shared the lunatic's vision. In the palm of the man's hand a livid fire was burning, its flames yellow and white. They leapt a foot high, eager for something to consume, their brilliance echoed in Hobart's eyes.

'Oh yes,' said Hobart. 'Give me fire —'

'It's yours, my friend.'

'— and I'll burn them away.'

Shadwell smiled.

'You and I together,' he proposed.


Thus began a marriage made in Hell.

# Part Six

# Back Among the Blind Men

'If a man could pass through
Paradise in a dream, and have
a flower presented to him as a
pledge that his soul had really
been there, and if he found that
flower in his hand when he
awoke – Aye, and what then?'

S. T. Coleridge
*Anima Poetae*

# I

## TIME'S GONE BY

### 1

The people of Chariot Street had witnessed some rare scenes in recent times, but they'd re-established the status quo with admirable zeal. It was just before eight in the morning when Cal got off the bus and began the short walk to the Mooney residence, and everywhere along the street the same domestic rituals that he'd witnessed here since his childhood were being played out. Radios announced the morning's news through open windows and doors: a Parliamentarian had been found dead in his mistress' arms; bombs had been dropped in the Middle East. Slaughter and scandal, scandal and slaughter. And was the tea too weak this morning, my dear?; and did the children wash behind their ears?

He let himself into the house, turning over yet again the problem of what to tell Brendan. Anything less than the truth might beg more questions than it answered; and yet to tell the whole story . . . was that even *possible*? Did the words exist to evoke more than an echo of the sights he'd seen, the feelings he'd felt?

The house was quiet, which was worrying. Brendan had been a dawn riser since his days working on the Docks; even during the worst of recent times he'd been up to greet his grief early.

Cal called his father's name. There was no response.

He went through to the kitchen. The garden looked like a battlefield. He called again, then went to search upstairs.

His father's bedroom door was closed. He tried the handle, but the door was locked from the inside, something he'd never known happen before. He knocked lightly.

'Dad?' he said. 'Are you there?'

He waited several seconds, listening closely, then repeated his enquiry. This time from within came a quiet sobbing.

'Thank God,' he breathed. 'Dad? It's Cal.' The sobbing softened. 'Will you let me in, Dad?'

There was a short interval; then he heard his father's footsteps as he crossed to the bedroom door. The key was turned; the door was opened a reluctant six inches.

The face on the other side was more shadow than man. Brendan looked neither to have washed nor shaved since the previous day.

'Oh God . . . Dad.'

Brendan peered at his son with naked suspicion. 'Is it really you?'

The comment reminded Cal of how he must look: his face bloodied and bruised.

'I'm all right, Dad,' he said, offering a smile. 'What about you?'

'Are all the doors closed?' Brendan wanted to know.

'The doors? Yes.'

'And the windows?'

'Yes.'

Brendan nodded. 'You're absolutely sure?'

'I told you, yes. What's wrong, Dad?'

'The rats,' said Brendan, his eyes scanning the landing behind Cal. 'I heard them all night. They came up the stairs, they did. Sat at the top of the stairs. I heard them. Size of cats they were. They sat there waiting for me to come out.'

'Well they're not here any longer.'

'Got in through the fence. Off the embankment. Dozens of them.'

'Why don't we go downstairs?' Cal suggested. 'I can make you some breakfast.'

'No. I'm not coming down. Not today.'

306

'Then I'll make something and bring it up, shall I?'

'If you like,' said Brendan.

As Cal started down the stairs again, he heard his father lock and bolt the door once more.

## 2

In the middle of the morning, a knock on the door. It was Mrs Vallance, whose house was opposite the Mooneys'.

'I was just passing,' she said, this fact belied by the slippers on her feet. 'I thought I'd see how your father was doing. He was very odd with the police, I heard. What did you do to your face?'

'I'm all right.'

'I had a very polite officer interview me,' the woman said. 'He asked me . . .' she lowered her voice, '. . . if your father was unbalanced.'

Cal bit back a retort.

'They wanted to talk to you too, of course,' she said.

'Well I'm here now,' said Cal. 'If they need me.'

'My boy Raymond said he saw you on the railway. Running off, he said.'

'Goodbye, Mrs Vallance.'

'And he's got good eyes has Raymond.'

'I said goodbye,' said Cal, and slammed the door in the woman's self-satisfied face.

## 3

Her visit was not the last of the day; several people called to see that all was well. There was clearly much gossip in the street about the Mooney household. Perhaps some bright spark had realized that it had been the centre of the previous day's drama.

Every time there was a knock on the door, Cal expected to see Shadwell on the step. But apparently the Salesman had

307

more urgent concerns than finishing the job he'd begun in the ruins of Shearman's house. Or perhaps he was simply waiting for more propitious stars.

Then, just after noon, while Cal was out at the loft feeding the birds, the telephone rang.

He raced inside and snatched it up. Even before she spoke Cal knew it was Suzanna.

'Where are you?'

She was breathless, and agitated.

'We have to get out of the city, Cal. They're after us.'

'Shadwell?'

'Not just Shadwell. The police.'

'Have you got the carpet?'

'Yes.'

'Well then tell me where you are. I'll come and —'

'I can't. Not on the 'phone.'

'It's not tapped, for God's sake.'

'Any bets?'

'I have to see you,' he said, somewhere between a request and a demand.

'Yes . . .' she replied, her voice softening. 'Yes, of course . . .'

'How?'

There was a long silence. Then she said: 'Where you made your confession.'

'What?'

'You remember.'

He thought about it. What confession had he ever made to her? Oh yes: *I love you.* How could he have forgotten that?

'Yes?' she said.

'Yes. When?'

'An hour.'

'I'll be there.'

'We don't have much time, Cal.'

He was going to tell her he knew that, but the line was already dead.

\*

308

The ache in his bruised bones improved miraculously after the conversation; his step was light as he went upstairs to check on Brendan.

'I have to go out for a while, Dad.'

'Have you locked all the doors?' his father asked.

'Yes, the house is locked and bolted. Nothing can get in. Is there anything else you need?'

Brendan took a moment to consider the question.

'I'd like some whisky,' he said finally.

'Do we have any?'

'In the book-case,' said the old man. 'Behind the Dickens.'

'I'll fetch it for you.'

He was sliding the bottle from its hiding place when the door-bell rang again. He was of half a mind not to answer it, but the visitor insisted.

'I'll be with you in a minute,' he called upstairs; then opened the door.

The man in the dark glasses said:

'Calhoun Mooney?'

'Yes.'

'My name's Inspector Hobart; this is Officer Richardson. We're here to ask you some questions.'

'Right now?' said Cal. 'I'm just about to go out.'

'Urgent business?' said Hobart.

Wiser to say no, Cal reasoned.

'Not exactly,' he said.

'Then you won't mind us taking up some time,' said Hobart, and the two of them were inside the house in seconds.

'Close the door,' Hobart instructed his colleague. 'You look flustered, Mooney. Have you got something to hide?'

'Why should . . . ? No.'

'We're in possession of information to the contrary.'

From above, Brendan called for his whisky.

'Who's that?'

'It's my father,' said Cal. 'He wanted a drink.'

Richardson plucked the bottle from Cal's hand and crossed to the bottom of the stairs.

'Don't go up,' said Cal. 'You'll frighten him.'

'Nervous family,' Richardson remarked.

'He's not been well,' said Cal.

'My men are like lambs,' said Hobart. 'As long as you're within the law.'

Again, Brendan's voice drifted down:

'Cal? Who is it?'

'Just someone who wants a word with me, Dad,' Cal said.

There was another answer in his throat, though. One which he swallowed unsaid. A truer answer.

*It's the rats, Dad. They got in after all.*

4

The minutes ticked by. The question came around and around, as if on a carousel. It was apparent from Hobart's probing that he'd spoken at length with Shadwell, so outright denials from Cal were fruitless. He was obliged to tell what little part of the truth he could. Yes, he did know a woman called Suzanna Parrish. No, he knew nothing of her personal history, nor had she spoken of her political affiliations. Yes, he had seen her in the last twenty-four hours. No, he did not know where she was now.

As he answered the questions he tried not to think of her waiting for him at the river; waiting and not finding him and going away. But the more he tried to put the thought from his head, the more it returned.

'Restless, Mooney?'

'I'm a little hot, that's all.'

'Got an appointment to keep, have you?'

'No.'

'Where is she, Mooney?'

'I don't know.'

'There's no sense in protecting her. She's the worst filth, Mooney. Believe me. I've seen what she can do. Things you wouldn't believe. Makes my stomach turn over to think of it.'

He spoke with complete conviction. Cal didn't doubt that he meant all he said.

'What are you, Mooney?'

'What do you mean?'

'Are you my friend or my enemy? There's no middle way, you see. No *maybe*. Friend or enemy. Which?'

'I've done nothing against the law.'

'I'll be the one to decide that,' said Hobart. 'I know the Law. I know it and love it. And I won't have it spat on, Mooney. Not by you or anybody.' He took a breath. Then stated: 'You're a liar, Mooney. I don't know how deep you're in this, or why, but I do know you're a liar.' A pause. Then: 'So we'll start over again, shall we?'

'I've told you everything I know.'

'We'll start from the beginning. How did you meet the terrorist Suzanna Parrish?'

5

After two and three quarter hours on the carousel, Hobart finally bored of the ride, and pronounced that he was finished with Cal for now. No charges would be pressed, at least not immediately, but Cal should consider himself under suspicion.

'You made yourself two enemies today, Mooney,' Hobart said. 'Me and the Law. You'll live to regret that.'

Then the rats left.

Cal sat in the back room for five minutes, trying to gather his thoughts, then went up to see how Brendan was faring. The old man was asleep. Leaving his father to his dreams, Cal went in search of his own.

6

She'd gone, of course; long ago.

He wandered around in the vicinity, searching amongst the warehouses, hoping she'd left some message for him, but there was none to be found.

Exhausted by all the day had brought, he headed home. As he stepped through the gate back onto the Dock Road he caught sight of someone watching him from a parked car. One of Hobart's clan, perhaps; one of the Law-lovers. Maybe Suzanna had been nearby after all, but unable to make her presence known for fear of being spotted. The thought of her being so close, frustrating as it was, cushioned the blow of not seeing her, at least a little. When things were safe, she'd call him and arrange another rendezvous.

In the evening, the wind got up, and it gusted through the night and the following day, bringing the first chill of autumn with it. But it brought no news.

# II

## DESPAIR

And so it went on for a week and a half: no
news, no news.

He returned to work, claiming his father's
illness as reason for his absence, and took up
where he'd left off amid the claim forms. At
lunchtimes he came back to the house to heat
up some food for Brendan – who, though he could be coaxed
from his room, was painfully anxious to return to it – and to
feed the birds. In the evenings he made some attempt to tidy
the garden; he even patched the fence. But these tasks received
only a fraction of his attention. However many diversions he
put between himself and his impatience, nine out of every ten
thoughts were of Suzanna and her precious burden.

But the more days that went by without word from her, the
more he began to think the unthinkable: that she wasn't going
to ring. Either she feared the consequences of trying to make
contact or, worse, she no longer could. Towards the end of
the second week, he decided to try and find the carpet by the
only means available to him. He set the pigeons free.

They rose up into the air in an aerial ovation, and circled
the house. The sight reminded him of that first day in Rue
Street, and his spirits lifted.

'Go on,' he willed them. '*Go on*.'

Round and round they flew, as if orienting themselves. His
heart beat a little faster each time it seemed one of them was
detaching itself from the flock to head off. Running shoes on,
he was ready to follow.

But after all too short a time they began to tire of their liberation. One by one they fluttered down again – even 33 – some landing in the garden, others on the gutters of the house. A few even flew straight back into the loft. Their perches were cramped, and doubtless the night trains disturbed their sleep, but for most of them it was the only habitat they'd ever known.

Though there were surely winds up there to tempt them, winds that smelt of places lusher than their loft beside the railway line, they had no wish to chance their wings on such currents.

He cursed them for their lack of enterprise; and fed them; and watered them; and finally returned despondently to the house, where Brendan was talking of rats again.

# III

# FORGETFULNESS

## 1

The third week of September brought rain. Not the torrents of August, which had poured from operatic skies, but drizzles and piddlings. The days grew greyer; and so, it seemed, did Brendan. Though Cal made daily attempts to persuade his father downstairs, he would no longer come. Cal also made two or three valiant efforts to talk about what had happened a month before, but the old man was simply not interested. His eyes became glazed as soon as he sensed the drift of the conversation, and if Cal persisted he grew irritable.

The professionals judged that Brendan was suffering from senile dementia, an irreversible process which would finally make him impossible for Cal to nurse. It might be best for all concerned, they advised, if a place were found in a Nursing Home, where Brendan could be cared for twenty-four hours a day.

Cal rejected the suggestion. He was certain that Brendan's cleaving to a room he knew – one he'd shared with Eileen for so many years – was all that was keeping him from total breakdown.

He was not alone in his attempts to nurse his father. Two days after he'd failed to set the pigeons flying, Geraldine had appeared at the house. There was ten minutes of hesitant apologies and explanations, then Brendan's condition entered the exchange and Geraldine's good sense came triumphantly to the fore. Forget our differences, she said, I want to help.

315

Cal was not about to refuse the offer. Brendan responded to Geraldine's presence as a child to a long-lost teat. He was cosseted and indulged, and with Geraldine in the house in Eileen's place, Cal found himself falling back into the old domestic routines. The affection he felt for Geraldine was painless, which was surely the most certain sign of how slight it was. When she was there he was happy to be with her. But he seldom, if ever, missed her.

As to the Fugue, he did his best to keep his memories of it sharp, but it was by no means easy. The Kingdom had ways to induce forgetfulness so subtle and so numerous he was scarcely aware of how they dulled him.

It was only when, in the middle of a dreary day, something reminded him – a scent, a shout – that he had once been in another place, and breathed its air and met its creatures, it was only then that he realized how tentative his recall was. And the more he went in pursuit of what he was forgetting the more it eluded him.

The glories of the Fugue were becoming mere words, the reality of which he could no longer conjure. When he thought of an orchard it was less and less that extraordinary place he'd slept in (slept, and dreamt that this life he was now living was the dream) and more a commonplace stand of apple trees.

The miracles were drifting from him, and he seemed to be unable to hold onto them.

Surely dying was like this, he thought; losing things dear and unable to prevent their passing.

Yes; this was a kind of dying.

2

Brendan, for his part, continued to continue. As the weeks passed, Geraldine managed to talk him into joining them downstairs, but he was interested in little but tea and television, and his conversation was now scarcely more than grunts. Sometimes Cal would watch Brendan's face as he sat slumped in front of the television – his expression unchanging whether the screen offered pundits or comedians – and wondered what had happened to the man he'd known. Was the old Brendan still in hiding somewhere, behind those addled eyes?, or had he been an illusion all along, a son's dream of his father's permanence which, like the letter from Eileen, had simply evaporated? Perhaps it was for the best, he thought, that Brendan was shielded from his pain, then drew himself up short at such a thought. Wasn't that what they said as the coffin was marched past: it was all for the best? Brendan wasn't dead yet.

As time went by, Geraldine's presence began to prove as comforting to Cal as to the old man. Her smiles were the brightest thing those dismal months could boast. She came and went, more indispensable by the day, until, in the first week of December, she suggested it might be more convenient all round if she slept at the house. It was a perfectly natural progression.

'I don't want to marry you,' she told him quite plainly. The sorry spectacle of Theresa's marriage – five months old and already rocky – had confirmed her worst suspicions of matrimony. 'I did want to marry you once,' she said. 'But now I'm happy just to be with you.'

She proved easy company; down-to-earth, unsentimental: as much companion as lover. She it was who made certain the bills were paid on time, and saw that there was tea in the caddy. She it was too who suggested that Cal sell the pigeons.

'Your father doesn't show any interest in them any longer,' she said on more than one occasion. 'He wouldn't even notice if they were gone.'

That was certainly true. But Cal refused to contemplate the sale. Come spring and the fine weather his father might well show fresh interest in the birds.

'You know that's not true,' she'd tell him when he put this point. 'Why do you want to keep them so much? They're just a burden.' Then she'd let the subject drop for a few days, only to raise it again when a cue was presented.

History was repeating itself. Often in the course of these exchanges, which gradually became more heated, Cal could hear echoes of his mother and father: the same routes were being trodden afresh. And, like his father, Cal – though malleable on almost every other issue – was immovable on this. He would not sell the birds.

The real reason for his bullishness was not, of course, hope of Brendan's rehabilitation, but the fact that the birds were his last concrete link with the events of the previous summer.

In the weeks after Suzanna's disappearance he'd bought a dozen newspapers a day, scanning each page for some report of her, or the carpet, or Shadwell. But there was nothing, and eventually – unable to bear the daily disappointment – he'd stopped looking. Nor was there any further visit from Hobart or his men – which was in its way bad news. He, Cal, had become an irrelevancy. The story, if it was still being written, was running on without him.

He became so frightened he'd forget the Fugue that he took the risk of writing down all that he could remember of the night there, which, when he set himself to the task, was depressingly little. He wrote the names down too: Lemuel Lo; Apolline Dubois; Frederick Cammell . . .; set them all down at the back of his diary, in the section reserved for telephone numbers, except that there were no numbers for these people; nor addresses either. Just uncommon names to which he was less and less able to attach faces.

3

On some nights he had dreams, from which he would wake with tears on his face.

Geraldine consoled him as best she could, given that he claimed not to recall these dreams when he woke. That was in a sense true. He brought nothing into consciousness that words could encapsulate: only an aching sadness. She would lie beside him then, and stroke his hair, and tell him that though these were difficult times things could be much worse. She was right, of course. And by and by the dreams dwindled, until they finally ceased altogether.

318

# 4

In the last week of January, with Christmas bills still outstanding and too little money to pay them with, he sold the pigeons, with the exception of 33 and his mate. This pair he kept, though the reason why was harder and harder to remember; and by the end of the following month had been forgotten entirely.

# IV

## THE NOMADS

### 1

The passage of winter was certainly weary for Cal, but for Suzanna it held perils far worse than boredom and bad dreams.

Those perils had begun the day after the night of the Fugue, when she and the Peverelli brothers had so narrowly escaped capture by Shadwell. Her life, and Jerichau's, with whom she'd been re-united in the street beyond Shearman's estate, had scarcely been out of danger since.

She had been warned of this at Capra's House, and a good deal else beside. But of all she'd learned, the subject that had left the deepest impression was the Scourge. The Councillors had grown pale talking of how close to extinction the Families had come. And though the enemies now snapping at her heels — Shadwell and Hobart — were of a different order entirely, she could not help but believe they and the Scourge sprang from the same poisonous earth. They were all, in their way, enemies of life.

And they were equally relentless. Staying one step ahead of the Salesman and his new ally was exhausting. She and Jerichau had been granted a few hours' grace on that first day, when a false trail laid by the brothers had successfully confused the hounds, but Hobart had picked up the scent again by noon. She'd had no choice but to leave the city that afternoon, in a second-hand car she'd bought to replace the police vehicle they'd stolen. Using her own car, she knew, would be like sending up smoke signals.

One fact surprised her: there was no sign, either on the day of re-weaving, or subsequently, of Immacolata. Was it possible that the Incantatrix and her sisters had elected to stay in the carpet; or even become trapped there against their will? Perhaps that was too much to hope for. Yet the menstruum – which she was increasingly able to control and use – never carried a tremor of Immacolata's presence.

Jerichau kept a respectful distance in those early weeks; made uneasy, perhaps, by her preoccupation with the menstruum. He could be of no use in her learning process: the force she owned was a mystery to him; his maleness feared it. But by degrees she convinced him that neither it nor she (if they could be defined as separate entities) bore him the slightest ill-will, and he grew a little easier with her powers. She was even able to talk with him about how she'd first gained access to the menstruum, and how it had subsequently delved into Cal. She was grateful for the chance to talk about these events – they'd remained locked up in her for too long, fretted over. He had few answers for her, but the very telling seemed to heal her anxieties. And the less anxious she became, the more the menstruum showed its worth. It gave her a power that proved invaluable in those weeks: a premonitory skill that showed her ghost-forms of the future. She'd see Hobart's face on the stairs outside the room where they were hiding, and know that he'd be standing in that very spot before too long. Sometimes she saw Shadwell too, but mostly it was Hobart, his eyes desperate, his thin mouth shaping her name. That was the signal to move on, of course, whatever the time of day or night. Pack up their bags, and the carpet, and go.

She had other talents too, all rooted in the menstruum. She could see the lights Jerichau had first shown her on Lord Street; and after a surprisingly short space they became quite unremarkable to her: merely another piece of information – like the expression on a face, or the tone of a voice – that she used to read a stranger's temperament. And there was another visionary skill she now possessed, somewhere between the premonitions and the haloes: that is, she could see the consequence of natural processes. It wasn't just the bud she saw, but the blossom it would become in spring, and if she stretched her sight a little further, the fruit that would come after it. This grasp of *potential* had several consequences. For one, she gave up eating eggs. For another, she found herself fighting off a beguiling fatalism, which, if she hadn't resisted it, might have left her adrift in a sea of inevitabilities, going whatever way the future chose to take her.

It was Jerichau who helped save her from this dangerous tide, with his boundless enthusiasm for being and doing. Though the blossom, and the withering of the blossom, were inevitable, Human and Seerkind had choices to make before death: roads to travel, roads to ignore.

One of those choices was whether to stay companions or become lovers. They chose to be lovers, though it happened so naturally Suzanna could not pinpoint the moment of decision. Certainly they never talked explicitly about it; though perhaps it had been in the air since the conversation in the field outside Capra's House. It just seemed right that they take that comfort from each other. He was a sophisticated bed-partner, responsive to subtle changes in mood; capable of raucous laughter one moment and great gravity the next.

He was also, much to her delight, a brilliant thief. Despite the vicissitudes of life on the run, they ate (and travelled) like royalty, simply because he was so light-fingered. She wasn't certain how he managed to be so successful – whether it was some subtle rapture he employed to divert a watcher's eye, or whether he was simply born a thief. Whatever his method, he could steal anything, large or small, and scarcely a day went by without their tasting some expensive delicacy, or indulging his new-found passion for champagne.

It made the chase easier in more practical ways too, for they were able to change cars as often as they liked, leaving a trail of abandoned vehicles along the route.

That route took them in no particular direction; they simply drove where their instincts suggested. Intentionality, Jerichau had said, was the easiest way to get caught. I never *intend* to steal, he explained to Suzanna one day as they drove, not until I've done it; so nobody ever knows what I'm up to, because I don't either. She liked this philosophy; it appealed to her sense of humour. If she ever got back to London – to her clay and her kiln – she would see if the notion made aesthetic as well as criminal sense. Maybe letting go was the only true control. What kind of pots would she make if she didn't try to *think* about it?

The trick, however, didn't dislodge their pursuers, merely kept them at a distance. And on more than one occasion that distance narrowed uncomfortably.

2

They had been two days in Newcastle, in a small hotel on Rudyard Street. The rain had been falling steadily for a week now, and they'd been talking over the possibility of leaving the country, going somewhere sunnier. Serious problems attended such an option however. For one, Jerichau had no passport, and any attempt to get him one would put them both under scrutiny; for another, it was possible Hobart had alerted ports and airports to their existence. And third, even if they could travel, the carpet would be more difficult to transport. They'd almost certainly be obliged to let it out of their sight, and this Suzanna was not willing to do.

The argument went back and forth while they ate their pizza and drank their champagne and the rain lashed against the window.

And then, the fluttering began in her lower belly, that she'd come to recognize as an omen. She looked towards the door, and for a sickening moment she thought the menstruum had been too late with its warning, for she saw the door open and there was Hobart, staring straight at her.

'What is it?' Jerichau said.

His words made her realize her error. The ghost she saw was more solid than she'd ever seen before, which probably meant the event it foreshadowed was imminent.

'Hobart,' she said. 'And I don't think we've got much time.'

323

He made a pained face, but didn't question her authority on the matter. If she said Hobart was near, then near he was. She'd become the augurer; the witch: reading the air, and always finding bad news.

Moving was an elaborate business, because of the carpet. At each stopping-place they had to convince either the proprietor or the manager that the carpet came with them to their room. When they left, it had to be manhandled back into whichever vehicle they'd commandeered that day. All of which drew unwelcome attention. There was no alternative however. Nobody had ever promised that Heaven would be a light load to carry.

## 3

Less than thirty minutes later, Hobart pushed the door of the hotel suite open. The room was still warm with the woman's breath. But she and her nigger had gone.

Again! How many times in the last months had he stood in their litter and breathed the same air she'd breathed, and seen the shape of her body left on the bed? But always too late. Always they were ahead of him, and away, and all he was left with was another haunted room.

There would be no restful nights for him, no, nor peaceful days, until she was caught and under his thumb. Her capture had become his obsession; and her punishment too.

He knew all too well that in this decadent age, when every perversion had its apologist, she would be eloquently defended once caught. That was why he came in search of her *personally*, he and his few, so that he might show her the true face of the Law before the liberals came pleading. She would suffer for what she'd done to his heroes. She would cry out for mercy, and he would be strong, and deaf to her pleas.

He had an ally in this of course: Shadwell.

There was not one amongst his superiors in the Force whom he trusted as he trusted that man; they were like twin souls. He took strength from that.

And, oddly, from the book too, the book of codes that he'd taken from her. He'd had the volume studied minutely; the paper and the binding, all analysed for some hidden significance. None had been found. Which left the words and the pictures. These too had been studied by experts. The stories were apparently quite straightforward faery-tales. The illustrations, like the text, also pretended innocence.

But he wasn't fooled. The book meant something more than *Once upon a time*, he didn't doubt that for an instant. When he finally had the woman to himself, he'd burn its meaning from her, and no faint-heart would stop him.

## 4

They'd been more cautious after the near-miss in Newcastle. Instead of visiting major cities, where the police presence was substantial, they started to find smaller communities. That had its own disadvantages, of course. The arrival of two strangers, and a carpet, aroused curiosity and questions.

But the change of tactics worked. Never staying in any place more than thirty-six hours, and moving irrationally from town to town, village to village, the trail grew colder behind them. Days free of the hounds turned to weeks, and weeks became months, and it was almost as if their pursuers had given up the chase.

In that time Suzanna's thoughts turned often to Cal. So much had happened since that day beside the Mersey, when he'd professed love to her. She'd often wondered how much of what he'd felt had been some unconscious knowledge of how the menstruum had touched him, entered him, and how much had been love as it was conventionally understood. Sometimes she longed to pick up the 'phone and speak to him; indeed on several occasions she'd tried to do just that. Was it paranoia that prevented her from speaking, or was there – as her instinct intimated – another presence on the line, monitoring the call? On the fourth and fifth occasions it wasn't even Cal who answered, but a woman who demanded to know who this was, and when Suzanna remained silent threatened to report her. She didn't call again; it simply wasn't worth the risk.

Jerichau had an opinion on the matter.

'Mooney's a Cuckoo,' he said, when Cal's name came up in conversation. 'You should forget him.'

'If you're a Cuckoo, you're worth nothing, is that it?' she said. 'What about me?'

'You belong with us now,' he said. 'You're Seerkind.'

'There's so much you don't know about me,' she said. 'Years and years of just being an ordinary girl –'

'You were never ordinary.'

'Oh yes,' she said. 'Believe me, I was. Still am. *Here.*' She tapped her forehead. 'Sometimes I wake up and I can't believe what's happened . . . *happening* . . . to me. When I think of the way I was.'

'It's no use to look back,' said Jerichau. 'No use thinking of what could have been.'

'You don't do that any more, do you? I've noticed. You don't even talk about the Fugue.'

Jerichau smiled. 'Why should I?' he said. 'I'm happy as I am. With you. Maybe it'll be different tomorrow. Maybe it was different yesterday, I forget. But today, *now*, I'm happy. I even begin to like the Kingdom.'

She remembered him lost in the crowd on Lord Street; how he'd changed.

'So what if you never saw the Fugue again?'

He pondered this a moment. 'Who knows? Better not to think about it.'

It was an improbable romance. She, learning all the time from the power inside her a new vision. He, daily more seduced by the very world whose trivialities she was seeing with clearer and clearer eyes. And with that comprehension, so unlike the simplifications she'd been ruled by hitherto, she became even more certain that the carpet they carried was a last hope, while he – whose home the Weave contained – seemed increasingly indifferent to its fate, living *in* the moment and *for* the moment, touched scarcely at all by hope or regret.

He talked less and less of finding a safe place for the Fugue to reside, more and more of something tantalizing he'd seen in the street or on the television.

Often now, though he stayed with her and told her she could always rely upon him, she felt she was alone.

5

And somewhere behind her, Hobart was also alone; even amongst his men, or with Shadwell, alone: dreaming of her and the scent she left to mock him, and of the brutalities he'd deliver upon her.

In these dreams his hands would be flaming, as they'd been once before, and as she fought him the flames would lick up the walls of the room, and crawl across the ceiling, until the chamber was an oven. And he'd wake with his hands in front of his face, running not with fire but sweat, glad of the Law to keep him from panic, and glad too that he was on the side of the angels.

# OUR LADY OF THE BONES

1

These were dark days for Shadwell.

He had emerged from the Fugue in high spirits – possessed of a new breadth of purpose – only to have the world he wished so much to rule snatched from beneath his nose. Not only that, but Immacolata, to whom he might have looked for assistance, had apparently elected to remain in the Weave. She was, after all, one of the Seerkind, even though they'd spurned her. Perhaps he shouldn't be so surprised that once back on soil she'd once pretended to she'd been moved to remain there.

He was not completely bereft of company. Norris, the Hamburger King, was still at his beck and call, still content with servitude. And of course there was Hobart. The Inspector was probably insane, but that was all to the good. And he had one particular aspiration which Shadwell knew he might one day need to turn to his own ends. That was, to lead – as Hobart put it – a righteous crusade.

There was little use of a crusade, however, with nothing to mount it against. Five long months had passed, and every day that went by with the carpet unfound his desperation grew. Unlike others who'd stepped from the Fugue that night, he remembered the experience in the finest detail. The jacket – charged with the raptures of the realm – kept the memories fresh. All too fresh. Scarcely an hour passed without his craving to be there.

There was more to his hunger than simply the desire to

possess the Fugue. In these long weeks of waiting he'd come to a yet profounder ambition. If, and when, that soil was once more his to tread, he'd do what none of the Seerkind had ever dared; he'd go into the Gyre. This notion, once conceived, tormented his every waking moment. Penalties might have to be paid for such trespass, but would they not be worth the risk? Hidden behind that mask of cloud, the Mantle, was a concentration of magic unequalled in the history of the Seerkind, and therefore, in the history of the world.

Creation held court in the Gyre. To walk there, and see its secrets for himself, would that not be a kind of Godhood?

## 2

And today, he had the setting to match the tenor of these thoughts: this small church dedicated to St Philomena and St Callixtus, hidden away in the concrete wasteland of the City of London. He had not come here for the good of his soul; he had been invited here, by the priest who was presently conducting the lunchtime mass for a handful of office workers. A man he'd never met, who had written saying he had important news; news Shadwell could profit by. The Salesman had come without hesitation.

Shadwell had been brought up a Catholic; and though he'd long neglected his faith there was no forgetting the rituals he'd learned as a child. He listened to the Sanctus, his lips running with the rhythm of the words, though it was twenty years since he'd attended them. Then the Eucharistic Prayer — something short and sweet, so as not to keep the accountants from their calculations — and on to the Consecration.

. . . *Take this all of you and eat it. This is my body which will be given up for you* . . .

Old words; old rituals. But they still made sound commercial sense.

Talk of Power and Might would always attract an audience. Lords never went out of fashion.

329

Lost in thought he wasn't even aware that the mass had ended until the priest appeared at his side.

'Mr Shadwell?'

He looked up from his calf-skin gloves. The church was empty, but for the two of them.

'We've been waiting for you,' said the priest, not waiting for confirmation that he had the right man. 'You're most welcome.'

Shadwell got to his feet.

'What's this about?'

'Perhaps you'll come with me?' came the response.

Shadwell saw no reason not to comply. The priest led him across the nave, and into a wood-panelled room which smelt like a brothel, sweat and perfume mingled. At the far end of the room, a curtain, which he drew aside, and another door.

Before turning the key he said:

'You must stay close by me, Mr Shadwell, and not approach the Shrine . . .'

The Shrine? For the first time since coming here, Shadwell had an inkling of what was going on.

'I understand,' he said.

The priest opened the door. There was a steep flight of stone steps before them, lit only by the meagre light shed from the room they were leaving. He lost count of the steps after thirty; they were descending in almost total darkness after the first ten, and he kept his hands stretched to the wall, which was dry and chilly, in order to maintain his balance.

But now below, a light. The priest glanced over his shoulder, his face a pale ball in the murk.

'Stay by me,' he cautioned. 'It's dangerous.'

At the bottom, the priest took hold of his arm, as though not trusting Shadwell to obey his instructions. They had arrived in the centre of a labyrinth, it seemed; galleries ran off in all directions, twisting and turning unpredictably. In some, candles burned. Others were in darkness.

It was only as the guide led him down one of these corridors that Shadwell realized they were not alone here. The walls

330

were lined with niches, each of which contained a coffin. He shuddered. The dead were on every side; it was their dust that he could taste on his tongue. There was only one person, he knew, who would willingly keep such company.

Even as he formed this thought the priest's hand dropped from his arm, and the man withdrew down the passageway at some speed, murmuring a prayer as he went. The reason: a veiled figure, dressed from head to foot in black, approaching him down the tunnel, like a mourner who'd lost their way amongst the caskets. She did not have to speak or raise her veil for Shadwell to know that it was Immacolata.

She stood a little way from him, saying nothing. Her breath shook the folds of her veil.

Then she said:

'Shadwell.'

Her voice was slurred: even laboured.

'I thought you'd stayed in the Weave,' he said.

'I was almost detained there,' she replied.

'Detained?'

Behind him, Shadwell heard the priest's feet on the stairs as he made his exit.

'Friend of yours?' he asked.

'They worship me,' she told him. 'Call me Goddess; Mother of the Night. They emasculate themselves in order to better show their adulation.' Shadwell grimaced. 'That's why you're not allowed in the vicinity of the Shrine. They consider it desecration. If their Goddess hadn't spoken, they would not have let you this far.'

'Why'd you put up with them?'

'They gave me a hiding-place, when I needed one. Somewhere to heal.'

'Heal what?'

At this, the veil slowly lifted, untouched by Immacolata. The sight beneath was enough to make Shadwell's gorge rise. Her once exquisite features were wounded beyond recognition, a mass of raw tissue and seeping scars.

'. . . how . . . ?' he managed to say.

'The Custodian's husband,' she replied, her mouth so

twisted out of true it was difficult for her to form words properly.

'He did *that*?'

'He came with lions,' she said. 'And I was careless.'

Shadwell didn't want to hear any more.

'It offends you,' she said. 'You're a man of sensibility.'

This last word was pronounced with the subtlest irony.

'You can mask it, can't you?' he said, thinking of her skills with disguise. If she could imitate others, why not copy her perfect self?

'Would you have me a whore?' she said to him. 'Painting myself for *vanity*? No, Shadwell. I'll wear my wounds. They're more myself than beauty ever was.' She made a terrible smile. 'Don't you think?'

Despite her defiance, her voice trembled. She was pliable, he sensed; despairing even. Fearing insanity might claim her again.

'I've missed your company,' he said, attempting to look steadily at her face. 'We worked well together.'

'You've got new allies now,' she replied.

'You heard?'

'My sisters have been with you now and then.' The thought did not comfort him. 'Do you trust Hobart?'

'He serves his purpose.'

'Which is?'

'To find the carpet.'

'Which he hasn't done.'

'No. Not yet.' He tried to stare straight at her; tried to give her a loving look. 'I miss you,' he said. 'I need your help.'

Her palate made a soft hissing sound, but she didn't reply.

'Isn't that why you brought me here?' he said, 'so that we could begin again?'

'No,' she replied. 'I'm too weary for that.'

Hungry as he was to walk in the Fugue once again, the thought of picking up the chase where they'd left it – moving from city to city whenever the wind carried a rumour of the Weave – did not enthrall him either.

'Besides . . .' she said, '. . . you've changed.'

332

'No,' he protested. 'I still want the Weave.'

'But not to sell it,' she said. 'To rule it.'

'Where did you get that notion from?' he protested, offering an ingenuous smile. He could not read the ruin before him well enough to know whether his pretence worked. 'We had a pact, Goddess,' he said. 'We were going to bring them into the dust.'

'And you want that still?'

He hesitated, knowing that he risked everything with a lie. She knew him well – she could probably see into his skull if she chose to; he might lose more than her company if she sensed deceit in him. But then, she was changed, wasn't she? She came before him as spoiled goods. Her beauty, the one ungovernable power she had always had over him, was gone. She was the supplicant here, though she was trying to pretend otherwise. He risked the lie.

'What I want is what I've always wanted,' he said. 'Your enemies are my enemies.'

'Then we'll lay them low,' she said. 'Once and for all.'

Somewhere in the maze of her face a light ignited, and the human dust on the shelves at his side began to dance.

# VI

## THE BRITTLE MACHINE

### 1

On the morning of the second of February, Cal found Brendan dead in bed. He had died, the doctor reported, an hour before dawn; simply given up and slipped away in his sleep.

His mental processes had begun to deteriorate rapidly, about a week before Christmas. On some days he'd call Geraldine by his wife's name, and take Cal for his brother. The prognosis had not been good, but nobody had expected this sudden exit. No opportunity for explanations or fond farewells. One day he was here, the next he could only be mourned.

Much as Cal had loved Brendan, he found grief difficult. It was Geraldine who wept; Geraldine who had all the proper sentiments to hand out when the neighbours came to offer their condolences. Cal could only play the part of the grieving child, not feel it. All he felt was ill at ease.

That feeling grew stronger as the cremation approached. He was increasingly detached from himself, viewing his absence of emotion with a disbelieving eye. It seemed suddenly there were two Cals. One, the public mourner, dealing with the business of death as propriety demanded, the other a coruscating critic of the first, calling the bluff of every cliché and empty gesture. It was Mad Mooney's voice, this second: the scourge of liars and hypocrites. 'You're not real at all,' the poet would whisper. 'Look at you! Sham that you are!'

This dislocation brought strange side-effects; most significantly, the dreams that now returned to him. He dreamt himself floating in air as clear as love's eyes; dreamt trees heavy with golden fruit; dreamt animals that spoke like people, and people who roared. He dreamt of the pigeons too, several times a night, and on more than one occasion he woke certain that 33 and his mate had spoken to him, in their bird way, though he could make no sense of their advice.

The idea was still with him by day, and – though he knew the notion was laughable – he found himself quizzing the birds as he fed them their daily bread, asking them, half in jest, to give up what they knew. They just winked their eyes, and grew fat.

The funeral came and went. Eileen's relatives came across from Tyneside, and Brendan's from Belfast. There was whisky, and Guinness for Brendan's brothers, and ham sandwiches with the crusts cut off, and when the glasses and the plates were empty they all went home.

## 2

'We should have a holiday,' Geraldine suggested a week after the funeral. 'You haven't been sleeping well.'

He was sitting at the dining-room window, watching the garden.

'We need to do some work on the house,' he said. 'It's depressing me.'

'We can always sell it,' she replied.

It was a simple solution, and one his torpid mind hadn't conceived of. 'That's a bloody good idea,' he said. 'Find somewhere without a railway at the bottom of the garden.'

They started searching for another house immediately, before the better weather inflated prices. Geraldine was in her element, leading him round the properties with a seamless outpouring of observations and ideas. They found a modest terraced house in Wavertree which they both liked, and put an offer in for it, which was accepted. But the Chariot Street house proved more difficult to move. Two purchasers came to the brink of signing contracts, then withdrew. Even Geraldine's high spirits lost buoyancy as the weeks drew on.

They lost the Wavertree house at the beginning of March, and were obliged to begin the search over again. But their enthusiasm was much depleted, and they found nothing they liked.

And still, in dreams, the birds spoke. And still he couldn't interpret their wisdom.

# VII

## TALES OF SPOOK CITY

### 1

Five weeks after Brendan's remains had been scattered on the Lawn of Remembrance, Cal opened the door to a man with a wry, ruddy face, sparse hair brushed ear to ear to shelter his pate, and the stub of a hefty cigar between his fingers.

'Mr Mooney?' he said, and without waiting for confirmation, went on: 'You don't know me. My name's Gluck.' Transferring his cigar from right to left he gripped Cal's hand and shook it vigorously. 'Anthony Gluck,' he said. The man's face was vaguely familiar; from where, Cal wracked his brain to remember. 'I wonder,' Gluck said, 'if I may have a word with you?'

'I vote Labour,' said Cal.

'I'm not canvassing. I'm interested in the house.'

'Oh,' said Cal, beaming. 'Then come on in,' and he led Gluck through into the dining-room. The man was at the window in an instant, peering into the garden.

'Ah!' he said. 'So this is it.'

'It's chaos at the moment,' said Cal with faint apology.

'You left it untouched?' said Gluck.

'Untouched?'

'Since the events in Chariot Street.'

'Do you really want to buy the house?' said Cal.

'*Buy?*' said Gluck. 'Oh no, I'm sorry. I didn't even realize it was for sale.'

'You said you were interested —'

337

'So I am. But not to buy. No, I'm interested in the place because it was the centre of the disturbances last August. Am I right?'

Cal had only a patchwork memory of the events of that day. Certainly he remembered the freak whirlwind that had done so much damage in Chariot Street. He remembered the interview with Hobart quite clearly too; and how it had prevented his meeting with Suzanna. But there was much else – the Rake, the death of Lilia, indeed everything that sprang from the matter of the Fugue – that his mind had eclipsed.

Gluck's enthusiasm intrigued him however.

'That was no natural event,' he said. 'Not by a long chalk. It was a perfect example of what we in the business call anomalous phenomena.'

'Business?'

'You know what some people are calling Liverpool these days?'

'No.'

'Spook City.'

'Spook City?'

'And with good reason, believe me.'

'What did you mean when you said *business*?'

'In essence it's very simple. I document events that defy explanation; events that fall outside the comprehension of the scientific community, which people therefore choose *not to see*. Anomalous phenomena.'

'This has always been a windy city,' Cal pointed out.

'Believe me,' said Gluck, 'there was more to what happened here last summer than a high wind. There was a house on the other side of the river simply reduced to rubble overnight. There were mass hallucinations that took place in broad daylight. There were lights in the sky – brilliant lights – witnessed by hundreds of people. All that and more happened in the vicinity of this city, over a two or three day time period. Does that sound like coincidence to you?'

'No. If you're sure it all –'

'All happened? Oh, it happened Mr Mooney. I've been collecting this kind of material for twenty years and more,

338

collecting and collating it, and there are patterns in these phenomena.'

'They don't just happen here, then?'

'Good God, no. I get reports sent to me from all over Europe. After a while, you begin to see some kind of picture emerge.'

As Gluck spoke Cal remembered where he'd seen the man before. On a television programme, talking – if he remembered rightly – about governmental silence on visits from alien ambassadors.

'What happened in Chariot Street,' he was saying, 'and all over this city, is part of a pattern which is perfectly apparent to those of us who study these things.'

'What does it mean?'

'It means we're watched, Mr Mooney. We're scrutinized the live-long day.'

'Who by?'

'Creatures from another world, with a technology which beggars our own. I've only seen fragments of their artifacts, left behind by careless voyagers. But they're enough to prove we're less to them than household pets.'

'Really?'

'I recognize that look, Mr Mooney,' said Gluck, without irritation. 'You're humouring me. But I've seen the evidence with my own eyes. Especially in this past year. Either they're getting more careless, or they simply don't mind if we're wise to them any longer.'

'Which means what?'

'That their plans for us are entering some final phase. That their installations on our planet are in place, and we'll be defeated before we begin.'

'They mean to invade us?'

'You may scoff –'

'I'm not scoffing. Really I'm not. I can't say it's easy to believe, but . . .' He thought, for the first time in many months, of Mad Mooney. '. . . I'm interested to hear what you have to say.'

'Well,' said Gluck, his fierce expression mellowing. 'That makes a refreshing change. I'm usually thought of as comic

339

relief. But let me tell you: I'm scrupulous in my researches.'

'I believe it.'

'I've no need to massage the truth,' he said proudly. 'It's quite convincing enough as it is.'

He talked on, of his recent investigations, and what they'd turned up. Britain, it seemed, was alive from end to end with events prodigious and bizarre. Had Cal heard, he enquired, of the rain of deep-sea fish that had fallen on Halifax?; or the village in Wiltshire that boasted its own Borealis?; or of the three-year-old in Blackpool whose grasp of hieroglyphics had been picture-perfect since birth? All true stories, he claimed; all verifiable. And they were the least of it. The island seemed to be ankle-deep in miracles to which most of its inhabitants turned a blind eye.

'The truth's in front of our noses,' said Gluck. 'If we could only see it. The visitors are *here*. In England.'

It was an attractive notion – an apocalypse of fishes and wise children, to turn England inside out; and nonsensical as the facts appeared, Gluck's conviction was powerfully persuasive. But there was something wrong with his thesis. Cal couldn't work out what – and he certainly wasn't in any position to argue the point – but his gut told him that somewhere along the road Gluck had taken a wrong turning. What was so unsettling was the process this fabulous litany had begun in his head; a scrabbling for some fact he'd once possessed and now forgotten. Just beyond his fingertips.

'Of course, there's been an official cover-up,' Gluck was saying, 'here in Spook City.'

'Cover-up?'

'Certainly. It wasn't just houses that disappeared. People went too. Lured here, at least that's what my information suggests. Moneyed people; people with important friends, who came here and never left. Or at least not of their own accord.'

'Extraordinary.'

'Oh, I could tell you tales that would make the disappearance of a plutocrat seem small beer.' Gluck re-kindled his cigar, which had died each time he'd taken off on some fresh tack.

He puffed on it until he was veiled in smoke. 'But we know so little,' he said. 'That's why I keep searching, keep asking. I would have been on your doorstep a lot earlier, but that things have been so hectic.'

'I don't think there's much I can tell you,' said Cal. 'That whole period's sort of vague —'

'Yes,' said Gluck. 'It would be. I've had this happen repeatedly. Witnesses simply *forgetting*. I believe it's something our friends —' he pointed the wet end of his cigar skyward, '— are able to induce: this forgetfulness. Was there anybody else in the house that day?'

'My father. I think.'

He couldn't even be perfectly certain of that.

'Might I have a word with him?'

'He's dead. He died last month.'

'Oh. My condolences. Was it sudden?'

'Yes.'

'You're selling the house then. Leaving Liverpool to its own devices?'

Cal shrugged. 'I don't think so,' he said. Gluck peered at him out of the smoke. 'I just can't seem to make up my mind about much these days,' Cal confessed. 'It's like I'm living in a dream.'

*You never spoke a truer word,* said a voice at the back of his head.

'I understand,' said Gluck. 'Truly I do.'

He unbuttoned his jacket, and opened it. Cal's heartbeat unaccountably quickened, but all the man was doing was fishing in his inside pocket for his visiting card.

'Here,' he said. 'Please. Take it.'

*A. V. Gluck,* the card announced, and below the Birmingham address a phrase, in red ink:

*What is now proved was once only imagined.*

'Who's the quote from?'

'William Blake,' said Gluck. '*The Marriage of Heaven and Hell*. Would you keep the card? If anything should occur to you; anything . . . anomalous . . . I'd like to hear from you.'

'I'll keep it in mind,' Cal said. He looked at the card again. 'What does V. stand for?' he asked.

'Virgil,' Gluck confided. 'Well,' he said, 'everybody should have *some* little secret, don't you think?'

## 2

Cal kept the card, more as a keepsake of the encounter than in the expectation of using it. He'd enjoyed the man's company, in its off-beat way, but it was probably a performance best enjoyed once only. Twice might stale its eccentric charm.

When Geraldine got back he began to tell her about the visit, then thought better of it, and diverted the conversation to another subject entirely. He knew she'd laugh at his giving the fellow a minute of his attention, and, outlandish as Gluck and his theories were, he didn't want to hear the man mocked, however gently.

Maybe the man had taken the wrong turning, but at least he'd travelled some extraordinary roads. Though Cal could no longer remember why, he had the suspicion that they had that in common.

# Part Seven

# The Demagogue

*'All rising to great place is by a winding stair.'*

Sir Francis Bacon
*Essays*

# I

## THE MESSENGER

### 1

Spring was late that year, the March days murky, the nights frost-bitten. It sometimes seemed winter would never end; that the world would go on like this, grey upon grey, until entropy claimed its little life entirely.

The weeks brought bad times for Suzanna and Jerichau. It wasn't Hobart that caused them: indeed she even got to thinking that a reminder of their jeopardy might usefully shake them from their complacency.

But, while *she* suffered from lethargy and ennui, Jerichau's response to these weeks was in its way far more alarming. The pleasure he took in the inconsequentia of the Kingdom, which had been a source of amusement to them both, now took on the quality of an obsession. He lost entirely his capacity for stillness, which had initially drawn her to him. Now he was full of spurious energy, spouting advertising catch-phrases and jingles which he soaked up – Babu that he was – like a sponge, his talk an imitation of the flipness of television detectives and game-show hosts. They argued often, sometimes bitterly; he'd more often than not walk out in the middle of such exchanges, as if anger were not worth his sweat, only to return with some booty – usually drink – which he'd consume in sullen solitude if he couldn't get Suzanna to join him.

She tried to satisfy his restlessness by keeping them on the move, but it only exacerbated the disease.

Privately she began to despair, as she pictured history repeating itself two generations on, with her cast in Mimi's role.

And then, not a moment too soon, the weather began to improve, and her spirits started to rise. She even dared entertain the hope that the chase had actually stopped; their pursuers given up and gone home. In a month or so, perhaps, they could with some confidence go in search of a haven to begin the unweaving again.

But then came the glad tidings.

## 2

They were in a small town outside Coventry, rejoicing in the name of Fatherless Barn; as good a reason as any to be there. The day being bright, and the sun almost warm, they'd decided to risk leaving the carpet in storage at the boarding house they'd found, and take the air together.

Jerichau had just emerged from a confectioner's, his pockets full of white chocolate, his current passion, when somebody brushed past Suzanna, saying: 'Left and left', then hurried on without looking back.

Jerichau had heard the words too, and he instantly followed both stranger and instructions. She called after him, but he wasn't about to be waylaid. He turned left at the first intersection. Suzanna went in pursuit, cursing his indiscretion, which had already drawn some attention. Left and left again brought her into the narrowest of streets, where the sun surely seldom came. There Jerichau was embracing the stranger like a long lost brother.

It was Nimrod.

## 3

'You were so difficult to find,' he said, when they returned to the seclusion of the boarding house, taking a dog's leg so that Jerichau could steal a bottle of celebratory champagne. 'I almost caught up with you in Hull, then lost you. But some-

346

body remembered you at your hotel. Said you'd got drunk, Jerichau, is that right? And been helped to bed.'

'Could be,' said Jerichau.

'Anyhow, here I am, and with great news.'

'What?' said Suzanna.

'We're going back home. Very soon.'

'How do you know?'

'Capra says so.'

'*Capra?*' said Jerichau. It was enough to make him neglect his glass. 'How can that be?'

'The Prophet says so. It's all planned. Capra speaks to him –'

'Wait. Wait!' said Suzanna. 'What Prophet?'

'He says we have to spread the word,' said Nimrod, his enthusiasm boundless. 'Find the ones who left the Weave, and tell them liberation's at hand. I've been all over, doing just that. It was by chance I got wind of you. What luck, eh? Nobody knew where you were –'

'And that was the way it was meant to stay,' said Suzanna. 'I was to make contact in *my* time, when *I* judged the trail had grown cold.'

'It *is* cold,' said Nimrod. 'Stone cold. Surely you must have noticed that?' Suzanna kept her silence. 'Our enemies have given up the chase,' he went on. 'The Prophet knows that. He tells us what Capra says, and Capra says our Suppression is at an end.'

'Who is this Prophet?' said Suzanna.

Nimrod's excited flow ceased. He frowned as he stared at her.

'The Prophet is the Prophet,' he said. No further explanation was necessary, it seemed.

'You don't even know his name?' she said.

'He lived near the Gyre,' said Nimrod. 'That much I do know. A hermit, he was, until the weaving. That night, last summer, Capra called him. He left the Weave, to begin his teachings. The tyranny of the Cuckoos is nearly at an end –'

'I'll believe that when I see it,' said Suzanna.

'You will,' said Nimrod, with the unshakeable fervour of a true convert. 'This time, the earth will rise with us. That's

347

what people are saying. The Cuckoos have made too much mischief. Their Age is over.'

'Sounds like wish-fulfilment to me.'

'You may doubt –' said Nimrod.

'I do.'

'– but I've seen the Prophet. I've heard his words. And they come from Capra.' His eyes glittered with evangelical glee. 'I was in the gutter when the Prophet found me. Broken in pieces. Prey to every Cuckoo sickness. Then I heard the Prophet's voice, and went to him. Now look at me.'

Suzanna had argued with zealots before – her brother had been born again at twenty-three, and given his life to Christ – she knew from experience there was no gainsaying the bigotry of faith. Indeed there was part of her wanted to join the happy throng of believers Nimrod described; throw off the burden of the carpet and let the Fugue begin its life afresh. She was weary of being afraid to meet anybody's eye, of forever passing through. Any pleasure she might have taken in being an outsider, possessed of a wonderful secret, had long since soured. Now she wanted to have her fingers in clay again, or sit flirting with friends. But tempting as it was, she couldn't accept this cant and be silent. It stank.

'How do you know he doesn't mean us all harm?' she said.

'Harm? What harm is there in being free? You have to give the Weave back, Suzanna. I'll take you to him –' He snatched hold of her hand as he spoke, as if he was prepared to do it now. She pulled her fingers from his grip.

'What's the problem?' he said.

'I'm not just going to give the carpet up because you heard the Word,' she said fiercely.

'You *must*,' he said, as much disbelief as anger in his tone.

'When does this Prophet speak again?' said Jerichau.

'The day after tomorrow,' Nimrod replied, his eyes still on Suzanna. 'The chase is over,' he said to her. 'You must give the carpet back.'

'And if I don't, he'll come and get it?' she said. 'Is that the implication?'

'You Cuckoos –' Nimrod sighed. 'Always making things so damn difficult. He's come to give us Capra's wisdom. Why can't you see that?' He halted a moment. When he spoke again he'd modulated his strident tone. 'I respect your doubts,' he said. 'But you must understand the situation's changed.'

'I think we should see this Prophet for ourselves,' said Jerichau. He cast a glance at Suzanna. 'Yes?'

She nodded.

'Yes!' Nimrod grinned. 'Yes, he'll make everything clear to you.'

She longed for that promise to be made true.

'The day after tomorrow,' said Nimrod. 'There'll be an end to chases.'

# II

## SEEING THE LIGHT

### 1

That night, with Nimrod gone, and Jerichau sleeping off his champagne, she did something she'd never done before. She evoked the menstruum, simply for company. It had shown her many sights in recent weeks, and it had saved her from Hobart and his malice, but she was still suspicious of its power. She still couldn't quite work out whether she controlled it, or vice versa. Tonight, however, she decided that that was a Cuckoo's way of thinking, always making divisions: the viewer from the viewed; the peach from the taste it left on the tongue.

Such compartments were useful only as tools. At some point they had to be left behind. For better or worse, she *was* the menstruum, and the menstruum was her. She and it, indivisible.

Bathing in its silver light, her thoughts turned again to Mimi, who'd lived a life of waiting, her years growing dusty while she hoped for a miracle that was too late in coming. Thinking of that, she began to cry, quietly.

Not quietly enough, for she woke Jerichau. She heard his footsteps outside, then his tapping on the bathroom door.

'Lady?' he said. It was the name he only used when there was an apology in the air.

'I'm all right,' she said.

She had neglected to lock the door, and he pushed it open. He was dressed only in the long vest he always slept in. Seeing her misery, his face dropped.

'Why so sad?' he asked.

'It's all wrong,' were the only words she could find to express her confusion.

Jerichau's eyes had found the dregs of the menstruum, which moved across the floor between them, their brightness flickering out as they left her immediate vicinity. He kept a respectful distance.

'I'll go to the meeting place with Nimrod,' he said. 'You stay with the Weave. Yes?'

'Suppose they demand it?'

'Then we'll have to decide,' he said. 'But we shall see this Prophet first. He could be a charlatan.' He paused, not looking at her, but at the empty floor between them. 'A lot of us are,' he said after a moment. 'Me, for instance.'

She stared at him as he loitered in the doorway. It wasn't the dying glamour of the menstruum that kept him at bay, she now realized. She spoke his name, very quietly.

'Not you,' she said.

'Oh yes,' he replied.

There was another aching silence.

Then he said: 'I'm sorry, lady.'

'There's nothing to be sorry for.'

'I failed you,' he said. 'I wanted to be so much to you, and look how I failed.'

She stood up and went to him. His misery was so heavy he could not raise his head beneath its weight. She took hold of his hand and held it tight.

'I couldn't have survived these months without you,' she said. 'You've been my dearest friend.'

'Friend,' he said, his voice small. 'I never wanted to be your *friend*.'

She felt his hand tremble in hers, and the sensation brought back their adventure on Lord Street, when she'd held him in the crowd, and shared his visions, his terrors. Since then, they'd shared a bed as well, and it had been pleasurable, but little more. She'd been too obsessed with the beasts on their heels to think of much else; both too close and too distant from him to see how he suffered. She saw it now, and it frightened her.

351

'I love you, lady,' he murmured, his throat almost swallowing the words before they were said. Then he extricated his hand from hers and retreated from her. She went after him. The room was dark, but there was sufficient illumination to etch his anxious face, his jittering limbs.

'I didn't understand,' she said, and reached out to touch his face.

Not since the first night they'd met had she thought of him as unhuman; his hunger to soak up the trivialities of the Kingdom had further obscured that fact. Now she remembered it. Saw before her another species; another history. The thought made her heart pound. He sensed – or saw – the arousal in her, and his earlier hesitancy evaporated. He took a half step towards her, until his tongue could run along her lips. She opened her mouth to taste him, embracing him as she did so. The mystery embraced her in return.

Their previous coupling had been comforting, but unremarkable. Now – as though released by the statement of his love – he took a new lead, undressing her almost ritualistically, kissing her over and over and between the kisses whispering words in a language he must have known she couldn't understand, but which he spoke in a voice of infinite dexterity so that, uncomprehending, she understood. It was his love he spoke; erotic rhymes and promises; words that were the shape of his desire.

His phallus, a word; his semen, a word; her cunt, which he poured his poems into, a dozen words or more.

She closed her eyes and felt his recital consuming her. She answered him, in her way, sighs and nonsenses that found their place in the swell of his magic. When her eyes flickered open again she found the exchange had ignited the very air about them, their words – and the feelings they conveyed – writing a lexicon of light which flattered their nakedness.

It was as if the room was suddenly filled with lanterns, made of smoke and paper. They drifted up on the heat of their makers' bodies, their lights bringing every part of the room to exquisite life. She saw the tightly curled hairs he'd shed on the pillow, describing their own alphabet; saw the simple weave of the sheet extolled; saw everywhere a subtle inter-course of form with form: the walls' congress with the space they contained; the curtains' passion for the window; the chair for the coat that lay upon it, and the shoes beneath.

But mostly she saw him, and he was a wonder.

She caught the minute fluctuations of his iris when his gaze moved from the darkness of her hair to the pillow upon which it was spread; saw the pulse of his heart in the corrugation of his lips, and at his throat. The skin of his chest had an almost eerie smoothness to it, but was deeply muscled; his arms were sinewy, and would not countenance unbinding her a moment, but held her as tight as she held him. There was no show of machismo in this possessiveness, only an urgency which she more than equalled.

Outside, darkness was upon the hemisphere, but they were bright.

And though he had no breath for words now, their tender-ness fuelled the lights that cradled them, and they didn't dim, but echoed the lovers – marrying colour to colour, light to light, until the room blazed.

They loved, and slept, and loved again, and the words kept vigil around them, mellowing their show to a soothing flicker as sleep came a second time.

When she woke the next morning, and opened the curtains on another anxious day, she remembered the previous night as a vision of pure spirit.

2

'I was beginning to forget, lady,' he said that day. 'You kept what you were doing clear in your head. But I was letting it slip. The Kingdom is so strong. It can take your mind away.'

'You wouldn't have forgotten,' she said.

He touched her face, ran his finger-tip down the rim of her ear.

'Not you.'

Later, he said:

'I wish you could come with me to see the Prophet.'
'I do too; but it's not wise.'
'I know.'
'I'll be here, Jerichau.'
'That'll make me quick.'

# III

## CHARISMA

N imrod was waiting for him at the rendezvous they'd arranged two days before. It seemed to Jerichau his fervour had intensified in the intervening time.

'It's going to be the biggest meeting so far . . .' he said. 'Our numbers are growing all the time. The day's at hand, Jerichau. Our people are ready and waiting.'

'I'll believe it when I see it.'

See it he did.

As evening fell Nimrod took him by an elaborate route to a vast ruin of a building, far from any sign of human habitation. The place had been a foundry in its prime; but its heroic scale had doomed it when times got leaner. Now its walls would supposedly see the kindling of another heat entirely.

As they drew closer, it became apparent that there were lights burning in the interior, but there was no sound or sign of the immense gathering Nimrod had promised. A few solitary figures lurked amongst the rubble of service buildings; otherwise the place seemed to be deserted.

Once through the door, however, Jerichau faced the first shock of a night that would bring many: the vast building was filled to capacity with hundreds of the Kind. He saw members of every Root, Babu and Ye-me, Lo and Aia; he saw old men and women, he saw babes in arms. Some he knew had been in the Weave at the beginning, and had apparently elected the previous summer to try their luck in the Kingdom; others he guessed were descendants of those who'd rejected the Weave at the outset; they had a look about them which marked them out as strangers to their homeland. Many of them stood quite separately from their fellow devotees, as if nervous of rejection.

It was disorienting to see physiognomies that carried the subtle signature of his fellow Seerkind primped and painted *a la mode*; Seerkind dressed in jeans and leather jackets, in print dresses and high heels. To judge by their condition many of them had survived well enough in the Kingdom; perhaps even prospered. Yet they were here. A whisper of liberation had found them in their hiding places amongst the Cuckoos, and they'd come, bringing their children and their prayers. Kind who could only know of the Fugue from rumour and hearsay, drawn by the hope of seeing a place their hearts had never forgotten.

Despite his initial cynicism, he could not help but be moved by this silent and expectant multitude.

'I told you,' Nimrod whispered, as he led Jerichau through the throng. 'We'll get as close as we can, eh?'

At the end of the vast hall a rostrum had been set up, littered with flowers. Lights hovered in the air, Babu raptures, throwing a flickering luminescence on the stage beneath.

'He'll come soon,' said Nimrod.

Jerichau didn't doubt it. Even now there was some movement at the far end of the hall; several figures, dressed in the same dark blue, were ordering the crowd a few yards back from the vicinity of the rostrum. The devotees obeyed the instruction without question.

'Who are they?' said Jerichau, nodding towards the uniformed figures.

'The Prophet's Elite,' Nimrod returned. 'They're with him night and day. To keep him from harm.'

Jerichau had no time to ask any further questions. A door was opening in the bare brick wall at the back of the platform, a tremor of excitement passing through the hall. The congregation started to surge towards the platform. The swell of emotion was contagious; try as he might to keep his critical faculties sharp Jerichau found his heart pounding with excitement.

One of the Elite had appeared through the open door, carrying a plain wooden chair. This he set at the front of the platform. The crowd was pressing at Jerichau's back; he was hemmed in to right and left. Every face but his was turned towards the stage. Some had tears on their cheeks: the tension of waiting had been too much. Others were speaking silent prayers.

And now, two more Elite stepped through the door, parting to reveal a figure in pale yellow, the sight of whom brought a tide of sound from the crowd. It was not the jubilant shout of welcome Jerichau had been anticipating, but an intensification of the murmur that had begun a while earlier; a soft, yearning sound which stirred the gut.

Above the platform, the floating flames became brighter. The murmur grew in depth and resonance. Jerichau had to make a fierce effort not to join in.

The lights had reached a white heat, but the Prophet did not step forward and bathe in this blaze of glory. He hung back at the edge of the pool, teasing the crowd, which begged him with their moans to show himself. Still he resisted; still they summoned him, their wordless prayers growing feverish.

Only after three or four minutes of this holding back did he consent to answer their appeal, and step into the light. He was a sizeable man – a fellow Babu, Jerichau guessed – but some infirmity slowed his footsteps. His features were benign, even slightly effeminate; his hair, fine as a baby's, was a white mane.

Reaching the chair, he sat down – apparently with some pain – and surveyed the gathering. Little by little the murmuring grew softer. He did not speak, however, until it had ceased entirely. And when he did speak it was not with the voice Jerichau had expected from a Prophet: strident, possessed. It was a small, musical voice; its tone gentle, even hesitant.

'My friends . . .' he said. 'We're assembled here in the name of Capra . . .'

'Capra . . .' The name was whispered from wall to wall.

'I've heard Capra's words. They say the time is very, very close.' He spoke, Jerichau thought, almost reluctantly, as though he were the vessel of this knowledge, but far from comfortable with it.

'If there are many doubters amongst you –' the Prophet said, '– prepare to shed your doubts.'

Nimrod cast Jerichau a glance as if to say: he means you.

'We are greater by the day . . .' the Prophet said. 'Capra's word is everywhere finding its way to the forgotten and the forgetful. It stirs the sleeping into wakefulness. It makes the dying dance.' He spoke very quietly, letting the rhetoric substitute for volume. His congregation attended like children. 'Very soon we'll be home,' he said. 'We'll be back amongst our loved ones, walking where our mothers and fathers walked. We won't have to hide any longer. This Capra tells us. We will rise, my friends. Rise and be bright.'

There were barely stifled sobs from around the hall. He heard them, and hushed them with an indulgent smile.

'No need to weep,' he said. 'I see an end to weeping. An end to *waiting*.'

'Yes,' said the crowd, as one. 'Yes. Yes.'

Jerichau felt the swell of affirmation picking him up. He had no desire to resist. He was a part of these people wasn't he? Their tragedy was his tragedy; and their longing his too.

'Yes . . .' he found himself saying, 'yes . . . yes . . .'

At his side Nimrod said: 'Now do you believe?' then joined the chant himself.

The Prophet raised his gloved hands to subdue the voices. It took longer for the crowd to be hushed this time, but when the Prophet spoke again his voice was stronger, as though nourished by this display of fellow-feeling.

'My friends. Capra loves peace as we all love it, but let us not deceive ourselves. We have enemies. Enemies amongst Humankind, and yes, amongst our own Kind too. There are many who have cheated us. Conspired with the Cuckoos to keep our lands in sleep. This Capra has seen, with his own eyes. Treachery and lies, my friends; *everywhere*.' He bowed his head a moment, as if the effort of those words was close to defeating him. 'What shall we do?' he said, his voice despairing.

'*Lead us!*' somebody shouted.

The Prophet raised his head at this, his face troubled.

'I can only show you the way,' he protested.

But the cry had been taken up by others around the hall, and was growing.

'*Lead us!*' they called to him. '*Lead us!*'

Slowly, the Prophet got to his feet. Again, he raised his hands to silence the congregation, but this time they would not be subdued so readily.

'Please —' he said, obliged for the first time to raise his voice. 'Please. Listen to me!'

'We'll follow you!' Nimrod was shouting. 'We'll follow!'

Was it Jerichau's imagination, or had the lights above the platform begun to burn with fresh brilliance, the Prophet's hair a halo above his benevolent features? To judge by his expression the call to arms that rose from the floor distressed him; the vox populi wanted more than his vague promises.

'Listen to me,' he appealed. 'If you want me to lead you —'

'*Yes!*' roared five hundred throats.

'If that's what you want I have to warn you, it will not be easy. We would have to put away tenderness. We would have to be hard as stone. *Blood will flow*.'

His warning didn't chasten the crowd a jot. If anything it spurred their enthusiasm to new heights.

'We must be cunning —' said the Prophet, '— as those who've conspired against us have been cunning.'

The crowd was raising the roof now, Jerichau along with them.

'The Fugue calls us home!'

'*Home! Home!*'

'And its voice will not be denied. We must *march*!'

The door at the back of the platform had been opened a little, presumably so that the Prophet's entourage could hear

359

the speech. Now a movement there caught Jerichau's eye. There was somebody in the doorway, whose shadowy face he seemed to know –

'*We will go into the Fugue together,*' the Prophet was saying, his voice finally losing its frailty, its reluctance.

Jerichau looked past the speaker, trying to divide the watcher at the door from the darkness that concealed him.

'We will take the Fugue back from our enemies in the name of Capra.'

The man Jerichau was watching moved a step, and for an instant a fugitive beam of light caught him. Jerichau's stomach convulsed as he silently put a name to the face he saw. It bore a smile, but he knew there was no humour in it, for its owner knew no humour. Or love either; or mercy –

'Shout, my Kind! *Shout!*'

It was Hobart.

'Make them hear us, in their sleep. Hear us and fear our judgment!'

There could be no doubt of it. The time Jerichau had spent in the Inspector's company was burned into his memory forever. Hobart it was.

The voice of the Prophet was finding new strength with every syllable. Even his face seemed to have altered in some subtle fashion. Any sham of kindliness had been dropped; it was all righteous fury now.

'Spread the word –' he was saying. 'The exiles are returning!'

Jerichau watched the performance with fresh eyes, keeping up a pretence of enthusiasm, while questions fretted his thumping head.

Chief amongst them: who was this man, stirring the Kind with promises of Deliverance? A hermit, as Nimrod had described him, an innocent, being used by Hobart for his own ends? That was the best hope. The worst, that he and Hobart were in cahoots; a conspiracy of Kind and Humankind, created with what could only be one intention: possessing and perhaps destroying the Fugue.

The voices around him were deafening, but Jerichau was

no longer buoyed up by this tide, he was drowning in it. They were fodder, these people; Hobart's dupes. It made him sick to think of it.

'Be ready,' the Prophet was telling the assembly. 'Be ready. The hour is near.'

With that promise, the lights above the platform went out. When they came on again, moments later, the voice of Capra had gone, leaving an empty chair and a congregation ready to follow him wherever he chose to lead them.

There were cries from around the hall for him to speak to them again, but the door at the back of the stage was closed and not reopened. Gradually, realizing they wouldn't persuade their leader to appear again, the crowd began to disperse.

'Didn't I tell you?' said Nimrod. He stank of sweat, as did they all. 'Didn't I say?'

'Yes, you did.'

Nimrod seized hold of Jerichau's arm.

'Come with me now,' he said, eyes gleaming. 'We'll go to the Prophet. We'll tell him where the carpet is.'

'Now?'

'Why not? Why give our enemies any more time to prepare themselves?'

Jerichau had vaguely anticipated this exchange. He had his excuses prepared.

'Suzanna must be persuaded of the wisdom of this,' he said. 'I can best do that. She trusts me.'

'Then I'll come with you.'

'No. I'll do it alone.'

Nimrod looked wary; perhaps even suspicious.

'I watched over you once,' Jerichau reminded him, 'when you were a babe in arms.' This was his ace card. 'Remember that?'

Nimrod couldn't keep a smile from his face. 'Such times,' he said.

'You're going to have to trust me the way you trusted me then,' Jerichau said. He didn't much like the deception, but this was no time for ethical niceties. 'Let me go to Suzanna, and together we'll bring the carpet here. Then we can all go to the Prophet; the three of us.'

'Yes,' said Nimrod. 'I suppose there's sense in that.'

They walked to the door together. The throng of devotees was already dispersing into the night. Jerichau made his farewells and his promises to Nimrod, and headed away. When he'd gained sufficient cover of distance and darkness, he made a long arc around the building, and headed back towards it.

# IV

## AS GOOD MEN GO

I t began to rain while he kept watch at the rear of the foundry, but after twenty minutes his waiting was rewarded. A door opened, and two of the Prophet's Elite Guard emerged. So eager were they for the shelter of their car – there were several parked behind the building – that they left the door behind them ajar. Jerichau lingered in the shelter of the dripping undergrowth until they'd driven away, then crossed at speed to the door, and stepped inside.

He was in a dirty, brick-lined corridor, off which several small passageways ran. A lamp burned at the end of the corridor where he stood; the rest of the place was in darkness.

Once away from the outside door – and the sound of the rain – he could hear voices. He followed them, the passageway becoming darker as he left the vicinity of the bulb. Words came and went.

'. . . the smell of them . . .' somebody said. There was laughter. Using it as cover, Jerichau moved more swiftly towards the sound. Now another light, albeit dim, reached his straining eyes.

'They're making a fool of you,' a second voice said. It was Hobart who replied.

'We're close, I tell you,' he said. 'I'll have her.'

'Never mind the woman . . .' came the response. The voice was perhaps that of the Prophet, though it had changed timbre.

'. . . I want the carpet. All the armies in the world are worth fuck-all if we've got nothing to conquer.'

The vocabulary was less circumspect than his words from the platform had been: there was no reluctance to lead the army here; no false modesty. Jerichau pressed close to the door from beyond which the voices came.

'Get this filth off me will you?' said the Prophet. 'It smothers me.'

No sooner had he spoken than all conversation on the other side of the door abruptly ceased. Jerichau held his breath, fearful he was missing some whispered exchange. But he could hear nothing.

Then, the Prophet again.

'We shouldn't have secrets . . .' he said, apparently apropos of nothing. 'Seeing is believing, don't they *say*!'

At this, the door was flung wide. Jerichau had no chance to retreat, but stumbled forward into the room. He was instantly seized by Hobart, who wrenched his captive's arm behind his back until the bones threatened to snap, at the same time seizing Jerichau's head so hard he could not move it.

'You were right,' said the Prophet. He was standing stark naked in the middle of the room, legs apart, arms spread wide, the sweat dripping from him. A bare bulb threw its uncharitable light upon his pale flesh, from which steam rose.

'I can sniff them out,' said a voice Jerichau recognized, and the Incantatrix Immacolata stepped into his line of vision. Despite his situation the terrible maiming of her face gave him some satisfaction. Harm had been done to this creature. That was cause for rejoicing.

'How long were you listening?' the Prophet asked Jerichau. 'Did you hear anything interesting? Do tell.'

Jerichau looked back towards the man. Three members of the Elite were working about his body, wiping him down with towels. It wasn't just his sweat they were removing; parts of his flesh – at the neck and shoulders, on the arms and hands – were coming away too. This was the smothering filth Jerichau had heard him complain of; he was sloughing off the skin of the Prophet. The air was rank with the stench of venomous raptures: the corrupt magic of the Incantatrix.

'Answer the man,' said Hobart, twisting Jerichau's arm to within a fraction of breaking.

'I heard nothing,' Jerichau gasped.

The steaming man snatched a towel from one of his attendants.

'Jesus,' he said, as he rubbed at his face. 'This stuff is a trial.'

Pieces of flesh fell from beneath the towel, and hit the floor, hissing. He threw the dirtied towel down with them, and looked back up at Jerichau. Remnants of the illusion clung to his features here and there, but the actor beneath was quite recognizable: Shadwell the Salesman, naked as the day he was born. He tore off the white wig he'd worn, and tossed that down too, then snapped his fingers. A cigarette, already lit, was placed in his hand. He drew on it deeply, wiping a glob of ectoplasm from beneath his eye with the ball of his hand.

'Were you at the meeting?' he asked.

'Of course he was,' Immacolata said, but she was silenced with a sharp look from Shadwell. He pulled at his foreskin, quite unselfconsciously.

'Was I good?' he said. 'No, no, of course I was.'

He peered at his pudenda over his shiny gut. 'Who the fuck are you?' he said.

Jerichau kept his mouth shut.

'I asked you a question,' said Shadwell. He put the cigarette between his lips and spread his arms, so that his dressers could finish his toilet. They proceeded to towel the remaining ectoplasm from his face and body, then began to powder his bulk.

'I know him,' said Hobart.

'Do you indeed?'

'He's the woman's partner. He's with Suzanna.'

'Really?' said Shadwell. 'Did you come to make a sale, is that it? See what we'd pay you for her?'

'I haven't seen her . . .' Jerichau said.

365

'Oh yes you have,' said Shadwell. 'And you're going to tell us where to find her.'

Jerichau closed his eyes. Oh Gods, make this end, he thought; don't let me suffer. I'm not strong. I'm not strong.

'It won't take long,' Shadwell murmured.

'Tell him,' said Hobart. Jerichau cried out as his bones creaked.

'Stop that!' Shadwell said. The grip relaxed a little. 'Keep your brutalities out of my sight,' said the Salesman. His voice rose. 'Understand me?' he said. 'Do you? *Do you understand?*'

'Yes, sir.'

Shadwell grunted, then turned to Immacolata, his sudden fury just as suddenly dissipated.

'I think your sisters might enjoy him,' he said. 'Get them here, will you?'

The Incantatrix uttered a summons, which came from her misshapen lips like breath on an icy morning. Shadwell returned his attention to Jerichau, speaking as he dressed.

'There's more than pain to be suffered,' he said lightly, 'if you don't tell me where I may find the carpet.'

He hoisted up his trousers, and buttoned up the fly, throwing an occasional glance in Jerichau's direction.

'What are you waiting for?' he said to the prisoner. 'Some bargain or other?'

He put on his tie, while his attenders tied his shoe-laces.

'You'll wait a long time, my friend. I don't barter these days. I don't offer treats. My days as a Salesman are numbered.'

He took the jacket from his attendant, and slipped it on. The lining shimmered. Its powers were familiar to Jerichau from Suzanna's stories; but it seemed Shadwell had no desire to win a confession from him by that means.

'Tell me where the carpet can be found,' he said, 'or the sisters and their children will undo you nerve by nerve. Not a difficult choice, I would have thought.'

Jerichau made no reply.

There was a chill wind from the corridor.

'Ah, the ladies,' said Shadwell; and Death flew in at the door.

# V

## THE HOURS PASS

### 1

And still he didn't return.

It was three-thirty in the morning. She had stood by the window as the hour grew late; watched drunkards brawl, and two unlikely whores ply their desperate trade, until a police vehicle cruised by and they were either arrested or hired. Now the street was deserted, and all she had to watch were the lights changing at the crossroads – green, red, amber, green – without a vehicle passing in either direction. And still he didn't return.

She turned over a variety of explanations. That the meeting was still going on, and he couldn't slip away without arousing suspicion; that he'd found friends amongst the audience, and was talking over old times with them. That this; that that. But none of her excuses quite convinced her. Something was wrong. She and the menstruum both knew it.

They had made no contingency plans, which was stupid. How could they have been so stupid, she asked herself over and over. Now she was left pacing the narrow room not knowing what to do for the best; not wanting to leave in case he returned the minute after and discovered her gone, yet fearful of staying in case he'd been captured and was even now being beaten into telling them where she could be found.

Time was she would have believed the best. Contented herself that he would come back in a while, and waited patiently for him. But experience had changed her view of things. Life was not that kind.

At four-fifteen she started to pack. The very fact that she'd accepted that something was amiss, that she and the Weave were in jeopardy, made the adrenalin flow. At four-thirty she began to take the carpet downstairs. It was a lengthy and cumbersome business, but in recent months she'd shed every ounce of fat, and in the process discovered muscles she'd never known she had. And again the menstruum was with her, a body of will and light that made possible in minutes what should have taken hours.

Even so there was a hint of dawn in the sky by the time she threw their bags (she had packed for him too) into the back of the car. He would not come back now, she told herself. Something had detained him, and if she wasn't quick it would detain her too.

Fighting tears, she drove away, leaving another unpaid bill behind her.

2

It might have given Suzanna some small satisfaction if she could have seen the look on Hobart's face when, less than twenty minutes after her departure, he arrived at the hotel the prisoner had named.

He'd spilled a good deal while the beasts had their way with him: blood and words in equal measure. But the words were incoherent; a babble from which Hobart wrestled to extract any sense. There was talk of the Fugue, of course, amongst the sobs and the bleatings; and of Suzanna too. *Oh my lady*, he kept saying, *oh my lady*; then fresh sobbing. Hobart let him weep, and bleed, and weep some more, until the man was near to death. Then he asked the simple question: where *is* your lady? And the fool answered, his mind past knowing who asked the question, or indeed if he'd answered it.

And here, in the place the man had spoken of, Hobart now stood. But where was the woman of his dreams? Where was *Suzanna*? Gone again: flitted away, leaving the door-handle warm and the threshold still mourning her shadow.

It had been very close this time, though. He'd almost taken her. How long before he had her mystery netted, once and for all, her silver light between his fingers? Hours. Days at the most.

'Nearly mine,' he said to himself. He clutched the book of faery-tales close to his chest, so that none of its words could slip away, then left his lady's chamber to go whip up the hunt.

# VI

## HELLO, STRANGER

### 1

She hated leaving the city, knowing she was also leaving Jerichau behind somewhere, but whatever she felt for him – and that was a difficulty in itself – she knew better than to linger. She had to go, and go quickly.

But alone? How long would she, *could* she, survive like this? A car, a carpet and woman who sometimes was not even certain she was human . . .

She had friends around the country, and relatives too, but none she knew well enough to really trust. Besides, they'd ask questions, inevitably, and there was no part of this story she'd dare begin to explain. She thought about going back to London; to the flat in Battersea, where her old life – Finnegan and his out of season Valentines, the pots, the damp in the bathroom – would be waiting for her. But again there would be questions, and more questions. She needed the company of someone who would simply accept her, silence and all.

It had to be Cal.

Thinking of him, her spirits lightened. His eager grin came to mind, his soft eyes, his softer words. There was probably more danger in seeking him out than in returning to London, but she was tired of calculating risks.

She would do what her instincts told her to do; and her instincts said:

'Cal?'

There was a long silence at the other end of the telephone line, when she thought contact had been broken.

'Cal, are you there?'

Then he said: 'Suzanna?'

'Yes. It's me.'

'Suzanna . . .'

She felt tears close, hearing him speak her name.

'I have to see you, Cal.'

'Where are you?'

'In the middle of the city. Near some monument of Queen Victoria.'

'The end of Castle Street.'

'If you say so. Can I see you? It's very urgent.'

'Yes, of course. I'm not far from there. I'll slip away now. Meet you on the steps in ten minutes.'


He was there in seven, dressed in a charcoal-grey work suit, collar turned up against the drizzle, one of a hundred similar young men — accountant's clerks and junior managers — she'd seen pass by as she waited under Victoria's imperious gaze.

He did not embrace her, nor even touch her. He simply came to a halt two yards from where she stood, and looked at her with a mixture of pleasure and puzzlement, and said:

'Hello.'

'Hello.'

The rain was coming on more heavily by the moment.

'Shall we talk in the car?' she said. 'I don't like to leave the carpet on its own.'

At the mention of the carpet, the puzzled look on his face intensified, but he said nothing.

In his head Cal had a vague image of himself rummaging

through a dirty warehouse for a carpet, *this* carpet presumably – but his grasp on the whole story was slippery.

The car was parked in Water Street, a stone's throw from the monument. The rain beat a tattoo on the roof of the vehicle as they sat side by side.

Her precious cargo, which she'd been so loath to leave, was stored in the back of the car, doubled up and roughly covered with a sheet. Try as he might, he still couldn't get a fix on why the carpet was so important to her; or indeed why this woman – with whom he could only remember spending a few hours – was so important to him. Why had the sound of her voice on the telephone brought him running? Why had his stomach begun churning at the sight of her? It was absurd and frustrating, to feel so much and know so little.

Things would become clear, he reassured himself, once they began to talk.

But he was wrong in that assumption. The more they talked, the more bewildered he became.

'I need your help,' she said to him. 'I can't explain everything – we haven't got time now – but apparently there's some kind of Prophet appeared, promising a returning to the Fugue. Jerichau went to one of the meetings, and he didn't come back –'

'Wait,' said Cal, hands up to stem the rush of information. 'Hold on a moment. I'm not following this. Jerichau?'

'You remember Jerichau,' she said.

It was an unusual name, not easily forgotten. But he could put no face to it.

'Should I know him?' he said.

'Good God, Cal –'

'To be honest . . . a lot of things . . . are blurred.'

'You remember me well enough.'

'Yes. Of course. Of course I do.'

'And Nimrod. And Apolline. The night in the Fugue.'

She could see even before he murmured 'No' that he remembered nothing.

Perhaps there was a natural process at work here; a means by which the mind dealt with experiences that contradicted a lifetime's prejudices about the nature of reality. People simply *forgot*.

'I have strange dreams,' Cal said, his face full of confusion.

'What sort of dreams?'

He shook his head. He knew his vocabulary would prove woefully inadequate.

'It's hard to describe,' he said. 'Like I'm a child, you know? Except that I'm not. Walking somewhere I've never been. Not lost, though. Oh *shit* –' He gave up, angered by his fumblings. 'I can't describe it.'

'We were *there* once,' she told him calmly. 'You and I. We were there. What you're dreaming about *exists*, Cal.'

He stared at her for long moments. The confusion didn't leave his face, but it was mellowed now by the smallest of smiles.

'Exists?' he said.

'Oh yes. Truly.'

'Tell me,' he said softly. 'Please tell me.'

'I don't know where to begin either.'

'Try,' he said. 'Please.' There was such a yearning in his eyes; such a need to know.

'The carpet –' she began.

He glanced back at it. 'Is it yours?' he asked.

She couldn't help but laugh.

'No,' she said. 'The place you dream of . . . it's here. It's in this carpet.'

She could see incredulity sparring with his faith in her.

'*Here?*' he said.

Sometimes she almost found it difficult to comprehend that fact herself, and she had an advantage over Cal, or even poor Jerichau: she had the menstruum as a touchstone of the miraculous. She didn't blame him for his doubt.

'You have to trust me,' she said. 'However impossible it sounds.'

'I know this,' he said, his voice tight. 'Somewhere in me, *I know this.*'

'Of course you do. And you'll remember. I'll help you remember. But for now I need help from you.'

'Yes. Whatever you want.'

'There are people chasing me.'

'Why? Who?'

'I'll tell you about them, when we get the chance. The point is, they want to destroy the land you dream about, Cal. The world hidden in that carpet. The Fugue.'

'You want to hide back at my place?'

She shook her head. 'I risked a call there to get your work number. They could be waiting there already.'

'Geraldine wouldn't tell them anything.'

'I can't risk that.'

'We could go to Deke's place, out in Kirkby. Nobody'll find us there.'

'You trust him?'

'Sure.'

She switched on the engine. 'I'll drive,' she said. 'You direct.'

3

They turned into James Street, the fury of the rain monsoonal now. They didn't get far. A few yards down the road the traffic had come to a halt.

Cal wound down his window, and ducked his head out to see what the problem was. It was difficult to be certain of anything through the curtain of rain, but there seemed to have been a collision, and the traffic was backing up behind it. A few of the more impatient drivers in the queue were attempting to nose their way out into the city-bound lane, and failing, thus adding to the confusion. Horns began to blare; one or two drivers got out of their cars, their coats as makeshift umbrellas, to see what was up.

Cal laughed quietly.

'What's funny?' she asked him.

'An hour ago I was sitting in the Claims Department up to my elbows in paperwork –'

'Now you've got a fugitive for company.'

'The deal's fine by me,' he grinned.

'Why the hell aren't we moving?'

'I'll go look,' he said, and before she could prevent him he was out of the car and threading his way through the maze of vehicles, pulling his jacket up in a vain attempt to keep the rain off his head.

She watched him go, her fingers drumming on the wheel. She didn't like this situation. She was too visible: and visible was vulnerable.

As Cal reached the opposite side of the street, her attention was claimed by a flash of blue lights in the wing mirror. She glanced round to see several police motor-cycles cruising along the queue towards the accident. Her heart jumped a beat.

She looked towards Cal, hoping he was on his way back, but he was still studying the traffic. Come on out of the rain, damn you, she willed him; I need you here.

There were more officers, these on foot, making their way up the street, and they were speaking to the occupants of each car. Diversionary advice, no doubt; innocent enough. All she had to do was keep smiling.

Up ahead, cars were beginning to move off. The riders were directing the traffic around an accident site, bringing a halt to the contrary flow to do so. She looked over towards Cal, who was staring off down the street. Should she get out of the car; call him back? As she weighed the options, an officer appeared at her side, rapping on the window. She wound it down.

'Wait for the signal,' he told her. 'And take it slowly.'

He stared at her, rain dripping off his helmet and his nose. She offered a smile.

'Fine,' she said. 'I'll be careful.'

Though he'd delivered his instructions, he didn't move from the window, but stared at her.

'I know your face,' he said.

'Really?' she said, trying for light flirtatiousness, and missing by a mile.

'What's your name?'

Before she had time to lie, one of the officers up ahead called to her interrogator. He stood up, giving her an opportunity to glance back in Cal's direction. He was standing on the edge of the pavement, staring across at the car. She made a small shake of her head, hoping he'd read her signal through the rain-blurred window. The officer caught her warning.

'Something wrong?' he said.

'No,' she told him. 'Not at all.'

Another of the officers was approaching the car, shouting something over the din of rain and idling engines. The longer I stay here, she thought, the worse this is going to get; and she wrenched the wheel round. The officer at the window yelled for her to stop, but the die was cast. As the car bolted forward she chanced the briefest of glances in Cal's direction. She saw to her distress that he was engaged in trying to wind his way between the cars. Though she shouted his name, he was oblivious to her. She shouted again. Too late, he looked up; the officer in the front was running towards the car. He'd reached it before Cal was half way across the road. She had no choice but to make her escape, while she still had a prayer.

She accelerated, the officer in front of her throwing himself out of her path with inches to spare. There was no time to look back for Cal; she skirted the collision site at speed, hoping he'd used the diversion to pick up his heels and run.

She'd travelled no more than four hundred yards when she heard the sound of sirens rising behind her.

### 4

It took Cal half a dozen seconds to work out what had happened, and another two to curse his sloth. There was a moment of confusion, when none of the officers seemed certain whether to wait for instructions or give chase, during which pause Suzanna was away around the corner.

The officer who'd been at the car window instantly made his way in Cal's direction, his pace picking up with every step.

Cal pretended he hadn't seen the man, and began to walk

speedily back up towards the monument. There was a shouted summons, and then the sound of pursuit. He ran, not looking behind him. His pursuer was heavily dressed against the rain; Cal was much lighter footed. He made a left into Lower Castle Street, and another onto Brunswick Street, then a right onto Drury Lane. The sirens had begun by now; the bikes were in pursuit of Suzanna.

On Water Street he chanced a backward glance. His pursuer was not in sight. He didn't slow his pace, however, until he'd put half a mile between himself and the police. Then he hailed himself a taxi and headed back to the house, his head full of questions, and of Suzanna's face. She'd come and gone too quickly; already he was mourning her absence.

In order to better hold onto her memory, he fumbled for the names she'd spoken; but damn it, they were gone already.

# VII

_____

## LOST CAUSES

### 1

The blinding rain proved to be Suzanna's ally; so, perhaps, did her ignorance of the city. She took every turn she could, only avoiding cul-de-sacs, and the lack of any rationale in her escape route seemed to flummox her pursuers. Her path brought her out into Upper Parliament Street; at which point she put on some speed. The sirens faded behind her.

But it would not be for long, she knew. The noose was tightening once more.

There were breaks in the rain-bellied clouds as she drove from the city, and shafts of sun found their way between, leaving a sheen of gold on roof and tarmac. But for moments only. Then the clouds sealed their wound, and the benediction ceased.

She drove and drove, as the afternoon grew late, and once more she was alone.

### 2

Cal stood at the kitchen door. Geraldine – who was peeling an onion – looked up and said:

'Did you forget your umbrella?'

And he thought: she doesn't know who I am or what I am,

and how could she?, because God in Heaven I don't know either. I forget myself. Oh Jesus, why do I forget myself?

'Are you all right?' she was asking him, putting down the onion and the knife now and crossing the kitchen towards him. 'Look at you. You're soaked.'

'I'm in trouble,' he said flatly.

She stopped in her tracks. 'What, Cal?'

'I think the police may come here looking for me.'

'Why?'

'Don't ask. It's too complicated.'

Her face tightened a little.

'There was a woman on the 'phone this afternoon,' she said, 'asking for your work number. Did she get through to you?'

'Yes.'

'And is she something to do with this?'

'Yes.'

'Tell me, Cal.'

'I don't know where to begin.'

'Are you having a fling with this woman?'

'No,' he said. Then thought: *At least not that I remember*.

'Tell me then.'

'Later. Not now. Later.'

He left the kitchen to the smell of onions.

'Where are you going?' she called after him.

'I'm soaked to the skin.'

'*Cal.*'

'I have to get changed.'

'How bad is this trouble you're in?'

He stopped half way up the stairs, pulling off his tie.

'I can't remember,' he replied, but a voice at the back of his head – a voice he hadn't heard in a long while – said: *Bad son, bad*, and he knew it spoke the bitter truth.

She followed him as far as the bottom of the stairs. He went into the bedroom, and peeled off his wet clothes, while she continued to ply him with questions for which he had no replies, and with every unanswered question he could hear her voice get closer to tears. He knew he'd call himself a louse for this tomorrow (what was tomorrow?; another dream), but

379

he had to be away from the house again quickly, in case the police came looking for him. He had nothing to tell them of course — at least he could remember nothing. But they had ways, these people, of making a man speak.

He rummaged through the wardrobe, looking for a shirt, jeans and a coat, not giving a conscious thought to the choice. As he slipped on the thread-bare jacket he glanced out of the window. The street-lights had just come on; the rain was a silver torrent in their glare. A chilly night for a jaunt, but it couldn't be helped. He dug in his work suit for his wallet, which he transferred to his pocket, and that was it.

Geraldine was still at the bottom of the stairs, looking up at him. She had successfully fought off tears.

'And what am I supposed to tell them,' she demanded, 'if they come looking for you?'

'Say I came and went. Tell them the truth.'

'Maybe I won't be here,' she said. Then, warming to the idea. 'Yes. I don't think I'll be here.'

He had neither the time nor the words to offer any genuine solace.

'Please trust me,' was all he could find to say. 'I don't know what's happening any more than you do.'

'Maybe you should see a doctor, Cal,' she said as he came downstairs. 'Maybe . . .' — her voice softened — '. . . you're ill.'

He stopped his descent.

'Brendan told me things —' she went on.

'Don't bring Dad into this.'

'No, *listen to me*,' she insisted. 'He used to talk to me, Cal. Told me things in confidence. Things he thought he'd seen.'

'I don't want to hear.'

'He said he'd seen some woman killed in the back garden. And some monster on the railway track.' She smiled gently at the lunacy of this.

Cal stared down at her, suddenly sick to his stomach. Again, he thought: *I know this*.

'Maybe *you're* having hallucinations too.'

380

'He was telling stories to keep you amused,' said Cal. 'He used to like to make stuff up. It was the Irish in him.'

'Is that what you're doing, Cal?' she said, pleading for some reassurance. 'Tell me it's a joke.'

'I wish to God I could.'

'Oh, Cal —'

He went to the bottom of the stairs and softly stroked her face.

'If anyone comes asking —'

'I'll tell them the truth,' she said. 'I don't know anything.'

'Thank you.'

As he crossed to the front door she said:

'Cal?'

'Yes?'

'You're not in love with this woman are you? Only I'd prefer you to tell me if you are.'

He opened the door. The rain slapped the doorstep.

'I can't remember,' he said, and made a dash to the car.

3

After half an hour on the motorway the effects of a night without sleep, and all that the subsequent day had brought, began to catch up with Suzanna. The road in front of her blurred. She knew it was only a matter of time before she fell asleep at the wheel. She turned off the motorway at the first service stop, parked the car and went in search of a caffeine fix.

The cafeteria and amenities were thronged with customers, which she was thankful for. Amongst so many people, she was insignificant. Anxious about leaving the Weave a moment longer than she needed to, she purchased coffee from the vending machine rather than wait in a serpentine queue, then bought chocolate and biscuits from the shop and went back to the car.

Switching on the radio, she settled down to her stopgap meal. As she unwrapped the chocolate her thoughts went

381

again to Jerichau, the thief-magician, producing stolen goods from every pocket. Where was he now? She toasted him with her coffee, and told him to be safe.

At eight, the news came on. She waited for some mention of herself, but there was none. After the bulletin there was music; she let it play. Coffee drunk, chocolate and biscuits devoured, she slid down in the seat and her eyes closed to a jazz lullaby.

She was woken, mere seconds later, by a knocking on the window. There was a period of confusion while she worked out where she was, then she was wide awake, and staring with sinking heart at the uniform on the other side of the rain-streaked glass.

'Please open the door,' the policeman said. He seemed to be alone. Should she just turn on the engine and drive away? Before she could reach any decision the door was wrenched open from the outside.

'Get out,' the man said.

She complied. Even as she stepped from the car she heard the sound of soles on gravel on all sides of her.

Against the glare of the neon, a man stood silhouetted.

'Yes,' was all he said, and suddenly there were men coming at her from all sides. She was about to dig for the menstruum, but the silhouette was approaching her, with something in its hand. Somebody tore the sleeve from her arm, she felt the needle slide into her exposed skin. The subtle body rose, but not quickly enough. Her will grew sluggish, her sight narrowed to a well-shaft. At the end of it, Hobart's mouth. She tumbled towards the man, her fingers gouging the slime on the walls, while the beast at the bottom roared its hosannas.

# VIII

## NEW EYES FOR OLD

The Mersey was high tonight, and fast; its waters a filthy brown, its spume grey. Cal leaned on the promenade railing and stared across the churning river to the deserted shipyards on the far bank. Once this waterway had been busy with ships, arriving weighed down with their cargo and riding high as they headed for faraway. Now, it was empty. The docks silted up, the wharfs and warehouses idle. Spook City; fit only for ghosts.

He felt like one himself. An insubstantial wanderer. And cold too, the way the dead must be cold. He put his hands in his jacket pocket to warm them, and his fingers found there half a dozen soft objects, which he took out and examined by the light of a nearby lamp.

They looked like withered plums, except that the skin was much tougher, like old shoe-leather. Clearly they were fruit, but no variety he could name. Where and how had he come by them? He sniffed at one. It smelt slightly fermented, like a heady wine. And appetizing; tempting even. Its scent reminded him that he'd not eaten since lunchtime.

He put the fruit to his lips, his teeth breaking through the corrugated skin with ease. The scent had not deceived; the meat inside did indeed have an alcoholic flavour, the juice burning his throat like cognac. He chewed, and had the fruit to his lips for a second bite before he'd swallowed the first, finishing it off, seeds and all, with a fierce appetite.

Immediately, he began to devour another of them. He was

suddenly ravenous. He lingered beneath the wind-buffeted lamp, the pool of light he stood in dancing, and fed his face as though he'd not eaten in a week.

He was biting into the penultimate fruit when it dawned on him that the rocking of the lamp above couldn't entirely account for the motion of the light around him. He looked down at the fruit in his hand, but he couldn't quite focus on it. God alive! Had he poisoned himself? The remaining fruit dropped from his hand and he was about to put his fingers down his throat to make himself vomit up the rest when the most extraordinary sensation overtook him.

*He rose up*; or at least some part of him did.

His feet were still on the concrete, he could feel it solid beneath his soles, but he was still floating up, the lamp shining *beneath* him now, the promenade stretching out to right and left of him, the river surging against the banks, wild and dark.

The rational fool in him said: *you're intoxicated; the fruits have made you drunk.*

But he felt neither sick nor out of control; his sight (sights) were clear. He could still see from the eyes in his head, but also from a vantage point high above him. Nor was that all he could see. Part of him was with the litter too, gusting along the promenade; another part was out in the Mersey, gazing back towards the bank.

This proliferation of viewpoints didn't confuse him: the sights mingled and married in his head, a pattern of risings and fallings; of looking out and back and far and near.

He was not *one* but *many*.

He Cal; he his father's son; he his mother's son; he a child buried in a man, and a man dreaming of being a bird.

*A bird!*

And all at once it *all* came back to him; all the wonders he'd forgotten surged back with exquisite particularity. A thousand moments and glimpses and words.

A bird, a chase, a house, a yard, a carpet, a flight (and he the bird; *yes! yes!*); then enemies and friends; Shadwell, Immacolata; the monsters; and Suzanna, his beautiful

384

Suzanna, her place suddenly clear in the story his mind was telling itself.

He remembered it all. The carpet unweaving, the house coming apart; then into the Fugue, and the glories that the night there had brought.

It took all his new-found senses to hold the memories, but he was not overwhelmed. It seemed he dreamed them all at once; held them in a moment that was sweet beyond words: a reunion of self and secret self which was an heroic remembering.

And after the recognition, tears, as for the first time he touched the buried grief he felt at losing the man who'd taught him the poem he'd recited in Lo's orchard: his father, who'd lived and died and never once known what Cal knew now.

Momentarily, sorrow and salt drew him back into himself, and he was single-sighted once more, standing under the uncertain light, bereft –

Then his soul soared again, higher now, and higher, and this time it reached escape velocity.

Suddenly he was up, *up* above England.

Below him moonlight fell on bright continents of cloud, whose vast shadows moved over hill-side and suburb like silent ushers of sleep. He went too, carried on the same winds. Over tracts of land which pylons strode in humming lines; and city streets the hour had emptied of all but felons and wild dogs.

And this flight, gazing down like a lazy hawk, stars at his back, the isle beneath him, this flight was companion to that other he'd taken, over the carpet, over the Fugue.

No sooner had his mind turned to the Weaveworld than he seemed to sniff it – seemed to know where it lay beneath him. His eye was not sharp enough to pick out its place, but he knew he could find it, if he could only keep this new sense intact when he finally returned to the body beneath him.

The carpet was North-North-East of the city, that he *was* certain of; many miles away and still moving. Was it in Suzanna's hands?; was she fleeing to some remote place where she prayed their enemies wouldn't come? No, the news was worse than that, he sensed. The Weaveworld and the woman who carried it were in terrible jeopardy, somewhere below him –

At that thought his body grew possessive of him once more. He felt it around him – its heat, its weight – and he exalted in its solidity. Flying thoughts were all very well, but what were they worth without muscle and bone to act upon them?

A moment later he was standing beneath the light once more, and the river was still churning and the clouds he'd just seen from above moved in mute flotillas before a wind that smelt of the sea. The salt he tasted was not sea-salt; it was the tears he'd shed for the death of his father, and for his forgetting, and for his mother too perhaps – for it seemed all loss was one loss, all forgetting one forgetting.

But he'd brought new wisdom from the high places. He knew now that things forgotten might be recalled; things lost, found again.

That was all that mattered in the world: to search and find.

He looked North-North-East. Though the many sights he'd had were once more narrowed to one, he knew he could still find the carpet.

He saw it with his heart. And seeing it, started in pursuit.

# IX

## A SECRET PLACE

**S**uzanna stirred from her drugged sleep only slowly. At first the effort to keep her lids open for more than a few seconds was too much for her, and her consciousness struggled in darkness. But by degrees her body was cleansing itself of whatever Hobart had put into her veins. She just had to let it do that job in its own good time.

She was in the back of Hobart's car; that much was clear. Her enemy was in the front seat beside the driver. At one point he looked round, and saw that she was waking, but said nothing. He just stared at her for a little time, then returned his attentions to the road. There was something uncomfortably lazy about the look in his eyes, as if he was certain now of what the future would bring and had no need to hurry towards it.

In her drowsy state it was difficult to calculate time, but surely hours passed as they drove. Once she opened her eyes to find them passing through a sleeping city – she did not know which – then the remnants of the drug won her over again and when next she woke they were travelling a winding country road, lightless hills rising to either side. Only now did she realize that Hobart's car was leading a convoy; there were headlamps shining through the back window from the vehicles behind. She summoned up strength enough to turn round. There was a Black Maria following, and several vehicles behind that.

Again, drowsiness overtook her for a timeless while.

It was cold air that woke her again. The driver had opened

the window, and the air had brought goose-pimples to her arms. She sat up and breathed deeply, letting the chill slap her to wakefulness. The region they were driving through was mountainous. The Scottish Highlands, she presumed; where else would there still be snowy peaks in the middle of spring? They took a route now that led them off the road onto a rocky track, which slowed their pace considerably. The track rose, winding. The engine of the van behind laboured; but the road got rougher and steeper still before it delivered them to the top of the hill.

'There,' said Hobart to the driver. 'We found it. There!'

Suzanna peered from the window. There was neither moon nor stars to illuminate the scene, but she could see the black bulk of the mountains all around, and far below, lights burning.

The convoy followed the hill top for half a mile, then began a steady descent into the valley.

The lights she'd seen were car headlamps, the vehicles parked in a large circle, so that the lights created an arena. The arrival of Hobart's convoy was clearly expected; as they came within fifty yards of the circle she saw figures coming to greet them.

The car came to a halt.

'Where are we?' she slurred.

'Journey's end,' was all Hobart would say. Then, to the driver: 'Bring her.'

The legs beneath her were rubber-jointed; she had to hold onto the car for a while before she could persuade them to behave. With the driver keeping firm hold of her, she was then taken towards the arena. Only now did she realize the scale of the gathering. There were dozens of cars in the ring, and many more in the darkness beyond. The drivers and passengers, who amounted to hundreds, were not Human but Seerkind. Amongst them were anatomies and colorations that must have made them outcasts in the Kingdom.

She scanned the faces, looking for any that she knew, and one in particular. But Jerichau was not amongst them.

Hobart now stepped into the ring of light, and as he did so from the shadows on the opposite side of the arena stepped a figure Suzanna assumed was that of the Prophet. His appearance was greeted with a soft swell of murmuring from the Seerkind. Some pushed their way forward to get a better look at their Saviour; others fell to their knees.

He *was* impressive, Suzanna conceded to herself.

His deep-set eyes were fixed on Hobart, and a small smile of approval found his lips as the Inspector bowed his head before his master. So, that was the way of it. Hobart was in the Prophet's employ, which fact scarcely covered the latter with glory. Words were exchanged between them, the breath of the speakers visible on the cold air. Then the Prophet put his gloved hand on Hobart's shoulder and turned to announce to the assembly the return of the Weaveworld. Suddenly the air was full of shouts.

Hobart turned towards the Black Maria and beckoned. From its recesses came two of the Inspector's cohorts, carrying the carpet. They entered the ring of light, and, at Hobart's instruction, laid the carpet at the Prophet's feet. The crowd was hushed utterly in the presence of their sleeping homeland; and the Prophet, when he spoke, did not need to raise his voice.

'*Here*,' he said, almost casually. '*Did I not promise?*'

. . . and so saying he put his heel to the carpet. It unrolled in front of him. The silence held; all eyes were on the design; two hundred minds and more sharing the same thought . . .

*Open Sesame* . . .

. . . the call of all eager visitors, set before closed doors, and desiring access.

Open; show yourself . . .

Whether it was that collective act of will that began the unweaving, or whether the Prophet had previously plotted the mechanism, Suzanna could not know. Sufficient that it began. Not at the centre of the carpet, as at Shearman's house, but from the borders.

The last unweaving had been more accident than design, a

389

wild eruption of threads and pigment, the Fugue breaking into sudden and chaotic life. This time there was clearly system at work in the process, the knots decoding their motifs in a pre-arranged sequence. The dance of threads was no less complex than before, but there was a consummate grace about the spectacle, the strands describing the most elegant manœuvres as they filled the air, trailing life as they went. Forms were clothing themselves in flesh and feather, rock was flowing, trees taking flight towards their rooting place.

Suzanna had seen this glory before, of course, and was to some extent prepared for it. But to the Seerkind, and even more to Hobart and his bully-boys, the sight awoke fear and awe in equal measure.

Her guard utterly forgot his duty, and stood like a child before his first firework display, unsure of whether to run or stay. She took her chance while it was offered, and slipped from his custody, away from the light that would reveal her, glancing back long enough to see the Prophet, his hair rising like white fire from his scalp, standing in the midst of the unweaving while the Fugue burst into life all around him.

It was difficult to draw her gaze away, but she ran as best her legs would allow towards the darkness of the slopes. She moved twenty, thirty, forty yards from the circle. Nobody came after her.

A particularly bright blossoming at her back momentarily lit the terrain before her like a falling star. It was rough, uncultivated ground, interrupted only by the occasional outcrop of rock; a valley chosen for its remoteness, most likely, where the Fugue could be stirred from sleep uninterrupted by Humankind. How long this miracle would remain hidden, with summer on its way, was a moot point, but perhaps they had plans for a rapture to divert the inquisitive.

Again, the land ahead of her was lit, and momentarily she glimpsed a figure up ahead. It was there and gone so quickly she could not trust her eyes.

Another yard however, and she felt a chill on her cheek that was no natural wind. She guessed its source the instant it touched her, but she had no time to retreat or prepare herself before the darkness unfolded and its mistress stepped into her path.

# X

## FATALITIES

### 1

The face was mutilated beyond recognition, but the voice, colder than the chill the body gave off, was indisputably that of Immacolata. Nor was she alone: her sisters were with her, darker than the dark.

'Why are you running?' said the Incantatrix. 'There's nowhere to escape to.'

Suzanna halted. There was no ready way past the three.

'Turn around,' said Immacolata, another splendour from the Weave uncharitably lighting the wound of her face. 'See where Shadwell stands? That'll be the Fugue in moments.'

'Shadwell?' said Suzanna.

'Their beloved Prophet,' came the reply. 'Beneath that show of holiness I lent him, there beats a Salesman's heart.'

So Shadwell was the Prophet. What a perfect irony, that the seller of encyclopaedias should end up peddling hope.

'It was *his* idea,' said the Incantatrix, 'to give them a Messiah. Now they've got a righteous crusade, as Hobart calls it. They're going to claim their promised land. And destroy it in the process.'

'They won't fall for this.'

'They already have, sister. Holy wars are easier to start than rumours, amongst your Kind or mine. They believe every sacred word he tells them, as though their lives depended upon it. Which in a sense they do. They've been conspired against and cheated — and they're ready to tear the Fugue apart to get their hands on those responsible. Isn't that perfect?

The Fugue'll die at the very hands of those who've come to save it.'

'And that's what Shadwell wants?'

'He's a man: he wants adoration.' She gazed over Suzanna's shoulder towards the unweaving, and the Salesman, still in its midst. 'And that's what he's got. So he's happy.'

'He's pitiful,' said Suzanna. 'You know that as well as I do. Yet you give him power. Your power. *Our* power.'

'For my own ends, sister.'

'You gave him the jacket.'

'It was of my making, yes. Though there've been times I've regretted the gift.'

The ragged muscle of Immacolata's face was incapable of its former deceptions. As she spoke she couldn't mask the sorrow in her.

'You should have taken it back,' said Suzanna.

'A gift of rapture can't be *lent*,' said Immacolata, 'only given, and given in perpetuity. Did your grandmother teach you *nothing*? It's time you learned, sister. I'll give you those lessons.'

'And what do you get in return?'

'A distraction from Romo's gift to me.' She touched her face. 'And from the stench of men.' She paused, her maimed face darkening. 'They'll destroy you for your strength. Men like Hobart.'

'I wanted to kill him once,' Suzanna said, remembering the hatred she'd felt.

'He knows that. That's why he dreams of you. Death the maiden.' A laugh broke from her. 'They're all mad, sister.'

'Not *all*,' said Suzanna.

'What must I do to persuade you?' the Incantatrix said. 'Make you understand how you'll be betrayed. Have *already* been betrayed.'

Without seeming to take a step, she moved away from Suzanna. Flickering strands of light were moving past them now, as the Fugue spread from its hiding place. But Suzanna scarcely noticed. Her eyes were fixed on the sight revealed when Immacolata stood aside.

The Magdalene was there, sumptuously clothed in folds of

lacy ectoplasm: a wraith bride. And from beneath the creature's skirts a pitiful figure was emerging, and turning its face up towards Suzanna.

'Jerichau . . .'

The man's eyes were clouded; though they settled on Suzanna there was no recognition in them.

'See?' said Immacolata. 'Betrayed.'

'What have you *done* to him?' Suzanna demanded.

There was nothing left of the Jerichau she'd known. He looked like something already dead. His clothes were in tatters, his skin mottled and seeping from dozens of vicious wounds.

'He doesn't know you,' said the Incantatrix. 'He has a new wife now.'

The Magdalene stretched her hand out and touched Jerichau's head, stroking it as if he were a lap-dog.

'He went to my sister's arms willingly —' Immacolata said.

'Leave him be,' Suzanna yelled at the Magdalene. Enfeebled by the drugs, her self-control was perilously thin.

'But this is love,' Immacolata goaded. 'There'll be children in time. Many children. His lust knows no bounds.'

The thought of Jerichau coupling with the Magdalene made Suzanna shudder. Again, she called his name. This time his mouth opened, and it seemed his tongue was seeking to form a word. But no. All his palate could produce was a dribble of saliva.

'You see how quickly they turn to fresh pleasures?' said Immacolata. 'As soon as your back is turned he's ploughing another furrow.'

Rage leapt up in Suzanna, bettering her disgust. Nor did it come alone. Though the remnants of the drug still made any focus difficult, she felt the menstruum ambitious in her belly.

Immacolata knew it.

'Don't be perverse . . .' she said, her voice seeming to whisper at Suzanna's ear though they stood yards apart. 'We are more alike than not.'

As she spoke Jerichau raised his hands from the ground towards Suzanna, and now she realized why there was no

394

recognition in his eyes. He could not see her. The Magdalene had blinded her consort, to keep him close. But he knew she was there: he heard her, he reached for her.

'Sister . . .' Immacolata said to the Magdalene, '. . . bring your husband to heel.'

The Magdalene was quick to obey. The hand she had on Jerichau's head grew longer, the fingers pouring down over his face, entering his mouth and nostrils. Jerichau attempted to resist, but the Magdalene pulled on him, and he tumbled backwards amongst her pestilential petticoats.

Without warning, Suzanna felt the menstruum spill from her and fly towards Jerichau's tormentor. It happened in the time it took to see it. She caught a glimpse of the Magdalene's features, stretched into a shriek, then the stream of silver light struck her. The wraith's cry broke into pieces, fragments of sound spiralling off − a sobbing complaint, a howl of anger − as the assault lifted her into the air.

As usual, Suzanna's thoughts were a beat behind the menstruum. Before she was fully aware of what she was doing the light was tearing at the wraith, gaping holes opening in its matter. The Magdalene retaliated, the stream of the menstruum carrying the attack back into Suzanna's face. She felt blood splash down her neck, but the barbs only spurred her fury; she was tearing her enemy as though the wraith were a sheet of tissue paper.

Immacolata had not been a passive spectator in this, but had flung her own attack against Suzanna. The ground at Suzanna's feet shuddered, then rose around her as if to bury her alive, but the subtle body pitched the earth wall back, then went at the Magdalene with redoubled fury. Though the menstruum seemed to have a life of its own, that was an illusion. She owned this power, she knew; now more than ever. It was *her* anger that fuelled it, that deafened it to mercy or apology; it was she who would not be satisfied until the Magdalene was undone.

And all at once, it was over. The Magdalene's cries stopped dead.

*Enough*, Suzanna instructed. The menstruum let the few

fragments of rotted ectoplasm drop to the spattered ground, and withdrew its light into its mistress. From attack to counter-attack to *coup de grace* had taken maybe a dozen seconds.

Suzanna looked towards Immacolata, whose wretched features were all disbelief. She was trembling from head to foot, as if she might fall to the ground in a fit. Suzanna took her chance. She'd no way of knowing if she could survive a sustained attack from the Incantatrix, and now was certainly no time to put the problem to the test. As the third sister threw herself amongst the Magdalene's litter, and began to wail, Suzanna took to her heels.

The tide of the Fugue was lapping all around them now, and the brilliant air camouflaged her flight. Only after she'd covered ten yards or more did she come to her senses and remember Jerichau. There had been no sign of him in the vicinity of the dead Magdalene. Praying that he had found his way off the battlefield, she ran on, the Hag's harrowing din loud in her ears.

2

She ran and ran, believing over and over that she felt the chill of the Virgin on her neck. But it seemed she imagined the pursuit, for she ran unhindered for a mile or more, up the slope of the valley and over the crest of a hill, until the light of the Weave's forthcoming was dim behind her.

It would only be a short time before the Fugue reached her, and when it did she would need to have some strategy. But first she had to catch her breath.

The gloom nursed her awhile. She stood trying not to think too hard of what she'd just done. But a certain ungovernable elation filled her. She had killed the Magdalene; destroyed one of the Three: it was no minor feat. Had the power in her always been so dangerous?; ripening behind her ignorance, growing wise, growing lethal?

For some reason she remembered Mimi's book, which presumably Hobart still had in his possession. Now more than ever she hoped it could teach her something of what she was, and how to profit by it. She would have to get the volume back, even if it meant confronting Hobart once more.

As she formulated this thought she heard her name uttered, or an approximation of it. She looked in the direction of the voice, and there, standing a few yards from her, was Jerichau.

He had indeed escaped the Magdalene's grasp, though his face was scored by the sister's ethereal fingers. His wracked frame was on the verge of collapse, and even as he called Suzanna's name a second time, and threw his withered arms out towards her, his legs gave way beneath him and he fell face down on the ground.

She was kneeling by his side in moments, and turning him over. He was feather-light. The sisters had drained him of all but the spark of purpose that had sent him stumbling after her. Blood they could take; and seed and muscle. Love he'd kept.

She drew him up towards her. His head lolled against her breasts. His breathing was fast and shallow, his cold body full of tremors. She stroked his head; the diminishing light around it playing about her fingers.

He was not content simply to be cradled, however, but pushed himself away from her body a few inches in order to reach up and touch her face. The veins in his throat throbbed as he tried to speak. She hushed him, saying there would be time to talk later. But he made a tiny shake of his head, and she could feel as she held him how close the end was. She did him no kindness to pretend otherwise. It was time to die, and he had sought out her arms as a place to perform that duty.

'Oh my sweet . . .' she said, her chest aching. '. . . sweet man . . .'

Again he strove for words, but his tongue cheated him. Only soft sounds came, which she could make no sense of.

She leaned closer to him. He no longer resisted her comforting, but took hold of her shoulder and drew himself closer still to speak to her. This time she made a sense of the words, though they were scarcely more than sighs.

'I'm not afraid,' he said, expelling the last word on a breath that had no brother, but came against her cheek like a kiss.

Then his hand lost its strength, and slipped from her shoulder, his eyes closed, and he was gone from her.

A bitter thought came visiting: that his last words were as much a plea as a statement. Jerichau had been the only one she'd ever told about how at the warehouse the menstruum had stirred Cal from unconsciousness. Was that *I'm not afraid* his way of saying: leave me to death?; I wouldn't thank you for resurrection?

Whatever he'd meant she'd never find out now.

She laid him gently on the earth. Once, he'd spoken words of love that had defied their condition, and become light. Were there others he knew, that defied Death, or was he already on his way to that region Mimi had left for, all contact with the world Suzanna still occupied broken?

It seemed so. Though she watched the body 'til her eyes ached, it made no murmur. He had left it to the earth, and her with it.

# XI

## CAL, TRAVELLING NORTH

### 1

C al's journey North dragged on through the night, but he didn't weary. Perhaps it was the fruit that kept his senses so preternaturally clear; either that or a new-found sense of purpose that pressed him forward. He kept his analytic faculties on hold, making decisions as to his route instinctively.

Was it the same sense the pigeons had possessed that he now navigated by? A dream-sense, beyond the reach of intellect or reason: a *homing*? That was how it felt. That he'd become a bird, orienting himself not by the stars (they were blotted by clouds), nor by the magnetic pole, but by the simple urge to go home; back to the orchard, where he'd stood in a ring of loving faces and spoken Mad Mooney's verse.

As he drove he ransacked his head for other such fragments, so that he'd have something fresh to perform next time. Little rhymes came back from childhood, odd lines that he'd learned more for their music than their meaning.

> '*Naked Heaven comes and goes,*
> *Spits out seas and dyes the rose,*
> *Puts on coats of wind and rain*
> *And simply takes them off again.*'

He was no more certain of what some were about now than he'd been as a child, but they came to his lips as if fresh-minted, secure in their rhythms and rhymes.

Some had a bitter sting:

> *'The pestilence of families*
> *Is not congenital disease*
> *But feet that follow where the foot*
> *That has proceeeded them was put.'*

Others were fragments from poems which he'd either forgotten or never been taught in their entirety. One in particular kept coming back to him.

> *'How I love the pie-bald horses!*
> *Best of all, the pie-bald horses!'*

That was the closing lines of something, he presumed, but of what he couldn't remember.

There were plenty of other fragments. He recited the lines over and over as he drove, polishing his delivery, finding a new emphasis here, a fresh rhythm there.

There was no prompting from the back of his head; the poet was quite silent. Or was it that he and Mad Mooney were finally speaking with a single voice?

## 2

He crossed the border into Scotland about two-thirty in the morning and continued to drive North, the landscape becoming hillier and less populated as he drove. He was getting hungry, and his muscles were beginning to ache after so many hours of uninterrupted driving, but nothing short of Armageddon would have coaxed him to slow down or stop. With every mile he came nearer to Wonderland, in which a life too long delayed was waiting to be lived.

# XII

## RESOLUTION

### 1

Suzanna sat beside Jerichau's body for a long while, thinking, while trying all the time not to think. Down the hill the unweaving was still going on; the tide of the Fugue approaching her. But she couldn't face the beauty of it, not at the moment. When the threads started to come within fifty yards of her she retreated, leaving Jerichau's body where it lay.

Dawn was paling the clouds overhead. She decided to climb to higher ground so as to have an overview when day came. The higher she went the windier it became; a bitter wind, from the North. But it was worth the shivering, for the promontory she stood upon offered her a fine panorama, and as the day strengthened she realized just how cannily Shadwell had selected this valley. It was bounded on all sides by steep hills, whose slopes were bereft of any building, however humble. Indeed the only sign of human presence was the primitive track the convoy had followed to get here, which had most likely been used more in the last twenty-four hours than it had in its entire span hitherto.

It was on that road, as dawn brought colour to the hills, that she saw the car. It crept along the ridge of the hill a little way, then came to a halt. Its driver, minuscule from Suzanna's vantage point, got out and surveyed the valley. It seemed the Fugue below was not visible to such a casual witness, for the driver got back into the car almost immediately as if realizing that he'd taken a wrong turning. He didn't drive away how-

401

ever, as she'd expected. Instead he took the vehicle off the track, parking it out of sight amongst the gorse bushes. Then he got out again and began to walk in her direction, following a zig-zag route along the boulder-strewn hillside.

And now she began to think she recognized him; began to hope that her eyes did not deceive her, and that it was indeed Cal who was making his way towards her.

Had he seen her? It seemed not, for he was now starting to descend. She ran a little way to close the gap between them, and then climbed onto a rock and waved her arms. Her signal went unnoticed for several seconds, until by chance he glanced her way. He stopped, cupping his hand over his eyes. Then he changed directions and began to bound back up the slope towards her, and yes! it *was* Cal. Even then she feared some self-deception, until the sound of his raw breath reached her ears, and the squeak of his heels on the dewy grass.

He covered the last few yards between them stumbling more than running, and suddenly he was a moment away and she was crossing to meet his open arms, hugging him to her.

And this time it was she who said, 'I love you,' and answered his smiles with kisses and kisses.

2

They exchanged the bones of their stories as quickly as they could, leaving the meat for less urgent times.

'Shadwell doesn't want to sell the Fugue any longer,' said Suzanna. 'He wants to possess it.'

'And play the Prophet forever?' said Cal.

'I doubt that. He'll drop the pretence once he's in control.'

'Then we have to prevent him *seizing* control,' said Cal. 'Unmask him.'

'Or simply kill him,' she said.

He nodded. 'Let's not linger then,' he said.

They stood up and looked down at the world that now occupied the length and breadth of the valley beneath them. The unweaving was still not completed; filaments of light crept through the grass, spreading flora and fauna as they went.

Beyond the interface of Kingdom and Weaveworld the promised land gleamed. It was as if the Fugue had brought from sleep its own season, and that season was an everlasting spring.

There was a light in the shimmering trees, and in the fields, and rivers, that didn't come from the sky overhead, which was sullen, but broke from every bud and droplet. Even the most ancient stone was remade today. Like the poems Cal had rehearsed as he'd driven. Old words, new magic.

'It's waiting for us,' he said.

Together, they went down the hill.

## Part Eight

# The Return

*'You were about to tell me
something, child – but you
left off before you began.'*

William Congreve
*The Old Bachelor*

# I

## STRATEGY

S hadwell's army of deliverance consisted of three main battalions.

The first, and by far the largest, was the mass of the Prophet's followers, the converts whose fervour he had whipped to fanatical proportions, and whose devotion to him and to his promise of a new age knew no bounds. He had warned them that there would be bloodshed, and bloodshed they would have, much of it their own. But they were prepared for such sacrifice; indeed the wilder faction amongst them, chiefly Ye-me, the most hot-headed of the Families, were fairly itching to break some bones.

It was an enthusiasm Shadwell had already used – albeit discreetly – when occasional members of his congregation had called his preaching into question, and he was ready to use it again if there was any sign of softening in the ranks. He would of course do what he could to subdue the Fugue by rhetoric, but he didn't much fancy his chances. His followers had been easily duped: their lives in the Kingdom had so immersed them in half-truths that they were ready to believe any fiction if it was properly advertised. But the Seerkind who had remained in the Fugue would not be so easily misled. That was when the truncheons and the pistols would be called into play.

The second part of his army was made up of Hobart's confederates, choice members of the Squad Hobart had diligently prepared for a day of revolution that had never come. Shadwell had introduced them to the pleasures of his jacket, and they had all found something in the folds worth selling their souls for. Now they were his Elite, ready to defend his person to the death should circumstance demand.

The third and final battalion was less visible than the other two, but no less powerful for that. Its soldiers were the by-blows, the sons and daughters of the Magdalene: an unnumbered and unordered rabble whose resemblance to their fathers was usually remote, and whose natures ranged from the subtly lunatic to the beserk. Shadwell had made sure the sisters had kept their charges well hidden, as they were evidence of a corruption the Prophet could scarcely be associated with, but they were waiting, scrabbling at the veils Immacolata had flung around them, ready for release should the campaign demand such terrors.

He had planned his invasion with the precision of a Napoleon.

The first phase, which he undertook within an hour of dawn, was to go to Capra's House, there to confront the Council of the Families before it had time to debate the situation. The approach was made as a triumphal march, with the Prophet's car, its smoked glass windows concealing the passengers from the eyes of the inquisitive, leading a convoy of a dozen vehicles. In the back of the car Shadwell sat with Immacolata at his side. As they drove he offered his condolences on the death of the Magdalene.

'I'm most distressed . . .' he said quietly. '. . . we've lost a valued ally.'

Immacolata said nothing.

Shadwell took a crumpled pack of cigarettes from his jacket pocket and lit up. The cigarette, and the covetous way he had of smoking it, as if any moment it would be snatched from his lips, was utterly out of synch with the mask he wore. 'I think we're both aware of how this changes things,' he said, his tone colourless.

'What does it change?' she said. How he liked the unease that was plain on her face.

'You're vulnerable,' he reminded her. 'Now more than ever. That concerns me.'

'Nothing's going to happen to me,' she insisted.

'Oh but it might,' he said softly. 'We don't know how much resistance we're going to meet. It might be wise if you withdrew from the Fugue entirely.'

'No! I want to see them *burn*.'

'Understandable,' Shadwell said. 'But you're going to be a target. And if we lose you, we lose access to the Magdalene's children as well.'

Immacolata looked across at Shadwell. 'Is that what this is about? You want the by-blows?'

'Well . . . I think there's some tactical –'

'Have them,' she interrupted. 'Take them, they're yours. My gift to you. I don't want to be reminded of them. I despised her appetites.'

Shadwell offered a thin smile.

'My thanks,' he said.

'You're welcome to them. Just let me watch the fires, that's all I ask.'

'Oh certainly. Absolutely.'

'And I want the woman found. Suzanna. I want her found and given to me.'

'She's yours,' said Shadwell, as though nothing were simpler. 'One thing though. The children. Is there some particular word I use to bring them to me?'

'There is.'

He drew on his cigarette. 'I'd best have it,' he said. 'As they're mine.'

'Just call them by the names she gave them. That'll unleash them.'

'And what *are* their names?' he said, reaching into his pocket for a pen.

He scribbled them on the back of the cigarette pack as he recited them, so as not to forget them. Then, the business concluded, they continued their drive in silence.

# II

## THE BURIAL PARTY

Suzanna and Cal's first duty was to locate Jerichau's body, which took fully half an hour. The landscape of the Fugue had long since invaded the place where she'd left him, and it was more by luck than system that they found him.

Luck, and the sound of children; for Jerichau had not remained unaccompanied. Two women, and a half dozen of their offspring, from two years to seven or so, were standing (and playing) around the corpse.

'Who is he?' one of the women wanted to know when they approached.

'His name is Jerichau,' said Suzanna.

'*Was*,' one of the children corrected her.

'Was.'

Cal posed the inevitable, and delicate, question. 'What happens to bodies here? I mean . . . where do we take him?'

The woman grinned, displaying an impressive absence of teeth.

'Leave him here,' she said. 'He's not going to mind, is he? Bury him.'

She looked down lovingly on her smallest boy, who was naked and filthy, his hair full of leaves.

'What do *you* think?' she asked him.

He took his thumb from his mouth, and shouted: '*Bury him!*' – a chant which was immediately taken up by the other children. *'Bury him! Bury him!'* they yelled, and instantly one of them fell to her knees and began to dig at the earth like a mongrel in search of a bone.

'Surely there must be some formalities,' Cal said.

'Are you a Cuckoo then?' one of the mothers enquired.

'Yes.'

'And him?' She pointed to Jerichau.

'No,' said Suzanna. 'He was a Babu; and a great friend.'

The children had all taken to digging now, laughing and throwing handfuls of earth at each other as they laboured.

'Seems to me he was about ready to die,' said the woman to Suzanna. 'Judging by the look of him.'

She murmured: 'He was.'

'Then you should put him in the ground and be done with it,' came the response. 'They're just bones.'

Cal winced at this, but Suzanna seemed moved by the woman's words.

'I know,' she said. 'I *do* know.'

'The children'll help you dig a hole. They like to dig.'

'Is this right?' said Cal.

'Yes,' said Suzanna with a sudden certainty: 'Yes it is,' and she and Cal went down on their knees alongside the children and dug.

It was not easy work. The earth was heavy, and damp; they were both quickly muddied. But the sheer sweat of it, and the fact of getting to grips with the dirt they were going to put Jerichau's body beneath, made for healthy, and strangely rewarding, labour. It took a long time, during which the women watched, supervising the children and sharing a pipe of pungent tobacco as they did so.

As they worked Cal mused on how often the Fugue and its peoples had confounded his expectations. Here they were on their knees digging a grave with a gaggle of children: it was not what his dreams of being here had prepared him for. But in its way it was more real than he'd ever dared hope – dirt under the fingernails and a snotty-nosed child at his side blithely eating a worm. Not a dream at all, but an awakening.

When the hole was deep enough for Jerichau to be decently

concealed, they set about moving him. At this point Cal could no longer countenance the children's involvement. He told them to stand away as they went to assist in lifting the corpse.

'Let them help,' one of the women chided him. 'They're enjoying themselves.'

Cal looked up at the row of children, who were mud-people by now. They were clearly itching to be pall-bearers, all except for the worm-eater, who was still sitting on the lip of the grave, his feet dangling into the hole.

'This isn't any business for kids,' Cal said. He was faintly repulsed by the mothers' indifference to their off-springs' morbidity.

'Is it not?' said one of the women, refilling the pipe for the umpteenth time. 'You know something more about it than they do, then?'

He looked at her hard.

'Go on,' she challenged him. 'Tell them what you know.'

'Nothing,' he conceded reluctantly.

'Then what's to fear?' she enquired gently. 'If there's nothing to fear, why not let them play?'

'Maybe she's right, Cal,' said Suzanna, laying her hand on his. 'And I think he'd like it,' she said. 'He was never one for solemnity.'

Cal wasn't convinced, but this was no time to argue. He shrugged, and the children lent their small hands to the task of lifting Jerichau's body and laying it in the grave. As it was, they showed a sweet tenderness in the act, untainted by formality or custom. One of the girls brushed some dirt from the dead man's face, her touch feather-light, while her siblings straightened his limbs in the bed of earth. Then they withdrew without a word, leaving Suzanna to lay a kiss on Jerichau's lips. It was only then, at the very last, that she let go a small sob.

Cal picked up a handful of soil and threw it down into the grave. At this the children took their cue, and began to cover the body up. It was quickly done. Even the mothers came to the graveside and pitched a handful of earth in, as a gesture

412

of farewell to this fellow they'd only known as a subject of debate.

Cal thought of Brendan's funeral, of the coffin shunted off through faded curtains while a pallid young priest led a threadbare hymn. This was a better end, no doubt of it, and the children's smiles had been in their way more appropriate than prayers and platitudes.

When it was all done, Suzanna found her voice, thanking both the grave-diggers and their mothers.

'After all that digging,' said the eldest of the girls, 'I just hope he grows.'

'He will,' said her mother, with no trace of indulgence. 'They always do.'

On that unlikely remark, Cal and Suzanna went on their way, with directions to Capra's House. Where, had they but known it, the flies were soon to be feasting.

# III

## THE HORSE UNHARNESSED

### 1

**N**orris the Hamburger Billionaire had long ago forgotten what it was like to be treated as a man. Shadwell had other uses for him. First, of course, during the Weave's first waking, as his horse. Then, when man and mount returned to the Kingdom and Shadwell took on the mantle of Prophet, as footstool, foodtaster and fool, the butt of the Salesman's every humiliating whim. To this, Norris put up no resistance. As long as he was in thrall to the raptures of Shadwell's jacket he was utterly dead to himself.

But tonight, Shadwell had tired of his creature. He had new vassals on every side, and mistreating the sometime plutocrat had become a tired joke. Before the unweaving, he'd left Norris to the untender mercies of his Elite, to be their lackey. That unkindness was nothing, however, to his other: the withdrawal of the illusion that had won Norris' compliance.

Norris was not a stupid man. When the shock of waking to find himself bruised from head to foot had worn off he soon put the pieces of his recent history together. He couldn't know how much time had passed since he'd fallen for Shadwell's trick, (he'd been declared dead in his home town in Texas, and his wife had already married his brother), nor could he recall more than vaguely the discomforts and abuse that had been heaped upon him in his period of servitude. But he was quite certain of two things. One, that it was Shadwell who had reduced him to his present abjection, and two, that Shadwell would pay for the privilege.

His first task was to escape his new masters, which, during the spectacle of the unweaving, was easily done. They didn't even notice that he'd slipped away. The second objective was to find the Salesman, and this he reasoned was best done with the aid of whatever police force this peculiar country boasted. To that end he approached the first group of Seerkind he came across and demanded to be taken to somebody in authority. They were apparently unimpressed by his demands, but suspicious nevertheless. They called him a Cuckoo, which he took some exception to, and then accused him of trespassing. One of the women even suggested he might be a spy, and should be taken post haste to somebody in authority, at which point Norris reminded her that he'd been requesting that all along.

So they took him.

## 2

Which is how, a short while later, Shadwell's discarded horse was brought to Capra's House, which was at the time the centre of considerable commotion. The Prophet had arrived at the House half an hour before, at the end of his triumphal march, but the Councillors had refused him access to the sacred ground until they'd first debated the ethics of it.

The Prophet declared himself willing to accede to their metaphysical caution (after all was he not Capra's mouthpiece?, he understood absolutely the delicacy of this), and so stayed behind the black windows of his car until the Councillors had sorted the matter out.

Crowds had gathered, eager to see the Prophet in the flesh, and fascinated by the cars. There was an air of innocent excitement. Envoys ferried messages back and forth between the occupants of the House and the leader of the convoy that waited on its threshold, until it was at last announced that the Prophet would indeed be given access to Capra's House, on the understanding that he went bare-foot, and alone. This the

415

Prophet apparently agreed to, because mere minutes after this announcement the car door was opened and the great man indeed stepped forth, his feet naked, and approached the doorstep. The throng pressed forward to see him better – this Saviour who'd brought them to safety.

Norris, who was towards the back of the crowd, caught only a glimpse of the figure. He saw nothing of the man's face. But he saw the jacket well enough, and he recognized it on the instant. It was the same garment with which the Salesman had tricked him. How could he ever forget the iridescent fabric? It was Shadwell's jacket. It followed therefore that the wearer was Shadwell.

The sight of the jacket brought back an echo of the humiliations he'd endured at Shadwell's hands. He remembered the kicks and curses; he remembered the contempt. Filled with just fury, he shrugged off the hold of the man at his side, and squirmed his way through the pack of spectators towards the door of Capra's House.

At the front of the crowd he glimpsed the jacket and the man who wore it stepping inside. He made to follow, but a guard at the doorway blocked his path. He was pitched backwards, the throng laughing and applauding his antics, idiots that they were.

'*I know him!*' he yelled, as Shadwell disappeared from view. '*I know him!*'

He got to his feet, and ran at the door a second time, veering away at the last moment. The guard took the bait and gave chase, pursuing him into the crowd. Norris' life as a lackey had taught him something of strategy; he avoided the guard's grasp and made a dive for the unprotected doorway, flinging himself over the threshold before his pursuer could bring him down.

'*Shadwell!*' he yelled.

In the chamber of Capra's House the Prophet froze in mid-platitude. The words he'd been speaking were all conciliation, all understanding, but even the blindest of the assembly could not have failed to read the flicker of anger in the peace-bringer's eyes as that name was called.

416

'*Shadwell!*'

He turned towards the door. Behind him he heard the Councillors exchange whispered remarks. Then there was a commotion in the passageway outside, the door was flung open, and Norris was standing there, yelling his name.

The horse faltered as it set eyes on the Prophet. Shadwell could see doubt registering. This wasn't the face Norris had expected to see. He might yet escape with his masquerade unchallenged.

'Shadwell?' he said to Norris. 'I'm afraid I don't know anybody by that name.' He turned to the Councillors. 'Do you know the gentleman?' he enquired.

They regarded him with open suspicion, especially an old man at the heart of the gaggle, who hadn't taken his baleful eyes off the Prophet since Shadwell had entered this hovel. Now the canker of doubt had spread, damn it.

'The jacket . . .' said Norris.

'Who is this man?' the Prophet demanded. 'Will somebody please have him taken out?' He tried to make a joke of it. 'I think he's a little mad.'

Nobody moved; nobody except the horse. Norris stepped towards the Prophet, yelling as he came.

'I know what you did to me!' he said. 'Don't think I don't. Well I'm going to sue your ass off, Shadwell. Or whoever the hell you are.'

There was a further disturbance at the front door, and Shadwell glanced up to see two of Hobart's finest knocking the guard aside and coming to his aid. He opened his mouth to instruct them he could handle the situation, but before the words were off his lips Norris, his face all fury, flung himself at his enemy.

The Prophet's Elite had strict orders in such circumstances. Nobody, but *nobody*, was to lay hands on their beloved leader. Without a second's hesitation the two men had their pistols from their holsters, and they shot Norris dead in his tracks.

He fell forward at Shadwell's feet, blood coming from his wounds in bright spurts.

'Jesus God,' said Shadwell, through gritted teeth.

The echoes of the executioners' shots took longer to die than Norris had. It was as if the walls disbelieved the sound, and were playing it back and forth, back and forth, until they'd verified the transgression. Outside, the crowd had fallen absolutely silent; silent too, the assembly behind him. He could feel their accusing eyes.

'That was stupid,' he murmured to the killers. Then his arms outspread, he turned to the councillors.

'I do apologize for this unfortunate –'

'You're not welcome here,' one of the number said. 'You've brought death into Capra's House.'

'It was a misunderstanding,' he replied softly.

'No.'

'I *insist* you hear me out.'

Again: 'No.'

Shadwell offered a tiny smile.

'You call yourselves wise,' he said. 'Believe me, if that's true then you'll listen to what I've got to say. I didn't come here alone. I've got people – *your* people, Seerkind – with me. They love me, because I want to see the Fugue prosper, as they do. Now ... I'm prepared to let you *share* my vision, and the triumph that'll come with it, if you want to. But believe me, I'm going to liberate the Fugue with or without your support. Do I make myself clear?'

'Get out of here,' said the old man who'd been watching him.

'Be careful, Messimeris,' one of the others whispered.

'You don't seem to understand,' Shadwell said. 'I'm bringing you freedom.'

'You're not Seerkind,' Messimeris replied. 'You're a Cuckoo.'

'What if I am?'

'You cheated your way in here. You don't hear Capra's voice.'

'Oh I hear voices,' said Shadwell. 'I hear them loud and clear. They tell me that the Fugue's defenceless. That its leaders have spent too much time in hiding. That they're weak and frightened.'

418

He surveyed the faces in front of him, and saw, it had to be admitted, little of the weakness or the fear he spoke of: only a stoicism that would take longer to erode than he had time to waste. He glanced round at the men who'd shot Norris.

'It seems we have no choice,' he said. The men perfectly understood the signal. They withdrew. Shadwell turned back to the Councillors.

'We want you to leave,' Messimeris re-stated.

'Is that your final word?'

'It is,' said the other.

Shadwell nodded. Seconds ticked by, during which neither side moved a muscle. Then the front door opened again, and the gunmen returned. They had brought four more of the Elite with them, which made up a firing squad of six.

'I request you, one final time,' said Shadwell, as the squad formed a line to either side of him, 'don't resist me.'

The Councillors looked more incredulous than afraid. They had lived their lives in this world of wonders, but here before them was an arrogance that finally brought disbelief to their faces. Even when the gunmen raised their weapons they made no move, spoke no protest. Only Messimeris asked:

'Who is Shadwell?'

'A salesman I once knew,' said the man in the fine jacket. 'But he's dead and gone.'

'No,' said Messimeris. '*You're* Shadwell.'

'Call me what you like,' said the Prophet. 'Only bow your heads to me. Bow your heads and all's forgiven.'

Still there was no movement. Shadwell turned to the gunman at his left and claimed the pistol from his hand. He pointed it at Messimeris' heart. The two were standing no more than four yards apart; a blind man could not have failed to kill at that range.

'I say again: *bow your heads.*'

At last, a few of the assembly seemed to comprehend the seriousness of their situation, and did as he requested. Most just stared, however, pride, stupidity or plain disbelief keeping them from acquiescence.

Shadwell knew the crisis point was upon him. He either

pulled the trigger now, and in so doing bought himself a world, or else he left the salesroom and never looked back. In that instant he remembered standing on a hill-top, the Fugue laid before him. The memory tipped the balance. He shot the man.

The bullet entered Messimeris' chest, but there was no flow of blood; nor did he fall. Shadwell fired again, and a third time for good measure. Each shot hit home, but the man still failed to fall.

The Salesman felt a tremor of panic run through the six gunmen that stood around him. The same question was on their lips as on his: why wouldn't the old man die?

He fired his pistol a fourth time. As the bullet struck him the victim took a step towards his would-be executioner, raising his arm as he did so, as if he intended to snatch the smoking weapon from Shadwell's hand.

The motion was enough to push one of the six beyond the limits of his self-control. With a high-pitched cry he started to fire into the crowd. His hysteria instantly ignited the rest. Suddenly they were all firing, emptying their guns in their hunger to close the accusing eyes in front of them. In moments the chamber was filled with smoke and din.

Through it all, Shadwell saw the man he'd first fired upon complete the motion he'd begun with his salute. Then Messimeris fell forward, dead. His collapse didn't silence the guns; they blazed on. There were a few Councillors who'd fallen to their knees, heads bowed as Shadwell had demanded, and there were others who were taking refuge in the corners of the room. But most were simply gunned down where they stood.

Then, just as suddenly as it had begun, it was over.

Shadwell threw down his gun, and – though he had no taste for abattoirs – forced himself to survey the carnage before him. It was, he knew, the responsibility of one aspiring to Godhood never to look away. Wilful ignorance was the last refuge of humanity, and that was a condition he would soon have transcended.

And, when he studied the scene, it wasn't so unbearable.

He could look at the tumble of corpses and see them for the empty sacks they were.

But, as he turned to the door, something *did* make him flinch. Not a sight, but a memory: of Messimeris' last act. That stepping forward, that raised hand. He hadn't realized what it had signified until now. The man had been seeking payment. Try as he might to find some other explanation, Shadwell could not.

He, the sometime Salesman, had finally become a purchaser; and Messimeris' dying gesture had been to remind him of that.

He would have to start the campaign moving. Subdue the opposition and get access to the Gyre as speedily as possible. Once he'd drawn back the veil of cloud he'd be a God. And Gods were beyond the claims of creditors, alive or dead.

# IV

## THE ROPE-DANCERS

### 1

Cal and Suzanna walked as swiftly as curiosity would allow. There was much, despite the urgency of their mission, that slowed their steps. Such fecundity in the world around them, and a razor-sharp wit in its shaping, that they found themselves remarking on the remarkable so frequently they had to give it up and simply look. Amid the spectacle of flora and fauna surrounding them they saw no species entirely without precedent in the Kingdom of the Cuckoo, but nothing here – from pebble to bird, nor anything the eye could admire between – was untouched by some transforming magic.

Creatures crossed their path that belonged distantly to the family of fox, hare, cat and snake; but only distantly. And amongst the changes wrought in them was a total lack of timidity. None fled before the newcomers; only glanced Cal and Suzanna's way in casual acknowledgement of their existence, then went about their business.

It might have been Eden – or an opium dream of same – until the sound of a radio being ineptly tuned broke the illusion. Fragments of music and voices, interspersed with piercing whines and white noise, all punctuated by whoops of pleasure, drifted from beyond a small stand of silver birches. The whoops were rapidly replaced, however, by shouting and threats, which escalated as Cal and Suzanna made their way through the trees.

On the other side was a field of tall, sere grass. In it, three youths. One was balanced on a rope slung loosely between posts, watching the other two as they fought. The source of the acrimony was self-evident: the radio. The shorter of the pair, whose hair was so blond it was almost white, was defending his possession from his bulkier opponent, with little success. The aggressor snatched it from the youth's grip and threw it across the field. It struck one of several weather-worn statues that stood half lost in the grass, and the song it had been playing abruptly ceased. Its owner threw himself at the destroyer, yelling his fury:

'You bastard! Your broke it! You damn well broke it.'

'It was Cuckoo-shite, de Bono,' the other youth replied, easily fending off the blows. 'You shouldn't mess with shite. Didn't your Mam tell you that?'

'It was *mine*!' de Bono shouted back, giving up on his attack and going in search of his possession. 'I don't want your scummy hands on it.'

'God, you're pathetic, you know that?'

'Shut up, dickhead!' de Bono spat back. He couldn't locate the radio in the shin-high grass, which merely fuelled his fury.

'Galin's right,' the rope-percher piped up.

De Bono had fished a pair of wire-rimmed spectacles from the breast pocket of his shirt, and had crouched down to scrabble around for his prize.

'It's corruption,' said the youth on the rope, who had now taken to performing a series of elaborate steps along its length: hops, skips and jumps. 'Starbrook would have your balls if he knew.'

'Starbrook *won't* know,' de Bono growled.

'Oh yes he will,' said Galin, casting a look up at the rope-dancer. 'Because you're going to tell him, aren't you, Toller?'

'Maybe,' came the reply; and with it a smug smile.

De Bono had found the radio. He picked it up and shook it. There was no music forthcoming.

'You shit-head,' he said, turning to Galin. 'Look what you did.'

He might have renewed his assault at this juncture, if Toller, from his perch on the rope, hadn't set eyes on their audience.

'Who the hell are you?' he said.

All three stared at Suzanna and Cal.

'This is Starbrook's Field,' said Galin, his tone threatening. 'You shouldn't be here. He doesn't like women here.'

'Mind you, he's a damn fool,' said de Bono, putting his fingers through his hair and grinning at Suzanna. 'And you can tell him that, too, if he ever comes back.'

'I will,' said Toller, grimly. 'Depend on it.'

'Who is this Starbrook?' said Cal.

'Who's Starbrook?' Galin said. 'Everybody knows . . .' His voice trailed away; comprehension dawned. 'You're Cuckoos,' he said.

'That's right.'

'Cuckoos?' said Toller, so aghast he almost lost his balance. 'In the Field?'

De Bono's grin merely became more luminous at this revelation.

'Cuckoos,' he said. 'Then you can mend the machine –'

He crossed towards Cal and Suzanna, proffering the radio.

'I'll give it a try,' said Cal.

'Don't you *dare*,' said Galin, either to Cal, or de Bono, or both.

'It's just a radio, for God's sake,' Cal protested.

'It's Cuckoo-shite,' said Galin.

'Corruption,' Toller announced once more.

'Where did you get it?' Cal asked de Bono.

'None of your business,' said Galin. He took a step towards the trespassers. 'Now I told you once: you're not welcome here.'

'I think he's made his point, Cal,' Suzanna said. 'Leave it be.'

'Sorry,' Cal said to de Bono. 'You'll have to mend it yourself.'

'I don't know how,' the youth replied, crest-fallen.

'We've got work to do,' Suzanna said, one eye on Galin. 'We have to go.'

She pulled on Cal's arm. 'Come on,' she said.

'That's it,' said Galin. 'Damn Cuckoos.'

'I want to break his nose,' Cal said.

'We're not here to spill blood. We're here to *stop* it being spilled.'

'I know. I know.'

With an apologetic shrug to de Bono, Cal turned his back on the field, and they started away through the birches. As they reached the other side they heard footsteps behind them. Both turned. De Bono was following them, still nursing his radio.

'I'll come with you,' he said, without invitation. 'You can mend the machine as we go.'

'What about Starbrook?' Cal said.

'Starbrook's not coming back,' de Bono replied. 'They'll wait 'til the grass grows up their backsides and he still won't come back. I've got better things to do.'

He grinned.

'I heard what the machine said,' he told them. '*It's going to be a fine day.*'

## 2

De Bono proved an instructive fellow-traveller. There wasn't a subject he wasn't prepared to speculate upon, and his enthusiasm for talk did something to coax Suzanna from the melancholy that had come in the wake of Jerichau's death. Cal let them talk. He had his hands full trying to walk and repair the radio at the same time. He did, however, manage a repeat of his earlier question, as to where de Bono had got the item in the first place.

'One of the Prophet's men,' de Bono explained. 'Gave it to me this morning. He had boxes of them.'

'Did he indeed,' said Cal.

'It's a bribe,' said Suzanna.

'You think I don't know that?' said de Bono. 'I know you get nothing for nothing. But I don't believe everything a Cuckoo gives me's corruption. That's Starbrook's talk. We've lived with Cuckoos before, and survived —' He broke off, and turned his attention to Cal. 'Any luck?'

'Not yet. I'm not very good with wires.'

'Maybe I'll find somebody in Nonesuch,' he said, 'who can do it for me. It's only spitting distance now.'

'We're going to Capra's House,' said Suzanna.

'And I'll go with you. Only *via* the town.'

Suzanna began to argue.

'A man's got to eat,' said de Bono. 'My stomach thinks my throat's cut.'

'No detours,' said Suzanna.

'It's not a detour,' de Bono replied, beaming. 'It's on our way.' He cast her a sideways glance. 'Don't be so suspicious,' he said. 'You're worse than Galin. I'm not going to lead you astray. Trust me.'

'We haven't got time for sight-seeing. We've got urgent business.'

'With the Prophet?'

'Yes . . .'

'*There's* a piece of Cuckoo-shite,' Cal commented.

'Who? The Prophet?' said de Bono. 'A Cuckoo?'

'I'm afraid so,' said Suzanna.

'See, Galin wasn't entirely wrong,' Cal said. 'The radio's a little piece of corruption.'

'I'm safe,' said de Bono. 'It can't touch me.'

'Oh no?' said Suzanna.

'Not here,' de Bono replied, tapping his chest. 'I'm sealed.'

'Is that how it has to be?' said Suzanna, sighing. 'You sealed up in your assumptions, and us in ours?'

'Why not?' said de Bono. 'We don't need you.'

'You want the radio,' she pointed out.

He snorted. 'Not *that* much. If I lose it I won't weep. It's worthless. All Cuckoo stuff is.'

'Is that what Starbrook says?' Suzanna remarked.

'Oh very clever,' he replied, somewhat sourly.

'I dreamt of this place —' Cal said, breaking into the debate. 'I think a lot of Cuckoos do.'

'*You* may dream of *us*,' de Bono replied ungraciously. 'We don't of you.'

'That's not true,' Suzanna said. 'My grandmother loved one

426

of your people, and he loved her back. If you can love us, you can dream of us too. The way we dream of you, given the chance.'

She's thinking of Jerichau, Cal realized: she's talking in the abstract, but that's who she's thinking of.

'Is that so?' said de Bono.

'Yes, that's so,' Suzanna replied, with sudden fierceness. 'It's all the same story.'

'What story?' Cal said.

'*We* live it and *they* live it,' she said, looking at de Bono. 'It's about being born, and being afraid of dying, and how love saves us.' This she said with great certainty, as though it had taken her a good time to reach this conclusion and she was unshakeable on it.

It silenced the opposition awhile. All three walked on without further word for two minutes or more, until de Bono said:

'I agree.'

She looked up at him.

'You do?' she said, plainly surprised.

He nodded. 'One story?' he said. 'Yes, that makes sense to me. Finally, it's the same for you as it is for us, raptures or no raptures. Like you say. Being born, dying: and love between.' He made a small murmur of appreciation, then added: 'You'd know more about the last part, of course,' he said, unable to suppress a giggle. 'Being the older woman.'

She laughed; and as if in celebration the radio leapt into life once more, much to its owner's delight and Cal's astonishment.

'Good man,' de Bono whooped. 'Good man!'

He claimed it from Cal's hands, and began to tune it, so that it was with musical accompaniment that they entered the extraordinary township of Nonesuch.

427

# V

## NONESUCH

### 1

As they stepped into the streets de Bono warned them that the township had been put together in considerable haste, and that they shouldn't expect a paradigm of civil planning. But the warning went little way to preparing them for the experience ahead. There seemed to be no sign whatsoever of order in the place. The houses had been laid cheek by jowl in hapless confusion, the tunnels between – the terms *streets* flattered them – so narrow, and so thick with citizens, that wherever the eye went it found faces and facades ranging from the primitive to the baroque.

Yet it wasn't dark here. There was a shimmering in the stone, and in the paving at their feet, that lit the passages, and turned the humblest wall into an accidental masterpiece of bright mortar and brighter brick.

Any glamour the town could lay claim to was more than matched by its inhabitants. Their clothes had in them that same amalgam of the severe and the dazzling which the visitors had come to recognize as quintessentially Seerkindish; but here, in the Fugue's closest approximation to an urban environment, the style had been taken to new extremes. Everywhere there were remarkable garments and accoutrements on view. A formal waistcoat that rang with countless tiny bells. A woman whose clothes, though buttoned up to the throat, so matched the colour of her skin she was dressed as if naked. On a window sill a young girl sat cross-legged, ribbons of every colour lifting around her face on no discernible breeze.

428

Further down the same alley a man whose fedora seemed to have been woven from his hair was talking with his daughters, while in an adjacent doorway, a man in a rope suit sang to his dog. And style, of course, bred anti-style, like that of the negress and the white woman who whistled past naked but for pantaloons held up with string.

Though all took pleasure in how they appeared, it was not an end in itself. They had business to do this new morning; there was no time for posturing.

The only sights that seemed to be drawing any significant attention were the few items of late twentieth-century bric-à-brac that a few of the citizens were playing with. More gifts from the Prophet's Elite, no doubt. Toys that would tarnish in days, the way all Shadwell's promises would. There was no time to try and persuade the owners of these glittering non-senses to discard them; they would find out soon enough how frail any gift from that source truly was.

'I'll take you to *The Liars*,' said de Bono, leading the way through the crowd. 'We'll eat there, then get on our way.'

From every direction sights and sounds claimed the attention of the Cuckoos. Snatches of conversation came at them from doorstep and window; and songs (some from radios); and laughter. A baby bawled in its mother's arms; something barked above them, and Cal looked up to see a peacock parading on a high balcony.

'Where's he gone, for God's sake?' said Suzanna, as de Bono disappeared into the crowd for the third or fourth time. 'He's too damn quick.'

'We have to trust him. We need a guide,' said Cal. He caught sight of de Bono's blond head. 'There —'

They turned a corner. As they did so a cry went up from somewhere in the packed alleyway ahead, so piercing and so grief-stricken it seemed murder must have been committed. The sound didn't silence the crowd, but hushed it enough for Cal and Suzanna to catch the words that followed, as the echo of the howl died.

'They burned Capra's House!'

'That can't be,' somebody said, a denial taken up on every

429

side, as the word spread. But the news-carrier was not about to be shouted down.

'They burned it!' he insisted. 'And killed the Council.'

Cal had pressed forward through the throng to within sight of the man, who indeed looked as if he'd witnessed some catastrophe. He was dirtied with smoke and mud, through which tears coursed as he repeated his story, or what few bones of it there were. The denials were quietening now: there could be no doubting that he spoke the truth.

It was Suzanna who asked the simple question:

'Who did it?'

The man looked her way.

'The Prophet . . .' he breathed. 'It was the Prophet.'

At this the crowd erupted, curses and imprecations filling the air.

Suzanna turned back to Cal.

'We weren't quick enough,' she said, tears in her eyes. 'Jesus, Cal, we should have been there.'

'We wouldn't have made it,' said a voice at their side. De Bono had reappeared. 'Don't blame yourselves,' he said. Then added: 'Or me.'

'What now?' said Cal.

'We find the bastard and we kill him,' Suzanna said. She took hold of de Bono's shoulder. 'Will you show us the way out?'

'Of course.'

He about-turned and led them away from the knot of citizens surrounding the weeping man. It was apparent as they went that the news had reached every ear and alleyway. The songs and the laughter had entirely vanished. A few people were staring up at the slice of sky between the roofs, as if waiting for lightning. The looks on their faces reminded Cal of how the people of Chariot Street had looked, the day of the whirlwind: full of unspoken questions.

To judge by the snatches of conversation they caught as they went, there was some argument as to what had precisely happened. Some were saying that all those in Capra's House had been murdered; others that there were survivors. But whatever the discrepancies, the broader points were undisputed: the Prophet had declared war on any who challenged his primacy; and to that end his followers were already sweeping the Fugue in search of unbelievers.

'We have to get out into open country,' said Suzanna. 'Before they reach here.'

'It's a small world,' de Bono observed. 'It won't take them long to purge it, if they're efficient.'

'They will be,' said Cal.

There was no sign of panic amongst the residents; no attempt to pack their bags and escape. This persecution, or events like it, had happened before, or so their furrowed faces seemed to say. And most likely it would all happen again. Should they be so surprised?

It took the trio a handful of minutes to wind their way out of the township, and into the open air.

'I'm sorry we have to part so quickly,' Suzanna said to de Bono, when they stood at the perimeter.

'Why should we have to part?'

'Because we came here to stop the Prophet,' Suzanna said, 'and we're going to do that.'

'Then I'll take you where he'll be.'

'Where?' said Cal.

'The Firmament,' de Bono replied with confidence. 'The old palace. That's what they were saying in the street. Didn't you hear them? And it stands to reason. He'd be bound to take the Firmament if he wants to be King.'

## 2

They'd not got far from Nonesuch when de Bono halted, and pointed across the valley to a pall of smoke.

'Something burning,' he said.

'Let's hope it's Shadwell,' said Cal.

'I think I ought to know something about this bastard,' said de Bono. 'If we're going to slaughter him in his boots.'

They told him what they knew, which was, when they came to summarize it, a piffling amount.

'It's odd,' said Cal. 'It seems like I've known him all my life. But, you know, it's less than a year since I first set eyes on him.'

'Shadows can be cast in any direction,' said de Bono. 'That's my belief. Starbrook used to say there were even places close to the Gyre where the past and the future overlap.'

'I think maybe I visited one of them,' said Cal, 'last time I was here.'

'What was it like?'

Cal shook his head.

'Ask me tomorrow,' he said.

Their route had taken them into marshy territory. They picked their way across the mud from stone to stone, any hope of conversation cancelled by the clamour of frogs which rose from the reeds. Half way across, the sound of car engines met their ears. Putting caution aside they crossed to firmer ground by the most direct route, sinking up to their ankles in the water-sodden ground while the frogs – thumb-nail small, and poppy red – leapt before them in their many hundreds.

On the other side Cal shinned up a tree to get a better view. The vantage point offered him sight of a convoy of cars, heading towards the township. It had no need of roads. It was forging its way by dint of wheel and horsepower. Flights of birds rose before it; animals – those that were fast enough – scattered.

Suzanna called up to him:

'What can you see?'

'It's Hobart's mob, at a guess.'

'Hobart?'

She was up the tree and beside him in seconds, edging out along the branch to be clear of the foliage.

'It's him,' he heard her say, almost to herself. 'My God, it's him.'

She turned back to Cal, and there was a wildness in her eyes he didn't much like.

'You're going to have to go on without me,' she said.

They climbed down again, and picked up the argument at ground level.

'I've got business with Hobart. You go on. I'll find you when I'm done.'

'Can't he wait?' Cal said.

'*No*,' she told him firmly. 'No he can't. He's got the book Mimi gave me, and I want it back.'

She saw the perplexed look on his face, and could hear before he delivered them every argument he'd make against their parting. Shadwell was their true objective, he'd say; this was no time to be diverted from facing him. Besides, a book was just a book wasn't it?; it'd still be there tomorrow. All of which was true, of course. But somewhere in her belly she sensed that Hobart's cleaving to the book had some perverse logic about it. Perhaps the pages contained some knowledge she could put to good use in the conflict ahead, encoded in those *Once upon a times*. That was certainly Hobart's conviction, and what the enemy believed of you was probably true, or else why were you enemies in the first place?

'I have to go back,' she said. 'And that's all there is to it.'

'Then I'll come with you.'

'I can deal with him myself, Cal,' she said. 'You two have to go on to the Firmament. I'll find my way to you once I've got the book.'

She spoke with unshakeable conviction; he sensed it would be fruitless to argue with her.

'Then take care,' he said, wrapping his arms around her. 'Be safe.'

'And you, Cal. For me.'

With that, she was away.

De Bono, who'd been out of this conversation while he toyed with his radio, now said:

'Aren't we going with her?'

'No,' said Cal. 'She wants to go alone.'

He pulled a quizzical face. 'Love-affair, is it?' he asked.

'Something like that.'

# 3

Suzanna retraced their steps to the township with an urgency, an enthusiasm even, she didn't entirely comprehend. Was it just that she wanted the confrontation over and done with? Or could it be that she was actually *eager* to see Hobart again; that he had become a kind of mirror in which she might know herself better?

As she stepped back into the streets — which the citizens, retreating behind their doors, had now left more or less deserted — she hoped he knew she was near. Hoped his heart beat a little faster at her proximity, and his palms sweated.

If not, she'd teach him how.

# VI

---

## THE FLESH IS WEAK

### 1

Though Shadwell had set his sights on occupying the Firmament – the only building in the Fugue worthy of one teetering on Godhood – once ensconced there he found it an unsettling residence. Each of the monarchs and matriarchs who'd occupied the place over the centuries had brought their own vision to its halls and ante-chambers, their one purpose to expand upon the previous occupant's mysteries. The result was part labyrinth, part mystical ghost-train ride.

He was not the first Cuckoo to explore the Firmament's miraculous corridors. Several members of Humankind had found their way into the palace down the years, and wandered there unchallenged by its makers, who had no desire to sour its tranquillity with hard words. Lost in its depths these lucky few had seen sights that they would take to their graves. A chamber in which the tiles on the walls had twice as many sides as a dice, and flipped forever over and over, each facet having its place in a fresco that never came to rest long enough for the eye to entirely comprehend it. Another room in which rain constantly fell, a warm spring night rain, and the floor gave off the smell of cooling pavements; and another which seemed at first quite plain, but was built with such sense-beguiling geometries a man might think his head swelled to fill it one moment, and the next be shrunk to the size of a beetle.

And after an hour, or a day, of trespassing amongst these

wonders, some invisible guide would lead them to the door, and they'd emerge as if from a dream. Later they'd try to speak of what they'd seen, but a failure of memory and tongue usually conspired to reduce their attempts to babble. In desperation, many went back in search of that delirium. But the Firmament was a movable feast, and it had always flitted away.

Shadwell was the first Cuckoo, therefore, who walked those rapturous corridors and called them his own. It gave him no pleasure, however. That was perhaps its most elegant revenge on its unwelcome occupant.

## 2

In the late afternoon, before the light dwindled too much, the Prophet made his way up to the top of the Firmament's watchtower, to survey his territories. Despite the demands of recent weeks – the masquerading, the rallies, the constant politicking – he didn't feel weary. All he'd promised his followers and himself had come true. It was as if his performance as a Prophet had lent him prophetic powers. He'd found the Weave, as he'd said he would, and claimed it from its guardians; he'd led his crusaders into the very heart of the Fugue, silencing with almost supernatural speed any and all who'd defied him. From his present elevated status there was no route to rise but towards Godhood, and the means to that advancement was visible from where he now stood.

The Gyre.

Its Mantle roiled and thundered, veiling its secrets from all eyes, even his. No matter. Tomorrow, when Hobart's battalion had finished its suppression of the natives, they would escort the Prophet to the doorway of the Gyre, the place the Kind called the Narrow Bright, and he would step inside.

Then?; *ah, then* . . .

A chill on his nape stirred him from speculation.

Immacolata was standing at the viewing-room door. The light did not indulge her. It showed her wounds in all their suppurating glory; showed her frailty too; and her rancour. It repulsed him to look at her.

'What do you want?' he demanded.

'I came to join you,' she said. 'I don't like this place. It stinks of the Old Science.'

He shrugged, and turned his back on her.

'I know what you're thinking, Shadwell,' she said. 'And believe me, it wouldn't be wise.'

He hadn't heard his name uttered in a long while, and he didn't like the way it sounded. It was a throwback to a biography he'd almost ceased to believe was his.

'*What* wouldn't be wise?' he said.

'Trying to breach the Gyre.'

He made no reply.

'That *is* what you intend isn't it?'

She could read him still, all too easily.

'Maybe,' he said.

'That'd be a cataclysmic mistake.'

'Oh, indeed?' he said, not taking his eyes off the Mantle. 'And why's that?'

'Even the Families don't understand what they created when they set the Loom to work,' she said. 'It's unknowable.'

'*Nothing's* unknowable,' he growled. 'Not to me. Not any more.'

'You're still a man, Shadwell,' she reminded him. 'You're vulnerable.'

'Shut up,' he said.

'Shadwell —'

'*Shut up!*' he repeated, and turned on her. 'I don't want to hear your defeatism any longer. I'm here, aren't I? I won the Fugue.'

'*We* won it.'

'All right, *we*. What do you want for that little service?'

'You know what I want,' she said. 'What I've always wanted. Slow *genocide*.'

He smiled. His reply was a long time coming, and when it came was spoken slowly.

'No,' he said. 'No, I don't think so.'

'Why did we follow them all those years?' she asked. 'It was so you could have profit, and I could be avenged.'

'Things have changed,' he said. 'You must see that.'

'You want to rule them. That's it, isn't it?'

'I want more than that,' he said. 'I want to know what creation tastes like. I want what's in the Gyre.'

'It'll tear you apart.'

'I doubt that,' he said. 'I've never been stronger.'

'At the Shrine,' she replied, 'you said we'd destroy them *together*.'

'I lied,' Shadwell said lightly. 'I told you what you wanted to hear, because I needed you. Now you disgust me. I'll have new women, when I'm a God.'

'A *God* now is it?' She seemed genuinely amused by the thought. 'You're a *salesman*, Shadwell. You're a shabby little salesman. I'm the one they worship.'

'Oh yes,' Shadwell replied. 'I've seen your Cult. A boneyard, and a handful of eunuchs.'

'I won't be cheated, Shadwell,' she said, moving towards him. 'Not by you, of all men.'

He'd known for many months that this time would come, when she finally understood how he'd manipulated her. He'd prepared himself for the consequences, quietly and systematically divesting her of her allies, and increasing his own store of defences. But she still had the menstruum — of that she could never be dispossessed — and it was formidable. He saw it burgeoning in her eyes even now, and couldn't help but want to flinch before it.

He governed the instinct however, and instead walked across to her, and putting his hand to her face, stroked the lesions and the scabs there.

'Surely . . .' he murmured, '. . . you wouldn't kill me?'

'I won't be cheated,' she said again.

'But dead is dead,' he said, his tone soothing. 'I'm just a Cuckoo. You know how weak we are. No Resurrections for us.'

His touch had become more rhythmic. She hated it, he knew. She, the perfect virgin; she, all ice and regret. In earlier

438

times she might have burned the skin from his fingertips for visiting this indignity upon her. But Mama Pus was dead, the Hag her useless lunatic self. The once mighty Incantatrix was weak and weary, and they both knew it.

'All these years, sweetheart . . .' he said, '. . . all these years you gave me just enough leash, just enough temptation . . .'

'We agreed –' she said, '– together –'

'No,' said Shadwell, as though correcting a child. 'You used me, to go amongst the Cuckoos, because if the truth be known they *frighten* you.' She made to contradict, but he put his hand across her throat. 'Don't interrupt,' he told her. She obeyed him. 'You've always held me in contempt,' he went on. 'I know that. But I was useful, and did as I was told, as long as I wanted to touch you.'

'Is that what you want now?' she said.

'Once . . .' he said, almost mourning the loss, '. . . once I would have killed to feel the pulse in your throat. Like this.' His hand tightened a little. 'Or to have stroked your flesh . . .'

He worked the palm of his other hand against her breast.

'Don't do that,' she said.

'The Magdalene's dead,' he reminded her. 'So who's going to produce children now? It can't be the old bitch; she's sterile. No, lover. No. I think it has to be you. You'll finally have to offer up that precious cunt of yours.'

At this she threw him off her, and might have struck him dead but that revulsion at his mauling distracted her from the act. She soon recovered her self-control. The killing power was mustering behind her eyes. He couldn't with safety delay his revenge any longer. She'd taken him for a fool, but he had ways to make her regret her arrogance. As she raised her head to spit the menstruum at him he called out the names he'd written, mere hours before, on his pack of cigarettes.

'Sousa! Vessel! Fairchild! Divine! Loss! Hannah!'

The by-blows came at his call, scrabbling up the stairs. They were no longer the wretched, love-lorn things that the Magdalene had suckled. Shadwell had treated them tenderly in the short time he'd owned them; fed them; made them mighty.

The light died in Immacolata's face as she heard them behind her. She turned as they spilled through the door.

'You bequeathed them to me,' he said.

She let out a cry at the sight of them, grown gross and meaty. They stank of the slaughterhouse.

'I gave them blood instead of milk,' said Shadwell. 'It makes them love me.'

He made a clucking sound with his tongue, and the creatures sidled over to him, trailing organs they had yet to find a purpose for.

'I warn you,' he said, 'try to harm me and they'll take it badly.'

As he spoke he realized that in these last moments Immacolata had summoned the Hag from the cooler regions of the Firmament. She was at the Incantatrix's shoulder now, a restive shadow.

'Leave him,' he heard her sigh in Immacolata's ear. He didn't for an instant think she'd take that advice, but she did, first spitting on the floor at Shadwell's feet, then turning to go. He could scarcely believe the battle had been so easily won. She'd been more demoralized by grief and mutilation than he'd dared hope. The showdown was over before it had even begun.

One of the by-blows at his side uttered a soulful wail of frustration. He took his eyes off the sisters and told it to hush itself. His doing so proved all but fatal, for in the instant his gaze dropped the wraith-sister came flying at him, her jaws wide, her teeth suddenly vast, ready to tear out his cheating heart.

At the door, Immacolata was turning back, the menstruum breaking from her.

He yelled for the beasts to come to his aid, but even as he did so the Hag was upon him. His breath burst from him as he was thrown back against the wall, claws raking at his chest.

The by-blows weren't about to see their blood-bringer laid low. They were upon the Hag before her nails could rip through Shadwell's jacket, and she was dragged from him, shrieking. She'd been midwife to these creatures; she'd de-

440

livered them into a world of lunacy and darkness. Perhaps for that very reason they showed her no mercy. They tore at her without pause or apology.

'*Stop them*,' Immacolata yelled.

The Salesman was examining the lacerations the Hag had made in his jacket. Another moment and her fingers would have clutched his heart.

'Call them off, Shadwell! *Please!*'

'She's dead already,' he said. 'Let them play.'

Immacolata moved to aid her sister, but as she did so the largest of the by-blows, with the tiny white eyes of a deep-sea fish and a mouth like a wound, came between her and rescue. She spat an arrow of the menstruum into its pulsing chest, but it took the hurt in its stride, and came at her unchecked.

Shadwell had seen these monstrosities murder amongst themselves for the sport of it. He knew they could sustain horrendous injury without slowing. This one, for instance, called Vessel, could take a hundred such wounds and still make merry. Nor was it stupid. It had learned the lessons he'd taught it well enough. Even now it leapt upon the Incantatrix, wrapping its arms around her neck, and its legs about her hips.

Such intimacy would, he knew, drive Immacolata to distraction. Indeed, as it put its face to hers, kissing her as best its malformations would allow, she started to scream, all control and calculation finally lost. The menstruum flew from her in all directions, wasting its potency on the ceiling and the walls. Those few barbs that found her attacker did nothing but arouse it further. Though it had no sexual anatomy to speak of, Shadwell had trained it in the basic moves. It worked itself against her like a dog in heat, howling into her face.

Opening its mouth was a mistake on its part, for a fragment of the menstruum found its way down into its throat, and blew it wide. Its neck erupted, and its head, no longer supported, fell backwards on greasy strings of matter.

Even so, it clung to her, its body moving in ragged spasms against hers. But its grip had loosened sufficiently for her to

441

tear its body from her, the struggle leaving her bloodied from head to foot.

Shadwell called the remaining by-blows from their vengeful play. They withdrew to his side. All that was left of the Hag was a litter that resembled the leavings on a fish-gutter's tiles.

Seeing the remains, Immacolata, her face slack to the point of imbecility, let out a low moan of loss.

'Get her out of here,' said Shadwell. 'I don't want to see her filthy face. Take her into the hills. Dump her.'

Two of the by-blows approached the Incantatrix, and took hold of her. There was not so much as a flicker in her eye, nor a finger raised in protest. She seemed no longer even to see them. Either the slaughter of her one remaining sister, or her own violation by the beast, or perhaps both, had undone something inside her. She was suddenly bereft of any power to enchant or terrify. A sack, which they hauled away through the door, and carried off down the stairs. Not once did she even raise her eyes in Shadwell's direction.

He listened to the slouching gait of the by-blows fade down the stairs, still half expecting her to come back for him, to mount one final attack. But no. It was over.

He crossed to the muck of the Hag. It smelt of something rotten.

'Have it,' he said to the remaining beasts, who fell upon the scraps and fought over them. Revolted by their appetite, he turned his gaze back towards the Gyre.

Very soon now night would be upon the Fugue; a last curtain on the events of a busy day. With tomorrow, a new act would begin.

Somewhere beyond the cloud he was watching lay a knowledge that would transform him.

After that, no night would fall, except at his word; nor day dawn.

# VII

## AN OPEN BOOK

### 1

T he Law had come to Nonesuch.

It had come to root out dissension: it had found none. It had come with truncheons, riot shields and bullets, prepared for armed rebellion: it had found no whisper of that either. All it had found was a warren of shadowy streets, most of them deserted, and a few pedestrians who bowed their heads at the first sign of a uniform.

Hobart had immediately ordered a house to house search. It had been greeted with a few sour looks, but little more than that. He was disappointed; it would have been gratifying to have found something to sharpen his authority upon. All too easy, he knew, to be lulled into a false sense of security, especially when an anticipated confrontation had failed to materialize. Vigilance was the key word now; unending vigilance.

That was why he'd occupied a house with a good view of the township from its upper storeys, where he could take up residence for the night. Tomorrow would bring the big push on the Gyre, which could surely not go unopposed. And yet, who could be certain with these people? They were so docile; like animals, rolling over at the first sign of a greater power.

The house he'd commandeered had little to recommend it, beyond its view. A maze of rooms; a collection of faded murals, which he didn't care to study too closely; spare and creaking furniture. The discomfort of the place didn't bother him: he liked spartan living. But the atmosphere did; the sense he had that the ousted tenants were still here, just out of sight. If he'd been a man who believed in ghosts, he'd have said the house was haunted. He wasn't, so he kept his fears to himself, where they multiplied.

Evening had fallen, and the streets below were dark. He could see little from his high window now, but he could hear laughter drifting up from below. He'd given his men the evening to enjoy themselves, warning them never to forget that the township was enemy territory. The laughter grew more riotous, then faded down the street. Let them indulge themselves, he thought. Tomorrow the crusade would take them onto ground the people here thought of as sacred: if they were going to show any resistance, it would be then. He'd seen the same happen in the world outside: a man who wouldn't lift a finger if his house were burned down throwing a fit if someone touched a trinket he called *holy*. Tomorrow promised to be a busy day, and a bloody one too.

Richardson had declined the opportunity to take the night off, preferring to stay in the house, and make a report of the day's events for his personal records. He kept a ledger of his every move, set down in a tiny, meticulous hand. He worked on it now, as Hobart listened to the laughter disappearing below.

Finally, he put down his pen.

'Sir?'

'What is it?'

'These people, sir. It seems to me –' Richardson halted, unsure of how best to voice a question that had been vexing him since they'd arrived, '– it seems to me they don't look quite *human*.'

Hobart studied the man. His hair was immaculately cut, his cheeks immaculately shaved, his uniform immaculately pressed.

'You may be right,' he said.

A flicker of distress crossed Richardson's face.

'I don't understand . . . sir.'

'While you're here, you should believe nothing you see.'

444

'*Nothing*, sir?'

'Nothing at all,' Hobart said. He put his fingers to the glass. It was cold; his body heat lent the tips misty haloes. 'The whole place is a mass of illusions. Tricks and traps. None of it's to be trusted.'

'It's not real?' Richardson said.

Hobart stared across the roofs of this little nowhere, and turned the question over. *Real* was a word he'd once had no problem using. Real was what made the world go round, what was solid and true. And its flip side, *un*real, that was what some lunatic in a cell shouted at four in the morning; unreal was dreams of power without the flesh to give them weight.

But his view of these matters had subtly changed since his first encounter with Suzanna. He had wanted her capture as he'd wanted no other, and his pursuit of her had led from one strangeness to another, until he was so fatigued he scarcely knew right from left. Real? What *was* real? Perhaps (this thought would have been unthinkable before Suzanna) real was merely what he *said* was real. He was the general, and the soldier needed an answer, for his sanity's sake. A plain answer, that would let him sleep soundly.

He gave it:

'Only the Law's real here,' he said. 'We have to hang onto that. All of us. Do you understand?'

Richardson nodded. 'Yes, sir.'

There was a long pause, during which somebody outside began whooping like a drunken Cherokee. Richardson closed his ledger, and went to the second window.

'I wonder . . .' he said.

'Yes?'

'Perhaps I *should* go out. Just for a while. To see these illusions face to face.'

'Maybe.'

'Now that I know it's all a lie –' he said, '– I'm safe, aren't I?'

'As safe as you're ever going to be,' said Hobart.

'Then, if you don't mind . . .'

'Go on. See for yourself.'

Richardson was away in seconds, and down the stairs. A few moments later Hobart caught sight of his shadowy form moving away down the street.

The Inspector stretched. He was tired to the marrow. There was a mattress in the next room, but he was determined not to avail himself of it. Laying his head on a pillow would offer the rumours of occupancy here an easy victim.

Instead he sat down in one of the plain chairs and took the book of faery-tales from his pocket. It had not left his presence since its confiscation; he'd lost count of the times he'd scanned its pages. Now he did the same again. But the lines of prose grew steadily hazier in front of him, and though he tried to check himself, his lids became heavier and heavier.

Long before Richardson had found himself an illusion to call his own, the Law that had come to Nonesuch had fallen asleep.

## 2

Suzanna didn't find it so difficult to avoid Hobart's men when she stepped back into the township. Though they swarmed through the alleyways the shadows had become unnaturally dense there, and she was always able to stay a few steps ahead of the enemy. Getting access to Hobart was another matter, however. Though she wanted to be finished with her work here as quickly as possible there was no use in risking arrest. She'd escaped custody twice; three times might be pressing her luck. Though impatience gnawed at her, she decided to wait until the light faded. The days were still short this early in the year; it would only be a few hours.

She found herself an empty house – availing herself of some plain food that the owners had left there – and wandered around the echoing rooms until the light outside began to dwindle. Her thoughts turned back, and back again, to Jerichau, and the circumstances of his death. She tried to remember the way he looked, and had some success with his eyes and hands, but couldn't create anything like a complete portrait. Her failure depressed her. He was so soon gone.

She had just about decided that it was dark enough to risk venturing out when she heard voices. She went to the bottom of the stairs, and peered through to the front of the house. There were two silhouetted figures on the threshold.

'Not here . . .' she heard a girl's voice whisper.

'Why not?' said her male companion, his words slurred. One of Hobart's company, no doubt. 'Why not? It's as good as any.'

'There's somebody here already,' said the girl, staring into the mystery of the house.

The man laughed. 'Dirty fuckers!' he called. Then he took the woman roughly by the arm. 'Let's find somewhere else,' he said. They moved away, into the street.

Suzanna wondered if Hobart had sanctioned such fraternization. She couldn't believe he had.

It was time she put an end to stalking him in her imagination; time to find him and get her business with him done. She slipped through the house, scanned the street, then stepped out into the night.

The air was balmy, and with so few lights burning in the houses, and those that did burn mere candle-flames, the sky was bright above, the stars like dew-drops on velvet. She walked a little way with her face turned skyward, entranced by the sight. But not so entranced she didn't sense Hobart's proximity. He was somewhere near. But where? She could still waste precious hours going from house to house, trying to find him.

When in doubt, ask a policeman. It had been one of her mother's favourite saws, and never more apt. A few yards from where she stood one of Hobart's horde was pissing against a wall, singing a ragged rendition of *Land of Hope and Glory* to accompany the flood.

Trusting that his inebriation would keep him from recognizing her, she asked Hobart's whereabouts.

'You don't need *him*,' the man said. 'Come on in. We've got a party going.'

'Maybe later. I've got to see the Inspector.'

'If you must,' the man said. 'He's in the big house with the white walls.' He pointed back the way she'd come, splashing his feet as he did so. 'Somewhere off to the right,' he said.

The instructions, despite the provider's condition, were good. Off to the right was a street of silent dwellings, and at the corner of the next intersection a sizeable house, its walls pale in the starlight. There was nobody standing sentry at the door; the guards had presumably succumbed to whatever pleasures Nonesuch could offer. She pushed the door open and stepped inside unchallenged.

There were riot-shields propped against the wall of the room she'd entered, but she needed no confirmation that this was indeed the house. Her gut already knew that Hobart was in one of the upper rooms.

She started up the stairs, not certain what she would do when she confronted him. His pursuit of her had made her life a nightmare, and she wanted to make him regret it. But she couldn't kill him. Despatching the Magdalene had been terrible enough; killing a human being was more than her conscience would allow. Best just to claim her book, and go.

At the top of the stairs was a corridor, at the end of which a door stood ajar. She went to it, and pushed it open. He was there, her enemy; alone, slumped in a chair, his eyes closed. In his lap lay the book of faery-tales. The very sight of it made her nerves flutter. She didn't hesitate in the doorway, but crossed the bare boards to where he slumbered.

In his sleep, Hobart was floating in a misty place. Moths flew around his head, and beat their dusty wings against his eyes, but he couldn't raise his arms to brush them away. Somewhere near he sensed danger, but from which direction would it come?

The mist moved to his left, then to his right.

'Who . . . ?' he murmured.

The word he spoke froze Suzanna in her tracks. She was a yard from the chair, no more. He muttered something else; words she couldn't comprehend. But he didn't wake.

Behind his eyelids Hobart glimpsed an unfixable form in

448

the mist. He struggled to be free of the lethargy that weighed him down; fought to waken, and defend himself.

Suzanna took another step towards the sleeper.

He moaned again.

She reached for the book, her fingers trembling. As they closed around it, his eyes sprang wide open. Before she could snatch the book away from him, his grip on it tightened. He stood up.

'*No!*' he shouted.

The shock of his waking almost made her lose her hold, but she wasn't going to give her prize up now: the book was *her* property. There was a moment of struggle between them, as they fought for possession of the volume.

Then – without warning – a veil of darkness rose from their hands, or more correctly from the book they held between them.

She looked up into Hobart's eyes. He was sharing her shock at the power that was suddenly released from between their woven fingers. The darkness rose between them like smoke, and blossomed against the ceiling, immediately tumbling down again, enclosing them both in a night within a night.

She heard Hobart loose a yell of fear. The next moment words seemed to rise from the book, white forms against the smoke, and as they rose they became what they meant. Either that or she and Hobart were falling, and becoming symbols as the book opened to receive them. Whichever; or both; it was all one in the end.

Rising or falling, as language or life, they were delivered into storyland.

# VIII

## THE ESSENTIAL DRAGON

I t was dark in the state they'd entered; dark, and full of rumour. Suzanna could see nothing in front of her, not even her fingertips, but she could hear soft whispers, carried to her on a warm, pine-scented wind. Both touched her face, whispers and wind; both excited her. They knew she was here, the people that inhabited the stories in Mimi's book: for it was there, *in the book*, that she and Hobart now existed.

Somehow, in the act of struggling, they'd been transformed – or at least their thoughts had. They'd entered the common life of words.

Standing in the darkness, and listening to the whispers all around her, she didn't find the notion so difficult to comprehend. After all hadn't the author of this book turned his thoughts into words, in the act of writing it, knowing his readers would decode them as they read, making thoughts of them again? More: making an imagined life. So here was she now, living that life. Lost in *Geschichten der Geheimen Orte*; or found there.

There were hints of light moving to either side of her she now realized; or was it *she* that was moving: running perhaps, or flying? Anything was possible here: this was faery land. She concentrated, to get a better grasp of what these flashes of light and darkness meant, and realized all at once that she was travelling at speed through avenues of trees, vast primeval trees, and the light between them was growing brighter.

Somewhere up ahead, Hobart was waiting for her, or for the thing she'd become as she flew through the pages.

For she was not Suzanna here; or rather, not *simply* Suzanna. She could not simply be herself here, any more than he could be simply Hobart. They were grown mythical in this absolute forest. They had drawn to themselves the dreams that this state celebrated: the desires and faiths that filled the nursery stories, and so shaped all subsequent desires and faiths.

There were countless characters to choose from, wandering in the Wild Woods; sooner or later every story had a scene played here. This was the place orphaned children were left to find either their deaths or their destinies: where virgins went in fear of wolves, and lovers in fear of their hearts. Here birds talked, and frogs aspired to the throne, and every grove had its pool and well, and every tree a door to the Netherworld.

What, amongst these, was *she*? The Maiden, of course. Since childhood she'd been the Maiden. She felt the Wild Woods grow more luminous at this thought, as though she'd ignited the air with it.

*I'm the Maiden . . .*
she murmured,
*. . . and he's the Dragon.*

Oh yes. That was it; of course that was it.

The speed of her flight increased; the pages flipped over and over. And now ahead she saw a metallic brightness between the trees, and there the Great Worm was, its gleaming coils wrapped around the roots of a Noahic tree, its vast, flat-snouted head laid on a bed of blood-red poppies as it bided its terrible time.

Yet, perfect as it was, in every scaly detail, she saw Hobart there too. He was woven with the pattern of light and shade, and so – most oddly – was the word DRAGON. All three occupied the same space in her head: a living text of man, word and monster.

The Great Worm Hobart opened its one good eye. A broken arrow protruded from its twin, the work of some hero or other no doubt, who'd gone his tasselled and shining way in the belief that he'd dispatched the beast. It was not so easily destroyed. It lived still, its coils no less tremendous for the scars they bore, its glamour untarnished. And the living eye? It held enough malice for a tribe of dragons.

It saw her, and raised its head a little. Molten stone seethed between its lips, and murdered the poppies.

Her flight towards it faltered. She felt its glance pierce her. Her body began to tremble in response. She tumbled towards the dark earth like a swatted moth. The ground beneath her was strewn with words; or were they bones? Whichever, she fell amongst them, shards of nonsense thrown up in all directions by her flailing arms.

She got to her feet, and looked about her. The colonnades were empty in every direction: there was no hero to call upon, nor mother to take comfort with. She was alone with the Worm.

It raised its head a few feet higher, this minor motion causing a slow avalanche of coils.

It was a beautiful worm, there was no denying that, its iridescent scales glittering, the elegance of its malice enchanting. She felt, looking at it, that same combination of yearning and anxiety which she remembered so well from childhood. Its presence *aroused* her, there was no other word for it. As if in response to that confession, the Dragon roared. The sound it made was hot and low, seeming to begin in its bowels and winding down its length to break from between the countless needles of its teeth, a promise of greater heat to come.

All light had gone from between the trees. No birds sang or spoke, no animal, if any lived so close to the Dragon, dared move a whisker in the undergrowth. Even the bone-words and the poppies had disappeared, leaving these two elements, Maiden and Monster, to play out their legend.

'*It finishes here*,' Hobart said, with the Dragon's laval tongue. Each syllable he shaped was a little fire, which cremated the specks of dust around her head. She was not afraid of all this; rather, exhilarated. She had only ever been an observer of these rites; at last she was a performer.

'Have you nothing more *to tell me*?' the Dragon demanded,

452

spitting the words from between its serried teeth. *'No blessings? No explanations?'*

'Nothing,' she said defiantly. What was the purpose of talk, when they were so perfectly transparent to each other? They knew who they were, didn't they?; knew what they meant to one another. In the final confrontation of any great tale dialogue was redundant. With nothing left to say, only action remained: a murder or a marriage.

'Very well,' said the Dragon, and it moved towards her, drawing its length over the wasteland between them with vestigial forelegs.

*He means to kill me*, she thought; *I have to act quickly*. What did the Maiden do to protect herself in such circumstances as this? Did she flee, or try to sing the beast to sleep?

The Dragon was towering over her now. But it didn't attack. Instead it threw back its head, exposing the pale, tender flesh of its throat.

*'Please be quick,'* it growled.

She was bewildered by this.

'Be quick?' she said.

*'Kill me and be done,'* it instructed her.

Though her mind didn't fully comprehend this *volte face*, the body she occupied did. She felt it changing in response to the invitation; felt a new ripeness in it. She'd thought to live in this world as an innocent; but that she couldn't be. She was a grown woman; a woman who'd changed in the last several months, sloughed off years of dead assumptions; found magic inside herself; suffered loss. The role of Maiden – all milk and soft sighs – didn't fit.

Hobart knew that better than she. He hadn't come into these pages as a child, but as the man he was, and he'd found a role here that suited his most secret and forbidden dreams. This was no place for pretence. She was not the virgin, he was not the devouring worm. He, in his private imaginings, was power besieged, and seduced, and finally – painfully – *martyred*. That was why the Dragon before her raised its milky throat.

*Kill me and be done*, he said, lowering his head a little to look at her. In his surviving eye she saw for the first time how

453

wounded he was by his obsession with her; how he'd come to be in thrall to her, sniffing after her like a lost dog, hating her more with every day that passed for the power she had over him.

In the other reality – in the room from which they'd stepped, which was in turn hidden in a larger Kingdom (worlds within worlds) he would be brutal with her. Given the chance he'd kill her for fear of the truth he could only admit in the sacred grove of his dreams. But here there was no story to tell except the true one. That was why he raised his palpitating throat, and fluttered his heavily lidded eye. He was the virgin, frightened and alone, ready to die rather than sacrifice his tattered virtue.

And what did that make her? The beast, of course. She was the beast.

*No sooner thought than felt.*

She sensed her body growing larger, and larger, and larger still. Her blood-stream ran colder than a shark's. A furnace flared up in her belly.

In front of her Hobart was shrinking. The dragon-skin fell away from him in silky folds, and he was revealed, naked and white: a human male, covered in wounds. A chaste knight at the end of a weary road, bereft of strength or certitude.

She had claimed the skin he'd lost; she felt it solidify around her, its armour glittering. The size of her body was a joy to her. She exulted in the way it felt to be so dangerous and so impossible. This was how she *truly* dreamt of herself; this was the real Suzanna. She was a Dragon.

With that lesson learned, what was she to do? Finish the story as the man before her wished? Burn him? Swallow him?

Looking down at his insipidity from her rearing height, smelling the dirt off him, the sweat off him – she could easily find it in her heart to do her Dragon's duty, and *devour*. It would be easy.

She moved towards him, her shadow engulfing him. He was weeping, and smiling up at her with gratitude. She opened her vast jaws. Her breath singed his hair. She would cook him and swallow him in one swift motion. But she was not quick enough. As she was about to devour him she was distracted by a voice nearby. Was there somebody else in the grove? The sounds certainly belonged in these pages. They were far from human, though there were words attempting to surface through the barking and grunting. Pig; dog; man: a combination of all three, and all panicking.

The Knight Hobart opened his eyes, and there was something new in them, something besides tears and fatigue. He too had heard the voices; and hearing them, he was reminded of the place that lay beyond these Wild Woods.

The Dragon's moment of triumph was already sliding away. She roared her frustration, but there was nothing to be done. She felt herself shedding her scales, dwindling from the mythical to the particular, while Hobart's scarred body fluttered like a flame in a breeze, and went out.

Her instant of questioning would surely cost her dearly. In failing to finish the story, to satisfy her victim's desire for death, she'd given him fresh motive for hatred. What change might it have wrought in Hobart to have dreamed himself devoured?; to have made a second womb in the Worm's belly until he was born back into the world?

Too late, damn it; far too late. The pages could contain them no longer. Leaving their confrontation unfinished they broke from the words in a burst of punctuation. They didn't leave the din of the animals behind them: it grew louder as the darkness of the Wild Woods lifted.

Her only thought was for the book. She felt it in her hands once more, and took fiercer hold of it. But Hobart had the same idea. As the room appeared around them in all its solidity she found his fingers clawing at hers, tearing at her skin in his eagerness to claim the prize back.

'You should have killed me,' she heard him murmur.

She glanced up at his face. He looked even sicklier than the knight he'd been, sweat running down his sallow cheeks, gaze desperate. Then he seemed to realize himself, and the eyes grew arctic.

Somebody was beating on the other side of the door, from which the pained cacophony of animals still came.

'Wait!' Hobart yelled to his visitors, whoever they were. As he shouted he took one hand from the book and drew a gun from the inside of his jacket, digging the muzzle into Suzanna's abdomen.

'Let the book go, or I'll kill you.'

She had no choice but to comply. The menstruum would not be swift enough to incapacitate him before he pulled the trigger.

As her hands slipped from the volume, however, the door was thrown open, and all thought of books was eclipsed by what stood on the threshold.

Once, this quartet had been amongst the pride of Hobart's Squad: the smartest, the hardest. But their night of drinking and seduction had unbuttoned more than their trousers. It had undone their minds as well. It was as if the splendours Suzanna had first seen on Lord Street, the haloes that sainted Human and Seerkind alike, had somehow been drawn *inside* them, for the skin of their limbs and faces was swollen and raw, bubbles of darkness scurrying around their anatomies like rats under sheets.

In their panic at this disease, they'd clawed their clothes to tatters; their torsos shone with sweat and blood. And from their throats came the cacophony that had called the Dragon and the Knight out of the book; a bestiality that was echoed in a dozen horrid details. The way this one's face had swollen to lend him a snout; the way another's hands were fat as paws.

This, she presumed, was how the Seerkind had opposed the occupation of their homeland. They'd feigned passivity to seduce the invading army into their raptures, and this nightmare menagerie was the result. Apt as it was, she was appalled.

One of the pack now staggered into the room, his lips and forehead swollen to the brink of bursting. He was clearly trying to address Hobart, but all his spellbound palate could produce was the complaint of a cat having its neck wrung.

Hobart had no intention of deciphering the mewls, but instead levelled his gun at the wreckage shambling towards him.

'Come no closer,' he warned.

The man, spittle running from his open mouth, made a incoherent appeal.

'Get out!' was Hobart's response. He took a step towards the quartet.

The leader retreated, as did those in the doorway. Not for the gun's sake, Suzanna thought, but because Hobart was their master. These new anatomies only confirmed what their training had long ago taught them: that they were unthinking animals, in thrall to the Law.

'*Out!*' said Hobart again.

They were backing off along the corridor now, their din subdued by their fear of Hobart.

In a matter of moments his attention would no longer be diverted, Suzanna knew. He'd turn on her again, and the slim advantage gained by this interruption would have been squandered.

She had to let her instinct lead; she might have no other opportunity.

Seizing the moment, she ran at Hobart and snatched the book from his hand. He shouted out, and glanced her way, his gun still keeping the howling quartet at bay. With his eye off them, the creatures set up their racket afresh.

'There's no way out –' Hobart said to her, '– except by this door. Maybe you'd like to go that way . . . ?'

The creatures clearly sensed that something was in the air, and redoubled their din. It was like feeding time at the zoo. She'd not get two steps down the passage before they were upon her. Hobart had her trapped.

At that realization, she felt the menstruum rise in her, coming with breath-snatching suddenness.

Hobart knew instantly she was gathering strength. He crossed quickly to the door, and slammed it on the howling breed outside, then turned on her again.

'We saw some things, didn't we?' he said. 'But it's a story you won't live to tell.'

He aimed the gun at her face.

It wasn't possible to analyse what happened next. Perhaps

457

he fired and the shot miraculously went wide, shattering the window behind her. Whatever, she felt the night air invade the room, and the next moment the menstruum was bathing her from head to foot, turning her on her heel, and she was running towards the window with no time to consider the sense of this escape route until she was up on the sill and hurling herself out.

The window was three storeys up. But it was too late for such practicalities. She was committed to the leap, or fall, or – *flight!*

The menstruum scooped her up, throwing its strength against the wall of the house opposite, and letting her slide from window to roof on its cool back. It wasn't true flight, but it felt like the real thing.

The street reeled beneath her as she tumbled on solid air to meet the eaves of the other house, only to be scooped up a second time and carried over the roof, Hobart's shouts diminishing behind her.

She could not be held aloft for long, of course; but it was an exhilarating ride while it lasted. She slid helter skelter down another roof, catching sight in that moment of a streak of dawn light between the hills, then over gables and chimney stacks and down, swooping, into a square where the birds were already tuning up for the day.

As she flew down they scattered, startled by the twist evolution had taken to produce such a bird as this. Her landing must have reassured them that there was much design work still to do. She skidded across the paving stones, the menstruum cushioning the worst of the impact, and came to a halt inches from a mosaiced wall.

Shaking, and faintly nauseous, she stood up. The entire flight had probably lasted no more than twenty seconds, but already she heard voices raising the alarm in an adjacent street.

Clutching Mimi's gift, she slipped from the square and out of the township by a route that took her once in a circle and twice almost threw her into the arms of her pursuers. Every step of the way she discovered a new bruise, but she was at least alive, and wiser for the night's adventures.

Life and wisdom. What more could anybody ask?

# IX

# THE FIRE

The day and night that Suzanna spent in Nonesuch, and in the Wild Woods, stalking Hobart, took Cal and de Bono to no less remarkable places. They too had their griefs, and revelations; they too came closer to death than either wanted to come again.

Upon parting from her, they'd resumed their journey to the Firmament in silence, until out of nowhere de Bono had said:

'Do you love her?'

Oddly enough, that very thought had been on Cal's mind, but he hadn't replied to the question. It had frankly embarrassed him.

'You damn fool,' de Bono said. 'Why are you Cuckoos so afraid of your feelings? She's worth loving; even I can see that. So why don't you say it?'

Cal grunted. De Bono was right, but it rankled to be lectured on the matter by someone younger.

'You're afraid of her, is that it?' de Bono said.

The remark added insult to injury.

'Christ no,' Cal said. 'Why the fuck should I be afraid of her?'

'She's got powers,' said de Bono, taking off his spectacles and surveying the terrain ahead. 'Most women have, of course. That's why Starbrook wouldn't have them in the Field. It threw him off balance.'

'And what have we got?' Cal asked, kicking a stone ahead of him.

'We've got our pricks.'

'Starbrook, again?'

'De Bono,' came the reply, and the boy laughed. 'I tell you what,' he said. 'I know this place where we could go –'

'No detours,' said Cal.

'What's an hour or two?' said de Bono. 'Have you ever heard of Venus Mountain?'

'I said no detours, de Bono. If you want to go, then go.'

'Jesus, you're boring,' de Bono sighed. 'I just might leave you to it.'

'I'm not much enjoying your damn fool questions, either,' Cal said. 'So if you want to go pick flowers, do it. Just point me to the Firmament.'

De Bono fell silent. They walked on. When they did start talking again de Bono began to parade his knowledge of the Fugue, more for the pleasure of belittling his fellow traveller than out of any genuine desire to inform. Twice, in the middle of a diatribe, Cal dragged them into hiding as one of Hobart's patrols came within sighting distance of them. On the second occasion they were pinned down for two hours while the Squad got progressively drunker within yards of their hiding place.

When they finally moved on, they progressed much more slowly. Their cramp-ridden limbs felt leaden; they were hungry, thirsty and irritated by each other's company. Worst of all, dusk was creeping on.

'Just how far is it from here?' Cal wanted to know. Once, looking down on the Fugue from Mimi's wall, the confusion of its landscape had promised unending adventure. Now, immersed in that confusion, he would have given his eye-teeth for a good map.

'It's quite a distance yet,' de Bono replied.

'Do you know where the hell we are?'

De Bono's lip curled. 'Of course.'

'Name it.'

'Huh?'

'*Name it!*'

'I'll be damned if I will. You just have to trust me, Cuckoo.'

The wind had got up in the last half hour, and now it brought with it the sound of cries, which halted the escalating war of words between them.

'I smell a bonfire burning,' de Bono said. It was true. Besides its burden of pain, the wind brought the scent of burning wood. De Bono was already bounding off in search of its source. Nothing would have given Cal more satisfaction at that moment than leaving the rope-dancer to his own devices, but – much as he doubted de Bono's value as a guide – he was better than nothing. Cal followed him through the gathering darkness, up a small ridge. From there – across a space of fields littered with arches – they had a fine view of the fire. What looked to be a small copse was burning lustily, the flames fanned by the wind. On the outskirts of this sizeable blaze a number of cars were parked, their owners – more of Shadwell's army of deliverance – running riot.

'Bastards,' said de Bono, as several of them hounded down a victim and laid into him with cudgels and boots. 'Cuckoo bastards.'

'It's not just my people –' Cal began. But before he could finish the defence of his tribe, the words died on his tongue, as he recognized the place that was being destroyed in front of his eyes.

This was no wood. The trees weren't arbitrarily scattered, but planted in ordered avenues. Once, beneath the awning of those trees, he'd spoken Mad Mooney's verses. Now the orchard of Lemuel Lo was ablaze from end to end.

He started down the slope towards the conflagration.

'Where are you going?' de Bono asked him. 'Calhoun? What do you think you're doing?'

De Bono came after him, and took hold of his arm.

'Calhoun! Listen to me!'

'Let me alone,' Cal said, attempting to throw de Bono off. In the violence of that attempt the soil of the incline gave way beneath his heel and he lost balance, taking de Bono with him. They slid down the hill, dirt and stones showering them, and came to a halt in a waist-deep ditch of stagnant water at

461

the bottom. Cal began to haul himself out the other side, but de Bono had hold of his shirt.

'You can't do anything, Mooney,' he said.

'Get the fuck off me.'

'Look, I'm sorry about the Cuckoo remark, right? *We* breed vandals too.'

'Forget it,' said Cal, his eyes still on the fire. He detached de Bono's hand. 'I know this place,' he said. 'I can't just let it burn.'

He pulled himself up out of the ditch and started towards the blaze. He'd kill the bastards who'd done this, whoever they were. Kill them, and call it justice.

'*It's too late!*' de Bono called after him. 'You can't help.'

There was truth in what the youth said. Tomorrow there'd be nothing left of the orchard but ashes. Still he couldn't bring himself to turn his back on the spot where he'd first tasted the Fugue's raptures. Vaguely aware that de Bono was padding after him, and completely indifferent to the fact, he headed on.

As the scene before him became clearer he realized that the Prophet's troops (the word flattered them; it was a *rabble*) were not going unresisted. In several places around the fire figures were locked in hand-to-hand combat. But the orchard's defenders were easy meat for the fire-raisers, for whom these barbarities were little more than sport. They'd come into the Fugue armed with weapons that could decimate the Seerkind in hours. Even as Cal watched he saw one of the Kind felled with a pistol shot. Somebody went to the wounded man's aid, but was in her turn brought down. The soldiers went from body to body to see that the job was done. The first of the victims was not dead. He raised his hand towards his executioner, who pointed his gun at the man's head and fired.

A spasm of nausea convulsed Cal's system, as the smell of cooking flesh mingled with the smoke. He couldn't control his revulsion. His knees buckled, and he fell to the ground, retching on his empty stomach. At that moment his misery seemed complete: the wet clothes icy on his spine; the taste of his stomach in his throat; the paradise orchard burning nearby.

The horrors the Fugue was showing him were as profound as its visions had been elevated. He could fall no further.

'Come away, Cal.'

De Bono's hand was on his shoulder. He put a handful of freshly torn grass in front of Cal.

'Wipe your face,' he said softly. 'There's nothing to be done here.'

Cal pressed the grass beneath his nose, inhaling its cool sweetness. The nausea was passing. He chanced one more look up at the burning orchard. His eyes were watering, and at first glance he couldn't trust what they now told him. He wiped them with the back of his hand, sniffing. Then he looked again, and there – moving through the smoke in front of the fire – he saw Lem.

He spoke the man's name.

'Who?' said de Bono.

Cal was already getting up, though his legs were jittery.

'There,' Cal said, pointing towards Lo. The orchard-keeper was crouching beside one of the bodies, his hand extended to the face of the corpse. Was he closing the dead man's eyes, offering a blessing as he did so?

Cal had to make his presence known; had to speak to the man, even if it was just to say that he too had witnessed the horrors here, and that they wouldn't go unrevenged. He turned to de Bono. The blaze, reflected in the rope-dancer's spectacles, hid his eyes, but it was clear from the way his face was set that what he'd seen had not left him untouched.

'Stay here,' Cal said. 'I have to speak to Lem.'

'You're insane, Mooney,' de Bono said.

'Probably.'

He began back towards the fire, calling Lem's name. The rabble seemed to have tired of their hunt. Several had returned to their cars; another was pissing into the fire; yet others were simply watching the blaze, stupefied by drink and destruction.

Lem had done with his blessings, and was walking away from the remains of his orchard. Cal called his name again, but the sound of the fire drowned it out. He began to pick up his pace, and as he did so Lem caught sight of him from the corner of his eye. He seemed not to recognize Cal, however. Instead, alarmed by the approaching figure, he turned and started to run. Again, Cal yelled his name, and this time drew the man's attention. He stopped running and glanced back, squinting through the smoke and smuts.

'Lem! It's me!' Cal yelled. 'It's Mooney!'

Lo's grimy face was not capable of a smile, but he opened his arms in welcome to Cal, who crossed the last yards between them fearful that at any moment the curtain of smoke would part them again. It didn't. They embraced like brothers.

'Oh my poet,' said Lo, his eyes reddened with tears and smoke. 'What a place to find you.'

'I told you I wouldn't forget,' said Cal. 'Didn't I say that?'

'You did, by God.'

'Why did they do it, Lem? Why did they burn it down?'

'They didn't,' Lem replied. '*I* did.'

'You?'

'You think I'd give those bastards the pleasure of my fruit?'

'But, Lem . . . the trees. All those trees.'

Lo was digging in his pockets, and brought out handfuls of the Jude Pears. Many were bruised and broken, sap glistening as it ran over Lo's fingers. Their perfume pierced the filthy air, bringing back memories of lost times.

'There's seeds in every one of them, poet,' Lem said. 'And in every seed there's a tree. I'll find another place to plant.'

They were brave words, but he sobbed even as he spoke them.

'They won't defeat us, Calhoun,' he said. 'Whatever God's name they come in, we won't kneel to them.'

'You mustn't,' said Cal. 'Or everything's lost.'

As he spoke he saw Lo's gaze move off his face towards the rabble at the cars.

'We should be going,' he said, stuffing the fruit back into his pocket. 'Will you come with me?'

'I can't, Lem.'

'Well, I taught your verses to my daughters,' he said. 'I remembered them as you remembered me –'

'They're not mine,' Cal said. 'They're my grandfather's.'

'They belong to us all now,' Lo said. 'Planted in good ground —'

Suddenly, a shot. Cal turned. The three fire-watchers had seen them, and were coming their way. All were armed.

Lo snatched hold of Cal's hand for an instant, and squeezed it by way of farewell. Then contact was broken, as more shots followed on the first. Lo was heading off into the darkness, away from the light of the fire, but the ground was uneven, and he fell after only a few steps. Cal went after him, as the gunmen began a further round of shots.

'Get away from me —' Lo shouted. 'For God's sake *run*!'

Lo was scrabbling to pick up the fruit that he'd dropped from his pocket. As Cal reached him one of the gunman got lucky. A shot found Lo. He cried out, and clutched his side.

The gunmen were almost upon their targets now. They'd given up firing, to have better sport at close range. As they came within a half a dozen yards, however, the leader was felled by a missile hurled from the smoke. It struck his head, opening a substantial wound. He toppled, blinded by blood.

Cal had time to see the weapon that had brought the man down, and recognize it as a radio: then de Bono was weaving through the murky air towards the gunmen. They heard him coming: he was yelling like a wild man. A shot was fired in his direction; but went well wide. He threw himself past the hunters, and ran off in the direction of the fire.

The leader, his hand clamped to his head, was staggering to his feet, ready to give chase. De Bono's tactics, though they'd distracted the executioners, were as good as suicidal. The gunmen had him trapped against the wall of burning trees. Cal caught sight of him pelting through the smoke towards the fire, the killers in howling pursuit. A volley of shots was fired; he dodged them like the dancer he was. But there was no dodging the inferno ahead. Cal saw him glance round once, to take in the sight of his pursuers, then — idiot that he was — he plunged into the fire. Most of the trees were now no more than burning pillars, but the ground itself was a firewalker's heaven, hot ash

465

and charcoal. The air shimmered with the heat, corrupting de Bono's figure until it was lost between the trees.

There was no time to mourn him. His bravery had earned them a reprieve, but it would not last long. Cal turned back to aid Lemuel. The man had gone, however, leaving a splash of blood and a few fallen fruit to mark the place he'd been. Back at the fire, the gunmen were still waiting to mow de Bono down should he re-emerge. Cal had time to get to his feet and study the conflagration for any sign of the rope-dancer. There was none. Then he backed away from the pyre, and took off towards the slope on which he and de Bono had fought. As he did so a vague hope rose in him. He decided to change his route, and made a run that took him around to the other side of the orchard.

The air was clearer here; the wind was carrying the smoke in the opposite direction. He ran along the edge of the orchard, hoping against hope that maybe de Bono had outpaced the heat. Half way along the flank of the fire his horrified eyes found a pair of burning shoes. He kicked them over, then searched for their owner.

It was only when he turned his back on the flames that he saw the figure, standing in a field of high grass two hundred yards from the orchard. Even at that distance the blond head was recognizable. So, as he drew closer, was the smug smile.

He'd lost his eye-brows and his lashes; and his hair was badly singed. But he was alive and well.

'How did you do that?' Cal asked him, when he got within speaking distance of the fellow.

De Bono shrugged. 'I'd rather fire-walk than rope-dance any day of the week,' he said.

'I'd be dead without you,' Cal said. 'Thank you.'

De Bono was clearly uncomfortable with Cal's gratitude. He shooed it away with a wave of his hand, then turned his back on the fire and waded off through the grass, leaving Cal to follow.

'Do you know where we're going?' Cal called after him. It seemed they were striking off in another direction to the one they'd been following when they'd first come upon the fire, but he couldn't have sworn to it.

De Bono offered a reply, but the wind blew it away, and Cal was too weary to ask a second time.

# X

## UNEARTHLY DELIGHTS

### 1

The journey became a torment thereafter. Events at the orchard had drained Cal of what few reserves of strength he could still lay claim to. The muscles in his legs twitched as if they were about to go into spasm; the vertebrae in his lower back seemed to have lost their cartilage and were grinding against each other. He tried not to think of what would happen if and when they finally reached the Firmament. In the best of conditions he and de Bono would scarcely be Shadwell's equal. Like this, they'd be fodder.

The occasional wonders the starlight had uncovered – a ring of stones, linked by bands of whispering fog; what appeared to be a family of dolls, their identical faces pale, smiling beatifically from behind a silent waterfall – to these he gave no more than a cursory glance. The only sight that could have brought joy to his lips at that moment was a feather mattress.

But even the mysteries dwindled after a time, as de Bono led him up a dark hillside, with a soft wind moving in the grass around their feet.

The moon was rising through a bank of cumulus, making a ghost of de Bono as he forged on up the steep slope. Cal followed like a lamb, too weary to question their route.

But by degrees he became aware that the sighs he heard were not entirely the voice of the wind. There was an oblique music in them; a tune which came and fled again.

It was de Bono who finally came to a halt, and said:

'D'you hear them, Cal?'

'Yes. I hear them.'

'They know they've got visitors.'

'Is this the Firmament?'

'No,' said de Bono softly. 'The Firmament's for tomorrow. We're too tired for that. Tonight we stay here.'

'Where's here?'

'Can't you guess? Don't you smell the air?'

It was lightly perfumed; honeysuckle and night-blooming jasmine.

'And feel the earth?'

The ground was warm beneath his feet.

'This, my friend, is Venus Mountain.'

## 2

He should have known better than to trust de Bono; for all his heroics the fellow was wholly unreliable. And now they'd lost precious time.

Cal glanced behind him, to see if the route they'd come was discernible, but no; the moon had slipped into the cloud-bank for a little while, and the mountain-side was in darkness. When he looked back, de Bono had vanished. Hearing laughter a little way off, Cal called his guide's name. The laughter came again. It sounded too light to be de Bono, but he couldn't be certain.

'Where are you?' he asked, but there was no reply, so he went in the direction of the laughter.

As he advanced he stepped into a passage of warm air. Startled, he retreated, but the tropical warmth came with him, the honey scent now strong in his nostrils. It made him feel light-headed; his aching legs threatened to fold beneath him from the sheer swooning pleasure of it.

A little further up the incline he saw another figure, surely that of de Bono, moving in the gloom. Again he called the man's name, and this time he was granted a reply. De Bono turned and said:

'Don't fret, Cuckoo.'

His voice had taken on a dreamy quality.

'We've got no time —' Cal protested.

'Can't do . . . can't do anything . . .' de Bono's voice came and went, like a weak radio signal. 'Can't do anything tonight . . . except *love* . . .'

The last word faded, and so did de Bono, melting into the darkness.

Cal about-turned. He was certain that de Bono had been speaking from further up the mountain, which meant that if he turned his back on the spot, and walked, he'd be returning the way they'd come.

The warmth went with him as he about-turned. I'll get a new guide, he vaguely thought; get a guide and find the Firmament. He had an appointment to keep with somebody. Who was it? His thoughts were going the way of de Bono's voice. Oh yes: *Suzanna.*

At the mental formulation of her name the warmth somehow conspired with his limbs to draw him down to the ground. He wasn't sure how it happened — he didn't trip, he wasn't pushed — but in an instant he had his head on the ground, and oh, the comfort of it. It was like returning to a lover's bed on a morning of a frost. He stretched out, indulging his weary limbs, telling himself he'd just lie here long enough to gain some strength for the trials ahead.

He might well have fallen asleep, but that he heard his name called.

Not Cal, nor even Calhoun, but:

'*Mooney* . . .'

It was not de Bono's voice, but a woman's.

'Suzanna?'

He tried to sit up, but he was so heavy, so laden with the dirt of his journey he couldn't move. He wanted to slough the weight off like a snake its tired skin, but he lay there unable to move a finger joint, while the voice called him and called him, fading as it went searching for him in higher regions.

He so wanted to follow it; and without warning he felt that yearning realized, as his clothes fell away from him and he

470

began to travel over the grass, his belly to the earth's belly. How he was transported he wasn't certain, for he felt no movement in his limbs, and his breath was not quickened by the effort. Indeed he felt so removed from sensation it was as if he'd left body and breath behind him with his clothes.

One thing he had brought with him: light. A pale, cool light that illuminated the grass and the small mountain flowers nestling there; a light that travelled so close to him it might have been *of* him.

A few yards from where he journeyed he saw de Bono lying asleep on the grass, his mouth open like a fish's mouth. He moved towards the sleeper to question him, but before he reached the man something else drew his attention. Mere yards from where de Bono lay there were shafts of light springing up from the dark ground. He moved over his companion's body, his light almost stirring de Bono, then on towards this new mystery.

It was easily solved. There were several holes in the earth. He went to the lip of the nearest and peered down. The entire mountain, he now saw, was hollow. Below him was a vast cavern, with brightnesses moving in it. These were, presumably, the presences of which de Bono had spoken.

Now the suspicion that he'd left his body behind him somewhere along the way was confirmed, for he slipped down the hole – which would not have been wide enough to allow access to his head never mind his shoulders – and fell into the upper air of the cavern.

There he hovered, and gazed on the ritual being performed below.

At first sight the performers seemed to be spheres of luminous gas, perhaps forty of them, some large, some minute, their colours ranging from cool pastels through to livid yellows and reds. But as he drifted down from the dome of the cavern, claimed not by gravity but by the simple desire to know, he realized that the globes were far from blank. Within their confines forms were appearing, like ghosts in their perfect geometries. They were ephemeral, these visions, lasting seconds at most, before pale clouds veiled them and new

471

configurations took their place. But they lingered long enough for him to make sense of them.

In several of the spheres he saw shapes that resembled human foetuses, their heads vast, their thread-like limbs wrapped about their bodies. No sooner seen than gone; and in their place perhaps a splash of bright blue, that made the globe into a vast eyeball. In another, the gases were dividing and dividing, like a cell in love with itself; in a third the clouds had become a blizzard, in the depths of which he saw a forest and a hill.

He was certain these entities were aware of his being in the cavern, though none broke the regime of their motion to welcome him. He was not offended by this. Their dance was elaborate, and it would cause no little confusion if one of them were to move off its course. There was an exquisite inevitability about their motion – some of the spheres repeatedly moving within a hair's breadth of collision, then swinging wide an instant before disaster struck; others proceeding in families which described complex paths around each other while simultaneously moving in the great circle that was pivoted at the centre of the cavern.

There was more to fascinate him here than the tranquil majesty of the dance, however, for twice in the flux of one of the larger spheres he glimpsed an image which carried an extraordinary erotic charge. A naked woman, her limbs defying all the laws of anatomy, was floating on a pillow of cloud, her position one of pure sexual display. As Cal witnessed her she was gone, leaving him with the image of her invitation: her lips, her cunt, her buttocks. There was nothing whorish in her exhibition; the crime would have been in shame, which had no place in this charmed circle. The presences were too in love with being for such nonsenses.

They loved death too, and as unequivocally. One sphere had a corpse in its midst, rotted and crawling with flies, disclosed with the same delight as its companion glories.

But death did not interest Cal; the woman did.

*Can't do anything tonight* – de Bono had said – *except love*, and Cal knew it now to be true.

But love as he'd known it above ground was not appropriate here. The woman in the sphere needed no sweet-talk; her company was offered freely. The question was: how did he express his desire? He'd left his erection behind on Venus Mountain.

He needn't have concerned himself: she already knew his thoughts. As his eyes found her a third time, her glance seemed to draw him down into the midst of the dance. He found himself executing a slow, slow somersault, and settling into place beside his mistress.

As he attained this spot, he realized just what function he had here.

The voice on the mountain had called him *Mooney*, and that name had not been chosen in vain. He had come from above as light, as moonlight, and here he had found his orbit in a dance of planets and satellites.

Perhaps, of course, this was simply his interpretation. Perhaps the imperatives of this system pertained as much to love and snow-storms as to astronomy. In the face of such miracles conjecture was fruitless. Tonight, being was all.

The presences made another circuit, and he, lost in the sheer delight of this preordained journey, tumbling over and over (no heels or head here; only the pleasure of motion), was momentarily distracted from the woman he'd seen. But as his orbit took him out in a wide arc he once more set eyes on the planet she haunted. She emerged even as he watched, only to be lost in cloud again. Did he perform the same rites for her, turning from humanity to abstraction and back again at the blossoming of a milky cloud? He knew so little of himself, this Mooney, in his singular orbit.

All he could hope to comprehend of what he was he had to discover from the spheres upon whose faces he shed his borrowed light. That was perhaps the condition of moons.

It was enough.

He knew in that moment how moons made love. By bewitching the nights of planets; by stirring their oceans; by blessing the hunter and the harvester. A hundred ways that needed only the unbound anatomies of light and space.

473

As he thought this thought the woman opened to bathe in him, to spread her cunt and let his light pleasure her.

Entering, he felt the same heat, the same possessiveness, the same vanity as had ever marked the animal he'd been, but in place of labour there was ease, in place of ever imminent loss, sustenance; in place of urgency the sense that this could last forever, or rather that a hundred human lifetimes were a moment in the span of moons, and his ride on this empyrean carousel had made a nonsense of time.

At that thought a terrible sense of poignancy swept over him. Had all he'd left above on the mountain withered and died while these constellations moved steadily about their business?

He looked towards the centre of the system, the hub about which they all described their paths – eccentric or regular, distant or intimate; and there, in the place from which he drew his light, he saw himself, sleeping on a hillside.

I'm *dreaming*, he thought, and suddenly rose – like a bubble in a bottle – less moon than Mooney. The dome of the cavern – which he vaguely realized resembled the inside of a skull – was dark above him, and for an instant he thought he'd be dashed to death against it, but at the last moment the air grew bright around him and he woke, staring up at a sky streaked with light.

It was dawn on Venus Mountain.

3

Of the dream he'd had, one part was true. He *had* sloughed off two skins like a snake. One, his clothes, lay scattered around him in the grass. The other, the accrued grime of his adventures, had been bathed away in the night, either by dew or a fall of rain. Whichever, he was quite dry now; the warmth of the ground he lay upon (that part also had been no dream) had dried him off and left him sweet-smelling. He felt nourished too, and strong.

He sat up. Balm de Bono was already on his feet, scratching

his balls and staring up at the sky: a blissful combination. The grass had left an imprint on his back and buttocks.

'Did they please you?' he said, cocking an eye at Cal.

'Please me?'

'The Presences. Did they give you sweet dreams?'

'Yes they did.'

De Bono grinned lewdly.

'Want to tell me about it?' he said.

'I don't know how to –'

'Oh spare me the modesty.'

'No, it's just I . . . I dreamt I was . . . the moon.'

'You did *what*?'

'I dreamt –'

'I bring you to the nearest thing we've got to a whorehouse, and you dream about being the moon? You're a strange man, Calhoun.'

He picked up his vest, and put it on, shaking his head at Cal's bizarrity.

'What did *you* dream of?' Cal enquired.

'I'll tell you, one of these times,' said de Bono. 'When you're old enough.'

# 4

They dressed in silence, then set off down the gentle slope of the mountain.

# XI

## A WITNESS

### 1

T hough the day had dawned well for Suzanna, with her miraculous escape from Hobart, it had rapidly deteriorated. She'd felt oddly cocooned by night; with the dawn came nameless anxieties.

And some she *could* name. First off, the fact that she'd lost her guide. She had only the roughest idea of the direction in which the Firmament lay, so elected to make her way towards the Gyre, which was plainly visible at all times, and make what enquiries she could along the route.

Her second source of concern: the many signs that events in the Fugue were rapidly taking a turn for the worse. A great pall of smoke hung over the valley, and though there'd been rain in the night, fires still burned in many places. She came upon several battle sites as she went. In one place a fire-gutted car was perched in a tree like a steel bird, blown there presumably, or levitated. She couldn't know what forces had clashed the previous night, nor what weapons had been used, but the struggle had clearly been horrendous. Shadwell had divided the people of this once tranquil land with his prophetic talk – setting brother against brother. Those conflicts were traditionally the bloodiest. It should have come as no surprise then, to see bodies left where they'd fallen, for foxes and birds to pick at, denied the simple courtesy of burial.

If there was any sliver of comfort to be drawn from these scenes it was that Shadwell's invasion had not gone undefied. The destruction of Capra's House had been a massive miscalculation on his part. What chance he'd had of taking the Fugue with words alone had been squandered in that one tyrannical gesture. He could not now hope to win these territories by stealth and seduction. It was armed suppression or nothing.

Having seen for herself what damage the Seerkind's raptures were capable of, she nurtured some faint hope that any such suppression might be subverted. But what damage – perhaps irreversible – would be done to the Fugue while its inhabitants' freedom was being won? These woods and meadows weren't meant to host atrocities; their innocence of such horrors was a part of their power to enchant.

It was at such a spot – once untainted, now all too familiar with death – that she encountered the first living person in her travels that day. It was one of those mysterious snatches of architecture of which the Fugue could boast several; in this case a dozen pillars ranged around a shallow pool. On top of one of the pillars sat a stringy middle-aged man in a shabby coat – a large pair of binoculars around his neck – who looked up from the notebook in which he was scribbling as she approached.

'Looking for someone?' he enquired.

'No.'

'They're all dead anyway,' he said dispassionately. 'See?' The pavement around the pool was splashed with blood. Those that had shed it lay face up at the bottom of the water, their wounds white.

'Your handiwork?' she asked him.

'Me? Good God no. I'm just a witness. And what army are you with?'

'I'm with nobody,' she said. 'I'm on my own.'

This he wrote down.

'I don't necessarily believe you,' he said, as he wrote. 'But a good witness sets down what he sees and hears, even if he doubts it.'

'What *have* you seen?' she asked him.

'Confusion,' he said. 'People everywhere, and nobody sure who was who. And blood-letting the like of which I never thought to see here.' He peered at her. 'You're not Seerkind,' he said.

'No.'

'Just wandered in by chance, did you?'

'Something like that.'

'Well I'd wander back out again if I were you. Nobody's safe. A lot of folks have packed their bags and gone into the Kingdom rather than be slaughtered.'

'So who's left fighting?'

'Wild men. I know I shouldn't venture an opinion but that's the way it looks to me. Barbarians, raging around.'

Even as he spoke she heard shouting a little way off. With their breakfast done, the wild men were at work already.

'What can you see from up there?' she asked him.

'A lot of ruins,' he said. 'And occasional glimpses of the factions.' He put his binoculars to his eyes and made a sweep of the terrain, pausing here and there as he caught sight of some interesting detail. 'There's been a battalion out of Nonesuch in the last hour,' he said, 'looking much the worse for wear. There's rebels over towards the Steps, and another band to the North-West of here. The Prophet left the Firmament a little while ago – I can't say exactly when, my watch was stolen – and there's several squads of his evangelists preceding him, to clear the way.'

'The way where?'

'To the Gyre, of course.'

'The *Gyre*?'

'My guess is that was the Prophet's target from the outset.'

'He's not a Prophet,' said Suzanna. 'He's called Shadwell.'

'Shadwell?'

'Go on, write that down. He's a Cuckoo, and a salesman.'

'You know this for certain?' the man said. 'Tell me all.'

'No time,' Suzanna replied, much to his aggravation. 'I've got to get to him.'

'Oh. So he's a friend.'

'Far from it,' she said, her eyes straying back to the bodies in the pool.

'You'll never get near his throat, if that's what you're

478

hoping,' the man told her. 'He's guarded day and night.'

'I'll find a way,' she said. 'You don't know what he's capable of.'

'If he's a Cuckoo and he tries stepping into the Gyre, that'll be the end of us, *that* I do know. Still, it'll give me a last chapter, eh?'

'And who'll be left to read it?'

## 2

She left him up on his pillar, like some lonely penitent, pondering the remark. Her thoughts were grimmer for the conversation. Despite the presence of the menstruum in her system, she knew very little of how the forces that had made the Weaveworld worked, but it didn't take genius to see that for Shadwell to trespass on the rapturous ground of the Gyre would prove cataclysmic. He was all that rarefied region, and its makers, despised: he was Corruption. Perhaps the Gyre could destroy itself rather than give him access to its secrets. And if *it* ceased to exist wouldn't the Fugue – the unity of which was preserved by the power there – be lost to the maelstrom? That, she feared, was what the witness had meant with his pronouncements. If Shadwell entered the Gyre, the world would end.

There'd been no sign of animal or bird life since she'd left the vicinity of the pool. The trees and bushes were deserted; the undergrowth was hushed. She summoned the menstruum up until it brimmed in her, ready to be used in her defence should the occasion arise. There was no time left for niceties now. She would kill anyone who tried to prevent her from getting to Shadwell.

A noise from behind a partially demolished wall drew her attention. She stood her ground, and challenged the observer to make himself known. There was no reply forthcoming.

'I won't ask you again,' she said. *'Who's there?'*

At this there was a fall of brick shards, and a boy of four or

479

five, naked but for socks and dust, stood up and clambered over the rubble towards her.

'Oh my God,' she said, her heart going out to the child. In the instant her defences fell there was movement to right and left of her, and she found herself surrounded by a ragged selection of armed men.

The child's forlorn expression dropped, as one of the soldiers summoned him to his side. The man put a grimy hand through the boy's hair, and gave him a grim smile of approval.

'Name yourself,' someone demanded of her.

She had no idea of which side these men were on. If they were of Shadwell's army, admitting her name would be an instant death sentence. But, desperate as things were, she couldn't bring herself to unleash the menstruum against men – and a child – whose allegiance she didn't even know.

'Shoot her,' the boy said. 'She's with them.'

'Don't you dare,' said a voice at the back. 'I know her.'

She turned, as her saviour spoke her name, and there – of all people – was Nimrod. The last time they'd met he'd been a convert to Shadwell's unholy crusade: all talk of glorious tomorrows. Time and circumstance had humbled him. He was a picture of wretchedness, his clothes tattered, his face full of hurt.

'Don't blame me,' he said before she could even speak.

'I don't,' she said. There'd been times she'd cursed him, but they were history now. 'Truly I don't.'

'Help me –' he said suddenly, and came to her. She hugged him. He concealed his tears behind their embrace, until the others left off watching the reunion and slipped back into hiding.

Only then did he ask:

'Have you seen Jerichau?'

'He's dead,' she said. 'The sisters killed him.'

He drew away from her, and covered his face with his hands.

'It wasn't your fault,' she told him.

'I knew . . .' he said quietly. 'As soon as things went sour. I knew something terrible had happened to him.'

'You can't be blamed for not seeing the truth. Shadwell's a brilliant performer. And he was selling what people wanted to hear.'

'Wait,' said Nimrod, looking up at her. 'Are you telling me Shadwell's the Prophet?'

'Yes I am.'

He made a small shake of the head.

'A Cuckoo,' he said, his tone still half disbelieving. 'A Cuckoo.'

'It doesn't mean he isn't strong,' Suzanna cautioned. 'He's got raptures all his own.'

'You've got to come back to the camp,' Nimrod said, with fresh urgency. 'Talk to our commander before we leave for the Gyre.'

'Make it quick,' she said.

He was already away, leading her into the rockier terrain that concealed the rebels.

'There's only me and Apolline left alive,' he said, as they went, 'from the First Wakened. The rest are gone. My Lilia. Then Freddy Cammell. Now Jerichau.'

'Where's Apolline now?'

'She went out into the Kingdom, the last I heard. What about Cal? Is he with you?'

'We were going to meet up at the Firmament. But Shadwell's already on his way to the Gyre.'

'Which is as far as he'll get,' Nimrod said. 'Whatever raptures he's stolen, he's still just a man. And men bleed.'

So do we all, she thought, but left the thought unspoken.

481

# XII

## ONE FELL SWOOP

### 1

Nimrod's brave talk was undercut by what she found at the camp. It was more like a hospital than a military establishment. Well over three quarters of the fifty or so soldiers, men and women, who were gathered in the shelter of the rocks, had sustained some wound or other. Some were still capable of fighting, but many were clearly at death's door, tended with soft words in their failing minutes.

In one corner of the camp, out of sight of the dying, a dozen bodies were laid beneath make-shift shrouds. In another, a cache of captured armaments was being sorted through. It made a chilling display: machine-guns, flame-throwers, grenades. On this evidence Shadwell's followers had come prepared to destroy their homeland if it resisted their deliverance. Against these horrors, and the zeal with which they were wielded, the profoundest raptures were a frail defence.

If Nimrod shared her doubts he chose not to show them, but talked ceaselessly of the previous night's victories, as if to keep a telling silence at bay.

'We even took prisoners,' he boasted, leading Suzanna to a muddy pit amongst the boulders, where maybe a dozen captives sat, bound at ankles and wrists, guarded by a girl with a machine-gun. They were a forlorn mob. Some were wounded, all were distressed, weeping and muttering to themselves, as though Shadwell's lies no longer blinded them and they were waking up to the iniquity of what they'd done. She pitied them in their self-contempt. She knew all too well the powers of beguilement Shadwell possessed – in her time she'd almost succumbed to them herself. These were his *victims*, not his allies; they'd been sold a lie they'd had no power to refuse. Now, disabused of his teachings, they were left to brood on the blood they'd spilt, and despair.

'Has anybody talked with them?' she asked Nimrod. 'Maybe they've got some grasp of Shadwell's weaknesses.'

'The commander forbade it,' said Nimrod. 'They're diseased.'

'Don't talk nonsense,' Suzanna replied, and climbed down into the pit with the prisoners. Several turned their troubled faces towards her; one, at the sight of a face that bore some sign of lenience, started to sob loudly.

'I'm not here to accuse you,' she told them. 'I just want to talk with you.'

At her side a man with blood-caked features said:

'Are they going to kill us?'

'No,' she told him. 'Not if I can help it.'

'What happened?' another enquired, his voice slurred and dreamy: 'Is the Prophet coming?' Someone tried to shush him, but he rambled on. 'He must come soon, mustn't he? He must come, and take us into Capra's hands.'

'He isn't coming,' said Suzanna.

'We know that,' said the first prisoner. 'At least most of us do. We've been cheated. He told us –'

'I know what he told you,' Suzanna said. 'And I know how he cheated you. Now you've got to make good the damage, by helping me.'

'You can't overthrow him,' the man said. 'He's got powers.'

'Shut your mouth,' said one nearby, who was clutching a rosary so tightly his knuckles looked ready to pop. 'You mustn't say anything against him. He *hears*.'

'*Let him hear*,' the other spat back. 'Let him kill me if he chooses. I don't care.' He turned back to Suzanna: 'He's got demons with him. I've seen them. He feeds the dead to them.'

Nimrod, who was standing behind Suzanna listening to this evidence, now spoke up:

'Demons?' he said. 'You've seen them?'

'No,' said the white-faced man.

'*I* have,' said another.

'Describe them . . .' Nimrod demanded.

It was surely the by-blows the man spoke of, Suzanna thought, grown to monstrous proportions. But as the man began to tell what he knew she was distracted by the sight of a prisoner she hadn't previously noticed, squatting in the filthiest part of the compound, face turned to the rock. It was a woman, to judge by the hair that fell to the middle of her back, and she'd not been bound like the rest, simply left to grieve in the dirt.

Suzanna made her way through the captives towards her. As she approached she heard mutterings, and saw that the woman had her lips pressed to the stone, and was talking to it as if seeking comfort there. Her supplication faltered as Suzanna's shadow fell on the rock, and she turned.

It took a heart-beat only for Suzanna to see beyond the dried blood and excrement on the face that now looked up towards her; it was Immacolata. On her maimed face was the look of a tragedian. Her eyes were swollen with tears, and brimming now with a fresh flood; her hair was unbraided and thick with mud. Her breasts were bared for all to see, and in every sinew there was a terrible bewilderment. Nothing of her former authority remained. She was a madwoman, squatting in her own shit.

Contrary feelings fought in Suzanna. Here, trembling before her, was the woman who'd murdered Mimi in her own bed; part architect of the calamities which had overtaken the Fugue. The power behind Shadwell's throne, the source of countless deceits and sorrows; the Devil's inspiration. Yet she could not feel for Immacolata the hatred she'd felt for Shadwell or Hobart. Was it because the Incantatrix had first given her access to the menstruum, albeit unwillingly; or was it that they were – as Immacolata had always claimed – somehow *sisters*? Might *this*, under other skies, have been her fate; to be lost and mad?

'Don't . . . look at . . . me,' the woman said softly. There was no sign of recognition in her blood-shot eyes.

'Do you know who you are?' Suzanna asked her.

The woman's expression didn't change. After a few moments her answer came.

'The rock knows,' she said.

'The rock?'

'It'll be sand soon. I told it so, because it's true. It'll be sand.'

Immacolata took her gaze off her questioner and began to stroke the rock with her open palm. She'd been doing this for some while, Suzanna now saw. There were streaks of blood on the stone, where she'd rubbed the skin from her palm as if attempting to erase the lines.

'Why will it be sand?' Suzanna asked.

'It must come,' said Immacolata. 'I've seen it. The Scourge. It must come, and then we will all be sand.' She stroked more furiously. 'I told the rock.'

'Will you tell *me*?'

Immacolata glanced round, and then back to the rock. For a little while Suzanna thought the woman had forgotten the questioner until the words came again, haltingly.

'The Scourge must come,' she said. 'Even in its sleep, it knows.' She stopped wounding her hand. 'Sometimes it almost wakes,' she said. 'And when it does, we'll all be sand . . .'

She laid her cheek against the bloodied rock, and made a low sobbing sound.

'Where's your sister?' Suzanna said.

At this, the sobbing faltered.

'Is she here?'

'I have . . . no sisters,' Immacolata said. There was no trace of doubt in her voice.

'What about Shadwell? Do you remember Shadwell?'

'My sisters are dead. All gone to sand. Everything. Gone to sand.'

The sobs began again, more mournful than ever.

'What's your interest in her?' Nimrod, who'd been standing at Suzanna's shoulder for several seconds, wanted to know.

'She's just another lunatic. We found her amongst the corpses. She was eating their eyes.'

'Do you know who she is?' Suzanna said. 'Nimrod . . . that's Immacolata.'

His face grew slack with shock.

'Shadwell's mistress. I swear it.'

'You're mistaken,' he said.

'She's lost her mind, but I swear that's who it is. I was face to face with her less than two days ago.'

'So what's happened to her?'

'Shadwell, maybe . . .'

The name was echoed softly by the woman at the rock.

'Whatever happened, she shouldn't be here, not like this –'

'You'd better come speak to the commander. You can tell it all to her.'

## 2

It seemed it was to be a day of reunions. First Nimrod, then the Incantatrix, and now – leading this defeated troop – Yolande Dor, the woman who'd so vehemently fought the reweaving, back when Capra's House was still standing.

She too had changed. Gone, the strutting confidence of the woman. Her face looked pale and clammy; her voice and manner were subdued. She wasted no time with courtesies.

'If you've got something to tell me, spit it out.'

'One of your prisoners –' Suzanna began.

'I've no time to hear appeals,' came the reply. 'Especially from you.'

'This isn't an appeal.'

'I still won't hear it.'

'You *must*; and you *will*,' Suzanna responded. 'Forget how you feel about me –'

'I don't feel anything,' was Yolande's retort. 'The Council condemned themselves. You were just there to carry their burden for them. If it hadn't been you it would have been somebody else.'

This outburst seemed to pain her. She slipped her hand inside her unbuttoned jacket, clearly nursing a wound there. Her fingers came away bloody.

Suzanna persevered, but more softly.

'One of your prisoners,' she said, 'is Immacolata.'

Yolande looked across at Nimrod. 'Is that true?'

'It's true,' Suzanna said. 'I know her better than any of you. It's her. She's . . . lost; insane maybe. But if we could get some sense from her, we might use her to reach Shadwell.'

'Shadwell?'

'The Prophet. They were allies once; him and Immacolata.'

'I won't conspire with Corruption like that,' Yolande replied. 'We'll hang her when the proper time comes.'

'Well at least let me talk to her. Maybe I can coax something from her.'

'If she's lost her mind, why should we trust a word she says? No. Let her rot.'

'It's a wasted chance.'

'Don't tell me about wasted chances,' Yolande said bitterly. There was clearly no hope of persuading her. 'We move towards the Mantle in an hour,' she stated. 'If you want to swell our ranks, do so. Or else get about your business.'

This said, she turned her back on them both.

'Come on,' said Nimrod, and took his leave. But Suzanna lingered.

'For what it's worth,' she said, 'I hope we have time to talk, when all this is over.'

Yolande didn't turn back. 'Leave me alone,' she said.

Suzanna did just that.

3

For several minutes after Suzanna's departure from the prisoners' compound, Immacolata sat in the murk of her forgetfulness. Sometimes she wept. Sometimes she stared at the silent rock in front of her.

The violation Shadwell had visited upon her at the

Firmament, following as it had upon the destruction of her wraith-sisters, had driven her mind into a wilderness. But she'd not been alone there. Somewhere in those wastes she'd been reacquainted with the spectre that had haunted her so often in the past: the Scourge. She, who'd been happiest where the air was thickest with decay, who'd made necklaces of entrails, and soul-mates of the dead – she had found in the presence of that abomination nightmares even she'd prayed to wake from.

It still slept – which was some small consolation in her terror – but it would not sleep forever. It had tasks unfinished; ambitions unfulfilled. Very soon it would rise from its bed, and come looking to finish its business.

And on that day?

'. . . all sand . . .' she told the stone.

This time it didn't answer her. It was sulking, because she'd been indiscreet, talking to the woman with the grey eyes.

Immacolata rocked back and forth on her heels, and as she rocked the woman's words drifted back to her, tantalizing her. She only remembered a little of what the woman had said: a phrase, a name. Or rather, one name in particular. It echoed in her head now.

*Shadwell*.

It was like an itch beneath her scalp; an ache in her skull. She wanted to dig through her ear drum and pull it out, grind it underfoot. She rocked faster, to soothe the name away, but it wouldn't leave her head.

*Shadwell. Shadwell.*

And now there were other names rising to join the ranks of the remembered –

*The Magdalene.*

*The Hag.*

She saw them before her, as clear as the rock; *clearer*: her sisters, her poor, twice-slaughtered sisters.

And beneath their dead heels she saw a land; a somewhere she'd conspired to spoil for such a long, weary time. Its name came back to her, and she spoke it softly.

'The Fugue . . .'

That's what they'd called it, her enemies. How they'd loved it. How they'd fought for its safety, and in the process wounded her.

She put her hand out to the rock, and felt it tremble at her touch. Then she hauled herself to her feet, while the name that had begun this flood filled her head, washing forgetfulness away.

*Shadwell.*

How could she ever have forgotten her beloved Shadwell? She'd given him raptures. And what had he done in return? Betrayed and befouled her. Used her for as long as it had suited his purposes, then pitched her away, into the wilderness.

He hadn't thrown her far enough. Today, she'd found her way back, and she came with killing news.

# 4

The screams began suddenly, and mounted. Cries of disbelief, then shouts of horror the like of which Suzanna had never heard.

Ahead of her, Nimrod was already running towards the source of the din. She followed; and stepped into a scene of the bloodiest chaos.

'We're attacked!' Nimrod yelled at her, as rebels ran in all directions, many bearing fresh wounds. The ground was already littered with bodies; more were falling with every moment.

Before Nimrod could plunge into the fray, however, Suzanna took hold of his jacket.

'They're fighting each other!' she shouted to him, above the bedlam.

'What?'

'Look!' she said.

It took him only a few seconds to confirm what she'd seen. There was no sign of any outside attack. The rebels were at each others' throats. No quarter was being given on any side. Men were murdering men they'd moments ago been sharing a cigarette with. Some had even risen from their death-beds and were beating at the heads of those who'd nursed them.

Nimrod stepped on to the battlefield and dragged one of these sudden lunatics from the throat of another.

'What in God's name are you doing?' he demanded. The man was still struggling to reach his victim.

'That bastard!' the man shrieked. 'He raped my wife.'

'What are you talking about?'

'I saw him! Right there!' He jabbed his finger at the ground. '*There!*'

'Your wife's not here!' Nimrod yelled, shaking the man violently. 'She's not here!'

Suzanna scanned the battlefield. The same delusion, or something similar, had seized hold of all of these people. Even as they fought, they wept, and howled their accusations at each other. They'd seen their parents trampled underfoot, their wives abused and their children slaughtered: now they wanted to kill the culprits. Hearing this collective delusion voiced, she looked for its maker, and there – standing on a high rock, surveying the atrocities, was Immacolata. Her hair remained unbraided. Her breasts were still bare. But she was obviously no longer a stranger to her history. She'd remembered herself.

Suzanna began to move towards her, trusting that the menstruum would keep this terrible rapture from curdling her brains. It did so. Though she had to be nimble to avoid the brutalities on every side, she reached the vicinity of the rock without harm.

Immacolata seemed not to see her. Head back, teeth bared in a grin of appalling ferocity, her attention was entirely upon the mayhem she'd given birth to.

'*Forget them,*' Suzanna called up to her.

At these words the head dropped a fraction, and Suzanna felt the Incantatrix's gaze come to rest on her.

'Why are you doing this?' she said. 'They've done you no harm.'

'You should have left me to my emptiness,' the Incantatrix replied. 'You made me remember.'

490

'Then for *my* sake,' Suzanna said, 'leave them be.'

Behind her, the shouts had begun to wane, only to be replaced by the moans of the dying and the sobs of those who'd woken from this delusion to find their knives buried in the hearts of their friends.

Whether the rapture had faltered because Immacolata had done her worst, or because she'd responded to Suzanna's appeal, was neither here nor there. At least the death-dealing had stopped.

There was a moment's respite only, however, before a shot punctuated the sobs. The bullet struck the rock between Immacolata's bare feet. Suzanna turned to see Yolande Dor striding through the mortuary that had once been her little army, taking fresh aim at the Incantatrix as she did so.

Immacolata was not prepared to play target. As the second of the shots pealed against the rock, the Incantatrix rose into the air, and floated towards Yolande. Her shadow, passing over the battlefield like that of a carrion-bird, was fatal. At its touch the wounded, unable to run before it, turned their faces to the blood-sodden ground and breathed their last. Yolande didn't wait for the shadow to reach her, but fired at the creature over and over again. The same power that held Immacolata aloft simply threw the bullets aside.

Suzanna yelled for Yolande to retreat, but her warning went unheard or ignored. The Incantatrix swept down upon the woman and snatched her up – the menstruum wrapping them both in light – then threw her across the field. Her body hit the face of the rock upon which Immacolata had been standing, with a sickening thud, and dropped, broken, to the ground.

None of the surviving rebels made a move to go to their commander's aid. They stayed – frozen in terror – as the Incantatrix floated, a yard above the ground, across the arena of bodies, her shadow claiming those failing few who'd not been silenced by it on its outward journey.

Suzanna knew that what slim chance of mercy she'd won from the Incantatrix had been forfeited by Yolande's attack: she would now leave none living amongst her sometime captors. Without any time to formulate a defence, she threw the menstruum's living glance towards the woman. Its power was minuscule beside that of Immacolata, but she'd dropped her guard after killing Yolande, and the blow found her vulnerable. Struck in the small of the back she was flung forward. It took her seconds only to regain her equilibrium however, and turn, still hovering like some perverse saint, towards her attacker. There was no fury in her face; only mild amusement.

'Do you want to die?' she asked.

'No. Of course not.'

'Didn't I warn you how it would be, sister? Didn't I tell you? All grief, I said. All loss. Is that how it is?'

Suzanna wasn't entirely humouring the woman when she nodded her head. The Incantatrix made a long, soft sigh.

'You made me remember,' she said. 'I thank you for that. And in return –' She opened her hand, as if presenting some invisible gift '– your life.' The hand became a fist. 'And now, the debt's paid.'

As she spoke she began to descend once more, until her feet were on solid ground.

'There will come a time,' she said, looking at the bodies in whose midst they stood, 'when you will take comfort in the company of such as these. As I have. As I *do*.'

Then she turned her back on Suzanna and started to walk away. Nobody made any move to challenge her as she climbed the rocks and disappeared from sight. The survivors just watched, and gave up a prayer to whichever deities they held dear that the woman from the wilderness had passed them by.

# XIII

## A FLEETING GLIMPSE

### 1

Shadwell had not slept well; but then he supposed aspirant deities seldom did. With Godhood came a great burden of responsibility. Should he be so surprised then that his slumbers were uneasy?

Yet he'd known, from the time that he'd stood in the watchtower and studied the Mantle of the Gyre, that he had nothing to fear. He could feel the power hidden behind that cloud calling him by name, inviting him to step into its embrace, and be transformed.

A little before dawn however, as he was preparing to leave the Firmament, he was brought unsettling news: Hobart's forces in Nonesuch had been decimated by raptures that had driven most of them to lunacy. Nor was Hobart entirely free of the taint. When he arrived, an hour after the messenger, the Inspector had about him the air of a man who wasn't certain he could trust himself any longer.

From elsewhere, the news was better. Wherever the Prophet's forces had faced the native population in natural warfare, they had triumphed. It was only when the soldiers had failed to strike swiftly that the Seerkind had found a window through which to work their raptures, and when they had, the results were the same as they'd been in Nonesuch: men had either lost their minds, or woken from their evangelical zeal and joined the enemy.

Now that enemy was gathering at the Narrow Bright, warned either by rumour or rapture that the Prophet was intending to breach the Gyre, and prepared to defend its integrity to the death. There were several hundreds of them, but they scarcely constituted an army. They were, by all reports, an unarmed, unregimented collection of old men, women and children. The only problem they presented lay in the ethics of decimating them. But he'd decided, as his entourage left the Firmament for the Gyre, that such moral niceties were beneath him now. The greater crime by far would be to ignore the call he'd heard from beyond the Mantle.

When the moment came, as it soon would, he'd summon the by-blows, and let them devour the enemy, children and all. He would not shirk.

Godhood called, and he went, fleet-footed, to worship at his own altar.

2

The sense of physical and spiritual well-being Cal had felt when he woke on Venus Mountain did not falter as he and de Bono made their way down the slope towards the Firmament. But his fine mood was soon spoiled by the agitation in the landscape around them: a distressing, but unfixable, anxiety in every leaf and blade of grass. What shreds of bird-song there were sounded shrill; more alarms than music-making. Even the air buzzed around his head, as though for the first time he was alive to the news it carried.

Bad news no doubt. Yet there was not much of consequence to be seen. A few smouldering fires, little more, and even those signs of strife petered out as they approached the Firmament itself.

'This is it?' said Cal as de Bono led him through the trees towards a tall, but in truth quite unexceptional, building.

'It is.'

All the doors stood open; there was neither sound nor movement from within. They quickly scrutinized the exterior, searching for some sign of Shadwell's occupancy, but there was none visible.

After one circuit, de Bono spoke what Cal had been thinking: 'It's no use us waiting out here. We have to go in.'

Hearts hammering, they climbed the steps and entered.

Cal had been told to expect the miraculous, and he wasn't disappointed. Each room he put his head into showed him some new glory in tile and brick and paint. But that was all; only miracles.

'There's nobody here,' said de Bono, when they'd made a complete search of the lower floor. 'Shadwell's gone.'

'I'm going to try upstairs,' Cal said.

They climbed the flight, and separated, for speed's sake. At the end of one corridor Cal discovered a room whose walls were cunningly set with fragments of mirrors, reflecting the visitor in such a fashion that he seemed to see himself *behind* the walls, in some place of mist and shadow, peering out from between the bricks. That was strange enough; but by some further device – the method of which was beyond him – he seemed not to be alone in that other world, but sharing it with an assortment of animals – cats, monkeys and flying fish – all of which his reflection had apparently fathered, for they all had his face. He laughed to see it, and they all laughed with him, fish included.

Indeed it was not until his laughter died down that he heard de Bono summoning him, his shouts urgent. He left the room reluctantly, and went in search of the rope-dancer.

The call was coming from up a further flight of stairs.

'I hear you,' he yelled up to de Bono, and began to climb. The ascent was lengthy and steep, but delivered him into a room at the top of a watch-tower. Light poured through windows on every side, but the brightness couldn't dissuade him that the room had seen horrors; and recently. Whatever it had witnessed, de Bono had worse to show him.

'I've found Shadwell,' he announced, beckoning Cal over.

'Where?'

'At the Narrow Bright.'

Cal peered through the window adjacent to de Bono.

'Not that one,' he was told. 'This one brings it nearer.'

A telescopic window; and through it, a scene to make his pulse pick up its pace. Its backcloth: the seething Mantle cloud; its subject: massacre.

'He's going to breach the Gyre,' de Bono said.

It clearly wasn't just the conflict that had paled the youth; it was the thought of that act.

'Why would he want to do that?'

'He's a Cuckoo isn't he?' came the reply. 'What more reason does he need?'

'Then we have to stop him,' Cal said, ungluing his gaze from the window and heading back towards the stairs.

'The battle's already lost,' de Bono replied.

'I'm not going to stand and watch him occupy every damn inch of the Fugue. I'll go in after him, if that's what it takes.'

De Bono looked at Cal, a mixture of anger and despair on his face.

'You *can't*,' he said. 'The Gyre's forbidden territory, even to us. There are mysteries in there even Kind aren't allowed to set eyes on.'

'Shadwell's going in.'

'*Exactly*,' said de Bono. 'Shadwell's going in. And you know what'll happen? The Gyre will revolt. It'll destroy itself.'

'My God . . .'

'And if it does, the Fugue comes apart at the seams.'

'Then we stop him or we die.'

'Why do Cuckoos always reduce everything to such simple choices?'

'I don't know. You've got me there. But while you're thinking about it, here's another one: are you coming or staying?'

'Damn you, Mooney.'

'You're coming then?'

# XIV

## THE NARROW BRIGHT

### 1

There were less than a dozen individuals from amongst Yolande's rebel band who were firm enough of limb to make their way towards the Gyre. Suzanna went with them – Nimrod had requested that – though she told him in plain terms that any dream of overwhelming the enemy by force of arms was misbegotten. The enemy were many; they were few. The only hope remaining lay in her getting close to Shadwell, and dispatching him personally. If Nimrod's people could clear her route to the Prophet they might yet do service; otherwise, she advised them to preserve themselves, in the hope that there'd be a life worth living tomorrow.

They got within about two hundred yards of the battle, the sound of shots, and shouts, and car-engines, deafeningly loud, when she had her first sight of Shadwell. He'd found himself a mount – a vast, vile monster that could only be one of the Magdalene's children grown to a foul adulthood – and he was sitting astride its shoulders, surveying the battle.

'He's protected,' said Nimrod at her side. There were beasts, human and less than human, circling the Prophet. 'We'll divert them as best we can.'

There'd been a moment, as they'd approached the Gyre, when Suzanna's spirits had risen, despite the circumstance. Or perhaps because of it; because this confrontation promised to be the end-game – the war that would end all wars – after

497

which she'd have no more nights dreaming of loss. But the moment had passed quickly. Now all she felt – peering through the smoke at her enemy – was despondency.

It grew with every yard they covered. Wherever she looked, there were sights pitiful or nauseating. The struggle, it was clear, was already lost. The Gyre's defendants had been out-numbered and outarmed. Most had been laid low; the corpses food for Shadwell's creatures. The remnants, brave as they were, could not keep the Salesman from his prize any longer.

I was a dragon once, she found herself thinking, as she fixed her eye on the Prophet. If she could only remember how it had felt she might be one again. But this time there'd be no hesitation, no moment of doubt. This time, she'd *devour*.


2


The route to the Gyre took Cal through territory he remem-bered from his rickshaw ride; but its ambiguities had fled before the invading army, or else hidden their subtle heads.

And, he wondered, what of the old man he'd met at the end of that ride? Had he fallen prey to the marauders? Had his throat slit defending his little corner of Wonderland? Most likely Cal would never know. A thousand tragedies had wracked the Fugue in recent hours – the old man's fate was just part of a greater horror. A world was going to ash and dust around them.

And up ahead, the architect of these outrages. Cal saw the Salesman now, at the heart of the carnage, his face blazing with triumph. The sight made him put aside any thought of safety. With de Bono at his heels, he pitched into the thick of the battle.

There was scarcely a foot of clear ground between the bodies; the closer he got to Shadwell, the thicker the smell of blood and burning flesh became. He was soon separated from de Bono in the confusion, but it didn't matter any longer. His priority had to be the Salesman; every other consideration fell away. Maybe it was this purposefulness which got him through the blood-letting alive, though bullets filled the air like flies. His very indifference was a kind of blessedness. What he failed to notice, failed in turn to notice him. Thus he went unscathed through the heart of the battle, until he was within ten yards of Shadwell.

He cast around amongst the slain at his feet, in search of a weapon, and laid his hands on a machine-gun. Shadwell was dismounting from the beast he'd been riding, and turning his back on the conflict. There were a mere handful of defenders left between him and the Mantle, and they were already falling. He was seconds only from entering the Gyre. Cal raised the gun, and pointed it towards the Prophet.

But before his finger could find the trigger something rose up from feasting at his side, and came at him. One of the Magdalene's children, flesh between its teeth. He might have tried to kill it, but recognition slurred his intent. The creature that tore the gun from his hand was the self-same that had almost murdered him at the warehouse: his own child.

It had grown; it now stood half as tall again as Cal. But for all its bulk it was no sloth. Its fingers reached for him swift as lightning, and he only ducked them by the slimmest of margins, flinging himself down amid the corpses, where it doubtless intended to lay him permanently.

In desperation he sought the fallen gun, but before he could locate it the child came in fresh pursuit, its weight pulping the bodies it trod upon. Cal attempted to roll out from beneath it, but the beast was too quick, and snatched hold of his hair and throat. He clutched at the corpses, seeking purchase as the creature hauled him up, but his fingers slid over their gaping faces, and he was suddenly an infant in the embrace of his own monstrous off-spring.

His wild eyes caught fleeting sight of the Prophet. The Mantle's last defenders were dead. Shadwell was yards from the wall of the cloud. Cal struggled against the beast until his bones were about ready to break, but to no avail. This time the child intended to complete its task of patricide. Cal's last breath was steadily pressed from his lungs.

In extremis, he clawed at the polluted mirror before him,

and through the dusky air saw gobs of the child's flesh come away. There was a rush of bluish matter – like its mother's stuff – the chill of which slapped him back from dying, and he drove his fingers deeper into the beast's face. Its size had been gained at the price of durability. Its skull was wafer thin. He made a hook of his fingers, and pulled. The beast howled, and dropped him, the filth of its workings spilling out.

Cal dragged himself to his feet, in time to hear de Bono calling his name. He looked up towards the shout, vaguely aware that the ground beneath him was trembling, and that those who could were fleeing the battlefield. De Bono had an axe in his hand. He threw it towards Cal, as the by-blow, its head cratered, came for him again.

The weapon fell short, but Cal was over the bodies and to it in an instant, turning to face the beast at his back with a sideways blow that opened a wound in its flank. The carcass loosed a stinking froth of matter, but the child didn't fall. Cal swung again, opening the cut further; and again. This time the beast's hands went to the wound, and its head was lowered as it peered at the damage. Cal didn't hesitate. He raised the axe and brought it down on the child's skull. The blade divided the head to the neck, and the by-blow toppled forward, the axe still buried in its body.

Cal looked about him for a sign of de Bono, but the rope-dancer was nowhere to be seen. Nor was there any other living person, Kind or Cuckoo, visible through the smoke. The battle had ended. Those who'd survived it, on either side, had retreated; and with reason. The shuddering in the earth had intensified; it seemed the ground was ready to gape and swallow the field.

He turned his gaze back towards the Mantle. There was a raw-edged tear in the cloud. Beyond it, darkness. Shadwell, of course, had gone.

Without hesitating to compute the consequences, Cal stumbled through the devastation towards the cloud, and entered its darkness.

# 3

Suzanna had seen the conclusion of Cal's struggle with the by-blow from a distance, and might have reached him in time to prevent his going into the Gyre alone, but the tremors that rocked the Narrow Bright had Shadwell's army in sudden panic, and she came closer to being killed in their haste to get to safe ground than she'd been in the conflict itself. She was running against the tide, through smoke and confusion. By the time the air had cleared, and she'd oriented herself, Shadwell had dismounted and disappeared into the Gyre, and Cal was following.

She called to him, but the earth was in further convulsions, and her voice was lost beneath its roars. She cast one final look round to see Nimrod helping one of the wounded away from the Bright, then she began towards the wall of cloud, into which Cal had now vanished.

Her scalp tingled; the power of the place she stood before was immeasurable. There was every chance that it had already annihilated those foolhardy enough to trespass inside; but she couldn't be certain of that, and as long as there was a sliver of doubt she had to act. Cal was there, and whether he was dead or alive she had to go to him.

His name on her lips, as a keepsake and a prayer, she followed where he'd gone, into the living heart of Wonderland.

# Part Nine

# Into the Gyre

*'Upon our heels a fresh perfection treads.'*
John Keats
*Hyperion*

# I

## TRESPASSERS

### 1

Always, worlds within worlds.

In the Kingdom of the Cuckoo, the Weave; in the Weave, the Fugue; in the Fugue, the world of Mimi's book, and now this: the Gyre.

But nothing that she'd seen in the pages or places she'd visited could have prepared Suzanna for what she found waiting behind the Mantle.

For one thing, though it had seemed as she stepped through the cloud-curtain that there'd been only night awaiting her on the other side, that darkness had been an illusion.

The landscape of the Gyre was lit with an amber phosphorescence that rose from the very earth beneath her feet. The reversal upset her equilibrium completely. It was almost as if the world had turned over, and she was treading the sky. And the true heavens?; they were another wonder. The clouds pressed low, their innards in perpetual turmoil, as if at the least provocation they'd rain lightning on her defenceless head.

When she'd advanced a few yards she glanced behind her, just to be certain that she knew the route back. But the door, and the battlefield of the Narrow Bright beyond, had already disappeared; the cloud was no longer a curtain but a wall. A spasm of panic clutched her belly. She soothed it with the thought that she wasn't alone here. Somewhere up ahead was Cal.

But where? Though the light from the ground was bright

enough for her to walk by, it – and the fact that the landscape was so barren – conspired to make a nonsense of distance. She couldn't be certain whether she was seeing twenty yards ahead of her, or two hundred. Whichever, there was no sign of human presence within range of her eyesight. All she could do was follow her nose, and hope to God she was heading in the right direction.

And then, a fresh wonder. At her feet, a trail had appeared; or rather two trails, intermingled. Though the earth was impacted and dry – so much so that neither Shadwell nor Cal's footfalls had left an indentation, where the invaders had trodden the ground seemed to be vibrating. That was her first impression, at least. But as she followed their route the truth became apparent: the soil along the path pursuer and pursued had taken was *sprouting*.

She stopped walking and went down on her haunches to confirm the phenomenon. Her eyes weren't misleading her. The earth was cracking, and yellow-green tendrils, their strength out of all proportion to their size, were corkscrewing up out of the cracks, their growth so fast she could watch it happening. Was this some elaborate defence mechanism on the Gyre's part? Or had those ahead of her carried seeds into this sterile world, which the raptures here had urged into immediate life? She looked back. Her own route was similarly marked, the shoots only just appearing, while those in Cal and Shadwell's path – with a minute or more's headway – were already six inches high. One was uncurling like a fern; another had pods; a third was spiny. At this rate of growth they'd be trees within an hour.

Extraordinary as the spectacle was, she had no time to study it. Following this trail of proliferating life, she pressed on.

2

Though she'd picked up her pace to a trot, there was still no sign of those she was following. The flowering path was the only proof of their passing.

She was soon obliged to run well off the trail, for the plants, growing at exponential rate, were spreading laterally as well as vertically. As they swelled it became clear how little they had in common with the Kingdom's flora. If they had sprung from seeds brought in on human heels, the enchantments here had wrought profound changes in them.

Indeed the resemblance was less to a jungle than to some undersea reef, not least because the plants' prodigious growth made them sway as if moved by a tide. Their colours and their forms were utterly various; not one was like its neighbour. All they had in common was their enthusiasm for growth, for fruitfulness. Clouds of scented pollen were being expelled like breaths; pulsing blossoms were turning their heads to the clouds, as if the lightning was a kind of sustenance; roots were spreading underfoot with such violence the earth trembled.

Yet there was nothing threatening in this surge of life. The eagerness here was simply the eagerness of the new born. They grew for the pleasure of growing.

Then, from off to her right, she heard a cry; or something like a cry. Was it Cal? No; there was no sign of the trail dividing. It came again, somewhere between a sob and a sigh. It was impossible to ignore, despite her mission. Promising herself only the briefest of detours, she followed the sound.

Distance was so deceptive here. She'd advanced perhaps two dozen yards from the trail when the air unveiled the source of the sound.

It was a plant, the first living thing she'd seen here beyond the limits of the trail, with which it shared the same multiplicity of forms and brilliance of colour. It was the size of a small tree, its heart a knot of boughs so complex she suspected it must be several plants growing together in one spot. She heard rustling in the blossom-laden thicket, and amongst the serpentine roots, but she couldn't see the creature whose call had brought her here.

Something did become apparent, however: that the knot at the centre of the tree, all but lost amongst the foliage, was a human corpse. If she needed further confirmation it was in plain sight. Fragments of a fine suit, hanging from the boughs like the sloughed skins of executive snakes; a shoe, parcelled up in tendrils. The clothes had been shredded so that the dead flesh could be claimed by flora; green life springing up where red had failed. The corpse's legs had grown woody, and sprouted knotted roots; shoots were exploding from its innards.

There was no time to linger and look; she had work to do. She made one circuit of the tree, and was about to return to the path when she saw a pair of living eyes staring out at her from the leaves. She yelped. They blinked. Tentatively, she reached forward, and parted the twigs.

The head of the man she'd taken for dead was on almost back to front, and his skull had been cracked wide open. But everywhere the wounds had bred sumptuous life. A beard, lush as new grass, grew around a mossy mouth which ran with sap; floret-laden twigs broke from the cheeks.

The eyes watched her intently, and she felt moist tendrils reaching up to investigate her face and hair.

Then, its blossoms shaking as it drew breath, the hybrid spoke. One long, soft word.

'Amialive.'

Was it naming itself? When she'd overcome her surprise, she told it she didn't understand.

It seemed to frown. There was a fall of petals from its crown of flowers. The throat pulsed, and then regurgitated the syllables, this time better punctuated.

'Am ia live?'

'Are you alive?' she said, comprehending now. 'Of course. Of course you're alive.'

'I thought I was dreaming,' it said, its eyes wandering from its perusal of her a while, then returning. 'Dead, or dreaming. Or both. One moment . . . bricks in the air, breaking my head . . .'

'Shearman's house?' she said.

'Ah. You were there?'

'The Auction. You were at the Auction.'

It laughed to itself, and its humour tingled against her cheek.

'I always wanted . . . to be inside . . .' he said, '. . . inside . . .'

And now she understood the how and why of this. Though it was odd to think – odd? it was *incredible* – that this creature had been one of Shadwell's party, that was what she construed. Injured, or perhaps killed in the destruction of the house, he'd somehow been caught up in the Gyre, which had turned his broken body to this flowering purpose.

Her face must have registered her distress at his state, for the tendrils empathized, and grew jittery.

'So I'm not dreaming then,' the hybrid said.

'No.'

'Strange,' came the reply. 'I thought I was. It's so like paradise.'

She wasn't sure she'd heard correctly.

'Paradise?' she said.

'I never dared hope . . . life would be such pleasure.'

She smiled. The tendrils were soothed.

'This is Wonderland,' the hybrid said.

'Really?'

'Oh yes. We're near to where the Weave began; near to the Temple of the Loom. Here everything transforms, everything *becomes*. Me? I was lost. Look at me now. How I am!'

Hearing his boast her mind went back to the adventures she'd had in the book; how, in that no-man's-land between words and the world, everything had been transforming and becoming, and her mind, married in hatred with Hobart's, had been the energy of that condition. She the warp to his weft. Thoughts from different skulls, crossing, and making a material place from their conflict.

It was all part of the same procedure.

The knowledge was slippery; she wanted an equation in which she could fix the lesson, in case she could put it to use. But there were more pressing issues now than the higher mathematics of the imagination.

'I must go,' she said.

'Of course you must.'

'There are others here.'

'I saw,' said the hybrid. 'Passing overhead.'

'Overhead?'

'Towards the Loom.'

## 3

Towards the Loom.

She retraced her steps to the trail with fresh enthusiasm. The fact of the buyer's existence in the Gyre, apparently accepted by the forces here – even welcomed – gave her some hope that the mere presence of a trespasser was not sufficient to make the Gyre turn itself inside out. Its sensitivity had apparently been overestimated. It was strong enough to deal with an invading force in its own inimitable fashion.

Her skin had begun to itch, and there was a restlessness in her gut. She tried not to think too hard of what this signified, but the irritation increased as she again followed the trail. The atmosphere was thickening now; the world around her darkening. It wasn't night's darkness, coaxing sleep. The murk buzzed with life. She could taste it, sweet and sour. She could see it, busy behind her eyes.

She'd gone only a little way when something ran across her feet. She looked down to see an animal – an unlikely cross between squirrel and centipede, eyes bright, legs innumerable, cavorting between the roots. Nor, she now realized, was the creature alone. The forest was inhabited. Animals, as numerous and as remarkable as the plant-life, were spilling out from the undergrowth, changing even as they hopped and squirmed, more ambitious by the breath.

Their origins?: the plants. The flora had parented its own fauna; its buds flowering into insects, its fruits growing fur and scales. A plant opened, and butterflies rose in a flickering cloud; in a thorn thicket birds were fluttering into life; from a tree trunk, white snakes poured like sentient sap.

The air was so thick now she could have sliced it, new creatures crossing her path with every yard she advanced, only to be eclipsed by the murk. Something that was a distant relation of the armadillo waddled in front of her; three variations on the theme of ape came and went; a golden dog cavorted amongst the flowers. And so on. And so forth.

She had no doubt now why her skin itched. It longed to join this game of changes, to throw itself back into the melting pot and find a new design. Her mind, too, was half seduced by the notion. Amongst such joyous invention it seemed churlish to cleave to a single anatomy.

Indeed she might have succumbed in time to these temptations of the flesh, but that ahead of her a building now emerged from the fog: a plain brick building which she caught sight of for an instant before the air enclosed it again. Plain as it was, this could only be the Temple of the Loom.

A huge parrot swooped in front of her, speaking in tongues, then flitted away. She began to run. The golden dog had elected to keep pace with her; it panted at her heels.

Then, the shock wave. It came from the direction of the building, a force that convulsed the living membrane of the air, and rocked the earth. She was thrown off her feet amid sprawling roots, which instantly attempted to incorporate her into their design. She disengaged them from around about her, and pulled herself to her feet. Either the contact with the earth, or the wave of energy from the Temple, had sent her into paroxysms. Though she was standing quite still her whole body seemed to be *dancing*. There was no other word for it. Every part of her, from eye-lash to marrow, had caught the rhythm of power here; its percussion ordered her heart to a different beat; her blood sped then slowed; her mind soared and plummeted by turns.

But that was only flesh. Her other anatomy – the subtle body which the menstruum had quickened – was beyond the control of the forces here; or else was already in such accord with them it was left to its own work.

She occupied it now – telling it to keep her feet from rooting, and her head from sprouting wings and flying off. It soothed her. She'd been a dragon, and emerged again, hadn't she? This was no different.

Yes it is, said her fears. This is flesh and bone business; the dragon was all in my mind.

Haven't you learned yet? came the reply, there *is* no difference.

As the answer rang in her head, the second shock wave struck; and this time it was no *petit mal*, but the full fit. The ground beneath her began to roar. She started to run towards the Temple once more, as the noise mounted, but she'd got five yards at best when the roar became the hard din of breaking stone, and a zig-zag crack appeared to the right of her; and to the left another; and another.

The Gyre was tearing itself apart.

# II

## THE TEMPLE

### 1

Though Shadwell had a good lead on Cal, the thick air of the Gyre did not conceal him. The Salesman's jacket stood out like a beacon, and Cal followed it as fast as his jittery limbs would carry him. Though his struggle with the by-blow had left him weak, he was still much the fitter man, and steadily closed the gap between them. More than once he caught Shadwell glancing behind him, his face a smear of anxiety.

After all the chases and crusades, the beasts and the armies, it had come down to the two of them, racing towards a goal beyond the articulation of either. They were equals at last.

Or at least so Cal had thought. It was only when they came in sight of the Temple that the Salesman turned, and stood his ground. Either his fingers, or the air, had clawed his disguise from his face. He was the Prophet no longer. Fragments of the illusion clung to his chin, and around his hair line, but this was recognizably the man Cal had first confronted in that haunted room in Rue Street.

'Come no further, Mooney,' he instructed.

He was so breathless the words were barely audible, and the light from the earth made him look sick.

'I don't want to shed blood,' he told Cal. 'Not here. There are forces around us that wouldn't take kindly to that.'

Cal had stopped running. Now, as he listened to Shadwell's speech, he felt a twitching beneath the soles of his feet, and looked down to see shoots springing up between his toes.

'Go back, Mooney,' said Shadwell. 'My destiny isn't with you.'

Cal was only half-listening to the Salesman. The sudden growth beneath his feet intrigued him, and he saw now that it spread across the ground, following Shadwell's footsteps to where he stood. The barren soil had suddenly produced all manner of plant life, which was growing at a phenomenal rate. Shadwell had seen it too, and his voice was hushed as he said:

'*Creation*. See that, Mooney? Pure Creation.'

'We shouldn't be here,' said Cal.

Shadwell's face carried a lunatic grin.

'You have no place here,' he said. 'I grant you that. But I've waited all my life for this.'

An ambitious plant burst the earth beneath Cal's foot, and he stepped aside to let it grow. Shadwell read the movement as an attack. He opened his jacket. For an instant Cal thought he was going to try the old trick, but his solution was far simpler. He pulled a gun from his inside pocket, and pointed it at Cal.

'Like I said, I don't want to spill blood. So go back, Mooney. Go on. *Go on!* Back the way you came or so help me I'll blow your brains out.'

He meant it; of that Cal had not the least doubt. Raising his hands to chest height, he said:

'I hear you. I'm going.'

Before he could move however, three things happened in quick succession. First, something flew overhead, its passage almost hidden by the clouds that pressed upon the roof of the Temple. Shadwell looked up, and Cal, taking the chance, ran at the man, reaching to knock the gun from his grip.

The third event was the shot.

It seemed to Cal he saw the bullet break from the barrel on a plume of smoke; saw it cleave the space between the gun and his body. It was slow, as in a nightmare of execution. But he was slower still.

The bullet hit his shoulder, and he was thrown backwards, landing amongst flowers that had not existed thirty seconds before. He saw droplets of his blood rise over his head, as if claimed for the sky. He let the puzzle go. There was only energy enough to hold onto one problem at a time, and he had to make life his priority.

His hand went to the wound, which had shattered his clavicle. He put his palm against the hole to stop the blood coming, as the pain spread down across his body.

Above him, the clouds roiled on, thundering; or was the clamour he heard only in his head? Groaning, he rolled onto his side, to see if he could get a glimpse of what Shadwell was up to. The pain almost blinded him, but he fought to focus on the building up ahead.

Shadwell was entering the Temple. There was no guard at the threshold; just an archway in the brick, through which he was disappearing. Cal inched himself up onto two knees and a hand – the other still clamped to his shoulder – and from there got to his feet, and began to stagger towards the Temple door to claim the Salesman from his victory.


2


What Shadwell had told Mooney was true: he had no wish to shed blood in the Gyre. The secrets of Creation and Destruction dwelled here. If he'd needed confirmation of that fact he'd seen it spring up beneath their feet: a fabulous fecundity which brought with it the promise of heroic decay. That was the nature of any exchange – a thing gained, a thing lost. He, a salesman, had learned that lesson as a stripling. What he sought now was to stand beyond such commerce, inviolate. That was the condition of Gods. They had permanence, and purpose everlasting; they could not be spoiled in their prime, nor shown wonders only to have them snatched away. They were eternal, unchanging, and here inside this bald citadel he would join that pantheon.

It was dark over the threshold. No sign here of the shining

earth outside; just a shadowy passageway, its floor, walls and ceiling built of the same bare brick, without mortar between. He advanced a few yards, his fingertips running over the wall. It was an illusion, no doubt, but he had a curious sensation walking here: that the bricks were grinding upon each other, as his first mistress had ground her teeth in her sleep. He withdrew his fingers from the walls, advancing to the first turn in the passage.

At the corner, a welcome discovery. There was a light source somewhere up ahead; he would not have to stumble in darkness any further. The passage ran for forty-five yards or so, before making another ninety-degree turn.

Again, it was the same featureless brick; but half way down it he was presented with a second archway, and stepping through found himself in an identical corridor, but that it was shorter by twice the breadth of the first. He followed it, the light brightening, around one corner and along another bare passage, then around a second corridor which again had a door in it. Now he grasped the architect's design. The Temple was not one building but several, set within each other; a box containing a slightly smaller box which then contained a third.

The realization unnerved him. The place was like a maze. A simple one, perhaps, but nevertheless designed to confound or delay. Once again he heard the walls grinding, and pictured the whole construction closing in on him, and he suddenly unable to find his way out before the walls pressed him to bloody dust.

But he couldn't turn back now; not with the luminescence tempting him to turn one more corner. Besides, there were noises reaching him from the world outside: strange, disfigured voices, as if the inhabitants of some forgotten bestiary were prowling around the Temple, scraping at the brick, padding across the roof.

He had no choice but to press on. He'd sold his life away for a glimpse of Godhood; he had nothing to return to now but the bitterest defeat.

Forward then, and to Hell with the consequences.

# 3

As Cal came within a yard of the Temple door his strength gave out.

He could no longer command his legs to bear him up. He stumbled, throwing out his right arm to prevent his falling too heavily, and hit the ground.

Unconsciousness claimed him, and he was grateful for it. Escape lasted seconds only however, before the blackness lifted, and he was delivered back into nausea and agony. But now – and not for the first time in the Fugue – his blood-starved brain had lost its grasp on whether he was dreaming, or being dreamt.

That ambiguity had first visited him in Lemuel Lo's orchard, he remembered: waking from a dream of the life he'd lived to find himself in a paradise he'd only ever expected to encounter in sleep. And then later, on Venus Mountain, or beneath it, living the life of planets – and passing a millennium in that revolving state – only to wake a mere six hours older.

Now here was the paradox again, at death's door. Had he awoken to die?; or was dying true wakefulness? Round and round the thoughts went, in a spiral with darkness at its centre, and he fleeing into that darkness, wearier by the moment.

His head on the earth, which was trembling beneath him, he opened his eyes and looked back towards the Temple. He saw it upside down, the roof sitting in a foundation of clouds, while the bright ground shone around it.

Paradox upon paradox, he thought, as his eyes drifted closed again.

'Cal.'

Somebody called him.

'Cal.'

Irritated to be summoned this way, he opened his eyes only reluctantly.

It was Suzanna who was bending over him, saying his name. She had questions too, but his lazy mind couldn't grasp them.

Instead he said:

'Inside. Shadwell . . .'

'*Hold on,*' she told him. 'You understand me?'

She put his hand on her face. It was cool. Then she bent down and kissed him, and somewhere at the back of his skull he remembered this happening before; his lying on the ground, and her giving him love.

'I'll be here,' he said.

She nodded. 'You'd better be,' she replied, and crossed to the door of the Temple.

This time, he did not let his eyes close. Whatever dream waited beyond life, he would postpone its pleasure 'til he saw her face again.

# III

# THE MIRACLE OF THE LOOM

Outside the Temple, the quake tremors were worsening. Inside, however, an uneasy peace reigned. Suzanna started to advance down the darkened corridors, the itching in her body subdued now that she was out of the turbulence, in this, the eye of the hurricane.

There was light ahead. She turned a corner, and another, and finding a door in the wall, slipped through into a second passageway, as spartan as the one she'd left. The light was still tantalizingly out of reach. Around the next corner, it promised; just a little further, a little further.

The menstruum was quiet inside her, as though it feared to show itself. Was that the natural respect one miracle paid to a greater? If so, the raptures here were hiding their faces with no little skill; there was nothing about these corridors suggestive of revelation or power: just bare brick. Except for the light. That coaxed her still, through another door and along further passageways. The building, she now realized, was built on the principle of a Russian doll, one within another. *Worlds within worlds.* They couldn't diminish infinitely, she told herself. Or could they?

Around the very next corner she had her answer, or at least part of it, as a shadow was thrown up against the wall and she heard somebody shouting:

'*What in God's name?*'

For the first time since setting foot here, she felt the ground vibrate. There was a fall of brick dust from the ceiling.

'Shadwell,' she said.

As she spoke it seemed she could see the two syllables – *Shad Well* – carried along the corridor towards the next door. A fleeting memory came too: of Jerichau speaking his love to her; word as reality.

The shadow on the wall shifted, and suddenly the Salesman was standing in front of her. All trace of the Prophet had gone. The face revealed beneath was bloated and pale; the face of a beached fish.

'Gone,' he said.

He was shaking from head to foot. Sweat droplets decorated his face like pearls.

'It's all gone.'

Any fear she might once have had of this man had disappeared. He was here unmasked as ludicrous. But his words made her wonder. *What* had gone? She began to walk towards the door he'd stepped through.

'It was *you* –' he said, his shakes worsening. '*You* did this.'

'I did nothing.'

'Oh yes –'

As she came within a yard of him he reached for her, his clammy hands suddenly about her neck.

'*There's nothing there!*' he shrieked, pulling her close.

His grip intended harm, but the menstruum didn't rise to her aid. She was left with only muscle power to disengage him, and it was not enough.

'You want to see?' he screamed into her face. 'You want to see how I've been cheated? *I'll show you!*'

He dragged her towards the door, and pitched her through into the room at the heart of the Temple: the inner sanctum in which the miracles of the Gyre had been generated; the powerhouse which had held the many worlds of the Fugue together for so long.

It was a room some fifteen feet square, built of the same naked brick as the rest of the Temple, and high. She looked up to see that the roof had a skylight of sorts, open to the heavens. The clouds that swirled around the Temple roof shed a milky brightness down, as if the lightning from the Gyre was being kindled in the womb of troubled air above. The clouds were not the only movement overhead, however. As she gazed up she caught sight of a form in the corner of the roof. Before her gaze could focus on it, Shadwell was approaching her.

'Where is it?' he demanded. 'Where's the Loom?'

She looked around the sanctum, and discovered now that it was not entirely bare. In each of the four corners a figure was sitting, gazing towards the centre of the room. Her spine twitched. Though they sat bolt upright on their high-backed chairs, the quartet were long dead, their flesh like stained paper on their bones, their clothes hanging in rotted rags.

Had these guardians been murdered where they sat, so that thieves could remove the Loom unchallenged? So it seemed. Yet there was nothing in their posture that suggested a violent death; nor could she believe that this charmed place would have sanctioned bloodshed. No; something else had happened here – *was happening still, perhaps* – some essential point both she and Shadwell could not yet grasp.

He was still muttering to himself, his voice a decaying spiral of complaint. She was only half-listening; she was far more interested in the object she now saw lying in the middle of the floor. There it lay, the kitchen knife Cal had brought into the Auction Room all those months ago; the commonplace domestic tool which the look between them had somehow drawn into the Weave, to this very spot, the absolute centre of the Fugue.

Seeing it, pieces of the riddle began to slot together in her head. Here, where the glances of the sentinels intersected, lay the knife that *another* glance – between herself and Cal – had empowered. It had entered this chamber and somehow cut the last knot the Loom had created; and the Weave had released its secrets. All of which was well and good, except that the sentinels were dead, and the Loom, as Shadwell kept repeating, was gone.

'You were the one,' he growled. 'You knew all along.'

She ignored his accusations, a new thought forming. If the

521

magic *had* gone, she reasoned, why did the menstruum hide itself?

As she shaped the question Shadwell's fury drove him to attack.

'*I'll kill you!*' he yelled.

His assault caught her unawares, and she was flung back against the wall. The breath went out of her in a rush, and before she could defend herself his thumbs were at her throat, his bulk trapping her.

'Thieving bitch,' he said. 'You cheated me!'

She raised her hands to beat him off, but she was already growing weak. She struggled to draw breath, desperate for a mouthful of air even if it was the flatulent breath he was expelling, but his grip on her throat prevented so much as a mouthful reaching her. I'm going to die, she thought; I'm going to die looking into this curdled face.

And then her upturned eyes caught a glimpse of movement in the roof, and a voice said:

'The Loom is here.'

Shadwell's grip on Suzanna relaxed. He turned, and looked up at the speaker.

Immacolata, her arms spread out like a parachutist in free-fall, was hovering above them.

'Do you remember me?' she asked Shadwell.

'Jesus Christ.'

'I missed you, Shadwell. Though you were unkind.'

'Where's the Loom?' he said. 'Tell me.'

'There is no Loom,' she replied.

'But you just said —'

'The Loom is here.'

'Where then? *Where?*'

'There is no Loom.'

'You're out of your mind,' he yelled up at her. 'Either there *is* or there *isn't*!'

The Incantatrix had a skull's smile as she gazed down on the man below.

'*You're* the fool,' she said mildly. 'You don't understand, do you?'

Shadwell put on a gentler tone. 'Why don't you come down?' he said. 'My neck aches.'

She shook her head. It cost her effort to hang in the air that way, Suzanna could see; she was defying the sanctity of the Temple by working her raptures here. But she flew in the face of such edicts, determined to remind Shadwell of how earth-bound he was.

'Afraid, are you?' said Shadwell.

Immacolata's smile did not falter. 'I'm not afraid,' she said, and began to float down towards him.

Keep out of his way, Suzanna willed her. Though the Incantatrix had done terrible harm, Suzanna had no desire to see her felled by Shadwell's mischief. But the Salesman stood face to face with the woman and made no move. He simply said:

'You reached here before me.'

'I almost forgot you,' Immacolata replied. Her voice had lost any trace of stridency. It was full of sighs. 'But *she* reminded me,' she glanced at Suzanna. 'It was a fine service you did me, sister,' she said. 'To remind me of my enemy.'

Her eyes went back to Shadwell.

'You drove me mad,' she said. 'And I forgot you. But I remember now.'

Suddenly the smile and the sighs had gone entirely. There was only ruin, and rage.

'I remember very well.'

'Where's the Loom?' Shadwell demanded.

'You were always so *literal*,' Immacolata replied, contemptuously. 'Did you really expect to find a *thing*? Another object to be possessed? Is that your Godhood, Shadwell? Possession?'

'*Where the fuck is it?*'

She laughed then, though the sound from her throat had nothing to do with pleasure.

Her ridicule pressed Shadwell to breaking point; he flung himself at her. But she was not about to let herself be touched by his hands. As he snatched hold of her it seemed to Suzanna that her whole ruined face cracked open, spilling a force that might once have been the menstruum – that cool, bright river

523

Suzanna had first plunged into at Immacolata's behest – but was now a damned and polluted stream, breaking from the wounds like pus. It had force nevertheless. Shadwell was thrown to the ground.

Overhead, the clouds threw lightning across the roof, freezing the scene below by its scalpel light. The killing blow could only be a glance away, surely.

But it didn't come. The Incantatrix hesitated, the broken face leaking tainted power, and in that instant Shadwell's hand closed on the kitchen knife at his side.

Suzanna cried a warning, but Immacolata either failed to hear or chose not to. Then Shadwell was on his feet, his ungainly rise offering his victim a moment to strike him down, which was missed – and drove the blade up into her abdomen, a butcher's stroke which opened a traumatic wound.

At last she seemed to know he meant her death, and responded. Her face began to blaze afresh, but before the spark could become fire Shadwell's blade was dividing her to the breasts. Her innards slid from the wound. She screamed, and threw back her head, the unleashed force wasted against the sanctum walls.

On the instant, the room was filled with a roaring that seemed to come from both the bricks and the innards of Immacolata. Shadwell dropped the blood-slicked knife, and made to retreat from his crime, but his victim reached out and pulled him close.

The fire had entirely gone from Immacolata's face. She was dying, and quickly. But even in her failing moments her grip was strong. As the roaring grew louder she granted Shadwell the embrace she'd always denied him, her wound besmirching his jacket. He made a cry of repugnance, but she wouldn't let him go. He struggled, and finally succeeded in breaking her hold, throwing her off and staggering from her, his chest and belly plastered with blood. He cast one more look in her direction then started towards the door, making small moans of horror. As he reached the exit he looked up at Suzanna.

'I didn't . . .' he began, his hands raised, blood trickling between his fingers. 'It wasn't me . . .'

The words were as much appeal as denial.

'*It was magic!*' he said, tears starting to his eyes. Not of sorrow, she knew, but of a sudden righteous rage.

'*Filthy magic!*' he shrieked. The ground rocked to hear its glory denied.

He didn't wait to have the roof fall on his head, but fled from the chamber as the roars rose in intensity.

Suzanna looked back at Immacolata.

Despite the grievous wounding she'd sustained she was not yet dead. She was standing against one of the walls, clinging to the brick with one hand and keeping her innards from falling with the other.

'Blood's been spilt,' she said, as another tremor, more fierce than any that had preceded it, unknitted the foundations of the building. 'Blood's been spilt in the Temple of the Loom.'

She smiled that terrible, twisted smile.

'The Fugue's undone, sister –' she said.

'What do you mean?'

'I came here intending to spill his blood and bring the Gyre down. Seems it's me who's done the bleeding. It's no matter.' Her voice grew weaker. Suzanna stepped close, to hear her better. 'It's all the same in the end. *The Fugue is finished.* It'll be dust. All dust . . .'

She pushed herself off the wall. Suzanna reached and kept her from falling. The contact made her palm tingle.

'They're exiles forever,' Immacolata said, and frail as it was, there was triumph in her voice. 'The Fugue ends here. Wiped away as if it had never been.'

At this, her legs buckled beneath her. Pushing Suzanna away, she stumbled back against the wall. Her hand slipped from her belly; her guts unspooled.

'I used to dream . . .' she said, '. . . terrible emptiness . . .'

She stopped speaking, as she slid down the wall, strands of her hair catching on the brick.

'. . . sand and nothingness,' she said. 'That's what I dreamt. Sand and nothingness. And here it is.'

As if to bear out her remark the din grew cataclysmic.

525

Satisfied with her labours, Immacolata sank to the ground.

Suzanna looked towards her escape route, as the bricks of the Temple began to grind upon each other with fresh ferocity. What more could she do here? The mysteries of the Loom had defeated her. If she stayed she'd be buried in the ruins. There was nothing left to do but get out while she still could.

As she moved to the door, two pencil beams of light sliced through the grimy air, and struck her arm. Their brightness shocked her. More shocking still, their source. They were coming from the eye sockets of one of the sentinels. She stepped out of the path of the light, and as the beams struck the corpse opposite lights flared there too; then in the third sentinel's head, and the fourth.

These events weren't lost on Immacolata.

'The Loom . . .' she whispered, her breath failing.

The intersecting beams were brightening, and the fraught air was soothed by the sound of voices, softly murmuring words so unfixable they were almost music.

'You're too late,' said the Incantatrix, her comment made not to Suzanna but to the dead quartet. 'You can't save it now.'

Her head began to slip forward.

'Too late . . .' she said again.

Then a shudder went through her. The body, vacated by spirit, keeled over. She lay dead in her blood.

Despite her dying words, the power here was still building. Suzanna backed towards the door, to clear the beams' route completely. With nothing to bar their way they immediately redoubled their brilliance, and from the point of collision threw up new beams at every angle. The whispering that filled the chamber suddenly found a fresh rhythm; the words, though still alien to her, ran like a melodious poem. Somehow, they and the light were part of one system; the raptures of the four Families – Aia, Lo, Ye-me and Babu – working together: word music accompanying a woven dance of light.

This was the Loom; of course. *This was the Loom.*

No wonder Immacolata had poured scorn on Shadwell's literalism. Magic might be bestowed upon the physical, but it didn't *reside* there. It resided in the word, which was mind spoken, and in motion, which was mind made manifest; in the system of the Weave and the evocations of the melody: all *mind*.

Yet damn it, this recognition was not enough. Finally she was still only a Cuckoo, and all the puzzle-solving in the world wouldn't help her mellow the rage of this desecrated place. All she could do was watch the Loom's wrath shake the Fugue and all it contained apart.

In her frustration her thoughts went to Mimi, who had brought her into this adventure, but had died too soon to entirely prepare her for it. Surely even she would not have predicted this: the Fugue's failing, and Suzanna at its heart, unable to keep it beating.

The lights were still colliding and multiplying, the beams growing so solid now she might have walked upon them. Their performances transfixed her. She felt she could watch them forever, and never tire of their complexities. And still they grew more elaborate, more solid, until she was certain they would not be bound within the walls of the sanctum, but would burst out –

– into the Fugue, where she had to go. Out to where Cal was lying, to comfort him as best she could in the imminent maelstrom.

With this thought came another. That perhaps Mimi *had* known, or feared, that in the end it would simply be Suzanna and the magic – and that maybe the old woman had after all left a signpost.

She reached into her pocket, and brought out the book. *Secrets of the Hidden Peoples*. She didn't need to open the book to remember the epigraph on the dedication page:

*'What can be imagined need never be lost.'*

She'd tussled with its meaning repeatedly, but her intellect had failed to make much sense of it. Now she forsook her analytical thinking and let subtler sensibilities take over.

The light of the Loom was so bright it hurt her eyes, and as she stepped out of the sanctum she discovered that the beams were exploiting chinks in the brick – either that or eating at the wall – and breaking through. Needle-thin lines of light stratified the passageway.

Her thoughts as much on the book in her hand as on her safety, she made her way back via the route she'd come: door and passageway, door and passageway. Even the outer layers of corridor were not immune to the Loom's glamour. The beams had broken through three solid walls and were growing wider with every moment. As she walked through them, she felt the menstruum stir in her for the first time since she'd entered the Gyre. It rose not to her face, however, but through her arms and into her hands, which clasped the book, as though charging it.

*What can be imagined –*

The chanting rose; the light-beams multiplied.

*– need never be lost.*

The book grew heavier; warmer; like a living thing in her arms. And yet, so full of dreams. A thing of ink and paper in which another world awaited release. Not one world perhaps, but many; for as she and Hobart's time in the pages had proved, each adventurer reimagined the stories for themselves. There were as many Wild Woods as there were readers to wander there.

She was out into the third corridor now, and the whole Temple had become a hive of light and sound. There was so much energy here, waiting to be channelled. If she could only be the catalyst that turned its strength to better ends than destruction.

Her head was full of images, or fragments thereof:

she and Hobart in the forest of their story, exchanging skins and fictions;

she and Cal in the Auction Room, their glance the engine that turned the knife above the Weave.

And finally, the sentinels sitting in the Loom chamber. Eight eyes that had, even in death, the power to unmake the Weave. And . . . *make* it again?

Suddenly, she wasn't walking any longer. She was running, not for fear that the roof would come down on her head but because the final pieces of the puzzle were coming clear, and she had so little time.

Redeeming the Fugue could not be done alone. Of course not. *No* rapture could be performed alone. Their essence was in exchange. That was why the Families sang and danced and wove: their magic blossomed *between people*: between performer and spectator, maker and admirer.

And wasn't there rapture at work between her mind and the mind in the book she held?; her eyes scanning the page and soaking up another soul's dreams? It was like love. Or rather love was its highest form: mind shaping mind, visions pirouetting on the threads between lovers.

'*Cal!*'

She was at the last door, and flinging herself into the turmoil beyond.

The light in the earth had turned to the colour of bruises, blue-black and purple. The sky above writhed, ripe to discharge its innards. From the music and the exquisite geometry of light inside the Temple, she was suddenly in bedlam.

Cal was propped against the wall of the Temple. His face was white, but he was alive.

She went to him and knelt by his side.

'What's happening?' he said, his voice lazy with exhaustion.

'I've no time to explain,' she said, her hand stroking his face. The menstruum played against his cheek. 'You have to trust me.'

'Yes,' he said.

'Good. You have to think for me, Cal. Think of everything you remember.'

'Remember . . . ?'

As he puzzled at her a crack, fully a foot wide, opened in the earth, running from the threshold of the Temple like a messenger. The news it carried was all grim. Seeing it, doubts filled Suzanna. How could anything be claimed from this chaos? The sky shed thunder; dust and dirt were flung up from the crevasses that gaped on every side.

She endeavoured to hold onto the comprehension she'd found in the corridors behind her. Tried to keep the images of the Loom in her head. The beams intersecting. Thought over and under thought. Minds filling the void with *shared* memories and *shared* dreams.

'Think of everything you remember about the Fugue,' she said.

'Everything?'

'Everything. All the places you've seen.'

'Why?'

'Trust me!' she said. 'Please God, Cal, trust me. What do you remember?'

'Just bits and pieces.'

'Whatever you can find. Every little piece.'

She pressed her palm to his face. He was feverish, but the book in her other hand was hotter.

In recent times she'd shared intimacies with her greatest enemy, Hobart. Surely she could share knowledge with this man, whose sweetness she'd come to love.

'Please . . .' she said.

'For you . . .' he replied, seeming to know at last all she felt for him, '. . . anything.'

And the thoughts came. She felt them flow into her, and through her; she was a conduit, the menstruum the stream on which his memories were carried. Her mind's eye saw glimpses only of what he'd seen and felt here in the Fugue, but they were things fine and beautiful.

An orchard; firelight; fruit; people dancing; singing. A road; a field; de Bono and the rope-dancers. The Firmament (rooms full of miracles); a rickshaw; a house, with a man standing on the step. A mountain, and planets. Most of it came too fast for her to focus upon, but *her* comprehension of what he'd seen wasn't the point. She was just part of a cycle – as she'd been in the Auction Room.

Behind her, she felt the beams breaking through the last wall, as though the Loom was coming to meet her, its genius for transfiguration momentarily at her disposal. They hadn't got long. If she missed this wave there'd be no other.

'Go on,' she said to Cal.

He had his eyes closed now, and the images were still

pouring out of him. He'd remembered more than she'd dared hope. And she in her turn was adding sights and sounds to the flow –

The lake; Capra's House; the forest; the streets of Nonesuch –

– they came back, razor sharp, and she felt the beams pick them up and speed them on their way.

She'd feared the Loom would reject her interference, but not at all; it married its power to that of the menstruum, transforming all that she and Cal were remembering.

She had no control over these processes. They were beyond her grasp. All she could do was be a part of the exchange between meaning and magic, and trust that the forces at work here comprehended her intentions better than she did.

But the power behind her was growing too strong for her; she could not channel its energies much longer. The book was getting too hot to hold, and Cal was shuddering beneath her hand.

'Enough!' she said.

Cal's eyes flew open.

'I haven't finished.'

'*Enough I said.*'

As she spoke, the structure of the Temple began to shudder.

Cal said: 'Oh God.'

'Time to go,' said Suzanna. 'Can you walk?'

'Of course I can walk.'

She helped him to his feet. There were roars from within, as one after another the walls capitulated to the rage of the Loom.

They didn't wait to watch the final cataclysm, but started away from the Temple, brick-shards whining past their heads.

Cal was as good as his word: he could indeed walk, albeit slowly. But running would have been impossible in the waste-land they were now obliged to cross. As Creation had been the touchstone of the outward journey, wholesale Destruction marked their return. The flora and fauna that had sprung into being in the footsteps of the trespassers were now suffering a swift dissolution. Flowers and trees were withering, the stench of their rot carried on the hooligan winds that scoured the Gyre.

With the earth-light dimmed, the scene was murky, the gloom further thickened by dust and airborne matter. From the darkness animal cries rose as the earth opened and consumed the very creatures it had produced mere minutes before. Those not devoured by the bed from which they'd sprung were subject to a fate still more terrible, as the powers that had made them unknitted their children. Pale, skeletal things that had once been bright and alive now littered the landscape, breathing their last. Some turned their eyes up to Cal and Suzanna, looking for hope or help, but they had none to offer.

It was as much as they could do to keep the cracks in the earth from claiming them too. They stumbled on, arms about each other, heads bowed beneath a barrage of hailstones which the Mantle, as though to perfect their misery, had unleashed.

'How far?' Cal said.

They halted and Suzanna stared ahead; she could not be certain they were not simply walking in circles. The light at their feet was now all but extinguished. Here and there it flared up, but only to illuminate another pitiable scene: the last wracking moments of the glory that their presence here had engendered.

Then:

'*There!*' she said, pointing through the curtain of hail and dust. '*I see a light.*'

They set off again, as fast as the suppurating earth would allow. With every step, their feet sank deeper into a swamp of decaying matter, in which the remnants of life still moved; the inheritors of this Eden: worms and cockroaches.

But there was a distinct light at the end of the tunnel; she glimpsed it again through the thick air.

'Look up, Cal,' she said.

He did just that, though only with effort.

'Not far now. A few more steps.'

He was becoming heavier by the moment; but the tear in

the Mantle was sufficient to spur them on over the last few yards of treacherous earth.

And finally they stepped out into the light, almost spat from the entrails of the Gyre as it went into its final convulsions.

They stumbled away from the Mantle, but not far before Cal said:

'I can't . . .'

and fell to the ground.

She knelt beside him, cradling his head, then looked around for help. Only then did she see the consequences of events in the Gyre.

Wonderland had gone.

The glories of the Fugue had been shredded and torn, their tatters evaporating even as she watched. Water, wood and stone; living animal tissue and dead Seerkind: all gone, as though it had never been. A few remnants lingered, but not for long. As the Gyre thundered and shook, these last signs of the Fugue's terrain became smoke and threads, then empty air. It was horribly quick.

Suzanna looked behind her. The Mantle was receding too, now that it had nothing left to conceal, its retreat uncovering a wasteland of dirt and fractured rock. Even its thunder was diminishing.

'Suzanna!'

She looked back to see de Bono coming towards her.

'What happened in there?'

'Later,' she said. 'First, we have to get help for Cal. He's been shot.'

'I'll fetch a car.'

Cal's eyes flickered open.

'Is it gone?' he murmured.

'Don't think about it now,' she said.

'I want to know,' he demanded, with surprising vehemence, and struggled to sit up. Knowing he wouldn't be placated, Suzanna helped him.

He moaned, seeing the desolation before them.

Groups of Seerkind, with a few of Hobart's people scattered

amongst them, stood in the valley and up the slopes of the surrounding hills, neither speaking nor moving. They were all that remained.

'What about Shadwell?' said Cal.

Suzanna shrugged. 'I don't know,' she said. 'He escaped the Temple before me.'

The din of a revved car-engine cancelled further conversation, as de Bono drove one of the invaders' vehicles across the dead grass, bringing it to a halt a few feet from where Cal lay.

'I'll drive,' said Suzanna, once Cal had been laid on the back seat.

'What do we tell the doctors?' Cal said, his voice getting fainter. 'I've got a bullet in me.'

'We'll cross that bridge when we come to it,' said Suzanna. As she got into the driver's seat, which de Bono had only reluctantly vacated, somebody called her name. Nimrod was running towards the car.

'Where are you going?' he said to her.

She directed his attention to the passenger.

'My friend,' he said, seeing Cal, 'you look the worse for wear.' He tried a smile of welcome, but tears came instead.

'It's over,' he said, sobbing. 'Destroyed. Our sweet land . . .' He wiped his eyes and nose with the back of his hand. 'What do we do now?' he said to Suzanna.

'We get out of harm's way,' she told him. 'As quickly as we can. We still have enemies –'

'It doesn't matter any more,' he said. 'The Fugue's gone. Everything we ever possessed, *lost*.'

'We're alive, aren't we?' she said. 'As long as we're alive . . .'

'Where will we go?'

'We'll find a place.'

'You have to lead us now,' said Nimrod. 'There's only you.'

'Later. First, we have to help Cal –'

'Yes,' he said. 'Of course.' He'd taken hold of her arm, and was loath to let her go. 'You *will* come back?'

'Of course,' she said.

534

'I'll take the rest of them North,' he told her. 'Two valleys from here. We'll wait for you there.'

'Then *move*,' she said. 'Time's wasting.'

'You will remember?' he said.

She would have laughed his doubts off, but that remembering was all. Instead she touched his wet face, letting him feel the menstruum in her fingers.

It was only as she drove away that she realized she'd probably blessed him.

# IV

## SHADWELL

The Salesman had fled the Gyre as the first dissolution began in the Fugue outside. His escape had therefore not only gone unchallenged, but unseen. With the fabric of their homeland coming apart on every side, nobody paid the least attention to the shabby, blood-stained figure that stumbled away through the mayhem.

Once only was he obliged to stop, and find a place in the chaos where he could give vent to his nausea. The vomit splattered his once-fine shoes, and he spent a further moment cleaning them with a handful of leaves, which began to evaporate in his hands even as he put them to the task.

Magic! How it revolted him now! The Fugue had enticed him with its promises. It had flaunted its so-called enchantments in front of him until he — poor Cuckoo that he was — had been blinded to all sense. Then it had led him a merry dance. Made him dress in borrowed skin; made him deceive and manipulate: all for love of its lies. And *lies* they were; he saw that now. Even as he'd reached to embrace his prize it had evaporated, denying him ownership, and leaving him to look like the guilty party.

The fact that it had taken him so long to see how he'd been used, however, was proof positive of his innocence in all of this. He'd intended no harm to any living thing; he'd wanted only to bring truth and stability into a place sorely deficient in both. For his pains, he'd been cheated and connived against.

What could history accuse him of then, other than naïveté: a forgivable sin. No, the true villains in this tragedy were the Seerkind, the wielders of rapture and unreason. They it was who'd twisted his benign ambition out of true, and so invited these horrors upon them all. A grim spiral of destruction that had ended in the Gyre – with *him* – a victim of circumstance – driven to murder.

He made his way out through the decaying Fugue, and began to climb up from the valley. The wind was cleaner on the slopes, and it shamed him. He stank of fear and frustration, while it smelt of the sea. Inhaling it, he knew that in such cleanliness lay his only hope for sanity.

Disgusted by his condition, he pulled off his bloodied jacket. It was excrement: corrupted and corrupting. In accepting it from the Incantatrix he'd made his first error: from that all subsequent misdirections had sprung. In his repugnance he tried to tear at the lining, but it resisted his strength, so he simply bundled the jacket up and threw it, high into the air. It rose a little way, then fell again, tumbling down a rocky slope, its passage starting a minor avalanche of pebbles, and came to rest spreadeagled like a legless suicide. At last it was where it had belonged from the start: in the dirt.

The Seerkind belonged with it, he thought. But they were survivors. Deception was in their blood. Though their territories had been destroyed, he didn't put it past them to have another trick or two up their sleeves. As long as they lived, these defilers, he would not rest easy in his bed. They'd made a fool and a butcher of him, and there was no health for him now until every last one of them was laid low.

Standing on the hill, looking down into the valley below, he felt a breath of new purpose. He'd been tricked and humiliated, but he was at least *alive*. The battle was not yet over.

They had an enemy, these monsters. Immacolata had dreamt of it often, and spoken of the wilderness where it resided.

*The Scourge, she'd called it.*

If he was to destroy the Seerkind he would need an ally,

and what better than that nameless power from which they'd hidden, an age ago?

They could never hide again. They had no land to conceal themselves in. If he could find this Scourge – and wake it from its wilderness – it and he would cleanse them at a stroke.

*The Scourge.* He liked the sound of the word mightily.

But he'd like better the silence that would come when his enemies were ash.

# A FRAGILE PEACE

1

Cal was happy to sleep for a while; happy to be at ease in the embrace of gentle hands and gentle words. The nurses came and went; a doctor too, smiling down at him and telling him all would be well, while de Bono, at the man's side, nodded and smiled.

A night later, he woke to find Suzanna with him in the room, mouthing words which he was too weary to hear. He slept, happy that she was near, but when he woke again, she'd gone. He asked after her, and after de Bono too, and was told that they'd be back, and that he wasn't to concern himself. Sleep, the nurse told him. Sleep, and when you wake all will be well. He vaguely knew this advice had failed someone he knew and loved, but his drugged mind couldn't quite remember who. So he did as he was told.

It was a sleep rich with dreams, in many of which he had a starring role, though not always wearing his own skin. Sometimes he was a bird; sometimes a tree, his branches laden with fruits each of which were like little worlds. Sometimes he was the wind, or like the wind, and ran unseen but strong over landscapes made of upturned faces – rock faces, flower faces – and streams in which he knew every silver fish by name.

And sometimes he dreamt he was dead; was floating in an infinite ocean of black milk, while presences invisible but mighty distressed the stars above him, and threw them down in long arcs that sang as they fell.

Comfortable as it was, this death, he knew he was only

dreaming it, indulging his fatigue. The time would come soon when he'd have to wake again.

When he did, Nimrod was by his bed.

'You needn't worry,' he told Cal. 'They won't ask you any questions.'

Cal's tongue was sluggish, but he managed to say:

'How did you do that?'

'A little rapture,' Nimrod said, unsmiling. 'I can still manage the occasional deceiving.'

'How are things?'

'Bad,' came the reply. 'Everyone's grieving. I'm not a public griever myself, so I'm not very popular.'

'And Suzanna?'

He made an equivocal look. 'I like the woman myself,' he said. 'But she's having problems with the Families. When they're not grieving, they're arguing amongst themselves. I get sick of the din. Sometimes I think I'll go find Marguerite. Forget I was ever Seerkind.'

'You can't.'

'You watch me. It's no use being sentimental, Cal. The Fugue's gone; once and for all. We may as well make the best of it. Join the Cuckoos; let bygones be bygones. Good God, we won't even be noticed. There's stranger things than us in the Kingdom these days.' He pointed to the television in the corner of the room. 'Every time I turn it on, something new. Something different. I might even go to America.' He slipped off his sunglasses. Cal had forgotten how extraordinary his eyes were. 'Hollywood could use a man with my attributes,' he said.

Despite Nimrod's quiet despair, Cal couldn't help but smile at this. And indeed, perhaps the man was right; perhaps the Seerkind *had* no choice now but to enter the Kingdom, and make whatever peace they could with it.

'I must go,' he was saying. 'There's a big meeting tonight. Everyone has a right to have their say. We'll be talking all night, most likely.' He went to the door.

'I won't go to California without saying goodbye,' he remarked, and left the patient alone.

Two days passed, and nobody came. Cal was getting better quickly; and it seemed that whatever rapture Nimrod had worked on the staff had indeed diverted them from making any report of their patient's wound to the police.

By the afternoon of the third day Cal knew he was much improved, because he was getting restless. The television – Nimrod's new love – could provide only soap opera and a bad movie. The latter, the lesser of the two banalities, was playing when the door opened, and a woman dressed in black stepped into the room. It took Cal a moment before he recognized his visitor as Apolline.

Before he could offer a welcome she said:

'No time to talk, Calhoun –' and, approaching the bed, thrust a parcel at Cal.

'Take it!' she said.

He did so.

'I have to be away quickly,' she went on. Her face softened as she gazed at him. 'You look tired, my boy,' she said. 'Take a holiday!' And with that advice retreated to the door.

'Wait!' he called after her.

'No time! No time!' she said, and was away.

He took the string and brown paper from around his present, and discovered inside the book of faery-tales which Suzanna had found in Rue Street. With it, there was a scrawled note.

*Cal*, it read,

> *Keep hold of this for me, will you? Never let it out of your sight. Our enemies are still with us. When the time is safe, I'll find you.*
> *Do this for us all.*
> *I'm kissing you.*
> *Suzanna.*

He read the letter over and over, moved beyond telling by the way she'd signed off: *I'm kissing you*.

But he was confounded by her instructions: the book seemed an unremarkable volume, its binding torn, its pages yellowed. The text was in German, which he had no command of whatsoever. Even the illustrations were dark, and full of shadows, and he'd had enough shadows to hurt him a lifetime. But if she wanted him to keep it safe, then he'd do so. She was wise, and he knew better than to take her instructions lightly.

### 3

After the visit from Apolline, nobody else came. He was not altogether surprised. There'd been an urgency in the woman's manner, and yet more in the letter from Suzanna. *Our enemies are still with us*, she'd written. If she wrote that, then it was true.

They discharged him after a week, and he made his way back to Liverpool. Little had changed. The grass still refused to grow in the churned earth where Lilia Pellicia had died; the trains still ran North and South; the china dogs on the dining-room sill still looked for their master, their vigil rewarded only with dust.

There was dust too on the note that Geraldine had left on the kitchen table – a brief missive saying that until Cal learned to behave like a reasonable human being he could expect none of her company.

There were several other letters awaiting him – one from his section leader at the firm, asking him where the hell he was, and stating that if he wished to keep his job he'd better make some explanation of his absence post haste. The letter was dated the 11th. It was now the 25th. Cal presumed he was out of a job.

He couldn't find it in him to be much concerned by

unemployment; nor indeed by Geraldine's absence. He wanted to be alone; wanted the time to think through all that had happened. More significantly, he found feelings about anything hard to come by. As the days passed, and he made a stab at reassembling his life, he rapidly came to see that his time in the Gyre had left him wounded in more ways than one. It was as though the forces unleashed at the Temple had found their way into him, and left a little wilderness where there'd once been a capacity for tears and regret.

Even the poet was silent. Though Cal could still remember Mad Mooney's verses by heart they were just sounds to him now; they failed to move.

There was one comfort in this: that perhaps his new-found stoicism suited better the function of solitary librarian. He would be vigilant, but he would anticipate nothing, neither disaster nor revelation.

That was not to say he would give up looking to the future. True, he was just a Cuckoo: scared and weary and alone. But so, in the end, were most of his tribe: it didn't mean all was lost. As long as they could still be moved by a minor chord, or brought to a crisis of tears by scenes of lovers reunited; as long as there was room in their cautious hearts for games of chance, and laughter in the face of God, that must surely be enough to save them, at the last.

If not, there was no hope for any living thing.

# BOOK THREE

# OUT OF
# THE EMPTY
# QUARTER

# Part Ten

# The Search for the Scourge

*'. . . if you gaze for long
into an abyss, the abyss gazes
also into you.'*

Friedrich Nietzsche
*Beyond Good and Evil*

Part Ten

# The Search for the Scourge

# I

## NO REST FOR THE WICKED

### 1

**B**efore the explorers, the *Rub al Khali* had been a blank space on the map of the world. After them, it remained so.

Its very name, given to it by the Bedu, the desert nomads who'd lived for unnumbered centuries in the deserts of the Arab Peninsula, meant: The Empty Quarter. That they, familiar with wildernesses that would drive most men insane, should designate this place *empty* was the most profound testament to its nullity imaginable.

But amongst those Europeans for whom names were not proof enough, and who had, from the beginning of the nineteenth century, gone looking for places to test their mettle, the *Rub al Khali* rapidly acquired legendary status. It was perhaps the single greatest challenge the earth could offer to adventurers, its barrenness unrivalled by any wasteland, equatorial or arctic.

Nothing lived there, nor could. It was simply a vast nowhere, two hundred and fifty thousand square miles of desolation, its dunes rising in places to the height of small mountains, and elsewhere giving way to tracts of heat-shattered stone large enough to lose a people in. It was trackless, waterless and changeless. Most who dared its wastes were swallowed by it, its dust increased by the sum of their powdered bones.

But for that breed of man – as much ascetic as explorer – who was half in love with losing himself to such an end – the number of expeditions that had retreated in the face of the Quarter's maddening absence, or disappeared into it, was simply a spur.

Some challenged the wasteland in the name of cartology, determined to map the place for those who might come after them, only to discover that there was nothing *to* map but the chastening of their spirit. Others went looking for lost tombs and cities, where fabled wealth awaited that man strong enough to reach into Hell and snatch it out. Still others, a patient, secretive few, went in the name of Academe, seeking verification of theories geological or historical. Still others looked for the Ark there; or Eden.

All had this in common: that if they returned from the Empty Quarter – even though their journey might have taken them only a day's ride into that place – they came back changed men. Nobody could set his eyes on such a void and return to hearth and home without having lost a part of himself to the wilderness forever. Many, having endured the void once, went back, and back again, as if daring the desert to claim them; not content until it did. And those unhappy few who died at home, died with their eyes not on the loving faces at their bedside, nor on the cherry tree in blossom outside the window, but on that waste that called them as only the Abyss can call, promising the soul the balm of nothingness.

2

For years Shadwell had listened to Immacolata speak of the emptiness where the Scourge resided. Mostly she'd talked of it in abstract terms: a place of sand and terror. Though he'd comforted her in her fear as best he'd known how, he'd soon stopped listening to her babble.

But standing on the hill overlooking the valley which the Fugue had once occupied, blood on his hands and hatred in his heart, her words had come back to him. In subsequent months he'd set himself the task of discovering that place for himself.

550

He had chanced on pictures of the *Rub al Khali* early in his investigations, and had quickly come to believe that this was the wasteland she'd seen in her prophetic dreams. Even now, in the latter portion of the century, it remained largely a mystery. Commercial aircraft routes still gave it wide berth, and though a road now crossed it the desert swallowed the efforts of any who attempted to exploit its spaces. Shadwell's problem was therefore this: if indeed the Scourge *did* live somewhere in the Empty Quarter, how would he be able to find it in a void so vast?

He began by consulting the experts: in particular an explorer called Emerson, who had twice crossed the Quarter by camel. He was now a withered and bed-bound old man, who was at first contemptuous of Shadwell's ignorance. But after a few minutes' talk he warmed to the obsessive in his visitor, and offered much good advice. When he spoke of the desert it was as of a lover who'd left stripes upon his back, yet whose cruelty he ached to have again.

As they parted he said:

'I envy you, Shadwell. God alive, I envy you.'

3

Though Emerson had told him that the desert was always a solitary experience, Shadwell did not go alone to the *Rub al Khali*; he took Hobart with him.

The Law no longer called Hobart as it had. An investigation into the events that had all but destroyed his Division had found him criminally negligent; he might well have been imprisoned but that his masters concluded he was unbalanced – indeed probably always had been – and that exposing a system that would employ such a madman to the scrutiny of a court case would cover none of them in glory. Instead a complete story was fabricated – which made heroes of those men who'd gone into the Fugue with Hobart and died there, and retired on full pay those who'd emerged with their sanity in tatters. There was a valiant attempt by several bereaved wives to discredit this fiction, but when hints of the real explanation were uncovered it seemed infinitely more unlikely than the lie. Nor were the survivors able to give any coherent account of what they'd experienced. Those few details they did unburden themselves of merely served to confirm their lunacy.

Hobart, however, did not have madness as a place of retreat, having been in its hold for years. The vision of fire that Shadwell had given him – and which had first claimed him for the Salesman's faction – obsessed him still, despite the fact that the coat had been discarded. Knowing that in Shadwell's company his obsession would not be mocked, Hobart elected to remain there. With Shadwell, his dreams had come closest to being realized; and, though their shared ambitions had been defeated, the man still spoke a language Hobart's dementia understood. When the Salesman talked of the Scourge, Hobart knew it could only be the Dragon of his dreams by another name. Once, he half-remembered, he'd sought that monster in a forest, but he'd found only confusion there. It had been a sham, that Dragon; not the true beast he still longed to meet. He knew where that legend waited now: not in a forest but a desert, where its breath had reduced all living matter to ash and sand.

They went together, therefore, to a village on the Southern fringe of the Quarter; a place so inconsequential it couldn't even lay claim to a name.

Here they were obliged to leave their jeep, and, with their driver as interpreter, pick up guides and camels. It was not simply the practical problems of crossing the Quarter by vehicle that made Shadwell forsake wheel for hooves. It was a desire – encouraged by Emerson – to be as much a part of the desert as was possible. To go into that void not as conquerors but as penitents.

Locating their two guides for the expedition was the business of an hour, no more, there being so few either willing or able-bodied enough to make the journey. Both men were of *Ahl Murra* tribe, who alone of all the tribes claimed spiritual kinship with the Quarter. The first, a fellow called Mitrak ibn

Talaq, Shadwell chose because he boasted that he'd guided white men into the *Rub al Khali* (and back out again) on four previous occasions. But he would not go without the company of a younger man by the name of Jabir, whom he variously described as his cousin, half-cousin and brother-in-law. This other looked to be little more than fifteen, but had the scrawny strength and the worldly-wise glance of a man three times that age.

Hobart was left to haggle with them, though the terms of the arrangements took some time to sort out, as the Arabic he'd learned for this expedition was primitive, and the Arabs' English was bad. They seemed to know their profession however. The purchase of camels was the business of half a day; the purchasing of supplies another morning.

It was therefore the labour of a mere forty-eight hours to prepare for the crossing.

On the day of their departure, however, Shadwell — whose fastidiousness had not kept him from satisfying his belly — fell foul of an intestinal plague that turned his innards to water. With his gut in revolt he couldn't keep a morsel of food in his system long enough to profit by it, and he quickly became weak. Wracked by fever, and with access only to the most rudimentary medication, all he could do was take refuge in the hovel they'd hired, find the corner where the sun couldn't reach him, and there sweat the sickness out.

Two days passed, without his improving. He was not used to illness, but on those few occasions he *had* fallen sick he'd always hidden himself away, and suffered in private. Here, privacy was nearly impossible to find. All day he could hear scrabblings outside the door and window, as people fought for a chance to peer through the cracks at the infidel, moaning on his filthy sheet. And when the locals grew tired of the spectacle there were still the flies, watching over him, thirsty for the tainted waters at his lips and eyes. He'd long since learned the hopelessness of shooing them away. He simply lay in his sweat and let them drink, his fevered mind drifting off to cooler places.

On the third day Hobart suggested they postpone the journey, pay off Ibn Talaq and Jabir, and return to civilization. There Shadwell could regain his strength for another try. Shadwell protested at this, but the same thought had crept into his own head more than once. When the infection finally left his body, he'd be in no fit state to dare the Quarter.

That night, however, things changed. For one, there was a wind. It came not in gusts but as a steady assault, the sand it carried creeping in beneath the door and through the cracks in the window.

Shadwell had slept a little during the preceding day, and had benefited from his rest, but the wind prevented him from settling now. The disturbance got into his gut too, obliging him to spend half the night squatting over the bucket he'd been provided with, while his bowels gave vent.

That was where he was — squatting in misery in a cloud of flatulence — when he first heard the voice. It came out of the desert, rising and falling like the wail of some infernal widow. He'd never heard its like.

He stood up, soiling his legs in doing so, his body wracked with shudders.

It was the Scourge he was hearing, he had no doubt. The sound was muted, but indisputable. A voice of grief, and power; and *summoning*. It offered them a signpost. They would not have to go blindly into the wilderness, hoping luck would bring them to their destination. They'd follow the route the wind had come. Sooner or later wouldn't it lead them to the creature whose voice it carried?

He hoisted up his trousers and opened the door. The wind was running wild through the tiny town, depositing sand wherever it went, whining at the houses like a rabid dog. He listened again for the voice of the Scourge, praying that it was not some hallucination brought on by his hunger. It was not. It came again, the same anguished howl.

One of the villagers hurried past the spot where Shadwell stood. The Salesman stepped out of the doorway and took the man's arm.

'You hear?' he said.

The man turned his scarred face towards Shadwell. One of his eyes was missing.

'*Hear?*' said Shadwell, pointing to his head as the sound came again.

The man shook off Shadwell's grip.

'*Al hiyal,*' the man replied, practically spitting the words out.

'Huh?'

'*Al hiyal . . .*' he said again, backing away from Shadwell as from a dangerous idiot, his hand at the knife in his belt.

Shadwell had no argument with the man; he raised his hands, smiling, and left him to his troubles.

A curious exhilaration had seized hold of him, making his starved brain sing. They'd go tomorrow into the Quarter, and damn his intestines to Hell. As long as he could stay upright on a saddle he could make the journey.

He stood in the middle of the squalid street, his heart pounding like a jack-hammer, his legs trembling.

'I hear you,' he said; and the wind took the words from his lips as if by some perverse genius known only to desert winds it could return the way it had come, and deliver Shadwell's words back to the power that awaited him in the void.

# II

# OBLIVION

## 1

**N**othing, neither in the books he'd read nor the testimonies he'd listened to, nor even in the tormented voice he'd heard on the wind the previous night, had prepared Shadwell for the utter desolation of the *Rub al Khali*. The books had described its wastes as best words could, but they couldn't evoke the terrible nullity of the place. Even Emerson, whose mixture of understatement and passion had been persuasive in the extreme, hadn't come near to touching upon the blank truth.

The journey was hour upon relentless hour upon relentless hour of heat and bare horizons, the same imbecile sky overhead, the same dead ground beneath the camels' feet.

Shadwell had no energy to waste on conversation; and Hobart had always been a silent man. As for Ibn Talaq and the boy, they rode ahead of the infidels, occasionally whispering, but mostly keeping their counsel. With nothing to divert the attention, the mind turned to the body for its subject, and rapidly became obsessed with sensation. The rhythm of the thighs as they chafed against the saddle, or the taste of the blood from the lips and gums; these were thought's only fodder.

Even speculation about what might lie at this journey's end was lost in the dull blur of discomfort.

Seventy-two hours passed without incident: only the same curdling heat, the same rhythm of hoof on sand, hoof on sand, as they followed the bearing of the wind on which the

Scourge's voice had come. Neither of the Arabs made any enquiry as to the infidels' purpose, nor was any explanation offered. They simply marched, the void pressing upon them from all sides.

It was worse by far when they stopped, either to rest the camels, or to offer their sand-clogged throats a dribble of water. Then the sheer immensity of the silence came home to them.

Existence here was an irrational act, in defiance of all physical imperatives. What kind of creature had chosen to make its home in such an absence, Shadwell wondered at such moments: and what force of will must it possess, to withstand the void? Unless – and this thought came more and more – it was *of* the void: a part of the emptiness and silence. That possibility made his belly churn: that the power he sought *belonged* here – chose dunes for its bed and rock for its pillow. He finally began to understand why Immacolata's visions of the Scourge had brought sweat to her brow. In those nightmares she had tasted a terrible *purity*, one that had made her own pale by its light.

But he was not afraid; except of failing. Until he stepped into the presence of that creature – until he learned the source of its cleanliness, he could not be cleansed himself. That he longed for above all things.

And, as the night fell on their fourth day in the Quarter, that desire came still closer to being realized.

Jabir had just set the fire when the voice came again. There was little wind tonight, but it rose with the same solemn authority as before, tainting the air with its tragedy.

Ibn Talaq, who'd been cleaning his rifle, was the first to his feet, his eyes wide and wild, either an oath or a prayer on his lips. Hobart was on his feet seconds later, while Jabir went to soothe the camels, who had panicked at the sound and were tearing at their tethers. Only Shadwell stayed beside the fire, gazing into the flames as the howl – sustained as if on one monumental breath – filled the night.

It seemed to go on for minutes before it finally died away.

557

When it did it left the animals muttering, and the men silent. Ibn Talaq was first back to the fire, and the business of rifle-cleaning; the boy followed. Finally, Hobart too.

'We're not alone,' said Shadwell after a time, his gaze still on the flames.

'What was it?' said Jabir.

'*Al hiyal*,' Ibn Talaq said.

The boy pulled a face.

'*What is al hiyal?*' Shadwell said.

'They mean the noise the sand makes,' Hobart said.

'The sand?' said Shadwell. 'You think *that* was the sand?'

The boy shook his head.

'Of course not,' said Shadwell. 'That's the voice of the one we've come to meet.'

Jabir threw a handful of bone-white sticks onto the fire. It devoured them immediately.

'Do you understand?' Shadwell asked.

Ibn Talaq looked up from his work, and stared at Shadwell.

'They understand,' said Hobart.

'I thought maybe they'd lose their nerve.'

Ibn Talaq seemed to sense the implication of this remark.

'*Rub al Khali*,' he said, 'we know. All of it. We know.'

Shadwell grasped the point. They were Murra. Their tribe laid claim to this territory as its own. To retreat before the mysteries of the Empty Quarter would be tantamount to disinheritance.

'How close are we?' said Hobart.

'I don't know,' Shadwell replied. 'You heard it the same as me. Perhaps very near.'

'Do you think it knows we're here?' said Hobart.

'Perhaps,' said Shadwell. 'Does it matter?'

'I suppose not.'

'If it doesn't know tonight, it will by tomorrow.'


2


They set out at dawn the next day, to cover as much distance as they could before the sun mounted too high, following the same bearing as they'd followed on the previous four days.

For the first time in their journey the landscape they were crossing showed some subtle change, as the rhythmical rise and fall of the dunes gave way to much larger, irregular rises. The sand of these hills was soft, and collapsed in sibilant avalanches beneath the feet of animal and human alike. Nobody could ride. The travellers coaxed the animals, still jittery after the night before, up the ever steeper slopes with curses and kindness in equal measure, only to reach the top and find a yet larger dune ahead of them.

Without any words being exchanged, Ibn Talaq had relinquished his position at the head of the quartet, and it was Shadwell who now set the pace, leading the party up the faces of the dunes and down into the troughs between. There, the subtlest of winds blew, more distressing in its ingratiating way than any storm, for it seemed to whisper as it ran over the sand, its message just beyond the reach of comprehension.

Shadwell knew what words it carried, however:

*Climb*, it said, *climb if you dare. One more hill, and you'll find all you ever wanted waiting.*

– and with its coaxing he'd lead the way up the next slope, out of the cool shadow and into the blinding sunlight.

They were close, Shadwell knew; very close. Though, in the early afternoon, Jabir began to complain, demanding that they rest the animals, Shadwell would have none of it. He forced the pace, his mind divided from his body's discomfort; almost floating. Sweat was nothing; pain was nothing. All of it could be endured.

And then, at the top of a dune it had taken the better part of an hour to climb, the murmurs in the wind were confirmed. They had left the dunes behind them. Ahead the terrain was absolutely flat as far as the eye could see, though that wasn't many miles, for the wind carried a cargo of sand that veiled the horizon like smoke. Even in the *Rub al Khali* this wasteland was a new refinement of desolation: a connoisseur's nowhere.

559

'God Almighty,' said Hobart, as he climbed to where Shadwell stood.

The Salesman took hold of Hobart's arm. His breath was rapid and rasping; his sun-skinned face dripped sweat.

'Don't let me fall,' he murmured. 'We're close now.'

'Why don't we wait awhile before going any farther?' said Hobart. 'Maybe rest, until tomorrow?'

'Don't you want to meet your Dragon?' Shadwell asked.

Hobart said nothing to this.

'Then I'll go alone,' was Shadwell's response. He dropped the camel's reins and began to stagger down the slope to meet the plain.

Hobart scanned the sterility before him. What Shadwell said was true: they *were* close, he felt it. And that thought, which days ago had excited him, now put a terror into him. He'd seen enough of the Quarter to know that the Dragon that occupied it was not the glittering monster of his dreams. It defied his imagination to conjure the terror that nested in such a place.

But one thing he knew: it would care not at all for the Law, or its keepers.

He might turn from it still, he thought, if he were resolute. Persuade the guides that Shadwell was leading them to extinction, and that they'd all be wiser leaving the Salesman to his insanity. Already Shadwell was at the bottom of the slope, and marching away from the dune, not even bothering to glance behind him to see that the rest were following. Let him go, a part of Hobart said: let him have his Scourge if that's what he wants; and death too.

But fearful as he was he couldn't quite bring himself to turn his back on the wasteland. His mind, which was narrowed now to a tunnel, showed him again his hands alive with an unconsuming flame. In that rare moment of vision he'd tasted power he'd never quite been able to put words to, and nothing his subsequent experience had brought – the defeats and humiliations – could extinguish the memory.

Somewhere, far from here, those who'd defeated him – who'd perverted the Laws of the real and the righteous – still lived. To go back amongst them with fire at his fingertips and lay their wretched heads low – that was an ambition worth enduring the wasteland for.

Dreaming of flame, he took up the reins of Shadwell's camel, and followed in the Salesman's footsteps down onto the mirror-bright sand.

# III

---

# THE WALL

istance was impossible to judge on the plain they now crossed. The dunes at their backs were soon obscured by the sand-thickened air, and ahead, the same veil shut the vista from sight. Though the wind was insistent, it did nothing to alleviate the assault of the sun: it merely added misery to misery, dragging at the legs until every step was a torment. But nothing slowed Shadwell. He marched like a man possessed until – after an hour of this inferno – he stopped dead, and pointed through the blur of heat and wind.

'There,' he said.

Hobart, who'd come abreast of him, narrowed his dazzled eyes and followed the direction of Shadwell's finger. But the sand clouds defied his scrutiny.

'Nothing,' he said.

Shadwell seized hold of his arm.

'Damn you, *look*!'

And this time Hobart realized Shadwell was not deceived. Some distance from where they stood the ground seemed to rise up again.

'What is it?' Hobart shouted against the wind.

'A wall,' Shadwell said.

It looked more like a range of hills than a wall, Hobart thought, for it ran along the entire visible horizon. Yet, though there were breaks in its length here and there, its regularity suggested Shadwell's judgement was correct. It was indeed a wall.

Without further exchange, they began the march towards it.

There was no sign of any structure rising on the far side, but its builders must have valued whatever it had been made to enclose and protect, for with every yard they drew closer, its sheer scale became awesomely apparent. It rose fifty feet or more above the desert floor; yet such was the skill of the masons there was no visible sign of how it had been constructed.

Twenty yards from the wall the party halted, leaving Shadwell to approach it unaccompanied. He stretched his hand out to touch the stone, which was hot beneath his finger-tips, its surface so smooth it was almost silken. It was as if the wall had been raised out of molten rock, shaped by intelligences that could mould lava like cold clay. Clearly there was no practical way of scaling a surface so innocent of niche or scar, even if any of them had possessed the energy to do so.

'There must be a gate,' said Shadwell. 'We'll walk 'til we find it.'

The sun was well past its peak now, the day beginning to cool. But the wind was not about to give the travellers a moment's respite. It seemed to be keeping guard along the wall, lashing at their legs as though eager to throw them to the ground. But having got so far without being slaughtered, the party's fears had been replaced by curiosity as to what lay on the other side. The Arabs had found their voices again, and kept up a constant dialogue, doubtless planning how they'd boast of their find once home.

They walked for fully half an hour, the wall unbroken. There were places where cracks had appeared in it – though none low enough to offer hand-holds – and others where the top edge showed signs of crumbling, but there was neither window nor gate in its length, however small.

'Who built this?' said Hobart as they walked.

Shadwell was watching their shadow on the wall, as it kept pace with them.

'Ancients,' he said.

563

'To keep the desert out?'

'Or keep the Scourge in.'

The last few minutes had brought a subtle change in the wind. It had given up nipping at their legs, and gone about braver business. It was Ibn Talaq who first spotted what.

'There! There!' he said, and pointed along the wall.

A few hundred yards from where they stood a stream of sand was being carried out through the wall, bellowing as it went. As they approached, it became apparent that this was not a gate, but a breach in the wall. The stone had been thrown down in heaps of rubble. Shadwell was first to reach the scattered pieces, many the size of small houses, and began to scramble up over them, until at last he looked down into the place the walls had been raised to guard.

Behind him, Hobart called:

'What do you see?'

Shadwell didn't speak. He simply surveyed the scene behind the wall with disbelieving eyes, as the wind that roared through the breach threatened to throw him from his perch.

There were neither palaces nor tombs on the other side of the wall. Indeed there was no sign, however vestigial, of habitation; no obelisks, no colonnades. There was only sand, and more sand; endless sand. Another desert, rolling away from them, as empty as the void at their backs.

'Nothing.'

It wasn't Shadwell who spoke but Hobart. He too had scaled the boulders, and stood at Shadwell's side.

'Oh Jesus . . . nothing.'

Shadwell made no reply. He simply clambered down the other side of the breach, and stepped into the shadow of the wall. What Hobart said appeared to be true: there was nothing here. Why then did he feel certain that this place was somehow sacred?

He walked through the mire of sand that the wind had heaped against the rubble of the breach, and surveyed the dunes. Was it possible that the sand had simply *covered* the secret they'd come here to find? Was the Scourge concealed here, its howl that of something buried alive? If so, how could they ever hope to locate it?

He turned back, and squinted up at the wall. Then, on impulse, he began to climb the open edge of the breach. It was heavy going. His limbs were weary, and the wind had polished the stone in its many years of passage, but he eventually gained the summit.

At first it seemed his efforts had been for nothing. All he'd won for his sweat was a view of the wall, running off in both directions until distance claimed it.

But when he came to survey the scene below, he realized that there was a *pattern* visible in the dunes. Not the natural wave patterns that the wind created, but something more elaborate – vast geometrical designs laid out in the sand – with walkways or roads between them. He'd read, in his research on wastelands, of designs drawn by some ancient people on the plains of South America; pictures of birds and gods that could have made no sense from the earth, but had been drawn as if to enchant some heavenly spectator. Was that the case here? Had the sand been raised in these furrows and banks as a message to the sky? If so, what power had done it? A small nation would be needed to move so much sand; and the wind would undo tomorrow what had been done today. Whose work was this then?

Perhaps night would tell.

He climbed back down the wall to where Hobart and the others were waiting amid the boulders.

'We'll camp here tonight,' he said.

'Inside the walls or out?' Hobart wanted to know.

'Inside.'

# IV

## URIEL

Night came down like a dropped curtain. Jabir made a fire in the shelter of the wall, out of the remorseless assault of the wind, and there they ate bread and drank coffee. There was no conversation. Exhaustion had claimed their tongues. They simply sat hunched up, staring into the flames.

Though his bones ached, Shadwell couldn't sleep. As the fire burned low, and one by one the others succumbed to fatigue, he was left to keep watch. The wind dropped a little as the night deepened, its bellow becoming a moan. It soothed him like a lullaby, and at last, his eyelids dropped closed. Behind them, the busy patterns of his inner-eye. Then emptiness.

In sleep, he heard the boy Jabir's voice. It called him from darkness but he didn't want to answer. Rest was too sweet. It came again, however: a horrid shriek. This time he opened his lids.

The wind had died completely. Overhead the stars were bright in a perfect sky, trembling in their places. The fire had gone out, but their light was sufficient for him to see that both Ibn Talaq and Jabir were missing from their places. He got up, crossed to Hobart, and shook him awake.

As he did so, his eye caught sight of something on the ground a little way beyond Hobart's head. He stared—doubting what he saw.

There were *flowers* underfoot, or so he seemed to see. Clusters of blooms, set in abundant foliage. He looked up from the ground, and his parched throat unleashed a cry of astonishment.

The dunes had gone. In their place a jungle had risen up, a riot of trees that challenged the wall's height – vast, flower-laden species whose leaves were the size of a man. Beneath their canopy was a wilderness of vines and shrubs and grasses.

For a moment he doubted his sanity, until he heard Hobart say: '*My God*,' at his side.

'You see it too?' said Shadwell.

'I see it . . .' Hobart said, ' . . . a garden.'

'Garden?'

At first sight the word scarcely described this chaos. But further scrutiny showed that there was order at work in what had initially seemed anarchy. Avenues had been laid under the vast, blossom-laden trees; there were lawns and terraces. This was indeed a garden of sorts, though there would be little pleasure to be had walking in it, for despite the surfeit of species – plants and bushes of every size and shape – there was not amongst them a single variety that had colour. Neither bloom nor branch nor leaf nor fruit; all, down to the humblest blade, had been bled of pigment.

Shadwell was puzzling at this when a further cry issued from the depths. It was Ibn Talaq's voice this time; and it rose in a steep curve to a shriek. He followed it. The ground was soft beneath his feet, which slowed his progress, but the shriek went on, broken only by sobbing breaths. Shadwell ran, calling the man's name. There was no fear left in him; only an overwhelming hunger to see the Maker of this enigma face to face.

As he advanced down one of the shadowy boulevards, its pathway strewn with the same colourless plant-life, Ibn Talaq's cry stopped dead. Shadwell was momentarily disoriented. He halted, and scanned the foliage for some sign of movement. There was none. The breeze did not stir a single frond; nor – to further compound the mystery – was there a hint of perfume, however subtle, from the mass of blossoms.

Behind him, Hobart muttered a cautionary word. Shadwell

567

turned, and was about to condemn the man's lack of curiosity when he caught sight of the trail his own footsteps had made. In the Gyre, his heels had brought forth life. Here, they'd destroyed it. Wherever he'd set foot the plants had simply crumbled away.

He stared at the blank ground where there'd previously been grasses and flowers, and the explanation for this extraordinary growth became apparent. Ignoring Hobart now, he walked towards the nearest of the bushes, the blooms of which hung like censers from their branches. Tentatively, he touched his fingers to one of the flowers. Upon this lightest of contacts the blossom fell apart, dropping from the branch in a shower of sand. He brushed its companion with his thumb: it too fell away, and with it the branch, and the exquisite leaves it bore; *all* returned to sand at a touch.

The dunes hadn't disappeared in the night, to make way for this garden. They had *become* the garden; risen up at some unthinkable command to create this sterile illusion. What had at first sight seemed a miracle of fecundity was a mockery. It was sand. Scentless, colourless, lifeless: a dead garden.

A sudden disgust gripped him. This trick was all too like the work of the Seerkind: some deceitful rapture. He flung himself into the midst of the shrubbery, flailing to right and left of him in his fury, destroying the bushes in stinging clouds. A tree, brushed by his hand, collapsed like an extinguished fountain. The most elaborate blossoms fell apart at his merest touch. But he wasn't satisfied. He flailed on until he'd cleared a small grove amid the press of foliage.

'*Raptures!*' he kept yelling, as the sand rained down on him. '*Raptures!*'

He might have gone on to more ambitious destruction, but that the Scourge's howl – the same he'd first heard days before, as he'd squatted in shit – began. That voice had brought him through desolation and emptiness; and to what? More desolation, more emptiness. His anger unassuaged by the damage he'd done, he turned to Hobart.

568

'Which way's it coming from?'

'I don't know,' said Hobart, stumbling back a few steps. *'Everywhere.'*

*'Where are you?'* Shadwell demanded, yelling into the depths of the illusion. 'Show yourself!'

'Don't – ' said Hobart, his voice full of dread.

'This is your Dragon,' Shadwell said. 'We have to see it.'

Hobart shook his head. The power that had made this place was not one he wanted sight of. Before he could retreat, however, Shadwell had hold of him.

'We meet it together,' he said. 'It's cheated us *both*.'

Hobart struggled to be free of Shadwell's grip, but his violence ceased as his panicked eyes caught sight of the form that now appeared at the far end of the avenue.

It was as tall as the canopy; twenty-five feet or more, its long, bone-white head brushing the branches, sand-petals spiralling down.

Though it still howled, it lacked a mouth, or indeed any feature on its face but eyes, which it had in terrifying numbers, twin rows of lidless, lashless slits which ran down each side of its head. There were perhaps a hundred eyes in all, but staring an age at it would not have revealed their true number, for the thing, despite its solidity, defied fixing. Were those wheels that moved at its heart, tied with lines of liquid fire to a hundred other geometries which informed the air it occupied? Did innumerable wings beat at its perimeters, and light burn in its bowels, as though it had swallowed stars?

Nothing was certain. In one breath it seemed to be enclosed in a matrix of darting light, like scaffolding struck by lightning; in the next the pattern became flame confetti, which swarmed at its extremities before it was snatched away. One moment, ether; the next, juggernaut.

And then, as suddenly as it had begun, the wail it was unleashing died away.

The Scourge stopped moving.

Shadwell released Hobart, as the stench of shit rose from the man's trousers. Hobart fell to the ground, making small sobbing sounds. Shadwell left him where he lay, as the

Scourge's head, mazed in geometries, located the creatures that had trespassed in its garden.

He didn't retreat. What use was retreat? In every direction from this place lay thousands of square miles of wasteland. There was nowhere to run to. All he could do was stand his ground and share with this terror the news he brought.

But before he could utter a word, the sand at his feet began to move. For an instant he thought the Scourge intended to bury him alive, as the ground liquified. But instead the sand drew back like a sheet, and sprawled on the bed below – a few feet from where Shadwell stood – was the corpse of Ibn Talaq. The man was naked, and appalling torments had been visited upon him. Both his hands had been burned from his arms, leaving blackened stumps from which cracked bone protruded. His genitals had been similarly destroyed, and the eyes seared from his head. There was no use pretending the wounds had been delivered after death: his mouth still shaped his dying scream.

Shadwell was revolted, and averted his eyes, but the Scourge had more to show him. The sand moved again, to his right, and another body was uncovered. This time, Jabir, lying on his belly, his buttocks burned down to the bone, his neck broken and his head twisted round so that he stared up at the sky. His mouth was burned out.

'Why?' was the word on Shadwell's lips.

The Scourge's gaze made his bowels ache to empty themselves, but he still delivered the question.

'*Why?* We mean no harm here.'

The Scourge made no sign that it had even heard the words. Had it perhaps lost the power of communication after an age here in the wilderness, its only response to the pain of being, that howl?

Then – somewhere amid the legion eyes – a skittering light, which was snatched by the burning wheels and spat towards Shadwell. In the breath before it struck him he had time to hope his death would be quick; then the light was on him. The agony of its touch was blinding; at its caress his body folded up beneath him. He struck the ground, his skull ready

570

to split. But death didn't come. Instead the pain dropped away suddenly, and the burning wheel appeared in his mind's eye. The Scourge was in his head, its power circling in his skull.

Then the wheel went out, and in its place a vision, lent him by his possessor:

he was floating through the garden; high up in the trees. This is the Scourge's sight, he realized: he was sitting behind its eyes. Their shared gaze caught a motion on the ground below, and moved towards it.

There on the sand was Jabir — naked, and on all fours — with Ibn Talaq impaling him, grunting as he worked his flesh into the boy. To Shadwell's eyes the act looked uncomfortable, but harmless enough. He'd seen worse in his time; *done* worse, indeed. But it wasn't just sight he was sharing with the Scourge; its thoughts came too: and the creature saw a crime in this rutting, and judged it punishable by death.

Shadwell had seen the results of the Scourge's executions; he had no desire to watch them re-enacted. But he had no choice. The Scourge owned his mind's eye; he was obliged to watch every terrible moment.

Brightness reached down and tore the pair from each other, then scoured out the offending parts — mouth, and eyes, and groin and buttocks — erasing them with fire. It was not quick. They had time to suffer — he heard again the shrieks that had brought him into the garden — and time to beg. But the fire was unforgiving. By the time it had done its work Shadwell was sobbing for it to stop. Finally it did, and a shroud of sand was drawn over the bodies. Only when that was done did the Scourge grant him his own sight back. The ground he lay on — stinking of his vomit — reappeared in front of him.

He lay where he'd fallen, trembling. Only when he was certain he wouldn't collapse did he raise his head and look up at the Scourge.

It had changed shape. No longer a giant, it sat on a hill of sand it had raised beneath itself, its many eyes turned up towards the stars. It had gone from judge and executioner to contemplative in a matter of moments.

Though the images that had filled his head had faded,

Shadwell knew the creature still maintained its presence in his mind. He could feel the barbs of its thought. He was a human fish, and hooked.

It looked away from the sky, and down at him.

*Shadwell . . .*

He heard his name called, though in its new incarnation the Scourge still lacked a mouth. It needed none of course, when it could dabble in a man's head this way.

*I see you,*

it said. Or rather, that was the thought it placed in Shadwell's head, to which he put words.

*I see you. And I know your name.*

'That's what I want,' Shadwell said. 'I want you to know me. Trust me. *Believe* me.'

Sentiments like these had been part of his Salesman's spiel for more than half his life; he drew confidence from speaking them.

*You're not the first to come here,* the Scourge said. *Others have come. And gone.*

Shadwell knew all too well *where* they'd gone. He had a momentary glimpse – whether it was at the Scourge's behest or of his own making he couldn't be sure – of the bodies that were buried beneath the sand, their rot wasted on this dead garden. The thought should have made him afraid, but he'd felt all he was going to feel of fear, seeing the executions. Now, he would speak plainly, and hope the truth kept him from death.

'I came here for a reason,' he said.

*What reason?*

This was the moment. The customer had asked a question and he had to reply to it. No use to try and prevaricate or prettify, in the hope of securing a better sale. The plain truth was all he had to bargain with. On that, the sale was either won or lost. Best to simply state it.

'The Seerkind,' he said.

He felt the barbs in his brain twitch at the name, but there was no further response. The Scourge was silent. Even its wheels seemed to dim, as if at any moment the engine would flicker out.

Then, oh so quietly, it shaped the word in his head.

*Seer. Kind.*

And with the word came a spasm of energy, like lightning, that erupted in his skull. It was in the substance of the Scourge as well, this lightning. It flickered across the equation of its body. It ran back and forth in its eyes.

*Seerkind.*

'You know who they are?'

The sand hissed around Shadwell's feet.

*I had forgotten.*

'It's been a long time.'

*And you came here, to tell me?*

'To remind you.'

*Why?*

The barbs twitched again. It could kill me at any moment, Shadwell thought. It's nervous, and that makes it dangerous. I must be careful; play it cunningly. Be a salesman.

'They hid from you,' he said.

*Indeed.*

'All these years. Hid their heads so you'd never find them.'

*And now?*

'Now they're awake again. In the human world.'

*I had forgotten. But I'm reminded now. Oh yes. Sweet Shadwell.*

The barbs relaxed, and a wave of the purest pleasure broke over Shadwell, leaving him almost sick with the excess of it. It was a joy-bringer too, this Scourge. What power did not lie in its control?

'May I ask a question?' he said.

*Ask.*

'Who are you?'

The Scourge rose from its throne of sand, and in an instant it grew blindingly bright.

Shadwell covered his eyes, but the light shone through flesh and bone, and into his head, where the Scourge was pronouncing its eternal name.

*I am called Uriel,*

it said.

*Uriel, of the principalities.*

He knew the name, as he'd known by heart the rituals he'd heard at St Philomena's: and from the same source. As a child he'd learned the names of all the angels and archangels by heart: and amongst the mighty Uriel was of the mightiest. The archangel of salvation; called by some the flame of God. The sight of the executions replayed in his head – the bodies withering beneath that merciless fire: an *Angel's* fire. What had he done, stepping into the presence of such power? This was Uriel, of the principalities . . .

Another of the Angel's attributes rose from memory now, and with it a sudden shock of comprehension. Uriel had been the angel left to stand guard at the gates of Eden.

*Eden.*

At the word, the creature blazed. Though the ages had driven it to grief and forgetfulness, it was still an Angel: its fires unquenchable. The wheels of its body rolled, the visible mathematics of its essence turning on itself and preparing for new terrors.

*There were others here*, the Seraph said, *that called this place Eden. But I never knew it by that name.*

'What, then?' Shadwell asked.

*Paradise*, said the Angel, and at the word a new picture appeared in Shadwell's mind. It was the garden, in another age. No trees of sand then, but a lush jungle that brought to mind the flora that had sprung to life in the Gyre: the same profligate fecundity, the same unnamable species that seemed on the verge of defying their condition. Blooms that might at any moment take breath, fruit about to fly. There was none of the urgency of the Gyre here, however; the atmosphere was one of inevitable rising up, things aspiring at their own pace to some higher state, which was surely *light*, for everywhere between the trees brightnesses floated like living spirits.

*This was a place of making*, the Angel said. *For ever and ever. Where things came to be.*

'To be?'

*To find a form, and enter the world.*

'And Adam, and Eve?'

*I don't remember them,* Uriel replied.

'The first parents of humanity.'

*Humanity was raised from dirt in a thousand places, but not here. Here were higher spirits.*

'The Seerkind?' said Shadwell. 'Higher spirits?'

The Angel made a sour sound. The image of the paradise-garden convulsed, and Shadwell glimpsed furtive figures moving amongst the trees like thieves.

*They began here,* said the Angel; and in Shadwell's mind he saw the earth break open, and plants rise from it with human faces; and mist congeal . . . *But they were accidents. Droppings from greater stuff, that found life here. We did not know them, we spirits. We were about sublimer business.*

'And they grew?'

*Grew. And grew curious.*

Now Shadwell began to comprehend.

'They smelt the world,' he prompted.

The Angel shuddered, and again Shadwell was bombarded with images. He saw the forefathers of the Seerkind, naked, every one, their bodies all colours and sizes − a crowd of freakish forms − tails, golden eyes and cox-combs, flesh on one with the sheen of a panther; another with vestigial wings − he saw them scaling the wall, eager to be out of the garden −

'They escaped.'

*Nobody escapes me,* said Uriel. *When the spirits left, I remained here to keep watch until their return.*

That much, the Book of Genesis had been correct about: a guardian set at the gate. But little else, it seemed. The writers of that book had taken an image that mankind knew in its heart, and folded it into their narrative for their own moral purposes. What place God had here, if any, was perhaps as much a matter of definition as anything. Would the Vatican know this creature as an Angel, if it presented itself before the gates of that state? Shadwell doubted it.

'And the spirits?' he said. 'The others who were here?'

*I waited,* said the Angel.

And waited, and waited, thought Shadwell, until loneliness drove it mad. Alone in the wilderness, with the garden withering and rotting, and the sand breaking through the walls . . .

'Will you come with me now?' said Shadwell. 'I can lead you to the Seerkind.'

The Angel turned its gaze on Shadwell afresh.

*I hate the world,* it said. *I was there before, once.*

'But if I take you to them,' said Shadwell. 'You can do your duty, and be finished with it.'

Uriel's hatred of the Kingdom was like a physical thing; it chilled Shadwell's scalp. Yet the Angel didn't reject the offer, merely bided its time as it turned the possibility over. It wanted an end to its waiting, and soon. But its majesty was repulsed at the thought of contact with the human world. Like all pure things, it was vain, and easily spoiled.

*Perhaps . . .* it said.

Its gaze moved off Shadwell towards the wall. The Salesman followed its look, and there found Hobart. The man had taken the chance to creep away during the exchange with Uriel; but he'd not got far enough.

*. . . this time . . .* the Angel said, the light flickering in the concourse of its eyes, *. . . I will go . . .* The light was caught up by the wheels, and thrown out towards Hobart. *. . . in a different skin.*

With that, the entire engine flew apart, and not one but countless arrows of light fled towards Hobart. Uriel's gaze had bound him to the spot; he could not avoid the invasion. The arrows struck him from forehead to foot, their light entering him without breaking his skin.

In the space of a heart-beat all trace of the Angel had gone from the hill beside Shadwell; and with its disappearance into flesh came a new spectacle. A shudder ran through the ground from the wall where Hobart stood and through the garden. At its passage the sand forms began to decay, countless plants dropping into dust, avenues of trees shuddering and collapsing like arches in an earthquake. Watching the escalating destruction, Shadwell thought again of his first sight of the patterns in the dunes. Perhaps his assumptions then had been correct;

576

perhaps this place *was* in some way a sign to the stars. Uriel's pitiful way of recreating a lost glory, in the hope that some passing spirit would come calling, and remind it of itself.

Then the cataclysm grew too great, and he retreated before he was buried in a storm of sand.

Hobart was no longer on the garden's side of the breach, but had climbed the boulders, and stood looking out across the blank wastes of the desert.

There was no outward sign of Uriel's occupancy. To a casual eye this was the same Hobart. His gaunt features were as glacial as ever, and it was the same colourless voice that emerged when he spoke. But the question he posed told a different story.

'Am I the Dragon now?' he asked.

Shadwell looked at him. There was, he now saw, a brilliance in the hollows of Hobart's eyes that he'd not seen since he'd first seduced the man with promises of fire.

'Yes,' he said. 'You're the Dragon.'


They didn't linger. They began the trek back towards the border there and then, leaving the Empty Quarter emptier than ever.

## Part Eleven

# The Dream Season

'The sky is darkening like a stain,
Something is going to fall like rain
And it won't be flowers.'

W. H. Auden
*The Two*

# I

# PORTRAIT OF THE HERO
# AS A YOUNG LUNATIC

## 1

**W**hat's happened to Cal Mooney? the neighbours were saying: what an odd fellow he's become, full of half-smiles and sly glances. Mind you, weren't they always a peculiar family? The old man was related to a poet, I've heard, and you know what they say about poets: a little mad, all of them. And now the son's gone the same way. So sad. Funny the way people change isn't it?

The gossip rang true of course. Cal knew he *had* changed. And yes, he probably was a little mad. When he looked at himself in the mirror some mornings there was a wildness in his eyes which was no doubt distressing to the cashier at the supermarket, or the woman who tried to pry some potential scandal from him as they waited in line at the bank.

'Are you living alone then?'

'Yes,' he'd say.

'It's a big house for one. You must find it difficult cleaning.'

'No, not really.'

He'd get a quizzical look from the questioner. Then he'd say:

'I like dust,' knowing the remark would fuel the tittle-tattle, but unable to lie for their benefit. And he could see, as he spoke, the way they smiled inside, filing the remark away for regurgitation over the laundry.

Oh, he was Mad Mooney all right.

## 2

This time, there was no forgetting. His mind was too much a part of his lost Wonderland for it to slip away. The Fugue was with him all day, every day; and through the nights too.

But there was little joy in remembering. Only an all but unbearable ache of loss, knowing that a world which he'd longed for all his life was gone forever. He would never again tread its rapturous earth.

The how and why of this loss were somewhat hazy, particularly when it came to events in the Gyre. He recalled in some detail the battle at the Narrow Bright, and his plunging through the Mantle. But what had happened subsequently was just a series of disconnected images. Things sprouting, things dying; his blood, dancing down his arm in a little ecstasy; the brick at his back, trembling . . .

That was about all. The rest was so vague he could scarcely conjure a moment of it.

## 3

He knew he needed some diversion from his grief, or he'd simply dwindle into a melancholy from which there would be no emerging, so he looked around for a new job, and in early July got one: baking bread. The pay was not good, and the hours were anti-social, but he enjoyed the work – which was the antithesis of his labours at the insurance firm. He didn't have to talk much, or concern himself with office politics. There was no rising in the ranks here, just the plain business of dough and ovens. He was happy with the job. It gave him biceps like steel, and warm bread for his breakfast.

But the diversion was only temporary. His mind went back all too often to the source of his suffering, and suffered again. Such masochism was perhaps the nature of his species. Indeed that belief was supported by the reappearance of Geraldine in the middle of July. She turned up on the doorstep one day and stepped into the house as if nothing had ever happened between them. He was glad to see her.

This time, however, she didn't move in. They agreed that returning to that domestic status quo could only be a retrograde step. Instead she came and went through the summer on an almost daily basis, sometimes staying over at Chariot Street, more often not.

For nigh on five weeks she didn't ask him a single question about events the previous spring, and he in turn volunteered no information. When she eventually did raise the subject, however, it was in a manner and context he hadn't expected.

'Deke's telling everyone you've been in trouble with the police . . .' she said, ' . . . but I told him: not my Cal.'

He was sitting in Brendan's chair beside the window, watching the late summer sky. She was on the couch, amid a litter of magazines.

'I told them, you're no criminal. I know that. Whatever happened to you . . . it wasn't that kind of trouble. It was *deeper* than that, wasn't it?' She glanced across at him. Did she want a reply? It seemed not, for before he could open his mouth she was saying:

'I never understood what was going on, Cal, and maybe it's better I don't. But . . .' She stared down at the magazine open on her lap, then back up at him. 'You never used to talk in your sleep,' she said.

'And I do now?'

'All the time. You talk to people. You shout sometimes. Sometimes you just smile.' She was a little embarrassed confessing to this. She'd been watching him as he slept; and listening too. 'You've *been* somewhere, haven't you?' she said. 'You've seen something nobody else has.'

'Is that what I talk about?'

'In a sort of way. But that's not what makes me think you've seen things. It's the way you are, Cal. The way you look sometimes . . .'

That said, she seemed to reach an impasse, and returned her attention to the pages of the magazine, flipping the pages without really looking at them.

Cal sighed. She'd been so good with him, so protective: he owed her an explanation, however difficult it was.

'You want me to tell you?' he said.

'Yes. Yes, I do.'

'You won't believe it,' he warned.

'Tell me anyway.'

He nodded, and took up the story that he'd come so near to spilling the previous year, after his first visit to Rue Street.

'I saw Wonderland . . .' he began.

## 4

It took him three quarters of an hour to give her the outline of all that had happened since the bird had first flown from the loft; and another hour to try and fine-tune his account. Once begun, he found himself reluctant to leave anything out: he wanted to tell it all as best he could, as much for his own benefit as for Geraldine's.

She listened attentively, looking up at him sometimes, more often staring out of the window. Not once did she interrupt.

When he was finally finished, the wounds of bereavement reopened by the telling, she said nothing, not for a long time.

Finally he said: 'You don't believe me. I said you wouldn't.'

Again, there was silence. Then she said: 'Does it matter to you if I do or I don't?'

'Yes. Of course it matters.'

'Why, Cal?'

'Because then I'm not alone.'

She smiled at him, got up, and crossed to where he sat.

'You're not alone,' she said, and said no more.

Later, as they slipped into sleep together, she said:

'Do you love her? . . . Suzanna, I mean?'

He'd expected the question, sooner or later.

584

'Yes,' he said softly. 'In a way I can't explain; but yes.'

'I'm glad,' she murmured in the darkness. Cal wished he could read her features, and know from them if she was telling the truth, but he left any further questions unasked.

They didn't speak of it at all thereafter. She was no different with him than she'd been before he told her: it was almost as if she'd put the whole account out of her mind. She came and went on the same *ad hoc* basis. Sometimes they'd make love, sometimes not. And sometimes they'd be happy; or almost so.

The summer came and went without much disturbing the thermometer, and before the freckles had a chance to bloom on Geraldine's cheeks, it was September.

5

Autumn suits England; and that autumn, preceding as it would the worst winter since the late forties, came in glory. The winds were high, bringing passages of warm rain interspersed with stabs of liquid brightness. The city found a lost glamour. Clouds the colour of slate piled up behind its sunstruck houses; the wind brought the smell of the sea; brought gulls too, on its back, dipping and weaving over the roofs.

That month Cal felt his spirits rise again — seeing the King-dom of the Cuckoo shine, while above it the skies seemed charged with secret signs. He began to see faces in the shreds of clouds; heard codes tapped out by rain-drops on the sill. Something was surely imminent.

He remembered Gluck too, that month. Anthony Virgil Gluck, collector of anomalous phenomena. He even thought of contacting the man again, and went so far as to dig Gluck's card out from the pocket of his old trousers. He didn't make the call however, perhaps because he knew he was ripe to believe any pretty superstition if it promised miracles, and that wouldn't be wise.

Instead he kept his eye on the sky, day and night. He even bought himself a small telescope, and began to teach himself the whereabouts of the constellations. He found the process reassuring. It was good to look up during the day and know that the stars were still above his head, even though he couldn't see them. It was doubtless the same for countless other mysteries. That they shone, but the world shone more brightly, and blinded him to them.

And then, in the middle of October (the eighteenth, in fact; or rather, the early morning of the nineteenth) he had the first of the nightmares.

# II

## REPRESENTATIONS

### 1

Eight days after the destruction of the Fugue and all it had contained, the remnants of the Four Families – in all, maybe a hundred individuals – assembled to debate their future. Though they were survivors, they had little reason to celebrate the fact. With the Weaveworld's passing they'd lost their homes, their possessions, and in many cases their loved ones too. All they had, as reminders of their former happiness, was a handful of raptures, much weakened with the Fugue's defeat. These were small comfort. Raptures could not wake the dead, nor keep the corruptions of the Kingdom at bay.

So; what were they to do? There was a voluble faction – led by Balm de Bono – that argued to make their story public; to become, in essence, a *cause*. There was merit in the idea. Perhaps the safest place to be *was* in plain sight of the human world. But there was substantial opposition to the scheme, fuelled by the one possession circumstance could not take from these people: pride. Many of them stated bluntly that they'd rather die than throw themselves on the mercy of Cuckoos.

Suzanna had a further problem with the idea. Though her fellow humans might be persuaded to believe the Kind's tale, and sympathize, how long would their compassion last? Months?; a year, at most. Then they'd turn their attention to some new tragedy. The Seerkind would be yesterday's victims, tainted by celebrity but scarcely saved by it.

587

The combination of her argument and the widespread horror at humbling themselves to the Cuckoos was sufficient to outweigh the opposition. Determined to be civilized in defeat, de Bono conceded.

It was the last time the etiquette of debate shaped the night's proceedings, as the meeting grew steadily more heated. The escalation began with a call from a harried, grey-faced man that they put aside all pretence to bettering their lot and concentrate on revenging themselves on Shadwell.

'We've lost everything,' he said. 'The only satisfaction we've got left is seeing that bastard dead.'

There were voices raised in protest against this defeatism, but the man demanded the right to be heard.

'We're going to die out here,' he said, his face knotted up. 'All we've got left are a few *moments* . . . to destroy the ones who did this to us.'

'Seems to me this is no time for a vendetta,' Nimrod said. 'We have to think constructively. Plan for the future.'

There was some ironic laughter amongst the gathering, above which the voice of the would-be avenger rose:

'*What future?*' he said, almost triumphant in his despair. 'Look at us!' There were many downcast eyes at this; they knew all too well what a forlorn sight they made. 'We're the last of the few. There won't be any coming after us, and we all know it.' He turned on Nimrod. 'I don't want to talk about the future,' he said. 'That's just asking for more grief.'

'That's not true – ' Suzanna said.

'Easy for you to say,' he retorted.

'Shut your mouth, Hamel,' Nimrod shouted.

'I won't!'

'She came here to help us.'

'We've had enough help from her to kill us!' Hamel yelled back.

His pessimism had found a good number of supporters.

'She's a Cuckoo,' one of them now piped up. 'Why doesn't she go back where she belongs?'

Part of Suzanna was ready to do just that: she had no desire to be the target for so much bitterness. Their words stung.

More than that, they stirred another fear: that somehow she *could* have done more than she had; or at least done it differently. But she had to stay, for de Bono, and Nimrod, and all the others who looked to her for guidance in the Kingdom. The fact was that all Hamel had argued made a sad sense to her. She could see how easy it would be to take strength from hating Shadwell, and so be diverted from the losses they'd sustained. *They* more than she, of course; and that thought she had to keep uppermost in her mind. *She'd* lost a dream she'd had a few precious moments to indulge. They'd lost their world.

A new voice now entered the controversy; one she was surprised to hear: that of Apolline. Suzanna hadn't even been aware of the woman's presence in the room until she rose from a cloud of tobacco smoke and addressed the company.

'I'm not going to lie down and die for anyone,' she said. 'Especially not you, Hamel.'

Her defiance echoed that of Yolande Dor, back in Capra's House: it seemed always to be the women who argued most vehemently for life.

'What about Shadwell?' somebody said.

'What *about* him?' said Apolline. 'You want to go kill him, Hamel? I'll buy you a bow and arrow!'

The remark won over-enthusiastic laughter from some quarters, but only served to infuriate the opposition more.

'We're practically extinct, sister,' Hamel replied, his scorn lavish. 'And you're not too fertile these days.'

Apolline took the taunt in good humour.

'Want to try me?' she said.

Hamel's lips curled at the suggestion.

'I had a wife – ' he said.

Apolline, taking her usual pleasure in offending, jiggled her hips at Hamel, who spat in her direction. He should have known better. She spat back, only more accurately. Though the missile was harmless enough he responded as though he'd been stabbed, throwing himself towards Apolline with a cry of rage. Somebody got between them before he could land a blow, and he struck out instead at the peace-maker. The assault ended any lingering pretence to civilized debate: the whole assembly began shouting and arguing, while Hamel and the other man traded punches amongst the overturned chairs. It was Apolline's pimp who parted them. Though the fight had lasted no more than a minute, both had taken a beating, and were bleeding at mouth and nose.

Suzanna watched with a heavy heart as Nimrod attempted to calm proceedings. There was so much she wanted to talk with the Kind about: problems upon which she needed their advice; secrets – tender and difficult – which she wanted to share. But while things were so volatile she feared voicing these matters would simply be further fuel for dissension.

Hamel took his leave, cursing Suzanna, Apolline and all who – as he put it – 'sided with the shit'. He didn't go unaccompanied. Two dozen left with him.

There was no serious attempt to return to the debate after this eruption; the meeting had effectively been brought to a halt. No one was in any mood to make balanced decisions, nor were they likely to be so, at least until a little time had passed. It was concluded, therefore, that the survivors would disperse, and lie low in any safe place they could find. There were so few of them left that melting amongst the populous would not prove too difficult. They'd wait out the winter, until the reverberations had died down.

2

Suzanna parted from Nimrod after the meeting, leaving instructions with him as to her whereabouts in London. She was exhausted; she needed to rest her head awhile.

After two weeks back at home, however, she discovered that attempting to restore her energies by doing nothing was a sure route to lunacy, and instead returned to work at the studio. It proved a wise move. The problems of re-establishing a working rhythm distracted her from dwelling too much on the losses and failures of recent times; and the very fact of *making* something – even if it was only pots and plates –

590

answered the need she had to begin again. She'd never been so aware of clay's mythic associations as now, of its reputation as the first stuff, the base matter from which story-book nations had taken shape. Her skill could only manage pots not people, but worlds had to begin somewhere. She worked long hours, with just the radio and the smell of the clay for company, her thoughts never completely free of melancholy, but lighter than she'd dared hope.

Hearing that she was back in town, Finnegan appeared on her doorstep one afternoon, spruce as ever, to invite her out to dinner. It was strange to think of his waiting for her while she'd been adventuring; and touching too. She accepted his invitation, and was more thoroughly charmed by his company than she ever remembered being. He, forthright as ever, said that they were made for each other, and should marry immediately. She told him she made a rule of never marrying bankers. The next day he sent flowers, and a note saying that he'd relinquish his profession. They saw each other regularly thereafter. His warmth and easy manner were the perfect diversion from the darker thoughts that still threatened to intrude when she had time to think.

Every now and then, through the summer months and into the early autumn, she had some brief contact with members of the Kind, though they were kept to the minimum, for safety's sake. The news seemed to be good. Many of the survivors had returned to the vicinity of their ancestors' homes, and found niches there.

Better news still, there was no sign of either Shadwell or Hobart. There were rumours that Hamel had instigated a search for the Salesman, and had given up after failing to uncover a single clue as to the enemy's whereabouts. As for the remnants of his army – those Seerkind who'd embraced the Prophet's visions – they'd been the authors of their own punishment, waking from their evangelical nightmare to find it had destroyed all they held dear.

Some had sought forgiveness from their fellows, and had arrived, shamefaced and despairing, at that controversial meeting. Others, the grapevine confirmed, had been overcome by remorse, and had spiralled into dereliction. Some had even taken their own lives. There were yet others, she'd heard – the born blood-letters amongst the Kind – who'd left the battlefield regretting nothing, and gone out into the Kingdom in search of further violence. They would not have to look far.

But rumour and supposition apart, there was little to report. She got on with trying to make sense of her old life, while they made new lives for themselves. As to Cal, she followed his rehabilitation through Kind who'd gone to ground in Liverpool, but made no direct contact. This was in part a practical decision: it was wiser that they kept their distance from each other until they were certain the enemy had disappeared. But it was also an emotional consideration. They had shared much, in the Fugue and out. Too much to be lovers. The Weaveworld occupied the space between them – it had from the beginning. That fact made a nonsense of any thought of a domestic or romantic arrangement. They'd seen Hell and Heaven together. After that, surely everything else was bathos.

Presumably Cal felt the same, because he made no attempt at contacting her. Not that it was necessary. Though they neither saw nor spoke to each other she felt his constant presence. She had been the one to nip in the bud any possibility of physical love between them, and she had sometimes regretted that; but what they shared now was perhaps the highest aspiration of all lovers: between them they held a world.

3

In the middle of October her work started to take a new and completely uncharacteristic turn. For no particular reason she forsook her plates and bowls and began to work figuratively. The results gained her few admirers, but they satisfied some inner imperative which would not be gainsaid.

Meanwhile, Finnegan pressed his suit with dinners and flowers, his attentions redoubling each time she politely rejected him. She began to think there was more than a streak of the masochist in his nature, coming back as he did each time she sent him on his way.

Of all the extraordinary times she'd had since she'd first become part of the Fugue's story, these were in their way the strangest, as her experience of the Weaveworld and that of her present life did battle in her head for the right to be called real. She knew this was Cuckoo thinking; that they were *both* real. But her mind would not marry them – nor her place in them. What did the woman Finnegan proclaimed his love for – the smiling, clay beneath the fingers Suzanna – have to do with the woman who'd stood face to face with dragons? She came to wish she couldn't evoke those mythic times as well as she could, because afterwards she'd feel sick with the triviality of being herself.

For that reason she kept a rein on the menstruum, which was not difficult to do. Its once unpredictable nature was much tamed now; a consequence of the Fugue's demise, she assumed. It hadn't foresaken her entirely. Sometimes it seemed to get restless, and decided to stretch itself, usually – though it took her a little time to realize this – in response to some environmental cue. There were places in the Kingdom that were charged up; places where she sensed a spring beneath the earth, aching to fountain. The menstruum knew them. So, in some cases, did the Cuckoos, sanctifying the spots as best their myopia knew how: with steeples and monuments. Just as many of these territories remained unrecognized, however, and passing through some unremarkable street she'd feel a surge in her belly, and know power was buried there.

Most of her life she'd associated power with politics or money, but her secret self had learned better. Imagination was true power: it worked transformations wealth and influence never could. She saw its processes even in Finnegan. On the few occasions she coaxed him to talk about his past, particularly his childhood, she saw the colours around his head strengthen and ripen, as in the act of imagining he was reunited with himself; made a continuum. At those moments she'd remember the line from Mimi's book:

*That which is imagined need never be lost.*
And on those days she was even happy.

4

Then, early in the third week of December, any fragile hope of good times abruptly came to an end.

The weather turned icy that week. Not just bitter, but arctic. There was no snow as yet, just a cold so profound the nerve-endings couldn't tell it from fire. She still worked on in the studio, unwilling to give up her creating, though her paraffin heater could barely raise the temperature above zero, and she was obliged to wear two sweaters and three pairs of socks. She scarcely noticed. She'd never been so preoccupied with making as she was now, bullying the clay into the shapes in her mind's eye.

Then, on the seventeenth, completely without warning, Apolline came calling. The eternal widow, she was swathed in black from head to foot.

'We have to speak,' she said, as soon as the door was closed.

Suzanna escorted her through to the studio, and cleared a seat for her amid the chaos. She didn't want to sit, however, but wandered around the room, eventually ending up at the frost-scoured windows, peering out of them while Suzanna rinsed the clay from her hands.

'Are you being followed?' Suzanna asked her.

'I don't know,' came the reply. 'Maybe.'

'Do you want some coffee?'

'I'd prefer something stronger. What have you got?'

'Just brandy.'

'Just brandy will do.'

She sat. Suzanna located the bottle she kept for her occasional one-woman parties, and put an ample measure in a cup. Apolline drained it, filled it a second time, then said:

'Have you had the dreams?'

'What dreams?'

'We've all been having them,' Apolline said.

The way she looked – face sallow despite the cold, eyes ringed with darkness – Suzanna wondered that she'd had any sleep at all of late.

'Terrible dreams,' the widow went on, 'like the end of the world.'

'Who's been having them?'

'Who hasn't?' said Apolline. 'Everyone, the same thing. The same appalling thing.'

She'd drained her cup a second time, and now took the bottle from the bench for a further shot.

'Something bad's going to happen. We can all feel it. That's why I've come.'

Suzanna watched her while she poured herself more brandy, her mind posing two quite separate questions. First: were these nightmares simply the inevitable result of the horrors the Seerkind had endured, or something more? And – if the latter – why hadn't *she* had them too?

Apolline interrupted these thoughts, her words slightly slurred by her intake of alcohol.

'People are saying it's the Scourge. That it's coming for us again, after all this time. Apparently this is the way it first made its presence known before. In dreams.'

'And you think they're right?'

Apolline winced as she swallowed another throatful of brandy.

'Whatever it is, we have to protect ourselves.'

'Are you suggesting some kind of . . . offensive?'

Apolline shrugged. 'Don't know,' she said. 'Maybe. Most of them are so damn *passive*. It sickens me, how they lie back and take whatever comes their way. Worse than whores.'

She stopped, and sighed heavily. Then said:

'Some of the younger ones have got it into their heads that maybe we can raise the Old Science.'

'To what purpose?'

'To finish off the Scourge, of course!' she snapped, 'before it finishes us.'

'How do you estimate our chances?'

'A little better than zero,' Apolline grunted. 'Jesus, I don't know! At least we're wise to it this time. That's something. Some of us are going back to the places where there was some power, to see if we can dredge up anything useful.'

'After all these years?

'Who's counting?' she said. 'Raptures don't age.'

'So what are we looking for?'

'Signs. Prophecies. God knows.'

She put down her cup, and traipsed back to the window, rubbing at the frost with the ball of her gloved hand to clear a spy-hole. She peered out, then made a ruminative grunt before once more turning her narrowed eyes on Suzanna.

'You know what I think?' she announced.

'What?'

'I think you're keeping something from us.'

Suzanna said nothing, which won a second grunt from Apolline.

'I thought so,' she said. 'You think we're our own worst enemies, eh? Not to be trusted with secrets?' Her gaze was black and bright. 'You may be right,' she said. 'We fell for Shadwell's performance, didn't we? At least some of us did.'

'You didn't?'

'I had distractions,' she answered. 'Business in the Kingdom. Come to that, I still do . . .' Her voice trailed off. 'I thought I could turn my back on the rest of them, you see. Ignore them and be happy. But I can't. In the end . . . I think I must *belong* with them, God help me.'

'We came so close to losing everything,' said Suzanna.

'We *did* lose,' said Apolline.

'Not quite.'

The interrogating eyes grew sharper; and Suzanna teetered on the edge of pouring out all that had happened to Cal and herself in the Gyre. But Apolline's appraisal was accurate: she *didn't* trust them with their own miracles. Her instinct told her

596

to keep her account of the Loom to herself for a while longer. So instead of spilling the story she said:

'At least we're still alive.'

Apolline, undoubtedly sensing that she'd come close to a revelation and been denied it, spat on the floor.

'Small comfort,' she said. 'We're reduced to digging around in the Kingdom for some sniff of rapture. It's pitiful.'

'So what can I do to help?'

Apolline's expression was almost venomous; nothing would have given her greater satisfaction, Suzanna guessed, than walking out on this devious Cuckoo.

'We're not enemies,' said Suzanna.

'Are we not?'

'You *know* we're not. I want to do whatever I can for you.'

'So you say,' Apolline replied, without much conviction. She looked away towards the window, her tongue ferreting in her cheek for a polite word. 'Do you know this wretched city well?' she said finally.

'Pretty well.'

'So you could go looking, could you? Around and about.'

'I could. *I will.*'

Apolline dug a scrap of paper from her pocket, torn from a notebook.

'Here are some addresses,' she said.

'And where will you be?'

'Salisbury. There was a massacre there, back before the Weave. One of the cruellest, in fact; a hundred children died. I might sniff something out.'

Her attention had suddenly been claimed by the shelves on which Suzanna had put some of her recent work. She went to it, her skirts trailing in the clay dust.

'I thought you said you hadn't been dreaming?' she remarked.

Suzanna scanned the row of pieces. She'd been immersed in their making for so long she'd scarcely been conscious of their potency, or indeed the consistency of the obsession behind them. Now she saw them with fresh eyes. They were all human figures, but twisted out of true, as though (the thought came with a pricking of the scalp) they were at the heart of some devouring fire; caught in the instant before it erased their faces. Like all of her current work they were unglazed, and roughly rendered. Was that because their tragedy was as yet unwritten: simply an idea in the fermenting mind of the future?

Apolline took one of the figures down, and ran her thumb over its contorted features.

'You've been dreaming with your eyes open,' she commented, and Suzanna knew without a shadow of a doubt that it was true.

'It's a good likeness,' the widow said.

'Of whom?'

Apolline set the tragic mask back on the shelf.

'Of us all.'

# III

## NO LULLABIES

### 1

Cal had been sleeping alone when he had the first of the nightmares.

It began on Venus Mountain; he was wandering there, his legs ready to give out beneath him. But with that horrid foreknowledge of disaster that dreams grant he knew it would not be wise to close his eyes and sleep. Instead he stood on the warm ground while forms that were lit as if by a sun that had already set behind the mountain moved around him. A man was dancing nearby, his skirts like living tissue; a girl flew over, trailing the scent of her sex; there were lovers in the long grass, coupling. One of them cried out, whether in pleasure or alarm he wasn't certain, and the next moment he was running over the mountainside, and there was something coming after him, something vast and remorseless.

He shouted as he ran, to alert the lovers and the bird-girl and the dancer to the horror that had come for them all, but his voice was pitifully thin – the voice of a mouse – and the next moment the grass around him began to smoulder. Before his eyes the coupling bodies now burst into flames; an instant later the girl fell out of the sky, her body consumed by the same venomous fire. Again, he shouted, in terror this time, trying to leap over the flames as they advanced across the ground in his direction. But he wasn't agile enough. His heels caught fire, and he felt the heat creep up the back of his legs as he ran.

Howling now, he found an extra burst of speed, and suddenly Venus Mountain was gone, and he was running barefoot down streets he'd known since childhood. It was night, but the lamps along the street had been smashed, and the paving stones torn up beneath his feet made the going treacherous.

Still the pursuer came after him, sniffing his carbonized heels.

Knowing it would outpace him given time, he looked for some place of sanctuary as he ran, but the doors of the houses – even those of childhood friends – were nailed shut, the windows boarded up.

There was no help to be had here. All he could do was keep running, in the vain hope that the monster would be distracted by more tempting quarry.

An alleyway caught his eye; he ducked down it. Made a turn, made another turn. Ahead, a brick wall, and in it, a door, through which he hurled himself. Only then did he realize where this inevitable route had taken him.

He knew the yard at once, though the wall had grown twice as high since he'd last been here, and the gate through which he'd stepped a moment ago had sealed itself up. It was the yard behind Mimi Laschenski's house. Once, in another life, he'd stood on that wall, and toppled, and fallen, finally, into paradise.

But there was no carpet in the yard now, nor any presence, bird or man, to offer their consolation. Just him, and the four shadowy corners of the yard, and the sound of his pursuer approaching the hiding place.

He took refuge in one of the corners and crouched down. Though the heels beneath his buttocks had been extinguished, his panic had not; he felt sick with fear.

The monster approached. He smelt the heat off its hide. It wasn't the heat of *life* – not sweat or breath – but a dry, dead fire; ancient, merciless; an oven in which all the good of the world might be cremated. And it was close. Just beyond the wall.

He held his breath. There was a crippling ache in his bladder. He put his hands between his legs, cupping his prick and balls, shaking with terror. Make it go away, he silently pleaded to the darkness: make it leave me alone and I'll be good as gold forever: I swear I will.

Though he could scarcely believe his luck, his appeal was heard, for the presence on the other side of the wall gave up its pursuit and retreated. His spirits lifted a little, but he kept his cramped position until his dream-sense told him that the enemy had withdrawn entirely. Only then did he dare stand up again, his joints cracking.

The pressure in his bladder would no longer be denied. Turning to the wall, he unzipped himself. The brick was hot from the presence of the creature, and his piss hissed against it.

In mid-flow, the sun came out, suddenly, flooding the yard. No, it wasn't the sun. It was his pursuer, rising over the wall, its head hotter than a hundred noons, its oven-maw open wide.

He could not help but look into its face, though it would surely blind him. He saw enough eyes for a nation, pressed side by side, set on great wheels, their nerves drawn out like bright threads and knotted in the belly of the creature. There was more, much more, but he only glimpsed it before the heat set him alight from head to toe-nail.

He shrieked.

And with the cry, the yard disappeared, and he was travelling again on Venus Mountain, only this time the landscape beneath him was not earth and rock, but flesh and bone. It was his own body he was flying over, his substance become a world, and it was burning up, burning to extinction. His shriek was the land's shriek, and it rose and rose as he and it were utterly consumed.

*Too much!*

He woke suddenly to find himself curled up in the middle of the bed, a knot of dreamt agony. He was sweating so much surely the fire would have been extinguished.

But no. It burned on in his mind's eye for minutes afterwards, still bright.

## 2

It was more than a nightmare, he knew; it had the potency of a vision. After that first visit there was a blank night, then it came again, and again the night after. The particulars were altered somewhat (a different street, a different prayer) but it was in essence the same warning; or *prophecy*.

There was a gap of several days before the fourth dream, and this time Geraldine was with him. Though she made every attempt to wake him – he was howling, she said – he could not be roused until the dream was over. Only then did he open his eyes to find her sobbing with panic.

'I thought you were dying,' she said, and he half believed she was right; that his heart would not bear many more of these terrors before it burst.

It was not just *his* death the vision promised, however; it was that of the people on Venus Mountain, who seemed to occupy his very substance. A catastrophe was coming, that would lay waste those few Seerkind who had survived; who were, in their way, as intimate to him as his own flesh. That was what the dream told.


He lived through November in fear of sleep, and what it would bring. The nights were growing longer, the portions of light shrinking. It was as if the year itself was sliding into sleep, and in the mind of the night that would follow the substance of his dream was taking shape. A week into December, with the nightmare coming almost as soon as he closed his eyes, he knew he had to speak to Suzanna. Find her, and tell her what he was seeing.

But how? Her letter to him had been quite clear: she would contact him when it was safe to do so. He had no address for her; nor a telephone number.

In desperation, he turned to the only source of intelligence he had on the whereabouts of miracles.

He found Virgil Gluck's card, and rang the number on it. There was no reply.

# IV

## THE SHRINE OF THE MORTALITIES

### 1

The day after Apolline's visit – with polar conditions moving down across the country, and the temperature dropping hourly – Suzanna went out to look at the sites on the list. The first of them proved a disappointment: the house she'd come to see, and those adjacent to it, were in the process of being demolished. As she studied her map, to be certain she'd come to the correct address, one of the workmen left a fire of roof-timbers he was tending and sauntered across to her.

'There's nothing to see,' he said. There was a look of distaste on his face which she couldn't fathom.

'Is this where number seventy-two stood?' she asked.

'You don't look the type,' he replied.

'I'm sorry, I don't – '

'To come looking.'

She shook her head. He seemed to see that he'd made an error of some kind, and his expression mellowed.

'You didn't come to see the murder house?' he said.

'Murder house?'

'This is where that bastard did his three kiddies in. There've been people here all week, picking up bricks – '

'I didn't know.'

She vaguely remembered the grim headlines, however: an apparently sane man – and loving father – had murdered his children while they slept; then killed himself.

604

'My mistake,' said the fire-watcher. 'Couldn't believe some of these people, wanting souvenirs. It's unnatural.'

He frowned at her, then turned away and headed back to his duties.

*Unnatural.* That was the way Violet Pumphrey had condemned Mimi's house in Rue Street; Suzanna had never forgotten it. '*Some houses*,' she'd said, '*they're not quite natural.*' She'd been right. Perhaps the children who'd died here had been victims of that same unfocused fear; their killer moved either to preserve them forever from the forces he felt at work in his little sphere, or else wash his own fear away in their blood. Whichever, unless she could read auguries in smoke or rubble, there was no sense in lingering.

## 2

The second site, which was in the centre of the city, was neither house nor rubble, but a church, its dedicatees Saints Philomena and Callixtus, two names she was not at all familiar with. Minor martyrs, presumably. It was a charmless building of red brick and stone dressing, hedged in on every side by new office developments, the small accompanying graveyard littered and forsaken. In its way it looked as unpromising as the ruins that had been the murderer's house.

But before she even stepped over the threshold the menstruum told her that this was one of the *charged* places. Inside, that instinct was confirmed: she was delivered from a cold, bland street into a haven for mysteries. She didn't need to be a believer to find the candlelight and smell of incense persuasive; nor to be touched by the image of Madonna and Christ-child. Whether their story was history or myth was academic; the Fugue had taught her that. All that mattered was how loudly the image spoke, and today she found in it a hope for birth and transcendence her heart needed.

There were half a dozen people sitting in the pews, either praying or simply letting their pulses slow a little. Out of respect for their meditations she walked as quietly as the stone underfoot would allow down one of the side-aisles to the altar. As she approached the chancel rail her sense that there was power here intensified. She felt self-conscious as though somebody had their eyes on her. She looked round. None of the worshippers was looking her way. But as she turned back towards the altar, the floor beneath her feet grew insubstantial, then vanished entirely, and she was left standing on the air, staring down into the labyrinthine bowels of St Philomena's. There were catacombs laid out below; the power was sourced there.

The vision lasted two or three seconds only before it flickered out, leaving her hanging onto the rail until the vertigo it had brought with it passed. Then she looked about her for a door that would offer her access to the crypt.

There was only one likely option that she could see, off to the left of the altar. She climbed the steps, and was crossing to the door when it opened and a priest stepped through.

'Can I help you?' he wanted to know, offering up a wafer-thin smile.

'I want to see the crypt,' she said.

The smile snapped. 'There isn't one,' he replied.

'But I've seen it,' she told him, pressed to bluntness by the fact that the menstruum had risen in her as she'd crossed beneath Christ's gaze, unnerving her with its eagerness.

'Well, you can't go down. The crypt's sealed.'

'I have to,' she told him.

The heat of her insistence brought a stare of something like recognition from him. When he spoke again his voice was an anxious whisper.

'I've got no authority,' he said.

'*I* have,' she answered, the response coming not from her head, but from her belly.

'Couldn't you wait?' he murmured. The words were his last appeal, for when she chose not to reply he stood aside, and allowed her to walk past him into the room beyond.

'You want me to show you?' he said, his voice now barely audible.

'Yes.'

He led her to a curtain, which he drew aside. The key was in the lock of the door. He turned it, and pushed the door open. The air that rose from below was dry and stale, the stairway before her steep; but she was not afraid. The call she felt from below coaxed her down, whispering its encouragement. This was no grave they were entering. Or if it was, the dead had more than rot on their minds.

## 3

Her glimpse of the maze beneath the church hadn't prepared her for how far below ground level it actually lay. The light from the baptistery rapidly faded as the staircase wound its way down. After two dozen steps she could not see her guide at all.

'How much further?' she said.

At that moment, he struck a match and set it to a candle-wick. The flame was reluctant in the feeble air, but by its uncertain light she saw the priest's fretful face turned towards her. Beyond him were the corridors she'd first viewed from above, lined with niches.

'There's nothing here,' he said, with some sadness. 'Not any longer.'

'Show me anyway.'

He nodded weakly, as though he'd lost entirely the strength to resist her, and led her down one of the passageways, carrying the candle before him. The niches, she now saw, were all occupied: caskets piled from floor to ceiling. It was a pleasant enough way to decay, she supposed, cheek by jowl with your peers. The very civility of the sight lent greater force to the scene that awaited her when, at the end of the passageway, he opened a door, and – ushering her before him – said:

'This is what you came to see, isn't it?'

She stepped inside; he followed. Such was the size of the room they'd entered that the meagre candle-flame was not equal to illuminating it. But there were no caskets here, that much was apparent. There were only bones – and those there were in their thousands, covering every inch of the walls and ceiling.

The priest crossed the room and put the candle to a dozen wicks set in candelabra of femur and skull pan. As the flames brightened the full ambition of the bone-arranger's skills became apparent. The mortal remains of hundreds of human beings had been used to create vast symmetrical designs: baroque configurations of shin and rib, with clusters of skulls as their centre pieces; exquisite mosaics of foot and finger bones, set off with teeth and nails. It was all the more ghastly because it was so meticulously rendered, the work of some morbid genius.

'What is this place?' she asked.

He frowned at her, perplexed.

'You know what it is. The Shrine.'

' . . . shrine?'

He moved towards her.

'You *didn't* know?'

'No.'

Rage and fear suddenly ignited his face. 'You *lied* to me!' he said, his voice setting the candles fluttering. 'You said you knew – ' He snatched hold of her arm. 'Get out of here,' he demanded, dragging her back towards the door. 'You're trespassing –'

His grip hurt her. It was all she could do to stop the menstruum retaliating. As it was, there was no need, for the priest's gaze suddenly left her, and strayed to the candles. The flames had grown brighter, their jittering manic. His hand dropped from her arm, and he began to back away towards the door of the Shrine, as the flickering fires became incandescent. His short-cropped hair was literally standing on end; his tongue lolled in his open mouth, robbed of exclamation.

She didn't share his terror. Whatever was happening in the chamber, it felt *good* to her; she bathed in the energies that were loose in the air around her head. The priest had reached the door, and now fled down the passageway towards the stairs. As he did so the caskets began to rattle in their brick niches, as if their contents wanted to be up to meet the day that was dawning in the Shrine. Their drumming lent fervour to the spectacle before her. In the centre of the chamber a form was beginning to appear, drawing its substance from the dust-filled air, and the bone-shards that lay on the floor. Suzanna could feel it plucking flecks from her face and arms, to add to its sum. It was not one shape, she now saw, but three; the central figure towering over her. Common sense might have counselled retreat, but unlikely as it seemed, given that death surrounded her on all sides, she'd seldom felt safer.

That sense of ease didn't falter. The dust moved in front of her in a slow dance, more soothing than distressing, the two flanking shapes forsaking their creation before they became coherent and running into the central figure to lend it new solidity. Even then it was only a dust-ghost, barely able to hold itself together. But in the features that were taking shape before her Suzanna could see traces of Immacolata.

What more perfect place for the Incantatrix to keep her Shrine? Death had always been her passion.

The priest was scrabbling for a prayer in the passageway outside, but the grey, glittering smudge that hung in the air in front of Suzanna was unmoved. Its features had elements of not one but all three sisters. The Hag's senility; the Magdalene's sensuality; the exquisite symmetry of Immacolata. Unlikely as it seemed, the synthesis worked; the marriage of contradictions rendered both more tenuous and more pliant by the delicacy of its construction. It seemed to Suzanna that if she breathed too hard she'd undo it.

And then the voice. That, at least, was recognizably Immacolata's, but there was a softness in it now that it had previously lacked. Perhaps, even, a delicate humour?

'We're glad you came,' she said. 'Will you request the Adamatical to leave? We have business to do, you and I.'

'What sort of business?'

'It's not for his ears,' the mote ghost said. 'Please. Help him to his feet, will you? And tell him there's no harm done. They're so superstitious, these men . . .'

She did as Immacolata asked: went down the drumming corridor to where the man was cowering, and drew him to his feet.

'I think maybe you should leave,' she said. 'The Lady wants it.'

The priest gave her a sickened look.

'All this time – ' he said. ' – I never really believed.'

'It's all right,' she said. 'There's no damage done.'

'Are you coming too?'

'No.'

'I can't come back for you,' he warned her, tears spilling down his cheeks.

'I understand,' she said. 'You go on. I'm safe.'

He needed no further urging, but was off up the stairs like a jack rabbit. She returned down the passageway – the caskets still rattling – to face the woman.

'I thought you were dead,' she said.

'What's dead?' Immacolata replied. 'A word the Cuckoos use when the flesh fails. It's nothing, Suzanna; you know that.'

'Why are you here, then?'

'I've come to pay a debt to you. In the Temple, you kept me from falling, or have you forgotten?'

'No.'

'Nor I. Such kindnesses are not negligible. I understand that now. I understand many things. You see how I'm reunited with my sisters? Together we're as we could never be apart. A single mind, three-in-one. *I* am *we*; and we see our malice, and regret it.'

Suzanna might well have doubted this unlikely confession but that the menstruum, brimming at her eyes and throat, confirmed the truth of it. The wraith before her – and the power behind it – had no hatred on its mind. What *did* it have? There was the question. She didn't need to ask; it knew her question.

'I'm here with a warning,' it said.

'About what? Shadwell?'

'He's only a part of what you now face, sister. A fragment.'

610

'Is it the Scourge?'

The phantom shuddered at the name, though surely its state put it beyond the reach of such dangers. Suzanna didn't wait for confirmation. There was no use disbelieving the worst now.

'Is Shadwell something to do with the Scourge?' she asked.

'He raised it.'

'Why?'

'He thinks magic has tainted him,' the dust said. 'Corrupted his innocent salesman's soul. Now he won't be content until every rapture-maker's dead.'

'And the Scourge is his weapon?'

'So he believes. The truth may be more . . . complex.'

Suzanna ran her hand down over her face, her mind seeking the best route of enquiry. One simple question occurred:

'What kind of creature is this Scourge?'

'The answer's perhaps just another question,' said the sisters. 'It *thinks* that it's called Uriel.'

'Uriel?'

'An Angel.'

Suzanna almost laughed at the absurdity of this.

'That's what it believes, having read the Bible.'

'I don't follow.'

'Most of this is beyond even our comprehension, but we offer you what we know. It's a spirit. And it once stood guard over a place where magic was. A garden, some have said, though that may be simply another fiction.'

'Why should it want to wipe the Seerkind out?'

'They were made there, in that garden, kept from the eyes of Humankind, because they had raptures. But they fled from it.'

'And Uriel — '

' — was left alone, guarding an empty place. For centuries.'

Suzanna was by no means certain she believed any of this, but she wanted to hear the story completed.

'What happened?'

'It went mad, as any prisoner of duty must, left without

611

fresh instructions. It forgot itself, and its purpose. All it knew was sand and stars and emptiness.'

'You should understand . . .' said Suzanna. 'I find all this difficult to believe, not being a Christian.'

'Neither are we,' said the three-in-one.

'But you still think the story's true?'

'We believe there's truth *inside* it, yes.'

The reply made her think again of Mimi's book, and all it contained. Until she'd entered its pages the realm of Faery had seemed child's play. But facing Hobart in the forest of their shared dreams, she'd learned differently. There'd been truth inside *that* story: why not this too? The difference was that the Scourge occupied the same physical world as she did. Not metaphor, not dream-stuff; *real*.

'So it forgot itself,' she said to the phantom. 'How then did it remember?'

'Perhaps it never has,' said Immacolata. 'But its home was found, a hundred years back, by men who'd gone looking for Eden. In their heads it read the story of the paradise garden and took it for its own, whether it was or not. It found a name too. *Uriel, flame of God. The spirit who stood at the gates of lost Eden –*'

'And was it Eden? The place it guarded?'

'You don't believe that any more than I do. But Uriel does. Whatever its true name is – if it even has one – that name's forgotten. It believes itself an Angel. So, for better or worse, it is.'

The notion made sense to Suzanna, in its way. If, in the dream of the book, she'd believed herself a dragon, why shouldn't something lost in madness take an Angel's name?

'It murdered its discoverers, of course – ' Immacolata was saying, ' – then went looking for those who'd escaped it.'

'The Families.'

'Or their descendants. And it almost wiped them out. But they were clever. Though they didn't understand the power that pursued them, they knew how to *hide*. The rest you're familiar with.'

'And Uriel? What did it do when the Seerkind disappeared?'

'It returned to its fortress.'

'Until Shadwell.'

'Until Shadwell.'

Suzanna mused on this for a little time, then asked the one question this whole account begged.

'What about God?' she said.

The three-in-one laughed, her motes somersaulting.

'We don't need God to make sense of this,' she said. Suzanna wasn't certain if she spoke only for themselves or for her too. 'If there was a First Cause, a force of which this Uriel is a fragment, it's forsaken its sentinel.'

'So what do we do?' said Suzanna. 'There's been talk of mustering the Old Science.'

'Yes, I heard . . .'

'Would that defeat it?'

'I don't know. Certainly I made some miracles in my time that might have wounded it.'

'Then help us now.'

'That's beyond us, Suzanna. You can see our condition for yourself. All that's left is dust and will-power, haunting the Shrine we were worshipped at, until the Scourge comes to destroy it.'

'You're certain it'll do that?'

'This Shrine is sacred to magic. Shadwell will bring the Scourge here and destroy it the first chance he gets. And we're defenceless against it. All we can do is warn you.'

'Thank you for that.'

The wraith began to waver, as its power to hold its form diminished.

'There was a time, you know . . .' Immacolata said, 'when we had such raptures.' The dust she was made of was blowing away, the bone-shards dropping to the ground. 'When every breath was magic; and we were afraid of nothing.'

'It may come again.'

Within seconds the three had grown so tenuous they were barely recognizable. But the voice lingered a little while, to say:

'It's in your hands, sister . . .'

And then they were gone.

# V
## THE NAKED FLAME

### 1

The house that Mimi Laschenski had occupied for over half a century had been sold two months after her death. The new owners had been able to purchase it for a song, given its dilapidated condition, and put several weeks of hard labour into modernizing it before moving in. But that investment of time and money was not enough to persuade them to stay. A week later they left in a hurry, claiming the place was haunted. Sensible folks too, to look at them, talking of empty rooms that growled; of large invisible forms that brushed past them in darkened passageways; and, almost worse in its way, the pungent smell of cats that hung over the place, however hard they scrubbed the boards.

Once left empty, number eighteen Rue Street remained so. The property market was slow up that end of the city, and the rumours about the house were enough to deter the few who came to view. It was eventually taken over by squatters, who in the six days of their occupancy undid much of the work the previous owners had put in. But the twenty-four hour a day orgy which the neighbours suspected was going on came to an abrupt halt in the middle of the sixth night, and the tenants were gone by the following morning, exiting in some haste to judge by the litter of belongings they left on the steps.

After that, the house had no more occupants, legal or otherwise, and it didn't take long for gossip about number eighteen to be supplanted by talk of more lively scandals. The house simply became an unsaleable eye-sore: its windows boarded up, its paintwork deteriorating.

That was, until that night in December. What would happen that night would change the face of Rue Street entirely, and guarantee that the house in which Mimi Laschenski had lived out her lonely old age was never occupied again.

## 2

Had Cal set eyes on the five figures that entered number eighteen that night it would have taken him some time to recognize their leader as Balm de Bono. The rope-dancer's hair was cropped so short it was all but invisible; his face was thin, his features set. Even less recognizable, perhaps, was Toller, whom Cal had last seen perched on a rope in Starbrook's Field. Toller's ambitions as a rope-dancer had come to an abrupt end hours after that encounter, when he'd fallen foul of the Prophet's men. They'd broken his legs, and cracked his skull, leaving him for dead. He had at least survived. Starbrook's third pupil, Galin, had perished that night, in a vain attempt to protect his master's Field from desecration.

It had been de Bono's inspiration to visit the Laschenski house – where the Weave had lain for so long – in the hope of finding a pocket of the Old Science to arm themselves against the approaching cataclysm. He had three other allies in this, besides Toller: Baptista Dolphi, whose father had been shot down in Capra's House; her lover, Otis Beau; and a girl whom he'd first seen in Nonesuch, sitting on a window-ledge wearing paper wings. He'd seen her again, on Venus Mountain, in the reverie the presences there had granted him, and she'd shown him a world of paper and light that had kept him from total despair in the hours that followed. Her name was Leah.

Of the five, she was the most expert in the working of raptures; and the most sensitive to their proximity. It was she, therefore, who led the way through the Laschenski house in search of the room where the Weaveworld had lain. Her path-finding took them up the stairs and into the second-storey front room.

'The house is full of echoes,' she said. 'Some of the Custodian; some of animals. It takes time to sort them out – ' She went down on her knees in the middle of the room, and put her hands on the floor. ' – but the Weave lay here, I'm sure of it.'

Otis went across to where she knelt. He too crouched and put his palms to the ground.

'I don't feel a thing,' he said.

'Believe me,' said Leah. 'This is where it lay.'

'Why don't we get down to the bare boards?' Toller suggested. 'We may get a clearer signal.'

Plush, deep-pile carpeting had been laid in the room, only to be subsequently soiled by the squatters. They removed what remnants of furniture the room could boast, then tore the carpet up. The labour left them shaky: the training de Bono had devised for this expedition – refinement techniques culled from his old master's teachings – had kept sleep and food in recent days to the minimum. But it paid dividends when they laid their hands on the stripped boards. Their rarefied senses responded on the instant; even Otis could feel the echoes now.

'I can practically see the Weave,' Baptista said.

It was a sensation they all shared.

'What do we do now?' Otis asked Leah, but she was too involved in the echoes to hear his question. He turned to de Bono: 'Well?' he said.

De Bono had no answers. Though he'd theorized at length with any who'd debate on the subject, the plain fact was this: they were flying blind. There was no sure way of getting to the raptures whose memory they were evoking. His unspoken hope was that the ghosts of power here would come to *them*, sensing the urgency of their mission. If, however, the force beneath their fingertips was unmoved by the gravity of their cause, then they had no way to persuade it. They'd be obliged

616

to face their nightmares unprotected; which was — he didn't doubt — a sentence of death.

## 3

At two-fifty in the morning Cal woke from a dream which — though it resembled the terrors of previous nights — was in several significant ways different. For one thing, he'd not been alone on Venus Mountain; he'd had the company of de Bono. Together they'd fled the creature that came after them, into the same maze of alleyways that would lead — had the dream proceeded in its usual fashion — to the yard behind the Laschenski house. But it didn't. Somewhere in the alley he and de Bono were parted, and Cal, completely disoriented, took a route that led him into another street entirely.

There, the sense of pursuit waned, only to be replaced by a fresh anxiety. He was no longer the quarry, his dream-self knew, because the creature had gone after de Bono, leaving him in the role of helpless observer. The street seemed to be full of hiding places — doorways and garden walls — where it might wait, stoking its fires. But he'd misunderstood, once again. It had no need to hide. There it was now, crossing the intersection at the end of the street. Not a single pursuer this time, but two. One was human; a slouching shadowy form. The other — gigantic, as tall as a house, a cloud in which a furnace roared. He started to edge back towards the alleyway from which he'd stepped, moving slowly so as not to attract the monster or its companion's attention. A foolish hope. The refuge he sought had been sealed up, and as his fingers scrabbled at the brick the creature looked his way.

It had already devoured de Bono: he saw his friend's ashes in the cloud whose flame sight was on him.

*I don't want to burn!* he yelled, but the fire was coming at him —

*Please God!*

Before it struck him he flung himself up out of sleep.

Geraldine was not with him tonight; he lay in the middle

of the bed, trembling from gut to pores, until he was certain movement wouldn't make him vomit, then he got up, went to the window, and drew the curtains aside.

Chariot Street was perfectly quiet; the same icy hush that would be city-wide at this hour. Snow had begun to fall; its idling descent hypnotic. But the sight of neither street nor snow nor lamplight reassured him. There was a reason why the terrors that came in sleep were different tonight: because they weren't just in dreams any longer. He knew this without any trace of doubt. That somewhere near, in a street like this – all lamplight and peace – his nightmares were coming true.

### 4

There was mute but perceptible elation in the upper room of the Laschenski house: the call had been answered. It had begun slowly, with lights moving back and forth through the echoes of the Weave, as the Old Science rose from its hiding places in the carpet and came to meet those who longed for it. The process was still slow, and demanding – they could not afford distraction from the task for fear of losing contact. But they were prepared for such rigours, and as the power beneath their hands intensified they couldn't help but express their pleasure in soft words of welcome. The past was coming to fetch them.

A noise from the floor below drew de Bono's attention. Taking care not to disturb the others as they worked, he tip-toed to the door and stepped out onto the landing.

There was no encore to the sound that had brought him out here. He crossed the darkened landing to the top of the stairs, and studied the shadows below. Nothing moved there. He'd imagined it, he decided. His protein-starved brain was playing tricks on him. But just to be certain he went through to one of the back bedrooms and peered down into the yard. Snow was falling, the flakes tapping lightly on the glass. That was all he could see or hear.

He took his spectacles off and pressed his fingers to his eyes. The burst of energy that had come with the first intimations of success had faded. All he wanted now was sleep. But they had a good deal of work to do yet. Calling the Old Science up was just beginning; next came the problem of harnessing it.

He turned away from the window to make his way back to his companions. As he did so he saw two figures moving towards the Weave room. Had someone come out to search for him? He put his spectacles back on, to get a better look at them.

The sight before him brought a shouted warning to his lips, but it was old news by the time he raised it, falling on ears already deafened by their own screams. It was all so quick. One moment he was slipping the scene into focus; the very next, it erupted.

Before he could reach the landing the killers had stepped into the carpet room, and the door was flung off its hinges by the force unleashed inside. A body was flung out on a stream of molten light and held – as though spitted – in the middle of the landing, while darts of flame devoured it. He saw the victim clearly. It was Toller; poor Toller; his body closing into a blistered knot as the fire withered him.

The de Bono who'd been with Cal at Lemuel Lo's orchard would now have flung himself into the holocaust, and not considered the consequences. But bad times had taught him caution. There was no merit in suicide. If he tried to challenge the force that was running riot in the carpet room he'd die the way the rest were dying, and there'd be nobody left to testify to this atrocity. He knew the power whose labours he was witnessing: the worst predictions of his fellow Kind were here proved. This was the Scourge.

There was another explosion in the carpet room, and fresh fire blossomed onto the landing. The ceiling and floor were alight now; so were the bannisters and stairs. Very soon any escape route would be blocked, and he'd perish where he stood. He had to risk crossing the landing, and hope that the smoke would conceal him from the killing glance. There was no time to plot his route through the fire. Shielding his face he made a straight run for the stairs.

He almost got there too, but as he came within a pace of the top step he stumbled. He threw out his arms to save his fall and his hands gripped hold of the burning bannister. A cry escaped him, as the fire caught him; then he was up again and stumbling down the stairs towards the front door.

The Scourge came after him immediately, its first blow melting the brick where he'd stood two beats before. Eyes on the door, he pelted down the stairs, and was within five steps of the hallway when he heard a sound – like a titanic intake of breath – behind him. Why did he turn? He was a fool to turn. But he wanted a sight of the Scourge before it slaughtered him.

It was not the fire-bringer he saw at the top of the stairs however, but its slave. He'd never seen the Salesman dressed in his own skin, so he couldn't name this man. All he saw in that instant was a wasted, sweating face, regarding him with more desperation than malice. The sight made him hesitate, and as he did so this Cuckoo stood aside, and the Scourge came into view.

It was made of innumerable eyes; and bone that had never been clothed; and emptiness. He saw the fire in it too, of course: a fire from the bowels of a sun, in love with extinction. And he saw agony.

It would have been upon him – both fire and agony – had the ceiling above the stairs not given way at that moment, falling between him and his tormentors in a curtain of flame. He didn't escape its touch. Pieces of debris struck him: he smelt his skin burn. But while the deluge eclipsed him he was down the rest of the stairs and out – in three or four panicked paces – into the freezing air of the street.

There was a body burning in the gutter, having been thrown from the upper window, reduced by the Scourge's heat to the size of a child. It was beyond all recognition.

With sudden fury he turned back on the house and yelled at the beasts within:

'*Bastards! Bastards!*'

Then he took to his heels, before the fire came after him.

There were lights on all along the street, and doors opening as Cuckoos came out to see what it was that had disturbed their slumbers. Always the sight-seers: open-mouthed, disbelieving. There was a force for desolation loose in their midst which could consume their lives at a glance, surely they could see that? But they'd watch anyway, willing to embrace the void if it came with sufficient razzmatazz. In his rage and his despair de Bono found himself saying: let it come, let it come. There were no safe places left; nor powers to protect the vulnerable.

So let it do its worst, if that at the last was inevitable. Let the void come, and bring an end to the tyranny of hope.

# VI

## DEATH COMES HOME

As the dead hours between midnight and first light ticked by, the snowfall became heavier. Cal sat in his father's chair at the back window, and watched the flakes as they spiralled down, knowing from experience that trying to get back to sleep was a waste of effort. He would sit here and watch the night until the first train of the new day rattled by. The sky would begin to lighten an hour or so after that, though with the clouds so snow-laden the dawn would be subtler than usual. About seven-thirty he'd pick up the telephone and try calling Gluck, something he'd been doing regularly, both from the house and from the bakery, for several days, and always with the same result. Gluck didn't answer; Gluck wasn't home. Cal had even asked for the line to be checked, in case it was faulty. There was no technical problem, however: there was simply nobody to pick up the receiver at the other end. Perhaps the visitors Gluck had been spying on for so long had finally taken him to their bosom.

A knocking at the front door brought him to his feet. He looked at the clock: it was a little after three-thirty. Who the hell would come calling at this hour?

He stepped out into the hallway. There was a sliding sound from the far side of the door. Was somebody pushing against it?

'Who's there?' he said.

There was no reply. He took a few more steps towards the

door. The sliding sound had stopped, but the rapping – much fainter this time – was repeated. He unbolted the door, and took off the chain. The noises had ceased entirely now. Curiosity bettering discretion, he opened the door. The weight of the body on the other side threw it wide. Snow and Balm de Bono fell on the Welcome mat.

It wasn't until Cal went down on his haunches to help the man that he recognized the pain-contorted features. De Bono had cheated fire once; but this time it had caught him, and more than made up for its former defeat.

He put his hand to the man's cheek, and at his touch the eyes flickered open.

'Cal . . .'

'I'll get an ambulance.'

'*No*,' said de Bono. 'It's not safe here.'

The look on his face was enough to silence Cal's objections.

'I'll get the car-keys,' he said, and went in search of them. He was returning to the front door, keys in hand, when a spasm ran through him, as though his gut was trying to tie a knot in itself. He'd felt this sensation all too often of late, in dreams. There, it meant the beast was near.

He stared out into the spattered darkness. The street was deserted, as far as he could see; and silent enough to hear the snow-hooded lamps hum in the cold. But his heart had caught his belly's trepidation: it was thumping wildly.

When he knelt at de Bono's side again, the man had made a temporary peace with his pain. His face was expressionless and his voice flat, which gave all the more potency to his words.

'It's coming . . .' he said. ' . . . it's followed me . . .'

A dog had started to bark at the far end of the street. Not the whining complaint of an animal locked out in the cold, but raw alarm.

'What is it?' Cal said, looking out at the street again.

'The Scourge.'

' . . . oh Jesus . . .'

The barking had been picked up from kennels and kitchens

all along the row of houses. As in sleep, so waking: the beast was near.

'We have to get moving,' Cal said.

'I don't think I can.'

Cal put his arm beneath de Bono and lifted him gently into a sitting position. The wounds he'd received were substantial, but they weren't bleeding; the fire had sealed them up, blackening the flesh of his arms and shoulder and side. His face was the colour of the snow, his heat running out of him in breath and sweat.

'I'm going to take you to the car,' Cal said, and pulled de Bono to his feet. He wasn't quite dead weight; there was enough strength left in his legs to aid Cal in his efforts. But his head lolled against Cal's shoulder as they crept up the path.

'The fire touched me . . .' de Bono whispered.

'You'll survive.'

'It's eating me up . . .'

'Stop talking and walk.'

The car was parked only a few yards down the street. Cal leaned de Bono against the passenger side while he unlocked the doors, glancing up and down the street every few seconds while his inept fingers fumbled with the keys. The snow was still getting heavier, shrouding both ends of the street.

The door was open. He went round to help de Bono into the passenger seat, then returned to the driver's side.

As he stooped to get into the car, the dogs all stopped barking. De Bono made a small sound of distress. They'd done their duty as watch-dogs; self-preservation silenced them now. Cal got into the car and slammed the door. There was snow on the windscreen, but there wasn't time to start scraping it off: the wipers would have to take care of it. He turned on the ignition. The engine laboured, but failed to start.

At his side de Bono said, ' . . . it's near . . .'

Cal didn't need telling. He tried the key again; but still the engine resisted life.

'*Come on,*' he coaxed it, '*please.*'

His plea bore fruit; on the third attempt the engine caught. His instinct was to accelerate and get out of Chariot Street as quickly as possible, but the snow, falling as it did on several days' accumulation of ice, made the going treacherous. The wheels repeatedly threatened to lose their grip, the car sliding back and forth across the road. But yard by yard they crept through the pall of snow, which was so heavy now it reduced visibility to a car length. It was only as they approached the end of Chariot Street that the truth came clear. It wasn't just snow that was smothering them. There was a fog thickening the air, so dense that the car headlights had difficulty penetrating it.

Chariot Street was suddenly no longer part of the Kingdom. Though it had been Cal's stamping ground since childhood, it was alien territory now: its landmarks erased, its urbanity turned over to wasteland. It belonged to the Scourge, and they were lost in it. Unable to see any sign of a turning he trusted to instinct and made a right. As he swung the wheel over, de Bono sat bolt upright.

'*Go back!*' he yelled.

'What?'

'Back! Jesus! *Back!*'

He was gripping the dashboard with his wounded hands, staring into the fog ahead.

'It's there! *There!*'

Cal glanced up, as something huge moved in the fog ahead, crossing the path of the car. It came and went too quickly for him to gain more than a fleeting impression: but that was already too much. He'd underestimated it in his dreams. It was vaster than he'd imagined: and darker; and emptier.

He struggled to put the vehicle into reverse, panic making his every motion a farce. Off to his right the fog was folding upon itself, or unfolding. Which direction was the thing going to come from next?; or was it somehow *everywhere* around them, the fog its hatred made matter?

'*Calhoun.*'

He looked at de Bono, then through the windscreen at the sight that had de Bono rigid in his seat. The fog was dividing in front of them. From its depths the Scourge loomed.

625

What Cal saw befuddled him. There was not one form emerging from the murk, but two, locked in a grotesque union.

One was Hobart; albeit a Hobart much transfigured by the horror that now possessed him. His flesh was white, and there was blood running from the dozen places around his body where lines of force – connected by wheels and arcs of fire – entered his body and broke out the other side, revolving through him as they swung to meet the second form: the monstrous geometry that towered above him.

What Cal saw in that geometry was all paradox. It was bleached, yet black; a void, yet brimming; perfect in its beauty, yet more profoundly rotten than any living tissue could be. A living citadel of eyes and light, corrupt beyond words, and stinking to high heaven.

De Bono threw himself against the door and began to wrestle with the handle. The door opened, but Cal snatched hold of him before he could pitch himself out, at the same time putting his foot on the accelerator. As he did so a sheet of white flame erupted in front of the car, eclipsing the Scourge.

It was the briefest of respites. The car had backed up only five yards before the Scourge came at it again.

As it came, Hobart opened his mouth to a dislocating width, and a voice that was not his issued from his throat.

'*I see you,*' it said.

The next moment it seemed the ground beneath the car erupted, and the vehicle was flung over onto the driver's side.

There was total confusion within, as a hail of bric-a-brac tumbled from dashboard and glove compartment. Then de Bono was scrabbling at the passenger door once again, pushing it open. Despite his wounds some of a rope-dancer's agility was still in evidence, for he was out of the felled vehicle in two economical moves.

'*Get going!*' he yelled to Cal, who was still attempting to work out which way was up. As he stood, and levered himself out of the car, two sights were there to greet him. One, that of de Bono disappearing into the fog, which now seemed charged on every side with an empire of eyes. The other, a figure standing in the midst looking at him. It seemed it was a night for familiar faces, changed by circumstance. First, de Bono; then Hobart; and now – though for an instant Cal refused to believe it – *Shadwell*.

He'd seen the man play many roles. Avuncular salesman, wreathed in smiles and promises; tormentor and seducer; Prophet of Deliverance. But here was a Shadwell stripped of pretences, and the actor beneath was a vacant thing. His features, robbed of animation, hung on his bones like soiled linen. Only his eyes – which had always been small, but now seemed vestigial – still preserved a trace of fervour.

They watched Cal now, as he scrambled off the car and onto the ice-slick street.

'There's nowhere left to run,' he said. His voice was slurred, as though he needed sleep. 'It's going to find you, wherever you try to hide. It's an Angel, Mooney. It has God's eyes.'

'An Angel? *That?*'

The fog trembled to right and left of them, like living tissue. At any moment it might be back upon them. But the sight of Shadwell, and the riddle of his words, kept Cal glued to the spot. And another puzzle too; something about Shadwell's changed appearance which he couldn't put his finger on.

'It's called Uriel,' Shadwell said. 'The flame of God. And it's here to bring an end to magic. That's its only purpose. An end to rapture. Once and for all.'

The fog trembled again, but Cal still stared at Shadwell, too intrigued to retreat. It was perverse, to be vexed by trivia when a power of an Angel's magnitude was within spitting distance. But then the Mooneys had always been perverse.

'That's my gift to the world,' Shadwell was declaring. 'I'm going to destroy the magicians. Every one. I don't sell any longer you see. I do this for love.'

At this mention of selling, Cal recognized the change in the man. It was sartorial. Shadwell's jacket, the jacket of illusions which had broken Brendan's heart, and doubtless the hearts of countless others, had gone. In its place Shadwell wore a new coat, immaculately tailored but bereft of raptures.

'We're bringing an end to illusions and deceptions. An end to it all – '

As he spoke the fog shuddered, and from it there came a single shriek, which was cut off abruptly. De Bono: living and dying.

' . . . you *fucker* . . .' Cal said.

'I was deceived,' Shadwell replied, untouched by Cal's hostility. 'So terribly deceived. Seduced by their duplicity; willing to spill blood to have what they tantalized me with –'

'And what are you doing now?' Cal spat back. 'Still spilling blood.'

Shadwell opened his arms. 'I come empty-handed, Calhoun,' he replied. 'That's my gift. Emptiness.'

'I don't want your damn gifts.'

'Oh you do. In your bones you do. They've seduced you with their circus. But here's an end to that sham.'

There was such sanity in his voice; a politician's sanity, as he sold his flock the wisdom of the bomb. This soulless certainty was more chilling than hysteria or malice.

Cal realized now that his first impression had been mistaken. Shadwell the actor had not disappeared. He'd simply forsaken his patter and his hyperbole for a playing style so plain, so minimal, it scarcely seemed like a performance at all. But it was. This was his triumph: Shadwell the Naked.

The fog had begun to churn with fresh enthusiasm. Uriel was coming back.

Cal took one more look at Shadwell, to fix the mask in his mind once and for all, then he turned and started to run.

He didn't see the Scourge reappear, but he heard the car explode behind him, and felt the blast of heat which turned the snow to a warm drizzle around his head. He heard Shadwell's voice too – carried crisply on the cold air.

'*I see you . . .* '

he said.

That was a lie; he didn't and he couldn't. The fog was for the moment Cal's ally. He fled through it, not caring much in which direction he went as long as he outpaced the gift-giver's brute.

628

A house loomed up out of the murk. He didn't recognize it, but he followed the pavement until he reached the first crossroads. The intersection he knew, and took off back towards Chariot Street by a labyrinthine route designed to confuse his pursuers.

Shadwell would guess where he was headed, no doubt; the living fog that concealed the Scourge was probably half way down Chariot Street already. The thought gave speed to Cal's feet. He had to get to the house before the fire. Suzanna's book was there: the book she'd given into his hands for safe-keeping.

Twice the ice underfoot brought him down, twice he hauled himself up again – limbs and lungs aching – and ran on. At the railway bridge he clambered over the wire and up onto the embankment. The fog had thinned out here; there was just the snow, falling on the silent tracks. He could see the backs of the houses clearly enough to count them as he ran, until he reached the fence at the back of his father's house. He clambered over, realizing as he ran past the loft that he had another duty to perform here before he could make his escape. But first, the book.

Stumbling through the ruins of the garden he reached the back door and let himself in. His heart was a lunatic, beating against his ribs. Any moment the Scourge would be outside, and this – his home – would go the way of the Fugue. There was no time to retrieve anything of sentimental value, he had seconds only to gather the bare essentials: maybe not even that. He picked up the book, then a coat, and finally went in search of his wallet. A glance at the window showed him that the street outside had vanished; the fog was pressing its clammy face at the glass. Wallet secured he raced back through the house and left by the route he'd come: out of the door and through the tangle of bushes his mother had planted so many springs ago.

At the loft, he halted. He couldn't take 33 and his mate with him, but he could at least give them a chance to escape if they wanted to. They did. They were flying back and forth in the frost-proofed cage he'd built for them, perfectly alive to their jeopardy. As soon as he opened the door they were out and into the air, rising through the snow until they found the safety of the clouds.

As he started along the embankment – not back towards the bridge but in the opposite direction – he realized that he might never again see the house he was leaving behind. The ache that thought awoke made the cold seem benign. He paused, and turned to try and hold the sight in his memory: the roof, the windows of his parents' bedroom, the garden, the empty loft. This was the house in which he'd grown to adulthood; the house where he'd learned to be the man he was, for better or worse; here all his memories of Eileen and Brendan were rooted. But in the end it was just bricks and mortar; evil could take it as it had taken the Fugue.

As certain as he could be that he had the picture before him memorized, he headed off into the snow. Twenty yards on down the track a roar of destruction announced that he was a refugee.

## Part Twelve

# Stalking Paradise

'Western Wind, when wilt thou blow,
The small rain down can rain?
Christ if my love were in my arms
And I in my bed again!'

Anon, 16th Century

# I

## A CHAPTER OF ACCIDENTS

### 1

I f there was any pattern at all to the events of the day following, it was of reunions denied by chance, and of others just as capriciously granted.

Suzanna had decided the previous evening that she'd go up to Liverpool and re-establish contact with Cal. There was no use in circumspection now. Events were clearly approaching a crisis-point. Cal had to be warned, and plans made – the kind of plans that could only be made face to face – about how they could best protect Mimi's book, and their lives, in the coming storm. She tried calling him 'til about midnight, but nobody answered.

In the morning she rang Apolline, fresh from Salisbury, to tell her what she'd seen and learned at the Shrine of the Mortalities. She was prepared for Apolline to reject the information Immacolata's spirit had offered, out of contempt for its source, but that proved not to be the case.

'Why shouldn't we believe it?' she said. 'If the dead can't be honest, who can? Besides, it only confirms what we already knew.'

Suzanna told her she planned to go to Liverpool, and talk with Cal.

'You won't be alone up there,' Apolline informed her. 'Some people went looking for raptures in your grandmother's house. You might want to find out if they had any luck.'

'I'll do that. I'll call you when I've seen them.'

'Don't expect me to be sober.'

Before setting out Suzanna tried calling Chariot Street once more. This time her call received the number disconnected tone; the operator could not tell her why. The morning news bulletin would have answered the question, had she switched on the radio; the television would even have shown her pictures of the patch of blasted ground where the Mooney house had once stood. But she tuned in too late for the news, only catching the weather-report, which promised snow, and more snow.

Attempting the journey by car was, she knew, a certain disaster. Instead she took a taxi to Euston, and the mid-morning train North. Just about the time she was settling down for the four-hour trip to Liverpool Lime Street – which in fact took six – Cal was half way to Birmingham on the eight-twenty train via Runcorn and Wolverhampton.

## 2

He'd called Gluck from a telephone box at the Pier Head, where he'd gone following the confrontation in the fog. There was no particular plan in this: he'd just felt the need to go to the river, and the last night bus before dawn had taken him there. He'd slipped the Scourge, at least for the time being; he even entertained the thought that the creature might be satisfied with the devastation it had wrought. But his gut knew differently. The Angel – Shadwell's *flame of God* – had an insatiable appetite for death. It would not be satisfied until they were all dust: Shadwell included, he hoped. Indeed the only comfort he drew from the night's horrors was the sense he'd had that he'd been viewing the Salesman's farewell performance.

The wind off the river was bitter; the snow in it pricked his skin like needles. But he leaned on the railings and watched the water until his fingers and face were numb; then, with the clocks on the Liver Building all offering times in the vicinity of six, he went in search of sustenance. He was in luck. A small cafe was open, serving breakfast to the early-run bus drivers. He bought himself a substantial meal, thawing out as he ate his eggs and toast, still trying to sort out what was for the best. Then, around six-thirty, he tried to get through to Gluck. He hadn't really expected any reply, but luck was with him, at least in this, for just as he was about to put the receiver down, the 'phone at the other end was picked up.

'Hello?' said a sleep-thickened voice. Though Cal knew Gluck scarcely at all, he'd seldom, if ever, been so happy to make contact with someone.

'Mr Gluck? It's Cal Mooney. You probably won't remember me, but – '

' – of course I remember. How are things on the Mersey?'

'I have to talk to you. It's urgent.'

'I'm all ears.'

'I can't on the 'phone.'

'Well, come and see me. Do you have my address?'

'Yes. I've still got your card.'

'Then come. I'd enjoy the company.'

These welcoming words, coming after the losses of the night, were almost too much; Cal felt his eyes pricking.

'I'll get the first train down,' he said.

'I'll be here.'

Cal stepped out of the telephone box into the biting air. Daylight was still a while away; the snow-bound streets were almost deserted as he trudged up towards the station. A truck laboured through the gloom, spreading grit on the icy road; a newspaper vendor was laying out the early morning edition in the dubious shelter of a doorway; otherwise, he saw nobody. It was difficult to imagine, as he trudged, that there would ever be another spring in Spook City.

3

Suzanna stood at the end of Chariot Street and stared at the sight before her. There were too many people milling around for her to advance any further – her suspicion of uniforms had not mellowed; nor had that of Cuckoos in large numbers

– but she could see clearly from where she stood that the Mooney house no longer existed. It had been razed literally *to the ground*, and the fire that had consumed it had spread along the row in both directions. The Scourge had come visiting in the night.

Trembling, she left the scene, and made her way to Rue Street, fearing the worst. She found there nothing she hadn't anticipated. Mimi's house had been gutted.

What was she to do now?; return to London and leave Cal – if he'd survived – to his own devices? She had no way of tracing him; she could only trust that somehow he'd find his way to her. Things were so damn chaotic, with the Kind spread across the country, and Cal missing, and the book?; she didn't dare think too hard about that. She just turned her back on the ruins of Mimi's house and walked away down Rue Street, what little store of optimism she'd possessed defeated by what she'd seen.

As she turned the corner, a kerb-crawler drew up alongside her, and a round face, wearing sun-glasses, leaned out of the window.

'You're going to get cold,' he said.

'Go to Hell,' she told him, and quickened her step. He kept pace with her.

'I told you to go to Hell,' she said, throwing him a look intended to leave him limp. He slid his glasses down his nose, and stared at her. The eyes revealed beneath were bright gold.

'Nimrod?'

'Who else?'

Had it not been for the eyes she'd never have recognized him. His face had filled out, all but a hint of his good looks gone.

'I need feeding,' he said. 'How about you?'

4

His appetite seemed to have expanded in direct proportion to the direness of their jeopardy. She sat across the table of the

Chinese restaurant where he took her, and watched him wade through the menu, devouring not only his food but most of hers too.

It didn't take long for them to provide each other with outlines of their recent investigations. Most of her news was stale stuff now: the Scourge was amongst them. But Nimrod had more current information, gleaned from conversations overheard and questions asked. At Chariot Street – he was able to report – no bodies had been found, so it might be safely assumed that Cal had not perished there. Remains had however been found in Rue Street.

'I didn't know any of them personally,' he said. 'But I'm afraid you did.'

'Who?'

'Balm de Bono.'

' – de Bono?'

'He was at Rue Street last night.'

She fell silent, thinking of the brief time she'd spent with de Bono, and of their debates together. Now he was gone. And how soon would the rest of them follow?

'What do we do, Nimrod?' she murmured. 'Do we try and hide again? Another Weave?'

'There aren't enough of us to fill a prayer mat,' Nimrod said mournfully. 'Besides, we don't have the raptures. There's very little power left between us.'

'So we sit back and wait for the Scourge to pick us off? Is that what you're saying?'

Nimrod drew his hand over his face.

'I've fought about as hard as I can . . .' he said. 'I think we all have.'

He fetched a tobacco tin from his pocket, and began to roll himself a cigarette. 'I've made my mistakes,' he said. 'I fell for Shadwell's lies . . . I even fell in love.'

'You did?'

He made a slight smile, which reminded Suzanna of the irrepressible creature he'd once been. 'Oh yes . . .' he said. '. . . I've had my adventures in the Kingdom. But they didn't last long. There was always a part of me that never left the

637

Fugue. That still *hasn't* left.' He lit the match-thin cigarette he'd rolled. 'I suppose that's ludicrous,' he said, 'given that the place doesn't exist any longer.'

He'd forsaken his dark glasses as soon as the waiter had retired. His eyes, their gold untarnished, were on her now, looking for some sliver of hope.

'You can remember it?' she said.

'The Fugue? Of course.'

'So can I. Or at least I think I can. So maybe it isn't lost.'

He shook his head.

'Don't be sentimental,' he chided. 'Memories aren't enough.'

It was fruitless to argue the niceties of that: he was telling her that he was in pain; he didn't want platitudes or metaphysics.

She turned over in her head the problem of whether she should tell him what she knew: that she had reason to hope that all was not lost; that the Fugue might *be* again, one day. It was, she knew, a slender hope – but he needed a life-line, however tenuous.

'It's not over,' she said.

'Dream on,' he replied. 'It's finished.'

'I tell you the Fugue's not gone.'

He looked up from his cigarette.

'What do you mean?'

'In the Gyre . . . I used the Loom.'

'*Used* the Loom? What are you saying?'

'Or *it* used *me*. Maybe a bit of both.'

'How? Why?'

'To keep everything from being lost.'

Nimrod was leaning across the table now.

'I don't understand,' he said.

'Neither do I, fully,' she replied. 'But something happened. Some force . . .'

She sighed. She didn't have the words to describe those moments. Part of her wasn't even sure it had happened. But of one thing she was certain:

'I don't believe in defeat, Nimrod. I don't care what this fucking Scourge is. I won't lie down and die because of it.'

'You don't have to,' he said. 'You're a Cuckoo. You can walk the other way.'

'You should know better than that,' she said, sharply. 'The Fugue belongs to anyone who'll die for it. Me . . . Cal . . .'

He looked chastened.

'I know,' he said. 'I'm sorry.'

'It's not just you who needs the Fugue, Nimrod. We all do.'

She glanced towards the window. Through the bamboo blinds she could see that the snow was coming down again with fresh vehemence. 'I never believed in Eden,' she said softly. 'Not the way the Bible tells it. Original sin and all that crap. But maybe the story's got an echo somewhere in it.'

'An echo?'

'Of the way things really were. A place of miracles, where magic was made. And the Scourge ended up believing the Eden story, because it was a corrupted version of the truth.'

'Does it matter?' Nimrod sighed. 'Whether the Scourge is an Angel or not; whether it comes from Eden, or not, how does that alter anything? The point is, it *believes* it's Uriel. And that means it'll destroy us.'

The point was incontestable. When the world was coming to an end, what did names matter?

'I think we should be together,' he said, after a pause, 'instead of spread across the country. Perhaps we can muster something if we're all in one place.'

'I see the sense in that.'

'Better than the Scourge picking us off!'

'But where?'

'There was a place . . .' he said, 'where it never came. I remember it vaguely. Apolline will tell us better.'

'What kind of place?'

'A hill, I think it was,' he said, his unblinking stare on the white paper tablecloth between them. 'Some kind of hill . . .'

'We'll go there then, shall we?'

'It's as good a place to die as any.'

# II

## DUST AND ASHES

The saints on the facade of the Church of St Philomena and St Callixtus had long since lost their faces to the rain. They had no eyes to see the visitors that came to the door in the early evening of 21st December; nor did they have ears to hear the debate on the step. Even if they had heard, and seen – even if they'd stepped off their pedestals and gone out to warn England that it had an Angel in its midst – their alarms would have gone unheeded. England had no need of saints tonight, nor any night: it had martyrs enough.

Hobart stood on the threshold, the Scourge's light visible through the flesh of his throat and darting from the corners of his mouth. He had hold of Shadwell's arm, and would not let him step out of the snow.

'This is a *church* . . .' he said, not with Uriel's voice but with his own. Sometimes the Angel seemed to give him the right to self-government for a while, only to pull the leash tight again if its host grew fractious.

'Yes, it's a church,' said Shadwell. 'And we're here to destroy it.'

Hobart shook his head.

'No,' he said. 'I won't do that.'

Shadwell was too tired for argument. This was not the first of the day's visits. Since leaving Chariot Street the Angel had led them to several sites around the country, where it remembered the Seerkind taking refuge during the last holocaust. All had been wasted journeys: the places – when they were still recognizable – were devoid of magic or its makers. The weather had deteriorated by the hour. Snow now blanketed the country from one end to the other, and Shadwell was weary of both the trek and the chill. He'd become anxious too, as each pursuit ended in disappointment; anxious that Uriel would grow impatient, and his control of the creature would begin the slip. That was why he'd brought the Angel here, where he knew there was magic, or its leavings. This was where Immacolata had made the Rake: a place part shrine, part womb. Here Uriel's hunger for destruction would be assuaged, for tonight at least.

'We have work to do inside,' he told Uriel's host. 'The Scourge's work.'

But Hobart still refused to cross the threshold.

'We can't destroy it . . .' he said, ' . . . God's house.'

There was irony aplenty in the fact that he, Shadwell – raised a Catholic – and Uriel, God's fire, should be ready to demolish this pitiful temple; while Hobart – whose only religion had been the Law – refused. This was the man who kept not the Bible close to his heart, but a book of faery-tales. So why this sudden fastidiousness? Did he sense that death was close, and it was time to repent his Godlessness? If so, Shadwell was unmoved.

'You're the Dragon, Hobart,' he said. 'You can do what you like.'

The man shook his head, and at his denial the light in his throat brightened.

'You wanted fire, you've got it,' Shadwell went on.

'I *don't* want it,' Hobart said, his words becoming choked. 'Take . . . it . . . away . . .'

The last syllables were forced through chattering teeth. Smoke came too, up from his belly. And after it, Uriel's voice.

'*No more argument,*' it demanded.

Though it seemed to have reclaimed the reins of Hobart's body, the man still fought to keep control for himself. The conflict made him shake violently, a display Shadwell was certain would draw unwelcome attention if they didn't soon step out of public view.

'There are Seerkind inside,' he said. 'Your enemies.'

His coaxing went unheard by either Uriel or Hobart. Either the Angel was losing its grip on its vessel, or Hobart had developed new powers of resistance, for Uriel was having to fight hard to regain total possession. One or other of them began to beat the body's fist against the portico, perhaps to distract its opponent. The flesh, caught between man and Angel, burst and bled.

Shadwell tried to avoid being spattered, but the Inspector's grip was fiercer than ever, holding him close. The wasted head turned in Shadwell's direction. From the smoky cavern between his teeth Hobart's voice emerged, barely decipherable.

'Get . . . it . . . out of me,' he pleaded.

'I can do nothing,' Shadwell said, wiping a fleck of blood from his upper lip with his free hand. 'It's too late.'

'*He knows that*,' came the reply. Not Hobart's voice this time, but Uriel's. '*He's the Dragon forever*.'

Hobart had begun to sob, his snot and tears boiling away as they reached the furnace of his mouth.

'*Don't be afraid*,' said Uriel, its tone a parody of Shadwell at his silkiest. '*Do you hear me, Hobart?*'

The head nodded loosely, as if the muscle of the neck it was carried on was half cut through.

'Shall we go inside?' said Shadwell.

Again, that dislocated nodding. The body was free of twitches now; the face a blank. As final proof of the Angel's triumph, Hobart dropped his hold on Shadwell, then turned and went ahead of the Salesman into the church.

It was deserted, the candles cold, the smell of incense souring.

'*There are raptures here*,' said Uriel.

'Indeed there are,' said Shadwell, following the creature down the aisle to the chancel rail. He had expected the crucifix above the altar to win some response from the Angel, but

Uriel passed it by without a glance, and crossed to the baptistery door. It laid Hobart's broken hand upon the wood. The boards smouldered, the door flew open. It was the same procedure at the second door. With Uriel-in-Hobart leading the way they descended into the crypt.

They were not alone there; a light was burning at the far end of the passage along which Immacolata had come to meet Shadwell: from the Shrine, presumably. Without further word Uriel began along the corridor, ribbons of its hidden self flowing from Hobart's torso and grazing the caskets in the walls, pleasuring in their stillness, their silence. It was half way between stairs and Shrine when a priest stepped from an intersecting passageway and blocked the path. His face was pale, as if powdered, a streak of blue dirt – some sign of obsequience – daubed in the centre of his forehead.

'Who are you?' he demanded.

'Step aside,' said Shadwell.

'You're trespassing,' the man retorted. 'Get out of here!'

Uriel had stopped a yard or two from where the priest stood, and now threw its hand out and snatched hold of one of the casket ledges, its other hand taking hold of Hobart's hair and dragging the man's face towards the wall as if to beat its own skull open. This was not the Angel's doing, Shadwell realized, but Hobart's. Using the distraction of the priest's appearance, he was again attempting to seize control. The contested body immediately became epileptic, a throttled roar emerging from its throat, which may have been intended as a warning to the priest. If so, it went uncomprehended. The man stood his ground as Uriel twisted Hobart's head back in his direction – bone and cartilage audibly grinding upon each other. A moment passed: priest and Angel face to face. Then Uriel's flame erupted from Hobart's mouth.

The effect, in the confined space of the passage, was more impressive than anything Shadwell had witnessed in Rue Street. The shock-wave threw him backwards, but he was too much the voyeur to be denied the spectacle, and hauled himself upright to watch Uriel's lethal theorems proved on its victim. The priest's body was lifted against the ceiling and pinned there until the flames had devoured it.

It was over in seconds, and Shadwell squinted through the smoke to see Uriel moving off towards the Shrine, with Hobart loosing a sobbing howl of horror at what had been done. Shadwell followed, dwindling motes of fiery ash falling around him. The fire had not just caught the priest, but was eating at the very brick of the passageway, and consuming the caskets in the niches. The lead of their inner linings dripped from the ledges, and the bodies came with it, shrouds burning around their illustrious bones.

As he approached the door of the Shrine Shadwell's feet slowed. This had been Immacolata's domain. Here she'd been all-powerful, worshipped by unmanned men whose abeyance to Christ and his Mother had been a sham; men who'd believed her a Goddess. He'd never believed that himself. So why did he have this sudden fear upon him?: a desecrator's fear?

He stepped inside the Shrine, and there had his answer. As he surveyed the bones on the walls he knew as only a lover could know that the creature he'd lusted after, and finally betrayed, was still holding court here. Death had no hold on her. She was in the walls, or in the air: somewhere near.

'Goddess . . .' he heard himself say.

There was no time to warn Uriel. A second priest, younger than his dead brother, appeared from the shadows and ran at the Angel, knife in hand. Hobart's cry stopped, and he turned his mutinous hands to the task of preventing a second slaughter, clamping them to his face to dam the coming fire. The device gave the attacker time to deliver a cut, the knife entering Hobart's side. But as the priest withdrew it for a second stab Uriel's benediction spurted between Hobart's fingers, then broke out entirely, taking the flesh and bone of his hands with it. The fire caught the priest head on and flung him across the Shrine. He danced against the bones for a heart-beat, then he, like his brother, was ash.

He'd done serious damage to Hobart, but it took Uriel less time to cauterize the wound with its glance than it had taken the knife to deliver it. The task done, it turned its gaze on

Shadwell. For a breathless moment the Salesman thought it meant to burn him where he stood. But no.

'*Don't be afraid,*' it said.

It had offered the same meagre comfort to Hobart mere minutes before. The sentiment had sounded hollow then, but more so now, in the light of the way it had maimed its host. Hobart's hands, which he'd once envisaged burning with righteous fire, had been reduced to withered claws in the act of trying to prevent that fire from doing its work. Hobart was sobbing again, as he or the Angel held the stumps up to be examined. Had Uriel left him with the burden of pain his nerve-endings must be suffering, or did he sob that his body was an instrument in these abominations?

The arms dropped, and Uriel turned his attention to the walls.

'*I like these bones,*' it said, and wandered over to the most elaborate of the designs. Tendrils, thin as sewing-thread and lightning bright, skipped from its borrowed torso and face, and ran over the skulls and rib-cages.

There was a moment of hiatus, the fire roaring in the niches outside, the ashes of the second priest still hanging in the air. In that moment Shadwell heard Immacolata's voice. It was the most intimate of whispers, a lover's whisper.

'What have you done?' she said.

He glanced across at Uriel, who was still entranced by the macabre symmetry of the wall. It made no sign of having heard the Incantatrix. Again, the question.

'What have you done?' she said. 'It knows no mercy.'

He did not need to voice his response. Thought was enough.

'And you did?' he answered.

'I didn't know myself,' Immacolata told him. 'I think this Scourge is the same.'

'It's called Uriel,' Shadwell reminded her, 'it's an Angel.'

'Whatever it is, you have no power over it.'

'I freed it.' Shadwell responded. 'It obeys me.'

'Why lie?' Immacolata said. 'I know when you're afraid.'

The din of destruction broke the exchange. Shadwell looked up from his thoughts to see Uriel, its tendrils extended across the wall, sweep all the bones from their places like so much crockery from a piled table. They fell around it in a dusty litter, the remains of fully half a hundred people.

Uriel laughed – another trick it had caught from Shadwell – the sound made more distressing by its artificiality. It had found a game it liked. Turning to the next wall it proceeded to vandalize that in the same manner; then on to the third.

'Tell it to stop . . .' Immacolata's ghost whispered, as bones large and small joined the myriad on the ground. 'If you're not afraid: tell it to stop.'

But Shadwell simply watched as the Angel cleared the fourth wall at a stroke, then turned its attention to the ceiling.

'You'll be next,' Immacolata said.

Shadwell flattened himself against the now naked brick as remains rained down.

'No . . .' he murmured.

The bones stopped falling; there were none left on either walls or ceiling. Slowly, the dust began to settle. Uriel turned to Shadwell.

'Why do you whisper behind my back?' it enquired lightly.

Shadwell glanced towards the door. How far would he get if he tried to run now? A yard or two, probably. There was no escape. It knew; it heard.

'Where is she?' Uriel demanded. The demolished chamber was hushed from one end to the other. 'Make her show herself.'

'She used me,' Shadwell began. 'She'll tell you lies. Tell you I loved raptures. I didn't. You must believe me, I didn't.'

He felt the Angel's countless eyes upon him; their stare silenced him.

'You can hide nothing from me,' the Angel pronounced. 'I know what you've desired, in all its triviality, and you needn't fear me.'

'No?'

'No. I enjoy the dust you are, Shadwell. I enjoy your futility, your meaningless desires. But the other that's here – the woman whose raptures I can smell – she I want to kill. Tell her to show herself and be done with it.'

'She's dead already.'

'So why does she hide?'

646

'I don't,' came Immacolata's voice, and the bones on the floor churned like a sea as the ghost rose from them. Not simply *from* them but *of* them, defying Uriel's destruction as her will made a new anatomy from the fragments. The result was far more than a sum of its parts. It was, Shadwell saw, not one but all of the sisters, or a projection of their collective spirit.

'Why should I hide from you?' the monument said. Every shard in its body revolved as she spoke.

'Are you happy now?' she asked.

*'What is happy?'* Uriel wanted to know.

'Don't bother to protest your innocence,' the phantom said. 'You know you don't belong in this world.'

*'I came here before.'*

'And you left. Do so again.'

*'When I'm done,'* Uriel replied. *'When the rapture-makers are extinguished. That's my duty.'*

'Duty?' Immacolata said, and her bones laughed.

*'Why do I amuse you?'* Uriel demanded.

'You are so deceived. You think you're alone – '

*'I am alone.'*

'No. You've forgotten yourself; and so you've been forgotten.'

*'I am Uriel. I guard the gate.'*

'You are not alone. Nobody – nothing – is alone. You're part of something more.'

*'I am Uriel. I guard the gate.'*

'There's nothing left to guard,' Immacolata said. 'But your duty.'

*'I am Uriel. I –'*

'Look at yourself. I dare you. Throw the man you're wearing away, and look at yourself.'

Uriel did not speak its reply, but shrieked it.

*'I WILL NOT!'*

And with its words it unleashed its fury against the body of bones. The statue flew apart as the fire struck it, burning fragments shattering against the walls. Shadwell shielded his face as Uriel's flame ran back and forth across the chamber to eradicate the Incantatrix's image completely. It was not satisfied for a long while, scouring each corner of the Shrine until every last offending shard was chased to ash.

Only then did that same sudden tranquillity descend that Shadwell loathed so much. The Angel sat Hobart's wretched body on a pile of bones, and picked up a skull between the fire-blackened hands.

*'Might it not be cleaner . . .'* the Angel said, its words measured, *' . . . if we emptied the whole world of living things?'*

The suggestion was floated so delicately, its tone so perfectly a copy of Shadwell's Reasonable Man, that it took him a moment to comprehend the ambition of what it proposed.

*'Well?'* it said. *'Might it not?'*

It looked up at Shadwell. Though its features were still in essence Hobart's, all trace of the man had been banished from them. Uriel shone from every pore.

*'I asked a question,'* it said. *'Would that not be fine?'*

Shadwell murmured that it would.

*'Then we should see such a fire, shouldn't we?'* it said, rising from its seat of bones. It went to the door, and stared off down the passageway, where the caskets still burned.

*'Oh . . .'* it said with yearning in its voice. *'. . . such a fire.'*

Then, eager not to delay its goal's consummation by a moment, it started back towards the stairs, and the sleeping Kingdom beyond.

# III

## THE SECRET ISLE

### I

The train was an hour late reaching Birmingham. When it finally arrived the snow was still falling, and taxis couldn't be had for love nor money. Cal asked for directions to Harborne, and waited in line for twenty-five minutes to board the bus, which then crawled from stop to stop, taking on further chilled passengers until it was so overburdened it could carry no more. Progress was slow. The city-centre was snarled with traffic, reducing everything to a snail's pace. Once out of the centre the roads were hazardous – dusk and snow conspiring to cut visibility – and the driver never risked more than ten miles an hour. Everyone sat in wilful cheerfulness, avoiding each others' eyes for fear of having to make conversation. The woman who'd seated herself beside Cal was nursing a small terrier, encased in a tartan coat, and a picture of misery. Several times he caught its doleful eyes regarding him, and returned its gaze with a consoling smile.

He'd eaten on the train, but he still felt lightheaded, utterly divorced from the dismal scenes their route had to offer. The wind slapped him from his reverie, however, once he stepped out of the bus on Harborne Hill. The woman with the tartan dog had given him directions to Waterloo Road, assuring him that it was a three-minute trot at the outside. In fact it took him almost half an hour to find, during which time the chill had clawed its way through his clothes and into his marrow.

Gluck's house was a large, double-fronted building, its

facade dominated by a monkey-puzzle tree which rose to challenge the eaves. Twitching with cold, he rang the bell. He didn't hear it sound in the house, so he knocked, hard, then harder. A light was turned on in the hallway, and after what seemed an age the door was opened, to reveal Gluck, the remains of a chewed cigar in his hand, grinning and instructing him to get in out of the cold before his balls froze. He didn't need a second invitation. Gluck closed the door after him, and threw a piece of carpet against it to keep out the draught, then led Cal down the hallway. It was a tight squeeze. The passage was all but choked by cardboard boxes, piled to well above head height.

'Are you moving?' Cal asked, as Gluck ushered him into an idyllically warm kitchen which was similarly littered with boxes, bags and piles of paperwork.

'Good God, no,' Gluck replied. 'Take off your wet stuff. I'll fetch you a towel.'

Cal skinned off his soaked jacket and equally sodden shirt, and was taking off his shoes, which oozed water like sponges, when Gluck returned with not only a towel but a sweater and a pair of balding corduroys.

'Try these,' he said, slinging the clothes into Cal's lap. 'I'll make some tea. You like tea?' He didn't wait for an answer. 'I live on tea. Sweet tea and cigars.'

He filled the kettle and lit the antiquated gas cooker. That done he fetched a pair of hiker's socks from the radiator, and gave them to Cal.

'Getting warmer?' he asked.

'Much.'

'I'd offer you something stronger,' he said, as he produced tea-caddy, sugar and a chipped mug from a cupboard. 'But I don't touch it. My father died of drink.' He put several heaped spoons of tea into the pot. 'I must tell you,' he said, wreathed in steam. 'I never expected to hear from you again. Sugar?'

'Please.'

'Pick up the milk, will you? We'll go through to the study.'

Taking the pot, sugar and mug, he led Cal out of the kitchen and upstairs to the first landing. It was in the same condition as the floor below: its decoration neglected, its lamps without shades, and heaped everywhere the same prodigious amount of paperwork, as though some mad bureaucrat had willed Gluck his life's work.

He pushed open one of the doors and Cal followed him into a large, cluttered room – more boxes, more files – which was hot enough to grow orchids in, and reeked of stale cigar smoke. Gluck set the tea down on one of the half-dozen tables, claiming his own mug from beside a heap of notes, then drew two armchairs up beside the electric fire.

'Sit. Sit,' he exhorted Cal, whose gaze had been drawn to the contents of one of the boxes. It was full, to brimming, with dried frogs.

'Ah,' said Gluck. 'No doubt you're wondering . . .'

'Yes,' Cal confessed. 'I am. Why frogs?'

'Why indeed?' Gluck replied. 'It's one of the countless questions we're trying to answer. It isn't *just* frogs, of course. We get cats; dogs; a lot of fish. We've had tortoises. Aeschylus was killed by a tortoise. That's one of the first recorded falls.'

'Falls?'

'From the heavens,' said Gluck. 'How many sugars?'

'Frogs? From the sky?'

'It's very common. *Sugars?*'

'Two.'

Cal peered into the box again, and took a trio of frogs out. Each was tagged; on the tag was written the date it fell, and where. One had come down in Utah, one in Dresden, a third in County Cork.

'Are they dead on arrival?' he asked.

'Not always,' said Gluck, handing Cal his tea. 'Sometimes they arrive unharmed. Other times, in pieces. There's no pattern to it. Or rather, there *is*, but we've still to find it.' He sipped his tea noisily. 'Now – ' he said, ' – you're not here to talk about frogs.'

'No, I'm not.'

'What *are* you here to talk about?'

'I don't know where to begin.'

651

'Those are always the best tales,' Gluck declared, his face glowing. 'Begin with the most preposterous.'

Cal smiled; here was a man ready for a story.

'Well – ' he said, taking a deep breath. And he began.

He'd intended to keep the account short, but after ten minutes or so Gluck began to interrupt his story with disgressionary questions. It consequently took several hours to tell the whole thing, during which Gluck smoked his way through an heroic cigar. At last, the narrative reached Gluck's doorstep, and it became shared memory. For two or three minutes Gluck said nothing, nor did he even look at Cal, but studied the debris of stubs and matches in the ashtray. It was Cal who broke the silence.

'Do you believe me?' he said.

Gluck blinked, and frowned, as though he'd been stirred from thoughts of something entirely different.

'Shall we make some more tea?' he said.

He tried to stand up, but Cal took fierce hold of his arm.

'*Do you believe me?*' he demanded.

'Of course,' said Gluck, with a trace of sadness in his voice. 'I think I'm obliged to. You're sane. You're articulate. You're damnably particular. Yes, I believe you. But you must understand, Cal, that in doing so I deliver a mortal blow to several of my fondest illusions. You are looking at a man in mourning for his theories.' He stood up. 'Ah well . . .' he picked up the pot from the table, then set it down again. 'Come next door,' he said.

There were no curtains at the window of the next room. Through it Cal saw that the snow had thickened to near-blizzard proportions while he'd been talking. The garden at the back of the house, and the houses beyond, had become a white nowhere.

But Gluck hadn't brought him in to show him the view; it was the walls he was directing Cal's attention to. Every available inch was covered with maps, most of which looked to have been up there since the world was young. They were stained with an accrual of cigar smoke, scrawled over in a dozen different pens, and infested with countless coloured pins, each presumably marking a place where some anomalous phenomenon had occured. And on the fringes of these maps, tacked up in mind-boggling profusion, were photographs of the events: grainy, thumb-nail pictures, foot-wide enlargements, strips of sequential images lifted from a home movie. There were many he could make no sense of, and others that looked patently fake. But for every blurred or phony photograph there were two that pictured something genuinely startling, like the frumpy woman standing in a domestic garden up to her ankles in what seemed to be a trawler's deep-sea catch; or the policeman standing guard outside a three-storey house which had fallen over on its face, though not a single brick was out of place; or the car bonnet which bore the imprint of two human faces, side by side. Some of the pictures were comical in their casual weirdness, others had a grim authenticity about them – the witnesses sometimes distressed, sometimes shielding their faces – that was anything but amusing. But all, whether ludicrous or alarming, went to support the same thesis: that the world was stranger than most of Humankind ever assumed.

'This is just the tip of the iceberg – ' said Gluck. 'I've got thousands of these photographs. Tens of thousands of testimonies.'

Some of the pictures, Cal noted, were linked by threads of various colours to pins in the maps.

'You think there's a pattern here?' said Cal.

'I believe so. But now, after hearing what you've told me, I begin to think maybe I was looking in the wrong place for it. Some of my evidence, you see, overlaps with your account. For the last three weeks – while you were trying to contact me – Max and I were up in Scotland, looking at a site we just found in the Highlands. We picked up some very strange articles there. I'd assumed it was a landing place of some kind for our visitors. I think now I was wrong. It was probably the valley your unweaving took place in.'

'What did you find?'

'The usual debris. Coins, clothing, personal effects of one kind or another. We boxed them all up, and brought them back down with us to examine at leisure. We could have made them fit our pet theories, you know . . . but now I think much of that's in ruins.'

'I'd like to see that stuff,' Cal said.

'I'll unpack it for you,' said Gluck. His expression, since Cal had told his story, had been that of a deeply perplexed man. Even now he surveyed the map room with something akin to despair. In the past few hours he'd seen his whole world-view thrown into disarray.

'I'm sorry,' said Cal.

'What for?' Gluck replied. 'Telling me about miracles? Please don't be. I'll just as happily believe in your mystery as in mine. It'll just take a little time to adjust. All I ask is that the mystery be there.'

'Oh it is,' said Cal. 'Believe me, it is. I just don't know *where*.'

His attention strayed from Gluck's face to the window, and the blank scene beyond. More and more he feared for his beloved exiles. The night, the Scourge and the snow all seemed to be conspiring to erase them.

He crossed to the window; the temperature plummeted as he approached the icy glass.

'I have to find them,' he said. 'I have to be with them.'

He'd successfully kept his sense of desolation at bay until now; but sobs suddenly wracked him. He heard Gluck come to his side, but he didn't have sufficient mastery of himself to control his tears: they kept falling. Gluck put a comforting hand on his shoulder.

'It's good to see somebody so in need of the miraculous,' he said. 'We'll find your Seerkind, Mooney. Trust me. If there's a clue to their whereabouts, it's here.'

'We have to be quick,' Cal said softly.

'I know. But we'll find them. Not just for you, but for me. I want to meet your lost people.'

'They're not mine.'

'In a way they are. And you're theirs. I could see that on your face. That's why I believe you.'

654

# 2

'Where do we begin?'; that was Cal's question.

The house was packed with reports from basement to attic. Perhaps, as Gluck had said, there was somewhere amongst them a clue – a line in a report, a photograph – that would point to the Kind's location. But *where*? How many testimonies would they have to dig through before they uncovered some hint of the hiding place? That assumed, of course, that in this time of jeopardy they'd band together. If not – if they were spread across the Isles – then it was a completely lost cause, as opposed to one almost lost.

Cal chided himself for that thought. It was no use being defeatist. He had to believe that there was a chance of discovery; had to believe the task before them wasn't just a way to occupy the time before the cataclysm. He would take Gluck as his model. Gluck, who'd spent his life in pursuit of something he'd never really seen, not doubting for an instant the validity of that pursuit; Gluck, who even now was brewing tea and digging out files, behaving as though he believed to his core that the solution to their problem was close at hand.

They'd made a base in the study. Gluck had cleared the largest desk, and laid on it a map of Britain, so vast it hung over the top like a tablecloth.

'The Spectred Isle,' he said to Cal. 'Study it a while. See if any of the sites we've investigated down the years ring a bell.'

'All right.'

'I'll go sort through the reports; and break open the boxes we brought from Scotland.'

He got about his business, leaving Cal to peruse the map, which was even more heavily annotated than those in the next room, many of the symbols, crossed lines and clusters of dots, accompanied by cryptic acronyms. What the letters *UFO* signified needed no explanation, but what was a *Suspected TMD*? or a *Cirrus VS*? He decided to ignore the notes, which were only distracting him, and simply examine the map systematically, quarter inch by quarter inch, beginning at Land's End and working his way back and forth across the country. He was grateful that he need only examine the land, because the seas around Britain – those regions whose names had always enchanted him on the weather reports: Fastnet, Viking, Forties, Tiree – those too had their share of miracles. It stood to reason. If there were squid falling on suburbia perhaps there were rains of tyres and chimney stacks on the North Sea. He had moved to and fro across the country half a dozen times when Gluck reappeared.

'Any luck?' he wanted to know.

'Not so far,' said Cal.

Gluck put a foot-high heap of reports on one of the chairs.

'Maybe we'll find something here,' he said. 'I've started with events in the neighbourhood of Spook City, and we'll spread out from there.'

'Seems logical.'

'You dig in. Anything that seems faintly familiar, set aside. As long as you keep reading, I'll keep supplying.'

Gluck pinned the map up on the wall beside the desk, and left Cal to wade through the first collection of reports.

The work required concentration, which Cal found hard to come by. It was ten-thirty, and he already wanted sleep. But as he leafed through this catalogue of neglected wonders his weary eyes and wearier brain forgot their fatigue, re-invigorated by the startling stuff before them.

Many of the incidents were variations on by now familiar themes: events in defiance of laws geographical, temporal and metrological. Misplaced menageries; excursions from distant stars; houses larger inside than out; radios that picked up the voices of the dead; ice in midsummer trees; and hives that hummed the Lord's Prayer. All these things had taken place not in the faraway, but in Preston and Healey Bridge, in Scunthorpe and Windermere; solid, stoical places, inhabited by pragmatists not prone to hysteria. This country, which Gluck had called the Spectred Isle, was alive from one end to the other with delirious visions. It too was Wonderland.

Gluck came and went, supplying fresh files and fresh tea at

intervals, but otherwise doing as little as possible to disturb Cal's concentration. It was difficult, Cal found, not to be sidetracked by many of the more bizarre accounts, but by disciplining himself severely he sifted out the one in every hundred or so that contained some detail that might connect the event described with the Fugue or its inhabitants. Some he knew of already: the destruction of Shearman's house, for instance. But there were other reports – of words seen in the air, of a man whose pet monkey quoted the Psalms – which had occurred in places he'd never heard of. Perhaps the Kind were there now.

It was only when he decided to take a short break from his labours that Gluck mentioned he'd unpacked the boxes they'd brought from Scotland, and asked if Cal wanted to examine the contents. He followed Gluck back into the map room, and there – every item tagged and marked meticulously – was the litter events in the valley had left behind. There wasn't much; either the survivors had destroyed the bulk of it, or natural processes had done the job. But there were a few pitiful reminders of the disaster – personal belongings of no particular interest – and some weaponry. Into both categories, weapon and personal effects – fell the one item that made Cal's skin run with gooseflesh. There, laid across one of the boxes, was Shadwell's jacket. He stared at it nervously.

'Something you recognize?' said Gluck.

Cal told him what, and from where.

'My God,' said Gluck. 'That's the jacket?'

His incredulity was understandable; viewed by the light of a bare bulb there was nothing so remarkable about the garment. But it still took Cal a minute to pluck up the courage to pick it up. The lining, which had probably seduced hundreds in its time, seemed quite unexceptional. There was perhaps a gleam in the cloth that was not entirely explicable, but no more evidence than that of its powers. Perhaps they'd gone out of it, now that its owner had discarded it, but Cal wasn't willing to take the risk. He threw it down again, covering up the lining.

'We should take it with us,' Gluck said. 'When we go.'

657

'Go where?'

'To meet with the Seerkind.'

'No. I don't think so.'

'Surely it belongs with them,' Gluck said.

'Maybe,' Cal replied, without conviction. 'But we have to find them first.'

'Back to work then.'

He returned to the reports. Taking a break had been an error; he found it difficult to re-establish his rhythm. But he pushed on, using as a spur the sad remains next door, and the thought that they might soon represent his last keepsakes of the Kind.

At three-forty-five in the morning he finished going through the reports. Gluck had taken the opportunity to sleep for a while in one of the armchairs. Cal stirred him, and presented him with the nine key files he'd selected.

'Is this all?' said Gluck.

'There were others I wasn't sure about. I kept them aside, but I thought they might be red herrings.'

'True enough,' said Gluck. He went over to the map, and put pins in the nine locations. Then he stood back and looked. There was no discernible pattern to the sites; they were spread irregularly over the country. Not one was within fifty miles of another.

'Nothing,' said Cal.

'Don't be so hasty,' Gluck told him. 'Sometimes the connections take a little while to become apparent.'

'We don't *have* a while,' Cal reminded him wearily. The long hours of sleeplessness were catching up with him; his shoulder, where Shadwell's bullet had wounded him, ached; indeed his whole body ached.

'It's useless,' he said.

'Let me study it,' said Gluck. 'See if I can find the pattern.'

Cal threw up his hands in exasperation.

'There *is* no pattern,' he said. 'All I can do is go to those places one by one – ' (*in this weather?* he heard himself thinking, *you'll be lucky if you can step out of the door tomorrow morning.*)

658

'Why don't you go lay your head down for a few hours. I prepared a bed in the spare room. It's up one more flight, second on your left.'

'I feel so bloody useless.'

'You'll be even more useless if you don't get some sleep. Go on.'

'I think I'll have to. I'll get going first thing – '

He climbed the stairs. The upper landing was cold; his breath went before him. He didn't undress, but slung the blankets over him, and left it at that.

There were no curtains at the frost-encrusted window, and the snow outside cast a blue luminescence into the room, bright enough to read by. But it didn't keep him from sleep more than thirty seconds.

# IV

## PAST HOPE

### 1

They came at the summons, all of them; came in ones and twos sometimes, sometimes in families or groups of friends; they came with few suitcases (what did they have in the Kingdom worth weighing themselves down with?), the only possessions they cared about those they'd brought out of the Fugue, and carried upon their persons. Souvenirs of their lost world: stones, seeds, the keys of their houses.

And of course they brought their raptures, what few they had. Brought them to the place Nimrod had told Suzanna about, but had failed to name. Apolline had remembered it, however. It was a place, in the time before the Weave, that the Scourge had never found.

It was called Rayment's Hill.

Suzanna feared that the Cuckoos would have wrought some profound change on the area; dug it up or levelled it. But no. The Hill was untouched, and the copse below it, where the Families had spent that distant summer, had flourished, and become a wood.

She'd also questioned the wisdom of their taking refuge out of doors in such appalling weather – the pundits were already pronouncing this the bitterest December in living memory – but she was assured that beleaguered as they were the Kind had solutions to such simple problems.

They had been safe below Rayment's Hill once; perhaps they would be safe there again.

The sense of relief amongst them at being reunited was palpable. Though most had survived well enough in the Kingdom, circumstances had obviously required that they keep their grief hidden. Now, back amongst their own people, they could reminisce about the old country, and that was no small comfort. Nor were they entirely defenceless here. Though their powers were vastly reduced without the Fugue to fuel them, they still had one or two deceiving raptures to call into play. It was doubtful they'd keep the power that had destroyed Chariot Street at bay for long, but beggars couldn't be choosers.

And when they were finally gathered in the groves between the trees – their collective presence working a subtle transformation upon bush and branch – she felt the indisputable rightness of this decision. If the Scourge eventually found them, they'd at least be together at the end.

There were only two notable absentees. Cal was one, of course. The other was the book she'd given into his hands; a book whose living pages had contained echoes of this midwinter wood. She prayed they were both safe somewhere – the book and its keeper. Safe; and dreaming.

2

Perhaps it was the thought he'd been in the process of shaping when sleep came (that the snow-light was bright enough to read by) which prompted the dream he had.

He imagined that he woke, and reaching into the pocket of his jacket – which was unaccountably deep – took out the book which he'd saved from destruction back at Chariot Street. He tried to open it, but his fingers were numb and he fumbled like a fool. When eventually he got the trick, there was a shock waiting, for the pages were blank, every one of them, blank as the world outside the window. The stories and the illustrations had gone.

661

And the snow kept falling on the seas of Viking and Dogger Bank, and on the land too. It fell on Healey Bridge and Blackpool, on Bath and Devizes, burying the houses and streets, the factories and the cathedrals, filling the valleys until they were indistinguishable from the hills, blinding the rivers, smothering the trees, until at last the Spectred Isle was as blank as the pages of Suzanna's book.

All this made perfect sense to his dreaming self: for were they not part of the same story, the book and the world outside it? Warp and weft. *One world, indivisible.*

The sights made him afraid. Emptiness was inside and out; and he had no cure for it.

'*Suzanna . . .*' he murmured in his sleep, longing to put his arms around her, to hug her close to him.

But she wasn't near. Even in dreams he could not pretend she was near, couldn't bring her to his side. All he could do was hope she was safe; hope she knew more than he did about keeping nullity at bay.

'*I don't remember being happy,*' a voice out from the past whispered in his ear. He couldn't put a name to it, but he knew its owner was long gone. He pressed his dream into reverse, in pursuit of its identity. The words came again, more strongly.

'*I don't remember being happy.*'

Memory gave him the name this time, and a face too. It was Lilia Pellicia; and she was standing at the bottom of the bed, only it wasn't the bed he'd gone to sleep in. It wasn't even the same room.

He looked round. There were others here too, conjured from the past. Freddy Cammell was peering at his reflection; Apolline was straddling a chair, a bottle to her lips. At her side stood Jerichau, nursing a golden-eyed child. He knew now where he was, and when. This was his room in Chariot Street, the night the fragment of the carpet had come unwoven.

Without prompting, Lilia spoke again; the same line that had brought him here.

'*I don't remember being happy.*'

Why, of all the extraordinary sights he'd seen and

662

conversations he'd heard since that night had his memory chosen to replay this moment?

Lilia looked at him. Her distress was all too apparent; it was as though her second-sight had predicted the night of snow he was dreaming through; had known, even then, that all was lost. He wanted to comfort her, wanted to tell her that happiness was possible, but he had neither the conviction nor the will to misrepresent the truth.

Apolline was speaking now.

*'What about the hill?'* she said.

What *about* the hill?, he thought. If he'd once known what she'd been talking about, he'd forgotten since.

*'What was it called?'* she asked. *' . . . where we stayed –'*

Her words began to slide away.

*Go on*, he willed her. But the remembered warmth of the room was already fading. A chill from the present had crept over him, driving that balmy August night into retreat. He listened still, his heart beginning to thump in his head. His brain hadn't re-run this conversation arbitrarily: there was method in it. Some secret was about to be divulged, if he could only hold on long enough.

*'What was it called?'* Apolline's faltering voice repeated, *'. . . where we stayed, that last summer? I remember that as if it were yesterday . . .'*

She looked across at Lilia for a reply. Cal looked too.

*Answer her*, he thought.

But the chill was getting worse, summoning him back from the past into the bleak present. He desperately wanted to take with him the clue that was hovering on Lilia's lips.

*'I remember that . . .'* Apolline said again, her stridency growing thinner with every syllable, *' . . . as if it were yesterday.'*

He stared at Lilia, willing her to speak. She was already as transparent as cigarette smoke.

*Please God answer her*, he said.

As her image began to flicker out entirely, she opened her mouth to speak. For a moment, it seemed he'd lost her, but her reply came, so softly it hurt to listen for it.

'*Rayment's Hill* . . .' she said.

Then she'd gone.

'Rayment's Hill!'

He woke with the words on his lips. The blankets had slid off him as he slept, and he was so cold his fingers were numb. But he'd claimed the place from the past. That was all he needed.

He sat up. There was daylight at the window. The snow was still coming down.

'Gluck!' he called. 'Where are you?'

Kicking a box of notes downstairs in his haste, he went in search of the man, and found him slumped in the armchair where he'd sat to hear Cal tell his tale.

He shook Gluck's arm, telling him to wake up, but he was swimming in deep waters, and didn't surface until Cal said:

'*Virgil.*'

at which his eyes opened as though he'd been slapped.

'What?' he said. He squinted up at Cal. 'Oh, it's you. I thought I heard . . . my father . . .'

He ran his palm over his bleary features.

'What time is it?'

'I don't know. Morning sometime.'

'Want some tea?'

'Gluck, I think I know where they are.'

The words brought him round. He stood up.

'Mooney! You mean it? Where?'

'What do you know about a place called Rayment's Hill?'

'Never heard of it.'

'Then that's where they are.'

## Part Thirteen

# Magic Night

'The woods are lovely, dark and deep.
But I have promises to keep,
And miles to go before I sleep.'

Robert Frost
*Stopping by Woods on a Snowy Evening*

# I

---

# BLIZZARD

## 1

Ice had stopped the clocks of England.

Though the meteorologists had been predicting Siberian conditions for more than a week, the sudden drop in temperature found the country, as usual, unprepared. Trains had ceased to run; aircraft were grounded. Telephone and power lines were down in Yorkshire and Lincolnshire; villages and even small towns in the Southern Counties cut off by drifting snow. The plea from the media was to stay at home; advice that was widely taken, leaving industry and commerce to dwindle and – in some areas – stop entirely. Nobody was moving, and with good reason. Large sections of motorway were closed, either blocked by snow or stranded vehicles; the major roads were a nightmare, the minor roads impassable. To all intents and purposes the Spectred Isle had ground to a halt.

## 2

It had taken Cal some time to locate Rayment's Hill amongst Gluck's comprehensive supply of maps, but he found it eventually: it was in Somerset, South of Glastonbury. In ordinary conditions it was perhaps an hour's drive down the M5. Today, however, God alone knew how long it would take.

Gluck, of course, wanted to come with him, but Cal suspected that if the Seerkind were indeed in hiding at the hill they'd not take kindly to his bringing a stranger into their midst. He put the point to Gluck as gently as he could. Try as he might Gluck couldn't conceal his disappointment, but said he understood how delicate these encounters could be; he'd been preparing himself for just such a meeting all his life; he would not insist. And yes, of course Cal could take one of the cars, though neither was exactly reliable.

As Cal prepared to leave, bundled up as best they could devise against the cold, Gluck presented him with a parcel, roughly tied up with string.

'What is it?' he asked.

'The jacket,' Gluck replied. 'And some of the other evidence I picked up.'

'I don't want to take it. Especially not the jacket.'

'It's their magic, isn't it?' Gluck said. 'Take it, damn you. Don't make a thief of me.'

'Under protest.'

'I put some cigars in too. A little peace offering from a friend.' He grinned. 'I envy you, Cal; every frozen mile.'


He had time to doubt as he drove; time to call himself a fool for *hoping* again, for even daring to believe some memory he'd dredged up would lead him to the lost ones. But his dream, or a part of it at least, was validated as he drove. England *was* a blank page; the blizzard had blotted everything out. Somewhere beneath its shroud people were presumably about their lives, but there was little sign of that. Doors were locked and curtains closed against a day that had begun back towards night somewhere around noon. Those few hardy souls who were out in the storm hurried along the pavements as fast as the ice underfoot would allow, eager to be back beside their fires, where the television would be promising a Christmas of plastic snow and sentiment.

There was practically no traffic on the roads, which allowed Cal to take liberties with the Law: crossing intersections on red and ignoring one-way systems as he escaped the city. Gluck had helped him plan his route before he left, and the news bulletins kept him alerted to road closures, so he made reasonably good progress at first, joining the M5 South of Birmingham, and managing a steady forty miles an hour until – just North of the Worcester junction – the radio informed him that a fatal accident had closed the motorway between junctions eight and nine. Cursing, he was obliged to leave the motorway and take the A38 through Great Malvern, Tewkesbury and Gloucester. Going was much slower here. No attempt had been made to clear or grit the road, and several vehicles had simply been abandoned by drivers who'd decided that to press on was tantamount to suicide.

The weather worsened as he approached Bristol, obliging him to cut his speed to a crawl. Blinded by snow, he missed the turn for the A37 and had to retrace his route, the sky now almost pitch black though it was still only the middle of the afternoon. A mile or so short of Shepton Mallet he stopped for petrol and chocolate, to be told by a garage attendant that most of the roads south of the town were blocked. He began to feel plotted against. It was as though the weather was somehow part of the Scourge's masterplan; that it knew he was near and was throwing obstacles in his path to see just how hard he'd fight to reach his place of execution.

But if that were so then at least it meant he was on the right track; that somewhere in the wilderness ahead his loved ones were waiting.

3

The truth in the warning he'd been given at the garage became all too apparent when he turned off the A road at Lydford on Fosse, and onto a minor thoroughfare that would in theory carry him West to Rayment's Hill. He'd known before setting out that this would be the most problematic part of the journey, but there was no alternative. No main road fed this area; there were only narrow tracks and backwaters, most of which, he knew, would have been buried beneath the drifts.

He advanced maybe two miles, the road ahead white on

white, until the ice-clogged tread of the tyres would no longer grip, and the car came to a halt, its spinning wheels doing no more than kick up sheets of snow. He revved the engine, bullying it and coaxing it by turns, but the vehicle was not going to move without help. Reluctantly, he got out, and immediately sank to mid-shin in the snow. Gluck had lent him a pair of hiking boots and heavy socks, which protected his feet, but the chill soaked through his trousers in an instant. He put up the hood of his anorak – again, Gluck's gift – and trudged round to the back of the car. Having no shovel all he could do was clear the snow by hand. His efforts bore no fruit. After twenty minutes' work he hadn't succeeded in getting the car to move an inch either forward or backward.

He decided to give up on the task before his fingertips froze. Taking refuge in the car, the engine idling so as to keep the heat coming, he sat and considered the options available to him. The last sign of human habitation had been back at the turn into this road, two miles behind him; two miles of digging through the drifts – with the snow still falling – in near as damnit total darkness. Suppose, after that walk, he could get someone foolish or charitable enough to help him; hours would have been lost.

There were two other options. One – that he stay where he was and sit out the night. This he rejected without a second thought. The other, that he finish the journey to Rayment's Hill on foot. To judge by his map, which was not detailed, the road forked a little way on. If he were to take the left-hand track it would in principle take him to the vicinity of the hill. He'd be guided almost entirely by instinct, however, for virtually all distinguishing features of the landscape – ditches, hedgerows, the road itself – had disappeared. But what else could he do? It was better to travel blind than not at all.

With the decision made, his spirits rose, and he turned his attention to the problem of protecting himself against the elements. In the back of the car, upturned between the seats, and presumably overlooked, he found a box of Gluck's precious reports. Hoping he'd be forgiven this trespass he clambered over onto the back seat and proceeded to put several layers of paper and photographs between his skin and his clothing, insulating himself with tales of falling frogs and talking bees. The supply exhausted, he tore up the box itself and double lined his trousers – which would take the brunt of the cold – with cardboard. Finally, he ripped up two chamois leathers he found on the back window ledge and wrapped them around his face, pulling his anorak hood up, and tying its drawstring tight to seal himself in. With more paper lining his gloves, he was as ready for the onslaught as he'd ever be. Picking up the parcel Gluck had given him, he turned off the engine and stepped out to meet the snow.

This is the act of a lunatic, he thought as he slammed the door and began to trudge away from the car: I'm Mad Mooney to the bitter end.

It wasn't as dark outside as he'd anticipated. In the time it had taken to prepare for his march the fury of the blizzard had abated somewhat, and the landscape was suffused with a milky brightness, the canvas of snow more luminous than the laden sky above it. There were even breaks in the cloud; stars glimmered between. He began to think he might have a chance after all.

The first quarter-mile did nothing to dispel his optimism, but with the next quarter his makeshift insulation began to fail. The damp started to creep through the cardboard beneath his trousers, numbing his legs. It crept through his gloves and their lining too, making his fingers ache. Worse still, he couldn't find any sign of the fork in the road marked on the map, and became more certain with every dragging step that he'd missed the turning, his present route leading *away* from the hill rather than towards it.

He decided to take a risk and strike out across the fields. The land to his left rose steeply. Perhaps at the top he'd get a better grasp of the lay of the land. He glanced back in the direction of the car, but he could no longer see it. No matter; he was committed now. He made towards the white face of the hill and began to climb.

The break in the clouds had grown larger, and there was an

expanse of glittering sky above him, pin-pointed with stars. He'd learned the names of the major constellations when he bought his telescope, and he could name them easily; he, the Memory Man. They meant nothing of course, those names, except in the human perspective; they were just tags bestowed by some star-gazer who'd seemed to see a pattern in the scattering overhead: a bow and arrow, a bear, a plough. They meant nothing in the cosmic context. But it was a necessary comfort, to see the stars and call them by name, as if you knew them as friends. Without that courtesy the sight might break a man's heart.

The ache in his legs and hands was contagious; his arms and torso had caught it, so had his prick and balls, his ears and sinuses. Indeed there seemed to be no part of him that didn't give him pain. But there was no going back. Another thirty yards would bring him to the top of the hill, he estimated, and began to count them off. At eighteen he had to stop to gain some breath for the remaining twelve. Walking against both the snow and the incline was claiming more energy than he had to give. As he stood, gasping for air like an asthmatic, he glanced down at the tracks he'd left in the snow. He'd taken his path to be straight, but it wandered back and forth wildly.

Not wanting to think about what that signified, he turned back to his ascent. Every step now was a major challenge. He was obliged to lift his knees to groin height in order to step over the snow rather than try and drag through it. His freezing muscles protested every stride, but he finally got there, presented at the summit with a pure white panorama. It was a as though the house of England had been deserted, and a dust-sheet thrown over its furniture 'til the owners returned. *If* they returned. It was possible, standing on the rise looking down on the blankness below, the silence utter, to believe they would never come back to this forsaken place, and that he was alone.

But there *was* a hill, and it could only be the one he sought, because there was no other. Between it and the place he stood, however, lay an expanse of snow-covered fields. At the sight of the distance he had yet to cover his innards seemed to sink, but he knew that standing still would only make his muscles seize up, and so began to career down the slope, barely in control of his body.

Towards the bottom the snow became deeper and deeper still, until he was waist-high in it, and he was not so much walking as swimming. But as he started across the field towards the hill the crippling ache of cold began to fade, and a welcome deadness replaced it. Half way across his fingers let slip the package Gluck had given him, a fact his increasingly narrowed consciousness was barely aware of. His shrinking thoughts had turned to how comfortable the snow he was ploughing through looked. Maybe he should give up his trek for a while, and lay down on this pristine pillow. His head was heavier by the moment, and the snow would be oh so comfortable. Where was the harm in lying down in it 'til he felt stronger? But lazy as his thoughts were becoming he wasn't so far gone not to know sleep would kill him. If he stopped now he stopped forever.

He reached the bottom of Rayment's Hill on the verge of collapse, then drove himself, step by step, up the slope. It was longer than the first one, but not so steep. He couldn't think far enough ahead to wonder what he'd find on the other side; it took all his mental effort to instruct his limbs to move. But as he came within a few yards of the brow he raised his head in the dim hope of seeing the stars. The clouds had sealed them from sight, however; a fresh assault was mustering in the sky.

Two more steps and he reached the summit, turning his gaze on the landscape laid out below the hill. There was nothing to see. No sign of anything even resembling a hiding place, however vestigial, for as far as his appalled sight stretched. Only snow-covered fields, and more of the same, rolling away into the distance, deserted and silent. He was alone.

If he'd had the strength to weep he would have wept. Instead he let his exhaustion triumph, and he fell down in the snow. There was no way he could make the return journey to the car, even if he'd been able to find his way. That fatal sleep he'd kept denying himself would just have to claim him.

673

But as his lids began to close he caught a movement in the wastes at the base of the hill – something was running about in the snow. He tried to focus; failed; pressed his fingers to his face to stir himself; looked up and tried again. His eyes didn't deceive him. There *was* something moving on the blank page in front of him; an animal of some kind.

Could it be . . . a *monkey*?

He plunged his arms into the snow and hauled himself up, but as he did so he lost his balance and pitched forward. For several seconds earth and sky became a blur as he tumbled down the slope, coming to a halt encased in ice. It took him a moment to re-orient himself, but when he did he saw the animal – and yes, it *was* a monkey! – fleeing from him.

He stood up, more snow than man, and stumbled after it. Where in God's name was it running to? There were only open fields ahead of it.

Suddenly, the animal vanished. One moment it was plainly in front of him, and he was gaining on it. The very next it had disappeared from the field, as though it had fled through an open door and slammed it closed. He halted, not believing the evidence of his befuddled sight. Was the animal a mirage of some kind? Or had the cold simply undone his sanity?

He stared at the snow. There were distinctly tracks there – paw tracks, where the monkey had been playing. He followed them, and the testimony of his eyes was confirmed. The tracks stopped dead a few feet from where he stood. Beyond the spot there was simply clean, crisp snow; acres of it.

'All right,' he said to the empty field. 'Where are you?'

As he spoke he took another step towards the place where the monkey had pulled its disappearing trick, and asked his question again.

'Please . . .' he said, his voice failing, 'where are you?'

There was no answer, of course. Mirages were silent.

He stared at the tracks, and felt the last vestiges of hope go out of him.

Then a voice said:

'Don't stand in the cold.'

He looked up. There was nobody visible to right or left of him. But the instructions came again.

'Two paces forward. And be quick about it.'

He took one tentative step. As he was about to take the second an arm appeared from the air directly in front of him, and – seizing hold of his anorak – claimed him from the snow.

# SHELTER FROM THE STORM

1

There was a wood on the other side of the curtain through which Cal had been yanked, its thatch of branches so dense all but a sprinkling of snow had been kept from the ground, so that it was mossy and leaf-strewn underfoot. The place was dark, but he could see a fire burning some way off from him, its light welcome, its promise of warmth even more so. Of the man who'd dragged him out of the snow there was no sign; at least he failed to see anyone until a voice said:

'Terrible weather we're having,' and he turned to find the monkey Novello, and its human companion, standing no more than two yards from him, camouflaged by stillness.

'It was Smith who did it,' said the monkey, leaning towards Cal. 'Him who pulled you through. Don't let them blame me.'

The man threw the animal a sideways glance.

'He's not speaking to me,' Novello announced, 'because I strayed outside. Well, it's done now, isn't it? Why don't you come along to the fire? You'd better lie down before you fall down.'

'Yes,' Cal said, ' . . . please.'

Smith led the way. Cal followed, his stupefied brain still grappling with what he'd just experienced. The Kind might be cornered, but they weren't without a trick or two; the illusion that kept this wood from sight had survived close scrutiny. And once on the other side there was a second surprise: the season. Though the branches of the trees above him were bare, and it was last summer's moss he was walking on, there was a scent of spring in the air, as if the ice that gripped the Spectred Isle from end to end had no hold here. Sap was rising; buds were swelling; things on every side were turning their cells to the sweet labour of growth. The sudden clemency induced a mild euphoria in him, but his frozen limbs hadn't got the message. As he came within a few yards of the fire he felt his body lose its power to hold itself up. He reached out to one of the trees for support, but it stepped away from him – or so it seemed – and he fell forward.

He didn't hit the ground. There were arms to catch him, and he gave himself over to them. They carried him to the vicinity of the fire, and he was gently laid down. A hand touched his cheek and he looked away from the flames to see Suzanna kneeling at his side, firelight on her face.

He said her name – or at least hoped he did. Then he passed out.


2


It had happened before that he'd closed his eyes seeing her, only to wake and find her gone. But not this time. This time she was waiting for him, on the other side of sleep. Not just waiting, but holding him, and rocking him. The layers of clothes, paper pulp and photographs he'd been wearing had been peeled off him as he slept, and a blanket wrapped around his nakedness.

'I found my way home,' he said to her, when he could get his tongue to work again.

'I went to Chariot Street to fetch you,' she said, 'but the house had gone.'

'I know . . .'

'And Rue Street too.'

He nodded. 'De Bono came looking for me . . .' He halted, silenced by the memory. Even the fire, and her arms around him, couldn't prevent his shuddering as he stood again in the fog, and glimpsed what it had half concealed.

677

' . . . the Scourge came after us,' he said.

'And Shadwell,' she added.

'Yes. How did you know?'

She told him about the Shrine.

'So what happens now?' he said.

'We wait. We keep the rapture up, and we wait. We're all here now. You were the only one missing.'

'I'm found now,' he said softly.

She tightened her hold on him.

'And there'll be no more separations,' she said. 'We'll just have to pray they pass us by.'

'No praying *please*,' said a voice from behind Suzanna. 'We don't want angels hearing us.'

Cal craned his neck to see the newcomer. The lines on the face before him were deeper than they'd been, the beard a little more grizzled: but it was still Lem's face, Lem's smile.

'Poet,' Lo said, bending to put his hand through Cal's hair. 'We almost lost you.'

'No chance,' said Cal, with a slow smile. 'Have you still got the fruits?'

Lo patted the breast pocket of his coat, the modernity of which rather suited him. 'Got them here,' he said. 'Speaking of which: is the man hungry?'

'I can always eat,' said Cal.

'There's food to be had when you want it.'

'Thank you.'

Lem was about to depart, then turned back and very solemnly said:

'Will you help me plant, Calhoun? When the time comes?'

'You know I will.'

Lem nodded. 'I'll see you in a while,' he said, and withdrew from the circle of firelight.

'Are my clothes dry?' Cal asked. 'I can't wander around like this.'

'Let me see if I can borrow something for you,' Suzanna replied.

He sat up to let her rise, but before she did so she kissed him on the lips. It was not a casual kiss; its touch did more to warm him than a dozen fires. When she left his side he had to wrap the blanket around him to cover up the fact that more than sap was rising tonight.

Alone, he had time to think. Though he'd come within spitting distance of death it was already difficult to remember the pain he'd been in, such a short time ago; possible, even, to think there was no world at all beyond this enchanted wood, and that they could stay here forever and make magic. But seductive as that thought was he knew indulging it, even for a moment, was dangerous. If there was to be a life for the Kind after tonight – if by some miracle Uriel and its keeper *did* pass them by – then that life had to be lived as part of the Wonderland he'd found in Gluck's bureau of miracles. One world, indivisible.

After a dozing time, Suzanna returned with a collection of clothes, and laid them beside him.

'I'm going to make a round of the lookouts,' she said, 'I'll see you later.'

He thanked her for the clothes, and began to dress. This was his second borrowed skin in twenty-four hours, and it was – predictably, given its source – odder than anything Gluck had supplied. He took pleasure in the collision of styles: a formal waistcoat and a battered leather jacket; odd socks and pigskin shoes.

'Now that's the way a poet should dress,' Lemuel declared when he came back for Cal. 'Like a blind thief.'

'I've been called worse.' Cal replied. 'There was talk of food?'

'There was,' said Lem, and escorted him away from the fire. Once his flame-dazzled eyes had grown accustomed to the half-light he realized there were Kind everywhere; perched in the branches or sitting on the ground between the trees, surrounded by their earthly goods. Despite the wonders these people had been intimate with, tonight they resembled any band of refugees, their eyes dark and full of caution, their mouths tight. Some, it was true, had decided to make the best of what might well be their last night alive. Lovers lay in each others' arms exchanging whispers and kisses; a singer poured a lilt onto the air, to which three women were dancing, the stillness between their steps so profound they were lost amongst the trees. But most of the fugitives were inert, keeping themselves under lock and key for fear their dread show.

The smell of coffee came to greet Cal as Lem brought him into a clearing where another fire, smaller than the one he'd slept by, was burning. Half a dozen Kind were eating here. He knew none of them.

'This is Calhoun Mooney,' Lem announced. 'A poet.'

One of the number, who was sitting in a chair while a woman carefully shaved his head, said:

'I remember you from the orchard. You're the Cuckoo.'

'Yes.'

'Have you come to die with us?' said a girl crouching beside the fire, pouring herself coffee. The remark, which would have been judged an indiscretion in most company, drew laughter.

'If that's what it comes to,' said Cal.

'Well don't go on an empty stomach,' said the shaved man. As his barber towelled the last of the suds from his scalp Cal realized he'd grown his mane to conceal a skull decorated with rhythmic pigmentation from the gaze of the Kingdom. Now he could parade it again.

'We've only got bread and coffee,' Lem said.

'Suits me,' Cal told him.

'You saw the Scourge,' said another of the company.

'Yes,' Cal replied.

'Must we talk about that, Hamel?' said the girl at the fire.

The man ignored her. 'What was it like?' he asked.

Cal shrugged. 'Huge,' he said, hoping the subject would be dropped. But it wasn't just Hamel who wanted to know; all of them – even the girl who'd objected – were waiting for further details. 'It had hundreds of eyes . . .' he said. 'That's all I saw, really.'

'Maybe we could blind it,' Hamel said, drawing on his cigarette.

'How?' said Lem.

'The Old Science.'

'We don't have the power to keep the screen up much longer,' said the woman who'd been doing the shaving.

'Where are we going to get the strength to meet the Scourge?'

'I don't understand this Old Science business,' said Cal, sipping at the coffee Lem had brought him.

'It's all gone anyway,' said the shaved man.

'Our enemies kept it,' Hamel reminded him. 'That bitch Immacolata and her fancy-man – they had it.'

'And those who made the Loom,' said the girl.

'They're dead and gone,' Lem said.

'Anyway,' said Cal. 'You couldn't blind the Scourge.'

'Why not?' said Hamel.

'Too many eyes.'

Hamel wandered to the fire and threw the stub of his cigarette into its heart.

'All the better to see us with,' he said.

The flame the stub burned with was bright blue, which made Cal wonder what the man had been smoking. Turning his back on the fire Hamel disappeared between the trees, leaving silence in his wake.

'Will you excuse me, poet?' said Lem. 'I've got to go find my daughters.'

'Of course.'

Cal sat down to finish his meal, leaning his back against a tree to watch the comings and goings. His short sleep had only taken the edge off his fatigue; eating made him dozy again. He might have slept where he sat but that the strong coffee he'd drunk had gone straight to his bladder, and he needed to relieve himself. He got up and went in search of a secluded bush to do just that, rapidly losing his bearings amongst the trees.

In one grove he came upon a couple dancing to the late-night music from a small transistor radio – like lovers left on a dance floor after the place had closed, too absorbed in each other to be parted. In another place a child was being taught to count, its abacus a string of floating lights its mother had spoken into being. He found a deserted spot to unburden himself, and was fumbling to do the buttons of his borrowed trousers up again when somebody took hold of his arm. He turned to find Apolline Dubois at his side. She was in black, as ever, but was wearing lipstick and mascara, which didn't flatter her. Had he not seen the all but empty vodka bottle in her hand her breath would have told him she'd had a good night's drinking behind her.

'I'd offer you some,' she said, 'but it's all I've got left.'

'Don't worry,' he told her.

'Me?' she said. 'I never worry. It's all going to end badly whether I worry or not.'

Drawing herself closer to him, she peered at his face.

'You look sick,' she announced. 'When did you last have a shave?'

As he opened his mouth to answer her something happened to the air around them. A tremor ran through it, with darkness at its heels. She forsook her hold on him instantly, dropping the vodka bottle in the same moment. It struck his foot, but he managed to bite back his curse, and was thankful for it. Every sound from between the trees, music or mathematics, had ceased utterly. So had the noises in the undergrowth, and from the branches. The wood was suddenly death-bed quiet, the shadows thickening between the trees. He put his arm out and clutched hold of one of the trunks, fearful of losing all sense of geography. When he looked around Apolline was backing away from him, only her powdered face visible. Then she turned away, and that too was gone.

He wasn't entirely alone. Off to his right he saw somebody step from the cover of the trees and hurriedly kick earth over the small fire by which mother and child had been engaged in their lessons. They were there still, the woman's hand pressed over her off-spring's mouth, the child's eyes turned up to look at her, wide with fear. As the last light was snuffed out Cal saw her mouth ask a question of the man, who in answer jerked his thumb over his shoulder. Then the scene went to black.

For a few moments Cal stayed put, vaguely aware that there were people moving past him – purposefully, as if to their stations. Rather than remain where he was, clinging to the tree like a man in a flood, he decided to go in the direction the fire-smotherer had pointed, and find out what was going on. Hands extended to help him plot his course as he navigated his way between the trees. His every movement produced some unwelcome sound: his pigskin shoes creaked; his hands, touching a trunk, brought fragments of bark down in a pattering rain. But there was a destination in sight. The trees were thinning out, and between them he could see the brightness of snow. Its light made the going easier, and by it he came to within ten yards of the edge of the wood. He knew now where he was. Ahead lay the field where he'd seen Novello playing; and louring over it, the white slope of Rayment's Hill.

As he started to move closer somebody put their hand on his chest, halting him, and a nod from a dogged face at his side directed him back the way he'd come. But somebody crouched in the shrubbery closer to the edge of the trees turned to look at him, and with a raised hand signalled that he should be allowed passage. It was only when he came within a yard of her hiding-place that he saw it was Suzanna. Though they were very near the perimeter of the trees, and the snow-light was almost lurid, she was difficult to see. A rapture was wrapped around her like a veil, strengthening on her exhaled breaths, weakening on the intake. Her attention was on the field again, and the hill beyond. Snow was still falling without pause; it seemed to have erased his tracks, though not, perhaps, unaided.

'It's here,' she whispered, without looking his way.

He studied the scene before him. There was nothing out there but the hill and the snow.

'I don't see – ' he began.

She silenced him with a touch, and nodded towards the young trees at the outskirts of the wood.

'She sees it,' her whisper said.

He studied the saplings, and realized that one was flesh and blood. A young girl was standing at the very edge of the trees, her arms extended, her hands holding onto the branches of saplings to left and right.

Somebody moved out of the half-light and took up a position beside Suzanna.

'How close?' he said.

Cal knew the voice, though the man was much changed.

'Nimrod?'

The golden eyes glanced at Cal without registering anything, then looked away, before returning with recognition in them. Apolline had been right, Cal thought; he must look bad. Nimrod stretched his arm in front of Suzanna and clasped Cal's hand tightly. As he broke contact again the girl at the perimeter let out the tiniest exclamation, and Nimrod's question – '*How close?*' – was answered.

Shadwell and Hobart had appeared at the top of the hill. Though the sky at their backs was dark, they were darker still against it, their ragged silhouettes unmistakable.

'They found us,' Nimrod breathed.

'Not yet,' said Suzanna.

Very slowly, she stood up, and as if on that signal a tremor – the twin to the rumour that had first hushed the wood – ran through the trees. The air seemed to darken even further.

'They're strengthening the screen,' Nimrod whispered.

Cal wished he had some useful role to play in this, but all he could do was watch the hill and hope the enemy would turn its back and go searching elsewhere. He'd known Shadwell too long to believe this likely, however, and he wasn't surprised when the Salesman started down the slope towards the field. The enemy was obstinate. He'd come to give the gift of Death he'd spoken of in Chariot Street, and he wouldn't be satisfied until he'd done so.

Hobart, or the power inside him, was lingering on the brow of the hill, where it could better survey the terrain. Even at this distance the flesh of its face flared and darkened like embers in a high wind.

Cal glanced behind him. The Kind were just visible, standing at regular intervals between the trees, their concentration focused on the rapture that stood between them and slaughter. Its redoubled effect was strong enough to invade his eyes, though he stood within the walls. For a moment the darkness of the wood grew tenuous, and it seemed he could see through it, to the snow on the other side.

He looked back at Shadwell, who had reached the bottom of the slope and was scanning the landscape ahead of him. It was only now, seeing the man clearly, that Cal's thoughts returned to the jacket that Shadwell had lost or thrown away, and which he too had abandoned in his travels. It was out there somewhere in the field behind Rayment's Hill, where his frozen fingers had let it fall. As Shadwell started to walk towards the wood, he stood up, and whispered:

' . . . the jacket . . .'

Suzanna was close to him, her answer barely audible.

'What about it?'

Shadwell had stopped walking again, and was scrutinizing the snow in front of him. Was some vestige of Cal's and Novello's tracks still visible?

'Do you know where the jacket is?' Suzanna was saying.

'Yes,' he said. 'On the other side of the hill.'

The Salesman had raised his eyes once more, and was staring at the scene in front of him. Even from a distance it was clear the expression on his face was one of puzzlement, even suspicion. The illusion was apparently holding; but for how long? On the hill above him Uriel spoke, its words carrying on the snow-laden wind.

'*I smell them,*' it said.

Shadwell nodded, and took a pack of cigarettes from his pocket, lighting it beneath the flap of his coat. Then he returned his gaze to the scene in front of him. Was it the chill that made him squint, or was he seeing a ghost of something against the glare of snow?

'We're just going to get weaker,' said Suzanna. 'Unless we get help.'

'From the jacket?' Cal said.

'It had power once,' she replied. 'Maybe it still does. Can you find it?'

'I don't know.'

'That's not the answer we need.'

'Yes. I can find it.'

She looked back towards the hill. Shadwell had decided to rejoin Uriel, and was climbing the slope once more. The Angel had sat Hobart's body in the snow, and was staring up at the clouds.

'I'll go with you,' said Nimrod.

'They'll be able to see us from up there.'

'We'll make a detour. Get out round the back.' He looked at Suzanna. 'Yes?' he said.

'Yes,' she replied. 'Go on, while there's still time.'

He was away at speed, Cal in tow, weaving through the trees and the Kind standing between them. The strain of keeping the shield up against the sight of man and Angel was taking its toll; several of the rapturers had collapsed; others were plainly near it.

Nimrod's sense of direction was faultless; they came out on the far side of the wood, and instantly threw themselves face down in the snow. The depth of the fall was in their favour; they could practically tunnel through it, keeping the drifts between them and the hill as much as possible. But the snow could not protect them all the way; there were patches of open ground that had to be crossed if they weren't to follow a route so hopelessly circuitous they'd not reach their target before dawn. The wind was blowing sheets of loose snow before it, but in the gaps between them they had a clear view of the hill, and those on the summit – should they chance to look down – had a clear view of them. They'd caught the rhythm of the wind however, laying low when it died down and making a run when a gust gave them cover. By this means they crept within thirty yards of the flank of the hill unseen, and it seemed the most dangerous part of the route was over, when the wind suddenly dropped, and in the lull Cal heard Shadwell's triumphant voice.

'*You!*' he said, pointing down at them. '*I see you!*'

He stepped down the side of the hill a few yards, then went back up to alert Uriel, who was still gazing at the sky.

'Run for it!' Cal yelled to Nimrod, and giving up any attempt at concealment they both ploughed on through the snow, Cal leading now as he went in search of what he'd lost. A glance up at the summit showed him that Shadwell had roused Hobart, who had stood up. The man was stark naked –

indifferent to the blizzard – his body blackened by fire and smoke. Any moment, Cal knew, that same fire would find Nimrod and himself.

He began to run again, expecting the flame at any moment. Three stumbling steps, and still it didn't come. Now four, and five; six, seven. Still there was no avenging flame.

Bafflement made him look once more towards the hill. Shadwell was still at the summit, imploring the Angel to do its damnedest. But in the window between one gust of snow and the next Cal saw that Uriel had other business, distracting it from its role as executioner.

He started to run again, knowing that he and Nimrod had been granted a precious chance at life, but unable to stop himself mourning the sight of Suzanna, climbing the hill to meet the Angel's gaze.

# III

## ON THE HILL

### 1

S he had no plan in mind. But as she'd watched Nimrod and Cal creeping towards the hill it had become perfectly apparent that unless there was some diversion they'd be sighted and killed. She was not about to ask for volunteers. If anyone was going to distract the Angel's fire it surely had to be her; after all, she and Hobart had played this game of Dragons before; or a variation upon it.

Rather than step directly out through the screen, and so give Shadwell his target, she slipped through the trees and out at the flank, moving from drift to drift until she was some distance from the wood. Only then did she move out into full view of the Dragon.

Had she been faster she might have prevented Shadwell from seeing Cal and Nimrod at all; as it was she heard his accusing cry moments before she emerged from hiding. Twenty seconds later and Shadwell would have succeeded in rousing Hobart, and the death inside him, to action. But when the Salesman climbed back up the hill Hobart's eyes were already on her, and wouldn't be dislodged.

Before making this appearance she'd watched the two figures at the summit intently, to see if she could make any sense of the politics between them. But their behaviour – or more particularly Uriel's – confounded her. Surely the Scourge had as much appetite for the chase as Shadwell; but it seemed utterly distracted from the matter in hand, staring up at the sky as if mesmerized. Only once was it moved to show its fire, when – without any apparent cue – the body of the man it occupied spontaneously combusted, flames cocooning him until his clothes were burned from his back, and his flesh seared. He'd not moved an inch as the fire did its work, but had stood in the midst of his pyre like a martyr, gazing over the empty landscape until – again, without any apparent reason – the fire died.

Now, as she climbed to meet him, she saw just how traumatized Hobart's body was. The flames that had enveloped him were only the most recent of countless assaults his flesh had endured. He'd been wounded several times, some of the holes ineptly sealed; his hands were horribly maimed; his face – hair and brows burned away – was barely recognizable. But seeing the way his eyes stared from his blistered features one impression was confirmed: he, and perhaps the force within him, was somehow mesmerized. There was no sign that he felt pain from his wounds, nor shame that he stood naked before her, not the glorious victim of his dreams but a column of wretchedness, stinking of death and cooked meat.

Meeting that blank stare the fear necessity had kept at bay so far rose up in her. Was it possible she could get beyond this trance, to the Hobart with whom she'd shared that story of Maiden, Knight and Dragon? If she could, perhaps she might survive this confrontation; or at least waylay the enemy long enough for the Kind to prepare new defences.

Shadwell had seen her now. Beside Hobart the man looked positively dapper, but his face told another story. His features, which had pretended so much in their time, were manic now, the sham of courtesy he produced for her more pitiful than ironic.

'Well, well,' he said. 'And where did you appear from?'

His hands were plunged deep into his pockets to keep them warm, and they stayed there. He made no attempt to take hold of her, or even approach her. He knew, presumably, she could not escape the summit alive.

'I came to see Hobart,' she told him.

'I'm afraid he isn't here,' Shadwell replied.

'Liar,' she said.

Hobart's eyes were still on her. Was there a flicker of response in them?

'I'm telling you the truth,' Shadwell protested. 'Hobart's gone. This *thing* . . . it's just a shell. You know what's inside. And it isn't Hobart.'

'That's a pity,' she said, playing his civilized game while it gave her time to think.

'No loss,' said Shadwell.

'But we had unfinished business.'

'You and Hobart?'

'Oh yes.' She was looking straight at the burned man as she spoke. 'I was hoping he'd remember me.'

At this, Hobart's head sagged a little, then rose again: a primitive nod.

'You *do* remember,' she said.

The eyes didn't leave her for an instant.

'Are you the Dragon – ' she asked him.

'Shut up,' said Shadwell.

'Or the Knight?'

'I told you to be quiet!' He made a move towards her, but before he could get within striking distance Hobart raised his arm and put the black stump of his hand on Shadwell's chest. The Salesman stepped back from it.

*He's frightened*, Suzanna thought. The stain of fear she saw around his head only confirmed what his face already admitted. There was more power here than he knew to handle, and he was afraid. But he wasn't so cowed as to keep his silence.

'Burn her,' he said to Hobart. 'Make her tell us where they are.'

Her gut convulsed. She hadn't taken that possibility into account: that they'd torture her to make her tell. But it was too late for flight. Besides, Hobart showed no sign of obeying Shadwell's instructions. He simply watched her, the way the Knight in the book had watched her: a wounded creature at the end of his story. And she in her turn felt as she'd felt then: both afraid, and strong. The body before her was a receptacle for devestating power, but if she could just reach into it – oh

690

so gently – and speak with the Hobart whose secret heart she knew, perhaps, just *perhaps*, she could coax him into siding with her against the Scourge. Dragons had weaknesses; maybe Angels did too. Could she make him raise its throat to her?

'I . . . remember you,' he said.

The voice was faltering, and pained, but it was clearly that of Hobart, not his tenant. She glanced sideways at Shadwell, who was watching this encounter with bewilderment, then back at Hobart, catching sight, as she did so, of something flickering in the unsealed holes of his body. Her instinct was to step back, but he stopped her.

'Don't,' he said. 'Don't . . . leave me. It won't harm you.'

'You mean the Dragon?'

'Yes,' he said. 'The snow's made it slow. It thinks it's in the sand. Alone.'

Now the Scourge's inactivity began to make some vague sense. Perched on the hill, surveying the wilderness of snow, it had lost its grip on the present. It was back in the void it had occupied for the millennium, where it waited for fresh instructions from its Maker. Shadwell was not that Maker. He was dust; human dust. It no longer heard him.

But it knew the smell of the Kind; it had howled as much from this very spot. And when the raptures failed – as soon they must – the wilderness would no longer keep it from its duty. Seeing them, it would do what it had come to do, not for Shadwell's sake, but for its own. She had to get to it quickly.

'Do you remember the book?' she said to Hobart.

He took a moment to answer her. In the silence the furnace in his body brightened again. She began to fear that his words of comfort had been misplaced; that these two Law-givers were so much a part of each other that the breaking of one trance had alerted the other.

'Tell me . . .' she said. 'The book . . .'

'Oh yes,' he told her, and with his recognition the light intensified. 'We were there . . .' he said, ' . . . in the trees. You, and me, and – '

He stopped talking, and his face, which had been slack, suddenly contorted. There was panic there, as the fires rose

691

to the lips of his wounds. From the corner of her eyes she could see Shadwell stepping back slowly, as if from a ticking bomb. Her mind careered around for a delaying tactic, but none came.

Hobart was raising his broken hands to his face, and in the gesture she comprehended how they'd been destroyed. He'd tried to stymie the Scourge's fire once before, and his flesh had been forfeit.

'Burn her,' she heard Shadwell mutter.

Then the fire began to come. It didn't appear suddenly, as she'd expected, but oozed from the hurts he'd sustained, and from his nostrils, and mouth, and prick, and pores, running in fiery rivulets through which darts of the Angel's intention ran, still slothful, but growing stronger. She'd lost the race.

Hobart was not quite beaten, however; he was making one last, gallant attempt to speak his mind. The chattering ceased as he forced his mouth open. But before he could utter a word Uriel ignited his spittle. Fire licked up across his face, the geometries behind it sharpening. Through the flames Suzanna saw Hobart's eyes on her, and as their gaze met he threw back his head.

She knew the gesture, of old. He was offering her his throat.

*'Kill me and be done,'* the Dragon had said.

Hobart was demanding that same kindness now, in the only way left to him.

*Kill me and be done.*

In the book she'd hesitated, and lost her chance to fell her enemy. This time she wouldn't falter.

She had the menstruum as a weapon, and as ever it knew her intention better than she did. Even as her thoughts embraced the notion of murder it was flying from her, crossing the space between her and Hobart in a silver instant and snatching hold of him.

His throat was offered, but it was not his throat it took, it was his heart. She felt the heat of his body fly back along the river into her head, and with it the rhythm of his life. His heart was beating in her grasp; she clasped it tight, no trace of guilt touching her. He wanted death, and she had it to give: that was a fair exchange.

He shuddered. But his heart, for all its sins, was brave, and beat on.

Fire was coming from everywhere about him. He wept it, shat it, sweated it. She could smell her hair singeing; steam rose between them as the snow melted and was boiled away. The geometries were taking control of the fire now; shaping it, aiming it. Any moment, it would be upon her.

She gripped his heart tighter still, feeling it swell against her hold. Still beating, still beating.

Just as she thought it was beyond her, the muscle gave up its work, and stopped.

From somewhere in Hobart a noise rose which his lungs could not have made nor his mouth expelled. But she heard it clearly, and so did Shadwell: part sob, part sigh. It was his last word. The body in which she still had her mind's fingers was dead before the sound had faded.

She began to call the menstruum out of him, but the Scourge caught its tail and an echo of the void came to meet her along the stream. She had a taste of its lunacy, and its pain, before she snatched her lethal strength back to her.

There was an empty moment, while steam rose and snow fell. Then the sometime Knight and Dragon Hobart fell dead at her feet.

'What have you done?' Shadwell said.

She wasn't sure. Killed Hobart, certainly. But beyond that? The corpse face down in front of her showed no sign of occupancy; the fires from it were suddenly extinguished. Had Hobart's death driven Uriel out of the man, or was it simply biding its time?

'You killed him,' Shadwell said.

'Yes.'

'How? Jesus . . . how?'

She was readying herself to resist him if he attacked, but it wasn't murder in his look, it was disgust.

'You're one of the magicians, aren't you?' he said. 'You're here with them.'

693

'I was,' she told him. 'But they've gone, Shadwell. You've missed your chance.'

'You might trick me with your deceits,' he said, his voice full of pretended innocence. 'I'm only human. But you can't hide from the Angel.'

'You're right,' she said. 'I'm afraid. Like you.'

'Afraid?'

'It's got nowhere to hide now,' she reminded him, casting a look at Hobart's corpse. 'Won't it need somebody? It's either you or me, and I'm rotten with magic. You're clean.'

For a fraction of a second Shadwell's facade dropped, and she had her words confirmed; even amplified. He was not simply afraid; he was terrified.

'It won't touch me,' he protested, his throat constricted. 'I woke it. It owes me its life.'

'Do you think it cares?' she said. 'Aren't we all fodder to a thing like that?'

In the face of her questions his pretence to indifference failed him; he began to run his tongue over his lips, top then bottom, over and over.

'You don't want to die, do you?' she said. 'At least, not like *that*.'

This time it was his glance that went to the body on the ground.

'It wouldn't *dare*,' he said. But he dropped his volume as he spoke, as though fearful it would hear him.

'Help me,' she said to him. 'Together we might be able to control it.'

'It's not possible,' he replied.

As he spoke the body in the warm mud between them burst into incandescent flames. This time there was nothing left for Uriel's fire to devour but muscle and bone; Hobart had been stripped as naked as a man could get. The skin burst, blood boiling up in a hundred places. Suzanna stepped back to avoid being caught by the rain of heat, and in doing so put herself within Shadwell's reach. He took hold of her, placing her body between him and the fire.

But the Scourge had already left Hobart, and had taken itself

694

into the hill. The ground began to shake, the din of grinding rock and pulped earth rising from beneath them.

Whatever Uriel had gone underground to devise Suzanna wanted to run from it while there was time, but Shadwell still had hold of her, and much as she wished to let the menstruum strike him down he was the only ally she had left. He it was who'd woken the beast, and been its companion. If anyone knew its weaknesses, he was the man.

The roaring in the ground climbed to a crescendo, and with it, the whole hill *tipped*. She heard Shadwell cry out, then he fell, taking Suzanna with him. His hold probably saved her life, for as they rolled down the slope the ground at the summit of Rayment's Hill erupted.

Rock and frozen earth were carried skywards, then hailed down on their heads. She had no time to protect herself from its descent. She was still spitting snow from her mouth when something struck her on the back of the neck. She tried to keep hold of consciousness, but it slipped her, and she slid into the night behind her eyes.

2

Shadwell was still beside her when she came round, his hold on her so fierce it had deadened her arm from elbow to fingertip. At first she thought the blow she'd sustained had affected her sight, but it was a fog that had closed off the world around them; a cold, clinging fog that seemed to encompass the entire hill. Through it Shadwell watched her, his eyes two slits in his filthied face.

'You're alive – ' he said.

'How long have we been here?'

'A minute or two.'

'Where's the Scourge?' she asked him.

He shook his head. 'It's not reasoning any more,' he said. 'Hobart was right. It doesn't know where it is. You've got to help me – '

'That's why you stayed.'

' – or else we'll neither of us get out of here alive.'

'So how?' she said.

He gave her a small, twitching smile.

'Placate it,' he said.

'Again: *how*?'

'Give it what it wants. Give it the magicians.'

She laughed in his face.

'Try again,' she said.

'It's the only option. Once it's got them it'll be satisfied. It'll leave us alone.'

'I'm not going to give it anything.'

His grip strengthened. He crabbed his way through the muck to her side.

'It's going to find them anyway, sooner or later,' he said. He was on the verge of sobbing like a baby. 'There's no chance they can survive this. But *we* can. If we can just make the bastards show themselves. It won't want us once it's got them. It'll be satisfied.' His face was inches away; every tic and tear was hers to scrutinize. 'I know you hate me,' he said. 'I deserve it. So don't do it for me, do it for yourself. I can make it worth your while.' She looked at him with something close to awe, that even now he could bargain. 'I've got stuff stashed away,' he said. 'A fortune. You name your price. It's all yours. Whatever you want. Free, gratis and – '

He stopped.

'Oh sweet Jesus,' he said.

Somewhere in the fog, something had begun to howl: a rising wail which he recognized and feared. He seemed to decide that it was no use hoping she'd aid him, for he let her go and rose to his feet. The fog was equally dense on every side; it took him several seconds to elect an escape route. But once he had, he was away at a stumbling run, as the howl – which could only be Uriel – shook the hill.

Suzanna stood up, the fog and her aching head making the surroundings swim. The ground was so churned it was impossible to tell where the slope of the hill lay, so she couldn't orient herself to get back to the wood. All she could do was run, as fast as possible, away from the howl, blood coursing down the back of her neck. Twice she fell; twice her body made contact with an earth that seemed ready to open up beneath her.

She was on the verge of collapse when a figure loomed from the fog ahead of her, calling her name. It was Hamel.

'I'm here — ' she yelled to him, over the din of the Scourge. He was with her in seconds, leading her over the treacherous ground and back towards the wood.


3


Luck was on Shadwell's side. Once he was away from the hill itself the fog thinned and he realized that either by instinct or accident he'd chosen the best direction to run in. The road was not far from here; he'd be away down it before the Angel had finished on the hill; away to some safe place on the other side of the globe where he could lick his wounds and put this whole horror out of his head.

He chanced a look over his shoulder. His blessed flight had already put a good distance between himself and the scene of devastation. The only sign of the Angel was the fog; and that still clung to the hill. He was safe.

He slowed his pace as he came within sight of the hedgerow which bounded the road; all he had to do now was follow it until he came to a gate. The snow was still falling, but his sudden turn of speed had got him heated; sweat was running down his back and chest. Even as he unbuttoned his coat, however, he realized the warmth was not self-generated. The snow was turning to slush beneath his feet, as heat rose from the ground, and with it, a sudden spring, shoots bursting from the earth and rising like snakes towards his face. As they flowered he realized the depth of his error. They came with fire for sap, these blossoms, and at their hearts were Uriel's eyes, Uriel's countless eyes.

He could go neither forward nor back; they were all around him. To his horror he heard the Angel's voice in his head, as he had first heard it back in the *Rub al Khali*.

*Do I dare?*

– it said, mocking his boast to Suzanna.

*DO I DARE?*

And then it was upon him.

One moment he was only himself. A man; a history.

The next he was pressed to the lid of his creaking skull as the Angel of Eden claimed him.

His last act as a man with a body he could call his own was to shriek.

4

'Shadwell,' she said.

'No time to enjoy it,' Hamel remarked grimly. 'We've got to get back before they start to move out.'

'Move out?' she said. 'No, we mustn't do that. The Scourge is still here. It's in the hill.'

'No choice,' Hamel replied. 'The raptures are almost used up. See?'

They were within a few yards of the trees now, and there was indeed a smoky presence in the air; a hint of what was concealed behind the screen.

'No strength left,' Hamel said.

'Any sign of Cal?' she asked. 'Or Nimrod?'

He gave a short, dismissive shake of the head. They were gone, his look said, and not worth fretting for.

She glanced back at the hill, hoping for some sign that contradicted him, but there was no movement. Fog still held court at the summit; the upturned earth around it was still.

'Are you coming?' he wanted to know.

She followed him, her head throbbing, the first step taken through snow, the second through thicket. There was a child crying in the depths of the hideaway, its sobs inconsolable.

'See if you can keep her quiet, Hamel,' she said. 'But *gently*.'

'Are we going or aren't we?' he said.

'Yes,' she conceded. 'We have to. I just want to see Cal back first.'

'There's no *time*,' he insisted.

'All right,' she said. 'I heard you. We'll go.' He grunted, and turned away from her. 'Hamel?' she called after him.

'What?'

'Thank you for coming after me.'

'I want to be out of here,' he said plainly, and went in search of the sobbing, leaving her to return to the lookout post that offered the best view of the hill.

There were several Kind keeping watch there.

'Anything?' she asked one of them.

He didn't need to answer. A murmur amongst them drew her gaze to the hill.

The fog cloud was stirring. It was as if something in its midst had taken a vast breath, for the cloud folded upon itself, growing smaller and smaller, until the force that haunted it became visible.

Uriel had found the Salesman. Though it was Shadwell's body that stood in the mud of Rayment's Hill, the eyes burned with a seraphic light. From the purposeful way it surveyed the field there could be little doubt that the distraction which had made it mild had passed. The Angel was no longer lost in a remembered void. It knew both where it was and why. 'We've got to move!' she said. 'The children first.'

The order came not an instant too soon, for even as the message ran through the trees, and the fugitives began their last dash for safety, Uriel turned its murderous eyes on the field below Rayment's Hill, and the snow began to burn.

# IV

## SYMMETRY

### 1

**N**o trace of the route Cal had described across the field behind the hill was visible when he and Nimrod reached there; the blizzard had erased it. All they could do was guess at the path he would have followed, and dig in the vicinity in the hope of chancing upon the lost package. But it was nearly hopeless. His route to the hill had been far from direct – fatigue had made him reel and wander like a drunkard; and since then the wind had re-arranged the drifts so that in some places they were deep enough to bury a man upright.

The driving snow obscured the hill-top most of the time, so Cal could only guess at what was happening up there. What chance did anyone have of survival against Shadwell, and the Scourge?: little or none, probably. But then Suzanna had brought him out of the Gyre alive, hadn't she?, against all the odds. The thought of her on the hill, distracting Uriel's fatal gaze, made him dig with greater devotion to the task, without really believing they had a hope in hell of finding the jacket.

Their digging steadily took he and Nimrod further apart, until Cal could no longer see his fellow searcher through the veil of snow. But at one point he heard the man cry out in alarm, and turned to see a flickering brightness in the wastes behind him. Something was burning on the hill. He started back towards it, but sense prevailed over heroics. If Suzanna was alive, then she was alive. If she was dead, he was wasting her sacrifice turning his back on the search.

As he began again, any pretence to a system in the work forgotten, the roaring in the hill began, climaxing in the din of erupting earth. This time he didn't look back, didn't try to pierce the veil for news of love; he simply dug, and dug, turning his grief into fuel for the task.

In his haste he almost lost the treasure in the act of finding it, his hands already covering the glimpse of paper before his distracted brain had registered what it was. When it did he began to dig like a terrier, shovelling snow behind him, not quite daring to believe he'd found the package. As he dug the wind brought a voice to him, then whipped it away again, a cry for help, somewhere in the wilderness. It wasn't Nimrod, so he kept digging. The voice came back. He looked up, narrowing his eyes against the onslaught. Was there somebody wading through the snow some way off from him? Like the voice, the sight came and went.

The package was just as evasive. But even as he was thinking he'd been mistaken, and there was nothing to find, his frozen fingers closed on the thing. As he pulled it from the drift the paper, which was almost mush, tore, and the contents fell in the snow. A box of cigars; some trinkets; and the jacket. He picked it up. If it had looked unremarkable at Gluck's house it looked more so now. He hoped somebody in the wood had a clue as to how to unleash its powers, because he certainly didn't.

He looked around for Nimrod, to give him the news, and saw two figures trudging towards him, one holding the other up. The bearer was Nimrod; the man he was helping – the same Cal had heard and glimpsed presumably – so swathed in protective clothing he was unrecognizable. Nimrod had seen the prize Cal had lifted up to show him, however, and was coaxing the man to pick up his speed, yelling something to Cal as he approached. The wind stole the words away, but he yelled them again as he came closer.

'Is this a friend of yours?'

The man he was all but carrying lifted his snow-encrusted face, and fumbled with the scarf that was wrapped around its lower half. Before he'd pulled it down, however, Cal said:

701

'Virgil?'

The scarf came away, and Gluck was looking up at him with a mixture of shame and triumph on his face in equal measure.

'Forgive me,' he said. 'I had to be here. I had to see.'

'If there's anything *left* to see,' Nimrod shouted over the din of the wind.

Cal looked back towards Rayment's Hill. Between the gusts it was apparent that the top of the hill had been entirely blown open. Over it a pall of smoke was rising, its underbelly lit by flames.

'The wood . . .' he said. Forgetting Nimrod and Gluck, he began to plough through the snow, back towards the hill and what lay beyond.

2

There was nothing arbitrary in the Scourge's attack. It was systematically destroying the field and the surrounding region in the knowledge that sooner or later its eyes would find the creatures whose proximity it smelt. In the trees there was an organized retreat; the children, accompanied by either guardians or parents, moving through to the rear of the wood and out into the open air. Few others moved, but stayed at their stations, preserving the integrity of their hiding place. Suzanna wasn't certain if this was defiance or fatalism; perhaps a little of both. But however deep they dug, their store of raptures was all but exhausted. It was a matter of seconds rather than minutes now before Uriel-in-Shadwell's glance reached the trees. When it did so the woods would burn, invisible or no.

Hamel was at Suzanna's side as she watched the Angel's approach.

'Are you coming?' he said.

'In a moment.'

'It's now or never.'

Maybe it would be never, then. She was so transfixed by the formidable power being unleashed in front of her, she couldn't

702

avert her astonished gaze. It fascinated her that strength of this magnitude should be turned to the sordid business of atrocity; something was wrong with a reality that made that possible, and offered no cure for it, nor hope of cure.

'We have to go,' said Hamel.

'Then go,' she told him.

Tears were welling in her eyes. She resented them coming between her and seeing. But with them she felt the menstruum rising — not to protect her but to be with her at the last; to give her its little sum of joy.

The Angel raised its sights. She heard Hamel shout. Then the trees to the right of where she stood burst into flames.

There were cries from the depths of the wood as the screen was breached.

'*Scatter!*' somebody yelled.

Hearing its prey, the Scourge caused Shadwell's face to smile: a smile to end the world with. Then the light in the bloated body intensified, as Uriel mustered a final fire, to destroy the rapturers forever.

A beat before it broke, a voice said:

'*Shadwell?*'

It was the Salesman's name that had been called, but it was Uriel that looked round, its calamitous glance momentarily postponed.

Suzanna's gaze left the Scourge, and went to the speaker.

It was Cal. He was walking across the smoking ground that had once been the snow-covered field at the bottom of the hill; walking straight towards the enemy.

At the sight of him she didn't hesitate to break cover. She stepped out from the margin of the trees and into the open air. Nor did she come alone. Though she didn't take her eyes off Cal for an instant she heard whispers and footfalls at her side as the Kind appeared from hiding; a gesture of solidarity in the face of extinction which moved her profoundly. At the last, their appearance here said, we're together, Cuckoo and Kind, part of one story.

None of which prevented an awed voice, which she recognized as that of Apolline, from saying:

'Is he out of his fucking mind?'

as Cal continued to advance across the earth Uriel had laid waste.

Behind her, the crackling of flames mounted, as the fire, fanned by the wind, spread through the woods. Its glow washed the ground, throwing the shadows of the Kind towards the two figures in the field ahead. Shadwell, with his fine clothes torn and singed, his face paler than a dead man's. Cal in his pigskin shoes, the flame-light picking out threads in his jacket.

No; not *his* jacket: Shadwell's. The jacket of illusions.

How could she have been so slow as not to have noticed it earlier? Was it the fact that it fitted him so well, though it had been made for a man half his size again? Or was it simply that his face had claimed all her attention, that face which even now had about it a purposefulness she'd come to love.

He was within ten yards of the Scourge, and now stood still.

Uriel-in-Shadwell said nothing, but there was a restlessness in the Salesman's body that threatened to detonate at any moment.

Cal fumbled to unbutton the jacket, frowning at the ineptitude of his fingers. But he got the trick of it on the fourth attempt, and the jacket fell open.

That done, he spoke. His voice was thin, but it didn't shake.

'I've got something to show you,' he said.

At first Uriel-in-Shadwell offered no response. When it did it was not the possessor who replied but the possessed.

'There's nothing there I want,' the Salesman said.

'It's not *for* you,' Cal replied, his voice growing stronger. 'It's for the Angel of Eden. For Uriel.'

This time neither Scourge nor Salesman replied. Cal took hold of the front panel of the jacket, and opened it, exposing the lining.

'Don't you want to look?' he enquired.

Silence answered him.

'Whatever you see,' he went on. 'It's yours.'

Somebody at Suzanna's side whispered: 'What does he think he's doing?'

704

She knew; but didn't waste precious effort on a reply. Cal needed all the power she could will to him: all her hope, all her love.

Again, he addressed the Scourge.

'What do you see?' he said.

This time he got an answer.

'Nothing.'

It was Shadwell who spoke.

'I. See. Nothing.'

'Oh Cal,' Suzanna breathed, catching the flicker of despair that crossed his face. She knew exactly what he was thinking, and shared his doubt. Were the raptures in the jacket dead? Had they withered away without victims to nourish them, leaving him standing before Uriel unarmed?

A long moment passed. Then, from somewhere in the belly of the Angel there rose a low moan. As it came Shadwell's mouth opened, and he spoke again. But it was quietly this time, as if to himself; or the thing inside himself.

'*Don't look,*' he said.

Suzanna held her breath, not daring to believe his words were a warning. Yet how else could they be construed?

'You *do* see something,' Cal said.

'No,' Shadwell replied.

'Look,' said Cal, opening the jacket as wide as he could. 'Look and see.'

Suddenly, Shadwell began yelling.

'It's *lies*!' he screeched, his body shuddering now. 'It's all corruption!'

But the moan that was still rising from the creature inside him drowned his warnings out. This was not the howl Suzanna had heard in the rock of Rayment's Hill: not an insane cry of rage. This sound was sad, infinitely sad, and as if answering sound with light the jacket, whose threads she'd feared bankrupt, began to brighten.

Immediately Shadwell's warnings began again, tinged with a new hysteria.

'*Don't!*' he shouted. '*Don't, damn you!*'

The Scourge was deaf to the appeals of its host, however. It had its innumerable eyes on the lining of the jacket, willing forth from it a vision only it could see.

For Cal the moment carried terror and joy in such confusion he could not tell one from the other. Not that it mattered: events now were out of his hands. All he could do was stand his ground while the jacket performed whatever deceits it had power to perform.

He hadn't meant to put it on; that hadn't been a part of his plan at all. Indeed he'd *had* no plan; he'd just plunged through the snow, hoping he wasn't too late to intervene. But events had already outpaced him. Uriel's glance had found the Kind's refuge, and was destroying it. The jacket which he'd dug for was redundant; the Kind's bluff was called. But the sight of the Salesman put another thought into his head: that the jacket's raptures had worked when Shadwell had *worn* it, and that he had no better option now than to do the same.

No sooner had he slipped his arms into it than it fitted itself to him, snug as a surgeon's glove. He felt its embrace as a bargain made. Hereafter it was a part of him, and he of it.

Even now, as he stood before Uriel, he could feel it tapping into him, seeking his humanity to add spice to the illusion it was creating. The Angel's gaze was fixed on the lining, entranced, the face it wore becoming more distorted with every breath Shadwell wasted on his pleas and predictions.

'It'll deceive you!' he roared. 'It's magic! Do you hear me?'

If the Angel was aware of his panic, it didn't comprehend it. Or if it comprehended, it didn't care. The jacket's genius for seduction was rising to its greatest triumph. All it had enthralled hitherto were Cuckoos, whose hearts were malleable and sentimental, and whose desires scarcely rose above the pedestrian. But the dream-life of the entity which now gazed into it was of a different order entirely. Uriel had no halcyon childhood to mourn, nor lovers to pine for. Its mental powers, though they'd been long left to sterility, were immense, and the jacket's raptures were pressed to their limits to produce an image of what it most desired.

The garment had begun to writhe and ripple on Cal's back,

706

its seams creaking around him as though it could scarcely bear what was being asked of it, and was ready to fly apart. He felt he might do the same if this wasn't over soon. The jacket's demands upon him were becoming intolerable, as it dug deeper and ever deeper into him, trawling his soul for the inspiration to match the Angel's need. His torso and arms had grown numb; his hands no longer owned the strength to hold the jacket open. It was left to the forces loose in the lining to spread the coat wide, while he stood in the flux of power, his mind assaulted by fragments of whatever Uriel was yearning after. He could make only partial sense of them.

There was a planet of light he saw, turning over and over before him, its immensity grazing his lips. There was a flame sea, lapping at a beach of stone and cloud. There were forms his mind's eye couldn't endure to look at making riddles of their breath.

But they were all fugitive visions, and when they'd gone he was back standing on the same dead earth, his body being wasted by Uriel's hunger. The jacket had reached its limits. It had begun to disintegrate, threads being sucked from its warp and weft and burned away before him.

But Uriel wasn't about to be cheated; its eyes drew on the fabric, demanding it make good the promise Cal had voiced. Beneath this assault the jacket finally capitulated, but in its destruction Uriel's demand was answered. The lining burst, and from it rose the image Uriel's appetite had shaped, its brightness blinding Cal.

He heard Shadwell bellow, then his own cries rose over the din, pleading with the Angel to take its dream to its bosom.

Uriel didn't hesitate. It wanted this vision as much as Cal wanted rid of it. Through a haze of anguish Cal saw Shadwell's body begin to bloat as the Angel inside him prepared to show itself. The Salesman could only wail his despair as he felt himself plucked into the air, Uriel's geometries bearing him up. His skin was tight as a drum, stretched to the limits of its tolerance; his mouth a toothlined O as his cartilage tore and sinew snapped. Then he broke, his body bursting to release its captive, the fragments incinerated in the instant they flew by the glory his destruction unleashed.

Before him Cal saw plainly the incarnation he'd only glimpsed in the fog on Chariot Street: Uriel's eyes, Uriel's geometry, Uriel's hunger.

And then its magnetism drew the illusion its will had made out from the ruins of the jacket and up to meet it.

The vision stood revealed: as bright as Uriel, and as vast, as well it had to be, for the image the raptures had made was *another* Uriel, the Seraph's equal in every way. As it rose up the vestiges of the jacket fell away from Cal, but its degeneration did not compromise the creature it had parented. Uriel's mirror stood unbowed before the power that had summoned it into being.

Cal, robbed both of his strength and of the images he'd peeped on, tasted a terrible banality. He had no energy left to look up and wonder at the majesty above him. His eyes were turned inward, and he saw only emptiness there. A desert, in which his dust blew with the dust of all the things he'd ever loved and lost; blew to the end of time and knew neither rest nor meaning.

His body surrendered, and he fell as though he'd been shot, while the dust in his head whipped him away, into the void. He witnessed nothing of what followed. Suzanna saw his collapse. Ignoring the giants that towered over the burning wood, she went to his aid. Overhead the Angels hovered like twin suns, their energies filling the air with invisible needles. Careless of their stings she bent her back to the task of dragging Cal away from this rendezvous of spirit and spirit. She was beyond fear now, or hope. The first and only necessity was to have Cal safe in her arms. Whatever followed would follow. It was beyond her.

Others had come to her assistance: Apolline, Hamel, and from the far side of the field, Nimrod. Together they picked Cal up and took him out of the region of needles, laying him down gently where the ground was softest.

Above them, the confrontation was reaching a new plateau. Uriel's form had become impossibly complex, its anatomy transforming at the speed of its thought; part engine, part citadel; all meticulous fire. And its conjured companion was matching it change for change, darts passing between them like needles threaded with fire, drawing them closer and closer still, until they were locked like lovers.

If there had once been a distinction between Uriel the real and Uriel the imagined that no longer pertained. Such divisions were for Cuckoos, who believed they lived both inside their heads and out; to whom thought was only life's shadow, and not its own true self.

Uriel knew better. It had needed the Old Science to seduce it into confessing its profoundest desire: simply, to see its own true face, and seeing it know how it had been before loneliness had corrupted it.

Now it embraced that remembered self, and learned its lesson on the instant. The pit of its insanity had been as deep as the stars it had descended from were high. Unreminded of its nature it had sunk into obsession, devoted to a dead duty. But looking on itself – seeing the glory of its condition – it shed that lunacy, and shedding it, looked starward.

There were heavens it had business in, where the age it had wasted here was but a day, and its grief, *all* grief, an unknown state.

On the thought, it rose, it and itself one triumphant splendour.

There were clouds above. It was away between them in moments, leaving only a rain of dwindling light on the faces of those who watched it pass from sight.


'Gone,' said Lo, when even the light had died, and there was only a gruel of snow shed from above.

'Is it over then?' Apolline wanted to know.

'I think it is,' said Hamel. There were tears pouring down his cheeks.

A fresh gust of wind had lent new fervour to the flames that were devouring the wood. It did not matter much. They no longer had need to take refuge there. Perhaps tonight marked an end to refuges.

Suzanna looked down at Cal, whom she was cradling as

709

she'd once cradled Jerichau. But Jerichau had died in her arms: Cal would not; she swore he would not. He had not escaped the furnace of the jacket's destruction unmarked: the skin of his face and his chest were burned, or perhaps stained. But that was the only outward damage.

'How is he?' said a voice she didn't know.

She looked up to meet the harried gaze of a Cuckoo like herself, muffled up in several layers of clothing.

'Suzanna?' he said. 'My name is Gluck. I'm a friend of Calhoun's.'

'You're welcome,' said someone.

Gluck beamed.

'He's not going to die,' said Suzanna, stroking Cal's face. 'He's just sleeping awhile.'

'He's had a busy night,' said Nimrod, and there were tears on his stoical face too, pouring down.

# V

## THE SLEEPWALKER

### 1

There was a wilderness, and Cal was dust in the wilderness, and his hopes and dreams were dust in the wilderness, all driven before the same unforgiving wind.

He had tasted Uriel's condition, before its healing. He'd shared the spirit's loneliness and desolation, and his frail mind had been snatched up into the void and left there to die. He knew no way out. In the final arithmetic his life was a wasteland: of fire, of snow, of sand. All of it, a wasteland, and he would wander there 'til he could wander no more.

### 2

To those who were tending him, he seemed simply to be resting; at least at first. They let him sleep, in the belief that he'd wake healed. His pulse was strong, his bones unbroken. All he needed was time to recover his strength.

But when he woke the following afternoon, in Gluck's house, it was immediately clear that something was profoundly amiss. His eyes opened, but Cal was not in them. His gaze was devoid of recognition or response. It and he were as blank as an empty page.

Suzanna couldn't know – none of them could – what he'd shared with Uriel during their confrontation, but she could make an educated guess. If her experience of the menstruum had taught her anything it was that every exchange was a two-way street. Cal had conspired with Immacolata's jacket to give Uriel its vision, but what had the lunatic spirit given him in return?

When, after two days, there was no sign of improvement in his state, they called in expert help, but though the doctors exhausted their tests on him they could find nothing physiologically wrong. This was not a coma, they ventured, so much as a trance; and they knew no precedent for it, except perhaps sleepwalking. One of their number even went so far as to suggest the condition might be self-induced, a possibility Suzanna did not entirely dismiss.

There were no reasons they could find, they finally announced, as to why the patient wasn't up and awake and living a healthy life. There are plenty of reasons, Suzanna thought, but none that she could begin to explain. Perhaps he had simply seen too much; and the surfeit had left him indifferent to being.

### 3

And the dust rolled on.

Sometimes he thought he heard voices in the wind; very distant voices. But they disappeared as quickly as they came, and left him alone again. That was for the best, he knew, because if there was a place beyond this wasteland and the voices were trying to coax him back, it would bring him pain, and he was better off without it. Besides, sooner or later the inhabitants of that otherwhere would come to him. They'd wither and die and join the dust in the wilderness. That was how things happened; always had and always would.

Everything went to dust.

### 4

Each day Suzanna would spend several hours talking to him, telling him how the day had gone, and whom she'd met, mentioning the names of people he knew and places he'd been in the hope of stirring him from his inertia. But there was no response; not a glimmer.

Sometimes she'd get into a quiet rage at his apparent indifference to her, and tell him to his vacant face that he was being selfish. She loved him, didn't he know that? She loved him and she wanted him to know her again, and be with her. Other times she'd come close to despair, and however hard she tried she couldn't stem the tears of frustration and unhappiness. She'd leave his bedside then, until she'd composed herself again, because she was fearful that somewhere in his sealed head he'd hear her grief and flee even further into himself.

She even tried to reach him with the menstruum, but he was a fortress, and her subtle body could only gaze into him, not enter. What it saw gave her no cause for optimism. It was as if he was uninhabited.

5

Outside the window of Glück's home it was the same story: there were few signs of life. This was the hardest winter since the beginning of the century. Snow fell on snow; ice glazed ice.

As January crept to its dismal end people began not to ask after Cal as frequently. They had problems of their own in such a grim season, and it was relatively easy for them to put him out of their minds because he wasn't in pain; or at least in no pain he could express. Even Gluck tactfully suggested that she was giving too much of her time over to nursing him. She had her own healing to do; a life to be put in some sort of order; plans to be laid for the future. She'd done all that could be expected from a devoted friend, and more, he argued, and she should start to share the burden with others.

I can't, she told him.

Why not?, he asked.

I love him, she said, and I want to be with him.

713

That was only half the answer of course. The other half was the book.

There it lay in his room, where she'd put it the day they'd returned from Rayment's Hill. Though it had been Mimi's gift to Suzanna, the magic that it now contained meant she could no longer open it alone. Just as she'd needed Cal at the Temple, in order to use the Loom's power, and charge the book with their memories, so she needed him again if they were to reverse the process. The magic hung in the space between them. She could not reclaim on her own what they'd imagined together.

Until he woke the *Stories of the Secret Places* would remain untold. And if he didn't wake they'd remain that way forever.

## 6

In the middle of February, with the false hint of a thaw in the air, Gluck took himself off to Liverpool, and, by dint of some discreet enquiries in Chariot Street, located Geraldine Kellaway. She returned with him to Harborne to visit Cal. His condition shocked her, needless to say, but she had that brand of pragmatism that would find her the first brewing tea after Armageddon, and within an hour she'd taken it in her stride.

She returned to Liverpool after two days, back to the life she'd established in Cal's absence, promising to visit again soon.

If Gluck had hoped her appearance would do something to break the deadlock of Cal's stupor, he was disappointed. The sleepwalker went on in the same fashion, through February and early March, while outside the promised thaw was delayed and delayed.

During the day they'd move him from his bed to the window, and there he'd sit, overlooking the expanse of frost-gripped ground behind Gluck's house. Though he was fed well, chewing and swallowing with the mechanical efficiency of an animal; though he was shaved and bathed daily; though his legs were exercised to keep the muscles from wasting, it was apparent to those few who still came visiting, and especially to Suzanna and Gluck, that he was preparing die.

# 7

And the dust rolled on.

# VI

## RAPTURE

### 1

**I**f Finnegan hadn't called she would never have gone down to London. But he had, and she did, as much at Gluck's insistence than from any great enthusiasm for the trip.

As soon as she got out of the house, however, and started travelling, she began to feel the weight of recent weeks lift a little. Hadn't she once said to Apolline that there was comfort in their at least being alive? It was true. They would have to make the best they could of that, and not sigh for things circumstance had denied them.

She found Finnegan less than his usual spritely self. His career at the bank had floundered of late, and he needed a shoulder to curse upon. She supplied it happily, more than content to hear his catalogue of woes if they distracted her from her own. He reminded her, when he'd finished complaining and gnashing his teeth, of something she'd once said about never marrying a banker. As it seemed he'd soon be out of a job would she think again?, he wondered. It was clear from his tone he didn't expect yes for an answer, and he didn't get it, but she told him she hoped they'd always be friends.

'You're a strange woman,' he said as they parted, apropos of nothing in particular.

She took the remark as flattery.

## 2

It was late afternoon by the time she got back to Harborne. Another night of frost was on its way, pearling the pavements and roofs.

When she went upstairs she found the sleepwalker had not been put in his chair but was sitting against heaped pillows on the bed, his eyes as glazed as ever. He looked sick; the mark Uriel's revelation had left on his face was livid against his pallid skin. She'd left too early to shave him that morning, and it distressed her to see how close to utter dereliction such minor neglect had left him looking. Talking quietly to him about where she'd been, she led him from the bed over to the chair beside the window, where the light was a little better. Then she collected the electric razor from the bathroom and shaved his stubble.

At the beginning it had been an eerie business, ministering to him like this, and it had upset her. But time had toughened her, and she'd come to view the various chores of keeping him presentable as a means to express her affection for him.

Now, however, as dusk devoured the light outside, she felt those early anxieties rising in her again. Perhaps it was the day she'd spent out of the house, and out of Cal's company, that made her tender to this experience afresh. Perhaps it was also the sense she had that events were drawing to a close; that there would not be many more days when she would have to shave him and bathe him. That it was almost over.

Night was upon the house so quickly the room soon became too gloomy to work in. She went to the door and switched on the light.

His reflection appeared in the window, hanging in the glass against the darkness outside. She left him staring at it while she went for the comb.

*

There was something in the void ahead of him, though he couldn't see what. The wind was too strong, and he, as ever, was dust before it.

But the shadow, or whatever it was, persisted, and sometimes — when the wind dropped a little — it seemed he could almost see it studying him. He looked back at it and its gaze held him, so that instead of being blown on, and away, the dust he was made of momentarily stood still.

As he returned the scrutiny, the face before him became clearer. He knew it vaguely, from some place he'd gained and lost. Its eyes, and the stain that ran from hairline to cheek, belonged to somebody he'd known once. It irritated him, not being able to remember where he'd seen this man before.

It was not the face itself which finally reminded him, but the darkness it was set against.

The last time he'd seen this stranger, perhaps the *only* time, the man had been standing against another such darkness. A cloud, perhaps, shot with lightning. It had a name, this cloud, but he couldn't remember it. The place had a name too, but that was even further out of his reach. The moment of their meeting he did remember however; and some fragments of the journey that led up to it. He'd been in a rickshaw, and he'd passed through a region where time was somehow out of joint. Where today breathed yesterday's air, and tomorrow's too.

For curiosity's sake he wanted to know the stranger's name, before the wind caught him and moved him on again. But he was dust, so he couldn't ask. Instead he pressed his motes towards the darkness on which the mysterious face hovered, and reached to touch his skin.

It was not a living thing he made contact with, it was cold glass. His fingers fell from the window, the heat-rings they'd left shrinking.

If it was glass before him, he dimly thought, then he must be looking at himself surely. The man he'd met, standing against that nameless cloud: that was *him*.

A puzzle awaited Suzanna when she returned to the room.

She was almost certain she'd left Cal with his hands on his lap, but now his right arm hung at his side. Had he tried to move? If so it was the first independent motion he'd made since the trance had claimed him.

She started to speak to him, softly, asking him if he heard her, if he saw her, or knew her name. But as ever it was a one-way conversation. Either his hand had simply slipped from his lap or she'd been mistaken and it hadn't been there in the first place.

Sighing, she set to combing his hair.


He was still dust in a wilderness, but now he was dust with a memory.

It was enough to give him weight. The wind bullied him, wanting its way with him, but this time he refused to be moved. It raged against him. He ignored it, standing his ground in the nowhere while he tried to fit the pieces of his thoughts together.

He had met himself once, in a house near a cloud; he'd been brought there in a rickshaw while a world folded up around him.

What did it signify, that he'd come face to face with himself as an old man? What did that mean?

The question was not so difficult to answer, even for dust. It meant he would at some future time step into that world, and live there.

And from that, what followed? *What followed?*

That the place was not lost.

Oh yes! Oh God in Heaven, *yes*! That was it. He would be there. Not tomorrow maybe, or the day after that; but some-day, some future day: he would *be there*.

It was not lost. The Fugue was not lost.

It took only that knowledge, that certainty, *and he woke*.


'Suzanna,' he said.

# 3

'Where is it?' was the only question he voiced, when they'd finished with their reunion. 'Where's it hidden?'

She went to the table and put Mimi's book into his hands. 'Here,' she said.

He ran his palm over the binding, but declined to open it.

'How did we do that?' he said. He asked the question with such gravity; like a child.

'In the Gyre,' she said. 'You and I. And the Loom.'

'All of it?' he said. 'All of it, in here?'

'I don't know,' she told him in all honesty. 'We'll see.'

'Now.'

'No, Cal. You're very weak still.'

'I'll be strong –' he said simply, ' – once we open the book.'

She could not better such argument; instead she reached across and laid her hands on Mimi's gift. As her fingers laced with his the lamp above their heads flickered and went out. Immersed in darkness they held the book between them, as she and Hobart had once held it. On that occasion it had been hatred that had fuelled the forces in the pages; this time it was joy.

They felt the book begin to tremble in their custody, growing warm. Then it flew out of their hands towards the window. The icy glass shattered and it disappeared, tumbling away into the darkness.

Cal got to his feet, and hobbled to the window; but before he'd reached it the pages rose, unbound, like birds in the night outside, like pigeons, the thoughts the Loom had inscribed between the lines spilling light and life. Then they swooped down again, and out of sight.

Cal turned away from the window.

'The garden,' he said.

His legs felt as though they were made of cotton-wool; he needed Suzanna's support to get him to the door. Together they started down the flight.

720

Gluck had heard the sound of breaking glass, and was half way up the stairs to investigate, a mug of tea in his hand. He'd seen wonders in his time, but the sight of Cal, telling him to get outside, *outside*, left him open-mouthed. By the time he'd found a question to ask, Cal and Suzanna were already half way down the second flight of stairs. He followed; into the hallway, and through the kitchen to the back door. Suzanna was unbolting it, top and bottom.

Though there had been winter at the window, it was spring that awaited them on the threshold.

And in the garden itself, spreading even as they watched, the source of that season: the home of their joy forever; the place they'd fought and almost died to save:

*The Fugue.*

It was emerging from the book's scattered pages in all its singular majesty, defying ice and darkness as it had defied so much else. The months it had spent amongst the tales in the book had not been wasted. It came with fresh mysteries and enchantments.

Here, in time, Suzanna would rediscover the Old Science, and with it heal ancient breaches. Here too, in some unimaginable year, Cal would go to live in a house on the borders of the Gyre, to which one day a young man would come whose history he knew. It was all ahead, all they'd dreamed together, all waiting to be born.

Even at that moment, in sleeping cities across the Isle, the refugees were waking and rising from their pillows, and throwing open the doors and windows, despite the cold, to meet the news the night was bringing them: that what could be imagined need never be lost. That even here, in the Kingdom, rapture might find a home.

After tonight there would be only one world, to live in and to dream; and Wonderland would never be more than a step away, a thought away.

Together Cal, Suzanna and Gluck left the house and went walking in that magic night.

Ahead, there were such sights unfolding: friends and places

they'd feared gone forever coming to greet them, eager for shared rapture.

There was time for all their miracles now. For ghosts and transformations; for passion and ambiguity; for noon-day visions and midnight glory. Time in abundance.

For nothing ever begins.

And this story, having no beginning, will have no end.